THE CORRECTIONS

THE
CORRECTIONS

JONATHAN
FRANZEN

Harper*Flamingo*Canada

www.harpercanada.com

HarperCollins books may be purchased for educational, business, or sales
promotional use. For information please write: Special Markets
Department, HarperCollins Canada, 55 Avenue Road, Suite 2900, Toronto,
Ontario, Canada M5R 3L2.

Canadian Cataloguing in Publication Data

Franzen, Jonathan
The corrections

ISBN 0-00-200509-3

I. Title.

PS3556.R37C67 2001   C813'.54   C2001-901461-9

01 02 03 04 FSG 6 5 4 3 2

Printed and bound in the United States

To David Means and Genève Patterson

ST. JUDE

THE MADNESS of an autumn prairie cold front coming through. You could feel it: something terrible was going to happen. The sun low in the sky, a minor light, a cooling star. Gust after gust of disorder. Trees restless, temperatures falling, the whole northern religion of things coming to an end. No children in the yards here. Shadows lengthened on yellowing zoysia. Red oaks and pin oaks and swamp white oaks rained acorns on houses with no mortgage. Storm windows shuddered in the empty bedrooms. And the drone and hiccup of a clothes dryer, the nasal contention of a leaf blower, the ripening of local apples in a paper bag, the smell of the gasoline with which Alfred Lambert had cleaned the paintbrush from his morning painting of the wicker love seat.

Three in the afternoon was a time of danger in these gerontocratic suburbs of St. Jude. Alfred had awakened in the great blue chair in which he'd been sleeping since lunch. He'd had his nap and there would be no local news until five o'clock. Two empty hours were a sinus in which infections bred. He struggled to his feet and stood by the Ping-Pong table, listening in vain for Enid.

Ringing throughout the house was an alarm bell that no one but Alfred and Enid could hear directly. It was the alarm bell of anxiety. It was like one of those big cast-iron dishes with an electric clapper that send schoolchildren into the street in fire drills. By now it had been ringing for so many hours that the Lamberts no longer heard the message of "bell ringing" but, as with any sound that continues for so long that you have the leisure to learn its component sounds (as with any word you stare at until it resolves itself into a string of dead letters), instead heard a clapper rapidly striking a metallic resonator, not a pure tone but a granular sequence of percussions with a keening overlay of overtones; ringing for so many days that it simply blended into the background except at certain early-morning hours when one or the other of them awoke in a sweat and realized that a bell had been ringing in their heads for as long as they could remember; ringing for so many months that the sound had given way to a kind of metasound whose rise and fall was not the beating of compression waves but the much, much slower waxing and waning of their *consciousness* of the sound. Which consciousness was particularly acute when the weather itself was in an anxious mood. Then Enid and Alfred—she on her knees in the dining room opening drawers, he in the basement surveying the disastrous Ping-Pong table—each felt near to exploding with anxiety.

The anxiety of coupons, in a drawer containing candles in designer autumn colors. The coupons were bundled in a rubber band, and Enid was realizing that their expiration dates (often jauntily circled in red by the manufacturer) lay months and even years in the past: that these hundred-odd coupons, whose total face value exceeded sixty dollars (potentially one hundred twenty dollars at the Chiltsville supermarket that doubled coupons), had all gone bad. Tilex, sixty cents off. Excedrin PM, a dollar off. The dates were not even *close*. The dates were *historical*. The alarm bell had been ringing for *years*.

She pushed the coupons back in among the candles and shut the drawer. She was looking for a letter that had come by Registered mail some days ago. Alfred had heard the mailman knock on the door and had shouted, "Enid! Enid!" so loudly that he couldn't hear her shouting back, "Al, I'm getting it!" He'd continued to shout her name, coming closer and closer, and because the sender of the letter was the Axon Corporation, 24 East Industrial Serpentine, Schwenksville, PA, and because there were aspects of the Axon situation that Enid knew about and hoped that Alfred didn't, she'd quickly stashed the letter somewhere within fifteen feet of the front door. Alfred had emerged from the basement bellowing like a piece of earth-moving equipment, *"There's somebody at the door!"* and she'd fairly screamed, "The mailman! The mailman!" and he'd shaken his head at the complexity of it all.

Enid felt sure that her own head would clear if only she didn't have to wonder, every five minutes, what Alfred was up to. But, try as she might, she couldn't get him interested in life. When she encouraged him to take up his metallurgy again, he looked at her as if she'd lost her mind. When she asked whether there wasn't some yard work he could do, he said his legs hurt. When she reminded him that the husbands of her friends all had hobbies (Dave Schumpert his stained glass, Kirby Root his intricate chalets for nesting purple finches, Chuck Meisner his hourly monitoring of his investment portfolio), Alfred acted as if she were trying to distract him from some great labor of his. And what was that labor? Repainting the porch furniture? He'd been repainting the love seat since Labor Day. She seemed to recall that the last time he'd painted the furniture he'd done the love seat in two hours. Now he went to his workshop morning after morning, and after a month she ventured in to see how he was doing and found that all he'd painted of the love seat was the legs.

He seemed to wish that she would go away. He said that the brush had got dried out, that that was what was taking so long. He said that scraping wicker was like trying to peel a blueberry. He said that there were crickets. She felt a shortness of breath then, but perhaps it was only the smell of gasoline and of the dampness of the workshop that smelled like urine (but could not possibly be urine). She fled upstairs to look for the letter from Axon.

Six days a week several pounds of mail came through the slot in the front door, and since nothing incidental was allowed to pile up downstairs—since the fiction of living in this house was that no one lived here—Enid faced a substantial tactical challenge. She didn't think of herself as a guerrilla, but a guerrilla was what she was. By day she ferried matériel from depot to depot, often just a step ahead of the governing force. By night, beneath a charming but too-dim sconce at a too-small table in the breakfast nook, she staged various actions: paid bills, balanced checkbooks, attempted to decipher Medicare co-payment records and make sense of a threatening Third Notice from a medical lab that demanded immediate payment of $0.22 while simultaneously showing an account balance of $0.00 carried forward and thus indicating that she owed nothing and in any case offering no address to which remittance might be made. It would happen that the First and Second Notices were underground somewhere, and because of the constraints under which Enid waged her campaign she had only the dimmest sense of where those other Notices might be on any given evening. She might suspect, perhaps, the family-room closet, but the governing force, in the person of Alfred, would be watching a network newsmagazine at a volume thunderous enough to keep him awake, and he had every light in the family room burning, and there was a non-negligible possibility that if she opened the closet door a cascade of catalogues and *House Beautifuls* and miscellaneous Merrill Lynch statements would come toppling and sliding out, incurring Alfred's wrath. There was also the possibility that the Notices would not be there, since the governing force staged random raids on her depots, threatening to "pitch" the whole lot of it if she didn't take care of it, but she was too busy dodging these raids to ever quite take care of it, and in the succession of forced migrations and deportations any lingering semblance of order was lost, and so the random Nordstrom shopping bag that was camped behind a dust ruffle with one of its plastic handles semi-detached would contain the whole shuffled pathos of a refugee existence—non-consecutive issues of *Good Housekeeping*, black-and-white snapshots of Enid in the 1940s, brown recipes on high-acid paper that called for wilted lettuce, the current month's telephone and gas bills, the detailed First Notice from the medical lab instructing co-payers to ignore subsequent billings for less than fifty cents, a complimentary cruise ship photo of Enid and Alfred wearing leis and sipping beverages from hollow coconuts, and the only extant copies of two of their children's birth certificates, for example.

Although Enid's ostensible foe was Alfred, what made her a guerrilla was the house that occupied them both. Its furnishings were of the kind that brooked no clutter. There were chairs and tables by Ethan Allen. Spode and Waterford in the breakfront. Obligatory ficuses, obligatory Norfolk pines. Fanned copies of *Architectural Digest* on a glass-topped coffee table. Touristic plunder—enamelware from China, a Viennese music box that Enid out of a sense of duty and mercy every so often wound up and raised the lid of. The tune was "Strangers in the Night."

Unfortunately, Enid lacked the temperament to manage such a house, and Alfred lacked the neurological wherewithal. Alfred's cries of rage on discovering evidence of guerrilla actions—a Nordstrom bag surprised in broad daylight on the basement stairs, nearly precipitating a tumble—were the cries of a government that could no longer govern. He'd lately developed a knack for making his printing calculator spit columns of meaningless eight-digit figures. After he devoted the better part of an afternoon to figuring the cleaning woman's social security payments five different times and came up with four different numbers and finally just accepted the one number ($635.78) that he'd managed to come up with twice (the correct figure was $70.00), Enid staged a nighttime raid on his filing cabinet and relieved it of all tax files, which might have improved household efficiency had the files not found their way into a Nordstrom bag with some misleadingly ancient *Good House-keeping*s concealing the more germane documents underneath, which casualty of war led to the cleaning woman's filling out the forms herself, with Enid merely writing the checks and Alfred shaking his head at the complexity of it all.

It's the fate of most Ping-Pong tables in home basements eventually to serve the ends of other, more desperate games. After Alfred retired he appropriated the eastern end of the table for his banking and corre-spondence. At the western end was the portable color TV on which he'd intended to watch the local news while sitting in his great blue chair but which was now fully engulfed by *Good Housekeeping*s and the seasonal candy tins and baroque but cheaply made candle holders that Enid never quite found time to transport to the Nearly New consign-ment shop. The Ping-Pong table was the one field on which the civil war raged openly. At the eastern end Alfred's calculator was ambushed by floral print pot-holders and souvenir coasters from the Epcot Center and a device for pitting cherries which Enid had owned for thirty years and never used, while he, in turn, at the western end, for absolutely no reason that Enid could ever fathom, ripped to pieces a wreath made of pinecones and spray-painted filberts and brazil nuts.

To the east of the Ping-Pong table was the workshop that housed Alfred's metallurgical lab. The workshop was now home to a colony of mute, dust-colored crickets, which, when startled, would scatter across the room like a handful of dropped marbles, some of them misfiring at crazy angles, others toppling over with the weight of their own copious protoplasm. They popped all too easily, and cleanup took more than one Kleenex. Enid and Alfred had many afflictions which they believed to be extraordinary, outsized—shameful—and the crickets were one of them.

The gray dust of evil spells and the cobwebs of enchantment thickly cloaked the old electric arc furnace, and the jars of exotic rhodium and sinister cadmium and stalwart bismuth, and the hand-printed labels browned by the vapors from a glass-stoppered bottle of aqua regia, and the quad-ruled notebook in which the latest entry in Alfred's hand dated from a time, fifteen years ago, before the betrayals had begun. Something as daily and friendly as a pencil still occupied the random spot on the workbench where Alfred had laid it in a different decade; the passage of so many years imbued the pencil with a kind of enmity. Asbestos mitts hung from a nail beneath two certificates of U.S. patents, the frames warped and sprung by dampness. On the hood of a binocular microscope lay big chips of peeled paint from the ceiling. The only dust-free objects in the room were the wicker love seat, a can of Rust-Oleum and some brushes, and a couple of Yuban coffee cans which despite increasingly strong olfactory evidence Enid chose not to believe were filling up with her husband's urine, because what earthly reason could he have, with a nice little half-bathroom not twenty feet away, for peeing in a Yuban can?

To the west of the Ping-Pong table was Alfred's great blue chair. The chair was overstuffed, vaguely gubernatorial. It was made of leather, but it smelled like the inside of a Lexus. Like something modern and medical and impermeable that you could wipe the smell of death off easily, with a damp cloth, before the next person sat down to die in it.

The chair was the only major purchase Alfred had ever made without Enid's approval. When he'd traveled to China to confer with Chinese railroad engineers, Enid had gone along and the two of them had visited a rug factory to buy a rug for their family room. They were unaccustomed to spending money on themselves, and so they chose one of the least expensive rugs, with a simple blue design from the Book of

Changes on a solid field of beige. A few years later, when Alfred retired from the Midland Pacific Railroad, he set about replacing the old cow-smelling black leather armchair in which he watched TV and took his naps. He wanted something really comfortable, of course, but after a lifetime of providing for others he needed more than just comfort: he needed a monument to this need. So he went, alone, to a non-discount furniture store and picked out a chair of permanence. An engineer's chair. A chair so big that even a big man got lost in it; a chair designed to bear up under heavy stress. And because the blue of its leather vaguely matched the blue in the Chinese rug, Enid had no choice but to suffer its deployment in the family room.

Soon, however, Alfred's hands were spilling decaffeinated coffee on the rug's beige expanses, and wild grandchildren were leaving berries and crayons underfoot, and Enid began to feel that the rug was a mistake. It seemed to her that in trying to save money in life she had made many mistakes like this. She reached the point of thinking it would have been better to buy no rug than to buy this rug. Finally, as Alfred's naps deepened toward enchantment, she grew bolder. Her own mother had left her a tiny inheritance years ago. Interest had been added to principal, certain stocks had performed rather well, and now she had an income of her own. She reconceived the family room in greens and yellows. She ordered fabrics. A paperhanger came, and Alfred, who was napping temporarily in the dining room, leaped to his feet like a man with a bad dream.

"You're redecorating *again*?"

"It's my own money," Enid said. "This is how I'm spending it."

"And what about the money *I* made? What about the work *I* did?"

This argument had been effective in the past—it was, so to speak, the constitutional basis of the tyranny's legitimacy—but it didn't work now. "That rug is nearly ten years old, and we'll never get the coffee stains out," Enid answered.

Alfred gestured at his blue chair, which under the paperhanger's plastic dropcloths looked like something you might deliver to a power station on a flatbed truck. He was trembling with incredulity, unable to believe that Enid could have forgotten this crushing refutation of her arguments, this overwhelming impediment to her plans. It was as if all the unfreedom in which he'd spent his seven decades of life were embodied in this six-year-old but essentially brand-new chair. He was grinning, his face aglow with the awful perfection of his logic.

"And what about the chair, then?" he said. *"What about the chair?"*

Enid looked at the chair. Her expression was merely pained, no more. "I never liked that chair."

This was probably the most terrible thing she could have said to Alfred. The chair was the only sign he'd ever given of having a personal vision of the future. Enid's words filled him with such sorrow—he felt such pity for the chair, such solidarity with it, such astonished grief at its betrayal—that he pulled off the dropcloth and sank into its arms and fell asleep.

(It was a way of recognizing places of enchantment: people falling asleep like this.)

When it became clear that both the rug and Alfred's chair had to go, the rug was easily shed. Enid advertised in the free local paper and netted a nervous bird of a woman who was still making mistakes and whose fifties came out of her purse in a disorderly roll that she unpeeled and flattened with shaking fingers.

But the chair? The chair was a monument and a symbol and could not be parted from Alfred. It could only be relocated, and so it went into the basement and Alfred followed. And so in the house of the Lamberts, as in St. Jude, as in the country as a whole, life came to be lived underground.

Enid could hear Alfred upstairs now, opening and closing drawers. He became agitated whenever they were going to see their children. Seeing their children was the only thing he seemed to care about anymore.

In the streaklessly clean windows of the dining room there was chaos. The berserk wind, the negating shadows. Enid had looked everywhere for the letter from the Axon Corporation, and she couldn't find it.

Alfred was standing in the master bedroom wondering why the drawers of his dresser were open, who had opened them, whether he had opened them himself. He couldn't help blaming Enid for his confusion. For witnessing it into existence. For existing, herself, as a person who could have opened these drawers.

"Al? What are you doing?"

He turned to the doorway where she'd appeared. He began a sentence: "I am—" but when he was taken by surprise, every sentence became an adventure in the woods; as soon as he could no longer see the light of the clearing from which he'd entered, he would realize that the crumbs he'd dropped for bearings had been eaten by birds, silent deft darting things which he couldn't quite see in the darkness but which were so numerous and swarming in their hunger that it seemed as if *they* were the darkness, as if the darkness weren't uniform, weren't an absence of light but a teeming and corpuscular thing, and indeed when as a studious teenager he'd encountered the word "crepuscular" in *McKay's Treasury of English Verse*, the corpuscles of biology had bled into his understanding of the word, so that for his entire adult life he'd seen in twilight a corpuscularity, as of the graininess of the high-speed film necessary for photography under conditions of low ambient light, as of a kind of sinister decay; and hence the panic of a man betrayed deep in the woods whose darkness was the darkness of starlings blotting out the sunset or black ants storming a dead opossum, a darkness that didn't just exist but actively *consumed* the bearings that he'd sensibly established for himself, lest he be lost; but in the instant of realizing he was lost, time became marvelously slow and he discovered hitherto unguessed eternities in the space between one word and the next, or rather he became trapped in that space between words and could only stand and watch as time sped on without him, the thoughtless boyish part of him crashing on out of sight blindly through the woods while he, trapped, the grownup Al, watched in oddly impersonal suspense to see if the panic-stricken little boy might, despite no longer knowing where he was or at what point he'd entered the woods of this sentence, still manage to blunder into the clearing where Enid was waiting for him, unaware of any woods—"packing my suitcase," he heard himself say. This sounded right. Verb, possessive, noun. Here was a suitcase in front of him, an important confirmation. He'd betrayed nothing.

But Enid had spoken again. The audiologist had said that he was mildly impaired. He frowned at her, not following.

"It's *Thursday*," she said, louder. "We're not leaving until *Saturday*."

"Saturday!" he echoed.

She berated him then, and for a while the crepuscular birds retreated, but outside the wind had blown the sun out, and it was getting very cold.

THE FAILURE

DOWN THE LONG CONCOURSE they came unsteadily, Enid favoring her damaged hip, Alfred paddling at the air with loose-hinged hands and slapping the airport carpeting with poorly controlled feet, both of them carrying Nordic Pleasurelines shoulder bags and concentrating on the floor in front of them, measuring out the hazardous distance three paces at a time. To anyone who saw them averting their eyes from the dark-haired New Yorkers careering past them, to anyone who caught a glimpse of Alfred's straw fedora looming at the height of Iowa corn on Labor Day, or the yellow wool of the slacks stretching over Enid's out-slung hip, it was obvious that they were midwestern and intimidated. But to Chip Lambert, who was waiting for them just beyond the security checkpoint, they were killers.

Chip had crossed his arms defensively and raised one hand to pull on the wrought-iron rivet in his ear. He worried that he might tear the rivet right out of his earlobe—that the maximum pain his ear's nerves could generate was less pain than he needed now to steady himself. From his station by the metal detectors he watched an azure-haired girl overtake his parents, an azure-haired girl of college age, a very wantable stranger with pierced lips and eyebrows. It struck him that if he could have sex with this girl for one second he could face his parents confidently, and that if he could keep on having sex with this girl once every minute for as long as his parents were in town he could survive their entire visit. Chip was a tall, gym-built man with crow's-feet and sparse butter-yellow hair; if the girl had noticed him, she might have thought he was a little too old for the leather he was wearing. As she hurried past him, he pulled harder on his rivet to offset the pain of her departure from his life forever and to focus his attention on his father, whose face was brightening at the discovery of a son among so many strangers. In the lunging manner of a man floundering in water, Alfred fell upon

Chip and grabbed Chip's hand and wrist as if they were a rope he'd been thrown. "Well!" he said. "Well!"

Enid came limping up behind him. "Chip," she cried, "what have you done to your *ears*?"

"Dad, Mom," Chip murmured through his teeth, hoping the azure-haired girl was out of earshot. "Good to see you."

He had time for one subversive thought about his parents' Nordic Pleasurelines shoulder bags—either Nordic Pleasurelines sent bags like these to every booker of its cruises as a cynical means of getting inexpensive walk-about publicity or as a practical means of tagging the cruise participants for greater ease of handling at embarkation points or as a benign means of building esprit de corps; or else Enid and Alfred had deliberately saved the bags from some previous Nordic Pleasurelines cruise and, out of a misguided sense of loyalty, had chosen to carry them on their upcoming cruise as well; and in either case Chip was appalled by his parents' willingness to make themselves vectors of corporate advertising—before he shouldered the bags himself and assumed the burden of seeing LaGuardia Airport and New York City and his life and clothes and body through the disappointed eyes of his parents.

He noticed, as if for the first time, the dirty linoleum, the assassin-like chauffeurs holding up signs with other people's names on them, the snarl of wires dangling from a hole in the ceiling. He distinctly heard the word "motherfucker." Outside the big windows on the baggage level, two Bangladeshi men were pushing a disabled cab through rain and angry honking.

"We have to be at the pier by four," Enid said to Chip. "And I think Dad was hoping to see your desk at the *Wall Street Journal*." She raised her voice. "Al? Al?"

Though stooped in the neck now, Alfred was still an imposing figure. His hair was white and thick and sleek, like a polar bear's, and the powerful long muscles of his shoulders, which Chip remembered laboring in the spanking of a child, usually Chip himself, still filled the gray tweed shoulders of his sport coat.

"Al, didn't you say you wanted to see where Chip worked?" Enid shouted.

Alfred shook his head. "There's no time."

The baggage carousel circulated nothing.

"Did you take your pill?" Enid said.

"Yes," Alfred said. He closed his eyes and repeated slowly, "I took my pill. I took my pill. I took my pill."

"Dr. Hedgpeth has him on a new medication," Enid explained to Chip, who was quite certain that his father had not, in fact, expressed interest in seeing his office. And since Chip had no association with the *Wall Street Journal*—the publication to which he made unpaid contributions was the *Warren Street Journal: A Monthly of the Transgressive Arts*; he'd also very recently completed a screenplay, and he'd been working part-time as a legal proofreader at Bragg Knuter & Speigh for the nearly two years since he'd lost his assistant professorship in Textual Artifacts at D—— College, in Connecticut, as a result of an offense involving a female undergraduate which had fallen just short of the legally actionable and which, though his parents never learned of it, had interrupted the parade of accomplishments that his mother could brag about, back home in St. Jude; he'd told his parents that he'd quit teaching in order to pursue a career in writing, and when, more recently, his mother had pressed him for details, he'd mentioned the *Warren Street Journal*, the name of which his mother had misheard and instantly begun to trumpet to her friends Esther Root and Bea Meisner and Mary Beth Schumpert, and though Chip in his monthly phone calls home had had many opportunities to disabuse her he'd instead actively fostered the misunderstanding; and here things became rather complex, not only because the *Wall Street Journal* was available in St. Jude and his mother had never mentioned looking for his work and failing to find it (meaning that some part of her knew perfectly well that he didn't write for the paper) but also because the author of articles like "Creative Adultery" and "Let Us Now Praise Scuzzy Motels" was conspiring to preserve, in his mother, precisely the kind of illusion that the *Warren Street Journal* was dedicated to exploding, and he was thirty-nine years old, and he blamed his parents for the person he had become—he was happy when his mother let the subject drop.

"His tremor's much better," Enid added in a voice inaudible to Alfred. "The only side effect is that he *may* hallucinate."

"That's quite a side effect," Chip said.

"Dr. Hedgpeth says that what he has is very mild and almost completely controllable with medication."

Alfred was surveying the baggage-claim cavern while pale travelers angled for position at the carousel. There was a confusion of tread patterns on the linoleum, gray with the pollutants that the rain had brought down. The light was the color of car sickness. "New York City!" Alfred said.

Enid frowned at Chip's pants. "Those aren't *leather*, are they?"

"Yes."

"How do you wash them?"

"They're leather. They're like a second skin."

"We have to be at the pier no later than four o'clock," Enid said.

The carousel coughed up some suitcases.

"Chip, help me," his father said.

Soon Chip was staggering out into the wind-blown rain with all four of his parents' bags. Alfred shuffled forward with the jerking momentum of a man who knew there would be trouble if he had to stop and start again. Enid lagged behind, intent on the pain in her hip. She'd put on weight and maybe lost a little height since Chip had last seen her. She'd always been a pretty woman, but to Chip she was so much a personality and so little anything else that even staring straight at her he had no idea what she really looked like.

"What's that—wrought iron?" Alfred asked him as the taxi line crept forward.

"Yes," Chip said, touching his ear.

"Looks like an old quarter-inch rivet."

"Yes."

"What do you do—crimp that? Hammer it?"

"It's hammered," Chip said.

Alfred winced and gave a low, inhaling whistle.

"We're doing a Luxury Fall Color Cruise," Enid said when the three of them were in a yellow cab, speeding through Queens. "We sail up to Quebec and then we enjoy the changing leaves all the way back down. Dad so enjoyed the last cruise we were on. Didn't you, Al? Didn't you have a good time on that cruise?"

The brick palisades of the East River waterfront were taking an angry beating from the rain. Chip could have wished for a sunny day, a clear view of landmarks and blue water, with nothing to hide. The only colors on the road this morning were the smeared reds of brake lights.

"This is one of the great cities of the world," Alfred said with emotion.

"How are you feeling these days, Dad," Chip managed to ask.

"Any better I'd be in heaven, any worse I'd be in hell."

"We're excited about your new job," Enid said.

"One of the great papers in the country," Alfred said. "The *Wall Street Journal.*"

"Does anybody smell fish, though?"

"We're near the ocean," Chip said.

"No, it's you." Enid leaned and buried her face in Chip's leather sleeve. "Your jacket smells *strongly* of fish."

He wrenched free of her. "Mother. Please."

Chip's problem was a loss of confidence. Gone were the days when he could afford to *épater les bourgeois*. Except for his Manhattan apartment and his handsome girlfriend, Julia Vrais, he now had almost nothing to persuade himself that he was a functioning male adult, no accomplishments to compare with those of his brother, Gary, who was a banker and a father of three, or of his sister, Denise, who at the age of thirty-two was the executive chef at a successful new high-end restaurant in Philadelphia. Chip had hoped he might have sold his screenplay by now, but he hadn't finished a draft until after midnight on Tuesday, and then he'd had to work three fourteen-hour shifts at Bragg Knuter & Speigh to raise cash to pay his August rent and reassure the owner of his apartment (Chip had a sublease) about his September and October rent, and then there was a lunch to be shopped for and an apartment to be cleaned and, finally, sometime before dawn this morning, a long-hoarded Xanax to be swallowed. Meanwhile, nearly a week had gone by without his seeing Julia or speaking to her directly. In response to the many nervous messages he'd left on her voice mail in the last forty-eight hours, asking her to meet him and his parents and Denise at his apartment at noon on Saturday and also, please, if possible, not to mention to his parents that she was married to someone else, Julia had maintained a total phone and e-mail silence from which even a more stable man than Chip might have drawn disturbing conclusions.

It was raining so hard in Manhattan that water was streaming down façades and frothing at the mouths of sewers. Outside his building, on East Ninth Street, Chip took money from Enid and handed it through the cab's partition, and even as the turbaned driver thanked him he realized the tip was too small. From his own wallet he took two singles and dangled them near the driver's shoulder.

"That's enough, that's enough," Enid squeaked, reaching for Chip's wrist. "He already said thank you."

But the money was gone. Alfred was trying to open the door by pulling on the window crank. "Here, Dad, it's this one," Chip said and leaned across him to pop the door.

"How big a tip was that?" Enid asked Chip on the sidewalk, under his building's marquee, as the driver heaved luggage from the trunk.

"About fifteen percent," Chip said.

"More like twenty, I'd say," Enid said.

"Let's have a fight about this, why don't we."

"Twenty percent's too much, Chip," Alfred pronounced in a booming voice. "It's not reasonable."

"You all have a good day now," the taxi driver said with no apparent irony.

"A tip is for service and comportment," Enid said. "If the service and comportment are especially good I might give fifteen percent. But if you *automatically* tip—"

"I've suffered from depression all my life," Alfred said, or seemed to say.

"Excuse me?" Chip said.

"Depression years changed me. They changed the meaning of a dollar."

"An economic depression, we're talking about."

"Then when the service really *is* especially good or especially bad," Enid pursued, "there's no way to express it monetarily."

"A dollar is still a lot of money," Alfred said.

"Fifteen percent if the service is exceptional, really exceptional."

"I'm wondering why we're having this particular conversation," Chip said to his mother. "Why this conversation and not some other conversation."

"We're both terribly anxious," Enid replied, "to see where you work."

Chip's doorman, Zoroaster, hurried out to help with the luggage and installed the Lamberts in the building's balky elevator. Enid said, "I ran into your old friend Dean Driblett at the bank the other day. I never run into Dean but where he doesn't ask about you. He was impressed with your new writing job."

"Dean Driblett was a classmate, not a friend," Chip said.

"He and his wife just had their fourth child. I told you, didn't I, they built that *enormous* house out in Paradise Valley—Al, didn't you count eight bedrooms?"

Alfred gave her a steady, unblinking look. Chip leaned on the Door Close button.

"Dad and I were at the housewarming in June," Enid said. "It was spectacular. They'd had it catered, and they had *pyramids* of shrimp. It was solid shrimp, in pyramids. I've never seen anything like it."

"Pyramids of shrimp," Chip said. The elevator door had finally closed.

"Anyway, it's a beautiful house," Enid said. "There are at least six bedrooms, and you know, it looks like they're going to fill them. Dean's tremendously successful. He started that lawn care business when he decided the mortuary business wasn't for him, well, you know, Dale Driblett's his stepdad, you know, the Driblett Chapel, and now his billboards are everywhere and he's started an HMO. I saw in the paper where it's the fastest-growing HMO in St. Jude, it's called DeeDeeCare, same as the lawn care business, and there are billboards for the HMO now, too. He's quite the entrepreneur, *I'd* say."

"Slo-o-o-o-w elevator," Alfred said.

"This is a prewar building," Chip explained in a tight voice. "An extremely desirable building."

"But you know what he told me he's doing for his mother's birthday? It's still a surprise for her, but I can tell you. He's taking her to Paris for eight days. Two first-class tickets, eight nights at the Ritz! That's the kind of person Dean is, very family-oriented. But can you believe that kind of birthday present? Al, didn't you say the house alone probably cost a million dollars? Al?"

"It's a large house but cheaply done," Alfred said with sudden vigor. "The walls are like paper."

"All the new houses are like that," Enid said.

"You asked me if I was impressed with the house. I thought it was ostentatious. I thought the shrimp was ostentatious. It was poor."

"It may have been frozen," Enid said.

"People are easily impressed with things like that," Alfred said. "They'll talk for months about the pyramids of shrimp. Well, see for yourself," he said to Chip, as to a neutral bystander. "Your mother's still talking about it."

For a moment it seemed to Chip that his father had become a likable old stranger; but he knew Alfred, underneath, to be a shouter and a punisher. The last time Chip had visited his parents in St. Jude, four years earlier, he'd taken along his then-girlfriend Ruthie, a peroxided young Marxist from the North of England, who, after committing numberless offenses against Enid's sensibilities (she lit a cigarette indoors, laughed out loud at Enid's favorite watercolors of Buckingham Palace, came to dinner without a bra, and failed to take even one bite of the "salad" of water chestnuts and green peas and cheddar-cheese cubes in a thick mayonnaise sauce which Enid made for festive occasions), had needled and baited Alfred until he pronounced that "the blacks" would be the ruination of this country, "the blacks" were incapable of coexisting with whites, they expected the government to take care of them, they didn't know the meaning of hard work, what they lacked above all was *discipline*, it was going to end with slaughter in the streets, *with slaughter in the streets*, and he didn't give a damn what Ruthie thought of him, she was a visitor in *his* house and *his* country, and she had no right to criticize things she didn't understand; whereupon Chip, who'd already warned Ruthie that his parents were the squarest people in America, had smiled at her as if to say, *You see? Exactly as advertised.* When Ruthie had dumped him, not three weeks later, she'd remarked that he was more like his father than he seemed to realize.

"Al," Enid said as the elevator lurched to a halt, "you have to admit that it was a very, very nice party, and that it was *very* nice of Dean to invite us."

Alfred seemed not to have heard her.

Propped outside Chip's apartment was a clear-plastic umbrella that Chip recognized, with relief, as Julia Vrais's. He was herding the parental luggage from the elevator when his apartment door swung open and Julia herself stepped out. "Oh. Oh!" she said, as though flustered. "You're early!"

By Chip's watch it was 11:35. Julia was wearing a shapeless lavender raincoat and holding a DreamWorks tote bag. Her hair, which was long and the color of dark chocolate, was big with humidity and rain. In the tone of a person being friendly to large animals she said "Hi" to Alfred and "Hi," separately, to Enid. Alfred and Enid bayed their names at her and extended hands to shake, driving her back into the apartment, where Enid began to pepper her with questions in which Chip, as he followed with the luggage, could hear subtexts and agendas.

"Do you live in the city?" Enid said. *(You're not cohabiting with our son, are you?)* "And you work in the city, too?" *(You are gainfully employed? You're not from an alien, snobbish, moneyed eastern family?)* "Did you grow up here?" *(Or do you come from a trans-Appalachian state where people are warmhearted and down-to-earth and unlikely to be Jewish?)* "Oh, and do you still have family in Ohio?" *(Have your parents perhaps taken the morally dubious modern step of getting divorced?)* "Do you have brothers or sisters?" *(Are you a spoiled only child or a Catholic with a zillion siblings?)*

Julia having passed this initial examination, Enid turned her attention to the apartment. Chip, in a late crisis of confidence, had tried to make it presentable. He'd bought a stain-removal kit and lifted the big semen stain off the red chaise longue, dismantled the wall of wine-bottle corks with which he'd been bricking in the niche above his fireplace at a rate of half a dozen Merlots and Pinot Grigios a week, taken down from his bathroom wall the close-up photographs of male and female genitalia that were the flower of his art collection, and replaced them with the three diplomas that Enid had long ago insisted on having framed for him.

This morning, feeling as if he'd surrendered too much of himself, he'd readjusted his presentation by wearing leather to the airport.

"This room is about the size of Dean Driblett's bathroom," Enid said. "Wouldn't you say, Al?"

Alfred rotated his bobbing hands and examined their dorsal sides.

"I'd never seen such an enormous bathroom."

"Enid, you have no tact," Alfred said.

It might have occurred to Chip that this, too, was a tactless remark, since it implied that his father concurred in his mother's criticism of the apartment and objected only to her airing of it. But Chip was unable to focus on anything but the hair dryer protruding from Julia's Dream-Works tote bag. It was the hair dryer that she kept in his bathroom. She seemed, actually, to be heading out the door.

"Dean and Trish have a whirlpool *and* a shower stall *and* a tub, all separate," Enid went on. "The sinks are his-and-hers."

"Chip, I'm sorry," Julia said.

He raised a hand to put her on hold. "We're going to have lunch here as soon as Denise comes," he announced to his parents. "It's a very simple lunch. Just make yourselves at home."

"It was nice to meet you both," Julia called to Enid and Alfred. To Chip in a lower voice she said, "Denise will be here. You'll be fine."

She opened the door.

"Mom, Dad," Chip said, "just one second."

He followed Julia out of the apartment and let the door fall shut behind him.

"This is really unfortunate timing," he said. "Just really, really unfortunate."

Julia shook her hair back off her temples. "I'm feeling good about the fact that it's the first time in my life I've ever acted self-interestedly in a relationship."

"That's nice. That's a big step." Chip made an effort to smile. "But what about the script? Is Eden reading it?"

"I think maybe this weekend sometime."

"What about you?"

"I read, um." Julia looked away. "Most of it."

"My idea," Chip said, "was to have this 'hump' that the moviegoer has to get over. Putting something offputting at the beginning, it's a classic modernist strategy. There's a lot of rich suspense toward the end."

Julia turned toward the elevator and didn't reply.

"*Did* you get to the end yet?" Chip asked.

"Oh, Chip," she burst out miserably, "your script starts off with a six-page lecture about anxieties of the phallus in Tudor drama!"

He was aware of this. Indeed, for weeks now, he'd been awakening most nights before dawn, his stomach churning and his teeth clenched, and had wrestled with the nightmarish certainty that a long academic monologue on Tudor drama had no place in Act I of a commercial script. Often it took him hours—took getting out of bed, pacing around, drinking Merlot or Pinot Grigio—to regain his conviction that a theory-driven opening monologue was not only not a mistake but the script's most powerful selling point; and now, with a single glance at Julia, he could see that he was wrong.

Nodding in heartfelt agreement with her criticism, he opened the door of his apartment and called to his parents, "One second, Mom, Dad. Just one second." As he shut the door again, however, the old arguments came back to him. "You see, though," he said, "the entire story is prefigured in that monologue. Every single theme is there in capsule form—gender, power, identity, authenticity—and the thing is . . . Wait. Wait. Julia?"

Bowing her head sheepishly, as though she'd somehow hoped he wouldn't notice she was leaving, Julia turned away from the elevator and back toward him.

"The thing is," he said, "the girl is sitting in the front row of the classroom *listening* to the lecture. It's a crucial image. The fact that *he* is controlling the discourse—"

"And it's a little creepy, though," Julia said, "the way you keep talking about her breasts."

This, too, was true. That it was true, however, seemed unfair and cruel to Chip, who would never have had the heart to write the script at all without the lure of imagining the breasts of his young female lead. "You're probably right," he said. "Although some of the physicality there is intentional. Because that's the irony, see, that she's attracted to his mind while he's attracted to her—"

"But for a woman reading it," Julia said obstinately, "it's sort of like the poultry department. Breast, breast, breast, thigh, leg."

"I can remove some of those references," Chip said in a low voice. "I can also shorten the opening lecture. The thing is, though, I want there to be a 'hump'—"

"Right, for the moviegoer to get over. That's a neat idea."

"Please come and have lunch. Please. Julia?"

The elevator door had opened at her touch.

"I'm saying it's a tiny bit insulting to a person somehow."

"But that's not you. It's not even based on you."

"Oh, great. It's somebody else's breasts."

"Jesus. Please. One second." Chip turned back to his apartment door and opened it, and this time he was startled to find himself face to face with his father. Alfred's big hands were shaking violently.

"Dad, hi, just another minute here."

"Chip," Alfred said, "ask her to stay! Tell her we want her to stay!"

Chip nodded and closed the door in the old man's face; but in the few seconds his back had been turned the elevator had swallowed Julia. He punched the call button, to no avail, and then opened the fire door and ran down the spiral of the service stairwell. *After a series of effulgent lectures celebrating the unfettered pursuit of pleasure as a strategy of subverting the bureaucracy of rationalism,* BILL QUAINTENCE, *an attractive young professor of Textual Artifacts, is seduced by his beautiful and adoring student* MONA. *Their wildly erotic affair has hardly begun, however, when they are discovered by Bill's estranged wife,* HILLAIRE. *In a tense confrontation representing the clash of Therapeutic and Transgressive worldviews, Bill and Hillaire struggle for the soul of young Mona, who lies naked between them on tangled sheets. Hillaire succeeds in seducing Mona with her crypto-repressive rhetoric, and Mona publicly denounces Bill. Bill loses his job but soon discovers e-mail records proving that Hillaire has given Mona money to ruin his career. As Bill is driving to see his lawyer with a diskette containing the incriminating evidence, his car is run off the road into the raging D—— River, and the diskette floats free of the sunken car and is borne by ceaseless, indomitable currents into the raging, erotic/chaotic open sea, and the crash is ruled vehicular suicide, and in the film's final scenes Hillaire is hired to replace Bill on the faculty and is seen lecturing on the evils of unfettered pleasure to a classroom in which is seated her diabolical lesbian lover Mona:* This was the one-page précis that Chip had assembled with the aid of store-bought screenwriting manuals and had faxed, one winter morning, to a Manhattan-based film producer named Eden Procuro. Five minutes later he'd answered his phone to the cool, blank voice of a young woman saying, "Please hold for Eden Procuro," followed by Eden Procuro herself crying, "I love it, love it, love it, love it, *love* it!" But now a year and a half had passed. Now the one-page précis had become a 124-page script called "The Academy Purple," and now Julia Vrais, the chocolate-haired owner of that cool, blank personal-assistant's voice, was running away from him, and as he raced downstairs to intercept her, planting his feet sideways to take the steps three and four at a time, grabbing the newel at each landing and reversing his trajectory with a jerk, all he could see or think of was a damning entry in his nearly photographic mental concordance of those 124 pages:

3: bee-stung lips, high round **breasts**, narrow hips and
3: over the cashmere sweater that snugly hugs her **breasts**
4: forward raptly, her perfect adolescent **breasts** eagerly
8: (eyeing her **breasts**)
9: (eyeing her **breasts**)

9:   (his eyes drawn helplessly to her perfect **breasts**)
11:   (eyeing her **breasts**)
12:   (mentally fondling her perfect **breasts**)
13:   (eyeing her **breasts**)
15:   (eyeing and eyeing her perfect adolescent **breasts**)
23:   (clinch, her perfect **breasts** surging against his
24:   the repressive bra to unfetter her subversive **breasts**.)
28:   to pinkly tongue one sweat-sheened **breast**.)
29:   phallically jutting nipple of her sweat-drenched **breast**
29:   I like your **breasts**.
30:   absolutely adore your honeyed, heavy **breasts**.
33:   (HILLAIRE's **breasts**, like twin Gestapo bullets, can be
36:   barbed glare as if to puncture and deflate her **breasts**
44:   Arcadian **breasts** with stern puritanical terry cloth and
45:   cowering, ashamed, the towel clutched to her **breasts**.)
76:   her guileless **breasts** shrouded now in militaristic
83:   I miss your body, I miss your perfect **breasts**, I
117:   drowned headlights fading like two milk-white **breasts**

And there were probably even more! More than he could remember! And the only two readers who mattered now were women! It seemed to Chip that Julia was leaving him because "The Academy Purple" had too many breast references and a draggy opening, and that if he could correct these few obvious problems, both on Julia's copy of the script and, more important, on the copy he'd specially laser-printed on 24-pound ivory bond paper for Eden Procuro, there might be hope not only for his finances but also for his chances of ever again unfettering and fondling Julia's own guileless, milk-white breasts. Which by this point in the day, as by late morning of almost every day in recent months, was one of the last activities on earth in which he could still reasonably expect to take solace for his failures.

Exiting the stairwell into the lobby, he found the elevator waiting to torment its next rider. Through the open street door he saw a taxi extinguish its roof light and pull away. Zoroaster was mopping up inblown water from the lobby's checkerboard marble. "Goodbye, Mister Chip!" he quipped, by no means for the first time, as Chip ran outside.

Big raindrops beating on the sidewalk raised a fresh, cold mist of pure humidity. Through the bead-curtain of water coming off the marquee, Chip saw Julia's cab brake for a yellow light. Directly across the street, another cab had stopped to discharge a passenger, and it occurred to Chip that he could take this other cab and ask the driver to follow Julia. The idea was tempting; but there were difficulties.

One difficulty was that by chasing Julia he would arguably be committing the worst of the offenses for which the general counsel of D—— College, in a shrill, moralistic lawyer's letter, had once upon a time threatened to countersue him or have him prosecuted. The alleged offenses had included fraud, breach of contract, kidnap, Title IX sexual harassment, serving liquor to a student under the legal drinking age, and possession and sale of a controlled substance; but it was the accusation of *stalking*—of making "obscene" and "threatening" and "abusive" telephone calls and trespassing with intent to violate a young woman's privacy—that had really scared Chip and scared him still.

A more immediate difficulty was that he had four dollars in his wallet, less than ten dollars in his checking account, no credit to speak of on any of his major credit cards, and no prospect of further proofreading work until Monday afternoon. Considering that the last time he'd seen Julia, six days ago, she'd specifically complained that he "always" wanted to stay home and eat pasta and "always" be kissing her and having sex (she'd said that sometimes she almost felt like he used sex as a kind of medication, and that maybe the reason he didn't just go ahead and self-medicate with crack or heroin instead was that sex was free and he was turning into such a cheapskate; she'd said that now that she was taking an actual prescription medication herself she sometimes felt like she was taking it for both of them and that this seemed doubly unfair, because she was the one who paid for the medication and because the medication made her slightly less interested in sex than she used to be; she'd said that, if it were up to Chip, they probably wouldn't even go to movies anymore but would spend the whole weekend wallowing in bed with the shades down and then reheating pasta), he suspected that the minimum price of further conversation with her would be an overpriced lunch of mesquite-grilled autumn vegetables and a bottle of Sancerre for which he had no conceivable way of paying.

And so he stood and did nothing as the corner traffic light turned green and Julia's cab drove out of sight. Rain was lashing the pavement in white, infected-looking drops. Across the street, a long-legged woman in tight jeans and excellent black boots had climbed out of the other cab.

That this woman was Chip's little sister, Denise—i.e., was the only attractive young woman on the planet whom he was neither permitted nor inclined to feast his eyes on and imagine having sex with—seemed to him just the latest unfairness in a long morning of unfairnesses.

Denise was carrying a black umbrella, a cone of flowers, and a pastry box tied with twine. She picked her way through the pools and rapids on the pavement and joined Chip beneath the marquee.

"Listen," Chip said with a nervous smile, not looking at her. "I need to ask you a big favor. I need you to hold the fort for me here while I find Eden and get my script back. There's a major, quick set of corrections I have to make."

As if he were a caddie or a servant, Denise handed him her umbrella and brushed water and grit from the ankles of her jeans. Denise had her mother's dark hair and pale complexion and her father's intimidating air of moral authority. She was the one who'd instructed Chip to invite his parents to stop and have lunch in New York today. She'd sounded like the World Bank dictating terms to a Latin debtor state, because, unfortunately, Chip owed her some money. He owed her whatever ten thousand and fifty-five hundred and four thousand and a thousand dollars added up to.

"See," he explained, "Eden wants to read the script this afternoon sometime, and financially, obviously, it's critical that we—"

"You can't leave now," Denise said.

"It'll take me an hour," Chip said. "An hour and a half at most."

"Is Julia here?"

"No, she left. She said hello and left."

"You broke up?"

"I don't know. She's gotten herself medicated and I don't even trust—"

"Wait a minute. Wait a minute. Are you wanting to go to Eden's, or chasing Julia?"

Chip touched the rivet in his left ear. "Ninety percent going to Eden's."

"Oh, Chip."

"No, but listen," he said, "she's using the word 'health' like it has some kind of absolute timeless meaning."

"This is Julia?"

"She takes pills for three months, the pills make her unbelievably obtuse, and the obtuseness then defines itself as mental health! It's like blindness defining itself as vision. 'Now that I'm blind, I can see there's nothing to see.' "

Denise sighed and let her cone of flowers droop to the sidewalk. "What are you saying? You want to follow her and take away her medicine?"

"I'm saying the structure of the entire culture is flawed," Chip said. "I'm saying the bureaucracy has arrogated the right to define certain states of mind as 'diseased.' A lack of desire to spend money becomes a symptom of disease that requires expensive medication. Which medication then destroys the libido, in other words destroys the appetite for the one pleasure in life that's free, which means the person has to spend even *more* money on compensatory pleasures. The very definition of mental 'health' is the ability to participate in the consumer economy. When you buy into therapy, you're buying into buying. And I'm saying that I personally am losing the battle with a commercialized, medicalized, totalitarian modernity right this instant."

Denise closed one eye and opened the other very wide. Her open eye was like nearly black balsamic vinegar beading on white china. "If I grant that these are interesting issues," she said, "will you stop talking about them and come upstairs with me?"

Chip shook his head. "There's a poached salmon in the fridge. A crème fraîche with sorrel. A salad with green beans and hazelnuts.

You'll see the wine and the baguette and the butter. It's good fresh butter from Vermont."

"Has it occurred to you that Dad is sick?"

"An hour is all it's going to take. Hour and a half at most."

"I said has it occurred to you that Dad is sick?"

Chip had a vision of his father trembling and pleading in the doorway. To block it out, he tried to summon up an image of sex with Julia, with the azure-haired stranger, with Ruthie, with anyone, but all he could picture was a vengeful, Fury-like horde of disembodied breasts.

"The faster I get to Eden's and make those corrections," he said, "the sooner I'll be back. If you really want to help me."

An available cab was coming down the street. He made the mistake of looking at it, and Denise misunderstood him.

"I can't give you any more money," she said.

He recoiled as if she'd spat on him. "Jesus, Denise—"

"I'd like to but I can't."

"I wasn't asking you for money!"

"Because where does it end?"

He turned on his heel and walked into the downpour and marched toward University Place, smiling with rage. He was ankle-deep in a boiling gray sidewalk-shaped lake. He was clutching Denise's umbrella in his fist without opening it, and still it seemed unfair to him, it seemed *not his fault*, that he was getting drenched.

Until recently, and without ever giving the matter much thought, Chip had believed that it was possible to be successful in America without making lots of money. He'd always been a good student, and from an early age he'd proved unfit for any form of economic activity except buying things (this he could do), and so he'd chosen to pursue a life of the mind.

Since Alfred had once mildly but unforgettably remarked that he didn't see the point of literary theory, and since Enid, in the florid biweekly letters by means of which she saved many dollars on long-distance dialing, had regularly begged Chip to abandon his pursuit of an "impractical" doctorate in the humanities ("I see your old science fair trophies," she wrote, "and I think of what an able young man like you could be giving back to society as a medical doctor, but then, you see, Dad and I always hoped we'd raised children who thought of others, not just themselves"), Chip had had plenty of incentives to work hard and prove his parents wrong. By getting out of bed much earlier than his grad-school classmates, who slept off their Gauloise hangovers until noon or one o'clock, he'd piled up the prizes and fellowships and grants that were the coin of the academic realm.

For the first fifteen years of his adult life, his only experience with failure had come secondhand. His girlfriend in college and long after, Tori Timmelman, was a feminist theorist who'd become so enraged with the patriarchal system of accreditation and its phallometric yardsticks of achievement that she refused (or was unable) to finish her dissertation. Chip had grown up listening to his father pontificate on the topics of Men's Work and Women's Work and the importance of maintaining the distinction; in a spirit of correction, he stuck with Tori for nearly a decade. He did all of the laundry and most of the cleaning and cooking and cat care in the little apartment that he and Tori shared. He read secondary literature for Tori and helped her outline and reoutline the chapters of her thesis that she was too throttled by rage to write. Not until D—— College had offered him a five-year tenure-track appointment (while Tori, still minus a degree, took a two-year nonrenewable job at an agriculture school in Texas) did he fully exhaust his supply of male guilt and move on.

He arrived at D——, then, as an eligible and well-published thirty-three-year-old to whom the college's provost, Jim Leviton, had all but guaranteed lifelong employment. Within a semester he was sleeping with the young historian Ruthie Hamilton and had teamed up at tennis with Leviton and brought Leviton the faculty doubles championship that had eluded him for twenty years.

D—— College, with an elite reputation and a middling endowment, depended for its survival on students whose parents could pay full tuition. To attract these students, the college had built a $30 million recreation center, three espresso bars, and a pair of hulking "residence halls" that were less like dorms than like vivid premonitions of the hotels in which the students would book rooms for themselves in their well-remunerated futures. There were herds of leather sofas and enough computers to ensure that no prospective matriculant or visiting parent could enter a room and not see at least one available keyboard, not even in the dining hall or field house.

Junior faculty lived in semi-squalor. Chip was lucky to have a two-story unit in a damp cinderblock development on Tilton Ledge Lane, on the western edge of campus. His back patio overlooked a waterway known to college administrators as Kuyper's Creek and to everybody else as Carparts Creek. On the far side of the creek was a marshy automotive boneyard belonging to the Connecticut State Department of Corrections. The college had been suing in state and federal courts for twenty years to preserve this wetland from the "ecodisaster" of drainage and development as a medium-security prison.

Every month or two, for as long as things were good with Ruthie, Chip invited colleagues and neighbors and the occasional precocious student to dinner at Tilton Ledge and surprised them with langoustines, or a rack of lamb, or venison with juniper berries, and retro joke desserts like chocolate fondue. Sometimes late at night, presiding over a table on which empty Californian bottles were clustered like Manhattan high-rises, Chip felt safe enough to laugh at himself, open up a little, and tell embarrassing stories about his midwestern childhood. Like how his father not only had worked long hours at the Midland Pacific Railroad and read aloud to his children and done the yard work and home maintenance and processed a nightly briefcaseful of executive paper but had also found time to operate a serious metallurgical laboratory in the family basement, staying up past midnight to subject strange alloys to electrical and chemical stresses. And how Chip at the age of thirteen had developed a crush on the buttery alkali metals that his father kept immersed in kerosene, on the blushing crystalline cobalt, the buxom heavy mercury, the ground-glass stopcocks and glacial acetic acid, and had put together his own junior lab in the shadow of his dad's. How his new interest in science had delighted Alfred and Enid, and how, with their encouragement, he'd set his young heart on winning a trophy at the regional St. Jude science fair. How, at the St. Jude city library, he'd unearthed a plant-physiology paper both obscure enough and simple enough to be mistaken for the work of a brilliant eighth-grader. How he'd built a controlled plywood environment for growing oats and had photographed the young seedlings meticulously and then ignored them for weeks, and how, by the time he went to weigh the seedlings and determine the effects of *gibberellic acid* in concert with an *unidentified chemical factor*, the oats were dried-out blackish slime. How he'd gone ahead anyway and plotted the experiment's "correct" results on graph paper, working backward to fabricate a list of seedling weights with some artful random scatter and then forward to make sure that the fictional data produced the "correct" results. And how, as a first-place winner at the science fair, he'd won a three-foot-tall silver-plated Winged Victory and the admiration of his father. And how, a year later, around the time his father was securing his first of two U.S. patents (despite his many grievances with Alfred, Chip was careful to impress on his dinner guests what a giant, in his own way, the old man was), Chip had pretended to study migratory bird populations in a park near some head shops and a bookstore and the house of a friend with foosball and a pool table. And how in a ravine at this park he'd uncovered a cache of downmarket porn over the weather-swollen pages of which, back home in the basement lab where, unlike his father, he never performed a real experiment or felt the faintest twinge of scientific curiosity, he'd endlessly dry-chafed the head of his erection without ever figuring out that this excruciating perpendicular stroke was actively suppressing orgasm (his dinner guests, many of them steeped in queer theory, took special delight in this detail), and how, as a reward for his mendacity and self-abuse and general laziness, he'd won a second Winged Victory.

In the haze of dinner-party smoke, as he entertained his sympathetic colleagues, Chip felt secure in the knowledge that his parents could not have been more wrong about who he was and what kind of career he was suited to pursue. For two and a half years, until the fiasco of Thanksgiving in St. Jude, he had no troubles at D—— College. But then Ruthie dumped him and a first-year female student rushed in, as it were, to fill the vacuum that Ruthie left behind.

Melissa Paquette was the most gifted student in the intro theory course, Consuming Narratives, that he taught in his third spring at D——. Melissa was a regal, theatrical person whom other students conspicuously avoided sitting close to, in part because they disliked her and in part because she always sat in the first row of desks, right in front of Chip. She was long-necked and broad-shouldered, not exactly beautiful, more like physically splendid. Her hair was very straight and had the cherry-wood color of new motor oil. She wore thrift-store clothes that tended not to flatter her—a man's plaid polyester leisure suit, a paisley trapeze dress, gray Mr. Goodwrench coveralls with the name *Randy* embroidered on the left front pocket.

Melissa had no patience with people she considered fools. At the second meeting of Consuming Narratives, when an affable dreadlocked boy named Chad (every class at D—— had at least one affable dreadlocked boy in it) took a stab at summarizing the theories of Thorstein "Webern," Melissa began to smirk at Chip complicitly. She rolled her eyes and mouthed the word "Veblen" and clutched her hair. Soon Chip was paying more attention to her distress than to Chad's discourse.

"Chad, sorry," she interrupted finally. "The name is Veblen?"

"Vebern. Veblern. That's what I'm saying."

"No, you were saying Webern. It's Veblen."

"Veblern. OK. Thank you very much, Melissa."

Melissa tossed her hair and faced Chip again, her mission accomplished. She paid no attention to the dirty looks that came her way from Chad's friends and sympathizers. But Chip drifted to a far corner of the classroom to dissociate himself from her, and he encouraged Chad to continue with his summary.

That evening, outside the student cinema in Hillard Wroth Hall, Melissa came pushing and squeezing through a crowd and told Chip that she was loving Walter Benjamin. She stood, he thought, too close to him. She stood too close to him at a reception for Marjorie Garber a few days later. She came galloping across the Lucent Technologies Lawn (formerly the South Lawn) to press into his hands one of the weekly short papers that Consuming Narratives required. She materialized beside him in a parking lot that a foot of snow had buried, and with her mittened hands and considerable wingspan she helped him dig out his car. She kicked a path clear with her fur-trimmed boots. She wouldn't stop chipping at the underlayer of ice on his windshield until he took hold of her wrist and removed the scraper from her hand.

Chip had co-chaired the committee that drafted the college's stringent new policy on faculty-student contacts. Nothing in the policy prevented a student from helping a professor clear snow off his car; and since he was also sure of his self-discipline, he had nothing to be afraid of. And yet, before long, he was ducking out of sight whenever he saw Melissa on campus. He didn't want her to gallop over and stand too close to him. And when he caught himself wondering if the color of her hair was from a bottle, he made himself stop wondering. He never asked her if she was the one who'd left roses outside his office door on Valentine's Day, or the chocolate statuette of Michael Jackson on Easter weekend.

In class he called on Melissa slightly less often than he called on other students; he lavished particular attention on her nemesis, Chad. He sensed, without looking, that Melissa was nodding in comprehension and solidarity when he unpacked a difficult passage of Marcuse or Baudrillard. She generally ignored her classmates, except to turn on them in sudden hot disagreement or cool correction; her classmates, for their part, yawned audibly when she raised her hand.

One warm Friday night near the end of the semester, Chip came home from his weekly grocery run and discovered that someone had vandalized his front door. Three of the four utility lights at Tilton Ledge had burned out, and the college was apparently waiting for the fourth to burn out before investing in replacements. In the poor light, Chip could see that somebody had poked flowers and foliage—tulips, ivy—through the holes in his rotting screen door. "What is this?" he said. "Melissa, you are jailbait."

Possibly he said other things before he realized that his stoop was strewn with torn-up tulips and ivy, a vandalism still in progress, and that he was not alone. The holly bush by his door had produced two giggling young people. "Sorry, sorry!" Melissa said. "You were talking to yourself!"

Chip wanted to believe she hadn't heard what he said, but the holly wasn't three feet away. He set the groceries inside his house and turned a light on. Standing beside Melissa was the dreadlocked Chad.

"Professor Lambert, hello," Chad said earnestly. He was wearing Melissa's Mr. Goodwrench coveralls, and Melissa was wearing a *Free Mumia* T-shirt that might have belonged to Chad. She'd slung an arm around Chad's neck and fitted a hip over his. She was flushed and sweaty and lit up on something.

"We were decorating your door," she said.

"Actually, Melissa, it looks pretty horrible," Chad said as he examined it in the light. Beat-up tulips were hanging down at every angle. The ivy runners had clods of dirt in their hairy feet. "Kind of a stretch to say 'decorating.' "

"Well, you can't *see* down here," she said. "Where's the *light?*"

"There is no light," Chip said. "This is the Ghetto in the Woods. This is where your teachers live."

"Dude, that ivy is pathetic."

"Whose tulips are these?" Chip asked.

"College tulips," Melissa said.

"Dude, I'm not even sure why we were doing this." Chad turned to allow Melissa to put her mouth on his nose and suck it, which didn't seem to bother him, although he drew his head back. "Wouldn't you say this was sort of more your idea than mine?"

"Our tuition pays for these tulips," Melissa said, pivoting to press her body more frontally into Chad. She hadn't looked at Chip since he turned the outdoor light on.

"So then Hansel and Gretel came and found my screen door."

"We'll clean it up," Chad said.

"Leave it," Chip said. "I'll see you on Tuesday." And he went inside and shut the door and played some angry music from his college years.

For the last meeting of Consuming Narratives the weather turned hot. The sun was blazing in a pollen-filled sky, all the angiosperms in the newly rechristened Viacom Arboretum blooming hard. To Chip the air felt disagreeably intimate, like a warm spot in a swimming pool. He'd already cued up the video player and lowered the classroom shades when Melissa and Chad strolled in and took seats in a rear corner. Chip reminded the class to sit up straight like active critics rather than be passive consumers, and the students sat up enough to acknowledge his request without actually complying with it. Melissa, usually the one fully upright critic, today slumped especially low and draped an arm across Chad's legs.

To test his students' mastery of the critical perspectives to which he'd introduced them, Chip was showing a video of a six-part ad campaign called "You Go, Girl." The campaign was the work of an agency, Beat Psychology, that had also created "Howl with Rage" for G—— Electric, "Do Me Dirty" for C—— Jeans, "Total F***ing Anarchy!" for the W—— Network, "Radical Psychedelic Underground" for E—— .com, and "Love & Work" for M—— Pharmaceuticals. "You Go, Girl" had had its first airing the previous fall, one episode per week, on a prime-time hospital drama. The style was black-and-white cinema verité; the content, according to analyses in the *Times* and the *Wall Street Journal*, was "revolutionary."

The plot was this: Four women in a small office—one sweet young African American, one middle-aged technophobic blonde, one tough and savvy beauty named Chelsea, and one radiantly benignant gray-haired Boss—dish together and banter together and, by and by, struggle together with Chelsea's stunning announcement, at the end of Episode 2, that for nearly a year she's had a lump in her breast that she's too scared to see a doctor about. In Episode 3 the Boss and the sweet young African American dazzle the technophobic blonde by using the W—— Corporation's Global Desktop Version 5.0 to get up-to-the-minute cancer information and to hook Chelsea into support networks and the very best local health care providers. The blonde, who is fast learning to love technology, marvels but objects: "There's no way Chelsea can afford all this." To which the angelic Boss replies: "I'm paying every cent of it." By the middle of Episode 5, however—and this was the campaign's revolutionary inspiration—it's clear that Chelsea will not survive her breast cancer. Tear-jerking scenes of brave jokes and tight hugs follow. In the final episode the action returns to the office, where the Boss is scanning a snapshot of the departed Chelsea, and the now rabidly technophiliac blonde is expertly utilizing the W—— Corporation's

Global Desktop Version 5.0, and around the world, in rapid montage, women of all ages and races are smiling and dabbing away tears at the image of Chelsea on their own Global Desktops. Spectral Chelsea in a digital video clip pleads: "Help us Fight for the Cure." The episode ends with the information, offered in a sober typeface, that the W——Corporation has given more than $10,000,000.00 to the American Cancer Society to help it Fight for the Cure . . .

The slick production values of a campaign like "You Go, Girl" could seduce first-year students before they'd acquired the critical tools of resistance and analysis. Chip was curious, and somewhat afraid, to see how far his students had progressed. With the exception of Melissa, whose papers were written with force and clarity, none of them had persuaded him that they were doing more than parroting the weekly jargon. Each year, it seemed, the incoming freshmen were a little more resistant to hardcore theory than they'd been the year before. Each year the moment of enlightenment, of critical mass, came a little later. Now the end of a semester was at hand, and Chip still wasn't sure that anyone besides Melissa really *got* how to criticize mass culture.

The weather wasn't doing him any favors. He raised the shades and beach light poured into the classroom. Summerlust came wafting off the bared arms and legs of boys and girls alike.

A petite young woman named Hilton, a chihuahua-like person, offered that it was "brave" and "really interesting" that Chelsea had died of cancer instead of surviving like you might have expected in a commercial.

Chip waited for someone to observe that it was precisely this self-consciously "revolutionary" plot twist that had generated publicity for the ad. Normally Melissa, from her seat in the front row, could be counted on to make a point like this. But today she was sitting by Chad with her cheek on her desk. Normally, when students napped in class, Chip called on them immediately. But today he was reluctant to say Melissa's name. He was afraid that his voice might shake.

Finally, with a tight smile, he said, "In case any of you were visiting a different planet last fall, let's review what happened with these ads. Remember that Nielsen Media Research took the 'revolutionary' step of giving Episode Six its own weekly rating. The first rating ever given to an ad. And once Nielsen rated it, the campaign was all but guaranteed an enormous audience for its rebroadcast during the November sweeps. Also remember that the Nielsen rating followed a week of print and broadcast news coverage of the 'revolutionary' plot twist of Chelsea's death, plus the Internet rumor about Chelsea's being a real person who'd really died. Which, incredibly, several hundred thousand people actually believed. Beat Psychology, remember, having fabricated her medical records and her personal history and posted them on the Web. So my question for Hilton would be, how 'brave' is it to engineer a surefire publicity coup for your ad campaign?"

"It was still a risk," Hilton said. "I mean, death is a downer. It could have backfired."

Again Chip waited for someone, anyone, to take his side of the argument. No one did. "So a wholly cynical strategy," he said, "if there's a financial risk attached, becomes an act of artistic bravery?"

A brigade of college lawn mowers descended on the lawn outside the classroom, smothering discussion in a blanket of noise. The sunshine was bright.

Chip soldiered on. Did it seem realistic that a small-business owner would spend her own money on special health care options for an employee?

One student averred that the boss she'd had at her last summer job had been generous and totally great.

Chad was silently fighting off the tickling hand of Melissa while, with his free hand, he counterattacked the naked skin of her midriff.

"Chad?" Chip said.

Chad, impressively, was able to answer the question without having it repeated. "Like, that was just one office," he said. "Maybe another boss wouldn't have been so great. But that boss *was* great. I mean, nobody's pretending that's an average office, right?"

Here Chip tried to raise the question of art's responsibilities vis-à-vis the Typical; but this discussion, too, was DOA.

"So, bottom line," he said, "we like this campaign. We think these ads are good for the culture and good for the country. Yes?"

There were shrugs and nods in the sun-heated room.

"Melissa," Chip said. "We haven't heard from you."

Melissa raised her head from her desk, shifted her attention from Chad, and looked at Chip with narrowed eyes. "Yes," she said.

"Yes what?"

"Yes, these ads are good for the culture and good for the country."

Chip took a deep breath, because this hurt. "Great, OK," he said. "Thank you for your opinion."

"As if you care about my opinion," Melissa said.

"I beg your pardon?"

"As if you care about any of our opinions unless they're the same as yours."

"This is not about opinions," Chip said. "This is about learning to apply critical methods to textual artifacts. Which is what I'm here to teach you."

"I don't think it is, though," Melissa said. "I think you're here to teach us to hate the same things you hate. I mean, you hate these ads, right? I can hear it in every word you say. You totally hate them."

The other students were listening raptly now. Melissa's connection with Chad might have depressed Chad's stock more than it had raised her own, but she was attacking Chip like an angry equal, not a student, and the class ate it up.

"I do hate these ads," Chip admitted. "But that's not—"

"Yes it is," Melissa said.

"Why do you hate them?" Chad called out.

"Tell us why you hate them," the little Hilton yipped.

Chip looked at the wall clock. There were six minutes left of the semester. He pushed a hand through his hair and cast his eyes around the room as if he might find an ally somewhere, but the students had him on the run now, and they knew it.

"The W—— Corporation," he said, "is currently defending three separate lawsuits for antitrust violations. Its revenues last year exceeded the gross domestic product of Italy. And now, to wring dollars out of the one demographic that it doesn't yet dominate, it's running a campaign that exploits a woman's fear of breast cancer and her sympathy with its victims. Yes, Melissa?"

"It's not cynical."

"What is it, if not cynical?"

"It's celebrating women in the workplace," Melissa said. "It's raising money for cancer research. It's encouraging us to do our self-examinations and get the help we need. It's helping women feel like we own this technology, like it's not just a guy thing."

"OK, good," Chip said. "But the question is not whether we care about breast cancer, it's what breast cancer has to do with selling office equipment."

Chad took up the cudgels for Melissa. "That's the whole point of the ad, though. That if you have access to information, it can save your life."

"So if Pizza Hut puts a little sign about testicular self-exams by the hot-pepper flakes, it can advertise itself as part of the glorious and courageous fight against cancer?"

"Why not?" Chad said.

"Does *anybody* see anything wrong with that?"

Not one student did. Melissa was slouching with her arms crossed and unhappy amusement on her face. Unfairly or not, Chip felt as if she'd destroyed in five minutes a semester's worth of careful teaching.

"Well, consider," he said, "that 'You Go, Girl' would not have been produced if W—— had not had a product to sell. And consider that the goal of the people who work at W—— is to exercise their stock options and retire at thirty-two, and that the goal of the people who own W—— stock" (Chip's brother and sister-in-law, Gary and Caroline, owned a great deal of W—— stock) "is to build bigger houses and buy bigger SUVs and consume even more of the world's finite resources."

"What's wrong with making a living?" Melissa said. "Why is it *inherently* evil to make money?"

"Baudrillard might argue," Chip said, "that the evil of a campaign like 'You Go, Girl' consists in the detachment of the signifier from the signified. That a woman weeping no longer just signifies sadness. It now also signifies: 'Desire office equipment.' It signifies: 'Our bosses care about us deeply.' "

The wall clock showed two-thirty. Chip paused and waited for the bell to ring and the semester to end.

"Excuse me," Melissa said, "but that is just such bullshit."

"What is bullshit?" Chip said.

"This whole class," she said. "It's just bullshit every week. It's one critic after another wringing their hands about the state of criticism. Nobody can ever quite say what's wrong exactly. But they all know it's evil. They all know 'corporate' is a dirty word. And if somebody's having fun or getting rich—disgusting! Evil! And it's always the death of this and the death of that. And people who think they're free aren't 'really' free. And people who think they're happy aren't 'really' happy. And it's impossible to radically critique society anymore, although what's so radically wrong with society that we need such a radical critique, nobody can say exactly. *It is so typical and perfect that you hate those ads!*" she said to Chip as, throughout Wroth Hall, bells finally rang. "Here things are getting better and better for women and people of color, and gay men and lesbians, more and more integrated and open, and all you can think about is some stupid, lame problem with signifiers and signifieds. Like, the only way you can make something bad out of an ad that's great for women—which you have to do, because there has to be something wrong with everything—is to say it's evil to be rich and evil to work for a corporation, and yes, I know the bell rang." She closed her notebook.

"OK," Chip said. "On that note. You've now satisfied your Cultural Studies core requirement. Have a great summer."

He was powerless to keep the bitterness out of his voice. He bent over the video player and gave his attention to rewinding and re-cuing "You Go, Girl" and touching buttons for the sake of touching buttons. He sensed a few students lingering behind him, as if they wanted to thank him for teaching his heart out or to tell him they'd enjoyed the class, but he didn't look up from the video player until the room was empty. Then he went home to Tilton Ledge and started drinking.

Melissa's accusations had cut him to the quick. He'd never quite realized how seriously he'd taken his father's injunction to do work that was "useful" to society. Criticizing a sick culture, even if the criticism accomplished nothing, had always felt like useful work. But if the supposed sickness wasn't a sickness at all—if the great Materialist Order of technology and consumer appetite and medical science really *was* improving the lives of the formerly oppressed; if it was only straight white males like Chip who had a problem with this order—then there was no longer even the most abstract utility to his criticism. It was all, in Melissa's word, bullshit.

Lacking the spirit to work on his new book, as he'd planned to do all summer, Chip bought an overpriced ticket to London and hitchhiked to Edinburgh and overstayed his welcome with a Scottish performance artist who had lectured and performed at D—— the previous winter. Eventually the woman's boyfriend said, "Time to be off now, laddie," and Chip hit the road with a backpack full of Heidegger and Wittgenstein that he was too lonely to read. He hated to think of himself as a man who couldn't live without a woman, but he hadn't been laid since Ruthie dumped him. He was the only male professor in D—— history to have taught Theory of Feminism, and he understood how important it was for women not to equate "success" with "having a man" and "failure" with "lacking a man," but he was a lonely straight male, and a lonely straight male had no equivalently forgiving Theory of Masculinism to help him out of this bind, this key to all misogynies:

¶ To feel as if he couldn't survive without a woman made a man feel weak;

¶ And yet, without a woman in his life, a man lost the sense of agency and difference that, for better or worse, was the foundation of his manhood.

On many a morning, in green Scottish places splashed with rain, Chip felt close to escaping this spurious bind and regaining a sense of self and purpose, only to find himself at four in the afternoon drinking beer at a train station, eating chips and mayonnaise, and hitting on Yankee college girls. As a seducer, he was hampered by ambivalence and by his lack of the Glaswegian accent that made American girls go weak in the knees. He scored exactly once, with a young hippie from Oregon who had ketchup stains on her chemise and a scalpy smell so overpowering that he spent much of the night breathing through his mouth.

His failures seemed more funny than squalid, though, when he came home to Connecticut and regaled his misfit friends with stories at his own expense. He wondered if somehow his Scottish depression had been the product of a greasy diet. His stomach heaved when he remembered the glistening wedges of browned whateverfish, the glaucous arcs of lipidy chips, the smell of scalp and deep-fry, or even just the words "Firth of Forth."

At the weekly farmers' market near D—— he loaded up on heirloom tomatoes, white eggplants, and thin-skinned golden plums. He ate arugula ("rocket," the old farmers called it) so strong it made his eyes water, like a paragraph of Thoreau. As he remembered the Good and the Healthful, he began to recover his self-discipline. He weaned himself off alcohol, got better sleep, drank less coffee, and went to the college gym twice a week. He read the damned Heidegger and did his crunches every morning. Other pieces of the self-improvement puzzle fell into place, and for a while, as cool working weather returned to the Carparts Creek valley, he experienced an almost Thoreauvian well-being. Between sets on the tennis court, Jim Leviton assured him that his tenure review would be a mere formality—that he shouldn't worry about competing with the department's other young theorist, Vendla O'Fallon. Chip's fall course load consisted of Renaissance Poetry and Shakespeare, neither of which required him to rethink his critical perspectives. As he girded himself for the last stage of his ascent of Mount Tenure, he was relieved to be traveling light; almost happy, after all, not to have a woman in his life.

He was at home on a Friday in September, making himself a dinner of broccoli rabe and acorn squash and fresh haddock and looking forward to a night of grading papers, when a pair of legs sashayed past his kitchen window. He knew this sashay. He knew the way Melissa walked. She couldn't pass a picket fence without trailing her fingertips against it.

She stopped in hallways to do dance steps or hopscotch. She went backwards or sideways, or skipped, or loped.

Her knock on his screen door was not apologetic. Through the screen he saw that she had a plate of cupcakes with pink frosting.

"Yeah, what's up?" he said.

Melissa raised the plate on upturned palms. "Cupcakes," she said. "Thought you might be needing some cupcakes in your life right around now."

Not being theatrical, Chip felt disadvantaged around people who were. "Why are you bringing me cupcakes?" he said.

Melissa knelt and set the plate on his doormat among the pulverized remains of ivy and dead tulips. "I'll just leave them here," she said, "and you can do whatever you want with them. Goodbye!" She spread her arms and pirouetted off the doorstep and ran up the flagstone path on tiptoe.

Chip went back to wrestling with the haddock filet, through the center of which ran a blood-brown fault of gristle that he was determined to cut out. But the fish had a starchy grain and was hard to get a grip on. "Fuck you, little girl," he said as he threw the knife into the sink.

The cupcakes were full of butter and frosted with a butter frosting. After he'd washed his hands and opened a bottle of Chardonnay he ate four of them and put the uncooked fish in the refrigerator. The skins of the overbaked squash were like inner-tube rubber. *Cent Ans de Cinéma Erotique*, an edifying video that had sat on a shelf for months without making a peep, suddenly demanded his immediate and full attention. He lowered the blinds and drank the wine, and brought himself off again and again, and ate two more cupcakes, detecting peppermint in them, a faint buttery peppermint, before he slept.

The next morning he was up at seven and did four hundred crunches. He immersed *Cent Ans de Cinéma Erotique* in dishwater and rendered it, so to speak, non-combustible. (He'd done this with many a pack of cigarettes while kicking the habit.) He had no idea what he'd meant when he'd thrown the knife into the sink. His voice had sounded nothing like him.

He went to his office in Wroth Hall and graded papers. He wrote in a margin: *Cressida's character may inform Toyota's choice of product name; that Toyota's Cressida informs the Shakespearean text requires more argument than you present here.* He added an exclamation point to soften his criticism. Sometimes, when ripping apart especially feeble student work, he drew smiley faces.

Spell-check! he exhorted a student who'd written "Trolius" for "Troilus" throughout her eight-page paper.

And the ever-softening question mark. Beside the sentence "Here Shakespeare proves Foucault all too right about the historicity of morals," Chip wrote: *Rephrase? Perhaps: "Here the Shakespearean text seems almost to anticipate Foucault (better: Nietzsche?) . . ."?*

He was still grading papers five weeks later, ten or fifteen thousand student errors later, on a windy night just after Halloween, when he heard a scrabbling outside his office door. Opening the door, he found a dime-store trick-or-treat bag hanging from the hall-side doorknob. The leaver of this gift, Melissa Paquette, was backpedaling up the hall.

"What are you doing?" he said.

"Just trying to be friends," she said.

"Well, thanks," he said. "I don't get it."

Melissa came back down the hall. She was wearing white painter's overalls, a long-sleeve thermal undershirt, and hot-pink socks. "I went trick-or-treating," she said. "This was like one-fifth of my haul."

She stepped closer to Chip and he backed away. She followed him into his office and circled it on tiptoe, reading titles on his shelves. Chip leaned against his desk and folded his arms tightly.

"So I'm taking Theory of Feminism with Vendla," Melissa said.

"That would be the logical next step. Now that you've rejected the nostalgic patriarchal tradition of critical theory."

"Exactly my thinking," Melissa said. "Unfortunately, her class is so *bad*. People who took it with you last year said it was great. But Vendla's idea is that we should sit around and talk about our feelings. Because the Old Theory was about the head, see. And therefore the New True Theory has to be about the heart. I'm not convinced she's even read all the stuff she assigns us."

Through his open door Chip could see the door of Vendla O'Fallon's office. It was papered with healthful images and adages—Betty Friedan in 1965, beaming Guatemalan peasant women, a triumphant female soccer star, a Bass Ale poster of Virginia Woolf, SUBVERT THE DOMINANT PARADIGM—that reminded him, in a dreary way, of his old girlfriend Tori Timmelman. His feeling about decorating doors was: What are we, high-school kids? Are these our bedrooms?

"So basically," he said, "even though you thought my class was bullshit, it now seems like a superior brand of bullshit because you're taking hers."

Melissa blushed. "Basically! Except you're a much better teacher. I mean, I learned a ton from you. That's what I wanted to tell you."

"Consider me told."

"See, my mom and dad split up in April." Melissa flung herself down on Chip's college-issue leather sofa and assumed the full therapeutic position. "For a while it was kind of great that you were being so anti-corporate, and then suddenly it really, really irritated me. Like, my parents have a lot of money, and they're not evil people, although my dad did just move in with this character named Vicki who's like four years older than me. But he still loves my mom. I know he does. As soon as I was out of the house, things deteriorated a little, but I know he still loves her."

"The college has a lot of services," Chip said, arms folded, "for students going through these things."

"Thanks. On the whole I'm doing brilliantly, except for having been rude to you in class that time." Melissa hooked her heels on the arm of the sofa, pried her shoes off, and let them drop to the floor. Soft curves in thermal knitwear spilled out to either side of her overalls' bib, Chip noticed.

"I had an excellent childhood," she said. "My parents have always been my best friends. They homeschooled me till seventh grade. My mom was in med school in New Haven and my dad had this punk band, the Nomatics, that was touring, and at my mom's first ever punk show she went out with my dad and ended up in his hotel room. She quit school, he quit the Nomatics, and they were never apart after that. Totally romantic. See, and my dad had some money from a trust fund, and it was really brilliant what they did then. There were all these new IPOs, and my mom was up on all the biotech and reading *JAMA*, and Tom—my dad—could vet the numbers part of it, and they just made really great investments. Clair—my mom—stayed home with me and we hung out all day, you know, and I learned my times tables, et cetera, and it was always just the three of us. They were so, so in love. And parties every weekend. And finally it occurred to us, we *know* everybody, and we're really good *investors*, so why not start a mutual fund? Which we did. And it was incredible. It's still a great fund. It's called the Westportfolio Biofund Forty? We started some other funds, too, when the climate got more competitive. You kind of have to offer a full array of services. That's what the institutional investors were telling Tom, at any rate. So he started these other funds, which unfortunately have pretty much tanked. I think that's the big problem between him and Clair. Because her fund, the Biofund Forty, where *she* makes the picks, is still doing great. And now she's heartbroken and depressed. She's holed up in our house and she never goes out. Meanwhile Tom wants me to meet this Vicki person, who he says is 'lots of fun' and a roller blader. The thing is, we all know my mom and dad are *made* for each other. They complement each other perfectly. And I just think if you knew how cool it is to start a company, and how great it is when the money starts coming in, and how romantic it can be, you wouldn't be so harsh."

"Possibly," Chip said.

"Anyway, I thought you'd be somebody I could talk to. On the whole I'm coping brilliantly, but I could kind of use a friend."

"How's Chad?" Chip said.

"A sweet boy. Good for about three weekends." Melissa swung a leg off the sofa and planted a stockinged foot on Chip's leg, close to his hip. "It's hard to imagine two people less long-term compatible than him and me."

Through his jeans Chip could feel the deliberate flexing of her toes. He was trapped against his desk, and so, to escape, he had to take hold of her ankle and swing her leg back onto the sofa. Her pink feet immediately grasped his wrist and pulled him toward her. It was all very playful, but his door was open, and his lights were on, and his blinds were raised, and somebody was in the hall. "Code," he said, pulling free. "There's a code."

Melissa rolled off the sofa, stood up, and came closer. "It's a stupid code," she said. "If you care about somebody."

Chip retreated to the doorway. Up the hall, by the department office, a tiny blue-uniformed woman with a Toltec face was vacuuming. "There are good reasons to have it," he said.

"So I can't even give you a hug now."

"That's right."

"It's stupid." Melissa stepped into her shoes and joined Chip in the doorway. She kissed him on the cheek, near his ear. "So there."

He watched her slide-step and pirouette down the hall and out of sight. He heard a fire door bang shut. He carefully examined every word he'd said, and he gave himself an A for correctness. But when he returned to Tilton Ledge, where the last of the utility lights had burned out, he was swamped by loneliness. To erase the tactile memory of Melissa's kiss, and her lively warm feet, he phoned an old college friend in New York and made a date for lunch the next day. He took *Cent Ans de Cinéma Erotique* from the cabinet where, in expectation of a night like this, he'd stashed it after soaking it. The tape was still playable. The image was snowy, though, and during the first really hot bit, a hotel-room scene with a wanton chambermaid, the snow thickened to a blizzard and the screen went blue. The VCR made a dry, thin choking sound. *Air, need air*, it seemed to say. Tape had leaked out and wound itself around the machine's endoskeleton. Chip extracted the cassette and several handfuls of Mylar, but then something broke and the machine spat up a plastic spool. Which, all right, these things happened. But the trip to Scotland had been a financial Waterloo, and he couldn't afford a new VCR.

Nor was New York City, on a cold rainy Saturday, the treat he needed. Every sidewalk in lower Manhattan was dotted with the metallic squared spirals of antitheft badges. The badges were bonded to the wet pavement with the world's strongest glue, and after Chip had bought some imported cheeses (he did this every time he visited New

York to be sure of accomplishing at least one thing before returning to Connecticut, and yet it felt a little sad to buy the same baby Gruyère and Fourme d'Ambert at the same store; it brought him up against the more general failure of consumerism as an approach to human happiness), and after he'd lunched with his college friend (who had recently quit teaching anthropology and hired himself out to Silicon Alley as a "marketing psychologist" and who advised Chip, now, to wake up and do the same), he returned to his car and discovered that each of his plastic-wrapped cheeses was protected by its own antitheft badge and that, indeed, a fragment of antitheft badge had stuck to the bottom of his left shoe.

Tilton Ledge was glazed with ice and very dark. In the mail Chip found an envelope containing a short note from Enid lamenting Alfred's moral failures ("he sits in that chair *all day, every day*") and a lengthy profile of Denise, clipped from *Philadelphia* magazine, with a slavering review of her restaurant, Mare Scuro, and a full-page glamour photo of the young chef. Denise in the photo was wearing jeans and a tank top and was all muscled shoulders and satiny pecs ("Very young and very good: Lambert in her kitchen," the caption read), and this was just the kind of girl-as-object horseshit, Chip thought bitterly, that sold magazines. A few years ago Enid's letters had reliably contained a paragraph of despair about Denise and Denise's failing marriage, with phrases like *he is too OLD for her!* double-underlined, and a paragraph festooned with *thrilled*s and *proud*s apropos of Chip's hiring by D—— College, and although he knew that Enid was skilled at playing her children off against each other and that her praise was usually double-edged, he was dismayed that a woman as smart and principled as Denise had used her body for marketing purposes. He threw the clipping in the trash. He opened the Saturday half of the Sunday *Times* and—yes, he was contradicting himself, yes, he was aware of this—paged through the Magazine in search of ads for lingerie or swimwear to rest his weary eyes on. Finding none, he began to read the Book Review, where a memoir called *Daddy's Girl*, by Vendla O'Fallon, was declared "astonishing" and "courageous" and "deeply satisfying" on page 11. The name Vendla O'Fallon was rather unusual, but Chip had been so completely unaware that Vendla was publishing a book that he refused to believe she'd written *Daddy's Girl* until, near the end of the review, he encountered a sentence that began: "O'Fallon, who teaches at D—— College . . ."

He closed the Book Review and opened a bottle.

In theory both he and Vendla were in line for tenure in Textual Artifacts, but in practice the department was already overtenured. That Vendla commuted to work from New York (thus flouting the college's informal requirement that faculty live in town), and that she skipped important meetings and taught every gut she could, had been steady sources of comfort to Chip. He still had the edge in scholarly publications, student evaluations, and support from Jim Leviton; but he found that two glasses of wine had no effect on him.

He was pouring himself his fourth when his telephone rang. It was Jim Leviton's wife, Jackie. "I just wanted you to know," Jackie said, "that Jim's going to be OK."

"Was something wrong?" Chip said.

"Well, he's resting fine. We're over at St. Mary's."

"What happened?"

"Chip, I asked him if he thought he could play tennis, and do you know what? He nodded! I said I was going to call you, and he nodded, yes, he was good for tennis. His motor skills appear to be fully normal. Fully—normal. And he's lucid, that is the important thing. That is the really good news here, Chip. His eyes are bright. He's the same old Jim."

"Jackie, did he have a stroke?"

"There'll be some rehabilitation," Jackie said. "Obviously today will be his effective retirement date, which, Chip, as far as I'm concerned, is an absolute blessing. We can make some changes now, and in three years—well, it's not going to take any three years for him to rehabilitate. When all is said and done, we're going to be ahead of this game. His eyes are so bright, Chip. He's the same old Jim!"

Chip rested his forehead against his kitchen window and turned his head so that he could open one eye directly against the cold, damp glass. He knew what he was going to do.

"The same old lovable Jim!" Jackie said.

The following Thursday, Chip made dinner for Melissa and had sex with her on his red chaise longue. He'd taken a fancy to the chaise back in the days when dropping eight hundred dollars on an antique-store impulse was somewhat less suicidal financially. The chaise's backrest was angled in erotic invitation, its padded shoulders thrown back, its spine arching; the plush of its chest and belly looked ready to burst the fabric buttons that crisscrossed it. Breaking his initial clinch with Melissa, Chip excused himself for one second to turn off lights in the kitchen and stop in the bathroom. When he returned to the living room, he found her stretched out on the chaise wearing only the pants half of her plaid polyester leisure suit. In the dim light she could have been a hairless, heavy-titted man. Chip, who much preferred queer theory to queer practice, basically hated the suit and wished she hadn't worn it. Even after she'd taken off the pants there was a residue of gender confusion on her body, not to mention the rank b.o. that was the bane of synthetic fabrics. But from her underpants, which to his relief were delicate and sheer—distinctly gendered—an affectionate warm rabbit came springing, a kicking wet autonomous warm animal. It was almost more than he could handle. He hadn't slept two hours in the previous two nights, and he had a head full of wine and a gut full of gas (he couldn't remember why he'd made a cassoulet for dinner; possibly for no good reason), and he worried that he hadn't locked the front door—that there was a gap in the blinds somewhere, that one of his neighbors would drop by and try the door and find it unlocked or peer in through the window and see him flagrantly violating Sections I, II, and VI of a code that he himself had helped draft. Altogether for him it was a night of anxiety and effortful concentration, punctuated by little stabs of throttled pleasure, but at least Melissa seemed to find it exciting and romantic. Hour after hour, she wore a big crinkled U of a smile.

It was Chip's proposal, after a second extremely stressful tryst at Tilton Ledge, that he and Melissa leave campus for the week-long Thanksgiving break and find a cottage on Cape Cod where they wouldn't feel observed and judged; and it was Melissa's proposal, as they departed through D——'s little-used eastern gate under cover of darkness, that they stop in Middletown and buy drugs from a high-school friend of hers at Wesleyan. Chip waited in front of Wesleyan's impressively weatherproofed Ecology House and drummed on the steering wheel of his Nissan, drummed so hard his fingers throbbed, because it was important not to think about what he was doing. He'd left behind mountains of ungraded papers and exams, and he had not yet managed to visit Jim Leviton in the rehab unit. That Jim had lost his powers of speech and now impotently strained his jaw and lips to form words— that he'd become, according to reports from colleagues who'd visited him, an angry man—made Chip all the more reluctant to visit. He was in the mode now of avoiding anything that might make him experience an emotion. He beat on the steering wheel until his fingers were stiff and burning and Melissa came out of the Ecology House. She brought into the car a smell of woodsmoke and frozen flower beds, the smell of an affair in late autumn. She put into Chip's palm a golden caplet marked with what appeared to be the old Midland Pacific Railroad logo—

without the text. "Take this," she told him, closing the door.

"This is? Some kind of Ecstasy?"

"No. Mexican A."

Chip felt culturally anxious. Not long ago, there had been no drugs he hadn't heard of. "What does it do?"

"Nothing and everything," she said, swallowing one herself. "You'll see."

"How much do I owe you for this?"

"Never mind that."

For a while the drug did seem, as promised, to do nothing. But on the industrial outskirts of Norwich, still two or three hours from the Cape, he turned down the trip hop that Melissa was playing on his stereo and said, "We have to stop immediately and fuck."

She laughed. "I guess *so*."

"Why don't I pull over," he said.

She laughed again. "No, let's find a room."

They stopped at a Comfort Inn that had lost its franchise and now called itself the Comfort Valley Lodge. The night clerk was obese and her computer was down. She manually registered Chip with the labored breathing of someone lately stranded by a systems malfunction. Chip put his hand on Melissa's belly and was about to reach into her pants when it occurred to him that fingering a woman in public was inappropriate and might cause trouble. For similar, purely rational reasons he suppressed the impulse to pull his dick out of his pants and show it to the wheezing, perspiring clerk. But he did think the clerk would be interested in seeing it.

He took Melissa down on the cigarette-divoted carpeting of Room 23 without even shutting the door.

"It is so much better like this!" Melissa said, kicking the door shut. She yanked her pants down and practically wailed with delight, "This is *so* much better!"

He didn't dress all weekend. The towel he was wearing when he took delivery of a pizza fell open before the delivery man could turn away. "Hey, love, it's me," Melissa said into her cell phone while Chip lay down behind her and went at her. She kept her phone arm free and made supportive filial noises. "Uh-huh . . . Uh-huh . . . Sure, sure . . . No, that's hard, Mom . . . No, you're right, that is hard . . . Sure . . . Sure . . . Uh-huh . . . Sure . . . That's really, really hard," she said, with a twinkle in her voice, as Chip sought leverage for an extra sweet half inch of penetration while he shot. On Monday and Tuesday he dictated large chunks of a term paper on Carol Gilligan which Melissa was too annoyed with Vendla O'Fallon to write by herself. His near-photographic recall of Gilligan's arguments, his total mastery of theory, got him so excited that he began to tease Melissa's hair with his erection. He ran the head of it up and down the keyboard of her computer and applied a gleaming smudge to the liquid-crystal screen. "Darling," she said, "don't come on my computer." He nudged her cheeks and ears and tickled her armpits and finally backed her up against the bathroom door while she bathed him in her cherry-red smile.

Each night around dinnertime, for four nights running, she went to her luggage and got two more golden caplets. Then on Wednesday Chip took her to a cineplex and they sneaked into an extra movie and a half for the price of the original matinee bargain. Back at the Comfort Valley Lodge, after a late pancake dinner, Melissa called her mother and spoke at such length that Chip fell asleep without swallowing a caplet.

He awoke on Thanksgiving in the gray light of his undrugged self. For a while, as he lay listening to the sparse holiday traffic on Route 2, he couldn't place what was different. Something about the body beside him was making him uneasy. He considered turning and burying his face in Melissa's back, but it seemed to him she must be sick of him. He could hardly believe she hadn't minded his attacks on her, all his pushing and pawing and poking. That she didn't feel like a piece of meat that he'd been using.

In a matter of seconds, like a market inundated by a wave of panic selling, he was plunged into shame and self-consciousness. He couldn't bear to stay in bed a moment longer. He pulled on his shorts and snagged Melissa's toiletries kit and locked himself in the bathroom.

His problem consisted of a burning wish not to have done the things he'd done. And his body, its chemistry, had a clear instinctive understanding of what he had to do to make this burning wish go away. He had to swallow another Mexican A.

He searched the toiletries kit exhaustively. He wouldn't have thought it possible to feel dependent on a drug with no hedonic kick, a drug that on the evening of his fifth and final dose he hadn't even craved. He uncapped Melissa's lipsticks and removed twin tampons from their pink plastic holder and probed with a bobby pin down through her jar of skin cleanser. Nothing.

He took the kit back out to the main room, which was fully light now, and whispered Melissa's name. Receiving no answer, he dropped to his knees and rifled her canvas travel bag. Paddled his fingers in the empty cups of bras. Squeezed her sock balls. Touched the various private pouches and compartments of the bag. This new and different violation of Melissa was sensationally painful to him. In the orange light of his shame he felt as if he were abusing her internal organs. He felt like a surgeon atrociously fondling her youthful lungs, defiling her kidneys, sticking his finger in her perfect, tender pancreas. The sweetness of her little socks, and the thought of the even littler socks of her all too proximate girlhood, and the image of a hopeful bright romantic sophomore packing clothes for a trip with her esteemed professor—each sentimental association added fuel to his shame, each image recalled him to the unfunny raw comedy of what he'd done to her. The jismic grunting butt-oink. The jiggling frantic nut-swing.

By now his shame was boiling so furiously it felt liable to burst things in his brain. Nevertheless, while keeping a close eye on Melissa's sleeping form, he managed to paw her clothing a second time. Only after he'd resqueezed and rehandled each piece of it did he conclude that the Mexican A was in the big zippered outer pocket of her bag. This zipper he eased open tooth by tooth, clenching his own teeth to survive the noise of it. He'd worked the pocket open just far enough to push his hand through it (and the stress of this latest of his penetrations released fresh gusts of flammable memory; he felt mortified by each of the manual liberties he'd taken with Melissa here in Room 23, by the insatiable lewd avidity of his fingers; *he wished he could have left her alone*) when the cell phone on the nightstand tinkled and with a groan she came awake.

He snatched his hand from the forbidden place, ran to the bathroom, and took a long shower. By the time he came out, Melissa was dressed and had repacked her bag. She looked utterly uncarnal in the morning light. She was whistling a happy tune.

"Darling, a change of plans," she said. "My father, who really is a lovely man, is coming out to Westport for the day. I want to go be with them."

Chip wished he could fail to feel the shame that she was failing to feel; but to beg for another pill was acutely embarrassing. "What about our dinner?" he said.

"I'm sorry. It's just really important that I be there."

"So it's not enough to be on the phone with them for a couple of hours every day."

"Chip, I'm sorry. But we're talking about my best friends."

Chip had never liked the sound of Tom Paquette: a dilettante rocker and trust-fund baby who ditched his family for a roller blader. And in the last few days Clair's boundless capacity to yak about herself while Melissa listened had turned Chip against her, too.

"Great," he said. "I'll take you to Westport."

Melissa flipped her hair so that it fanned across her back. "Darling? Don't be mad."

"If you don't want to go to the Cape, you don't want to go to the Cape. I'll take you to Westport."

"Good. Are you going to get dressed?"

"It's just that, Melissa, you know, there's something a little sick about being so close to your parents."

She seemed not to have heard him. She went to the mirror and applied mascara. She put on lipstick. Chip stood in the middle of the room with a towel around his waist. He felt warty and egregious. He felt that Melissa was right to be disgusted by him. And yet he wanted to be clear.

"Do you understand what I'm saying?"

"Darling. Chip." She pressed her painted lips together. "Get dressed."

"I'm saying, Melissa, that children are not supposed to get along with their parents. Your parents are not supposed to be your best friends. There's supposed to be some element of rebellion. That's how you define yourself as a person."

"Maybe it's how *you* define yourself," she said. "But then you're not exactly an advertisement for happy adulthood."

He grinned and bore this.

"I like myself," she said. "But you don't seem to like yourself so much."

"Your parents seem very fond of themselves, too," he said. "You seem very fond of yourselves as a family."

He'd never seen Melissa really angry. "I love myself," she said. "What's wrong with that?"

He was unable to say what was wrong with it. He was unable to say what was wrong with anything about Melissa—her self-adoring parents, her theatricality and confidence, her infatuation with capitalism, her lack of good friends her own age. The feeling he'd had on the last day of Consuming Narratives, the feeling that he was mistaken about everything, that there was nothing wrong with the world and nothing wrong with being happy in it, that the problem was his and his alone, returned with such force that he had to sit down on the bed.

"What's our drug situation?"

"We're out," Melissa said.

"OK."

"I got six of them and you've had five."

"What?"

"And it was a big mistake, evidently, not to give you all six."

"What have you been taking?"

"Advil, darling." Her tone with this endearment had moved beyond the arch to the outright ironic. "For saddle soreness?"

"I never asked you to get that drug," he said.

"Not in so many words," she said.

"What do you mean by that?"

"Well, a fat lot of fun we were going to have without it."

Chip didn't ask her to explain. He was afraid she meant he'd been a lousy, anxious lover until he took Mexican A. He had, of course, been a lousy, anxious lover; but he'd allowed himself to hope she hadn't noticed. Under the weight of this fresh shame, and with no drug left in the room to alleviate it, he bowed his head and pressed his hands into his face. Shame was pushing down and rage was boiling up.

"Are you going to drive me to Westport?" Melissa said.

He nodded, but she must not have been looking at him, because he heard her flipping through a phone book. He heard her tell a dispatcher she needed a ride to New London. He heard her say: "The Comfort Valley Lodge. Room twenty-three."

"I'll drive you to Westport," he said.

She shut the phone. "No, this is fine."

"Melissa. Cancel the cab. I'll drive you."

She parted the room's rear curtains, exposing a vista of Cyclone fencing, stick-straight maples, and the back side of a recycling plant. Eight or ten snowflakes drifted dismally. In the eastern sky was a raw patch where the cloud cover was abraded, the white sun wearing through. Chip dressed quickly while Melissa's back was turned. If he hadn't been so strangely full of shame, he might have gone to the window and put his hands on her, and she might have turned and forgiven him. But his hands felt predatory. He imagined her recoiling, and he wasn't entirely convinced that some dark percentage of his being didn't really want to rape her, to make her pay for liking herself in a way he couldn't like himself. How he hated and how he loved the lilt in her voice, the bounce in her step, the serenity of her amour propre! She got to be her and he didn't. And he could see that he was ruined—that he didn't like her but would miss her disastrously.

She dialed another number. "Hey, love," she said into her cell phone. "I'm on my way to New London. I'll take the first train that comes . . . No, I just want to be with you guys . . . Totally . . . Yes, totally . . . OK, kiss kiss, I'll see you when I see you . . . Yep."

A car honked outside the door.

"There's my cab," she told her mother. "Right, OK. Kiss kiss. Bye."

She shrugged into her jacket, lifted her bag, and waltzed across the room. At the door she announced in a general way that she was leaving. "I'll see you later," she said, almost looking at Chip.

He couldn't figure out if she was immensely well adjusted or seriously messed up. He heard a cab door slam, an engine rumble. He went to the front window and got a glimpse of her cherrywood hair through the rear window of a red-and-white cab. He decided, after five years without, that the time had come to buy some cigarettes.

He put on a jacket and crossed expanses of cold asphalt indifferent to pedestrians. He pushed money through a slot in the bulletproof glass of a minimart.

It was the morning of Thanksgiving. The flurries had stopped and the sun was halfway out. A gull's wings rattled and clacked. The breeze had a ruffly quality, it didn't quite seem to touch the ground. Chip sat on a freezing guardrail and smoked and took comfort in the sturdy mediocrity of American commerce, the unpretending metal and plastic roadside hardware. The thunk of a gas-pump nozzle halting when a tank was filled, the humility and promptness of its service. And a *99¢ Big Gulp* banner swelling with wind and sailing nowhere, its nylon ropes whipping and pinging on a galvanized standard. And the black sanserif numerals of gasoline prices, the company of so many 9s. And American sedans moving down the access road at nearly stationary speeds like thirty. And orange and yellow plastic pennants shivering overhead on guys.

"Dad fell down the basement stairs again," Enid said while the rain came down in New York City. "He was carrying a big box of pecans to the basement and he didn't hold the railing and he fell. Well, you can imagine how many pecans are in a twelve-pound box. Those nuts rolled everywhere. Denise, I spent half a day on my hands and knees. And I'm still finding them. They're the same color as those crickets we can't get rid of. I reach down to pick up a pecan, and it jumps in my face!"

Denise was trimming the stems of the sunflowers she'd brought. "Why was Dad carrying twelve pounds of pecans down the basement stairs?"

"He wanted a project he could work on in his chair. He was going to shell them." Enid hovered at Denise's shoulder. "Is there something I can do here?"

"You can find me a vase."

The first cabinet that Enid opened contained a carton of wine-bottle corks and nothing else. "I don't understand why Chip invited us here if he wasn't even going to eat lunch with us."

"Conceivably," Denise said, "he didn't plan on getting dumped this morning."

Denise's tone of voice was forever informing Enid that she was stupid. Denise was not, Enid felt, a very warm or giving person. However, Denise was a daughter, and a few weeks ago Enid had done a shameful thing that she was now in serious need of confessing to somebody, and she hoped Denise might be that person.

"Gary wants us to sell the house and move to Philadelphia," she said. "Gary thinks Philadelphia makes sense because he's there and you're there and Chip's in New York. I said to Gary, I love my children, but St. Jude is where I'm comfortable. Denise, I'm a midwesterner. I'd be *lost* in Philadelphia. Gary wants us to sign up for assisted living. He doesn't understand that it's already too late. Those places won't let you in if you have a condition like Dad's."

"But if Dad keeps falling down the stairs."

"Denise, he doesn't hold the railing! He refuses to accept that he shouldn't be carrying things on the stairs."

Underneath the sink Enid found a vase behind a stack of framed photographs, four pictures of pinkish furry things, some sort of kooky art or medical photos. She tried to reach past them quietly, but she knocked over an asparagus steamer that she'd given Chip for Christmas once. As soon as Denise looked down, Enid could not pretend she hadn't seen the pictures. "What on earth?" she said, scowling. "Denise, what are these?"

"What do you mean, 'what are these?'?"

"Some sort of kooky thing of Chip's, I guess."

Denise had an "amused" expression that drove Enid crazy. "Obviously you know what they are, though."

"No. I don't."

"You don't know what they are?"

Enid took the vase out and closed the cabinet. "I don't *want* to know," she said.

"Well, that's something else entirely."

In the living room, Alfred was summoning the courage to sit down on Chip's chaise longue. Not ten minutes ago, he'd sat down on it without incident. But now, instead of simply doing it again, he'd stopped to think. He'd realized only recently that at the center of the act of sitting down was a loss of control, a blind backwards free fall. His excellent blue chair in St. Jude was like a first baseman's glove that gently gathered in whatever body was flung its way, at whatever glancing angle, with whatever violence; it had big helpful ursine arms to support him while he performed the crucial blind pivot. But Chip's chaise was a low-riding, impractical antique. Alfred stood facing away from it and hesitated, his knees bent to the rather small degree that his neuropathic lower legs permitted, his hands scooping and groping in the air behind him. He was afraid to take the plunge. And yet there was something obscene about standing half-crouched and quaking, some association with the men's room, some essential vulnerability which felt to him at once so poignant and degraded that, simply to put an end to it, he shut his eyes and let go. He landed heavily on his bottom and continued on over backwards, coming to rest with his knees in the air above him.

"Al, are you all right?" Enid called.

"I don't understand this furniture," he said, struggling to sit up and sound powerful. "Is this meant to be a sofa?"

Denise came out and put a vase of three sunflowers on the spindly table by the chaise. "It's like a sofa," she said. "You can put your legs up and be a French philosophe. You can talk about Schopenhauer."

Alfred shook his head.

Enid enunciated from the kitchen doorway, "Dr. Hedgpeth says you should only sit in *high, straight-backed* chairs."

Since Alfred showed no interest in these instructions, Enid repeated them to Denise when she returned to the kitchen. "*High, straight-backed* chairs only," she said. "But Dad won't listen. He insists on sitting in his leather chair. Then he shouts for me to come and help him get up. But if I hurt my back, then where are we? I put one of those nice old ladder-back chairs by the TV downstairs and told him *sit here*. But he'd rather sit in his leather chair, and then to get out of it he slides down the cushion until he's on the floor. Then he crawls on the floor to the Ping-Pong table and uses the Ping-Pong table to hoist himself up."

"That's actually pretty resourceful," Denise said as she took an armload of food from the refrigerator.

"Denise, he's *crawling across the floor*. Rather than sit in a nice, comfortable straight-backed chair which the doctor says it's important that he sit in, *he crawls across the floor*. He shouldn't be sitting so much to begin with. Dr. Hedgpeth says his condition is not at all severe if he would just get out and *do* a little. Use it or lose it, that's what every doctor says. Dave Schumpert has had ten times more health problems than Dad, he's had a colostomy for fifteen years, he's got one lung and a pacemaker, and look at all the things that he and Mary Beth are doing. They just got back from snorkeling in Fiji! And Dave *never* complains, *never* complains. You probably don't remember Gene Grillo, Dad's old friend from Hephaestus, but he has bad Parkinson's—much, much worse than Dad's. He's still at home in Fort Wayne but in a wheelchair now. He's really in awful shape, but, Denise, he's *interested* in things. He can't write anymore but he sent us an 'audio letter' on a cassette tape, really thoughtful, where he talks about each of his grandchildren in detail, because he knows his grandkids and takes an interest in them, and about how he's started to teach himself Cambodian, which he calls Khmer, from listening to a tape and watching the Cambodian (or Khmer, I guess) TV channel in Fort Wayne, because their youngest son is married to a Cambodian woman, or Khmer, I guess, and her parents don't speak any English and Gene wants to be able to talk to them a little. Can you believe? Here Gene is in a wheelchair, completely crippled, and he's still thinking about what he can do for somebody else! While Dad, who can walk, and write, and dress himself, does nothing all day but sit in his chair."

"Mother, he's depressed," Denise said in a low voice, slicing bread.

"That's what Gary and Caroline say, too. They say he's depressed and he should take a medication. They say he was a workaholic and that work was a drug which when he couldn't have it anymore he got depressed."

"So drug him and forget him. A convenient theory."

"That's not fair to Gary."

"Don't get me started on Gary and Caroline."

"*Golly*, Denise, the way you throw that knife around I don't see how you haven't lost a finger."

From the end of a French loaf Denise had made three little crust-bottomed vehicles. On one she set shavings of butter curved like sails full of wind, into another she loaded Parmesan shards packed in an excelsior of shredded arugula, and the third she paved with minced olive meat and olive oil and covered with a thick red tarp of pepper.

Enid spoke—"Mm, don't those look nice"—as she reached, cat-quick, for the plate on which Denise had arranged the snacks. But the plate eluded Enid.

"These are for Dad."

"Just a corner of one."

"I'll make some more for you."

"No, I just want one corner of his."

But Denise left the kitchen and took the plate to Alfred, for whom the problem of existence was this: that, in the manner of a wheat seedling thrusting itself up out of the earth, the world moved forward in time by adding cell after cell to its leading edge, piling moment on moment, and that to grasp the world even in its freshest, youngest moment provided no guarantee that you'd be able to grasp it again a moment later. By the time he'd established that his daughter, Denise, was handing him a plate of snacks in his son Chip's living room, the next moment in time was already budding itself into a pristinely ungrasped existence in which he couldn't absolutely rule out the possibility, for example, that his wife, Enid, was handing him a plate of feces in the parlor of a brothel; and no sooner had he reconfirmed Denise and the snacks and Chip's living room than the leading edge of time added yet another layer of new cells, so that he again faced a new and ungrasped world; which was why, rather than exhaust himself playing catch-up, he preferred more and more to spend his days down among the unchanging historical roots of things.

"Something to tide you while I get lunch," Denise said.

Alfred gazed with gratitude at the snacks, which were holding about ninety percent steady as food, flickering only occasionally into objects of similar size and shape.

"Maybe you'd like a glass of wine?"

"Not necessary," he said. As the gratitude spread outward from his heart—as he was moved—his clasped hands and lower arms began to bounce more freely on his lap. He tried to find something in the room that didn't move him, something he could rest his eyes on safely; but because the room was Chip's and because Denise was standing in it, every fixture and every surface—even a radiator knob, even a thigh-level expanse of faintly scuffed wall—was a reminder of the separate, eastern worlds in which his children led their lives and hence of the various vast distances that separated him from them; which made his hands shake all the more.

That the daughter whose attentions most aggravated his affliction was the person he least wanted to be seen by in the grip of this affliction was the sort of Devil's logic that confirmed a man's pessimism.

"I'll leave you alone for a minute," Denise said, "while I get the lunch going."

He closed his eyes and thanked her. As if waiting for a break in a downpour so that he could run from his car into a grocery store, he waited for a lull in his tremor so that he could reach out and safely eat what she'd brought him.

His affliction offended his sense of ownership. These shaking hands belonged to nobody but him, and yet they refused to obey him. They were like bad children. Unreasoning two-year-olds in a tantrum of selfish misery. The more sternly he gave orders, the less they listened and the more miserable and out of control they got. He'd always been vulnerable to a child's recalcitrance and refusal to behave like an adult. Irresponsibility and undiscipline were the bane of his existence, and it was another instance of that Devil's logic that his own untimely affliction should consist of his body's refusal to obey him.

If thy right hand offend thee, Jesus said, cut it off.

As he waited for the tremor to abate—as he watched his hands' jerking rowing motions impotently, as if he were in a nursery with screaming misbehaving infants and had lost his voice and couldn't make them quiet down—Alfred took pleasure in the imagination of chopping his hand off with a hatchet: of letting the transgressing limb know how deeply he was angry with it, how little he loved it if it insisted on disobeying him. It brought a kind of ecstasy to imagine the first deep bite of the hatchet's blade in the bone and muscle of his offending wrist; but along with the ecstasy, right beside it, was an inclination to weep for this hand that was his, that he loved and wished the best for, that he'd known all its life.

He was thinking about Chip again without noticing it.

He wondered where Chip had gone. How he'd driven Chip away again.

Denise's voice and Enid's voice in the kitchen were like a larger bee and a smaller bee trapped behind a window screen. And his moment came, the lull that he'd been waiting for. Leaning forward and steadying his taking hand with his supporting hand, he grasped the butter-sailed schooner and got it off the plate, bore it aloft without capsizing it, and then, as it floated and bobbed, he opened his mouth and chased it down and got it. Got it. Got it. The crust cut his gums, but he kept the whole thing in his mouth and chewed carefully, giving his sluggish tongue wide berth. The sweet butter melting, the feminine softness of baked leavened wheat. There were chapters in Hedgpeth's booklets that even Alfred, fatalist and man of discipline that he was, couldn't bring himself to read. Chapters devoted to the problems of swallowing; to the late torments of the tongue; to the final breakdown of the signal system . . .

The betrayal had begun in Signals.

The Midland Pacific Railroad, where for the last decade of his career he'd run the Engineering Department (and where, when he'd given an order, it was carried out, Mr. Lambert, right away, sir), had served hundreds of one-elevator towns in west Kansas and west and central Nebraska, towns of the kind that Alfred and his fellow executives had grown up in or near, towns that in their old age seemed the sicker for the excellent health of the Midpac tracks running through them. Although the railroad's first responsibility was to its stockholders, its Kansan and Missourian officers (including Mark Jamborets, the corporation counsel) had persuaded the Board of Managers that because a railroad was a pure monopoly in many hinterland towns, it had a civic duty to maintain service on its branches and spurs. Alfred personally had no illusions about the economic future of prairie towns where the median age was fifty-plus, but he believed in rail and he hated trucks, and he knew firsthand what scheduled service meant to a town's civic pride, how the whistle of a train could raise the spirits on a February morning at 41°N 101°W; and in his battles with the EPA and various DOTs he'd learned to appreciate rural state legislators who could intercede on your behalf when you needed more time to clean up your waste-oil tanks in the Kansas City yards, or when some goddamned bureaucrat was insisting that you pay for forty percent of a needless grade-separation project at Country Road H. Years after the Soo Line and Great Northern and Rock Island had stranded dead and dying towns all across the northern Plains, then, the Midpac had persisted in running short semiweekly or even biweekly trains through places like Alvin and Pisgah Creek, New Chartres and West Centerville.

Unfortunately, this program had attracted predators. In the early 1980s, as Alfred neared retirement, the Midpac was known as a regional carrier that despite outstanding management and lush profit margins on its long-haul lines had very ordinary earnings. The Midpac had already repulsed one unwelcome suitor when it came under the acquisitive gaze of Hillard and Chauncy Wroth, fraternal twin brothers from Oak Ridge, Tennessee, who had expanded a family meat-packing business into an empire of the dollar. Their company, the Orfic Group, included a chain of hotels, a bank in Atlanta, an oil company, and the Arkansas Southern Railroad. The Wroths had lopsided faces and dirty hair and no discernible desires or interests apart from making money; *Oak Ridge Raiders*, the financial press called them. At an early exploratory meeting that Alfred attended, Chauncy Wroth persisted in addressing the Midpac's CEO as "Dad": *I'm well aware it don't seem like "fair play" to you, DAD . . . Well, DAD, why don't you and your lawyers go ahead and have that little chat right now . . . Gosh, and here Hillard and myself was under the impression, DAD, that you're operating a business, not a charity . . .* This kind of anti-paternalism played well with the railroad's unionized workforce, which after months of arduous negotiations voted to offer the Wroths a package of wage and work-rule concessions worth almost $200 million; with these prospective savings in hand, plus twenty-seven percent of the railroad's stock, plus limitless junk financing, the Wroths made an irresistible tender offer and bought the railroad outright. A former Tennessee highway commissioner, Fenton Creel, was hired to merge the railroad with the Arkansas Southern. Creel shut down the Midpac's headquarters in St. Jude, fired or retired a third of its employees, and moved the rest to Little Rock.

Alfred retired two months before his sixty-fifth birthday. He was at home watching *Good Morning America* in his new blue chair when Mark Jamborets, the Midpac's retired corporation counsel, called with the news that a sheriff in New Chartres (pronounced "Charters"), Kansas, had had himself arrested for shooting an employee of Orfic Midland. "The sheriff's name is Bryce Halstrom," Jamborets told Alfred. "He got a call that some roughnecks were trashing Midpac signal wires. He went over to the siding and saw three fellows ripping down the wire, smashing signal boxes, coiling up anything copper. One of them took a county bullet in his hip before the others made Halstrom understand they were working for the Midpac. Hired for copper salvage at sixty cents a pound."

"But that's a good new system," Alfred said. "It's not three years since we upgraded the whole New Chartres spur."

"The Wroths are scrapping everything but the trunk lines," Jamborets said. "They're junking the Glendora cutoff! You think the Atchison, Topeka wouldn't make a bid on that?"

"Well," Alfred said.

"It's a Baptist morality gone sour," said Jamborets. "The Wroths can't abide that we admitted any principle but the ruthless pursuit of profit. I'm telling you: they hate what they can't comprehend. And now they're sowing salt in the fields. Close down headquarters in St. Jude? When we're twice the size of Arkansas Southern? They're punishing St. Jude for being the home of the Midland Pacific. And Creel's punishing the towns like New Chartres for being Midpac towns. He's sowing salt in the fields of the financially unrighteous."

"Well," Alfred said again, his eyes drawn to his new blue chair and its delicious potential as a sleep site. "Not my concern anymore."

But he'd worked for thirty years to make the Midland Pacific a strong system, and Jamborets continued to call him and send him news reports of fresh Kansan outrages, and it all made him very sleepy. Soon hardly a branch or spur in Midpac's western district remained in service, but apparently Fenton Creel was satisfied with pulling down the signal wires and gutting the boxes. Five years after the takeover, the rails were still in place, the right-of-way was undisposed of. Only the copper nervous system, in an act of corporate self-vandalism, had been dismantled.

"And now I'm worried about our health insurance," Enid told Denise. "Orfic Midland is switching all the old Midpac employees to managed care no later than April. I have to find an HMO that has some of Dad's and my doctors on their list. I'm *deluged* with prospectuses, where the differences are all in the fine print, and honestly, Denise, I don't think I can handle this."

As if to forestall being asked for help, Denise quickly said: "What plans does Hedgpeth accept?"

"Well, except for his old fee-for-service patients, like Dad, he's exclusive now with Dean Driblett's HMO," Enid said. "I told you about the big party at Dean's *gorgeous, huge* new house. Dean and Trish really are about the nicest young couple I know, but golly, Denise, I called his company last year after Dad fell down on the lawn mower, and you know what they wanted for cutting our little lawn? Fifty-five dollars a week! I'm not opposed to profit, I think it's *wonderful* that Dean's successful, I told you about his trip to Paris with Honey, I'm not saying anything against him. But fifty-five dollars a week!"

Denise sampled Chip's green-bean salad and reached for the olive oil. "What would it cost to stay with fee-for-service?"

"Denise, hundreds of dollars a month extra. Not one of our good friends has managed care, everybody has fee-for-service, but I don't see how we can afford it. Dad was so conservative with his investments, we're lucky to have any cushion for emergencies. And this is something else I'm very, very, very, very worried about." Enid lowered her voice. "One of Dad's old patents is finally paying off, and I need your advice."

She stepped out of the kitchen and made sure that Alfred couldn't hear. "Al, how are you doing?" she shouted.

He was cradling his second hors d'oeuvre, the little green boxcar, below his chin. As if he'd captured a small animal that might escape again, he shook his head without looking up.

Enid returned to the kitchen with her purse. "He finally has a chance to make some money, and he's not interested. Gary talked to him on the phone last month and tried to get him to be a little more aggressive, but Dad blew up."

Denise stiffened. "What was Gary wanting you to do?"

"Just be a little more aggressive. Here, I'll show you the letter."

"Mother, those patents are Dad's. You have to let him handle it however he wants."

Enid hoped that the envelope at the bottom of her purse might be the missing Registered letter from the Axon Corporation. In her purse, as in her house, lost objects did sometimes marvelously resurface. But the envelope she found was the original Certified letter, which had never been lost.

"Read this," she said, "and see if you agree with Gary."

Denise set down the can of cayenne pepper with which she'd dusted Chip's salad. Enid stood at her shoulder and reread the letter to make sure it still said what she remembered.

Dear Dr. Lambert:

On behalf of the Axon Corporation, 24 East Industrial Serpentine, Schwenksville, Pennsylvania, I'm writing to offer you a lump sum payment of five thousand dollars ($5000.00) for the full, exclusive, and irrevocable right to United States Patent #4,934,417 (THERAPEUTIC FERROACETATE-GEL ELECTRO-POLYMERIZATION), for which you are original and sole holder of license.

The management of Axon regrets that it cannot offer you a larger fee. The company's own product is in the earliest stages of testing, and there is no guarantee that its investment will bear fruit.

If the terms outlined in the attached Licensing Agreement are acceptable, please sign and have notarized all three copies and return them to me no later than September 30.

Sincerely yours,

Joseph K. Prager
Senior Associate Partner
Bragg Knuter & Speigh

When this letter had arrived in the mail in August and Enid had awakened Alfred in the basement, he'd shrugged and said, "Five thousand dollars won't change the way we live." Enid had suggested that they write to the Axon Corporation and ask for a larger fee, but Alfred shook his head. "We'll have soon spent five thousand dollars on a lawyer," he said, "and then where are we?" It didn't hurt to ask, though, Enid said. "I will not ask," Alfred said. But if he just wrote back, Enid said, and asked for ten thousand . . . She fell silent as Alfred fixed her with a look. She might as well have proposed that they make love.

Denise had taken a bottle of wine from the refrigerator, as if to underline her indifference to a matter of consequence to Enid. Sometimes Enid believed that Denise had disdain for every last thing she cared about. The sexual tightness of Denise's blue jeans, as she bumped a drawer shut with her hip, sent this message. The assurance with which she drove a corkscrew into the cork sent this message. "Do you want some wine?"

Enid shuddered. "It's so early in the day."

Denise drank it like water. "Knowing Gary," she said, "I'm guessing he said try to gouge them."

"No, well, see—" Enid reached toward the bottle with both hands. "Just a tiny drop, pour me just a swallow, honestly, I never drink this early in the day, never—you see, but Gary wonders why the company is even bothering with the patent if they're still so early in their development. I guess the usual thing is just to infringe on the other person's patent. —That's too much! Denise, I don't like so much wine! Because, see, the patent expires in six years, so Gary thinks the company must stand to make a lot of money soon."

"Did Dad sign the agreement?"

"Oh, yeah. He went over to the Schumperts' and had Dave notarize it."

"Then you have to respect his decision."

"Denise, he's being stubborn and unreasonable. I can't—"

"Are you saying this is an issue of competency?"

"No. No. This is fully in character. I just can't—"

"If he already *signed* the agreement," Denise said, "what is Gary imagining you're going to do?"

"Nothing, I guess."

"So what's the point here?"

"Nothing. You're right," Enid said. "There's nothing we can do," although in fact there was. If Denise had been a little less partisan in her support of Alfred, Enid might have confessed that after Alfred had given her the notarized agreement to mail at the post office on her way to the bank, she'd hidden the agreement in the glove compartment of their car, and had let the envelope sit and radiate guilt for several days; and that later, while Alfred was napping, she'd hidden the envelope more securely at the back of a laundry-room cabinet containing jars of undesirable jams and spreads going gray with age (kumquat-raisin, brandy-pumpkin, Korean barfleberry) and vases and baskets and cubes of florist's clay too good to throw away but not good enough to use; and that, as a result of this dishonest act, she and Alfred could still extract a big licensing fee from Axon, and that it was therefore crucial that she locate the second, Registered letter from Axon and hide it before Alfred found out that she'd deceived and disobeyed him. "Oh, but that reminds me," she said, emptying her glass, "there's something else I really need your help with."

Denise hesitated before replying with a polite and cordial "Yes?" This hesitation confirmed Enid's long-held belief that she and Alfred had taken a wrong turn somewhere in Denise's upbringing. Had failed to instill in their youngest child the proper spirit of generosity and cheerful service.

"Well, as you know," Enid said, "we've gone to Philadelphia for the last eight Christmases in a row, and Gary's boys are old enough now that they might like to have a memory of Christmas at their grandparents' house, and so *I* thought—"

"*Damn!*" came a cry from the living room.

Enid set down her glass and hurried from the kitchen. Alfred was sitting on the edge of the chaise in a somehow penal posture, his knees high and his back a little hunched, and was surveying the crash site of his third hors d'oeuvre. The gondola of bread had slipped from his fingers on its approach to his mouth and plunged to his knee, scattering wreckage and tumbling to the floor and finally coming to rest beneath the chaise. A wet pelt of roasted red pepper had adhered to the chaise's flank. Shadows of oil-soak were forming around each clump of olive morsels on the upholstery. The emptied gondola lay on its side with its yellow-soaked, brown-stained white interior showing.

Denise squeezed past Enid with a damp sponge and went and knelt by Alfred. "Oh, Dad," she said, "these are hard to handle, I should have realized."

"Just get me a rag and I'll clean it up."

"No, here," Denise said. Cupping one hand for a receptacle, she brushed the bits of olive from his knees and thighs. His hands shook in the air near her head as if he might have to push her away, but she did her work quickly, and soon she'd sponged the bits of olive up from the floor and was carrying the dirtied food back to the kitchen, where Enid had wanted a tiny extra splash of wine and in her hurry not to be conspicuous had poured a rather substantial tiny splash and downed it quickly.

"Anyway," she said, "I thought that if you and Chip were interested, we could all have one last Christmas in St. Jude. What do you think of that idea?"

"I'll be wherever you and Dad want to be," Denise said.

"No, I'm asking *you*, though. I want to know if it's something you're especially interested in doing. If you'd especially like to have one last Christmas in the house you grew up in. Does it sound like it might be fun for you?"

"I can tell you right now," Denise said, "there's no way Caroline's leaving Philly. It's a fantasy to think otherwise. So if you want to see your grandkids, you'll have to come east."

"Denise, I'm asking what *you* want. Gary says he and Caroline haven't ruled it out. I need to know if a Christmas in St. Jude is something that you really, really want for *yourself*. Because if all the rest of us are agreed that it's important to be together as a family in St. Jude one last time—"

"Mother, it's fine with me, if you think you can handle it."

"I'll need a little help in the kitchen is all."

"I can help you in the kitchen. But I can only come for a few days."

"You can't take a week?"

"No."

"Why not?"

"Mother."

"*Damn!*" Alfred cried again from the living room as something vitreous, maybe a vase containing sunflowers, hit the floor with a cracking-open sound, a gulp of breakage. "*Damn! Damn!*"

Enid's own nerves were so splintery she almost dropped her wine-glass, and yet a part of her was grateful for this second mishap, whatever it was, because it gave Denise a small taste of what she had to put up with every day, around the clock, at home in St. Jude.

The night of Alfred's seventy-fifth birthday had found Chip alone at Tilton Ledge pursuing sexual congress with his red chaise longue.

It was early January and the woods around Carparts Creek were soggy with melting snow. Only the shopping-center sky above central Connecticut and the digital readouts of his home electronics cast light on his carnal labors. He was kneeling at the feet of his chaise and sniffing its plush minutely, inch by inch, in hopes that some vaginal tang might still be lingering eight weeks after Melissa Paquette had lain here. Ordinarily distinct and identifiable smells—dust, sweat, urine, the dayroom reek of cigarette smoke, the fugitive afterscent of quim—became abstract and indistinguishable from oversmelling, and so he had to pause again and again to refresh his nostrils. He worked his lips down into the chaise's buttoned navels and kissed the lint and grit and crumbs and hairs that had collected in them. None of the three spots where he thought he smelled Melissa was unambiguously tangy, but after exhaustive comparison he was able to settle on the least questionable of the three spots, near a button just south of the backrest, and give it his full nasal attention. He fingered other buttons with both hands, the cool plush chafing his nether parts in a poor approximation of Melissa's skin, until finally he achieved sufficient belief in the smell's reality—sufficient faith that he still possessed some relic of Melissa—to consummate the act. Then he rolled off his compliant antique and slumped on the floor with his pants undone and his head on the cushion, an hour closer to having failed to call his father on his birthday.

He smoked two cigarettes, lighting the second off the first. He turned on his television to a cable channel that was running a marathon of old Warner Bros. cartoons. At the edge of the pool of tubal glow he could see the mail that for nearly a week he'd been dropping, unopened, on the floor. Three letters from the college's new acting provost were in the pile, also something ominous from the teachers' retirement fund, also a letter from the college housing office with the words NOTICE OF EVICTION on the front of the envelope.

Earlier in the day, while killing some hours by circling in blue ballpoint ink every uppercase M in the front section of a month-old *New York Times*, Chip had concluded that he was behaving like a depressed person. Now, as his telephone began to ring, it occurred to him that a depressed person ought to continue staring at the TV and ignore the ringing—ought to light another cigarette and, with no trace of emotional affect, watch another cartoon while his machine took whoever's message.

That his impulse, instead, was to jump to his feet and answer the phone—that he could so casually betray the arduous wasting of a day— cast doubt on the authenticity of his suffering. He felt as if he lacked the ability to lose all volition and connection with reality the way depressed people did in books and movies. It seemed to him, as he silenced the TV and hurried into his kitchen, that he was failing even at the miserable task of falling properly apart.

He zipped up his pants, turned on a light, and lifted the receiver. "Hello?"

"What's going on there, Chip?" Denise said without preliminaries. "I just talked to Dad and he said he hadn't heard from you."

"Denise. Denise. Why are you shouting?"

"I'm shouting," she said, "because I'm upset because it's Dad's seventy-fifth birthday and you haven't called him and you didn't send him a card. I'm upset because I've been working for twelve hours and I just called Dad and he's worried about you. What's going on there?"

Chip surprised himself by laughing. "What's going on is that I've lost my job."

"You didn't get tenure?"

"No, I was fired," he said. "They didn't even let me teach the last two weeks of classes. Somebody else had to give my exams. And I can't appeal the decision without calling a witness. And if I try to talk to my witness it's just further evidence of my crime."

"Who's the witness? Witness to what?"

Chip took a bottle from the recycling bin, double-checked its emptiness, and returned it to the bin. "A former student of mine says I'm obsessed with her. She says I had a relationship with her and wrote her a term paper in a motel room. And unless I get a lawyer, which I can't afford to do because they've cut my pay off, I'm not allowed to speak to this student. If I try to see her, it's considered stalking."

"Is she lying?" Denise said.

"Not that this is anything Mom and Dad need to know about."

"Chip, is she lying?"

Spread open on Chip's kitchen counter was the section of the *Times* in which he'd circled all the uppercase *M*'s. Rediscovering this artifact now, hours later, would have been like remembering a dream except that a remembered dream didn't have the power to pull a waking person back into it, whereas the sight of a heavily marked story about severe new curtailments in Medicare and Medicaid benefits induced in Chip the same feeling of unease and unrealized lust, the same longing for un-consciousness, that had sent him to the chaise to sniff and grope. He had to struggle now to remind himself that he'd already *gone* to the chaise, he'd already *taken* that route to comfort and forgetfulness.

He folded the *Times* and dropped it on top of his heaping trash can.

" 'I never had sexual relations with that woman,' " he said.

"You know I'm judgmental about a lot of things," Denise said, "but not about things like this."

"I said I didn't sleep with her."

"I'm stressing, though," Denise said, "that this is one area where absolutely anything you say to me will fall on sympathetic ears." And she cleared her throat pointedly.

If Chip had wanted to come clean to someone in his family, his little sister would have been the obvious choice. Having dropped out of college and having married badly, Denise at least had some acquaintance with darkness and disappointment. Nobody but Enid, however, had ever mistaken Denise for a failure. The college she'd dropped out of was better than the one that Chip had graduated from, and her early marriage and more recent divorce had given her an emotional maturity that Chip was all too aware of lacking himself, and he suspected that even though Denise was working eighty hours a week she still managed to read more books than he did. In the last month, since he'd embarked on projects like digitally scanning Melissa Paquette's face from a freshman facebook and suturing her head to obscene downloaded images and tinkering with these images pixel by pixel (and the hours did fly by when you were tinkering with pixels), he'd read no books at all.

"There was a misunderstanding," he told Denise dully. "And then it was like they could hardly wait to fire me. And now I'm being denied due process."

"Frankly," Denise said, "it's hard to see being fired as a bad thing. Colleges are nasty."

"This was the one place in the world I thought I fit in."

"I'm saying it's very much to your credit that you don't. Although what are you surviving on, financially?"

"Who said I was surviving?"

"Do you need a loan?"

"Denise, you don't have any money."

"Yes I do. I'm also thinking you should talk to my friend Julia. She's the one in film development. I told her about that idea you had for an East Village *Troilus and Cressida*. She said you should call her if you're interested in writing."

Chip shook his head as if Denise were with him in the kitchen and could see him. They'd talked on the phone, months ago, about modernizing some of Shakespeare's less famous plays, and he couldn't bear that Denise had taken that conversation seriously; that she still believed in him.

"What about Dad, though?" she said. "Did you forget it's his birthday?"

"I lost track of time here."

"I wouldn't push you," Denise said, "except that I was the person who opened your Christmas box."

"Christmas was a bad scene, no question."

"Which package went to whom was pretty much guesswork."

Outside, a wind from the south had picked up, a thawing wind that quickened the patter of snowmelt on the back patio. The sense that Chip had had when the phone rang—that his misery was optional—had left him again.

"So are you going to call him?" Denise said.

He replaced the receiver in its cradle without answering her, turned off the ringer, and pressed his face into the doorframe. He'd solved the problem of family Christmas gifts on the last possible mailing day, when, in a great rush, he'd pulled old bargains and remainders off his bookshelves and wrapped them in aluminum foil and tied them up with red ribbon and refused to imagine how his nine-year-old nephew Caleb, for example, might react to an Oxford annotated edition of *Ivanhoe* whose main qualification as a gift was that it was still in its original shrink-wrap. The corners of the books had immediately poked through the aluminum foil, and the foil he'd added to cover up the holes hadn't adhered well to the underlying layers, and the result had been a soft and peely kind of effect, like onion skin or phyllo dough, which he'd tried to mitigate by plastering each package with the National Abortion Rights

Action League holiday stickers that he'd received in his annual membership kit. His handiwork had looked so clumsy and childish, so mentally unbalanced really, that he tossed the packages into an old grapefruit carton just to get them out of sight. Then he FedExed the carton down to Gary's house in Philadelphia. He felt as if he'd taken an enormous dump, as if, no matter how smeary and disagreeable it had been, he at least was emptied out now and would not be back in this position soon. But three days later, returning home late on Christmas night after a twelve-hour vigil at the Dunkin' Donuts in Norwalk, Connecticut, he faced the problem of opening the gifts his family had sent him: two boxes from St. Jude, a padded mailer from Denise, and a box from Gary. He decided that he would open the packages in bed and that the way he would get them up to his bedroom would be to kick them up the stairs. Which proved to be a challenge, because oblong objects had a tendency not to roll up a staircase but to catch on the steps and tumble back down. Also, if the contents of a padded mailer were too light to offer inertial resistance, it was difficult to get any lift when you kicked it. But Chip had had such a frustrating and demoralizing Christmas—he'd left a message on Melissa's college voice mail, asking her to call him at the pay phone at the Dunkin' Donuts or, better yet, to come over in person from her parents' house in nearby Westport, and not until midnight had exhaustion compelled him to accept that Melissa probably wasn't going to call him and certainly wasn't going to come and see him—that he was now psychically capable neither of breaking the rules of the game he'd invented nor of quitting the game before he'd achieved its object. And it was clear to him that the rules permitted only genuine sharp kicks (prohibited, in particular, working his foot under the padded mailer and advancing it with any sort of pushing or lofting motion), and so he was obliged to kick his Christmas package from Denise with escalating savagery until it tore open and spilled its ground-newsprint stuffing and he succeeded in catching its ripped sheathing with the toe of his boot and launching the gift in a long clean arc that landed it one step shy of the second floor. From there, however, the mailer refused to be budged up over the lip of the final step. Chip trampled and kicked and shredded the mailer with his heels. Inside was a mess of red paper and green silk. He broke his own rule and scraped the mess up over the last step, kicked it down the hall, and left it by his bed while he went down for the other boxes. These, too, he pretty well destroyed before he developed a method of bouncing them off a low step and then, while they were airborne, punting them all the way upstairs. When he punted the box from Gary it exploded in a cloud of white Styrofoam saucers. A bubble-wrapped bottle fell out and rolled down the stairs. It was a bottle of vintage Californian port. Chip carried it up to his bed and worked out a rhythm whereby he swallowed one large mouthful of port for each gift that he succeeded in unwrapping. From his mother, who was under the impression that he still hung a stocking by his fireplace, he'd received a box marked *Stocking Stuffers* containing small individually wrapped items: a package of cough drops, a miniature second-grade school photo of himself in a tarnished brass frame, plastic bottles of shampoo and conditioner and hand lotion from a Hong Kong hotel where Enid and Alfred had stayed en route to China eleven years earlier, and two carved wooden elves with sentimentally exaggerated smiles and loops of silver string that penetrated their little craniums so they could be hung from a tree. For placement under this presumptive tree, Enid had sent a second box of larger gifts wrapped in Santa-faced red paper: an asparagus steamer, three pairs of white Jockey underwear, a jumbo candy cane, and two calico throw pillows. From Gary and his wife, in addition to the port, Chip received a clever vacuum-pump system for preserving leftover wine from oxidation, as if leftover wine were a problem Chip had ever had. From Denise, to whom he'd given *The Selected Letters of André Gide* after erasing from the flyleaf the evidence that he'd paid one dollar for this particularly tone-deaf translation, he received a beautiful lime-green silk shirt, and from his father a hundred-dollar check with the handwritten instruction to buy himself something he liked.

Except for the shirt, which he'd worn, and the check, which he'd cashed, and the bottle of port, which he'd killed in bed on Christmas night, the gifts from his family were still on the floor of his bedroom. Stuffing from Denise's mailer had drifted into the kitchen and mixed with splashed dishwater to form a mud that he'd tracked all over. Flocks of sheep-white Styrofoam pebbles had collected in sheltered places.

It was nearly ten-thirty in the Midwest.

Hello, Dad. Happy seventy-fifth. Things are going well here. How are things in St. Jude?

Chip felt he couldn't make the call without some kind of pick-me-up or treat. Some kind of energizer. But TV caused him such critical and political anguish that he could no longer watch even cartoons without smoking cigarettes, and he now had a lung-sized region of pain in his chest, and there was no intoxicant of any sort in his house, not even cooking sherry, not even cough syrup, and after the labor of taking his pleasure with the chaise his endorphins had gone home to the four corners of his brain like war-weary troops, so spent by the demands he'd made of them in the last five weeks that nothing, except possibly Melissa in the flesh, could marshal them again. He needed a little morale-booster, a little pick-me-up, but he had nothing better than the month-old *Times*, and he felt that he'd circled quite enough uppercase *M*'s for one day, he could circle no more.

He went to his dining table and confirmed the absence of dregs in the wine bottles on it. He'd used the last $220 of credit on his Visa card to buy eight bottles of a rather tasty Fronsac, and on Saturday night he'd thrown one last dinner party to rally his supporters on the faculty. A few years ago, after D——'s drama department had fired a popular young professor, Cali Lopez, for having claimed to have a degree she didn't have, outraged students and junior faculty had organized boycotts and candlelight vigils that had forced the college not only to rehire Lopez but to promote her to full professor. Granted, Chip was neither a lesbian nor a Filipina, as Lopez was, but he'd taught Theory of Feminism, and he had a hundred-percent voting record with the Queer Bloc, and he routinely packed his syllabi with non-Western writers, and all he'd really done in Room 23 of the Comfort Valley Lodge was put into practice certain theories (the myth of authorship; the resistant consumerism of transgressive sexual (trans)act(ion)s) that the college had hired him to teach. Unfortunately, the theories sounded somewhat lame when he wasn't lecturing to impressionable adolescents. Of the eight colleagues who'd accepted his invitation for dinner on Saturday, only four had shown up. And despite his efforts to steer the conversation around to his predicament, the only collective action his friends had taken on his behalf had been to serenade him, as they killed the eighth bottle of wine, with an a capella rendition of "Non, Je Ne Regrette Rien."

He hadn't had the strength to clear the table in the intervening days. He considered the blackened red leaf lettuce, the skin of congealed grease on an uneaten lamb chop, the mess of corks and ashes. The shame and disorder in his house were like the shame and disorder in his head. Cali Lopez was now the college's acting provost, Jim Leviton's replacement.

Tell me about your relationship with your student Melissa Paquette.

My former student?

Your former student.

I'm friendly with her. We've had dinner. I spent some time with her at the beginning of Thanksgiving break. She's a brilliant student.

Did you give Melissa any help with a paper she wrote last week for Vendla O'Fallon?

We talked about the paper in a general way. She had some areas of confusion that I was able to help her clear up.

Is your relationship with her sexual?

No.

Chip, what I think we'll do is suspend you with pay until we can have a full hearing. That's what we'll do. We'll have a hearing early next week, and in the meantime you should probably get a lawyer and talk to your union rep. I also have to insist that you not speak to Melissa Paquette.

What does she say? That I wrote that paper?

Melissa violated the honor code by handing in work that was not her own. She's facing a one-semester suspension, but we understand that there are mitigating factors. For example, your grossly inappropriate sexual relationship with her.

That's what she says?

My personal advice, Chip, is resign now.

That's what she says?

You have no chance.

The snowmelt was raining down harder on his patio. He lit a cigarette on the front burner of his stove, took two painful drags, and pressed the coal into the palm of his hand. He groaned through clenched teeth and opened his freezer and put his palm to its floor and stood for a minute smelling flesh smoke. Then, holding an ice cube, he went to the phone and dialed the ancient area code, the ancient number.

While the phone rang in St. Jude, he planted a foot on the section of *Times* in his trash and mashed it down deeper, got it out of sight.

"Oh, Chip," Enid cried, "he's already gone to bed!"

"Don't wake him," Chip said. "Just tell him—"

But Enid set the phone down and shouted *Al! Al!* at volumes that diminished as she moved farther from the phone and up the stairs toward the bedrooms. Chip heard her shout, *It's Chip!* He heard their upstairs extension click into action. He heard Enid instructing Alfred, "Don't just say hello and hang up. *Visit* with him a little."

There was a rustling transfer of the receiver.

"Yes," Alfred said.

"Hey, Dad, happy birthday," Chip said.

"Yes," Alfred said again in exactly the same flat voice.

"I'm sorry to call so late."

"I was not asleep," Alfred said.

"I was afraid I woke you up."

"Yes."

"Well, so happy seventy-fifth."

"Yes."

Chip hoped that Enid was motoring back down to the kitchen as fast as she could, ailing hip and all, to bail him out. "I guess you're tired and it's late," he said. "We don't have to talk."

"Thank you for the call," Alfred said.

Enid was back on the line. "I'm going to finish these dishes," she said. "We had a party here tonight! Al, tell Chip about the party we had! I'm getting off the phone now."

She hung up. Chip said, "You had a party."

"Yes. The Roots were here for dinner and bridge."

"Did you have a cake?"

"Your mother made a cake."

The cigarette had made a hole in Chip's body through which, he felt, painful harms could enter and vital factors painfully escape. Melting ice was leaking through his fingers. "How was the bridge?"

"My typical terrible cards."

"That doesn't seem fair on your birthday."

"I imagine," Alfred said, "that you are gearing up for another semester."

"Right. Right. Although actually not. Actually I'm deciding not to teach at all this semester."

"I didn't hear."

Chip raised his voice. "I said I've decided not to teach this semester. I'm going to take the semester off and work on my writing."

"My recollection is that you are due for tenure soon."

"Right. In April."

"It seems to me that a person hoping to be offered tenure would be advised to stay and teach."

"Right."

"If they see you working hard, they will have no reason not to offer you tenure."

"Right. Right." Chip nodded. "At the same time, I have to prepare for the possibility that I won't get it. And I've got a, uh. A very attractive offer from a Hollywood producer. A college friend of Denise's who produces movies. Potentially very lucrative."

"A great worker is almost impossible to fire," Alfred said.

"The process can get very political, though. I have to have alternatives."

"As you wish," Alfred said. "However, I've found that it's usually best to choose one plan and stick with it. If you don't succeed here, you can always do something else. But you've worked many years to reach this point. One more semester's hard work won't hurt you."

"Right."

"You can relax when you have tenure. Then you're safe."

"Right."

"Well, thank you for the call."

"Right. Happy birthday, Dad."

Chip dropped the phone, left the kitchen, and took a Fronsac bottle by the neck and brought its body down hard on the edge of his dining table. He broke a second bottle. The remaining six he smashed two at a time, a neck in each fist.

Anger carried him through the difficult weeks that followed. He borrowed ten thousand dollars from Denise and hired a lawyer to threaten to sue D—— College for wrongful termination of his contract. This was a waste of money, but it felt good. He went to New York and ponied up four thousand dollars in fees and deposits for a sublet on Ninth Street. He bought leather clothes and had his ears pierced. He borrowed more money from Denise and reconnected with a college friend who edited the *Warren Street Journal*. He conceived revenge in the form of a screenplay that would expose the narcissism and treachery of Melissa Paquette and the hypocrisy of his colleagues; he wanted the people who'd hurt him to see the movie, recognize themselves, and suffer. He flirted with Julia Vrais and asked her on a date, and soon he was spending two or three hundred dollars a week to feed and entertain her. He borrowed more money from Denise. He hung cigarettes on his lower lip and banged out a draft of a script. Julia in the back seat of cabs pressed her face against his chest and clutched his collar. He tipped waiters and cabbies thirty and forty percent. He quoted Shakespeare and Byron in funny contexts. He borrowed more money from Denise and decided that she was right, that getting fired was the best thing that had ever happened to him.

He wasn't so naïve, of course, as to take Eden Procuro's professional effusions at face value. But the more he saw of Eden socially, the more confident he became that his script would get a sympathetic reading. For one thing, Eden was like a mother to Julia. She was only five years older, but she'd undertaken a wholesale recalibration and improvement of her personal assistant. Although Chip never quite shook the feeling that Eden was hoping to cast someone else in the role of

Julia's love interest (she habitually referred to Chip as Julia's "escort," not her "boyfriend," and when she talked about Julia's "untapped potential" and her "lack of confidence" he suspected that mate selection was one area in which she hoped to see improvement in Julia), Julia assured him that Eden thought he was "really dear" and "extremely smart." Certainly Eden's husband, Doug O'Brien, was on his side. Doug was a mergers-and-acquisitions specialist at Bragg Knuter & Speigh. He'd set Chip up with a flextime proofreading job and had seen to it that Chip was paid the top hourly wage. Whenever Chip tried to thank him for this favor, Doug made pshawing motions with his hand. "You're the man with the Ph.D.," he said. "That book of yours is scary smart stuff." Chip had soon become a frequent guest at the O'Brien-Procuros' dinner parties in Tribeca and their weekend house parties in Quogue. Drinking their liquor and eating their catered food, he had a foretaste of a success a hundred times sweeter than tenure. He felt that he was really living.

Then one night Julia sat him down and said there was an important fact that she hadn't mentioned earlier, and would he promise not to be too mad at her? The important fact was that she sort of had a husband. The deputy prime minister of Lithuania—a small Baltic country—was a man named Gitanas Misevičius? Well, the fact was that Julia had married him a couple of years ago, and she hoped Chip wouldn't be too mad at her.

Her problem with men, she said, was that she'd grown up without. Her father was a manic-depressive boat salesman whom she remembered meeting once and wished she'd never met at all. Her mother, a cosmetics-company executive, had fobbed Julia off on her own mother, who'd enrolled her in a Catholic girls' school. Julia's first significant experience with men was at college. Then she moved to New York and embarked on the long process of sleeping with every dishonest, casually sadistic, terminally uncommitted really gorgeous guy in the borough of Manhattan. By the age of twenty-eight, she had little to feel good about except her looks, her apartment, and her steady job (which mainly consisted, however, of answering the phone). So when she met Gitanas at a club and Gitanas took her seriously, and by and by produced an actual not-small diamond in a white-gold setting, and seemed to love her (and the guy was, after all, an honest-to-God ambassador to the United Nations; she'd gone and heard him do his Baltic thundering at the General Assembly), she did her level best to repay his kindness. She was As Agreeable As Humanly Possible. She refused to disappoint Gitanas even though, in hindsight, it probably would have been better to disappoint him. Gitanas was quite a bit older and fairly attentive in bed (not like Chip, Julia hastened to say, but not, you know, terrible), and he seemed to know what he was doing with the marriage thing, and so one day she went to City Hall with him. She might even have gone by "Mrs. Misevičius" if it had sounded less idiotic. Once she was married, she realized that the marble floors and black lacquer furniture and heavy modern smoked-glass fixtures of the ambassador's apartment on the East River weren't as entertainingly campy as she'd thought. They were more like unbearably depressing. She made Gitanas sell the place (the chief of the Paraguayan delegation was delighted to get it) and buy a smaller, nicer place on Hudson Street near some good clubs. She found a competent hairstylist for Gitanas and taught him how to pick out clothes with natural fibers. Things seemed to be going great. But somewhere she and Gitanas must have misunderstood each other, because when his party (the VIPPPAKJRIINPB17: the One True Party Unswervingly Dedicated to the Revanchist Ideals of Kazimieras Jaramaitis and the "Independent" Plebiscite of April Seventeen) lost a September election and recalled him to Vilnius to join the parliamentary opposition, he took it for granted that Julia would come along with him. And Julia understood the concept of one flesh, wife cleaving to husband, and so forth; but Gitanas in his descriptions of post-Soviet Vilnius had painted a picture of chronic coal and electricity shortages, freezing drizzles, drive-by shootings, and heavy dietary reliance on horsemeat. And so she did a really terrible thing to Gitanas, definitely the worst thing she'd ever done to anybody. She agreed to go and live in Vilnius, and she sort of got on the plane with Gitanas and sat down in first class and then sneaked off the plane and sort of changed their home phone number and had Eden tell Gitanas, when he called, that she had disappeared. Six months later Gitanas returned to New York for a weekend and made Julia feel really, really guilty. And, yes, no argument, she'd disgraced herself. But Gitanas proceeded to call her certain rough names and he slapped her pretty hard. The upshot of which was that they couldn't be together anymore, but she continued to use their apartment on Hudson Street in exchange for staying married in case Gitanas needed quick asylum in the United States, because apparently things were going from bad to worse in Lithuania.

Anyway, that was the story of her and Gitanas, and she hoped that Chip wouldn't be too mad at her.

And Chip was not. Indeed, at first he not only didn't mind that Julia was married, he adored the fact. He was fascinated by her rings; he talked her into wearing them in bed. Down at the offices of the *Warren Street Journal*, where he sometimes felt insufficiently transgressive, as if his innermost self were still a nice midwestern boy, he took pleasure in alluding to the European statesman he was "cuckolding." In his doctoral thesis ("Doubtful It Stood: Anxieties of the Phallus in Tudor Drama") he'd written extensively about cuckolds, and under the cloak of his reproving modern scholarship he'd been excited by the idea of marriage as a property right, of adultery as theft.

Before long, though, the thrill of poaching on the diplomat's preserve gave way to bourgeois fantasies in which Chip himself was Julia's husband—her lord, her liege. He became spasmodically jealous of Gitanas Misevičius, who, though Lithuanian, and a slapper, was a successful politician whose name Julia now pronounced with guilt and wistfulness. On New Year's Eve Chip asked her point-blank if she ever thought about divorce. She replied that she liked her apartment ("Can't beat the rent!") and she didn't want to look for another one right now.

After New Year's, Chip returned to his rough draft of "The Academy Purple," which he'd completed in a euphoric twenty-page blaze of keyboard-pounding, and discovered that it had a lot of problems. It looked, in fact, like incoherent hackwork. During the month that he'd spent expensively celebrating its completion, he'd imagined that he could remove certain hackneyed plot elements—the conspiracy, the car crash, the evil lesbians—and still tell a good story. Without these hackneyed plot elements, however, he seemed to have no story at all.

In order to salvage his artistic and intellectual ambitions, he added a long theoretical opening monologue. But this monologue was so unreadable that every time he turned on his computer he had to go and tinker with it. Soon he was spending the bulk of each work session compulsively honing the monologue. And when he despaired of shortening it any further without sacrificing important thematic material, he started fussing with the margins and hyphenation to make the monologue end at the bottom of page 6 rather than the top of page 7. He replaced the word "continue" with "go on" to save three spaces, thus allowing the word "(trans)act(ion)s" to be hyphenated after the second *t*, which triggered a whole cascade of longer lines and more efficient hyphenations. Then he decided that "go on" had the wrong rhythm and that "(trans)act(ion)s" should not be hyphenated under any circumstances, and so he scoured the text for other longish words to replace with shorter synonyms, all the while struggling to believe that stars and producers in Prada jackets would enjoy reading six pages (but not seven!) of turgid academic theorizing.

Once, when he was a boy, there was a total eclipse of the sun in the Midwest, and a girl in one of the poky towns across the river from St. Jude had sat outside and, in defiance of myriad warnings, studied the dwindling crescent of the sun until her retinas combusted.

"It didn't hurt at all," the blinded girl had told the *St. Jude Chronicle*. "It felt like nothing."

Each day that Chip spent grooming the corpse of a dramatically dead monologue was a day in which his rent and food and entertainment expenses were paid for, in large part, with his little sister's money. And yet as long as the money lasted, his pain was not acute. One day led to another. He rarely got out of bed before noon. He enjoyed his food and his wine, he dressed well enough to persuade himself that he was not a quivering gelatinous mess, and he managed, on four out of five evenings, to hide the worst of his anxiety and foreboding and enjoy himself with Julia. Because the sum he owed Denise was large in comparison to his proofreading wage but small by Hollywood standards, he worked less and less at Bragg Knuter & Speigh. His only real complaint was with his health. On a summer day when his work session consisted of rereading Act I, being struck afresh by its irredeemable badness, and hurrying outside to get some air, he might walk down Broadway and sit on a bench at Battery Park City and let the breeze off the Hudson flow under his collar, and listen to the ceaseless fut-fut of copter traffic and the distant shouts of millionaire Tribeca toddlers, and be overcome with guilt. To be so vigorous and healthy and yet so *nothing*: neither taking advantage of his good night's sleep and his successful avoidance of a cold to get some work done, nor yet fully entering into the vacation spirit and flirting with strangers and knocking back margaritas. It would have been better, he thought, to do his getting sick and dying now, while he was failing, and save his health and vitality for some later date when, unimaginable though the prospect was, he would perhaps no longer be failing. Of all the things he was wasting—Denise's money, Julia's goodwill, his own abilities and education, the opportunities afforded by the longest sustained economic boom in American history—his sheer physical well-being, there in the sunlight by the river, hurt the worst.

He ran out of money on a Friday in July. Facing a weekend with Julia, who could cost him fifteen dollars at a cinema refreshments counter, he purged the Marxists from his bookshelves and took them to the Strand in two extremely heavy bags. The books were in their original jackets and had an aggregate list price of $3,900. A buyer at the Strand appraised them casually and delivered his verdict: "Sixty-five."

Chip laughed in a breathy way, willing himself not to argue; but his U.K. edition of Jürgen Habermas's *Reason and the Rationalization of Society*, which he'd found too difficult to read, let alone annotate, was in mint condition and had cost him £95.00. He couldn't help pointing this out by way of example.

"Try somewhere else, if you like," the buyer said, his hand hesitating above the cash register.

"No, no, you're right," Chip said. "Sixty-five is great."

It was pathetically obvious that he'd believed his books would fetch him hundreds of dollars. He turned away from their reproachful spines, remembering how each of them had called out in a bookstore with a promise of a radical critique of late-capitalist society, and how happy he'd been to take them home. But Jürgen Habermas didn't have Julia's long, cool, pear-tree limbs, Theodor Adorno didn't have Julia's grapy smell of lecherous pliability, Fred Jameson didn't have Julia's artful tongue. By the beginning of October, when Chip sent his finished script to Eden Procuro, he'd sold his feminists, his formalists, his structuralists, his poststructuralists, his Freudians, and his queers. To raise money for lunch for his parents and Denise, all he had left was his beloved cultural historians and his complete hardcover Arden Shakespeare; and because a kind of magic resided in the Shakespeare—the uniform volumes in their pale blue jackets were like an archipelago of safe retreats—he piled his Foucault and Greenblatt and hooks and Poovey into shopping bags and sold them all for $115.

He spent sixty dollars on a haircut, some candy, a stain-removal kit, and two drinks at the Cedar Tavern. Back in August, when he'd invited his parents, he'd hoped that Eden Procuro might have read his script and advanced him money before they arrived, but now the only accomplishment and the only gift he had to offer was a home-cooked meal. He went to an East Village deli that sold reliably excellent tortellini and crusty bread. He was envisioning a rustic and affordable Italian lunch. But the deli appeared to have gone out of business, and he didn't feel like walking ten blocks to a bakery that he was certain had good bread, and so he wandered the East Village randomly, trudging in and out of meretricious food stores, hefting cheeses, rejecting breads, examining inferior tortellini. Finally he abandoned the Italian idea altogether and fixed on the only other lunch he could think of—a salad of wild rice, avocado, and smoked turkey breast. The problem then was to find ripe avocados. In store after store he found either no avocados or walnut-hard avocados. He found ripe avocados that were the size of limes and cost $3.89 apiece. He stood holding five of them and considered what to do. He put them down and picked them up and put them down and couldn't pull the trigger. He weathered a spasm of hatred of Denise for having guilted him into inviting his parents to lunch. He had the feeling that he'd never eaten anything in his life but wild-rice salad and tortellini, so blank was his culinary imagination.

Around eight o'clock he ended up outside the new Nightmare of

Consumption ("Everything—for a Price!") on Grand Street. A humidity had stolen over the sky, a sulfurous uneasy wind from Rahway and Bayonne. The supergentry of SoHo and Tribeca were streaming through the Nightmare's brushed-steel portals. The men came in various shapes and sizes, but all the women were slim and thirty-six; many were both slim and pregnant. Chip had a collar rash from his haircut and felt unready to be seen by so many perfect women. But right inside the Nightmare's door he glimpsed a box of greens marked *SORREL from Belize $0.99.*

He entered the Nightmare, snagged a basket, and put one bunch of sorrel in it. Ninety-nine cents. Installed above the Nightmare's coffee bar was a screen that gave running ironic tallies of TODAY'S GROSS RE-CEIPTS and TODAY'S PROFIT and PROJECTED QUARTERLY PER-SHARE DIV-IDEND (Unofficial Non-Binding Estimate Based on Past Quarterly Performances / This Information Provided for Entertainment Purposes Only), and COFFEE SALES THIS STATION. Chip wove among strollers and cell phone antennae to the fish counter, where, as in a dream, he found WILD NORWEGIAN SALMON, LINE CAUGHT on sale at a reasonable price. He pointed at a midsize filet, and to the fishman's question, "What else?" he replied in a crisp tone, almost a smug tone, "That'll do it."

The price on the beautiful paper-wrapped filet that he was handed was $78.40. Luckily, this discovery knocked the wind out of him, otherwise he might have lodged a protest before realizing, as he did now, that the prices at the Nightmare were per quarter pound. Two years ago, two months ago, he would not have made a mistake like this.

"Ha, ha!" he said, palming the seventy-eight-dollar filet like a catcher's mitt. He dropped to one knee and touched his bootlaces and took the salmon right up inside his leather jacket and underneath his sweater and tucked the sweater into his pants and stood up again.

"Daddy, I want swordfish," a little voice behind him said.

Chip took two steps, and the salmon, which was quite heavy, escaped from his sweater and covered his groin, for one unstable moment, like a codpiece.

"Daddy! Swordfish!"

Chip put his hand to his crotch. The dangling filet felt like a cool, loaded diaper. He repositioned it against his abs and tucked in the sweater more securely, zipped his jacket to the neck, and strode purposefully toward the whatever. Toward the dairy wall. Here he found a selection of French crèmes fraîches at prices implying transport via SST. The less unaffordable domestic crème fraîche was blocked by a man in a Yankees cap who was shouting into his cell phone while a child, apparently his, peeled back the foil tops of half-liters of French yogurt. She'd peeled back five or six already. Chip leaned to reach behind the man, but his fish belly sagged. "Excuse me," he said.

Like a sleepwalker the man on the phone shuffled aside. "I said fuck him. Fuck him! Fuck that asshole! We never closed. There's no ink on the line. I'll take that asshole down another thirty, you watch me. Honey, don't tear those, if we tear those we have to pay for them. I said it is a fucking buyer's ball as of yesterday. We close on *nuffin* till this thing bottoms out. Nuffin! Nuffin! Nuffin! Nuffin!"

Chip was approaching the checkout lanes with four plausible items in his basket when he caught sight of a head of hair so new-penny bright it could only belong to Eden Procuro. Who was, herself, slim and thirty-six and hectic. Eden's little son, Anthony, was seated on the upper level of a shopping cart with his back to a four-figure avalanche of shellfish, cheeses, meats, and caviars. Eden was leaning over Anthony and letting him pull on the taupe lapels of her Italian suit and suck on her blouse while, behind his back, she turned the pages of a script that Chip could only pray was not his own. The line-caught Norwegian salmon was soaking through its wrapping, his body heat melting the fats that had given the filet a degree of rigidity. He wanted to escape the Nightmare, but he wasn't prepared to discuss "The Academy Purple" under the current circumstances. He veered down a frosty aisle where the gelati came in plain white cartons with small black lettering. A man in a suit was crouching beside a little girl with hair like copper in sunshine. The girl was Eden's daughter, April. The man was Eden's husband, Doug O'Brien.

"Chip Lambert, what's happening?" Doug said.

There seemed to be no ways but girly ways for Chip to hold his grocery basket while he shook Doug's square hand.

"April's picking out her treat for after dinner," Doug said.

"Three treats," April said.

"Her three treats, right."

"What's that one?" April said, pointing.

"That is a grenadine-nasturtium sorbetto, sugar bunny."

"Do I like it?"

"That I can't tell you."

Doug, who was younger and shorter than Chip, so persistently claimed to be in awe of Chip's intellect and so consistently tested free of any irony or condescension that Chip had finally accepted that Doug really did admire him. This admiration was more grueling than belittlement.

"Eden tells me you finished the script," Doug said, restacking some gelati that April had upset. "Man, I am psyched. This project sounds *phenomenal*."

April was cradling three rimed cartons against her corduroy jumper.

"What kind did you get?" Chip asked her.

April shrugged extremely, a beginner's shrug.

"Sugar bunny, run those up to Mommy. I'm going to talk to Chip."

As April ran back up the aisle Chip wondered what it would be like to father a child, to always be needed instead of always needing.

"Something I wanted to ask you," Doug said. "Do you have a second? Say somebody offered you a new personality: would you take it? Say somebody said to you, *I will permanently rewire your mental hardware in whatever way you want.* Would you pay to have that done?"

The salmon paper was sweat-bonded to Chip's skin and tearing open at the bottom. This was not the ideal time to be providing Doug with the intellectual companionship he seemed to crave, but Chip wanted Doug to keep thinking highly of him and encourage Eden to buy his script. He asked why Doug asked.

"A lot of crazy stuff crosses my desk," Doug said. "Especially now with all the money coming home from overseas. All the dot-com issues, of course. We're still trying our very hardest to persuade the average American to happily engineer his own financial ruin. But the biotech is fascinating. I've been reading whole prospectuses about genetically altered squash. Apparently people in this country are eating a lot more squash than I was aware of, and squashes are prone to more diseases than you'd infer from their robust exterior. Either that or . . . Southern Cucumtech is seriously overvalued at thirty-five a share. Whatever. But Chip, this brain thing, man, it caught my eye. Bizarre fact number one is that I'm allowed to talk about it. It's all public knowledge. Is this bizarre?"

Chip was trying to keep his eyes focused on Doug in an interested manner, but his eyes were like children, they wanted to skip up and down the aisles. He was ready, basically, to jump out of his skin. "Yeah. Bizarre."

"The idea," Doug said, "is your basic gut cerebral rehab. Leave the shell and roof, replace the walls and plumbing. Design away that useless dining nook. Put a modern circuit breaker in."

"Uh huh."

"You get to keep your handsome façade," Doug said. "You still look serious and intellectual, a little Nordic, on the outside. Sober, bookish. But inside you're more livable. A big family room with an entertainment console. A kitchen that's roomier and handier. You've got your In-Sink-Erator, your convection oven. An ice-cube dispenser on the refrigerator door."

"Do I still recognize myself?"

"Do you want to? Everybody else still will—at least, the outside of you."

The big glowing tally for TODAY'S GROSS RECEIPTS paused for a moment at $444,447.41 and then went higher.

"My furnishings are my personality," Chip said.

"Say it's a gradual rehab. Say the workmen are very tidy. The brain's cleaned up every night when you get home from work, and nobody can bother you on the weekend, per local ordinance and the usual covenantal restrictions. The whole thing happens in stages—you grow into it. Or it grows into you, so to speak. Nobody's making you buy new furniture."

"You're asking hypothetically."

Doug raised a finger. "The only thing is there might be some metal involved. It's possible you'd set off alarms at the airport. I'm imagining you might get some unwanted talk radio, too, on certain frequencies. Gatorade and other high-electrolyte drinks might be a problem. But what do you say?"

"You're joking, right?"

"Check out the Web site. I'll give you the address. *'The implications are disturbing, but there's no stopping this powerful new technology.'* That could be the motto for our age, don't you think?"

That a salmon filet was now spreading down into Chip's underpants like a wide, warm slug did seem to have everything to do with his brain and with a number of poor decisions that this brain had made. Rationally Chip knew that Doug would let him go soon and that eventually he might even escape the Nightmare of Consumption and find a restaurant bathroom where he could take the filet out and regain his full critical faculties—that there would come a moment when he was no longer standing amid pricey gelati with lukewarm fish in his pants, and that this future moment would be a moment of extraordinary relief—but for now he still inhabited an earlier, much less pleasant moment from the vantage point of which a new brain looked like just the ticket.

"The desserts were a foot tall!" Enid said, her instincts having told her that Denise didn't care about pyramids of shrimp. "It was elegant elegant. Have you ever seen anything like that?"

"I'm sure it was very nice," Denise said.

"The Dribletts really do things super-deluxe. I'd never seen a dessert that tall. Have you?"

The subtle signs that Denise was exercising patience—the slightly deeper breaths she took, the soundless way she set her fork down on her plate and took a sip of wine and set the glass back down—were more hurtful to Enid than a violent explosion.

"I've seen tall desserts," Denise said.

"Are they tremendously difficult to make?"

Denise folded her hands in her lap and exhaled slowly. "It sounds like a great party. I'm glad you had fun."

Enid had, true enough, had fun at Dean and Trish's party, and she'd wished that Denise had been there to see for herself how elegant it was. At the same time, she was afraid that Denise would not have found the party elegant at all, that Denise would have picked apart its specialness until there was nothing left but ordinariness. Her daughter's taste was a dark spot in Enid's vision, a hole in her experience through which her own pleasures were forever threatening to leak and dissipate.

"I guess there's no accounting for tastes," she said.

"That's true," Denise said. "Although some tastes are better than others."

Alfred had bent low over his plate to ensure that any salmon or haricots verts that fell from his fork would land on china. But he was listening. He said, "Enough."

"That's what everybody thinks," Enid said. "Everybody thinks their taste is the best."

"But most people are wrong," Denise said.

"Everybody's entitled to their own taste," Enid said. "Everybody gets one vote in this country."

"Unfortunately!"

"Enough," Alfred said to Denise. "You'll never win."

"You sound like a snob," Enid said.

"Mother, you're always telling me how much you like a good home-cooked meal. Well, that's what I like, too. I think there's a kind of Disney vulgarity in a foot-tall dessert. *You* are a better cook than—"

"Oh, no. No." Enid shook her head. "I'm a nothing cook."

"That's not true at all! Where do you think I—"

"Not from me," Enid interrupted. "I don't know where my children got their talents. But not from me. I'm a nothing as a cook. A big nothing." (How strangely good it felt to say this! It was like putting scalding water on a poison-ivy rash.)

Denise straightened her back and raised her glass. Enid, who all her life had been helpless not to observe the goings-on on other people's plates, had watched Denise take a three-bite portion of salmon, a small helping of salad, and a crust of bread. The size of each was a reproach to the size of each of Enid's. Now Denise's plate was empty and she hadn't taken seconds of anything.

"Is that all you're going to eat?" Enid said.

"Yes. That was my lunch."

"You've lost weight."

"In fact not."

"Well, don't lose any more," Enid said with the skimpy laugh with which she tried to hide large feelings.

Alfred was guiding a forkful of salmon and sorrel sauce to his mouth. The food dropped off his fork and broke into violently shaped pieces.

"I think Chip did a good job with this," Enid said. "Don't you think? The salmon is very tender and good."

"Chip has always been a good cook," Denise said.

"Al, are you enjoying this? Al?"

Alfred's grip on his fork had slackened. There was a sag in his lower lip, a sullen suspicion in his eyes.

"Are you enjoying the lunch?" Enid said.

He took his left hand in his right and squeezed it. The mated hands continued their oscillation together while he stared at the sunflowers in the middle of the table. He seemed to *swallow* the sour set of his mouth, to choke back the paranoia.

"Chip made all this?" he said.

"Yes."

He shook his head as though Chip's having cooked, Chip's absence now, overwhelmed him. "I am increasingly bothered by my affliction," he said.

"What you have is very mild," Enid said. "We just need to get the medication adjusted."

He shook his head. "Hedgpeth said it's unpredictable."

"The important thing is to keep doing things," Enid said, "to keep active, to always just *go*."

"No. You were not listening. Hedgpeth was very careful not to promise anything."

"According to what I read—"

"I don't give a damn what your magazine article said. I am not well, and Hedgpeth admitted as much."

Denise set her wine down with a stiff, fully extended arm.

"So what do you think about Chip's new job?" Enid asked her brightly.

"His—?"

"Well, at the *Wall Street Journal*."

Denise studied the tabletop. "I have no opinion about it."

"It's exciting, don't you think?"

"I have no opinion about it."

"Do you think he works there full-time?"

"No."

"I don't understand what kind of job it is."

"Mother, I know nothing about it."

"Is he still doing law?"

"You mean proofreading? Yes."

"So he's still at the firm."

"He's not a lawyer, Mother."

"I know he's not a lawyer."

"Well, when you say, 'doing law,' or 'at the firm'—is that what you tell your friends?"

"I say he works at a law firm. That's all I say. A New York City law firm. And it's the truth. He does work there."

"It's misleading and you know it," Alfred said.

"I guess I should just never say anything."

"Just say things that are true," Denise said.

"Well, I think he *should* be in law," Enid said. "I think the law would be perfect for Chip. He needs the stability of a profession. He needs structure in his life. Dad always thought he'd make an excellent lawyer. I used to think doctor, because he was interested in science, but Dad always saw him as a lawyer. Didn't you, Al? Didn't you think Chip could be an excellent lawyer? He's so quick with words."

"Enid, it's too late."

"I thought maybe working for the firm he'd get interested and go back to school."

"Far too late."

"The thing is, Denise, there are so *many* things you can do with law.

You can be a company president. You can be a judge! You can teach. You can be a journalist. There are so *many* directions Chip could go in."

"Chip will do what he wants to do," Alfred said. "I've never understood it, but he is not going to change now."

He marched two blocks in the rain before he found a dial tone. At the first twin phone bank he came to, one instrument was castrated, with colored tassels at the end of its cord, and all that remained of the other was four bolt holes. The phone at the next intersection had chewing gum in its coin slot, and the line of its companion was completely dead. The standard way for a man in Chip's position to vent his rage was to smash the handset on the box and leave the plastic shards in the gutter, but Chip was in too much of a hurry for this. At the corner of Fifth Avenue, he tried a phone that had a dial tone but did not respond when he touched the keypad and did not return his quarter when he hung up nicely or when he picked the handset up and slammed it down. The other phone had a dial tone and took his money, but a Baby Bell voice claimed not to understand what he'd dialed and did not return the money. He tried a second time and lost his last quarter.

He smiled at the SUVs crawling by in ready-to-brake bad-weather automotive postures. The doormen in this neighborhood hosed the sidewalks twice a day, and sanitation trucks with brushes like the mustaches of city cops scoured the streets three times a week, but in New York City you never had to go far to find filth and rage. A nearby street sign seemed to read *Filth Avenue*. Things cellular were killing public phones. But unlike Denise, who considered cell phones the vulgar accessories of vulgar people, and unlike Gary, who not only didn't hate them but had bought one for each of his three boys, Chip hated cell phones mainly because he didn't have one.

Under the scant protection of Denise's umbrella, he crossed back to a deli on University Place. Brown cardboard had been laid over the scuff rug at the door for traction, but the cardboard was soaked and trampled, its shreds resembling washed-up kelp. Headlines in wire baskets by the door reported yesterday's tanking of two more economies in South America and fresh plunges in key Far Eastern markets. Behind the cash register was a lottery poster: *It's not about winning. It's about fun.*™

With two of the four dollars in his wallet Chip bought some of the all-natural licorice that he liked. For his third dollar the deli clerk gave him four quarters in change. "I'll take a Lucky Leprechaun, too," Chip said.

The three-leaf clover, wooden harp, and pot of gold that he uncovered weren't a winning, or fun, combination.

"Is there a pay phone around here that works?"

"No pay phone," the clerk said.

"I'm saying, is there one close to here that works?"

"No pay phone!" The clerk reached under the counter and held up a cell phone. "This phone!"

"Can I make one quick call with that?"

"Too late for broker now. Should have call yesterday. Should have buy American."

The clerk laughed in a way that was the more insulting for being good-humored. But then, Chip had reason to be sensitive. Since D——— College had fired him, the market capitalization of publicly traded U.S. companies had increased by thirty-five percent. In these same twenty-two months, Chip had liquidated a retirement fund, sold a good car, worked half-time at an eightieth-percentile wage, and still ended up on the brink of Chapter 11. These were years in America when it was nearly impossible not to make money, years when receptionists wrote MasterCard checks to their brokers at 13.9% APR and still cleared a profit, years of Buy, years of Call, and Chip had missed the boat. In his bones he knew that if he ever did sell "The Academy Purple," the markets would all have peaked the week before and any money he invested he would lose.

Judging from Julia's negative response to his script, the American economy was safe for a while yet.

Up the street, at the Cedar Tavern, he found a working pay phone. Years seemed to have passed since he'd had two drinks here the night before. He dialed Eden Procuro's office and hung up when her voice mail kicked in, but the quarter had already dropped. Directory assistance had a residential listing for Doug O'Brien, and Doug actually answered, but he was changing a diaper. Several minutes passed before Chip was able to ask him if Eden had read the script yet.

"Phenomenal. Phenomenal-sounding project," Doug said. "I think she had it with her when she went out."

"Do you know where she went?"

"Chip, you know I can't tell people where she is. You know that."

"I think the situation qualifies as urgent."

Please deposit—eighty cents—for the next—two minutes—

"My God, a pay phone," Doug said. "Is that a pay phone?"

Chip fed the phone his last two quarters. "I need to get the script back before she reads it. There's a correction I—"

"This isn't about tits, is it? Eden said Julia had a problem with too many tits. I wouldn't worry about that. Generally there's no such thing as too many. Julia's having a really intense week."

Please deposit—an additional—thirty cents—now—

"you what," Doug said.

for the next—two minutes—now—

"most obvious place you—"

or your call will be terminated—now—

"Doug?" Chip said. "Doug? I missed that."

We're sorry—

"Yeah, I'm here. I'm saying, why don't you—"

Goodbye, the company voice said, and the phone went dead, the wasted quarters clanking in its gut. The text on its faceplate had Baby Bell coloration, but it read: ORFIC TELECOM, **3 MINUTES 25¢**, EACH ADD'L MIN. 40¢.

The most obvious place to look for Eden was at her office in Tribeca. Chip stepped up to the bar wondering if the new bartender, a streaky blonde who looked like she might front the kind of band that played at proms, remembered him well enough from the night before to take his driver's license as surety on a twenty-buck loan. She and two unrelated drinkers were watching murky football somewhere, Nittany Lion action, brown squiggling figures in a chalky pond. And near Chip's arm, oh, not six inches away, was a nest of singles. Just lying there. He considered how a tacit transaction (pocketing the cash, never showing his face in here again, anonymously mailing reimbursement to the woman later) might be safer than asking for a loan: might be, indeed, the transgression that saved his sanity. He crumpled the cash into a ball and moved closer to the really rather pretty bartender, but the struggling brown round-headed men continued to hold her gaze, and so he turned and left the tavern.

In the back of a cab, watching the wet businesses drift by, he stuffed licorice into his mouth. If he couldn't get Julia back, he wanted in the worst way to have sex with the bartender. Who looked about thirty-nine herself. He wanted to fill his hands with her smoky hair. He imagined that she lived in a rehabbed tenement on East Fifth, he imagined that she drank a beer at bedtime and slept in faded sleeveless tops and gym shorts, that her posture was weary, her navel unassumingly pierced, her pussy like a seasoned baseball glove, her toenails painted the plainest basic red. He wanted to feel her legs across his back, he wanted to hear the story of her forty-odd years. He wondered if she really might sing rock and roll at weddings and bar mitzvahs.

Through the window of the cab he read GAP ATHLETIC as GAL PATHETIC. He read *Empire Realty* as *Vampire Reality*.

He was half in love with a person he could never see again. He'd stolen nine dollars from a hardworking woman who enjoyed college football. Even if he went back later and reimbursed her and apologized, he would always be the man who ripped her off when her back was turned. She was gone from his life forever, he could never run his fingers through her hair, and it was not a good sign that this latest loss was making him hyperventilate. That he was too wrecked by pain to swallow more licorice.

He read *Cross Pens* as *Cross Penises*, he read ALTERATIONS as ALTERCATIONS.

An optometrist's window offered: HEADS EXAMINED.

The problem was money and the indignities of life without it. Every stroller, cell phone, Yankees cap, and SUV he saw was a torment. He wasn't covetous, he wasn't envious. But without money he was hardly a man.

How he'd changed since D—— College fired him! He no longer wanted to live in a different world; he just wanted to be a man with dignity in this world. And maybe Doug was right, maybe the **breasts** in his script didn't matter. But he finally understood—he finally got it—that he could simply cut the opening theoretical monologue *in its entirety*. He could do this correction in ten minutes at Eden's office.

In front of her building he gave the cabby all nine stolen dollars. Around the corner, a six-trailer crew was filming on a cobbled street, kliegs ablaze, generators stinking in the rain. Chip knew the security codes to Eden's building, and the elevator was unlocked. He prayed that Eden hadn't read the script yet. The newly corrected version in his head was the one true script; but the old opening monologue still unhappily existed on the ivory bond paper of the copy Eden had.

Through the glass outer door on the fifth floor he saw lights in Eden's office. That his socks were soaked and his jacket smelled like a wet cow at the seashore and he had no way to dry his hands or hair was certainly unpleasant, but he was still enjoying not having two pounds of Norwegian salmon in his pants. By comparison, he felt fairly well put together.

He knocked on the glass until Eden emerged from her office and peered out at him. Eden had high cheekbones and big watery blue eyes and thin translucent skin. Any extra calories she ate at lunch in L.A. or drank as martinis in Manhattan got burned on her home treadmill or at her private swim club or in the general madness of being Eden Procuro. She was ordinarily electric and flaming, a bundle of hot copper wire; but her expression now, as she approached the door, was tentative or flustered. She kept looking back at her office.

Chip gestured that he wanted in.

"She's not here," Eden said through the glass.

Chip gestured again. Eden opened the door and put her hand on her heart. "Chip, I'm *so* sorry about you and Julia—"

"I'm looking for my script. Have you read it?"

"I—? Very hastily. I need to read it again. Need to take some notes!" Eden made a scribbling motion near her temple and laughed.

"That opening monologue," Chip said. "I've cut it."

"Oh, good, I love a willingness to cut. Love it." She looked back at her office.

"Do you think, though, that without the monologue—"

"Chip, do you need money?"

Eden smiled up at him with such odd merry frankness that he felt as if he'd caught her drunk or with her pants down.

"Well, I'm not flat broke," he said.

"No, no, of course. But still."

"Why?"

"And how are you with the Web?" she said. "Do you know any Java? HTML?"

"God, no."

"Well, just, come back to my office for a second. Do you mind? Come on back."

Chip followed Eden past Julia's desk, where the only visible Julian artifact was a stuffed toy frog on the computer monitor.

"Now that you two have broken up," Eden said, "there's really no reason you can't—"

"Eden, it's not a breakup."

"No, no, trust me, it's over," Eden said. "It is absolutely over. And I'm thinking you might enjoy a little change of scenery, so you can start getting over it—"

"Eden, listen, Julia and I are having a momentary—"

"No, Chip, sorry, not momentary: permanent." Eden laughed again. "Julia may not be blunt, but I am. And so, when I think about it, there's really no reason for you not to meet . . ." She led Chip into her office. "Gitanas? Incredible stroke of luck here. I have, here, the perfect man for the job."

Reclining in a chair by Eden's desk was a man about Chip's age in a red ribbed leather jacket and tight white jeans. His face was broad and baby-cheeked, his hair a sculpted blond shell.

Eden was practically climaxing with enthusiasm. "Here I've been racking my brain, Gitanas, I can't think of anyone to help you, and probably the best-qualified man in New York City is knocking at the door! Chip Lambert, you know my assistant Julia?" She winked at Chip. "Well, this is *Julia's husband*, Gitanas Misevičius."

In almost every respect—coloration, shape of head, height and build, and especially the wary, shame-faced smile that he was wearing—Gitanas looked more like Chip than anybody Chip could remember meeting. He was like Chip with bad posture and crooked teeth. He nodded nervously without standing up or extending a hand. "How's it going," he said.

It was safe to say, Chip thought, that Julia had a type.

Eden patted the seat of an unoccupied chair. "Sit sit sit," she told him.

Her daughter, April, was on the leather sofa by the windows with a mess of crayons and a sheaf of paper.

"April, hey," Chip said. "How were those desserts?"

The question seemed not to April's liking.

"She'll try those tonight," Eden said. "Somebody was testing limits last night."

"I was not testing limits," April said.

The paper on April's lap was ivory-colored and had text on its reverse.

"Sit! Sit!" Eden exhorted as she retreated to her birch-laminate desk. The big window behind her was lensed with rain. There was fog on the Hudson. Blackish smudges suggestive of New Jersey. Eden's trophies, on the walls, were movie-ad images of Kevin Kline, Chloë Sevigny, Matt Damon, Winona Ryder.

"Chip Lambert," she told Gitanas, "is a brilliant writer, with a script in development with me right now, *and* he's got a Ph.D. in English, *and*, for the last two years, he's been working with my husband doing mergers and acquisitions, *and* he's brilliant with all the Internet stuff, we were just now talking about Java and HTML, and, as you see, he cuts a very impressive, uh—" Here Eden for the first time actually gave her attention to Chip's appearance. Her eyes widened. "It must be raining cats and *dogs* out there. Chip's not, well, ordinarily quite so wet. (My dear, you are very wet.) In all honesty, Gitanas, you won't find a better man. And Chip, I'm just—delighted—that you came by. (Although you are very wet.)"

A man by himself could weather Eden's enthusiasm, but two men together had to gaze at the floor to preserve their dignity in the face of it.

"I, unfortunately," Eden said, "am slightly pressed for time. Gitanas having dropped in somewhat unexpectedly. What I would love is if the two of you could go and use my conference room and work things out, and take as long as you like."

Gitanas crossed his arms in the wound-up European style, his fists jammed in his armpits. He didn't look at Chip but asked him: "Are you an actor?"

"No."

"Well, Chip," Eden said, "that's not strictly true."

"Yes, it is. I've never acted in my life."

"Ha-ha-ha!" Eden said. "Chip is being modest."

Gitanas shook his head and looked at the ceiling.

April's sheaf of paper was definitely a screenplay.

"What are we talking about?" Chip said.

"Gitanas is looking to hire someone—"

"An American actor," Gitanas said with disgust.

"To do, uh, corporate PR for him. And for more than an *hour* now"—Eden glanced at her watch and let her eyes and mouth distend in exaggerated shock—"I've been trying to explain that the actors I work with are more interested in film and stage than in, say, international investment schemes. And tend, also, to have wildly inflated notions of their own literacy. And what I'm trying to explain to Gitanas is that you, Chip, not only have an excellent command of language and jargon, but you don't have to pretend to be an investment expert. You *are* an investment expert."

"I'm a part-time legal proofreader," Chip said.

"An expert in the language. A gifted screenwriter."

Chip and Gitanas traded glances. Something about Chip's person, perhaps the shared physical traits, seemed to interest the Lithuanian. "Are you looking for work?" Gitanas said.

"Possibly."

"Are you a drug addict?"

"No."

"I've *got* to go to the bathroom," Eden said. "April, honey, come along. Bring your drawings."

April obediently hopped off the sofa and went to Eden.

"Bring your drawings, though, honey. Here." Eden gathered up the ivory pages and led April to the door. "You men talk."

Gitanas put a hand to his face and squeezed his round cheeks, scratched his blond stubble. He looked out the window.

"You're in government," Chip said.

Gitanas tilted his head. "Yes and no. I was for many years. But my party is kaput, I'm an entrepreneur now. Sort of a governmental entrepreneur, let's say."

One of April's drawings had fallen to the floor between the window and the sofa. Chip extended a toe and pulled the page toward him.

"We have so many elections," Gitanas said, "nobody reports them internationally anymore. We have three or four elections a year. Elections are our biggest industry. We have the highest annual per capita output of elections of any country in the world. Higher than Italy, even."

April had drawn a portrait of a man with a regular body of sticks and blobs and oblongs, but for a head he had a black and blue snarled vortex, a ratty scrabble, a scribbled mess. Through the ivory bond, Chip could see faint blocks of dialogue and action on the other side.

"Do you believe in America?" Gitanas said.

"Jesus, where to begin," Chip said.

"Your country which saved us also ruined us."

With his toe Chip lifted one corner of April's drawing and identified the words—

```
                    MONA

              (cradling the revolver)

     What's wrong with being in love with myself?

     Why is that a problem?
```

—but the page had grown very heavy or his toe very weak. He let the page lie flat again. He pushed it underneath the sofa. His extremities had gone cool and a little bit numb. He couldn't see well.

"Russia went bankrupt in August," Gitanas said. "Maybe you heard? Unlike our elections, this was widely reported. This was *economic* news. This mattered to the investor. It also mattered to Lithuania. Our main trading partner now has crippling hard-currency debts and a worthless ruble. One guess which they use, dollars or rubles, to buy our hens' eggs. And to buy our truck undercarriages from our truck-undercarriage plant, which is the one good plant we have: well, it would be rubles. But the rest of the truck is made in Volgograd, and that plant closed. So we can't even get rubles."

Chip was having trouble feeling disappointed about "The Academy Purple." Never to look at the script again, never to show it to a soul: this might be a relief even greater than his relief in the men's room of Fanelli's where he'd taken the salmon from his pants.

From an enchantment of **breasts** and hyphens and one-inch margins he felt himself awakening to a rich and varied world to which he'd been dead for who knew how long. Years.

"I'm interested in what you're telling me," he told Gitanas.

"It's interesting. It is interesting," Gitanas agreed, still hugging himself tensely. "Brodsky said, 'Fresh fish always smells, frozen smells only when it thaws.' So, and after the big thaw, when all the little fish came out of the freezer, we were passionate about this and that. I was part of it. Very much part of it. But the economy was mismanaged. I had my fun in New York, but back home—there was a depression, all right. Then, too late, 1995, we pegged the litas to the dollar and started privatizing, way too fast. It wasn't my decision, but I might have done the same. The World Bank had money that we wanted, and the World Bank said privatize. So OK, we sold the port. We sold the airline, sold the phone system. The highest bidder was usually American, sometimes Western European. This wasn't supposed to happen, but it did. Nobody in Vilnius had cash. And the phone company said, OK, we'll have foreign owners with deep pockets, but the port and the airline will still be a hundred percent Lithuanian. Well, the port and the airline were thinking the same. But still it was OK. Capital was flowing, better cuts of meat at the butcher, fewer brownouts. Even the weather seemed milder. Mostly criminals took the hard currency, but that's post-Soviet reality. After the thaw, you get the rot. Brodsky didn't live to see that. So OK, but then all the world economies started collapsing, Thailand, Brazil, Korea, and this was a problem, because all the capital ran home to the U.S. We found out, for example, that our national airline was sixty-four percent owned by the Quad Cities Fund. Which is? A no-load growth fund managed by a young guy named Dale Meyers. You never heard of Dale Meyers, but every adult citizen of Lithuania knows his name."

This tale of failure seemed to amuse Gitanas greatly. It had been a long time since Chip had had such a powerful sensation of *liking* somebody. His queer friends at D—— College and the *Warren Street Journal* were so frank and headlong in their confidences that they foreclosed actual closeness, and his responses to straight men had long fallen into one of two categories: fear and resentment of the successes, flight from the contagion of the failures. But something in Gitanas's tone appealed to him.

"Dale Meyers lives in eastern Iowa," Gitanas said. "Dale Meyers has two assistants, a big computer, and a three-billion-dollar portfolio. Dale Meyers says he didn't mean to acquire a controlling stake in our national airline. Dale says it was program trading. He says one of his assistants misentered data that caused the computer to keep increasing its position in Lithuanian Airlines without reporting the overall size of the accumulated stake. OK, Dale apologizes to all Lithuanians for the oversight. Dale says he understands the importance of an airline to a country's economy and self-esteem. But because of the crisis in Russia and the Baltics, nobody wants tickets on Lithuanian Airlines. So, and American investors are pulling money out of Quad Cities. Dale's only way to meet his obligations is liquidate Lithuanian Airlines' biggest asset. Which is its fleet. He's gonna sell three YAK40s to a Miami-based air freight company. He's gonna sell six Aerospatiale turboprops to a start-up commuter airline in Nova Scotia. In fact, he already did that, yesterday. So, whoops, no airline."

"Ouch," Chip said.

Gitanas nodded fiercely. "Yeah! Yeah! Ouch! Too bad you can't fly a truck undercarriage! OK, and then. Then an American conglomerate called Orfic Midland liquidates the Port of Kaunas. Again, overnight. Whoops! Ouch! And then sixty percent of the Bank of Lithuania gets eaten up by a suburban bank in Atlanta, Georgia. And your suburban bank then liquidates our bank's hard-currency reserves. Your bank doubles our country's commercial interest rates overnight—why? To cover heavy losses in its failed line of Dilbert affinity MasterCards. Ouch! Ouch! But interesting, huh? Lithuania's not being such a successful player, is it? Lithuania really fucked things up!"

"How are you men doing?" Eden said, returning to her office with April in tow. "Maybe you want to use the conference room?"

Gitanas put a briefcase on his lap and opened it. "I'm explaining to Cheep my gripe with America."

"April, sweetie, sit down here," Eden said. She had a big pad of newsprint which she opened on the floor near the door. "This is better paper for you. You can make *big* pictures now. Like me. Like Mommy. Make a *big* picture."

April crouched in the middle of the newsprint pad and drew a green circle around herself.

"We've petitioned the IMF and World Bank for assistance," Gitanas said. "Since they encouraged us to privatize, maybe they're interested in the fact that our privatized nation-state is now a zone of semi-anarchy, criminal warlords, and subsistence farming? Unfortunately, IMF is handling complaints of bankrupt client states in order of the size of their respective GDPs. Lithuania was twenty-six on the list last Monday. Now we're twenty-eight. Paraguay just beat us. Always Paraguay."

"Ouch," Chip said.

"Paraguay being for some reason the bane of my existence."

"Gitanas, I told you, Chip is perfect," Eden said. "But listen—"

"IMF says expect delays of up to thirty-six months before any rescue can begin!"

Eden slumped into her chair. "Do you think we can wrap this up fairly soon?"

Gitanas showed Chip a printout from his briefcase. "You see, here, this Web page? 'A service of the U.S. Department of State, Bureau of European and Canadian Affairs.' It says: Lithuanian economy severely depressed, unemployment nearly twenty percent, electricity and running water intermittent in Vilnius, scarce elsewhere. What kind of businessman is going to put money in a country like that?"

"A Lithuanian businessman?" Chip said.

"Yes, funny." Gitanas gave him an appreciative look. "But what if I need something different on this Web page and others like it? What if I need to erase what's here and put, in good American English, that our country escaped the Russian financial plague? Like, say, Lithuania now has an annual inflation rate less than six percent, per capita dollar reserves same as Germany, and a trade surplus of nearly one hundred million dollars, due to continued strong demand for Lithuania's natural resources!"

"Chip, you'd be perfect for this," Eden said.

Chip had quietly and firmly resolved never to look at Eden or say a word to her again for as long as he lived.

"What are Lithuania's natural resources?" he asked Gitanas.

"Chiefly sand and gravel," Gitanas said.

"Huge strategic reserves of sand and gravel. OK."

"Sand and gravel in abundance." Gitanas closed his briefcase. "However, so, here's a quiz for you. Why the unprecedented demand for these intriguing resources?"

"A construction boom in nearby Latvia and Finland? In sand-starved Latvia? In gravel-starved Finland?"

"And how did these countries escape the contagion of global financial collapse?"

"Latvia has strong, stable democratic institutions," Chip said. "It's the financial nerve center of the Baltics. Finland placed strict limits on the outflow of short-term foreign capital and succeeded in saving its world-class furniture industry."

The Lithuanian nodded, obviously pleased. Eden pounded her fists on her desk. "God, Gitanas, Chip's fantastic! He is *so* entitled to a signing bonus. Also first-class accommodations in Vilnius and a per diem in dollars."

"Vilnius?" Chip said.

"Yeah, we're selling a country," Gitanas said. "We need a satisfied U.S. customer on site. Also much, much safer to work on the Web over there."

Chip laughed. "You actually expect American investors to send you money? On the basis of, what. Of sand shortages in Latvia?"

"They're already sending me money," Gitanas said, "on the basis of a little joke I played. Not even sand and gravel, just a mean little joke I played. Tens of thousands of dollars already. But I want them to send me millions."

"Gitanas," Eden said. "Dear man. This is completely a point-incentive moment. There could not *be* a more perfect situation for an escalator clause. Every time Chip doubles your receipts, you give him another point of the action. Hm? Hm?"

"If I see a hundred-times increase in receipts, trust me, Cheep will be a wealthy man."

"But I'm saying let's have this in writing."

Gitanas caught Chip's eye and silently conveyed to him his opinion of their host. "Eden, this document," he said. "What is Cheep's job designation? International Wire Fraud Consultant? First Deputy Co-Conspirator?"

"Vice President for Willful Tortious Misrepresentation," Chip offered.

Eden gave a scream of pleasure. "I love it!"

"Mommy, look," April said.

"Our agreement is strictly oral," Gitanas said.

"Of course, there's nothing actually illegal about what you're doing," Eden said.

Gitanas answered her question by staring out the window for a longish while. In his red ribbed jacket he looked like a motocross rider. "Of course not," he said.

"So it isn't wire fraud," Eden said.

"No, no. Wire fraud? No."

"Because, not to be a scaredy-cat here, but wire fraud is what this almost sounds like."

"The collective fungible assets of my country disappeared in yours without a ripple," Gitanas said. "A rich powerful country made the rules we Lithuanians are dying by. Why should we respect these rules?"

"This is an essential Foucaultian question," Chip said.

"It's also a Robin Hood question," Eden said. "Which doesn't exactly reassure me on the legal front."

"I'm offering Cheep five hundred dollars American a week. Also bonuses as I see fit. Cheep, are you interested?"

"I can do better here in town," Chip said.

"Try a thousand a *day*, minimum," Eden said.

"A dollar goes a long way in Vilnius."

"Oh, I'm sure," Eden said. "It goes a long way on the moon, too. What's to buy?"

"Cheep," Gitanas said. "Tell Eden what dollars can buy in a poor country."

"I imagine you eat and drink pretty well," Chip said.

"A country where a young generation grew up in a state of moral anarchy, and are hungry."

"Probably not hard to find a good-looking date, if that's what you mean."

"If it doesn't break your heart," Gitanas said. "To see a sweet little girl from the provinces get down on her knees—"

"Uch, Gitanas," Eden said. "There's a child in the room."

"I'm on an island," April said. "Mommy, look at my island."

"I'm talking about children," Gitanas said. "Fifteen-year-olds. You have dollars? Thirteen. Twelve."

"Twelve years old is not a selling point with me," Chip said.

"You prefer nineteen? Nineteen comes even cheaper."

"This frankly, um," Eden said, flapping her hands.

"I want Cheep to understand why a dollar is a lot of money. Why my offer is a valid offer."

"My problem," Chip said, "is I'd be servicing American debts with those very same dollars."

"Believe me, we're familiar with this problem in Lithuania."

"Chip wants a base salary of a thousand a day, plus performance incentives," Eden said.

"One thousand per week," Gitanas said. "For lending legitimacy to my project. For creative work and reassuring callers."

"One percent of gross," Eden said. "One point minus his twenty-thousand-dollar monthly salary."

Gitanas, ignoring her, took a thick envelope from his jacket and, with hands that were stubby and unmanicured, began to count out hundreds. April was crouched on a patch of white newsprint surrounded by toothed monsters and cruel scribbles in several colors. Gitanas tossed a stack of hundreds on Eden's desk. "Three thousand," he said, "for the first three weeks."

"He gets business-class plane fare, too, of course," Eden said.

"Yes, all right."

"And first-class accommodations in Vilnius."

"There's a room in the villa, no problem."

"Also, who protects him from these criminal warlords?"

"Maybe I'm a criminal warlord myself, a little bit," Gitanas said with a wary, shame-faced smile.

Chip considered the mess of green on Eden's desk. Something was giving him a hard-on, possibly the cash, possibly the vision of corrupt and sumptuous nineteen-year-olds, or maybe just the prospect of getting on a plane and putting five thousand miles between himself and the nightmare of his life in New York City. What made drugs perpetually so sexy was the opportunity to be other. Years after he'd figured out that pot only made him paranoid and sleepless, he still got hard-ons at the thought of smoking it. Still lusted for that jailbreak.

He touched the hundreds.

"Why don't I get online and make plane reservations for you both," Eden said. "You can leave right away!"

"So, you gonna do this thing?" Gitanas asked. "It's a lot of work, lot of fun. Pretty low risk. No such thing as no risk, though. Not where there's money."

"I understand," Chip said, touching the hundreds.

In the pageantry of weddings Enid reliably experienced the paroxysmal love of *place*—of the Midwest in general and suburban St. Jude in particular—that for her was the only true patriotism and the only viable spirituality. Living under presidents as crooked as Nixon and stupid as Reagan and disgusting as Clinton, she'd lost interest in American flag-waving, and not one of the miracles she'd ever prayed to God for had come to pass; but at a Saturday wedding in the lilac season, from a pew of the Paradise Valley Presbyterian Church, she could look around and see two hundred nice people and not a single bad one. All her friends were nice and had nice friends, and since nice people tended to raise nice children, Enid's world was like a lawn in which the bluegrass grew so thick that evil was simply choked out: a miracle of niceness. If, for example, it was one of Esther and Kirby Root's girls coming down the Presbyterian aisle on Kirby's arm, Enid would remember how the little Root had trick-or-treated in a ballerina costume, vended Girl Scout cookies, and baby-sat Denise, and how, even after the Root girls had gone off to good midwestern colleges, they all still made a point, when home on holiday, of tapping on Enid's back door and filling her in on the doings chez Root, often sitting and visiting for *an hour or more* (and not, Enid knew, because Esther had told them to come over but just because they were good St. Jude kids who naturally took an interest in other people), and Enid's heart would swell at the sight of yet another sweetly charitable Root girl now receiving, as her reward, the vows of a young man with a neat haircut of the kind you saw in ads for menswear, a really super young fellow who had an upbeat attitude and was polite to older people and didn't believe in premarital sex, and who had a job that contributed to society, such as electrical engineer or environmental biologist, and who came from a loving, stable, traditional family and wanted to start a loving, stable, traditional family of his own. Unless Enid was very much deceived by appearances, young men of this caliber continued, even as the twentieth century drew to a close, to be *the norm* in suburban St. Jude. All the young fellows she'd known as Cub Scouts and users of her downstairs bathroom and shovelers of her snow, the many Driblett boys, the various Persons, the young Schumpert twins, all these clean-cut and *handsome* young men (whom Denise, as a teenager, to Enid's quiet rage, had dismissed with her look of "amusement"), had marched or would soon be marching down heartland Protestant aisles and exchanging vows with nice, normal girls and settling down, if not in St. Jude itself, then at least in the same time zone. Now, in her secret heart, where she was less different from her daughter than she liked to admit, Enid knew that tuxes came in better colors than powder blue and that bridesmaids' dresses could be cut from more interesting fabrics than mauve crepe de chine; and yet, although honesty compelled her to withhold the adjective "elegant" from weddings in this style, there was a louder and happier part of her heart that loved this kind of wedding best of all, because a lack of sophistication assured the assembled guests that for the two families being joined together there were values that mattered more than style. Enid believed in matching and was happiest at a wedding where the bridesmaids suppressed their selfish individual desires and wore dresses that matched the corsages and cocktail napkins, the icing on the cake, and the ribbons on the party favors. She liked a ceremony at Chiltsville Methodist to be followed by a modest reception at the Chiltsville Sheraton. She liked a more elegant wedding at Paradise Valley Presbyterian to culminate in the clubhouse at Deepmire, where even the complimentary matches (*Dean & Trish ♦ June 13, 1987*) matched the color scheme. Most important of all was that the bride and groom themselves match: have similar backgrounds and ages and educations. Sometimes, at a wedding hosted by less good friends of Enid's, the bride would be heavier or significantly older than the groom, or the groom's family would hail from a farm town upstate and be obviously overawed by Deepmire's elegance. Enid felt sorry for the principals at a reception like that. She just *knew* the marriage was going to be a struggle from day one. More typically, though, the only discordant note at Deepmire would be an off-color toast offered by some secondary groomsman, often a college buddy of the groom, often mustached or weak-chinned, invariably flushed with liquor, who sounded as if he didn't come from the Midwest at all but from some more eastern urban place, and who tried to show off by making a "humorous" reference to premarital sex, causing both groom and bride to blush or to laugh with their eyes closed (not, Enid felt, because they were amused but because they were naturally tactful and didn't want the offender to realize how offensive his remark was) while Alfred inclined his head deafly and Enid cast her eye around the room until she found a friend with whom she could exchange a reassuring frown.

Alfred loved weddings, too. They seemed to him the one kind of party that had a real purpose. Under their spell he authorized purchases (a new dress for Enid, a new suit for himself, a top-quality ten-piece teakwood salad-bowl set for a gift) that he ordinarily would have vetoed as unreasonable.

Enid had looked forward, some day when Denise was older and had finished college, to hosting a really elegant wedding and reception (though not, alas, at Deepmire, since, almost alone among their better friends, the Lamberts could not afford the astronomical Deepmire fees) for Denise and a tall, broad-shouldered, possibly Scandinavian young man whose flaxen hair would offset the defect of the too-dark and too-curly hair Denise had inherited from Enid but who would otherwise be her match. And so it just about broke Enid's heart when, one October night, not three weeks after Chuck Meisner had given his daughter Cindy the most lavish reception ever undertaken at Deepmire, with all the men in tails, and a champagne fountain, and a helicopter on the eighteenth fairway, and a brass octet playing fanfares, Denise called home with the news that she and her boss had driven to Atlantic City and gotten married in a courthouse. Enid, who had a very strong stomach (never got sick, never), had to hand the phone to Alfred and go kneel in the bathroom and take deep breaths.

The previous spring, in Philadelphia, she and Alfred had eaten a late lunch at the *noisy* restaurant where Denise was ruining her hands and wasting her youth. After their lunch, which was quite good but much too rich, Denise had made a point of introducing them to the "chef" under whom she'd studied and for whom she was now boiling and toiling. This "chef," Emile Berger, was a short, unsmiling, middle-aged Jew from Montreal whose idea of dressing for work was to wear an old white T-shirt (like a *cook*, not a chef, Enid thought; no jacket, no toque) and whose idea of shaving was to skip it. Enid would have disliked Emile and snubbed him even if she hadn't gathered, from Denise's way of hanging on his words, that he had an unhealthy degree of influence with her daughter. "Those are *such* rich crab cakes," she accused in the kitchen. "*One bite* and I was stuffed." To which, instead of apologizing and deprecating himself, as any polite St. Judean would have done, Emile responded by agreeing that, yes, if it could be managed, and the flavor was good, a "lite" crab cake would be a wonderful thing, but the question, Mrs. Lambert, was how to manage it? Eh? How to make crabmeat "lite"? Denise was following this exchange hungrily, as if she'd scripted it or were memorizing it. Outside the restaurant, before she returned to her fourteen-hour shift, Enid made sure to say to her: "He certainly is a short little man! *So* Jewish-looking." Her tone was less controlled than she might have wished, a little squeakier and thinner at the edges, and she could tell from the distant look in Denise's eyes and from a bitterness around her mouth that she'd bruised her daughter's feelings. Then again, all she'd done was speak the truth. And she never, not for a second, imagined that Denise—who, no matter how immature and romantic she was, and no matter how impractical her career plans, had just turned twenty-three and had a beautiful face and figure and her whole life ahead of her—would actually *date* a person like Emile. As to what exactly a young woman was supposed to do with her physical charms while she waited for the maturing years to pass, now that girls no longer got married quite so young, Enid was, to be sure, somewhat vague. In a general way she believed in socializing in groups of three or more; believed, in a word, in parties! The one thing she knew categorically, the principle she embraced the more passionately the more it was ridiculed in the media and popular entertainments, was that sex before marriage was immoral.

And yet, on that October night, as she knelt on the bathroom floor, Enid had the heretical thought that it might after all have been wiser, in her maternal homilies, to have laid less stress on marriage. It occurred to her that Denise's rash act might even have been prompted, in some tiny part, by her wish to do the moral thing and please her mother. Like a toothbrush in the toilet bowl, like a dead cricket in a salad, like a diaper on the dinner table, this sickening conundrum confronted Enid: that it might actually have been preferable for Denise to go ahead and commit adultery, better to sully herself with a momentary selfish pleasure, better to waste a purity that every decent young man had the right to expect from a prospective bride, than to marry Emile. Except that Denise should never have been attracted to Emile in the first place! It was the same problem Enid had with Chip and even Gary: her children didn't match. They didn't want the things that she and all her friends and all her friends' children wanted. Her children wanted radically, shamefully other things.

While observing peripherally that the bathroom carpet was more spotted than she'd realized and ought to be replaced before the holidays, Enid listened to Alfred offering to send Denise a pair of plane tickets. She was struck by the seeming calm with which Alfred took the news that his only daughter had made the biggest decision of her life without consulting him. But after he'd hung up the phone and she'd come out of the bathroom and he'd commented, simply, that life was full of surprises, she noticed how strangely his hands were shaking. The tremor was at once looser and more intense than the one he sometimes got from drinking coffee. And during the week that followed, while Enid made the best of the mortifying position in which Denise had placed her by (1) calling her best friends and sounding thrilled to announce that Denise was getting married soon! to a very nice Canadian man, yes, but she wanted *immediate family only* at the ceremony, so, and she was introducing her new husband at a simple, informal open house at Christmastime (none of Enid's friends believed that she was thrilled, but they gave her full credit for trying to hide her suffering; some were even sensitive enough not to ask where Denise had registered for gifts) and (2) ordering, without Denise's permission, two hundred engraved announcements, not only to make the wedding appear more conventional but also to shake the gift tree a little in hopes of receiving compensation for the dozens and dozens of teakwood salad sets that she and

Alfred had given in the last twenty years: during this long week, Enid was so continually aware of Alfred's strange new tremor that when, by and by, he agreed to see his doctor and was referred to Dr. Hedgpeth and diagnosed with Parkinson's, an underground branch of her intelligence persisted in connecting his disease with Denise's announcement and so in blaming her daughter for the subsequent plummeting of her own quality of life, even though Dr. Hedgpeth had stressed that Parkinson's was somatic in origin and gradual in its onset. By the time the holidays rolled around, and Dr. Hedgpeth had provided her and Alfred with pamphlets and booklets whose drab doctor's-office color schemes, dismal line drawings, and frightening medical photos presaged a drab and dismal and frightening future, Enid was pretty well convinced that Denise and Emile had ruined her life. She was under strict orders from Alfred, however, to make Emile feel welcome in the family. So at the open house for the newlyweds she painted a smile on her face and accepted, over and over, the sincere congratulations of old family friends who loved Denise and thought she was darling (because Enid in raising her had emphasized the importance of being kind to her elders) (although what was her marriage if not an instance of excessive kindness to an elder?) where she would have much preferred condolences. The effort she made to be a good sport and cheerleader, to obey Alfred and receive her middle-aged son-in-law cordially and not say *one single word* about his religion, only added to the shame and anger she felt five years later when Denise and Emile were divorced and Enid had to give this news, too, to all her friends. Having attached so much meaning to the marriage, having struggled so hard to accept it, she felt that the least Denise could have done was stay married.

"Do you ever hear from Emile anymore?" Enid asked.

Denise was drying dishes in Chip's kitchen. "Occasionally."

Enid had parked herself at the dining table to clip coupons from magazines she'd taken from her Nordic Pleasurelines shoulder bag. Rain was coming down erratically in gusts that slapped and fogged the windows. Alfred was sitting on Chip's chaise with his eyes closed.

"I was just thinking," Enid said, "that even if things had worked out, and you'd stayed married, you know, Denise, Emile's going to be an old man in not too many years. And that's so much work. You can't imagine what a huge responsibility."

"In twenty-five years he'll be younger than Dad is now," Denise said.

"I don't know if I ever told you," Enid said, "about my high-school friend Norma Greene."

"You tell me about Norma Greene literally every time I see you."

"Well, you know the story, then. Norma met this man, Floyd Voinovich, who was a perfect gentleman, quite a number of years older, with a high-paying job, and he swept her off her feet! He was always taking her to Morelli's, and the Steamer, and the Bazelon Room, and the only problem—"

"Mother."

"The only problem," Enid insisted, "was that he was married. But Norma wasn't supposed to worry about that. Floyd said the whole arrangement was temporary. He said he'd made a bad mistake, he had a terrible marriage, he'd never loved his wife—"

"Mother."

"*And* he was going to divorce her." Enid let her eyes fall shut in raconteurial pleasure. She was aware that Denise didn't like this story, but there were plenty of things about Denise's life that were disagreeable to Enid, too, so. "Well, this went on for years. Floyd was very smooth and charming, and he could afford to do things for Norma that a man closer to her own age couldn't have. Norma developed a real taste for luxuries, and then, too, she'd met Floyd at an age when a girl falls head over heels in love, and Floyd had sworn up and down that he was going to divorce his wife and marry Norma. Well, by then Dad and I were married and had Gary. I remember Norma came over once when Gary was a baby, and she just wanted to hold him and hold him. She *loved* little children, oh, she just loved holding Gary, and I felt terrible for her, because by then she'd been seeing Floyd for years, and he was still not divorced. I said, Norma, you can't wait forever. She said she'd tried to stop seeing Floyd. She'd gone on dates with other men, but they were younger and they didn't seem matoor to her—Floyd was fifteen years older and very matoor, and I do understand how an older man has a matoority that can make him attractive to a younger woman—"

"Mother."

"And, of course, these younger men couldn't always afford to be taking Norma to fancy places or buying her flowers and gifts like Floyd did (because, see, he could really turn on the charm when she got impatient with him), and then, too, a lot of those younger men were interested in starting families, and Norma—"

"Wasn't so young anymore," Denise said. "I brought some dessert. Are you ready for dessert?"

"Well, you know what happened."

"Yes."

"It's a heartbreaking story, because Norma—"

"Yes. I know the story."

"Norma found herself—"

"Mother: *I know the story*. You seem to think it has some bearing on my own situation."

"Denise, I don't. You've never even told me what your 'situation' is."

"Then why do you keep telling me the story of Norma Greene?"

"I don't see why it upsets you if it has nothing to do with your own situation."

"What upsets me is that you seem to think it does. Are you under the impression that I'm involved with a married man?"

Enid was not only under this impression but was suddenly so angry about it, so clotted with disapproval, that she had difficulty breathing.

"Finally, *finally*, going to get rid of some of these magazines," she said, snapping the glossy pages.

"Mother?"

"It's better not to talk about this. Just like the Navy, don't ask, don't tell."

Denise stood in the kitchen doorway with her arms crossed and a dish towel balled up in her hand. "Where did you get the idea that I'm involved with a married man?"

Enid snapped another page.

"Did Gary say something to give you that idea?"

Enid struggled to shake her head. Denise would be furious if she found out that Gary had betrayed a confidence, and though Enid spent much of her own life furious with Gary about one thing or another, she prided herself on keeping secrets, and she didn't want to get him in trouble. It was true that she'd been brooding about Denise's situation for many months and had accumulated large stores of anger. She'd ironed at the ironing board and raked the ivy beds and lain awake at night rehearsing the judgments—*That is the kind of grossly selfish behavior that I will never understand and never forgive* and *I'm ashamed to be the parent of a person who would live like that* and *In a situation like this, Denise, my sympathies are one thousand percent with the wife, one thousand percent*—that she yearned to pronounce on Denise's immoral lifestyle. And now she had an opportunity to pronounce these judgments. And yet, if Denise denied the charges, then all of Enid's anger, all of her refining and rehearsal of her judgments, would go wasted. And if, on the other hand, Denise admitted everything, it might still be wiser for Enid to swallow her pent-up judgments than to risk a fight. Enid needed Denise as an ally on the Christmas front, and she didn't want to set off on a luxury cruise with one son having vanished inexplicably, another son blaming her for betraying his trust, and her daughter perhaps confirming her worst fears.

With great humbling effort she therefore shook her head. "No, no, no. Gary never said a thing."

Denise narrowed her eyes. "Never said a thing about what."

"Denise," Alfred said. "Let her be."

And Denise, who obeyed Enid in nothing, promptly turned and went back into the kitchen.

Enid found a coupon offering sixty cents off I Can't Believe It's Not Butter! with any purchase of Thomas' English muffins. Her scissors cut the paper and with it the silence that had fallen.

"If I do one thing on this cruise," she said, "I'm going to get through all these magazines."

"No sign of Chip," Alfred said.

Denise brought slices of tart on dessert plates to the dining table. "I'm afraid we may have seen the last of Chip today."

"It's *very* peculiar," Enid said. "I don't understand why he doesn't at least call."

"I've endured worse," Alfred said.

"Dad, there's dessert. My pastry chef made a pear tart. Do you want to have it at the table?"

"Oh, that's much too big a piece for me," Enid said.

"Dad?"

Alfred didn't answer. His mouth had gone slack and sour again in the way that made Enid feel that something terrible was going to happen. He turned to the darkening, rain-spotted windows and gazed at them dully, his head hanging low.

"Dad?"

"Al? There's dessert."

Something seemed to melt in him. Still looking at the window, he raised his head with a tentative joy, as if he thought he recognized someone outside, someone he loved.

"Al, what is it?"

"Dad?"

"There are children," he said, sitting up straighter. "Do you see them?" He raised a trembling index finger. "There." His finger moved laterally, following the motion of the children he saw. "And there. And there."

He turned to Enid and Denise as if he expected them to be overjoyed to hear this news, but Enid was not the least bit overjoyed. She was about to embark on a very elegant fall color cruise on which it would be extremely important that Alfred not make mistakes like this.

"Al, those are *sunflowers*," she said, half angry, half beseeching. "You're seeing reflections in the window."

"Well!" He shook his head bluffly. "I thought I saw children."

"No, sunflowers," Enid said. "You saw sunflowers."

After his party was voted out of power and the Russian currency crisis had finished off the Lithuanian economy, Gitanas said, he'd passed his days alone in the old offices of the VIPPPAKJRIINPB17, devoting his idle hours to constructing a Web site whose domain name, lithuania.com, he'd purchased from an East Prussian speculator for a truckload of mimeograph machines, daisy-wheel printers, 64-kilobyte Commodore computers, and other Gorbachev-era office equipment—the party's last physical vestiges. To publicize the plight of small debtor nations, Gitanas had created a satiric Web page offering DEMOCRACY FOR PROFIT: BUY A PIECE OF EUROPEAN HISTORY and had seeded links and references in American news groups and chat rooms for investors. Visitors to the site were invited to send cash to the erstwhile VIPP-PAKJRIINPB17—"one of Lithuania's most venerable political parties," the "cornerstone" of the country's governing coalition for "three of the last seven years," the leading vote-getter in the April 1993 general election, and now a "Western-leaning pro-business party" reorganized as the "Free Market Party Company." Gitanas's Web site promised that, as soon as the Free Market Party Company had bought enough votes to win a national election, its foreign investors would not only become "equity shareholders" in Lithuania Incorporated (a "for-profit nation state") but would also be rewarded, in proportion to the size of their investment, with personalized memorials to their "heroic contribution" to the "market liberation" of the country. By sending just $100, for example, an American investor could have a street in Vilnius ("no less than two hundred meters in length") named after him; for $5,000 the Free Market Party Company would hang a portrait of the investor ("minimum size 60 cm × 80 cm; *includes ornate gilt frame*") in the Gallery of National Heroes at the historic Šlapeliai House; for $25,000 the investor would be awarded perpetual title to an eponymous town "of no fewer than 5,000 souls" and be granted a "modern, hygienic form of *droit du seigneur*" that met "most of" the guidelines established by the Third International Conference on Human Rights.

"It was a nasty little joke," Gitanas said from the corner of the taxicab into which he'd wedged himself. "But who laughed? Nobody laughed. They just sent money. I gave an address and the cashier checks started coming in. E-mail queries by the hundred. What products would Lithuania Inc. make? Who were the officers in the Free Market Party Company and did they have a strong track record as managers? Did I have records of past earnings? Could the investor alternatively have a Lithuanian street or village named after his children or his children's favorite Pokémon character? Everybody wanted more information. Everybody wanted brochures. And prospectuses! And stock certificates! And brokerage information! And are we listed on such and such exchange and so forth? People want to come and visit! *And nobody is laughing.*"

Chip was tapping on the window with a knuckle and checking out the women on Sixth Avenue. The rain was letting up, umbrellas coming down. "Are the proceeds going to you or to the Party?"

"OK, so my philosophy about that is in transition," Gitanas said. From his briefcase he took a bottle of akvavit from which he'd already poured deal-sealing shots in Eden's office. He rolled sideways and handed it to Chip, who took a healthy pull and gave it back.

"You were an English teacher," Gitanas said.

"I taught college, yeah."

"And where your people from? Scandinavia?"

"My dad's Scandinavian," Chip said. "My mom's sort of mongrel Eastern European."

"People in Vilnius will look at you and think you're one of us."

Chip was in a hurry to get to his apartment before his parents left. Now that he had cash in his pocket, a roll of thirty hundreds, he didn't care so much what his parents thought of him. In fact, he seemed to recall that a few hours earlier he'd seen his father trembling and pleading in a doorway. As he drank the akvavit and checked out the women on the sidewalk, he could no longer fathom why the old man had seemed like such a killer.

It was true that Alfred believed the only thing wrong with the death penalty was that it wasn't used often enough; true as well that the men whose gassing or electrocution he'd called for, over dinner in Chip's childhood, were usually black men from the slums on St. Jude's north side. ("Oh, Al," Enid would say, because dinner was "the family meal," and she couldn't understand why they had to spend it talking about gas chambers and slaughter in the streets.) And one Sunday morning, after he'd stood at a window counting squirrels and assessing the damage to his oak trees and zoysia the way white men in marginal neighborhoods took stock of how many houses had been lost to "the blacks," Alfred had performed an experiment in genocide. Incensed that the squirrels in his not-large front yard lacked the discipline to stop reproducing or pick up after themselves, he went to the basement and found a rat trap over which Enid, as he came upstairs with it, shook her head and made small negative noises. "Nineteen of them!" Alfred said. "Nineteen of them!" Emotional appeals were no match for the discipline of such an exact and scientific figure. He baited the trap with a piece of the same whole wheat bread that Chip had eaten, toasted, for breakfast. Then all five Lamberts went to church, and between the Gloria Patri and the Doxology a young male squirrel, engaging in the high-risk behavior of the economically desperate, helped itself to the bread and had its skull crushed. The family came home to find green flies feasting on the blood and brain matter and chewed whole-wheat bread that had erupted through the young squirrel's shattered jaws. Alfred's own mouth and chin were sewn up in the distaste that special exertions of discipline—the spanking of a child, the eating of rutabaga—always caused him. (He was quite unconscious of this distaste he betrayed for discipline.) He fetched a shovel from the garage and loaded both the trap and the squirrel corpse into the paper grocery bag that Enid had half filled with pulled crabgrass the day before. Chip was following all this from about twenty steps behind him, and so he saw how, when Alfred entered the basement from the garage, his legs buckled a little, sideways, and he pitched into the washing machine, and then he ran past the Ping-Pong table (it had always scared Chip to see his father run, he seemed too old for it, too disciplined) and disappeared into the basement bathroom; and henceforth the squirrels did whatever they wanted.

The cab was approaching University Place. Chip considered returning to the Cedar Tavern and reimbursing the bartender, maybe giving her an even hundred to make everything OK, maybe getting her name and address and writing to her from Lithuania. He was leaning forward to direct the driver to the Tavern when a radical new thought arrested him: *I stole nine bucks, that's what I did, that's who I am, tough luck for her.*

He sat back and extended his hand for the bottle.

　　　　　　　　　　　　　　　　　　　　　THE CORRECTIONS

Outside his building the cabby waved away his hundred—too big, too big. Gitanas dug something smaller out of his red motocross jacket.

"Why don't I meet you at your hotel?" Chip said.

Gitanas was amused. "You're joking, right? I mean, I trust you a lot. But maybe I'll wait down here. Pack your bag, take your time. Bring a warm coat and hat. Suits and ties. Think financial."

The doorman Zoroaster was nowhere to be seen. Chip had to use his key to get inside. On the elevator he took deep breaths to quell his excitement. He didn't feel afraid, he felt generous, he felt ready to embrace his father.

But his apartment was empty. His family must have left minutes earlier. Body warmth was hanging in the air, faint smells of Enid's White Shoulders perfume, and something bathroomy, something old-persony. The kitchen was cleaner than Chip had ever seen it. In the living room all the scrubbing and stowing he'd done was visible now as it hadn't been the night before. And his bookshelves were denuded. And Julia had taken her shampoos and dryer from the bathroom. And he was drunker than he'd realized. And nobody had left a note for him. There was nothing on the dining table except a slice of tart and a vase of sunflowers. He had to pack his bags, but everything around him and inside him had become so strange that for a moment he could only stand and look. The leaves of the sunflowers had black spots and were rimmed with pale senescences; the heads were meaty and splendid, heavy as brownies, thick as palms. In the center of a sunflower's Kansan face was a subtly pale button within a subtly darker areola. Nature, Chip thought, could hardly have devised a more inviting bed for a small winged insect to tumble into. He touched the brown velvet, and ecstasy washed over him.

The taxi containing three Lamberts arrived at a midtown pier where a white high-rise of a cruise ship, the *Gunnar Myrdal*, was blotting out the river and New Jersey and half the sky. A crowd mostly of old people had converged on the gate and reattenuated in the long, bright corridor beyond it. There was something netherworldly in their determined migration, something chilling in the cordiality and white raiment of the

Nordic Pleasurelines shore personnel, the rain clouds breaking up too late to save the day—the hush of it all. A throng and twilight by the Styx.

Denise paid the cab fare and got the luggage into the hands of handlers.

"So, now, where do you go from here?" Enid asked her.

"Back to work in Philly."

"You look darling," Enid said spontaneously. "I love your hair that length."

Alfred seized Denise's hands and thanked her.

"I just wish it had been a better day for Chip," Denise said.

"Talk to Gary about Christmas," Enid said. "And do think about coming for a whole week."

Denise raised a leather cuff and checked the time. "I'll come for five days. I don't think Gary will do it, though. And who knows what's up with Chip."

"Denise," Alfred said impatiently, as if she were speaking nonsense, "please talk to Gary."

"OK, I will. I will."

Alfred's hands bounced in the air. "I don't know how much time I have! You and your mother need to get along. You and Gary need to get along."

"Al, you have plenty of—"

"We all need to get along!"

Denise had never been a crier, but her face was crumpling up. "Dad, all right," she said. "I'll talk to him."

"Your mother wants a Christmas in St. Jude."

"I'll talk to him. I promise."

"Well." He turned abruptly. "That's enough of that."

His black raincoat was flapping and whipping in the wind, and still Enid managed to hope that the weather would be perfect for cruising, that the water would be calm.

In dry clothes, with a coat bag and a duffel and cigarettes—smooth lethal Murattis, five bucks a box—Chip rode out to Kennedy with

Gitanas Misevičius and boarded the Helsinki flight on which, in violation of his oral contract, Gitanas had bought coach-class, not business-class, tickets. "We can drink tonight, sleep tomorrow," he said.

Their seats were aisle and window. As Chip sat down, he recalled how Julia had ditched Gitanas. He imagined her walking quickly off the plane and then sprinting down the concourse and throwing herself into the back seat of a good old yellow cab. He felt a spasm of homesickness—terror of the other; love of the familiar—but, unlike Julia, he had no desire to bolt. He'd no sooner buckled his seat belt than he fell asleep. He awoke briefly during takeoff and went under again until the entire population of the plane, as one, lit cigarettes.

Gitanas took a computer from its case and booted up. "So Julia," he said.

For an alarmed, sleep-clouded moment Chip thought that Gitanas was addressing him as Julia.

"My wife?" Gitanas said.

"Oh. Sure."

"Yeah, she's on antidepressants. This was Eden's idea, I think. Eden kind of runs her life now, I think. You could see she didn't want me in her office today. Didn't want me in town! I'm inconvenient now. So, but, OK, so Julia started taking the drug, and suddenly she woke up and she didn't want to be with men with cigarette burns anymore. That's what she says. Enough men with cigarette burns. Time to move on. No more men with burns." Gitanas loaded a CD into the computer's CD drive. "She wants the flat, though. At least the divorce lawyer wants her to want it. The divorce lawyer that Eden's paying for. Somebody changed the locks on the flat, I had to pay the super to let me in."

Chip closed his left hand. "Cigarette burns?"

"Yeah. Oh, yeah, I got a few." Gitanas craned his neck to see if any neighbors were listening, but all the passengers around them, except for two children with their eyes shut tight, were busy smoking. "Soviet military prison," he said. "I'll show you my memento of a pleasant stay there." He peeled his red leather jacket off one arm and rolled up the sleeve of the yellow T-shirt he was wearing underneath. A poxy interlocking constellation of scar tissue extended from his armpit down the inside of his arm to his elbow. "This was my 1990," he said. "Eight months in a Red Army barracks in the sovereign state of Lithuania."

"You were a dissident," Chip said.

"Yeah! Yeah! Dissident!" He worked his arm back into its sleeve. "It was horrible, great. Very tiring, but it didn't feel tiring. The tiredness came later."

Chip's memories of 1990 were of Tudor dramas, interminable futile fights with Tori Timmelman, a secret unhealthy involvement with certain texts of Tori's that illustrated the dehumanizing objectifications of pornography, and little else.

"So, I'm kind of scared to look at this," Gitanas said. On his computer screen was a dusky monochrome image of a bed, viewed from above, with a body beneath the blankets. "The super says she's got a boyfriend, and I retrieved some data. I had my surveillance in there from the previous owner. Motion detector, infrared, digital stills. You can look if you want. Might be interesting. Might be hot."

Chip remembered the smoke detector on the ceiling of Julia's bedroom. Often enough he'd stared up at it until the corners of his mouth were dry and his eyes had rolled back in his head. It had always seemed to him a strangely complicated smoke detector.

He sat up straighter in his seat. "Maybe you don't want to look at those."

Gitanas pointed and clicked intricately. "I'll angle the screen. You don't have to look."

Thunderheads of tobacco smoke were gathering in the aisles. Chip decided that he needed to light a Muratti; but the difference between taking a drag and taking a breath proved negligible.

"What I mean," he said, blocking the computer screen with his hand, "is maybe you want to eject the CD and not look at it."

Gitanas was genuinely startled. "Why don't I want to look at it?"

"Well, let's think about why."

"Maybe you should tell me."

"No, well, let's just think about it."

For a moment the atmosphere was furiously cheerful. Gitanas considered Chip's shoulder, his knees, and his wrist, as though deciding where to bite him. Then he ejected the CD and thrust it in Chip's face. "Fuck you!"

"I know, I know."

"Take it. Fuck you. I don't want to see it again. Take it."

Chip put the CD in his shirt pocket. He felt pretty good. He felt all right. The plane had leveled off in altitude and the noise had the steady vague white burning of dry sinuses, the color of scuffed plastic airliner windows, the taste of cold pale coffee in reusable tray-table cups. The North Atlantic night was dark and lonely, but here, on the plane, were lights in the sky. Here was sociability. It was good to be awake and to feel awakeness all around him.

"So, what, you got cigarette burns, too?" Gitanas said.

Chip showed his palm. "It's nothing."

"Self-inflicted. You pathetic American."

"Different kind of prison," Chip said.

THE MORE HE THOUGHT ABOUT IT, THE ANGRIER HE GOT

GARY LAMBERT'S profitable entanglement with the Axon Corporation had begun three weeks earlier, on a Sunday afternoon that he'd spent in his new color darkroom, trying to enjoy reprinting two old photographs of his parents and, by enjoying it, to reassure himself about his mental health.

Gary had been worrying a lot about his mental health, but on that particular afternoon, as he left his big schist-sheathed house on Seminole Street and crossed his big back yard and climbed the outside stairs of his big garage, the weather in his brain was as warm and bright as the weather in northwest Philadelphia. A September sun was shining through a mix of haze and smallish, gray-keeled clouds, and to the extent that Gary was able to understand and track his neurochemistry (and he was a vice president at CenTrust Bank, not a shrink, let's remember) his leading indicators all seemed rather healthy.

Although in general Gary applauded the modern trend toward individual self-management of retirement funds and long-distance calling plans and private-schooling options, he was less than thrilled to be given responsibility for his own personal brain chemistry, especially when certain people in his life, notably his father, refused to take any such responsibility. But Gary was nothing if not conscientious. As he entered the darkroom, he estimated that his levels of Neurofactor 3 (i.e., serotonin: a very, very important factor) were posting seven-day or even thirty-day highs, that his Factor 2 and Factor 7 levels were likewise outperforming expectations, and that his Factor 1 had rebounded from an early-morning slump related to the glass of Armagnac he'd drunk at bedtime. He had a spring in his step, an agreeable awareness of his above-average height and his late-summer suntan. His resentment of his wife, Caroline, was moderate and well contained. Declines led advances in key indices of paranoia (e.g., his persistent suspicion that Caroline and his two older sons were mocking him), and his seasonally adjusted assessment of life's futility and brevity was consistent with the overall robustness of his mental economy. He was not the least bit clinically depressed.

He drew the velvet blackout curtains and shut the lightproof shutters, took a box of 8×10 paper from the big stainless refrigerator, and fed two strips of celluloid to the motorized negative cleaner—a sexily heavy little gadget.

He was printing images from his parents' ill-fated Decade of Connubial Golf. One showed Enid bending over in deep rough, scowling in her sunglasses in the obliterative heartland heat, her left hand squeezing the neck of her long-suffering five-wood, her right arm blurred in the act of underhandedly throwing her ball (a white smear at the image's margin) into the fairway. (She and Alfred had only ever played on flat, straight, short, cheap public courses.) In the other photo Alfred was wearing tight shorts and a billed Midland Pacific cap, black socks and prehistoric golf shoes, and was addressing a white grapefruit-sized tee marker with his prehistoric wooden driver and grinning at the camera as if to say, *A ball this big I could hit!*

After Gary had given the enlargements their sour baths, he raised the lights and discovered that both prints were webbed over with peculiar yellow blotches.

He cursed a little, not so much because he cared about the photographs as because he wanted to preserve his good spirits, his serotonin-rich mood, and to do this he needed a modicum of cooperation from the world of objects.

Outside, the weather was curdling. There was a trickle in the gutters, a rooftop percussion of drops from overhanging trees. Through the walls of the garage, while he shot a second pair of enlargements, Gary could hear Caroline and the boys playing soccer in the back yard. He heard footfalls and punting sounds, less frequent shouts, the seismic whump of ball colliding with garage.

When the second set of prints emerged from the fixer with the same yellow blotches, Gary knew he ought to quit. But there came a tapping on the outside door, and his youngest son, Jonah, slipped through the blackout curtain.

"Are you printing pictures?" Jonah said.

Gary hastily folded the failed prints into quarters and buried them in the trash. "Just starting," he said.

He remixed his solutions and opened a fresh box of paper. Jonah sat down by a safe light and whispered as he turned the pages of one of the Narnia books, *Prince Caspian*, that Gary's sister, Denise, had given him. Jonah was in second grade but was already reading at a fifth-grade level. Often he spoke aloud the written words in an articulate whisper that was of a piece with his general Narnian dearness as a person. He had shining dark eyes and an oboe voice and mink-soft hair and could seem, even to Gary, more sentient animal than little boy.

Caroline did not entirely approve of Narnia—C. S. Lewis was a known Catholic propagandist, and the Narnian hero, Aslan, was a furry, four-pawed Christ figure—but Gary had enjoyed reading *The Lion, the Witch and the Wardrobe* as a boy, and he had not, it was safe to say, grown up to be a religious nut. (In fact he was a strict materialist.)

"So they kill a bear," Jonah reported, "but it's not a talking bear, and Aslan comes back, but only Lucy sees him and the others don't believe her."

Gary tweezed the prints into the stop bath. "Why don't they believe her?"

"Because she's the *youngest*," Jonah said.

Outside, in the rain, Caroline laughed and shouted. She had a habit of running herself ragged to keep up with the boys. In the early years of their marriage she'd worked full-time as a lawyer, but after Caleb was born she'd come into family money and now she worked half days only, at a philanthropically low salary, for the Children's Defense Fund. Her real life centered on the boys. She called them her best friends.

Six months ago, on the eve of Gary's forty-third birthday, while he and Jonah were visiting his parents in St. Jude, a pair of local contractors had come and rewired, replumbed, and re-outfitted the second floor of the garage as a surprise birthday gift from Caroline. Gary had occasionally spoken of reprinting his favorite old family photos and collecting them in a leather-bound album, an All-Time Lambert Two Hundred. But commercial printing would have sufficed for that, and meanwhile the boys were teaching him computer pixel-processing, and if he'd still needed a lab he could have rented one by the hour. His impulse on his birthday, therefore—after Caroline had led him out to the garage and presented him with a darkroom that he didn't need or want—was to weep. From certain pop-psychology books on Caroline's nightstand, however, he'd learned to recognize the Warning Signs of clinical depression, and one of these Warning Signs, the authorities all agreed, was a proclivity to inappropriate weeping, and so he'd swallowed the lump in his throat and bounded around the expensive new darkroom and exclaimed to Caroline (who was experiencing both buyer's remorse and gift-giver's anxiety) that he was utterly delighted with the gift! And then, to reassure himself that he wasn't clinically depressed and to make sure that Caroline never suspected anything of the kind, he'd resolved to work in the darkroom twice a week until the All-Time Lambert Two Hundred album was complete.

The suspicion that Caroline, consciously or not, had tried to exile him from the house by putting the darkroom in the garage was another key index of paranoia.

When the timer pealed, he transferred the third set of prints to the fixer bath and raised the lights again.

"What are those white blobs?" Jonah said, peering into the tray.

"Jonah, I don't know!"

"They look like clouds," Jonah said.

The soccer ball slammed into the side of the garage.

Gary left Enid scowling and Alfred grinning in the fixative and opened shutters. His monkey puzzle tree and the bamboo thicket next to it were glossy with rain. In the middle of the back yard, in soaked soiled jerseys that stuck to their shoulder blades, Caroline and Aaron were gulping air while Caleb tied a shoe. Caroline at forty-five had the legs of a college girl. Her hair was nearly as blond as when Gary had first met her, twenty years earlier, at a Bob Seger concert at the Spectrum. Gary was still substantially attracted to his wife, still excited by her effortless good looks and by her Quaker bloodlines. By ancient reflex, he reached for a camera and trained the zoom telephoto on her.

The look on Caroline's face dismayed him. There was a pinch in her brow, a groove of distress around her mouth. She was limping as she pursued the ball again.

Gary turned the camera on his oldest son, Aaron, who was best photographed unawares, before he could position his head at the self-conscious angle that he believed most flattered him. Aaron's face was flushed and mud-flecked in the drizzle, and Gary worked the zoom to frame a handsome shot. But resentment of Caroline was overwhelming his neurochemical defenses.

The soccer had stopped now and she was running and limping toward the house.

Lucy buried her head in his mane to hide from his face, Jonah whispered.

There came a screaming from the house.

Caleb and Aaron reacted instantly, galloping across the yard like action-picture heroes and disappearing inside. A moment later Aaron reemerged and shouted, in his newly crack-prone voice, "Dad! Dad! Dad! Dad!"

The hysteria of others made Gary methodical and calm. He left the darkroom and descended the rain-slick stairway slowly. In the open space above the commuter-rail tracks, behind the garage, a kind of spring-shower self-improvement of the light was working through the humid air.

"Dad, Grandma's on the phone!"

Gary ambled across the yard, pausing to examine and regret the injuries that the soccer had visited on the grass. The surrounding neighborhood, Chestnut Hill, was not un-Narnian. Century-old maples and ginkgos and sycamores, many of them mutilated to accommodate power lines, grew in giant riot over patched and repatched city streets bearing the names of decimated tribes. Seminole and Cherokee, Navajo and Shawnee. For miles in every direction, despite high population densities and large household incomes, there were no fast roads and few useful stores. The Land That Time Forgot, Gary called it. Most of the houses here, including his own, were made of a schist that resembled raw tin and was exactly the color of his hair.

"Dad!"

"Thank you, Aaron, I heard you the first time."

"Grandma's on the phone!"

"I know that, Aaron. You just told me."

In the slate-floored kitchen he found Caroline slumped in a chair with both hands pressed to her lower back.

"She called this morning," Caroline said. "I forgot to tell you. The phone's been ringing every five minutes, and finally I was running—"

"Thank you, Caroline."

"I was running—"

"Thank you." Gary snagged the cordless and held it at arm's length, as if to keep his mother at bay, while he proceeded into the dining room. Here he was waylaid by Caleb, who had a finger buried in the slick leaves of a catalogue. "Dad, can I talk to you for a second?"

"Not now, Caleb, your grandmother is on the phone."

"I just want—"

"Not now, I said."

Caleb shook his head and smiled in disbelief, like a much-televised athlete who'd failed to draw a penalty.

Gary crossed the marble-floored main hall into his very large living room and said hello into the little phone.

"I *told* Caroline," Enid said, "that I would call you back if you weren't near the phone."

"Your calls cost seven cents a minute," Gary said.

"Or you could have called me back."

"Mother, we're talking about twenty-five cents."

"I've been trying to reach you all day," she said. "The travel agent needs an answer by tomorrow morning at the latest. And, you know, we're still hoping you'll come for one last Christmas, like I promised Jonah, so—"

"Hang on a second," Gary said. "I'll check with Caroline."

"Gary, you've had *months* to discuss this. I'm not going to sit here and wait while you—"

"One second."

He blocked the perforations in the phone's mouthpiece with his thumb and returned to the kitchen, where Jonah was standing on a chair with a package of Oreos. Caroline, still slumped at the table, was breathing shallowly. "I did something terrible," she said, "when I ran to catch the phone."

"You were out there slipping around in the rain for two hours," Gary said.

"No, I was fine until I ran to get the phone."

"Caroline, I saw you limping before you—"

"I was *fine*," she said, "until I ran to get the *phone*, which was ringing for the *fiftieth time*—"

"Good, all right," Gary said, "it's my mother's fault. Now tell me what you want me to say about Christmas."

"Well, whatever. They're welcome to come here."

"We'd talked about the possibility of going *there*."

Caroline shook her head thoroughly, as if erasing something. "No. You talked about it. I never talked about it."

"Caroline—"

"I can't discuss this when she's on the phone. Have her call back next week."

Jonah was realizing that he could take as many cookies as he wanted and neither parent would notice.

"She needs to make arrangements now," Gary said. "They're trying to decide if they should stop here next month, after their cruise. It depends on Christmas."

"It's like I slipped a disk."

"If you won't talk about it," he said, "I'll tell her we're considering coming to St. Jude."

"No way! That was not the agreement."

"I'm proposing a one-time exception to the agreement."

"No! No!" Wet tangles of blond hair lashed and twisted as Caroline registered refusal. "You can't change the rules like that."

"A one-time exception isn't changing the rules."

"God, I think I need an X-ray," Caroline said.

Gary could feel the buzzing of his mother's voice against his thumb. "A yes or a no here?"

Standing up, Caroline leaned into him and buried her face in his sweater. She knocked lightly on his sternum with a little fist. "Please," she said, nuzzling his collarbone. "Tell her you'll call her later. Please? I really hurt my back."

Gary held the phone out to one side, his arm rigid, as she pressed against him. "Caroline. They've come here eight years in a row. It's not extreme of me to propose a one-time exception. Can I at least say we're considering the possibility?"

Caroline shook her head woefully and sank onto the chair.

"OK, fine," Gary said. "I'll make my own decision."

He strode into the dining room, where Aaron, who'd been listening, stared at him as if he were a monster of spousal cruelty.

"Dad," Caleb said, "if you're not talking to Grandma, can I ask you something?"

"No, Caleb, I'm talking to Grandma."

"Then can I talk to you right afterward?"

"Oh, God, oh, God," Caroline was saying.

In the living room Jonah had settled onto the larger leather sofa with his tower of cookies and *Prince Caspian*.

"Mother?"

"I don't understand this," Enid said. "If it's not a good time to talk, all right, call me back, but to make me wait *ten minutes*—"

"Yes, but here I am."

"Well, so, and what have you decided?"

Before Gary could answer, there burst from the kitchen a piteous raw feline wailing, a cry such as Caroline had produced during intercourse fifteen years ago, before there were boys to hear her.

"Mom, sorry, one second."

"This is not right," Enid said. "This is not polite."

"Caroline," Gary called into the kitchen, "do you think we can behave like adults for a few minutes?"

"Ah, ah, uh! Uh!" Caroline cried.

"Nobody ever died of a backache, Caroline."

"Please," she cried, "call her later. I tripped on the last step when I was running inside, Gary, it *hurts*—"

He turned his back on the kitchen. "Sorry, Mom."

"What on earth is going on there?"

"Caroline hurt her back a little bit playing soccer."

"You know, I hate to say this," Enid said, "but aches and pains are a part of getting older. I could talk about pain all day long if I wanted to. My hip is always hurting. As you get older, though, hopefully you get a little more matoor."

"Oh! Ahh! Ahh!" Caroline cried out voluptuously.

"Yeah, that's the hope," Gary said.

"Anyhow, what did you decide?"

"The jury's still out on Christmas," he said, "but maybe you should plan on stopping here—"

"Ow! Ow! Ow!"

"It's getting awfully late to be making Christmas reservations," Enid said severely. "You know, the Schumperts made their Hawaii reservations back in April, because last year, when they waited until September, they couldn't get the seats they—"

Aaron came running from the kitchen. "Dad!"

"I'm on the phone, Aaron."

"Dad!"

"I'm on the telephone, Aaron, as you can see."

"Dave has a colostomy," Enid said.

"You've got to do something *right now*," Aaron said. "Mom is really hurting. She says you have to drive her to the hospital!"

"Actually, Dad," said Caleb, sidling in with his catalogue, "there's someplace you can drive me, too."

"No, Caleb."

"No, but there's a store I really actually do need to get to?"

"The affordable seats fill up early," Enid said.

"Aaron?" Caroline shouted from the kitchen. "Aaron! Where are you? Where's your father? Where's Caleb?"

"It certainly is noisy in here for a person trying to concentrate," Jonah said.

"Mother, sorry," Gary said, "I'm going someplace quieter."

"It's getting very *late*," Enid said, in her voice the panic of a woman for whom each passing day, each hour, signified the booking of more seats on late-December flights and thus the particle-by-particle disintegration of any hope that Gary and Caroline would bring their boys to St. Jude for one last Christmas.

"Dad," Aaron pleaded, following Gary up the stairs to the second floor, "what do I tell her?"

"Tell her to call 911. Use your cell phone, call an ambulance." Gary raised his voice: "Caroline? Call 911!"

Nine years ago, after a midwestern trip whose particular torments had included ice storms in both Philly and St. Jude, a four-hour runway delay with a whining five-year-old and a screaming two-year-old, a night of wild vomiting by Caleb in reaction (according to Caroline) to the butter and bacon fat in Enid's holiday cooking, and a nasty spill that Caroline took on her in-laws' ice-covered driveway (her back trouble dated from her field-hockey days at Friends' Central, but she now spoke of having "reactivated" the injury on that driveway), Gary had promised his wife that he would never again ask her to go to St. Jude for Christmas. But now his parents had come to Philly eight years in a row, and although he disapproved of his mother's obsession with Christmas—it seemed to him a symptom of a larger malaise, a painful emptiness in Enid's life—he could hardly blame his parents for wanting to stay home this year. Gary also calculated that Enid would be more willing to leave St. Jude and move east if she'd had her "one last Christmas." Basically, he was prepared to make the trip, and he expected a *modicum of cooperation* from his wife: a mature willingness to consider the special circumstances.

He shut himself inside his study and locked the door against the shouts and whimpers of his family, the barrage of feet on stairs, the pseudo-emergency. He lifted the receiver of his study phone and turned off the cordless.

"This is ridiculous," Enid said in a defeated voice. "Why don't you call me back?"

"We haven't quite decided about December," he said, "but we may very well come to St. Jude. In which case, I think you should stop here after the cruise."

Enid was breathing rather loudly. "We're not making two trips to Philadelphia this fall," she said. "And I want to see the boys at Christmas, and so as far as I'm concerned this means you're coming to St. Jude."

"No, Mother," he said. "No, no, no. We haven't decided anything."

"I *promised* Jonah—"

"Jonah's not buying the tickets. Jonah's not in charge here. So you make your plans, we'll make ours, and hopefully everything will work out."

Gary could hear, with strange clarity, the rustle of dissatisfaction from Enid's nostrils. He could hear the seashore of her respiration, and all at once he realized.

"Caroline?" he said. *"Caroline, are you on the line?"*

The breathing ceased.

"Caroline, are you eavesdropping? Are you on the line?"

He heard a faint electronic click, a spot of static.

"Mom, sorry—"

Enid: "What on earth?"

Unbelievable! Unfuckingbelievable! Gary dropped the receiver on his desk, unlocked the door, and ran down the hallway past a bedroom in which Aaron was standing at his mirror with his brow wrinkled and his head at the Flattering Angle, past the main staircase on which Caleb was clutching his catalogue like a Jehovah's Witness with a pamphlet, to the master bedroom where Caroline was curled up fetally on a Persian rug, in her muddy clothes, a frosty gelpack pressed into her lower back.

"Are you eavesdropping on me?"

Caroline shook her head weakly, perhaps hoping to suggest that she was too infirm to have reached the phone by the bed.

"Is that a no? You're saying no? You weren't listening?"

"No, Gary," she said in a tiny voice.

"I heard the click, I heard the breathing—"

"No."

"Caroline, there are three phones on this line, I've got two of them in my study, and the third one's right here. Hello?"

"I wasn't eavesdropping. I just picked up the phone—" She inhaled through gritted teeth. "To see if the line was free. That's all."

"And sat and listened! You were eavesdropping! Like we've talked and talked and talked about not doing!"

"Gary," she said in a piteous little voice, "I swear to you I wasn't. My back is killing me. I couldn't reach to put the phone back for a minute. I put it on the floor. I wasn't eavesdropping. Please be nice to me."

That her face was beautiful and that the agony in it was mistakable for ecstasy—that the sight of her doubled-over and mud-spattered and red-cheeked and vanquished and wild-haired on the Persian rug turned him on; that some part of him believed her denials and was full of tenderness for her—only deepened his feeling of betrayal. He stormed back up the hall to his study and slammed the door. "Mother, hello, I'm sorry."

But the line was dead. He had to dial St. Jude now at his own expense. Through the window overlooking the back yard he could see sunlit, clamshell-purple rain clouds, steam rising off the monkey puzzle tree.

Because she wasn't paying for the call, Enid sounded happier. She asked Gary if he'd heard of a company called Axon. "It's in Schwenksville, Pennsylvania," she said. "They want to buy Dad's patent. Here, I'll read you the letter. I'm a little upset about this."

At CenTrust Bank, where Gary now ran the Equities Division, he'd long specialized in large-cap securities and never much concerned himself with small fry. The name Axon was not familiar to him. But as he listened to his mother read the letter from Mr. Joseph K. Prager at Bragg Knuter & Speigh, he felt he knew these people's game. It was clear that the lawyer, in drafting a letter and sending it to an old man with a midwestern address, had offered Alfred no more than a tiny percentage of the patent's actual value. Gary knew the way these shysters worked. In Axon's position he would have done the same.

"I'm thinking we should ask for ten thousand, not five thousand," Enid said.

"When does that patent expire?" Gary said.

"In about six years."

"They must be looking at big money. Otherwise they'd just go ahead and infringe."

"The letter says it's experimental and uncertain."

"Mother, exactly. That's exactly what they want you to think. But if it's so experimental, why are they bothering with this at all? Why not just wait six years?"

"Oh, I see."

"It's very, very good that you told me about this, Mother. What you need to do now is write back to these guys and ask them for a $200,000 licensing fee up front."

Enid gasped as she'd done long ago on family car trips, when Alfred swung into oncoming traffic to pass a truck. "*Two hundred thousand!* Oh, my, Gary—"

"And a one percent royalty on gross revenues from their process. Tell them you're fully prepared to defend your legitimate claim in court."

"But what if they say no?"

"Trust me, these guys have no desire to litigate. There's no down-side to being aggressive here."

"Well, but it's Dad's patent, and you know how he thinks."

"Put him on the phone," Gary said.

His parents were cowed by authority of all kinds. When Gary wanted to reassure himself that he'd escaped their fate, when he needed to measure his distance from St. Jude, he considered his own fearlessness in the face of authority—including the authority of his father.

"Yes," Alfred said.

"Dad," he said, "I think you should go after these guys. They're in a very weak position and you could make some real money."

In St. Jude the old man said nothing.

"You're not telling me you're going to take that offer," Gary said. "Because that's not even an option. Dad. That's not even on the menu."

"I've made my decision," Alfred said. "What I do is not your business."

"Yes, it is, though. I have a legitimate interest in this."

"Gary, you do not."

"I have a legitimate interest," Gary insisted. If Enid and Alfred ever ran out of money, it would fall to him and Caroline—not to his under-capitalized sister, not to his feckless brother—to pay for their care. But he had enough self-control not to spell this out for Alfred. "Will you at least tell me what you're going to do? Will you pay me that courtesy?"

"You could pay me the courtesy of not asking," Alfred said. "However, since you ask, I will tell you. I'm going to take what they offer and give half of the money to Orfic Midland."

The universe was mechanistic: the father spoke, the son reacted.

"Well, now, Dad," Gary said in the low, slow voice he reserved for situations in which he was very angry and very certain he was right. "You can't do that."

"I can and I will," Alfred said.

"No, really, Dad, you have to listen to me. There is absolutely no legal or moral reason for you to split the money with Orfic Midland."

"I was using the railroad's materials and equipment," Alfred said. "It was understood that I would share any income from the patents. And Mark Jamborets put me in touch with the patent lawyer. I suspect I was given a courtesy rate."

"That was fifteen years ago! The company no longer *exists*. The people you had the understanding with are *dead*."

"Not all of them are. Mark Jamborets is not."

"Dad, it's a nice sentiment. I understand the feeling, but—"

"I doubt you do."

"That railroad was raped and eviscerated by the Wroth brothers."

"I will not discuss it any further."

"This is sick! This is sick!" Gary said. "You're being loyal to a corporation that screwed you and the city of St. Jude in every conceivable way. It's screwing you again, *right now*, with your health insurance."

"You have your opinion, I have mine."

"And I'm saying you're being irresponsible. You're being selfish. If you want to eat peanut butter and pinch pennies, that's your business, but it's not fair to Mom and it's not fair to—"

"I don't give a damn what you and your mother think."

"It's not fair to me! Who's going to pay your bills if you get in trouble? Who's your fallback?"

"I will endure what I have to endure," Alfred said. "Yes, and I'll eat peanut butter if I have to. I like peanut butter. It's a good food."

"And if that's what Mom has to eat, she'll eat it, too. Right? She can eat dog food if she has to! Who cares what *she* wants?"

"Gary, I know what the right thing to do is. I don't expect you to understand—I don't understand the decisions you make—but I know what's fair. So let that be the end of it."

"I mean, give Orfic Midland twenty-five hundred dollars if you absolutely have to," Gary said. "But that patent is worth—"

"Let that be the end of it, I said. Your mother wants to talk to you again."

"Gary," Enid cried, "the St. Jude Symphony is doing *The Nutcracker* in December! They do a beautiful job with the regional ballet, and it sells out *so* fast, tell me, do you think I should get nine tickets for the day of Christmas Eve? They have a two o'clock matinee, or we can go on the night of the twenty-third, if you think that's better. You decide."

"Mother, listen to me. Do not let Dad accept that offer. Don't let him do anything until I've seen the letter. I want you to put a copy of it in the mail to me tomorrow."

"OK, I will, but I'm thinking the important thing right now is *The Nutcracker*, to get nine tickets all together, because it sells out *so fast*, Gary, you wouldn't believe."

When he finally got off the phone, Gary pressed his hands to his eyes and saw, engraved in false colors on the darkness of his mental movie screen, two images of golf: Enid improving her lie from the rough (*cheating* was the word for this) and Alfred making light of his badness at the game.

The old man had pulled the same kind of self-defeating stunt fourteen years ago, after the Wroth brothers bought the Midland Pacific. Alfred was a few months shy of his sixty-fifth birthday when Fenton Creel, the Midpac's new president, took him to lunch at Morelli's in St. Jude. The top echelon of Midpac executives had been purged by the Wroths for having resisted the takeover, but Alfred, as chief engineer, had not been a part of this palace guard. In the chaos of shutting down the St. Jude office and moving operations to Little Rock, the Wroths needed somebody to keep the railroad running while the new crew, headed by Creel, learned the ropes. Creel offered Alfred a fifty percent raise and a block of Orfic stock if he would stay on for two extra years, oversee the move to Little Rock, and provide continuity.

Alfred hated the Wroths and was inclined to say no, but that night, at home, Enid went to work on him. She pointed out that the Orfic stock alone was worth $78,000, that his pension would be based on his last three full years' salary, and that here was a chance to increase their retirement income by fifty percent.

These irresistible arguments appeared to sway Alfred, but three nights later he came home and announced to Enid that he'd tendered his resignation that afternoon and that Creel had accepted it. Alfred was then seven weeks short of a full year at his last, largest salary; it made no sense at all to quit. But he gave no explanation, then or ever, to Enid or to anyone else, for his sudden turnabout. He simply said: *I have made my decision.*

At the Christmas table in St. Jude that year, moments after Enid had sneaked onto baby Aaron's little plate a bite of hazelnut goose stuffing and Caroline had grabbed the stuffing from the plate and marched into the kitchen and flung it in the trash like a wad of goose crap, saying, "This is pure grease—yuck," Gary lost his temper and shouted: *You couldn't wait seven weeks? You couldn't wait till you were sixty-five?*

Gary, I worked hard all my life. My retirement is my business, not yours.

And the man so keen to retire that he couldn't wait those last seven weeks: what had he done with his retirement? He'd sat in his blue chair.

Gary knew nothing of Axon, but Orfic Midland was the sort of conglomerate whose holdings and management structure he was paid to stay abreast of. He happened to know that the Wroth brothers had sold their controlling stake to cover losses in a Canadian gold-mining venture. Orfic Midland had joined the ranks of the indistinguishable bland megafirms whose headquarters dotted the American exurbs; its executives had been replaced like the cells of a living organism or like the letters in a game of Substitution in which SHIT turned to SHOT and SOOT and FOOT and FOOD, so that, by the time Gary had okayed the latest bulk purchase of **OrficM** for CenTrust's portfolio, no blamable human trace remained of the company that had shut down St. Jude's third-largest employer and eliminated train service to much of rural Kansas. Orfic Midland was out of the transportation business altogether now. What survived of the Midpac's trunk lines had been sold off to enable the company to concentrate on prison-building, prison management, gourmet coffee, and financial services; a new 144-strand fiber-optic cable system lay buried in the railroad's old right-of-way.

This was the company to which Alfred felt loyal?

The more Gary thought about it, the angrier he got. He sat by himself in his study, unable to stem his rising agitation or to slow the steam-locomotive pace at which his breaths were coming. He was blind to the pretty pumpkin-yellow sunset unfolding in the tulip trees beyond the commuter tracks. He saw nothing but the principles at stake.

He might have sat there obsessing indefinitely, marshaling evidence against his father, had he not heard a rustling outside the study door. He jumped to his feet and pulled the door open.

Caleb was cross-legged on the floor, studying his catalogue. "Can I talk to you now?"

"Were you sitting out here listening to me?"

"No," Caleb said. "You said we could talk when you were done. I had a question. I was wondering what room I could put under surveillance."

Even upside down Gary could see that the prices for the equipment in Caleb's catalogue—items with brushed-aluminum cases, color LCD screens—were three- and four-figure.

"It's my new hobby," Caleb said. "I want to put a room under surveillance. Mom says I can do the kitchen if it's OK with you."

"You want to put the kitchen under surveillance as a hobby?"

"Yeah!"

Gary shook his head. He'd had many hobbies when he was a boy, and for a long time it had pained him that his own boys seemed to have none at all. Eventually Caleb had figured out that if he used the word "hobby," Gary would green-light expenditures he otherwise might have forbidden Caroline to make. Thus Caleb's hobby had been photography until Caroline had bought him an autofocus camera, an SLR with a better zoom telephoto lens than Gary's own, and a digital point-and-shoot camera. His hobby had been computers until Caroline had bought him a palmtop and a notebook. But now Caleb was nearly twelve, and Gary had been around the block one too many times. His guard was up regarding hobbies. He'd extracted from Caroline a promise not to buy Caleb more equipment of any kind without consulting with him first.

"Surveillance is not a hobby," he said.

"Dad, yes it is! Mom was the one who suggested it. She said I could start with the kitchen."

It seemed to Gary another Warning Sign of depression that his thought was: *The liquor cabinet is in the kitchen.*

"Better let me talk about this with Mom, all right?"

"But the store's only open till six," Caleb said.

"You can wait a few days. Don't tell me you can't."

"But I've been waiting all afternoon. You said you'd talk to me, and now it's almost night."

That it was almost night gave Gary clear title to a drink. The liquor cabinet was in the kitchen. He took a step in its direction. "What equipment exactly are we talking about?"

"Just a camera and a microphone and servo controls." Caleb thrust the catalogue at Gary. "See, I don't even need the expensive kind. This one's just six fifty. Mom said it was OK."

Time and again Gary had the feeling that there was something disagreeable that his family wanted to forget, something only he insisted on remembering; something requiring only his nod, his go-ahead, to be forgotten. This feeling, too, was a Warning Sign.

"Caleb," he said, "this sounds like something you're going to get bored with very soon. It sounds expensive and like you won't stay interested."

"No! No!" Caleb said, anguished. "I'm *totally* interested. Dad, it's a *hobby.*"

"You've gotten bored, though, pretty quickly with some of the other things we've gotten you. Things you also said you were 'very interested in' at the time."

"This is different," Caleb pleaded. "This time I'm really, truly interested."

Clearly the boy was prepared to spend any amount of devalued verbal currency to buy his father's acquiescence.

"Do you see what I'm saying, though?" Gary said. "Do you see the pattern? That things look one way before you buy them and another way afterward? Your feelings change after you buy things. Do you see that?"

Caleb opened his mouth, but before he could utter another plea or complaint, a craftiness flickered in his face.

"I guess," he said with seeming humility. "I guess I see that."

"Well, do you think it's going to happen with this new equipment?" Gary said.

Caleb gave every appearance of giving the question serious thought. "I think this is different," he said finally.

"Well, OK," Gary said. "But I want you to remember we had this conversation. I don't want to see this become just another expensive toy you play with for a week or two and then neglect. You're going to be a teenager pretty soon, and I want to start seeing a little longer attention span—"

"Gary, that isn't fair!" Caroline said hotly. She was hobbling from the doorway of the master bedroom, one shoulder hunched and her hand behind her back, applying pressure to the soothing gelpack.

"Hello, Caroline. Didn't realize you were listening."

"Caleb is not neglecting things."

"Right, I'm not," Caleb said.

"What you don't understand," Caroline told Gary, "is that everything's getting used in this new hobby. That's what's so brilliant about it. He's figured out a way to use all that equipment together in one—"

"Good, well, I'm glad to hear it."

"He does something creative and you make him feel *guilty*."

Once, when Gary had wondered aloud if giving Caleb so many gadgets might be stunting his imagination, Caroline had all but accused him of slandering his son. Among her favorite parenting books was *The Technological Imagination: What Today's Children Have to Teach Their Parents*, in which Nancy Claymore, Ph.D., contrasting the "tired paradigm" of Gifted Child as Socially Isolated Genius with the "wired paradigm" of Gifted Child as Creatively Connected Consumer, argued that electronic toys would soon be so cheap and widespread that a child's imagination would no longer be exercised in crayon drawings and made-up stories but in the synthesis and exploitation of existing technologies—an idea that Gary found both persuasive and depressing. When he was a boy not much younger than Caleb, his hobby had been building models with Popsicle sticks.

"Does this mean we can go to the store now?" Caleb said.

"No, Caleb, not tonight, it's almost six," Caroline said.

Caleb stamped his foot. "This always happens! I wait and wait, and then it gets too late."

"We'll rent a movie," Caroline said. "We'll get whatever movie you want."

"I don't want a movie. I want to do surveillance."

"It's not going to happen," Gary said. "So start dealing with it."

Caleb went to his room and slammed the door. Gary followed and flung it open. "That's enough now," he said. "We don't slam doors in this house."

"You slam doors!"

"I don't want to hear another word from you."

"You slam doors!"

"Do you want to spend the whole week in your room?"

Caleb replied by crossing his eyes and sucking his lips into his mouth: not another word.

Gary let his gaze drift into corners of the boy's room that he ordinarily took care not to look at. Neglected in piles, like the loot in a thief's apartment, was new photographic and computer and video equipment with an aggregate retail value possibly exceeding the annual salary of Gary's secretary at CenTrust. Such a riot of luxury in the lair of an eleven-year-old! Various chemicals that molecular floodgates had been holding back all afternoon burst loose and flooded Gary's neural pathways. A cascade of reactions initiated by Factor 6 relaxed his tear valves and sent a wave of nausea down his vagus: a "sense" that he survived from day to day by distracting himself from underground truths that day by day grew more compelling and decisive. The truth that he was going to die. That heaping your tomb with treasure wouldn't save you.

The light in the windows was failing rapidly.

"You're really going to use all this equipment?" he said with a tightness in his chest.

Caleb, his lips still involuted, gave a shrug.

"Nobody should be slamming doors," Gary said. "Me included. All right?"

"Yeah, Dad. Whatever."

Emerging from Caleb's room into the shadowed hallway, he nearly collided with Caroline, who was hurrying on tiptoe, in her stockinged feet, back in the direction of their bedroom.

"Again? Again? I say don't eavesdrop, and what do you do?"

"I wasn't eavesdropping. I've got to go lie down." And she hurried, limping, into the bedroom.

"You can run but you can't hide," Gary said, following her. "I want to know why you're eavesdropping on me."

"It is your paranoia, not my eavesdropping."

"My paranoia?"

Caroline slumped on the oaken king-size bed. After she and Gary were married, she'd undergone five years of twice-weekly therapy which the therapist, at the final session, had declared "an unqualified success" and which had given her a lifelong advantage over Gary in the race for mental health.

"You seem to think everybody *except* you has a problem," she said. "Which is what your mother thinks, too. Without ever—"

"Caroline. Answer me one question. Look me in the eye and answer me one question. This afternoon, when you were—"

"God, Gary, not this again. Listen to yourself."

"When you were horsing around in the rain, running yourself ragged, trying to keep up with an eleven-year-old and a fourteen-year-old—"

"You're obsessed! You're obsessed with that!"

"Running and sliding and kicking in the rain—"

"You talk to your parents and then you take your anger out on us."

"Were you limping before you came inside?" Gary shook his finger in his wife's face. "Look me in the eye, Caroline, look me right in the eye. Come on! Do it! Look me in the eye and tell me you weren't *already limping.*"

Caroline was rocking in pain. "You're on the phone with them for the better part of an hour—"

"You can't do it!" Gary crowed in bitter triumph. "You're lying to me and you will not admit you're lying!"

"Dad! Dad!" came a cry outside the door. Gary turned and saw Aaron shaking his head wildly, beside himself, his beautiful face twisted and tear-slick. "Stop shouting at her!"

The remorse neurofactor (Factor 26) flooded the sites in Gary's brain specially tailored by evolution to respond to it.

"Aaron, all right," he said.

Aaron turned away and turned back and marched in place, taking big steps nowhere, as though trying to force the shameful tears out of his eyes and into his body, down through his legs, and stamp them out. "God, please, Dad, do—not—shout—at her."

"OK, Aaron," Gary said. "Shouting's over."

He reached to touch his son's shoulder, but Aaron fled back up the hall. Gary left Caroline and followed him, his sense of isolation deepened by this demonstration that his wife had strong allies in the house. Her sons would protect her from her husband. Her husband who was a shouter. Like his father before him. His father before him who was now depressed. But who, in his prime, as a shouter, had so frightened young Gary that it never occurred to him to intercede on his mother's behalf.

Aaron was lying face down on his bed. In the tornado aftermath of laundry and magazines on the floor of his room, the two nodes of order were his Bundy trumpet (with mutes and a music stand) and his enormous alphabetized collection of compact discs, including boxed-set complete editions of Dizzy and Satchmo and Miles Davis, plus great miscellaneous quantities of Chet Baker and Wynton Marsalis and Chuck Mangione and Herb Alpert and Al Hirt, all of which Gary had given him to encourage his interest in music.

Gary perched on the edge of the bed. "I'm sorry I upset you," he said. "As you know, I can be a mean old judgmental bastard. And sometimes your mother has trouble admitting she's wrong. Especially when—"

"Her. Back. Is. Hurt," came Aaron's voice, muffled by a Ralph Lauren duvet. "She is *not lying*."

"I know her back hurts, Aaron. I love your mother very much."

"Then don't *shout* at her."

"OK. Shouting's over. Let's have some dinner." Gary lightly judo-chopped Aaron's shoulder. "What do you say?"

Aaron didn't move. Further cheering words appeared to be called for, but Gary couldn't think of any. He was experiencing a critical shortage of Factors 1 and 3. He'd had the sense, moments earlier, that Caroline was on the verge of accusing him of being "depressed," and he was afraid that if the idea that he was depressed gained currency, he would forfeit his right to his opinions. He would forfeit his moral certainties; every word he spoke would become a symptom of disease; he would never again win an argument.

It was therefore all the more important now to resist depression— to fight it with the truth.

"Listen," he said. "You were out there with Mom, playing soccer. Tell me if I'm right about this. Was she limping before she went inside?"

For a moment, as Aaron roused himself from the bed, Gary believed that the truth would prevail. But the face Aaron showed him was a reddish-white raisin of revulsion and disbelief.

"You're horrible!" he said. "You're *horrible!*" And he ran from the room.

Ordinarily Gary wouldn't have let Aaron get away with this. Ordinarily he would have battled his son all evening if that was what it took to extract an apology from him. But his mental markets—glycemic, endocrine, over-the-synapse—were crashing. He was feeling ugly, and to battle Aaron now would only make him uglier, and the sensation of ugliness was perhaps the leading Warning Sign.

He saw that he'd made two critical mistakes. He should never have promised Caroline that there would be no more Christmases in St. Jude. And today, when she was limping and grimacing in the back yard, he should have snapped at least one picture of her. He mourned the moral advantages these mistakes had cost him.

"I am not clinically depressed," he told his reflection in the nearly dark bedroom window. With a great, marrow-taxing exertion of will, he stood up from Aaron's bed and sallied forth to prove himself capable of having an ordinary evening.

Jonah was climbing the dark stairs with *Prince Caspian*. "I finished the book," he said.

"Did you like it?"

"I loved it," Jonah said. "This is outstanding children's literature. Aslan made a door in the air that people walked through and disappeared. They went out of Narnia and back into the real world."

Gary dropped into a crouch. "Give me a hug."

Jonah draped his arms on him. Gary could feel the looseness of his youthful joints, the cublike pliancy, the heat radiating through his scalp and cheeks. He would have slit his own throat if the boy had needed blood; his love was immense in that way; and yet he wondered if it was only love he wanted now or whether he was also coalition-building. Securing a tactical ally for his team.

What this stagnating economy needs, thought Federal Reserve Board Chairman Gary R. Lambert, *is a massive infusion of Bombay Sapphire gin*.

In the kitchen Caroline and Caleb were slouched at the table drinking Coke and eating potato chips. Caroline had her feet up on another chair and pillows beneath her knees.

"What should we do for dinner?" Gary said.

His wife and middle son traded glances as if this were the stick-in-the-mud sort of question he was famous for. From the density of potato-chip crumbs he could see they were well on their way to spoiled appetites.

"Mixed grill, I guess," said Caroline.

"Oh, yeah, Dad, do a mixed grill!" Caleb said in a tone mistakable for either irony or enthusiasm.

Gary asked if there was meat.

Caroline stuffed chips into her mouth and shrugged.

Jonah asked permission to build a fire.

Gary, taking ice from the freezer, granted it.

Ordinary evening. Ordinary evening.

"If I put the camera over the table," Caleb said, "I'll get part of the dining room, too."

"You miss the whole nook, though," Caroline said. "If it's over the back door, you can sweep both ways."

Gary shielded himself with the door of the liquor cabinet while he poured four ounces of gin onto ice.

" 'Alt. eighty-five'?" Caleb read from his catalogue.

"That means the camera can look almost straight down."

Still shielded by the cabinet door, Gary took a hefty warmish gulp. Then, closing the cabinet, he held up the glass in case anyone cared to see what a relatively modest drink he'd poured himself.

"Hate to break it to you," he said, "but surveillance is out. It's not appropriate as a hobby."

"Dad, you said it was OK as long as I stayed interested."

"I said I would think about it."

Caleb shook his head vehemently. "No! You didn't! You said I could do it as long as I didn't get bored."

"That is exactly what you said," Caroline confirmed with an unpleasant smile.

"Yes, Caroline, I'm sure you heard every word. But we're not putting this kitchen under surveillance. Caleb, you do not have my permission to make those purchases."

"Dad!"

"That's my decision, it's final."

"Caleb, it doesn't matter, though," Caroline said. "Gary, it doesn't matter, because he's got his own money. He can spend it however he wants. Right, Caleb?"

Out of Gary's sight, below the level of the table, she gave Caleb some kind of hand signal.

"Right, I've got my own savings!" Caleb's tone again ironic or enthusiastic or, somehow, both.

"You and I will talk about this later, Caro," Gary said. Warmth and perversion and stupidity, all deriving from the gin, were descending from behind his ears and down his arms and torso.

Jonah came back inside smelling like mesquite.

Caroline had opened a second large bag of potato chips.

"Don't spoil your appetite, guys," Gary said in a strained voice, taking food from plastic compartments.

Again mother and son traded glances.

"Yeah, right," Caleb said. "Gotta save room for mixed grill!"

Gary energetically sliced meats and skewered vegetables. Jonah set the table, spacing the flatware with the precision that he liked. The rain had stopped, but the deck was still slippery when Gary went outside.

It had started as a family joke: Dad always orders the mixed grill in restaurants, Dad only wants to go to restaurants with mixed grill on the menu. To Gary there was indeed something endlessly delicious, something irresistibly *luxurious*, about a bit of lamb, a bit of pork, a bit of veal, and a lean and tender modern-style sausage or two—a classic mixed grill, in short. It was such a treat that he began to do his own mixed grills at home. Along with pizza and Chinese takeout and one-pot pasta meals, mixed grill became a family staple. Caroline helped out by bringing home multiple heavy blood-damp bags of meat and sausage every Saturday, and before long Gary was doing mixed grill two or even three times a week, braving all but the foulest weather on the deck, and loving it. He did partridge breasts, chicken livers, filets mignons, and Mexican-flavored turkey sausage. He did zucchini and red peppers. He did eggplant, yellow peppers, baby lamb chops, Italian sausage. He came up with a wonderful bratwurst–rib eye–bok choy combo. He loved it and loved it and loved it and then all at once he didn't.

The clinical term, ANHEDONIA, had introduced itself to him in a nightstand book of Caroline's called *Feeling GREAT!* (Ashley Tralpis, M.D., Ph.D.). He'd read the dictionary entry for ANHEDONIA with a shiver of recognition, a kind of malignant *yes, yes*: "a psychological condition characterized by inability to experience pleasure in normally pleasurable acts." ANHEDONIA was more than a Warning Sign, it was an out-and-out symptom. A dry rot spreading from pleasure to pleasure, a fungus spoiling the delight in luxury and joy in leisure which for so many years had fueled Gary's resistance to the poorthink of his parents.

The previous March, in St. Jude, Enid had observed that, for a bank vice president married to a woman who worked only part-time, pro bono, for the Children's Defense Fund, Gary seemed to do an *awful* lot of cooking. Gary had shut his mother up easily enough; she was married to a man who couldn't boil an egg, and obviously she was jealous. But on Gary's birthday, after he'd flown back from St. Jude with Jonah and received the expensive surprise of a color photo lab, after he'd mustered the will to exclaim, *A darkroom, fantastic, I love it, I love it,* Caroline handed him a platter of raw prawns and brutal swordfish steaks to grill, and he wondered if his mother had a point. On the deck, in the radiant heat, as he blackened the prawns and seared the swordfish, a weariness overtook him. The aspects of his life not related to grilling now seemed like mere blips of extraneity between the poundingly recurrent moments when he ignited the mesquite and paced the deck, avoiding smoke. Shutting his eyes, he saw twisted boogers of browning meats on a grille of chrome and hellish coals. The eternal broiling, broiling of the damned. The parching torments of compulsive repetition. On the inner walls of the grill a deep-pile carpet of phenolic black greases had accumulated. The ground behind the garage where he dumped the ashes resembled a moonscape or the yard of a cement plant. He was very, very, very sick of mixed grill, and the next morning he told Caroline: "I'm doing too much cooking."

"So do less," she said. "We'll eat out."

"I want to eat at home *and* I want to do less cooking."

"So order in," she said.

"It's not the same."

"You're the one who's bent on having these sit-down dinners. The boys couldn't care less."

"*I* care about it. It's important to *me*."

"Fine, but, Gary: it's not important to me, it's not important to the boys, and we're supposed to cook for you?"

He couldn't entirely blame Caroline. In the years when she'd worked full-time, he'd never complained about frozen or takeout or pre-prepared dinners. To Caroline it probably seemed that he was changing the rules on her. But to Gary it seemed that the nature of family life itself was changing—that togetherness and filiality and fraternity weren't valued the way they were when he was young.

And so here he was, still grilling. Through the kitchen windows he could see Caroline thumb-wrestling Jonah. He could see her taking Aaron's headphones to listen to music, could see her nodding to the beat. It sure *looked* like family life. Was there really anything amiss here but the clinical depression of the man peering in?

Caroline seemed to have forgotten how much her back hurt, but she remembered as soon as he went inside with the steaming, smoking platter of vulcanized animal protein. She seated herself sideways at the table, nudged her food with a fork, and whimpered softly. Caleb and Aaron regarded her with grave concern.

"Doesn't anyone else want to know how *Prince Caspian* ends?" Jonah said. "Isn't anyone curious at all?"

Caroline's eyelids were fluttering, her mouth hanging open miserably to let air trickle in and out. Gary struggled to think of something undepressed to say, something reasonably unhostile, but he was rather drunk.

"Jesus, Caroline," he said, "we know your back hurts, we know you're miserable, but if you can't even sit up straight at the table—"

Without a word she slid off her chair, hobbled to the sink with her plate, scraped her dinner into the garbage grinder, and hobbled upstairs. Caleb and Aaron excused themselves and ground up their own dinners and followed her. Altogether maybe thirty dollars' worth of meat went into the sewer, but Gary, trying to keep his Factor 3 levels off the floor, succeeded pretty well in forgetting about the animals that had died for this purpose. He sat in the leaden twilight of his buzz, ate without tasting, and listened to Jonah's impervious bright chatter.

"This is an excellent skirt steak, Dad, and I would love another piece of that grilled zucchini, please."

From the entertainment room upstairs came the woofing of prime time. Gary felt briefly sorry for Aaron and Caleb. It was a burden to have a mother need you so extremely, to be responsible for her bliss, Gary knew this. He also understood that Caroline was more alone in the world than he was. Her father had been a handsome, charismatic anthropologist who died in a plane crash in Mali when she was eleven. Her father's parents, old Quakers who intermittently said "thee," had left her half of their estate, including a well-regarded Andrew Wyeth, three Winslow Homer watercolors, and forty sylvan acres near Kennett Square for which a developer had paid an incredible sum. Caroline's mother, now seventy-six and in scarily good health, lived with her second husband in Laguna Beach and was a major benefactor of the California Democratic Party; she came east every April and bragged about not being "one of those old women" who were obsessed with their grandkids. Caroline's only sibling, a brother named Philip, was a patronizing, pocket-protected bachelor and solid-state physicist on whom her mother doted somewhat creepily. Gary hadn't known this kind of family in St. Jude. From the start, he'd loved and pitied Caroline for the misfortune and neglect she'd suffered growing up. He'd undertaken to provide a better family for her.

But after dinner, while he and Jonah were loading the dishwasher, he began to hear female laughter upstairs, actual loud laughter, and he decided that Caroline was doing something very bad to him. He was tempted to go up and crash the party. As the buzzing of the gin faded from his head, however, the clanging of an earlier anxiety was becoming audible. An Axon-related anxiety.

He wondered why a small company with a highly experimental process was bothering to offer his father money.

That the letter to Alfred had come from Bragg Knuter & Speigh, a firm that often worked closely with investment bankers, suggested *due diligence*—a dotting of *i*'s and crossing of *t*'s on the eve of something big.

"Do you want to go and be with your brothers?" Gary said to Jonah. "It sounds like fun up there."

"No, thank you," Jonah said. "I'm going to read the next Narnia book, and I thought I might go to the basement, where it's quiet. Will you come with me?"

The old playroom in the basement, still dehumidified and carpeted and pine-paneled, still *nice*, was afflicted with the necrosis of clutter that sooner or later kills a living space: stereo boxes, geometric Styrofoam packing solids, outdated ski and beach gear in random drifts. Aaron and Caleb's old toys were in five big bins and a dozen smaller bins. Nobody but Jonah ever touched them, and in the face of such a glut even Jonah, alone or with a play-date pal, took an essentially archaeological approach. He might devote an afternoon to unpacking half of one large bin, patiently sorting action figures and related props, vehicles, and model buildings by scale and manufacturer (toys that matched nothing he flung behind the sofa), but he rarely reached the bottom of even one bin before his play date ended or dinner was served and he reburied everything he'd excavated, and so the toys whose profusion ought to have been a seven-year-old's heaven went basically unplayed with, another lesson in ANHEDONIA for Gary to ignore as well as he could.

While Jonah settled down to read, Gary booted up Caleb's "old" laptop and went online. He typed the words axon and schwenksville in the **Search** field. One of the two resulting site matches was the Axon Corporation Home Page, but this site, when Gary tried to reach it, turned out to be UNDER RENOVATION. The other match led him to a deeply nested page in the Web site of Westportfolio Biofunds, whose listing of Privately Held Corporations to Watch was a cyberbackwater of drab graphics and misspellings. The Axon page had last been updated a year earlier.

Axon Corporation, 24 East Industrial Serpentine, Schwenksville, PA, a Limited Liability Corporation registered in the state of Delaware, holds wordwide rights to the Eberle Process of Directed Neurochemotaxis. The Eberle Process is profected by United States Patents 5,101,239, 5,101,599, 5,103,628, 5,103,629, and 5,105,996, for which the Axon Corporation is the sole and exclusive grantor of license. Axon engages in refinement, marketing and sales of the Eberle Process to hospitals and clinics worldwide, and in research and development of related technologies. Its founder and chairman is Dr. Earl H. Eberle, former Distinguished Lecturer in Applied Neurobiology at the Johns Hopkins School of Medicine.

The Eberle Process of Directed Neurochemotaxis, also known as Eberle Reverse-Tomographic Chemotherapy, hav4 revolutionized the treatment of inoperable neuroblastomas and a variety of other morphologic defects of the brain.

The Eberle Process utilizes computer-orchestrated RF radiation to direct powerful carcinocdies, mutagens, and certain nonspecific toxins to diseased cerebral tissues and locally activate them without harm to surrounding healthy tissue.

At present, due to limitations in computing power, the Eberle Process requires sedating and immobilizing the patient in an Eberle Cylinder for up to thirfy-six hours while minutely orchestrated fields direct therapeutically active ligands and their inert "piggyback" carriers to the sight of disase. The next generation of Eberle Cylinders is expected to reduce maximum total treatment time to less two hours.

The Eberle Process received full FDA approval as a "safe and effective" therapy in October 1996. Widespread clincial use throughout the world in the years since then, as detailed in the numerous publications listed below, hav4 only confirmed its safety and effectiveness.

Gary's hopes of extracting quick megabucks from Axon were withering in the absence of online hype. Feeling a bit e-weary, fighting an e-headache, he ran a word search for earl eberle. The several hundred matches included articles with titles like NEW HOPE FOR NEUROBLASTOMA and A GIANT LEAP FORWARD and THIS CURE REALLY MAY BE A MIRACLE. Eberle and collaborators were also represented in professional journals with "Remote Computer-Aided Stimulation of Receptor

Sites 14, 16A and 21: A Practical Demonstration," "Four Low-Toxicity Ferroacetate Complexes That Cross the BBB," "In-Vitro RF Stimulation of Colloidal Microtubules," and a dozen other papers. The reference that most interested Gary, however, had appeared in *Forbes ASAP* six months earlier:

> Some of these developments, such as the Fogarty balloon catheter and Lasik corneal surgery, are cash cows for their respective corporate patent holders. Others, with esoteric names like the **Eberle Process** of Directed Neurochemotaxis, enrich their inventors the old-fashioned way: one man, one fortune. The **Eberle Process,** which as late as 1996 lacked regulatory approval but today is recognized as the gold standard for the treatment of a large class of cerebral tumors and lesions, is estimated to net its inventor, Johns Hopkins neurobiologist Earl H. ("Curly") Eberle, as much as $40 million annually in licensing fees and other revenues worldwide.

Forty million dollars annually was more like it. *Forty million dollars annually* restored Gary's hopes and pissed him off all over again. Earl Eberle earned *forty million dollars annually* while Alfred Lambert, also an inventor but (let's face it) a *loser* by temperament—one of the meek of the earth—was offered five thousand for his trouble. And planned to split this pea with Orfic Midland!

"I'm loving this book," Jonah reported. "This may be my favorite book yet."

So why, Gary wondered, why the rush-rush to get Dad's patent, eh, Curly? Why the big push-push? Financial intuition, a warm tingling in his loins, told him that perhaps, after all, a piece of inside information had fallen into his lap. A piece of inside information from an accidental (and therefore perfectly lawful) source. A juicy piece of private meat.

"It's like they're on a luxury cruise," Jonah said, "except they're trying to sail to the end of the world. See, that's where Aslan lives, at the end of the world."

In the SEC's Edgar Database Gary found an unapproved prospectus, a so-called red-herring prospectus, for an initial public offering of

Axon stock. The offering was scheduled for December 15, three-plus months away. The lead underwriter was Hevy & Hodapp, one of the elite investment banks. Gary checked certain vital signs—cash flow, size of issue, size of float—and, loins tingling, hit the **Download Later** button.

"Jonah, nine o'clock," he said. "Run up and take your bath."

"I would love to go on a luxury cruise, Dad," Jonah said, climbing the stairs, "if that could ever be arranged."

In a different **Search** field, his hands a little parkinsonian, Gary entered the words beautiful, nude, and blond.

"Shut the door, please, Jonah."

On the screen an image of a beautiful nude blonde appeared. Gary pointed and clicked, and a nude tan man, photographed mainly from the rear but also in close-up from his knees to his navel, could be seen giving his fully tumid attention to the beautiful nude blonde. There was something of the assembly line in these images. The beautiful nude blonde was like fresh raw material that the nude tan man was extremely keen to process with his tool. First the material's colorful fabric casing was removed, then the material was placed on its knees and the semi-skilled worker fitted his tool into its mouth, then the material was placed on its back while the worker orally calibrated it, then the worker clamped the material into a series of horizontal and vertical positions, crimping and bending the material as necessary, and very vigorously processed it with his tool . . .

The pictures were softening rather than hardening Gary. He wondered if he'd reached the age where money excited him more than a beautiful nude blonde engaging in sex acts, or whether ANHEDONIA, the solitary father's depression in a basement, might be encroaching even here.

Upstairs the doorbell rang. Adolescent feet came pounding down from the second floor to answer it.

Gary hastily cleansed the computer screen and went upstairs in time to see Caleb returning to the second floor with a large pizza box. Gary followed him and stood for a moment outside the entertainment room, smelling pepperoni and listening to the wordless munching of his sons and wife. On TV something military, a tank or a truck, was roaring to the accompaniment of war-movie music.

"Ve increase ze pressure, Lieutenant. Now you vill talk? Now?"

In *Hands-Off Parenting: Skills for the Next Millennium*, Dr. Harriet L. Schachtman warned: *All too often, today's anxious parents "protect" their children from the so-called "ravages" of TV and computer games, only to expose them to the far more damaging ravages of social ostracization by their peers.*

To Gary, who as a boy had been allowed half an hour of TV a day and had not felt ostracized, Schachtman's theory seemed a recipe for letting a community's most permissive parents set standards that other parents were forced to lower their own to meet. But Caroline subscribed to the theory wholeheartedly, and since she was the sole trustee of Gary's ambition not to be like his father, and since she believed that kids learned more from peer interaction than from parental instruction, Gary deferred to her judgment and let the boys watch nearly unlimited TV.

What he hadn't foreseen was that he himself would be the ostracized.

He retreated to his study and dialed St. Jude again. The kitchen cordless was still on his desk, a reminder of earlier unpleasantnesses and of fights still to come.

He was hoping to speak to Enid, but Alfred answered the telephone and said that she was over at the Roots' house, socializing. "We had a street-association meeting tonight," he said.

Gary considered calling back later, but he refused to be cowed by his father. "Dad," he said, "I've done some research on Axon. We're looking at a company with a *lot* of money."

"Gary, I said I didn't want you monkeying with this," Alfred replied. "It is moot now anyway."

"What do you mean, 'moot'?"

"I mean moot. It's taken care of. The documents are notarized. I'm recouping my lawyer's fees and that's the end of it."

Gary pressed two fingers into his forehead. "My God. Dad. You had it notarized? On a Sunday?"

"I will tell your mother that you called."

"Do *not* put those documents in the mail. Do you hear me?"

"Gary, I've had about enough of this."

"Well, too bad, because I'm just getting started!"

"I've asked you not to speak of it. If you will not behave like a decent, civilized person, then I have no choice—"

"Your decency is bullshit. Your civilization is bullshit. It's weakness! It's fear! It's bullshit!"

"I have no wish to discuss this."

"Then forget it."

"I intend to. We'll not speak of it again. Your mother and I will visit for two days next month, and we will hope to see you here in December. It's my wish that we can all be civil."

"Never mind what's going on underneath. As long as we're all 'civil.' "

"That is the essence of my philosophy, yes."

"Well, it ain't mine," Gary said.

"I'm aware of that. And that's why we will spend forty-eight hours and no more."

Gary hung up angrier than ever. He'd hoped his parents would stay for an entire week in October. He'd wanted them to eat pie in Lancaster County, see a production at the Annenberg Center, drive in the Poconos, pick apples in West Chester, hear Aaron play the trumpet, watch Caleb play soccer, take delight in Jonah's company, and generally see how good Gary's life was, how worthy of their admiration and respect; and forty-eight hours was not enough time.

He left his study and kissed Jonah good night. Then he took a shower and lay down on the big oaken bed and tried to interest himself in the latest *Inc*. But he couldn't stop arguing with Alfred in his head.

During his visit home in March he'd been appalled by how much his father had deteriorated in the few weeks since Christmas. Alfred seemed forever on the verge of derailing as he lurched down hallways or half slid down stairs or wolfed at a sandwich from which lettuce and meat loaf rained; checking his watch incessantly, his eyes wandering whenever a conversation didn't engage him directly, the old iron horse was careering toward a crash, and Gary could hardly stand to look. Because who else, if not Gary, was going to take responsibility? Enid was hysterical and moralizing, Denise lived in a fantasyland, and Chip hadn't been to St. Jude in three years. Who else but Gary was going to say: *This train should not be running on these tracks?*

The first order of business, as Gary saw it, was to sell the house. Get top dollar for it, move his parents into someplace smaller, newer, safer, cheaper, and invest the difference aggressively. The house was Enid and Alfred's only large asset, and Gary took a morning to inspect the whole property slowly, inside and out. He found cracks in the grouting, rust lines in the bathroom sinks, and a softness in the master bedroom ceiling. He noticed rain stains on the inner wall of the back porch, a beard of dried suds on the chin of the old dishwasher, an alarming thump in the forced-air blower, pustules and ridges in the driveway's asphalt, termites in the woodpile, a Damoclean oak limb dangling above a dormer, finger-wide cracks in the foundation, retaining walls that listed, whitecaps of peeling paint on window jambs, big emboldened spiders in the basement, fields of dried sow bug and cricket husks, unfamiliar fungal and enteric smells, everywhere he looked the sag of entropy. Even in a rising market, the house was beginning to lose value, and Gary thought: We've got to sell this fucker *now*, we can't lose another *day*.

On the last morning of his visit, while Jonah helped Enid bake a birthday cake, Gary took Alfred to the hardware store. As soon as they were on the road, Gary said it was time to put the house on the market.

Alfred, in the passenger seat of the gerontic Olds, stared straight ahead. "Why?"

"If you miss the spring season," Gary said, "you'll have to wait another year. And you can't afford another year. You can't count on good health, and the house is losing value."

Alfred shook his head. "I've agitated for a long time. One bedroom and a kitchen is all we need. Somewhere your mother can cook and we have a place to sit. But it's no use. She doesn't want to leave."

"Dad, if you don't put yourself someplace manageable, you're going to hurt yourself. You're going to wind up in a nursing home."

"I have no intention of going to a nursing home. So."

"Just because you don't intend to doesn't mean it won't happen."

Alfred looked, in passing, at Gary's old elementary school. "Where are we going?"

"You fall down the stairs, you slip on the ice and break your hip, you're going to end up in a nursing home. Caroline's grandmother—"

"I didn't hear where we were going."

"We're going to the hardware store," Gary said. "Mom wants a dimmer switch for the kitchen."

Alfred shook his head. "She and her romantic lighting."

"She gets pleasure from it," Gary said. "What do you get pleasure from?"

"What do you mean?"

"I mean you've just about worn her out."

Alfred's active hands, on his lap, were gathering nothing—raking in a poker pot that did not exist. "I'll ask you again not to meddle," he said.

The midmorning light of a late-winter thaw, the stillness of a weekday nonhour in St. Jude, Gary wondered how his parents stood it. The oak trees were the same oily black as the crows perching in them. The sky was the same color as the salt-white pavement on which elderly St. Judean drivers obeying barbiturate speed limits were crawling to their destinations: to malls with pools of meltwater on their papered roofs, to the arterial that overlooked puddled steel yards and the state mental hospital and transmission towers feeding soaps and game shows to the ether; to the beltways and, beyond them, to a million acres of thawing hinterland where pickups were axle-deep in clay and .22s were fired in the woods and only gospel and pedal steel guitars were on the radio; to residential blocks with the same pallid glare in every window, besquirreled yellow lawns with a random plastic toy or two embedded in the dirt, a mailman whistling something Celtic and slamming mailboxes harder than he had to, because the deadness of these streets, at such a nonhour, in such a nonseason, could honestly kill you.

"Are you happy with your life?" Gary said, waiting for a left-turn arrow. "Can you say you're ever happy?"

"Gary, I have an affliction—"

"A lot of people have afflictions. If that's your excuse, fine, if you want to feel sorry for yourself, fine, but why drag Mom down?"

"Well. You'll be leaving tomorrow."

"Meaning what," Gary said. "That you'll sit in your chair and Mom will cook and clean for you?"

"There are things in life that simply have to be endured."

"Why bother staying alive, if that's your attitude? What do you have to look forward to?"

"I ask myself that question every day."

"Well, and what's your answer?" Gary said.

"What's *your* answer? What do *you* think I should look forward to?"

"Travel."

"I've traveled enough. I spent thirty years traveling."

"Time with family. Time with people you love."

"No comment."

"What do you mean, 'no comment'?"

"Just that: no comment."

"You're still sore about Christmas."

"You may interpret it however you like."

"If you're sore about Christmas, you might have the consideration to say so—"

"No comment."

"Instead of insinuating."

"We should have come two days later and left two days earlier," Alfred said. "That's all I have to say on the topic of Christmas. We should have stayed forty-eight hours."

"It's because you're depressed, Dad. You are clinically depressed—"

"And so are you."

"And the responsible thing would be to get some treatment."

"Did you hear me? I said so are you."

"What are you talking about?"

"Figure it out."

"Dad, really, no, what are you talking about? *I'm* not the one who sits in a chair all day and sleeps."

"Underneath, you are," Alfred pronounced.

"That's simply *false*."

"One day you will see."

"I will not!" Gary said. "My life is on a fundamentally different basis than yours."

"Mark my words. I look at your marriage, I see what I see. Someday you'll see it, too."

"That's empty talk and you know it. You're just pissed off with me, and you have no way to deal with it."

"I've told you I don't want to discuss this."

"And I have no respect for that."

"Well, there are things in your life that I have no respect for either."

It shouldn't have hurt to hear that Alfred, who was wrong about almost everything, did not respect things in Gary's life; and yet it did hurt.

At the hardware store he let Alfred pay for the dimmer switch. The old man's careful plucking of bills from his slender wallet and his faint hesitation before he offered them were signs of his respect for a dollar—of his maddening belief that each one mattered.

Back at the house, while Gary and Jonah kicked a soccer ball, Alfred gathered tools and killed the power to the kitchen and set about installing the dimmer. Even at this late date it didn't occur to Gary not to let Alfred handle wiring. But when he came inside for lunch he found that his father had done no more than remove the old switch plate. He was holding the dimmer switch like a detonator that made him shake with fear.

"My affliction makes this difficult," he explained.

"You've got to sell this house," Gary said.

After lunch he took his mother and his son to the St. Jude Museum of Transport. While Jonah climbed into old locomotives and toured the dry-docked submarine and Enid sat and nursed her sore hip, Gary compiled a mental list of the museum's exhibits, hoping the list would give him a feeling of accomplishment. He couldn't deal with the exhibits themselves, their exhausting informativeness, their cheerful prose-for-the-masses. THE GOLDEN AGE OF STEAM POWER. THE DAWN OF FLIGHT.

A CENTURY OF AUTOMOTIVE SAFETY. Block after block of taxing text. What Gary hated most about the Midwest was how unpampered and unprivileged he felt in it. St. Jude in its optimistic egalitarianism consistently failed to accord him the respect to which his gifts and attainments entitled him. Oh, the sadness of this place! The earnest St. Judean rubes all around him seemed curious and undepressed. Happily filling their misshapen heads with facts. As if facts were going to save them! Not one woman half as pretty or as well dressed as Caroline. Not one other man with a decent haircut or an abdomen as flat as Gary's. But, like Alfred, like Enid, they were all extremely deferential. They didn't jostle Gary or cut in front of him but waited until he'd drifted to the next exhibit. Then they gathered round and read and learned. God, he hated the Midwest! He could hardly breathe or hold his head up. He thought he might be getting sick. He took refuge in the museum's gift shop and bought a silver belt buckle, two engravings of old Midland Pacific trestles, and a pewter hip flask (all for himself), a deerskin wallet (for Aaron), and a CD-ROM Civil War game (for Caleb).

"Dad," Jonah said, "Grandma says she'll buy me two books that cost less than ten dollars each or one book for less than twenty dollars, is that OK?"

Enid and Jonah were a lovefest. Enid had always preferred little kids to big kids, and Jonah's adaptive niche in the family ecosystem was to be the perfect grandchild, eager to scramble up on laps, unafraid of bitter vegetables, underexcited by television and computer games, and skilled at cheerfully answering questions like "Are you loving school?" In St. Jude he was luxuriating in the undivided attention of three adults. He declared St. Jude the nicest place he'd ever been. From the back seat of the Oldfolksmobile, his elfin eyes wide, he marveled at everything Enid showed him.

"It's so easy to park here!

"No traffic!

"The Transport Museum is better than any museums *we* have, Dad, don't you agree?

"I love the legroom in this car. I think this is the nicest car I've ever ridden in.

"All the stores are so close and handy!"

That night, after they'd returned from the museum and Gary had gone out and done more shopping, Enid served stuffed pork chops and a chocolate birthday cake. Jonah was dreamily eating ice cream when she asked him if he might like to come and have Christmas in St. Jude.

"I would love that," Jonah said, his eyelids drooping with satiety.

"You could have sugar cookies, and eggnog, and help us decorate the tree," Enid said. "It'll probably snow, so you can go sledding. And, Jonah, there's a *wonderful* light show every year at Waindell Park, it's called Christmasland, they have the whole park lit up—"

"Mother, it's March," Gary said.

"Can we come at Christmas?" Jonah asked him.

"We'll come again very soon," Gary said. "I don't know about Christmas."

"I think Jonah would love it," Enid said.

"I would *completely* love it," Jonah said, hoisting another spoonload of ice cream. "I think it might turn out to be the best Christmas I ever had."

"I think so, too," Enid said.

"It's March," Gary said. "We don't talk about Christmas in March. Remember? We don't talk about it in June or August, either. Remember?"

"Well," Alfred said, standing up from the table. "I am going to bed."

"St. Jude gets my vote for Christmas," Jonah said.

Enlisting Jonah directly in her campaign, exploiting a little boy for leverage, seemed to Gary a low trick on Enid's part. After he'd put Jonah to bed, he told his mother that Christmas ought to be the last of her worries.

"Dad can't even install a light switch," he said. "And now you've got a leak upstairs, you've got water coming in around the chimney—"

"I love this house," Enid said from the kitchen sink, where she was scrubbing the pork-chop pan. "Dad just needs to work a little on his attitude."

"He needs shock treatments or medication," Gary said. "And if you want to dedicate your life to being his servant, that's your choice. If you want to live in an old house with a lot of problems, and try to keep everything just the way you like it, that's fine, too. If you want to wear yourself out trying to do both, be my guest. Just don't ask me to make Christmas plans in March so you can feel OK about it all."

Enid upended the pork-chop pan on the counter beside the overloaded drainer. Gary knew he ought to pick up a towel, but the jumble of wet pans and platters and utensils from his birthday dinner made him weary; to dry them seemed a task as Sisyphean as to repair the things wrong with his parents' house. The only way to avoid despair was not to involve himself at all.

He poured a smallish brandy nightcap while Enid, with unhappy stabbing motions, scraped waterlogged food scraps from the bottom of the sink.

"What do *you* think I should do?" she said.

"Sell the house," Gary said. "Call a realtor tomorrow."

"And move into some cramped, modern condominium?" Enid shook the repulsive wet scraps from her hand into the trash. "When I have to go out for the day, Dave and Mary Beth invite Dad over for lunch. He loves that, and I feel so comfortable knowing he's with them. Last fall he was out planting a new yew, and he couldn't get the old stump out, and Joe Person came over with a pickax and the two of them worked all afternoon together."

"He shouldn't be planting yews," Gary said, regretting already the smallness of his initial pour. "He shouldn't be using a pickax. The man can hardly stand up."

"Gary, I know we can't be here forever. But I want to have one last *really nice* family Christmas here. And I want—"

"Would you consider moving if we had that Christmas?"

New hope sweetened Enid's expression. "Would you and Caroline consider coming?"

"I can't make any promises," Gary said. "But if you'd feel more comfortable about putting the house on the market, we would certainly consider—"

"I would adore it if you came. *Adore* it."

"Mother, though, you have to be realistic."

"Let's get through this year," Enid said, "let's think about having Christmas here, like Jonah wants, and then we'll see!"

Gary's ANHEDONIA had worsened when he returned to Chestnut Hill. As a winter project, he'd been distilling hundreds of hours of home videos into a watchable two-hour *Greatest Lambert Hits* compilation that he could make quality copies of and maybe send out as a "video Christmas card." In the final edit, as he repeatedly reviewed his favorite family scenes and re-cued his favorite songs ("Wild Horses," "Time After Time," etc.), he began to *hate* these scenes and *hate* these songs. And when, in the new darkroom, he turned his attention to the All-Time Lambert Two Hundred, he found that he no longer enjoyed looking at still photographs, either. For years he'd mentally tinkered with the All-Time Two Hundred, as with an ideally balanced mutual fund, listing with great satisfaction the images that he was sure belonged in it. Now he wondered whom, besides himself, he was trying to impress with these pictures. Whom was he trying to persuade, and of what? He had a weird impulse to *burn* his old favorites. But his entire life was set up as a correction of his father's life, and he and Caroline had long agreed that Alfred was clinically depressed, and clinical depression was known to have genetic bases and to be substantially heritable, and so Gary had no choice but to keep resisting ANHEDONIA, keep gritting his teeth, keep doing his best to *have fun* . . .

He came awake with an itching hard-on and Caroline beside him in the sheets.

His nightstand light was still burning, but otherwise the room was dark. Caroline lay in sarcophagal posture, her back flat on the mattress and a pillow beneath her knees. Through the screens on the bedroom windows came seeping the coolish, humid air of a summer grown tired. No wind stirred the leaves of the sycamore whose lowest branches hung outside the windows.

On Caroline's nightstand was a hardcover copy of *Middle Ground: How to Spare Your Child the Adolescence YOU Had* (Caren Tamkin, Ph.D., 1998).

She seemed to be asleep. Her long arm, kept flabless by thrice-weekly swims at the Cricket Club, rested at her side. Gary gazed at her little nose, her wide red mouth, the blond down and the dull sheen of sweat on her upper lip, the tapering strip of exposed blond skin between the hem of her T-shirt and the elastic of her old Swarthmore College gym shorts. Her nearer breast pushed out against the inside of the T-shirt, the carmine definition of its nipple faintly visible through the fabric's stretched weave . . .

When he reached out and smoothed her hair, her entire body jerked as if the hand were a defibrillator paddle.

"What's going on here?" he said.

"My back is killing me."

"An hour ago you were laughing and feeling great. Now you're sore again?"

"The Motrin's wearing off."

"The mysterious resurgence of the pain."

"You haven't said a sympathetic word since I hurt my back."

"Because you're lying about how you hurt it," Gary said.

"My God. *Again*?"

"Two hours of soccer and horseplay in the rain, that's not the problem. It's the ringing phone."

"Yes," Caroline said. "Because your mother won't spend ten cents to leave a message. She has to let it ring three times and then hang up, ring three times and then hang up—"

"It has nothing to do with anything *you* did," Gary said. "It's my mom! She magically flew here and kicked you in the back because she wants to hurt you!"

"After listening to it ring and stop and ring and stop all afternoon, I'm a nervous wreck."

"Caroline, *I saw you limping before you ran inside*. I saw the look on your face. Don't tell me you weren't in pain already."

She shook her head. "You know what this is?"

"And then the eavesdropping!"

"Do you know what this is?"

"You're listening on the only other free phone in the house, and you have the gall to tell me—"

"Gary, you're *depressed*. Do you realize that?"

He laughed. "I don't think so."

"You're brooding, and suspicious, and obsessive. You walk around with a black look on your face. You don't sleep well. You don't seem to get pleasure out of anything."

"You're changing the subject," he said. "My mother called because she had a reasonable request regarding Christmas."

"Reasonable?" Now Caroline laughed. "Gary, she is *bonkers* on the topic of Christmas. She is a *lunatic*."

"Oh, Caroline. Really."

"I mean it!"

"Really. Caroline. They're going to be selling that house soon, they want us all to visit one more time before they *die*, Caroline, before my parents *die*—"

"We've always agreed about this. We agreed that five people with busy lives should not have to fly at the peak holiday season so that two people *with nothing in their lives* wouldn't have to come here. And I've been more than happy to have them—"

"The hell you have."

"Until suddenly the rules change!"

"You have not been happy to have them here. Caroline. They're at the point where they won't even stay for more than forty-eight hours."

"And this is my fault?" She was directing her gestures and facial expressions, somewhat eerily, at the ceiling. "What you don't understand, Gary, is that this is an emotionally healthy family. I am a loving and deeply involved mother. I have three intelligent, creative, and emotionally healthy children. If you think there's a problem in this house, you better take a look at yourself."

"I'm making a reasonable proposal," Gary said. "And you're calling me 'depressed.' "

"So it's never occurred to you?"

"The minute I bring up Christmas, I'm 'depressed.' "

"Seriously, are you telling me it's never occurred to you, in the last six months, that you might have a clinical problem?"

"It is extremely hostile, Caroline, to call another person crazy."

"Not if the person potentially has a clinical problem."

"I'm proposing that we go to St. Jude," he said. "If you won't talk about it like an adult, I'll make my own decision."

"Oh, yeah?" Caroline made a contemptuous noise. "I guess Jonah might go with you. But see if you can get Aaron and Caleb on the plane with you. Just ask them where they'd rather be for Christmas."

Just ask them whose team they're on.

"I was under the impression that we're a family," Gary said, "and that we do things together."

"You're the one deciding unilaterally."

"Tell me this is not a marriage-ending problem."

"You're the one who's changed."

"Because, no, Caroline, that is, no, that is ridiculous. There are good reasons to make a one-time exception this year."

"You're depressed," she said, "and I want you back. I'm tired of living with a depressed old man."

Gary for his part wanted back the Caroline who just a few nights ago had clutched him in bed when there was heavy thunder. The Caroline who came skipping toward him when he walked into a room. The semi-orphaned girl whose most fervent wish was to be on *his* team.

But he'd also always loved how tough she was, how unlike a Lambert, how fundamentally unsympathetic to his family. Over the years he'd collected certain remarks of hers into a kind of personal Decalogue, an All-Time Caroline Ten to which he privately referred for strength and sustenance:

1. You're nothing at all like your father.
2. You don't have to apologize for buying the BMW.
3. Your dad emotionally abuses your mom.
4. I love the taste of your come.
5. Work was the drug that ruined your father's life.
6. Let's buy both!
7. Your family has a diseased relationship with food.
8. You're an incredibly good-looking man.

9. Denise is jealous of what you have.

10. There's absolutely nothing useful about suffering.

He'd subscribed to this credo for years and years—had felt deeply indebted to Caroline for each remark—and now he wondered how much of it was true. Maybe none of it.

"I'm calling the travel agent tomorrow morning," he said.

"And I'm telling you," Caroline replied immediately, "call Dr. Pierce instead. You need to talk to somebody."

"I need somebody who tells the truth."

"You want the truth? You want me to tell you why I'm not going?" Caroline sat up and leaned forward at the funny angle that her backache dictated. "You really want to know?"

Gary's eyes fell shut. The crickets outside sounded like water running interminably in pipes. From the distance came a rhythmic canine barking like the downthrusts of a handsaw.

"The truth," Caroline said, "is that forty-eight hours sounds just about right to me. I don't want my children looking back on Christmas as the time when everybody screamed at each other. Which basically seems to be unavoidable now. Your mother walks in the door with three hundred sixty days' worth of Christmas mania, she's been obsessing since the previous January, and then, of course, *Where's that Austrian reindeer figurine—don't you like it? Don't you use it? Where is it? Where is it? Where is the Austrian reindeer figurine?* She's got her food obsessions, her money obsessions, her clothes obsessions, she's got the whole ten-piece set of baggage which my husband *used* to agree is *kind of a problem*, but now suddenly, out of the blue, he's taking *her* side. We're going to turn the house inside out looking for a piece of thirteen-dollar gift-store kitsch because it has sentimental value to your mother—"

"Caroline."

"And when it turns out that Caleb—"

"This is not an honest version."

"Please, Gary, let me finish, when it turns out that Caleb did the kind of thing that *any normal boy* might do to a piece of gift-store crap that he found in the basement—"

"I can't listen to this."

"No, no, the problem is not that your eagle-eyed mother is obsessed with some garbagey piece of Austrian kitsch, no, that's not the problem—"

"It was a hundred-dollar hand-carved—"

"I don't care if it's a thousand dollars! Since when do you punish *him*, your *own son*, for your mother's craziness? It's like you're suddenly trying to make us act like it's 1964 and we're all living in Peoria. 'Clean your plate!' 'Wear a necktie!' 'No TV tonight!' And you wonder why we're fighting! You wonder why Aaron rolls his eyes when your mom walks in the room! It's like you're *embarrassed* to let her see us. It's like, for as long as she's here, you're trying to pretend we live some way that she approves of. But I'm telling you, Gary, we have *nothing* to be ashamed of. Your mother's the one who should be embarrassed. She follows me around the kitchen scrutinizing me, like, as if I roast a turkey every week, and if I turn my back for one second she's going to pour a quart of oil into whatever I'm making, and as soon as I leave the room she's going to *root through the trash* like some fucking Food Police, she's going to take food from the trash and *feed it to my children*—"

"The potato was in the sink, not the trash, Caroline."

"And you defend her! She goes outside to the trash barrels to see what other dirt she can dig up, and disapprove of, and she's asking me, literally every ten minutes, How's your back? How's your back? How's your back? Is your back any better? How'd you hurt it? Is your back any better? How's your back? She goes *looking* for things to disapprove of, and then she tries to tell *my* children how to dress for dinner in *my* house, and you don't back me up! You don't back me up, Gary. You start apologizing, and I don't get it, but I'm not doing it again. Basically, I think your brother's got the right idea. Here's a sweet, smart, funny man who's honest enough to say what he can and can't tolerate in the way of get-togethers. And your mother acts like he's this huge embarrassment and failure! Well, you wanted the truth. The truth is I cannot stand another Christmas like that. If we absolutely have to see your parents, we're doing it on our own turf. Just like you promised we always would."

A pillow of blue blackness lay on Gary's brain. He'd reached the point on the post-martini evening downslope where a sense of complication weighed on his cheeks, his forehead, his eyelids, his mouth. He understood how much his mother infuriated Caroline, and at the same time he found fault with almost everything that Caroline had said. The rather beautiful wooden reindeer, for example, had been stored in a well-marked box; Caleb had broken two of its legs and hammered a roofing nail through its skull; Enid had taken an uneaten baked potato from the sink and sliced it and fried it for Jonah; and Caroline hadn't bothered to wait until her in-laws had left town before depositing in a trash barrel the pink polyester bathrobe that Enid had given her for Christmas.

"When I said I wanted the truth," he said, not opening his eyes, "I meant I saw you limping before you ran inside."

"Oh, my God," Caroline said.

"My mother didn't hurt your back. You hurt your back."

"Please, Gary. Do me a favor and call Dr. Pierce."

"Admit that you're lying, and I'll talk about anything you want. But nothing's going to change until you admit that."

"I don't even recognize your voice."

"Five days in St. Jude. You can't do that for a woman who, like you say, has nothing else in her life?"

"Please come back to me."

A jolt of rage forced Gary's eyes open. He kicked the sheet aside and jumped out of bed. "This is a marriage-ender! I can't believe it!"

"Gary, please—"

"We're going to split up over a trip to St. Jude!"

And then a visionary in a warm-up jacket was lecturing to pretty college students. Behind the visionary, in a pixilated middle distance, were sterilizers and chromatography cartridges and tissue stains in weak solution, long-necked medicoscientific faucets, pinups of spread-eagled chromosomes, and diagrams of tuna-red brains sliced up like sashimi. The visionary was Earl "Curly" Eberle, a small-mouthed fifty-year-old in dime-store glasses, whom the creators of the Axon Corporation's promotional video had done their best to make glamorous. The camera work was nervous, the lab floor pitched and lurched. Blurry zooms zeroed in on female student faces aglow with fascination. Curiously obsessive attention was paid to the back of the visionary head (it was indeed curly).

"Of course, chemistry, too, even brain chemistry," Eberle was saying, "is basically just manipulation of electrons in their shells. But compare this, if you will, to an electronics that consists of little two- and three-pole switches. The diode, the transistor. The brain, by contrast, has several dozen kinds of switches. The neuron either fires or it doesn't; but this decision is regulated by receptor sites that often have shades of offness and on-ness between plain Off and plain On. Even if you could build an artificial neuron out of molecular transistors, the conventional wisdom is that you can still never translate all that chemistry into the language of yes/no without running out of space. If we conservatively estimate twenty neuroactive ligands, of which as many as eight can operate simultaneously, and each of these eight switches has five different settings—not to bore you with the combinatorics, but unless you're living in a world of Mr. Potato Heads, you're going to be a pretty funny-looking android."

Close-up of a turnip-headed male student laughing.

"Now, these are facts so basic," Eberle said, "that we ordinarily wouldn't even bother spelling them out. It's just the way things are. The only workable connection we have with the electrophysiology of cognition and volition is chemical. That's the received wisdom, part of the gospel of our science. Nobody in their right mind would try to connect the world of neurons with the world of printed circuits."

Eberle paused dramatically.

"Nobody, that is, but the Axon Corporation."

Ripples of buzz crossed the sea of institutional investors who'd come to Ballroom B of the Four Seasons Hotel, in central Philadelphia, for the road show promoting Axon's initial public offering. A giant video screen had been set up on the dais. On each of the twenty round tables in the semidark ballroom were platters of satay and sushi appetizers with the appropriate dipping sauces.

Gary was sitting with his sister, Denise, at a table near the door. He had hopes of transacting business at this road show and he would rather have come alone, but Denise had insisted on having lunch, today being Monday and Monday being her one day off, and had invited herself along. Gary had figured that she would find political or moral or aesthetic reasons to deplore the proceedings, and, sure enough, she was watching the video with her eyes narrowed in suspicion and her arms crossed tightly. She was wearing a yellow shift with a red floral print, black sandals, and a pair of Trotskyish round plastic glasses; but what really set her apart from the other women in Ballroom B was the bareness of her legs. Nobody who dealt in money did not wear stockings.

WHAT IS THE CORECKTALL PROCESS?

"Corecktall," said the cutout image of Curly Eberle, whose young audience had been digitally pureed into a uniform backdrop of tuna-red brain matter, "is a revolutionary neurobiological therapy!"

Eberle was seated on an ergonomic desk chair in which, it now developed, he could float and swerve vertiginously through a graphical space representing the inner-sea world of the intracranium. Kelpy ganglia and squidlike neurons and eellike capillaries began to flash by.

"Originally conceived as a therapy for sufferers of PD and AD and other degenerative neurological diseases," Eberle said, "Corecktall has proved so powerful and versatile that its promise extends not only to therapy but to an outright *cure*, and to a cure not only of these terrible degenerative afflictions but also of a host of ailments typically considered psychiatric or even psychological. Simply put, Corecktall offers for the first time the possibility of renewing and *improving* the hard wiring of an adult human brain."

"Ew," Denise said, wrinkling her nose.

Gary by now was quite familiar with the Corecktall Process. He'd scrutinized Axon's red-herring prospectus and read every analysis of the company he could find on the Internet and through the private services that CenTrust subscribed to. Bearish analysts, mindful of recent gut-wrenching corrections in the biotech sector, were cautioning against investing in an untested medical technology that was at least six years from market. Certainly a bank like CenTrust, with its fiduciary duty to be conservative, wasn't going to touch this IPO. But Axon's fundamentals were a lot healthier than those of most biotech startups, and to Gary the fact that the company had bothered to buy his father's patent at such an early stage in Corecktall's development was a sign of great corporate confidence. He saw an opportunity here to make some money and avenge Axon's screwing of his father and, more generally, be *bold* where Alfred had been *timid*.

It happened that in June, as the first dominoes of the overseas currency crises were toppling, Gary had pulled most of his playing-around money out of Euro and Far Eastern growth funds. This money was available now for investment in Axon; and since the IPO was still three months away, and since the big sales push for it had not begun, and since the red herring contained such dubieties as give non-insiders pause, Gary should have had no trouble getting a commitment for five thousand shares. But trouble was pretty much all he'd had.

His own (discount) broker, who had barely heard of Axon, belatedly did his homework and called Gary back with the news that his firm's allocation was a token 2,500 shares. Normally a brokerage wouldn't commit more than five percent of its allocation to a single customer this early in the game, but since Gary had been the first to call, his man was willing to set aside 500 shares. Gary pushed for more, but the sad fact was that he was not a big-time customer. He typically invested in multiples of a hundred, and to save on commissions he executed smaller trades himself online.

Now, Caroline was a big investor. With Gary's guidance she often bought in multiples of a thousand. Her broker worked for the largest house in Philadelphia, and there was no doubt that 4,500 shares of Axon's new issue could be found for a truly valued customer; this was how the game was played. Unfortunately, since the Sunday afternoon when she'd hurt her back, Gary and Caroline had been as close to not speaking as a couple could be and still function as parents. Gary was keen to get his full five thousand shares of Axon, but he refused to sacrifice his principles and crawl back to his wife and beg her to invest for him.

So instead he'd phoned his large-cap contact at Hevy & Hodapp, a man named Pudge Portleigh, and asked to be put down for five thousand shares of the offering on his own account. Over the years, in his fiduciary role at CenTrust, Gary had bought a lot of stock from Portleigh, including some certifiable turkeys. Gary hinted now to Portleigh that CenTrust might give him an even larger portion of its business in the future. But Portleigh, with weird hedginess, had agreed only to pass along Gary's request to Daffy Anderson, who was Hevy & Hodapp's deal manager for the IPO.

There had then ensued two maddening weeks during which Pudge Portleigh failed to call Gary back and confirm an allocation. Online buzz about Axon was building from a whisper to a roar. Two related major papers by Earl Eberle's team—"Reverse-Tomographic Stimulation of Synaptogenesis in Selected Neural Pathways" and "Transitory Positive Reinforcement in Dopamine-Deprived Limbic Circuits: Recent Clinical Progress"—appeared in *Nature* and the *New England Journal of Medicine* within days of each other. The two papers received heavy coverage in the financial press, including a front-page notice in the *Wall Street Journal*. Analyst after analyst began to flash strong Buys for Axon, and still Portleigh did not return Gary's messages, and Gary could feel the advantages of his insiderly head start disappearing hour by hour . . .

1. HAVE A COCKTAIL!

". . . Of ferrocitrates and ferroacetates specially formulated to cross the blood-brain barrier and accumulate interstitially!"

Said the unseen pitchman whose voice had joined Earl Eberle's on the video sound track.

"We also stir in a mild, non-habit-forming sedative *and* a generous squirt of Hazelnut Moccacino syrup, courtesy of the country's most popular chain of coffee bars!"

A female extra from the earlier lecture scene, a girl with whose neurological functions there was clearly nothing in the slightest wrong, drank with great relish and sexily pulsing throat muscles a tall, frosty glass of Corecktall electrolytes.

"What was Dad's patent?" Denise whispered to Gary. "Ferroacetate gel something-something?"

Gary nodded grimly. "Electropolymerization."

From his correspondence files at home, which contained, among other things, every letter he'd ever received from either of his parents, Gary had dug out an old copy of Alfred's patent. He wasn't sure he'd ever really looked at it, so impressed was he now by the old man's clear account of "electrical anisotropy" in "certain ferro-organic gels" and his proposal that these gels be used to "minutely image" living human tissues and create "direct electrical contact" with "fine morphologic structures." Comparing the wording of the patent with the description of Corecktall at Axon's newly renovated Web site, Gary was struck by the depth of similarity. Evidently Alfred's five-thousand-dollar process was at the *center* of a process for which Axon now hoped to raise upward of $200 million: as if a man didn't have enough in his life to lie awake at night and fume about!

"Yo, Kelsey, yuh, Kelsey, get me twelve thousand Exxon at one-oh-four max," the young man sitting to Gary's left said suddenly and too loudly. The kid had a palmtop stock-quoter, a wire in his ear, and the schizophrenic eyes of the cellularly occupied. "Twelve thousand Exxon, upper limit one zero four," he said.

Exxon, Axon, better be careful, Gary thought.

2. PUT ON A HEADSET & TURN ON THE RADIO!

"You won't hear a thing—not unless your dental fillings pick up ball games on the AM dial," the pitchman joked as the smiling girl lowered onto her camera-friendly head a metal dome reminiscent of a hair dryer, "but radio waves are penetrating the innermost recesses of your skull. Imagine a kind of global positioning system for the brain: RF radiation pinpointing and *selectively stimulating* the neural pathways associated with particular skills. Like signing your name. Climbing stairs. Remembering your anniversary. Thinking positively! Clinically tested at scores of hospitals across America, Dr. Eberle's reverse-tomographic methods have now been further refined to make this stage of the Corecktall process as simple and painless as a visit to your hairstylist."

"Until recently," Eberle broke in (he and his chair still drifting through a sea of simulated blood and gray matter), "my process required overnight hospitalization and the physical screwing of a calibrated steel ring into the patient's cranium. Many patients found this inconvenient; some also experienced discomfort. Now, however, enormous increases in computing power have made possible a process that is *instantaneously self-correcting* as to the location of the individual neural pathways under stimulation . . ."

"Kelsey, you da man!" young Mr. Twelve Thousand Shares of Exxon said loudly.

In the first hours and days following Gary's big Sunday blowout with Caroline, three weeks ago, both he and she had made overtures of peace. Very late on that Sunday night she'd reached across the demilitarized zone of the mattress and touched his hip. The next night he'd offered an almost-complete apology in which, although he refused to concede the central issue, he conveyed sorrow and regret for the collateral damage he'd caused, the bruised feelings and willful misrepresentations and hurtful imputations, and thus gave Caroline a foretaste of the rush of tenderness that awaited her if she would only admit that, regarding the central issue, he was in the right. On Tuesday morning she'd made an actual breakfast for him—cinnamon toast, sausage links, and a bowl of oatmeal topped with raisins arranged to resemble a face with a comically downturned mouth. On Wednesday morning he'd given her a compliment, a simple statement of fact ("You're beautiful") which, although it fell short of an outright avowal of love, did serve as a reminder of an objective basis (physical attraction) on which love could be restored if she would only admit that, regarding the central issue, he was in the right.

But each hopeful overture, each exploratory sally, came to naught. When he squeezed the hand she offered him and he whispered that he was sorry that her back hurt, she was unable to take the next step and allow that possibly (a simple "possibly" would have sufficed!) her two hours of soccer in the rain had contributed to her injury. And when she thanked him for his compliment and asked him how he'd slept, he was powerless to ignore a tendentious critical edge in her voice; he understood her to be saying, *Prolonged disturbance of sleep is a common symptom of clinical depression, oh, and, by the way, how did you sleep, dear?* and so he didn't dare admit that, as a matter of fact, he'd slept atrociously; he averred that he'd slept extremely well, thank you, Caroline, extremely well, *extremely* well.

Each failed overture of peace made the next overture less likely to succeed. Before long, what at first glance had seemed to Gary an absurd possibility—that the till of their marriage no longer contained sufficient funds of love and goodwill to cover the emotional costs that going to St. Jude entailed for Caroline or that *not* going to St. Jude entailed for him—assumed the contours of something terribly actual. He began to hate Caroline simply for continuing to fight with him. He hated the newfound reserves of independence she tapped in order to resist him. Especially, devastatingly hateful was her hatred of *him*. He could have ended the crisis in a minute if all he'd had to do was forgive her; but to see mirrored in her eyes how repellent she found him—it made him crazy, it poisoned his hope.

Fortunately, the shadows cast by her accusation of depression, long and dark though they were, did not yet extend to his corner office at CenTrust and to the pleasure he took in managing his managers, analysts, and traders. Gary's forty hours at the bank had become the only hours he could count on enjoying in a week. He'd even begun to toy with the idea of working a fifty-hour week; but this was easier said than done, because at the end of his eight-hour day there was often literally no work left on his desk, and he was all too aware, besides, that spending long hours at the office to escape unhappiness at home was exactly the trap his father had fallen into; was undoubtedly how Alfred had begun to self-medicate.

When he married Caroline, Gary had silently vowed never to work later than five o'clock and never to bring a briefcase home at night. By signing on with a mid-sized regional bank, he'd chosen one of the least ambitious career paths that a Wharton School M.B.A. could take. At first his intention was simply to avoid his father's mistakes—to give himself time to enjoy life, cherish his wife, play with his kids—but before long, even as he was proving to be an outstanding portfolio manager, he became more specifically allergic to ambition. Colleagues far less capable than he were moving on to work for mutual funds, to be freelance money managers, or to start their own funds; but they were also working twelve- or fourteen-hour days, and every single one of them had the perspiring manic style of a *striver*. Gary, cushioned by Caroline's inheritance, was free to cultivate nonambition and to be, as a boss, the perfect strict and loving father that he could only halfway be at home. He demanded honesty and excellence from his workers. In return he offered patient instruction, absolute loyalty, and the assurance that he would never blame them for his own mistakes. If his large-cap manager, Virginia Lin, recommended upping the percentage of energy stocks in the bank's boilerplate trust portfolio from six percent to nine percent and Gary (as was his wont) decided to leave the mix alone, and if the energy sector then proceeded to enjoy a couple of banner quarters, he pulled his big ironic I'm-a-jerk grimace and publicly apologized to Lin. Fortunately, for each of his bad decisions he made two or three good ones, and in the history of the universe there had never been a better six years for equities investment than the six years he'd run CenTrust's Equities Division; only a fool or a crook could have failed. With success guaranteed, Gary could then make a game of being unawed by his boss, Marvin Koster, and by Koster's boss, Marty Breitenfeld, the chairman of CenTrust. Gary never, ever kowtowed or flattered. Indeed, both Koster and Breitenfeld had begun to defer to *him* in matters of taste and protocol, Koster all but asking Gary's permission to enroll his eldest daughter in Abington Friends instead of Friends' Select, Breitenfeld buttonholing Gary outside the senior-executive pissoir to inquire if he and Caroline were planning to attend the Free Library benefit ball or if Gary had spun off his tickets to a secretary . . .

3. RELAX—IT'S ALL IN YOUR HEAD!

Curly Eberle had reappeared in his intracranial desk chair with a plastic model of an electrolyte molecule in each hand. "A remarkable property of ferrocitrate/ferroacetate gels," he said, "is that under low-level radio stimulation at certain resonant frequencies the molecules may spontaneously polymerize. More remarkably yet, these polymers turn out to be fine conductors of electrical impulses."

The virtual Eberle looked on with a benign smile as, in the bloody animated moil around him, eager waveforms came squiggling through. As if these waves were the opening strains of a minuet or reel, all the ferrous molecules paired off and arranged themselves in long, twinned lines.

"These transient conductive microtubules," Eberle said, "make thinkable the previously unthinkable: direct, quasi-real-time digital-chemical interface."

"But this is good," Denise whispered to Gary. "This is what Dad's always wanted."

"What, to screw himself out of a fortune?"

"To help other people," Denise said. "To make a difference."

Gary could have pointed out that, if the old man really felt like helping somebody, he might start with his wife. But Denise had bizarre and unshakable notions of Alfred. There was no point in rising to her bait.

4. THE RICH GET RICHER!

"Yes, an idle corner of the brain may be the Devil's workshop," the pitchman said, "but every idle neural pathway gets ignored by the Corecktall process. Wherever there's action, though, Corecktall is there to make it stronger! *To help the rich get richer!*"

From all over Ballroom B came laughter and applause and whoops of appreciation. Gary sensed that his grinning, clapping left-hand neighbor, Mr. Twelve Thousand Shares of Exxon, was looking in his direction. Possibly the guy was wondering why Gary wasn't clapping. Or possibly he was intimidated by the casual elegance of Gary's clothes.

For Gary a key element of not being a striver, a perspirer, was to dress as if he didn't have to work at all: as if he were a gentleman who just happened to enjoy coming to the office and helping other people. As if noblesse oblige.

Today he was wearing a caper-green half-silk sport coat, an ecru linen button-down, and pleatless black dress pants; his own cell phone was turned off, deaf to all incoming calls. He tipped his chair back and scanned the ballroom to confirm that, indeed, he was the only male guest without a necktie, but the contrast between self and crowd today left much to be desired. Just a few years ago the room would have been a jungle of blue pinstripe, ventless Mafiawear, two-tone power shirts, and tasseled loafers. But now, in the late maturing years of the long, long boom, even young suburban galoots from New Jersey were buying hand-tailored Italian suits and high-end eyewear. So much money had flooded the system that twenty-six-year-olds who thought Andrew Wyeth was a furniture company and Winslow Homer a cartoon character were able to dress like Hollywood aristocracy . . .

Oh, misanthropy and sourness. Gary wanted to enjoy being a man of wealth and leisure, but the country was making it none too easy. All around him, millions of newly minted American millionaires were engaged in the identical pursuit of feeling extraordinary—of buying the perfect Victorian, of skiing the virgin slope, of knowing the chef personally, of locating the beach that had no footprints. There were further tens of millions of young Americans who didn't have money but were nonetheless chasing the Perfect Cool. And meanwhile the sad truth was that not everyone could be extraordinary, not everyone could be extremely cool; because whom would this leave to be ordinary? Who would perform the thankless work of being comparatively *un*cool?

Well, there was still the citizenry of America's heartland: St. Judean minivan drivers thirty and forty pounds overweight and sporting pastel sweats, pro-life bumper stickers, Prussian hair. But Gary in recent years had observed, with plate-tectonically cumulative anxiety, that population was continuing to flow out of the Midwest and toward the cooler coasts. (He was part of this exodus himself, of course, but he'd made his escape early, and, frankly, priority had its privileges.) At the same time, all the restaurants in St. Jude were suddenly coming up to European speed (suddenly cleaning ladies knew from sun-dried tomatoes, suddenly hog farmers knew from crème brûlée), and shoppers at the mall near his parents' house had an air of entitlement offputtingly similar to his own, and the electronic consumer goods for sale in St. Jude were every bit as powerful and cool as those in Chestnut Hill. Gary wished that all further migration to the coasts could be banned and all midwesterners encouraged to revert to eating pasty foods and wearing dowdy clothes and playing board games, in order that a strategic national reserve of cluelessness might be maintained, a wilderness of taste which would enable people of privilege, like himself, to feel extremely civilized in perpetuity—

But *enough*, he told himself. A too-annihilating will to specialness, a wish to reign supreme in his superiority, was yet another Warning Sign of clinical D.

And Mr. Twelve Thousand Shares of Exxon wasn't looking at him anyway. He was looking at Denise's naked legs.

"The polymer strands," Eberle explained, "chemotactically associate with active neural pathways and so facilitate the discharge of electrical potential. We don't yet fully understand the mechanism, but the effect is to make any action the patient is performing easier *and more enjoyable* to repeat and to sustain. Producing this effect even transiently would be an exciting clinical achievement. Here at Axon, however, we have found a way to render that effect *permanent*."

"Just watch," the pitchman purred.

5. NOW IT'S YOUR TURN TO WORK A LITTLE!

As a cartoon human figure shakily raised a teacup to its mouth, certain shaky neural pathways lit up inside its cartoon head. Then the figure drank Corecktall electrolytes, donned an Eberle helmet, and raised the cup again. Little glowing microtubules hued to the active pathways, which began to blaze with light and strength. Steady as a rock the cartoon hand that lowered the teacup to its saucer.

"We've got to get Dad signed up for testing," Denise whispered.

"What do you mean?" Gary said.

"Well, this is for Parkinson's. It could help him."

Gary sighed like a tire losing air. How could it be that such an incredibly obvious idea had never occurred to him? He felt ashamed of himself and, at the same time, obscurely resentful of Denise. He aimed a bland smile at the video screen as if he hadn't heard her.

"Once the pathways have been identified and stimulated," Eberle said, "we are only a short step away from actual morphologic correction. And here, as everywhere in medicine today, *the secret is in the genes.*"

6. REMEMBER THOSE PILLS YOU TOOK LAST MONTH?

Three days ago, on Friday afternoon, Gary had finally got through to Pudge Portleigh at Hevy & Hodapp. Portleigh had sounded harried in the extreme.

"Gare, sorry, it's a rave scene here," Portleigh said, "but listen, my friend, I did talk to Daffy Anderson per your request. Daffy says, sure, no problem, we will definitely allocate five hundred shares for a good customer at CenTrust. So, are we OK, my friend? Are we good?"

"No," Gary said. "We said five thousand, not five hundred."

Portleigh was silent for a moment. "Shit, Gare. Big mix-up. I thought you said five hundred."

"You repeated it back to me. You said five thousand. You said you were writing it down."

"Remind me—this is on your own account or CenTrust's?"

"My account."

"Look, Gare, here's what you do. Call Daffy yourself, explain the situation, explain the mix-up, and see if he can rustle up another five hundred. I can back you up that far. I mean, it was my mistake, I had no idea how hot this thing would be. But you gotta realize, Daffy's taking food from somebody else's mouth to feed you. It's the Nature Channel,

Gare. All the little birdies with their beaks open wide. Me! Me! Me! I can back you up for another five hundred, but you gotta do your own squawking. All right, my friend? Are we good?"

"No, Pudge, we aren't good," Gary said. "Do you remember I took twenty thousand shares of refinanced Adelson Lee off your hands? We also took—"

"Gare, Gare, don't do this to me," Pudge said. "I'm aware. Have I forgotten Adelson Lee? Christ, please, it haunts my every waking hour. All I'm trying to say to you is that five hundred shares of Axon, it may sound like a dis, but it's not a dis. It's the best Daffy's going to do for you."

"A refreshing breath of honesty," Gary said. "Now tell me again if you forgot I said five thousand."

"OK, I'm an asshole. Thank you for letting me know. But I can't get you more than a thousand total without going all the way upstairs. If you want five thousand, Daffy needs a direct order from Dick Hevy. And since you mention Adelson Lee, Dick's going to point out to me that CoreStates took forty thousand, First Delaware took thirty thousand, TIAA-CREF took fifty, and so on down the line. The calculus is that crude, Gare. You helped us to the tune of twenty, we help you to the tune of five hundred. I mean, I'll try Dick if you want. I can also probably get another five hundred out of Daffy just by telling him you'd never guess he used to be shiny on top, to see him now. Whuff, the miracle of Rogaine. But basically this is the kind of deal where Daffy gets to play Santa Claus. He knows if you've been bad or good. In particular, he knows for whom you work. To be honest, for the kind of consideration you're looking for, what you really need to do is triple the size of your institution."

Size, oh, did it matter. Short of promising to buy some arrant turkeys with CenTrust money at a later date (and he could lose his job for this), Gary had no further leverage with Pudge Portleigh. However, he still had *moral* leverage in the form of Axon's underpayment for Alfred's patent. Lying awake last night, he'd honed the wording of the clear, measured lecture that he intended to deliver to Axon's brass this afternoon: *I want you to look me in the eye and tell me that your offer to my father was reasonable and fair. My father had personal reasons for accepting that offer; but I know what you did to him. Do you understand me? I'm not an old man in the Midwest. I know what you did. And I think you realize that it is not an option for me to leave this room without a firm commitment for five thousand shares. I could also insist on an apology. But I'm simply proposing a straightforward transaction between adults. Which, by the way, costs you n o t h i n g. Zero. Nada. Niente.*

"Synaptogenesis!" Axon's video pitchman exulted.

7. NO, IT'S NOT A BOOK OF THE BIBLE!

The professional investors in Ballroom B laughed and laughed.

"Could this possibly be a hoax?" Denise asked Gary.

"Why license Dad's patent for a hoax?" Gary said.

She shook her head. "This makes me want to, like, go back to bed."

Gary understood the feeling. He hadn't had a good night's sleep in three weeks. His circadian schedule was 180 degrees out of phase, he was revved all night and sandy-eyed all day, and he found it ever more arduous to believe that his problem wasn't neurochemical but personal.

How right he'd been, all those months, to conceal the many Warning Signs from Caroline! How accurate his intuition that a putative deficit of Neurofactor 3 would sap the legitimacy of his moral arguments! Caroline was now able to camouflage her animosity toward him as "concern" about his "health." His lumbering forces of conventional domestic warfare were no match for this biological weaponry. He cruelly attacked her *person*; she heroically attacked his *disease*.

Building on this strategic advantage, Caroline had then made a series of brilliant tactical moves. When Gary drew up his battle plans for the first full weekend of hostilities, he assumed that Caroline would circle the wagons as she'd done on the previous weekend—would adolescently pal around with Aaron and Caleb and incite them to make fun of Clueless Old Dad. Therefore on Thursday night he ambushed her. He proposed, out of the blue, that he and Aaron and Caleb go mountain-biking in the Poconos on Sunday, leaving at dawn for a long day of older-male bonding in which Caroline could not participate *because her back hurt*.

Caroline's countermove was to endorse his proposal enthusiastically. She urged Caleb and Aaron to go and *enjoy the time with their father*. She laid curious stress on this phrase, causing Aaron and Caleb to pipe up, as if on cue, "Mountain-biking, yeah, Dad, great!" And all at once Gary realized what was going on. He realized why, on Monday night, Aaron had come and unilaterally apologized for having called him "horrible," and why Caleb on Tuesday, for the first time in months, had invited him to play foosball, and why Jonah, on Wednesday, had brought him, unbidden, on a cork-lined tray, a second martini that Caroline had poured. He saw why his children had turned agreeable and solicitous: *because Caroline had told them that their father was struggling with clinical depression*. What a brilliant gambit! And not for a second did he doubt that a gambit was what it was—that Caroline's "concern" was purely bogus, a wartime tactic, a way to avoid spending Christmas in St. Jude—because there continued to be no warmth or fondness for him, not the faintest ember, in her eyes.

"Did you tell the boys that I'm depressed?" Gary asked her in the darkness, from the far margin of their quarter-acre bed. "Caroline? Did you lie to them about my mental state? Is that why everybody's suddenly being so agreeable?"

"Gary," she said. "They're being agreeable because they want you to take them mountain-biking in the Poconos."

"Something about this doesn't smell right."

"You know, you are getting seriously paranoid."

"Fuck, fuck, fuck!"

"Gary, this is frightening."

"You're fucking with my head! And there is no lower trick than that. There's no meaner trick in the book."

"Please, please, listen to yourself."

"Answer my question," he said. "Did you tell them I'm 'depressed'? 'Having a hard time'?"

"Well—aren't you?"

"Answer my question!"

She didn't answer his question. She said nothing more at all that night, although he repeated his question for half an hour, pausing for a minute or two each time so that she could answer, but she didn't answer.

By the morning of the bike trip, he was so destroyed by lack of sleep that his ambition was simply to function physically. He loaded three bikes onto Caroline's extremely large and safe Ford Stomper vehicle and drove for two hours, unloaded the bikes, and pedaled mile after mile on rutted trails. The boys raced on far ahead. By the time he caught up with them, they'd taken their rest and were ready to move again. They volunteered nothing but wore expressions of friendly expectation, as if Gary might have a confession to make. His situation was neurochemically somewhat dire, however; he had nothing to say except "Let's eat our sandwiches" and "One more ridge and then we turn around." At dusk he loaded the bikes back onto the Stomper, drove two hours, and unloaded them in an access of ANHEDONIA.

Caroline came out of the house and told the older boys what great fun she and Jonah had had. She declared herself a convert to the Narnia books. All evening, then, she and Jonah chattered about "Aslan" and "Cair Paravel" and "Reepicheep," and the online kids-only Narnia chat room that she'd located on the Internet, and the C. S. Lewis Web site that had cool online games to play and tons of cool Narnian products to order.

"There's a *Prince Caspian* CD-ROM," Jonah told Gary, "that I'm very much looking forward to playing with."

"It looks like a really interesting and well-designed game," Caroline said. "I showed Jonah how to order it."

"There's a Wardrobe?" Jonah said. "And you point and click and go through the Wardrobe into Narnia? And then there's all this cool stuff inside?"

Profound was Gary's relief the next morning as he bumped and glided, like a storm-battered yacht, into the safe harbor of his work week. There was nothing to do but patch himself up as well as he could, stay the course, *not be depressed*. Despite serious losses, he remained confident of victory. Since his very first fight with Caroline, twenty years earlier, when he'd sat alone in his apartment and watched an eleven-inning Phillies game and listened to his phone ring every ten minutes, every five minutes, every two minutes, he'd understood that at the ticking heart of Caroline was a desperate insecurity. Sooner or later, if he withheld his love, she came knocking on his chest with her little fist and let him have his way.

Caroline showed no sign of weakening, however. Late at night, when Gary was too freaked out and angry to shut his eyes, let alone sleep, she politely but firmly declined to fight with him. She was particularly adamant in her refusal to discuss Christmas; she said that listening to Gary on the topic was like watching an alcoholic drink.

"What do you need from me?" Gary asked her. "Tell me what you need to hear from me."

"I need you to take responsibility for your mental health."

"Jesus, Caroline. Wrong, wrong, wrong answer."

Meanwhile Discordia, the goddess of marital strife, had pulled strings with the airline industry. There appeared in the *Inquirer* a full-page ad for a slasheroo sale on Midland Airlines tickets, including a $198 round-trip fare between Philly and St. Jude. Only four dates in late December were blacked out; by staying just one extra day at Christmastime Gary could take the whole family to and from St. Jude (nonstop!) for under a thousand bucks. He had his travel agent hold five tickets for him, renewing the option daily. Finally, on Friday morning, with the sale due to end at midnight, he'd announced to Caroline that he was buying tickets. In accordance with her strict no-Christmas policy, Caroline turned to Aaron and asked him if he'd studied for his Spanish test. From his office at CenTrust, in a spirit of trench warfare, Gary called his travel agent and authorized the purchase. Then he called his doctor and requested a sleep aid, a short-term prescription, something a little more potent than the nonprescription stuff. Dr. Pierce replied that a sleep aid didn't sound like such a good idea. Caroline, Pierce said, had mentioned that Gary might be depressed, and a sleep aid certainly wasn't going to help with *that*. Maybe, instead, Gary would like to come in and talk about how he was feeling?

For a moment, after he hung up, Gary let himself imagine being divorced. But three glowing and idealized mental portraits of his children, shadowed by a batlike horde of fears regarding finances, chased the notion from his head.

At a dinner party on Saturday he'd rifled the medicine chest of his friends Drew and Jamie, hoping to find a bottle of something in the Valium class, but no such luck.

Yesterday Denise had called him and insisted, with ominous steeliness, that he have lunch with her. She said she'd seen Enid and Alfred in New York on Saturday. She said that Chip and his girlfriend had flaked on her and vanished.

Gary, lying awake last night, had wondered if stunts like this were what Caroline meant when she described Chip as a man "honest enough" to say what he could and couldn't "tolerate."

"The cells are genetically reprogrammed to release nerve-growth factor only when locally activated!" Earl Eberle's video facsimile said cheerfully.

A fetching young model, her skull in an Eberle Helmet, was strapped into a machine that retrained her brain to instruct her legs to walk.

A model wearing a wintry look, a look of misanthropy and sourness, pushed up the corners of her mouth with her fingers while magnified cutaway animation revealed, within her brain, the flowering of dendrites, the forging of new synaptic links. In a moment she was able to smile, tentatively, without using her fingers. In another moment, her smile was dazzling.

CORECKTALL: IT'S THE FUTURE!

"The Axon Corporation is fortunate to hold five U.S. patents protecting this powerful platform technology," Earl Eberle told the camera. "These patents, and eight others that are pending, form an insurmountable fire wall protecting the hundred-fifty million dollars that we have spent to date on research and development. Axon is the recognized world leader in this field. We have a six-year track record of positive cash flows and a revenue stream that we expect to top eighty million dollars in the coming year. Potential investors may rest assured that every penny of every dollar we raise on December 15 will be spent on developing this marvelous and potentially historic product.

"Corecktall: It's the Future!" Eberle said.

"It's the Future!" intoned the pitchman.

"It's the Future!" chorused the crowd of really good-looking students in nerdy glasses.

"I liked the past," Denise said, uptilting her complimentary half-liter of imported water.

In Gary's opinion, too many people were breathing the air in Ballroom B. A ventilation problem somehow. As the lights came up to full strength, silent wait-personnel fanned in among the tables bearing luncheon entrées under chafing lids.

"My first guess is salmon," Denise said. "No, my only guess is salmon."

Rising from talk-show chairs and moving to the front of the dais now were three figures who reminded Gary, oddly, of his honeymoon in Italy. He and Caroline had visited a cathedral somewhere in Tuscany, maybe Siena, in the museum of which were big medieval statues of saints that had once stood on the roof of the cathedral, each with an arm raised like a waving presidential candidate and each wearing a saintly grin of *certainty*.

The eldest of the three beatific greeters, a pink-faced man with rimless glasses, extended a hand as if to bless the crowd.

"All right!" he said. "All right, everybody! My name is Joe Prager, I'm the lead deal attorney at Bragg Knuter. To my left is Merilee Finch, CEO of Axon, to my right Daffy Anderson, the all-important deal manager at Hevy and Hodapp. We were hoping Curly himself might deign to join us today, but he is the man of the hour, he is being interviewed by CNN as we speak. So let me do a little caveating here, wink-wink-wink, and then turn the floor over to Daffy and Merilee."

"Yo, Kelsey, talk to me, baby, talk to me," Gary's young neighbor shouted.

"Caveat A," Prager said, "is please everyone take note that I'm stressing that Curly's results are extremely preliminary. This is all Phase

One research, folks. Anybody not hear me? Anybody in the back?" Prager craned his neck and waved both arms at the most distant tables, including Gary's. "Full disclosure: this is *Phase One* research. Axon does not yet have, in no way is it representing that it has, FDA approval for Phase Two testing. And what comes after Phase Two? Phase Three! And after Phase Three? A multistage review process that can delay the product launch by as much as three more years. Folks, hello, we are dealing with clinical results that are *extremely interesting* but *extremely preliminary*. So caveat emptor. All righty? Wink wink wink. All righty?"

Prager was struggling to keep his face straight. Merilee Finch and Daffy Anderson were sucking on smiles as if they, too, had guilty secrets or religion.

"Caveat B," Prager said. "An inspirational video presentation is not a prospectus. Daffy's representations here today, likewise Merilee's representations, are impromptu and, again, *not a prospectus* . . ."

The waitstaff descended on Gary's table and gave him salmon on a bed of lentils. Denise waved away her entrée.

"Aren't you going to eat?" Gary whispered.

She shook her head.

"Denise. Really." He felt inexplicably wounded. "You can surely have a couple of bites with me."

Denise looked him square in the face with an unreadable expression. "I'm a little sick to my stomach."

"Do you want to leave?"

"No. I just don't want to eat."

Denise at thirty-two was still beautiful, but long hours at the stove had begun to cook her youthful skin into a kind of terra-cotta mask that made Gary a little more anxious each time he saw her. She was his baby sister, after all. Her years of fertility and marriageability were passing with a swiftness to which he was attuned and she, he suspected, was not. Her career seemed to him an evil spell under the influence of which she worked sixteen-hour days and had no social life. Gary was afraid—he claimed, as her oldest brother, the *right* to be afraid—that by the time Denise awakened from this spell she would be too old to start a family.

He ate his salmon quickly while she drank her imported water.

On the dais the CEO of Axon, a fortyish blonde with the intelligent pugnacity of a college dean, was talking about side effects. "Apart from headaches and nausea, which are to be expected," said Merilee Finch, "we haven't tracked anything yet. Remember, too, that our platform technology has been widely used for several years now, with no significant deleterious effects reported." Finch pointed into the ballroom. "Yes, gray Armani?"

"Isn't Corecktall the name of a laxative?"

"Ah, well," Finch said, nodding violently. "Different spelling, but yes. Curly and I considered approximately ten thousand different names before we realized that branding isn't really an issue for the Alzheimer's patient, or the Parkinson's sufferer, or the massively depressed individual. We could call it Carcino-Asbesto, they'd still knock doors down to get it. Curly's big vision here, though, and the reason he's willing to risk the poopy jokes, and so forth, is that twenty years from now there's not going to be a prison left standing in the United States, because of this process. I mean, realistically, we live in the age of medical breakthroughs. There's no question we'll have competing therapies for AD and PD. Some of these therapies will probably come on line before Corecktall. So, for most disorders of the brain, our product will be just one weapon in the arsenal. Clearly the *best* weapon, but still, just one among many. On the other hand, when it comes to social disease, the brain of the criminal, there's no other option on the horizon. It's Corecktall or prison. So it's a forward-looking name. We're laying claim to a whole new hemisphere. We're planting the Spanish flag right on the beach here."

There was a murmur at a distant table where a tweedy, homely contingent was seated, maybe union fund managers, maybe the endowment crowd from Penn or Temple. One stork-shaped woman stood up from this table and shouted, "So, what's the idea, you reprogram the repeat offender to enjoy pushing a broom?"

"That is within the realm of the feasible, yes," Finch said. "That is one potential fix, although possibly not the best."

The heckler couldn't believe it. "Not the *best*? It's an ethical *nightmare*."

"So, free country, go invest in alternative energy," Finch said, for a laugh, because most of the guests were on her side. "Buy some geothermal penny stocks. Solar-electricity futures, very cheap, very righteous. Yes, next, please? Pink shirt?"

"You guys are dreaming," the heckler persisted at a shout, "if you think the American people—"

"Honey," Finch interrupted with the advantage of her lapel mike and amplification, "the American people support the death penalty. Do you think they'll have a problem with a socially constructive alternative like this? Ten years from now we'll see which of us is dreaming. Yes, pink shirt at Table Three, yes?"

"Excuse me," the heckler persisted, "I'm trying to remind your potential investors of the Eighth Amendment—"

"Thank you. Thank you very much," Finch said, her emcee's smile tightening. "Since you bring up cruel and unusual punishment, let me suggest that you walk a few blocks north of here to Fairmount Avenue. Go take a look at the Eastern State Penitentiary. World's first modern prison, opened in 1829, solitary confinement for up to twenty years, astonishing suicide rate, zero corrective benefit, and, just to keep this in mind, *still the basic model for corrections in the United States today*. Curly's not talking about this on CNN, folks. He's talking about the million Americans with Parkinson's and the four million with Alzheimer's. What I'm telling you now is not for general consumption. But the fact is, a one-hundred-percent voluntary alternative to incarceration is the opposite of cruel and unusual. Of all the potential applications of Corecktall, this is the most humane. This is the liberal *vision*: genuine, permanent, voluntary self-melioration."

The heckler, shaking her head with the emphasis of the unconvinceable, was already exiting the ballroom. Mr. Twelve Thousand Shares of Exxon, at Gary's left shoulder, cupped his hands to his mouth and booed her.

Young men at other tables followed suit, booing and smirking, having their sports-fan fun and lending support, Gary feared, to Denise's disdain for the world he moved in. Denise had leaned forward and was staring at Twelve Thousand Shares of Exxon in open-mouthed amazement.

Daffy Anderson, a linebacker type with thick glossy sideburns and a texturally distinct stubblefield of hair higher up, had stepped forward to answer money questions. He spoke of being *gratifyingly oversubscribed.* He compared the heat of this IPO to *Vindaloo curry* and *Dallas in July.* He refused to divulge the price that Hevy & Hodapp planned to ask for a share of Axon. He spoke of *pricing it fairly* and—wink, wink—*letting the market do its job.*

Denise touched Gary's shoulder and pointed to a table behind the dais, where Merilee Finch was standing by herself and putting salmon in her mouth. "Our prey is feeding. I say we pounce."

"What for?" Gary said.

"To get Dad signed up for testing."

Nothing about the idea of Alfred's participation in a Phase II study appealed to Gary, but it occurred to him that by letting Denise broach the topic of Alfred's affliction, by letting her create sympathy for the Lamberts and establish their moral claim on Axon's favors, he could increase his chances of getting his five thousand shares.

"You do the talking," he said, standing up. "Then I'll have a question for her, too."

As he and Denise moved toward the dais, heads turned to admire Denise's legs.

"What part of 'no comment' didn't you understand?" Daffy Anderson asked a questioner for a laugh.

The cheeks of Axon's CEO were puffed out like a squirrel's. Merilee Finch put a napkin to her mouth and regarded the accosting Lamberts warily. "I'm *so* starving," she said. It was a thin woman's apology for being corporeal. "We'll be setting up some tables in a couple of minutes, if you don't mind waiting."

"This is a semi-private question," Denise said.

Finch swallowed with difficulty—maybe self-consciousness, maybe insufficient chewing. "Yeah?"

Denise and Gary introduced themselves and Denise mentioned the letter that Alfred had been sent.

"I had to *eat* something," Finch explained, shoveling up lentils. "I think Joe was the one who wrote to your father. I'm assuming we're all square there now. He'd be happy to talk to you if you still had questions."

"Our question is more for you," Denise said.

"Sorry. One more bite here." Finch chewed her salmon with labored jawstrokes, swallowed again, and dropped her napkin on the plate. "As far as that patent goes, I'll tell you frankly, we considered just infringing. That's what everybody else does. But Curly's an inventor himself. He wanted to do the right thing."

"Frankly," Gary said, "the right thing might have been to offer more."

Finch's tongue was probing beneath her upper lip like a cat beneath blankets. "You may have a somewhat inflated idea of your father's achievement," she said. "A lot of researchers were studying those gels in the sixties. The discovery of electrical anisotropy is generally, I believe, credited to a team at Cornell. Plus I understand from Joe that the wording of that patent is unspecific. It doesn't even refer to the brain; it's just 'human tissues.' Justice is the right of the stronger, when it comes to patent law. I think our offer was rather generous."

Gary made his I'm-a-jerk face and looked at the dais, where Daffy Anderson was being mobbed by well-wishers and supplicants.

"Our father was fine with the offer," Denise assured Finch. "And he'll be happy to know what you guys are doing."

Female bonding, the making of nice, faintly nauseated Gary.

"I forget which hospital he's with," Finch said.

"He's not," Denise said. "He was a railroad engineer. He had a lab in our basement."

Finch was surprised. "He did that work as an amateur?"

Gary didn't know which version of Alfred made him angrier: the spiteful old tyrant who'd made a brilliant discovery in the basement and cheated himself out of a fortune, or the clueless basement amateur who'd unwittingly replicated the work of real chemists, spent scarce family money to file and maintain a vaguely worded patent, and was now being tossed a scrap from the table of Earl Eberle. Both versions incensed him.

Perhaps it was best, after all, that the old man had ignored Gary's advice and taken the money.

"My dad has Parkinson's," Denise said.

"Oh, I'm very sorry."

"Well, and we were wondering if you might include him in the testing of your—product."

"Conceivably," Finch said. "We'd have to ask Curly. I do like the human-interest aspect. Does your dad live around here?"

"He's in St. Jude."

Finch frowned. "It won't work if you can't get him to Schwenksville twice a week for at least six months."

"Not a problem," Denise said, turning to Gary. "Right?"

Gary was hating everything about this conversation. Health health, female female, nice nice, easy easy. He didn't answer.

"How is he mentally?" Finch said.

Denise opened her mouth, but at first no words came out.

"He's fine," she said, rallying. "Just—fine."

"No dementia?"

Denise pursed her lips and shook her head. "No. He gets a little confused sometimes, but—no."

"The confusion could be from his meds," Finch said, "in which case it's fixable. But Lewy-body dementia is beyond the purview of Phase Two testing. So is Alzheimer's."

"He's pretty sharp," Denise said.

"Well, if he's able to follow basic instructions, and he's willing to travel east in January, Curly might try to include him. It would make a good story."

Finch produced a business card, warmly shook Denise's hand, less warmly shook Gary's, and moved into the mob surrounding Daffy Anderson.

Gary followed her and caught her by the elbow. She turned around, startled.

"Listen, Merilee," he said in a low voice, as if to say, *Let's be realistic now, we adults can dispense with the nicey-nice crap.* "I'm glad you think my dad's a 'good story.' And it's very generous of you to give him five thousand dollars. But I believe you need us more than we need you."

Finch waved to somebody and held up one finger; she would be there in one second. "Actually," she said to Gary, "we don't need you at all. So I'm not sure what you're saying."

"My family wants to buy five thousand shares of your offering."

Finch laughed like an executive with an eighty-hour work week. "So does everybody in this room," she said. "That's why we have investment bankers. If you'll excuse me—"

She broke free and got away. Gary, in the crush of bodies, was having trouble breathing. He was furious with himself for having *begged*, furious for having let Denise attend this road show, furious for being a Lambert. He strode toward the nearest exit without waiting for Denise, who hurried after him.

Between the Four Seasons and the neighboring office tower was a corporate courtyard so lavishly planted and flawlessly maintained that it might have been pixels in a cybershopping paradise. The two Lamberts were crossing the courtyard when Gary's anger found a fault through which to vent itself. He said, "I don't know where the hell you think Dad's going to stay if he comes out here."

"Partly with you, partly with me," Denise said.

"You're never home," he said. "And Dad's on record as not wanting to be at *my* house for more than forty-eight hours."

"This wouldn't be like last Christmas," Denise said. "Trust me. The impression I got on Saturday—"

"Plus how's he going to get out to Schwenksville twice a week?"

"Gary, what are you saying? Do you not want this to happen?"

Two office workers, seeing angry parties bearing down, stood up and vacated a marble bench. Denise perched on the bench and folded her arms intransigently. Gary paced in a tight circle, his hands on his hips.

"For the last ten years," he said, "Dad has done *nothing* to take care of himself. He's sat in that fucking blue chair and wallowed in self-pity. I don't know why you think he's suddenly going to start—"

"Well, but if he thought there might actually be a cure—"

"What, so he can be depressed for an extra five years and die miserable at eighty-five instead of eighty? That's going to make all the difference?"

"Maybe he's depressed because he's sick."

"I'm sorry, but that is bullshit, Denise. That is a crock. The man has been depressed since before he even retired. He was depressed when he was still in perfect health."

A low fountain was murmuring nearby, generating medium-strength privacy. A small unaffiliated cloud had wandered into the quadrant of private-sphere sky defined by the encompassing rooflines. The light was coastal and diffuse.

"What would you do," Denise said, "if you had Mom nagging you seven days a week, telling you to get out of the house, watching every move you make, and acting like the kind of chair you sit in is a moral issue? The more she tells him to get up, the more he sits there. The more he sits there, the more she—"

"Denise, you're living in fantasyland."

She looked at Gary with hatred. "Don't patronize me. It's just as much a fantasy to act like Dad's some worn-out old machine. He's a person, Gary. He has an interior life. And he's nice to me, at least—"

"Well, he ain't so nice to me," Gary said. "And he's an abusive selfish bully to Mom. And I say if he wants to sit in that chair and sleep his life away, that's just fine. I love that idea. I'm one-thousand-percent a fan of that idea. But first let's yank that chair out of a three-floor house that's falling apart and losing value. Let's get Mom some kind of quality of life. Just do that, and he can sit in his chair and feel sorry for himself until the cows come home."

"She loves that house. That house *is* her quality of life."

"Well, she's in a fantasyland, too! A lot of good it does her to love the house when she's got to keep an eye on the old man twenty-four hours a day."

Denise crossed her eyes and blew a wisp of hair off her forehead. "You're the one in a fantasy," she said. "You seem to think they're going to be happy living in a two-room apartment in a city where the only people they know are you and me. And do you know who that's convenient for? For *you*."

He threw his hands in the air. "So it's convenient for me! I'm sick of worrying about that house in St. Jude. I'm sick of making trips out there. I'm sick of hearing how miserable Mom is. A situation that's convenient for you and me is better than a situation that's convenient for *nobody*. Mom's living with a guy who's a physical wreck. He's *had it*, he's *through*, finito, end of story, take a charge against earnings. And still she's got this idea that if he would only try harder, everything would be fine and life would be just like it used to be. Well, I got news for everybody: *it ain't ever gonna be the way it used to be*."

"You don't even want him to get better."

"Denise." Gary clutched his eyes. "They had five years before he even got sick. And what did he do? He watched the local news and waited for Mom to cook his meals. This is the real world we're living in. And *I* want them out of that house—"

"Gary."

"*I* want them in a retirement community out here, and *I'm* not afraid to say it."

"Gary, listen to me." Denise leaned forward with an urgent goodwill that only irritated him the more. "Dad can come and stay with me for six months. They can both come and stay, I can bring home meals, it's not that big a deal. If he gets better, they'll go back home. If he doesn't get better, they'll have had six months to decide if they like living in Philly. I mean, *what* is wrong with this?"

Gary didn't know what was wrong with it. But he could already hear Enid's invidious descants on the topic of Denise's wonderfulness. And since it was impossible to imagine Caroline and Enid amicably sharing a house for six days (never mind six weeks, never mind six months), Gary could not, even ceremonially, offer to put his parents up himself.

He raised his eyes to the intensity of whiteness that marked the sun's proximity to a corner of the office tower. The beds of mums and begonias and liriope all around him were like bikinied extras in a music video, planted in full blush of perfection and fated to be yanked again before they had a chance to lose petals, acquire brown spots, drop leaves. Gary had always enjoyed corporate gardens as backdrops for the pageant of privilege, as metonymies of pamperment, but it was vital not to ask too much of them. It was vital not to come to them in need.

"You know, I don't even care," he said. "It's a great plan. And if you want to do the legwork, that would be great."

"OK, I'll do the 'legwork,' " Denise said quickly. "Now what about Christmas? Dad really wants you guys to come."

Gary laughed. "So he's involved now, too."

"He wants it for Mom's sake. And she really, really wants it."

"Of course she wants it. She's Enid Lambert. What does Enid Lambert want if not Christmas in St. Jude?"

"Well, I'm going to go there," Denise said, "and I'm going to try to get Chip to go, and I think the five of you should go. I think we should all just get together and do that for them."

The faint tremor of virtue in her voice set Gary's teeth on edge. A lecture about Christmas was the last thing he needed on this October afternoon, with the needle of his Factor 3 gauge bumping on the bright red *E*.

"Dad said a strange thing on Saturday," Denise continued. "He said, 'I don't know how much time I have.' Both of them were talking like this was their last chance for a Christmas. It was kind of intense."

"Well, count on Mom," Gary said a little wildly, "to phrase the thing for maximum emotional coercion!"

"Right. But I also think she means it."

"I'm sure she means it!" Gary said. "And I will give it some thought! But, Denise, it is *not so easy* getting all five of us out there. It is not so easy! Not when it makes so much sense for us all to be here! Right? Right?"

"I know, I agree," Denise persisted quietly. "But remember, this would be a strictly one-time-only thing."

"I said I'd think about it. That's all I can do, right? I'll think about it! I'll think about it! All right?"

Denise seemed puzzled by his outburst. "OK. Good. Thank you. But the thing is—"

"Yeah, what's the thing," Gary said, taking three steps away from her and suddenly turning back. "Tell me what the thing is."

"Well, I was just thinking—"

"You know, I'm half an hour late already. I really need to get back to the office."

Denise rolled her eyes up at him and let her mouth hang open in mid-sentence.

"Let's just *finish* this conversation," Gary said.

"OK, well, not to sound like Mom, but—"

"A little too late for that! Huh? Huh?" he found himself shouting with crazy joviality, his hands in the air.

"Not to sound like Mom, but—you don't want to wait too long before you decide to buy tickets. There, I said it."

Gary began to laugh but checked the laugh before it got away from him. "Good plan!" he said. "You're right! Gotta decide soon! Gotta buy those tickets! Good plan!" He clapped his hands like a coach.

"Is something wrong?"

"No, you're right. We should all go to St. Jude for one last Christmas before they sell the house or Dad falls apart or somebody dies. It's a no-brainer. We should all be there. It is so obvious. You're absolutely right."

"Then I don't understand what you're upset about."

"Nothing! Not upset about anything!"

"OK. Good." Denise gazed up at him levelly. "Then let me ask you one other thing. I want to know why Mom is under the impression that I'm having an affair with a married man."

A pulse of guilt, a shock wave, passed through Gary. "No idea," he said.

"Did you tell her I'm involved with a married man?"

"How could I tell her that? I don't know the first thing about your private life."

"Well, did you suggest it to her? Did you drop a hint?"

"Denise. Really." Gary was regaining his parental composure, his aura of big-brotherly indulgence. "You're the most reticent person I know. On the basis of what could I say anything?"

"Did you drop a hint?" she said. "Because *somebody* did. *Somebody* put that idea in her head. And it occurs to me that I said one little thing to you, once, which you might have misinterpreted and passed on to her. And, Gary, she and I have enough problems without your giving her ideas."

"You know, if you weren't so mysterious—"

"I'm not 'mysterious.' "

"If you weren't so secretive," Gary said, "maybe you wouldn't have this problem. It's almost like you *want* people whispering about you."

"It's pretty interesting that you're not answering my question."

He exhaled slowly through his teeth. "I have no idea where Mom got that idea. I didn't tell her anything."

"All right," Denise said, standing up. "So I'll do that 'legwork.' You think about Christmas. And we'll get together when Mom and Dad are in town. I'll see you later."

With breathtaking decision she headed toward the nearest exit, not moving so fast as to betray anger but fast enough that Gary couldn't have caught up with her without running. He waited for a minute to see if she would return. When she didn't, he left the courtyard and bent his steps toward his office.

Gary had been flattered when his little sister had chosen a college in the very city where he and Caroline had lately bought their dream house. He'd looked forward to introducing Denise (showing her off, really) to all his friends and colleagues. He'd imagined that she would come to Seminole Street for dinner every month and that she and Caroline would be like sisters. He'd imagined that his whole family, even Chip, would eventually settle in Philadelphia. He'd imagined nieces and nephews, house parties and parlor games, long snowy Christmases on Seminole Street. And now he and Denise had lived in the same city for fifteen years, and he felt as if he hardly knew her. She never asked him for anything. No matter how tired she was, she never came to Seminole Street without flowers or dessert for Caroline, sharks' teeth or comic books for the boys, a lawyer joke or a lightbulb joke for Gary. There was no way around her properness, no way to convey to her the depth of his disappointment that, of the rich family-filled future that he'd imagined, almost *nothing* had come to pass.

A year ago, over lunch, Gary had told her about a married "friend" of his (actually a colleague, Jay Pascoe) who was having an affair with his daughters' piano teacher. Gary said that he could understand his friend's recreational interest in the affair (Pascoe had no intention of leaving his wife) but that he didn't see why the piano teacher was bothering.

"So you can't imagine," Denise said, "why a woman would want to have an affair with you?"

"I'm not talking about me," Gary said.

"But you're married and you have kids."

"I'm saying I don't understand what the woman sees in a guy she knows to be a liar and a sneak."

"Probably she disapproves of liars and sneaks in general," Denise said. "But she makes an exception for the guy she's in love with."

"So it's a kind of self-deception."

"No, Gary, it's the way love works."

"Well, and I guess there's always a chance she'll get lucky and marry into instant money."

This puncturing of Denise's liberal innocence with a sharp economic truth seemed to sadden her.

"You see a person with kids," she said, "and you see how happy they are to be a parent, and you're attracted to their happiness. Impossibility is attractive. You know, the safety of dead-ended things."

"You sound like you know something about it," Gary said.

"Emile is the only man I've ever been attracted to who *didn't* have kids."

This interested Gary. Under cover of fraternal obtuseness, he risked asking: "So, and who are you seeing now?"

"Nobody."

"You're not into some married guy," he joked.

Denise's face went a shade paler and two shades redder as she reached for her water glass. "I'm seeing nobody," she said. "I'm working very hard."

"Well, just remember," Gary said, "there's more to life than cooking. You're at a stage now where you need to start thinking about what you really want and how you're going to get it."

Denise twisted in her seat and signaled to the waiter for the check. "Maybe I'll marry into instant money," she said.

The more Gary thought about his sister's involvement with married men, the angrier he got. Nevertheless, he should never have mentioned the matter to Enid. The disclosure had come of drinking gin on an empty stomach while listening to his mother sing Denise's praises at Christmastime, a few hours after the mutilated Austrian reindeer had come to light and Enid's gift to Caroline had turned up in a trash can like a murdered baby. Enid extolled the generous multimillionaire who was bankrolling Denise's new restaurant and had sent her on a luxury two-month tasting tour of France and Central Europe, she extolled Denise's long hours and her dedication and her thrift, and in her backhandedly comparative way she carped about Gary's "materialism" and "ostentation" and "obsession with money"—as if she herself weren't dollar-sign-headed! As if she herself, given the opportunity, wouldn't have bought a house like Gary's and furnished it very much the same way he had! He wanted to say to her: *Of your three children, my life looks by far the most like yours! I have what you taught me to want! And now that I have it, you disapprove of it!*

But what he actually said, when the juniper spirits finally boiled over, was: "Why don't you ask Denise who she's sleeping with? Ask her if the guy's married and if he has any kids."

"I don't think she's dating anybody," Enid said.

"I'm telling you," the juniper spirits said, "ask her if she's ever been involved with somebody married. I think honesty compels you to ask that question before you hold her up as a paragon of midwestern values."

Enid covered her ears. "I don't want to know about this!"

"Fine, go ahead, stick your head in the sand!" the sloppy spirits raged. "I just don't want to hear any more crap about what an angel she is."

Gary knew that he'd broken the sibling code of honor. But he was glad he'd broken it. He was glad Denise was taking heat again from Enid. He felt surrounded, imprisoned, by disapproving women.

There was, of course, one obvious way of breaking free: he could say *yes* instead of *no* to one of the dozen secretaries and female pedestrians and sales clerks who in any given week took note of his height and his schist-gray hair, his calfskin jacket and his French mountaineering pants, and looked him in the eye as if to say *The key's under the doormat*. But there was still no pussy on earth he'd rather lick, no hair he'd rather gather in his fist like a golden silk bellpull, no gaze with which he'd rather lock his own at climax, than Caroline's. The only guaranteed result of having an affair would be to add yet another disapproving woman to his life.

In the lobby of the CenTrust Tower, on Market Street, he joined a crowd of human beings by the elevators. Clerical staff and software specialists, auditors and keypunch engineers, returning from late lunches.

"The lion he ascendant now," said the woman standing closest to Gary. "Very good time to shop now. The lion he often preside over bargains in the store."

"Where is our Savior in this?" asked the woman to whom the woman had spoken.

"This also a good time to remember the Savior," the first woman answered calmly. "Time of the lion very good time for that."

"Lutetium supplements combined with megadoses of partially hydrogenated Vitamin E!" a third person said.

"He's programmed his clock radio," a fourth person said, "which it says something about something I don't know that you can even do this, but he's programmed it to wake him up to WMIA at eleven past the hour every hour. Whole night through."

Finally an elevator came. As the mass of humanity moved onto it, Gary considered waiting for a less populated car, a ride less pullulating with mediocrity and body smells. But coming in from Market Street now was a young female estate planner who in recent months had been giving him talk-to-me smiles, touch-me smiles. To avoid contact with her, he darted through the elevator's closing doors. But the doors bumped his trailing foot and reopened. The young estate planner crowded on next to him.

"The prophet Jeremiah, girl, *he* speak of the lion. It tell about it in the pamphlet here."

"Like it's 3:11 in the morning and the Clippers lead the Grizzlies 146–145 with twelve seconds left in triple overtime."

Absolutely no reverb on a full elevator. Every sound was deadened by clothes and flesh and hairdos. The air prebreathed. The crypt over-warm.

"This pamphlet is the Devil's work."

"Read it over coffeebreak, girl. What the harm in that?"

"Both last-place teams looking to improve their odds in the college draft lottery by losing this otherwise meaningless late-season game."

"Lutetium is a rare-earth element, very rare and from the earth, and it's pure because it's elemental!"

"Like and if he set the clock for 4:11 he could hear all the late scores and only have to wake up once. But there's Davis Cup action in Sydney and it's updated hourly. Can't miss that."

The young estate planner was short and had a pretty face and hennaed hair. She smiled up at Gary as if inviting him to speak. She looked midwestern and happy to be standing next to him.

Gary fixed his gaze on nothing and attempted not to breathe. He was chronically bothered by the *T* erupting in the middle of the word CenTrust. He wanted to push the *T* down hard, like a nipple, but when he pushed it down he got no satisfaction. He got cent-rust: a corroded penny.

"Girl, this ain't replacement faith. This *supplemental.* Isaiah mention that lion, too. Call it the lion of Judah."

"A pro-am thing in Malaysia with an early leader in the clubhouse, but that could change between 2:11 and 3:11. Can't miss *that.*"

"My faith don't need no replacing."

"Sheri, girl, you got a wax deposit in your ear? Listen what I saying. This. Ain't. No. Replacement. Faith. This *supplemental.*"

"It guarantees silky vibrant skin plus an eighteen percent reduction in panic attacks!"

"Like I'm wondering how Samantha feels about the alarm clock going off next to her pillow eight times a night every night."

"All I saying is now's the time to shop is all I saying."

It occurred to Gary, as the young estate planner leaned into him to let a raft of sweltering humanity leave the elevator, as she pressed her hennaed head against his ribs more intimately than seemed strictly necessary, that another reason he'd remained faithful to Caroline through twenty years of marriage was his steadily growing aversion to physical contact with other human beings. Certainly he was in love with fidelity; certainly he got an erotic kick out of adhering to principle; but somewhere between his brain and his balls a wire was also perhaps coming loose, because when he mentally undressed and violated this little red-haired girl his main thought was how stuffy and undisinfected he would find the site of his infidelity—a coliform-bacterial supply closet, a Courtyard by Marriott with dried semen on the walls and bedspreads, the cat-scratch-feverish back seat of whatever adorable VW or Plymouth she no doubt drove, the spore-laden wall-to-wall of her boxlike starter apartment in Montgomeryville or Conshohocken, each site overwarm and underventilated and suggestive of genital warts and chlamydia in its own unpleasant way—and what a struggle it would be to breathe, how smothering her flesh, how squalid and foredoomed his efforts not to condescend . . .

He bounded out of the elevator on sixteen, taking big cool lungfuls of centrally processed air.

"Your wife's been calling," said his secretary, Maggie. "She wants you to call her right away."

Gary retrieved a stack of messages from his box on Maggie's desk. "Did she say what it is?"

"No, but she sounds upset. Even when I told her you weren't here, she kept calling."

Gary shut himself inside his office and flipped through the messages. Caroline had called at 1:35, 1:40, 1:50, 1:55, and 2:10; it was now 2:25. He pumped his fist in triumph. Finally, finally, some evidence of desperation.

He dialed home and said, "What's up?"

Caroline's voice was shaking. "Gary, something's wrong with your cell phone. I've been trying your cell phone and it doesn't answer. What's wrong with it?"

"I turned it off."

"How long has it been off? I've been trying you for an hour, and now I've got to go get the boys but I don't want to leave the house! I don't know what to do!"

"Caro. Tell me what's wrong."

"There's somebody across the street."

"Who is it?"

"I don't know. Somebody in a car, I don't know. They've been sitting there for an hour."

The tip of Gary's dick was melting like the flame end of a candle. "Well," he said, "did you go see who it is?"

"I'm afraid to," Caroline said. "And the cops say it's a city street."

"They're right. It is a city street."

"Gary, somebody stole the Neverest sign again!" She was practically sobbing. "I came home at noon and it was gone. And then I looked out and this car was there, and there's somebody in the front seat right now."

"What kind of car?"

"Big station wagon. It's old. I've never seen it before."

"Was it there when you came home?"

"I don't know! But now I've got to go get Jonah and I don't want to leave the house, with the sign missing and the car out there—"

"The alarm system is working, though, right?"

"But if I come home and they're still in the house and I surprise them—"

"Caroline, honey, calm down. You'd hear the alarm—"

"Broken glass, an alarm going off, somebody cornered, these people have guns—"

"Look, look, look. Caroline? Here's what you do. Caroline?" The fear in her voice and the need the fear suggested were making him so hot that he had to give himself a squeeze through the fabric of his pants, a pinch of reality. "Call me back on your cell phone," he said. "Keep me on the line, go out and get in the Stomper, and drive down the driveway. You can talk to whoever through the window. I'll be there with you the whole time. All right?"

"OK. OK. I'm calling you right back."

As Gary waited, he thought of the heat and the saltiness and the peach-bruise softness of Caroline's face when she'd been crying, the sound of her swallowing her lachrymal mucus, and the wide-open readiness of her mouth, then, for his. To feel nothing, not the feeblest pulse in the dead mouse from which his urine issued, for three weeks, to believe that she would never again need him and that he would never again want her, and then, on a moment's notice, to become light-headed with lust: this was marriage as he knew it. His telephone rang.

"I'm in the car," Caroline said from the cockpit-like aural space of mobile phoning. "I'm backing up."

"You can get his license number, too. Write it down before you pull up next to him. Let him see you getting it."

"OK. OK."

In tinny miniature he heard the big-animal breathing of her SUV, the rising *om* of its automatic transmission.

"Oh, fuck, Gary," she wailed, "he's gone! I don't see him! He must have seen me coming and driven away!"

"Good, though, that's good, that's what you wanted."

"No, because he'll circle the block and come back when I'm not here!"

Gary calmed her down and told her how to approach the house safely when she returned with the boys. He promised to keep his cell phone on and come home early. He refrained from comparing her mental health with his.

Depressed? He was not depressed. Vital signs of the rambunctious American economy streamed numerically across his many-windowed television screen. Orfic Midland up a point and three-eighths for the day. The U.S. dollar laughing at the euro, buggering the yen. Virginia Lin dropped in and proposed selling a block of Exxon at 104. Gary could see out across the river to the floodplain landscape of Camden, New Jersey, whose deep ruination, from this height and distance, gave the impression of a kitchen floor with the linoleum scraped off. The sun was proud in the south, a source of relief; Gary couldn't stand it when his parents came east and the eastern seaboard's weather stank. The same sun was shining on their cruise ship now, somewhere north of Maine. In a corner of his TV screen was the talking head of Curly Eberle. Gary upsized the picture and raised the sound as Eberle concluded: "A body-building machine for the brain, that's not a bad image, Cindy." The all-business-all-the-time anchors, for whom financial risk was merely the boon companion of upside potential, nodded sagely in response. "Body-building machine for the brain, ho-*kay*," the female anchor segued, "and coming up, then, a toy that's all the rage in Belgium (!) and its maker says *this* product could be bigger than the *Beanie Babies!*" Jay Pascoe dropped in to kvetch about the bond market. Jay's little girls had a new piano teacher now and the same old mother. Gary caught about one word of every three Jay spoke. His nerves were jangling as on the long-ago afternoon before his fifth date with Caroline, when they were so ready to finally be unchaste that each intervening hour was like a granite block to be broken by a shackled prisoner . . .

He left work at 4:30. In his Swedish sedan he wound his way up Kelly Drive and Lincoln Drive, out of the valley of the Schuylkill and its haze and expressway, its bright flat realities, up through tunnels of shadow and gothic arches of early-autumn leaves along the Wissahickon Creek, and back into the enchanted arboreality of Chestnut Hill.

Caroline's fevered imaginings notwithstanding, the house appeared to be intact. Gary eased the car up the driveway past the bed of hostas and euonymus from which, just as she'd said, another SECURITY BY NEVEREST sign had been stolen. Since the beginning of the year, Gary had planted and lost five SECURITY BY NEVEREST signs. It galled him to be flooding the market with worthless signage, thereby diluting the value of SECURITY BY NEVEREST as a burglary deterrent. Here in the heart of Chestnut Hill, needless to say, the sheet-metal currency of the Neverest and Western Civil Defense and ProPhilaTex signs in every front yard was backed by the full faith and credit of floodlights and retinal scanners, emergency batteries, buried hot lines, and remotely securable doors; but elsewhere in northwest Philly, down through Mount Airy into Germantown and Nicetown where the sociopaths had their dealings and their dwellings, there existed a class of bleeding-heart homeowners who hated what it might say about their "values" to buy their own home-security systems but whose liberal "values" did not preclude stealing Gary's SECURITY BY NEVEREST signs on an almost weekly basis and planting them in their own front yards . . .

In the garage he was overcome by an Alfred-like urge to recline in the car seat and shut his eyes. Turning off the engine, he seemed to switch off something in his brain as well. Where had his lust and energy disappeared to? This, too, was marriage as he knew it.

He made himself leave the car. A constrictive band of tiredness ran from his eyes and sinuses to his brain stem. Even if Caroline was ready to forgive him, even if he and she could somehow slip away from the kids and fool around (and, realistically, there was no way that they could do this), he was probably too tired to perform now anyway. Stretching out ahead of him were five kid-filled hours before he could be alone with her in bed. Simply to regain the energy he'd had until five minutes ago would require sleep—eight hours of it, maybe ten.

The back door was locked and chained. He gave it the firmest, merriest knock he could manage. Through the window he saw Jonah come trotting over in flip-flops and a swimsuit, enter security code, and unbolt and unchain the door.

"Hello there, Dad, I'm making a sauna in the bathroom," Jonah said as he trotted away again.

The object of Gary's desire, the tear-softened blond female whom he'd reassured on the phone, was sitting next to Caleb and watching a galactic rerun on the kitchen TV. Earnest humanoids in unisex pajamas.

"Hello!" Gary said. "Looks like everything's OK here."

Caroline and Caleb nodded, their eyes on a different planet.

"I guess I'll go put another sign out," Gary said.

"You should nail it to a tree," Caroline said. "Take it off its stick and nail it to a tree."

Nearly unmanned by disappointed expectation, Gary filled his chest with air and coughed. "The idea, Caroline, is that there be a certain classiness and subtlety to the message we're projecting? A certain word-to-the-wise quality? When you have to *chain* your sign to a tree to keep it from getting stolen—"

"I said nail."

"It's like announcing to the sociopaths: We're whipped! Come and get us! Come and get us!"

"I didn't say chain. I said nail."

Caleb reached for the remote and raised the TV volume.

Gary went to the basement and from a flat cardboard carton took the last of the six signs that a Neverest representative had sold to him in bulk. Considering the cost of a Neverest home-security system, the signs were unbelievably shoddy. The placards were unevenly painted and attached by fragile aluminum rivets to posts of rolled sheet metal too thin to be hammered into the ground (you had to dig a hole).

Caroline didn't look up when he returned to the kitchen. He might have wondered if he'd hallucinated her panicked calls to him if there were not a lingering humidity in his boxer shorts and if, during his thirty seconds in the basement, she hadn't thrown the dead bolt on the back door, engaged the chain, and reset the alarm.

He, of course, was mentally ill, whereas she! She!

"Good Christ," he said as he punched their wedding date into the numeric keypad.

Leaving the door wide open, he went to the front yard and planted the new Neverest sign in the old sterile hole. When he came back a minute later, the door was locked again. He took his keys out and turned the dead bolt and pushed the door open to the extent the chain permitted, triggering the excuse-me-please alarm inside. He shoved on the door, stressing its hinges. He considered putting his shoulder to it and ripping out the chain. With a grimace and a shout Caroline jumped up and clutched her back and stumbled over to enter code within the thirty-second limit. "Gary," she said, "just knock."

"I was in the front yard," he said. "I was fifty feet away. Why are you setting the alarm?"

"You don't understand what it was like here today," she muttered as, limping, she returned to interstellar space. "I'm feeling pretty alone here, Gary. Pretty alone."

"Here I am, though. Right? I'm home now."

"Yes. You're home."

"Hey, Dad, what's for dinner?" Caleb said. "Can we have mixed grill?"

"Yes," Gary said. "I will make dinner *and* I will do the dishes *and* I may also trim the hedge, because I, for one, am feeling good! All right, Caroline? Does that sound OK to you?"

"Yes, please, sure, make dinner," she murmured, staring at the TV.

"Good. I will make dinner." Gary clapped his hands and coughed. He felt as if, in his chest and his head, worn-out gears were falling off their axles, chewing into other parts of his internal machinery, as he demanded of his body a bravado, an undepressed energy, that it was simply not equipped to give.

He needed to sleep well tonight for at least six hours. To accomplish this, he planned to drink two vodka martinis and hit the sack before ten. He upended the vodka bottle over a shaker of ice and brazenly let it glug and glug, because he, a veep at CenTrust, had nothing to be ashamed of in relaxing after a hard day's work. He started a mesquite fire and drank the martini down. Like a thrown coin in a wide, teetering orbit of decay, he circled back into the kitchen and managed to get the meat ready, but he felt too tired to cook it. Because Caroline and Caleb had paid no attention to him when he made the first martini, he now made a second, for energy and general bolsterment, and officially considered it his first. Battling the vitreous lensing effects of a vodka buzz, he went out and threw meat on the grill. Again the weariness, again the deficit of every friendly neurofactor overtook him. In plain view of his entire family he made a third (officially: a second) martini and drank it down. Through the window he observed that the grill was in flames.

He filled a Teflon skillet with water and spilled only some of it as he rushed out to pour it on the fire. A cloud of steam and smoke and aerosol grease went up. He flipped all the meat scraps, exposing their charred, glossy undersides. There was a smell of wet burnedness such as firemen leave behind. Not enough life remained in the coals to do more than faintly color the raw sides of the meat scraps, though he left them on for another ten minutes.

His miraculously considerate son Jonah had meanwhile set the table and put out bread and butter. Gary served the less burned and less raw bits of meat to his wife and children. Wielding his knife and fork clumsily, he filled his mouth with cinders and bloody chicken that he was too tired to chew and swallow and also too tired to get up and spit out. He sat with the unchewed bird-flesh in his mouth until he realized that saliva was trickling down his chin—a poor way indeed to demonstrate good mental health. He swallowed the bolus whole. It felt like a tennis ball going down. His family was looking at him.

"Dad, are you feeling OK?" Aaron said.

Gary wiped his chin. "Fine, Aaron, thank you. Ticken's a little chuff. A little tough." He coughed, his esophagus a column of flame.

"Maybe you want to go lie down," Caroline said, as to a child.

"I think I'll trim that hedge," Gary said.

"You seem pretty tired," Caroline said. "Maybe you should lie down instead."

"Not tired, Caroline. Just got some smoke in my eyes."

"Gary—"

"I know you're telling everybody I'm depressed, but, as it happens, I'm not."

"Gary."

"Right, Aaron? Am I right? She told you I'm clinically depressed—right?"

Aaron, caught off guard, looked to Caroline, who shook her head at him slowly and significantly.

"Well? Did she?" Gary said.

Aaron lowered his eyes to his plate, blushing. The spasm of love that Gary felt then for his oldest son, his sweet honest vain blushing son, was intimately connected to the rage that was now propelling him, before he understood what was happening, away from the table. He was cursing in front of his kids. He was saying, "*Fuck* this, Caroline! *Fuck* your whispering! I'm going to fucking go trim that fucking hedge!"

Jonah and Caleb lowered their heads, ducking as if under fire. Aaron seemed to be reading the story of his life, in particular his future, on his grease-smeared dinner plate.

Caroline spoke in the calm, low, quavering voice of the patently abused. "OK, Gary, good," she said, "just please then let us enjoy our dinner. Please just go."

Gary went. He stormed outside and crossed the back yard. All the foliage near the house was chalky now with outpouring indoor light, but there was still enough twilight in the western trees to make them silhouettes. In the garage he took the eight-foot stepladder down from its brackets and danced and spun with it, nearly knocking out the windshield of the Stomper before he got control. He hauled the ladder around to the front of the house, turned on lights, and came back for the electric trimmer and the hundred-foot extension cord. To keep the dirty cord from contact with his expensive linen shirt, which he belatedly realized he was still wearing, he let the cord drag behind him and get destructively tangled up in flowers. He stripped down to his T-shirt but didn't stop to change his pants for fear of losing momentum and lying down on the dayheat-radiating lawn and listening to the crickets and the ratcheting cicadas and nodding off. Sustained physical exertion cleared his head to some extent. He mounted the ladder and lopped the lime-green lolling tops off yews, leaning out as far as he dared. Probably, finding himself unable to reach the twelve inches of hedge nearest the house, he should have turned off the clipper and come down and moved the ladder closer, but since it was a matter of twelve inches and he didn't have infinite reserves of energy and patience, he tried to *walk* the ladder toward the house, to kind of swing its legs and *hop* with it, while continuing to grip, in his left hand, the running clipper.

The gentle blow, the almost stingless brush or bump, that he then delivered to the meaty palm part of his right thumb proved, on inspection, to have made a deep and heavily bleeding hole that in the best of all possible worlds an emergency physician would have looked at. But Gary was nothing if not conscientious. He knew he was too drunk to drive himself to Chestnut Hill Hospital, and he couldn't ask Caroline to drive him there without raising awkward questions regarding his decision to climb a ladder and operate a power tool while intoxicated, which would collaterally entail admitting how much vodka he'd drunk before dinner and in general paint the opposite of the picture of Good Mental Health that he'd intended to create by coming out to trim the hedge. So while a swarm of skin-biting and fabric-eating insects attracted by the porch lights flew into the house through the front door that Gary, as he hurried inside with his strangely cool blood pooling in the cup of both hands, had neglected to kick shut behind him, he closeted himself in the downstairs bathroom and released the blood into the sink, seeing pomegranate juice, or chocolate syrup, or dirty motor oil, in its ferric swirls. He ran cold water on the gash. From outside the unlocked bathroom door, Jonah asked if he had hurt himself. Gary assembled with his left hand an absorptive pad of toilet paper and pressed it to the wound and one-handedly applied plastic surgical tape that the blood and water immediately made unsticky. There was blood on the toilet seat, blood on the floor, blood on the door.

"Dad, bugs are coming in," Jonah said.

"Yes, Jonah, why don't you shut the door and then go up and take a bath. I'll come up soon and play checkers."

"Can we play chess instead?"

"Yes."

"You have to give me a queen, a bishop, a horse, and a rook, though."

"Yes, go take a bath!"

"Will you come up soon?"

"Yes!"

Gary tore fresh tape from the fanged dispenser and laughed at himself in the mirror to be sure he could still do it. Blood was soaking through the toilet paper, trickling down around his wrist, and loosening the tape. He wrapped the hand in a guest towel, and with a second guest towel, well dampened, he wiped the bathroom clean of blood. He opened the door a crack and listened to Caroline's voice upstairs, to the dishwasher in the kitchen, to Jonah's bathwater running. A trail of blood receded up the central hall toward the front door. Crouching and moving sideways in crab fashion, with his injured hand pressed to his belly, Gary swabbed up the blood with the guest towel. Further blood was spattered on the gray wooden floor of the front porch. Gary walked on the sides of his feet for quiet. He went to the kitchen for a bucket and a mop, and there, in the kitchen, was the liquor cabinet.

Well, he opened it. By holding the vodka bottle in his right armpit he was able to unscrew the cap with his left hand. And as he was raising the bottle, as he was tilting his head to make a late small withdrawal from the rather tiny balance that remained, his gaze drifted over the top of the cabinet door and he saw the camera.

The camera was the size of a deck of cards. It was mounted on an altazimuth bracket above the back door. Its casing was of brushed aluminum. It had a purplish gleam in its eye.

Gary returned the bottle to the cabinet, moved to the sink, and ran water in a bucket. The camera swept thirty degrees to follow him.

He wanted to rip the camera off the ceiling, and, failing that, he wanted to go upstairs and explain to Caleb the dubious morality of spying, and, failing that, he at least wanted to know how long the camera had been in place; but since he had something to hide now, any action he took against the camera, any objection he made to its presence in his kitchen, was bound to strike Caleb as self-serving.

He dropped the bloody, dusty guest towel in the bucket and approached the back door. The camera reared up in its bracket to keep him centered in its field. He stood directly below it and looked into its eye. He shook his head and mouthed the words *No, Caleb.* Naturally, the camera made no response. Gary realized, now, that the room was probably miked for sound as well. He could speak to Caleb directly, but he was afraid that if he looked up into Caleb's proxy eye and heard his own voice and let it be heard in Caleb's room, the result would be an intolerably strong upsurge in the reality of what was happening. He therefore shook his head again and made a sweeping motion with his left hand, a film director's Cut! Then he took the bucket from the sink and swabbed the front porch.

Because he was drunk, the problem of the camera and Caleb's witnessing of his injury and his furtive involvement with the liquor cabinet didn't stay in Gary's head as an ensemble of conscious thoughts and anxieties but turned in on itself and became a kind of physical presence inside him, a hard tumorous mass descending through his stomach and coming to rest in his lower gut. The problem wasn't going anywhere, of course. But, for the moment, it was impervious to thought.

"Dad?" came Jonah's voice through an upstairs window. "I'm ready to play chess now."

By the time Gary went inside, having left the hedge half-clipped and the ladder in an ivy bed, his blood had soaked through three layers of toweling and bloomed on the surface as a pinkish spot of plasma filtered of its corpuscles. He was afraid of meeting somebody in the hallway, Caleb or Caroline certainly, but especially Aaron, because Aaron had asked him if he was feeling all right, and Aaron had not been able to lie to him, and these small demonstrations of Aaron's love were in a way the scariest part of the whole evening.

"Why is there a towel on your hand?" Jonah asked as he removed half of Gary's forces from the chessboard.

"I cut myself, Jonah. I'm keeping some ice on the cut."

"You smell like al-co-hol." Jonah's voice was lilting.

"Alcohol is a powerful disinfectant," Gary said.

Jonah moved a pawn to K4. "I'm talking about the al-co-hol you drank, though."

By ten o'clock Gary was in bed and thus arguably still in compliance with his original plan, arguably still on track to—what? Well, he didn't exactly know. But if he got some sleep he might be able to see his way forward. In order not to bleed on the sheets he'd put his injured hand, towel and all, inside a Bran'nola bread bag. He turned out the nightstand light and faced the wall, his bagged hand cradled against his chest, the sheet and the summer blanket pulled up over his shoulder. He slept hard for a while and was awakened in the darkened room by the throbbing of his hand. The flesh on either side of the gash was twitching as if it had worms in it, pain fanning out along five carpi. Caroline breathed evenly, asleep. Gary got up to empty his bladder and take four Advils. When he returned to bed, his last, pathetic plan fell apart, because he could not get back to sleep. He had the sensation that blood was running out of the Bran'nola bag. He considered getting up and sneaking out to the garage and driving to the emergency room. He added up the hours this would take him and the amount of wakefulness he would have to burn off upon returning, and he subtracted the total from the hours of night remaining until he had to get up and go to work, and he concluded that he was better off just sleeping until six and then, if need be, stopping at the ER on his way to work; but this was all contingent on his ability to fall back asleep, and since he couldn't do this, he reconsidered and recalculated, but now there were fewer minutes remaining of the night than when he'd first considered getting up and sneaking out. The calculus was cruel in its regression. He got up again to piss. The problem of Caleb's surveillance lay, indigestible, in his gut. He was mad to wake up Caroline and fuck her. His hurt hand pulsed. It felt elephantine; he had a hand the size and weight of an armchair, each finger a soft log of exquisite sensitivity. And Denise kept looking at him with hatred. And his mother kept yearning for her Christmas. And he slipped briefly into a room in which his father had been strapped into an electric chair and fitted with a metal helmet, and Gary's own hand was on the old-fashioned stirrup-like power switch, which he'd evidently already thrown, because Alfred came leaping from the chair fantastically galvanized, horribly smiling, a travesty of enthusiasm, dancing around with rigid jerking limbs and circling the room at double-speed and then falling hard, face down, wham, like a ladder with its legs together, and lying prone there on the execution-room floor with every muscle in his body galvanically twitching and boiling—

Gray light was in the windows when Gary got up to piss for the fourth or fifth time. The morning's humidity and warmth felt more like July than October. A haze or fog on Seminole Street confused—or disembodied—or refracted—the cawing of crows as they worked their way up the Hill, over Navajo Road and Shawnee Street, like local teenagers heading to the Wawa Food Market parking lot ("Club Wa" they called it, according to Aaron) to smoke their cigarettes.

He lay down again and waited for sleep.

"—day the fifth of October, among the top news stories we're following this morning, with his execution now less than twenty-four hours away, lawyers for Khellye—" said Caroline's clock radio before she swatted it silent.

In the next hour, while he listened to the rising of his sons and the sound of their breakfasts and the blowing of a trumpet line by John Philip Sousa, courtesy of Aaron, a radical new plan took shape in Gary's brain. He lay fetally on his side, very still, facing the wall, with his Bran'nola-bagged hand against his chest. His radical new plan was to do absolutely nothing.

"Gary, are you awake?" Caroline said from a medium distance, the doorway presumably. "Gary?"

He did nothing; didn't answer.

"Gary?"

He wondered if she might be curious about why he was doing nothing, but already her footsteps were receding up the hall and she was calling, "Jonah, come on, you're going to be late."

"Where's Dad?" Jonah said.

"He's still in bed, let's go."

There was a patter of little feet, and now came the first real challenge to Gary's radical new plan. From somewhere closer than the doorway Jonah spoke. "Dad? We're leaving now. Dad?" And Gary had to do nothing. He had to pretend he couldn't hear or wouldn't hear, he had to inflict his general strike, his clinical depression, on the one creature he wished he could have spared. If Jonah came any closer—if, for example, he came and gave him a hug—Gary doubted he would be able to stay silent and unmoving. But Caroline was calling from downstairs again, and Jonah hurried out.

Distantly Gary heard the beeping of his anniversary date being entered to arm the perimeter. Then the toast-smelling house was silent and he shaped his face into the expression of bottomless suffering and self-pity that Caroline wore when her back was hurting. He understood, as he never had before, how much comfort this expression yielded.

He thought about getting up, but he didn't need anything. He didn't know when Caroline was coming back; if she was working at the

CDF today, she might not return until three. It didn't matter. He would be here.

As it happened, Caroline came back in half an hour. The sounds of her departure were reversed. He heard the approaching Stomper, the disarming code, the footsteps on the stairs. He sensed his wife in the doorway, silent, watching him.

"Gary?" she said in a lower, more tender voice.

He did nothing. He lay. She came over to him and knelt by the bed. "What is it? Are you sick?"

He didn't answer.

"What is this bag for? My God. What did you do?"

He said nothing.

"Gary, say something. Are you depressed?"

"Yes."

She sighed then. Weeks of accumulated tension were draining from the room.

"I surrender," Gary said.

"What do you mean?"

"You don't have to go to St. Jude," he said. "Nobody who doesn't want to go has to go."

It cost him a lot to say this, but there was a reward. He felt Caroline's warmth approaching, its radiance, before she touched him. The sun rising, the first brush of her hair on his neck as she leaned over him, the approach of her breath, the gentle touching-down of her lips on his cheek. She said, "Thank you."

"I may have to go for Christmas Eve but I'll come back for Christmas."

"Thank you."

"I'm extremely depressed."

"Thank you."

"I surrender," Gary said.

An irony, of course, was that as soon as he'd surrendered—possibly as soon as he'd confessed to his depression, almost certainly by the time he showed her his hand and she put a proper bandage on it, and absolutely no later than the moment at which, with a locomotive as long and hard and heavy as an O-gauge model railroad engine, he tunneled up into wet and gently corrugated recesses that even after twenty years of traveling through them still felt unexplored (his approach was spoon-style, from behind, so that Caroline could keep her lower back arched outward and he could harmlessly drape his bandaged hand across her flank; the screwing wounded, the two of them were)—he not only no longer felt depressed, he felt euphoric.

The thought came to him—inappropriately, perhaps, considering the tender conjugal act that he was now engaged in; but he was who he was, he was Gary Lambert, he had inappropriate thoughts and he was sick of apologizing!—that he could now safely ask Caroline to buy him 4,500 shares of Axon and that she would gladly do it.

She rose and dipped like a top on a tiny point of contact, her entire, sexual being almost weightless on the moistened tip of his middle finger.

He spent himself gloriously. Spent and spent and spent.

They were still lying naked at the hooky-playing hour of nine-thirty on a Tuesday when the phone on Caroline's nightstand rang. Gary, answering, was shocked to hear his mother's voice. He was shocked by the reality of her existence.

"I'm calling from the ship," Enid said.

For one guilty instant, before it registered with him that phoning from a ship was expensive and that his mother's news could therefore not be good, Gary believed that she was calling because she knew that he'd betrayed her.

AT SEA

TWO HUNDRED HOURS, darkness, the *Gunnar Myrdal*: all around the old man, running water sang mysteriously in metal pipes. As the ship sliced open the black sea east of Nova Scotia, the horizontal faintly pitched, bow to stern, as if despite its great steel competence the ship were uneasy and could solve the problem of a liquid hill only by cutting through it quickly; as if its stability depended on such a glossing over of flotation's terrors. There was another world below—this was the problem. Another world below that had volume but no form. By day the sea was blue surface and whitecaps, a realistic navigational challenge, and the problem could be overlooked. By night, though, the mind went forth and dove down through the yielding—the violently lonely—nothingness on which the heavy steel ship traveled, and in every moving swell you saw a travesty of grids, you saw how truly and forever lost a man would be six fathoms under. Dry land lacked this z-axis. Dry land was like being awake. Even in chartless desert you could drop to your knees and pound land with your fist and land didn't give. Of course the ocean, too, had a skin of wakefulness. But every point on this skin was a point where you could sink and by sinking disappear.

As things pitched, so they trembled. There was a shivering in the *Gunnar Myrdal*'s framework, an endless shudder in the floor and bed and birch-paneled walls. A syncopated tremor so fundamental to the ship, and so similar to Parkinson's in the way it constantly waxed without seeming ever to wane, that Alfred had located the problem within himself until he overheard younger, healthier passengers remarking on it.

He lay approximately awake in Stateroom B11. Awake in a metal box that pitched and trembled, a dark metal box moving somewhere in the night.

There was no porthole. A room with a view would have cost hundreds of dollars more, and Enid had reasoned that since a stateroom was mainly used for sleeping who needed a porthole, at that price? She might look through it six times on the voyage. That was fifty dollars a look.

She was sleeping now, silently, like a person feigning sleep. Alfred asleep was a symphony of snoring and whistling and choking, an epic of Z's. Enid was a haiku. She lay still for hours and then blinked awake like a light switched on. Sometimes at dawn in St. Jude, in the long minute it took the clock-radio to flip a digit, the only moving thing in the house was the eye of Enid.

On the morning of Chip's conception she'd merely looked like she was shamming sleep, but on the morning of Denise's, seven years later, she really was pretending. Alfred in middle age had invited such venial deceptions. A decade-plus of marriage had turned him into one of the overly civilized predators you hear about in zoos, the Bengal tiger that forgets how to kill, the lion lazy with depression. To exert attraction, Enid had to be a still, unbloody carcass. If she actively reached out, actively threw a thigh over his, he braced himself against her and withheld his face; if she so much as stepped from the bathroom naked he averted his eyes, as the Golden Rule enjoined the man who hated to be seen himself. Only early in the morning, waking to the sight of her small white shoulder, did he venture from his lair. Her stillness and self-containment, the slow sips of air she took, her purely vulnerable object-hood, made him pounce. And feeling his padded paw on her ribs and his meat-seeking breath on her neck she went limp, as if with prey's instinctive resignation ("Let's get this dying over with"), although in truth her passivity was calculated, because she knew passivity inflamed him. He had her, and to some extent she wanted to be had, like an animal: in a mute mutual privacy of violence. She, too, kept her eyes shut. Often didn't even roll from the side she'd been lying on but simply flared her hip, brought her knee up in a vaguely proctologic reflex. Then without showing her his face he departed for the bathroom, where he washed and shaved and emerged to see the bed already made and to hear, downstairs, the percolator gulping. From Enid's perspective in the kitchen maybe a lion, not her husband, had voluptuously mauled her, or maybe one of the men in uniform she ought to have married had slipped into her bed. It wasn't a wonderful life, but a woman could sub-sist on self-deceptions like these and on her memories (which also now curiously seemed like self-deceptions) of the early years when he'd been mad for her and had looked into her eyes. The important thing was to keep it all tacit. If the act was never spoken of, there would be no reason to discontinue it until she was definitely pregnant again, and even after pregnancy no reason not to resume it, as long as it was never men-tioned.

She'd always wanted three children. The longer nature denied her a third, the less fulfilled she felt in comparison to her neighbors. Bea Meisner, though fatter and dumber than Enid, publicly smooched with her husband, Chuck; twice a month the Meisners hired a sitter and went dancing. Every October without fail Dale Driblett took his wife, Honey, someplace extravagant and out of state for their anniversary, and the many young Dribletts all had birthdays in July. Even Esther and Kirby Root could be seen at barbecues patting each other's well-marbled bottoms. It frightened and shamed Enid, the loving-kindness of other couples. She was a bright girl with good business skills who had gone directly from ironing sheets and tablecloths at her mother's board-inghouse to ironing sheets and shirts chez Lambert. In every neighbor woman's eyes she saw the tacit question: Did Al at least make her feel super-special in that special way?

As soon as she was visibly pregnant again, she had a tacit answer. The changes in her body were incontrovertible, and she imagined so vividly the flattering inferences about her love life that Bea and Esther and Honey might draw from these changes that soon enough she drew the inferences herself.

Made happy in this way by pregnancy, she got sloppy and talked about the wrong thing to Alfred. Not, needless to say, about sex or ful-fillment or fairness. But there were other topics scarcely less forbidden, and Enid in her giddiness one morning overstepped. She suggested he buy shares of a certain stock. Alfred said the stock market was a lot of dangerous nonsense best left to wealthy men and idle speculators. Enid suggested he nonetheless buy shares of a certain stock. Alfred said he remembered Black Tuesday as if it were yesterday. Enid suggested he nonetheless buy shares of a certain stock. Alfred said it would be highly improper to buy that stock. Enid suggested he nonetheless buy it. Alfred said they had no money to spare and now a third child coming. Enid suggested that money could be borrowed. Alfred said no. He said no in a much louder voice and stood up from the breakfast table. He said no so loudly that a decorative copper-plate bowl on the kitchen wall briefly hummed, and without kissing her goodbye he left the house for eleven days and ten nights.

Who would have guessed that such a *little* mistake on her part could change everything?

In August the Midland Pacific had made Alfred its assistant chief engineer for track and structures, and now he'd been sent east to inspect every mile of the Erie Belt Railroad. Erie Belt district managers shuttled him around in dinky gas-powered motor cars, darting in bug fashion onto sidings while Erie Belt megalosaurs thundered past. The Erie Belt was a regional system whose freight business trucks had damaged and whose passenger business private automobiles had driven into the red. Although its trunk lines were still generally hale, its branches and spurs were rotting like you couldn't believe. Trains poked along at 10 mph on rails no straighter than limp string. Mile upon mile of hopelessly buckled Belt. Alfred saw crossties better suited to mulching than to gripping spikes. Rail anchors that had lost their heads to rust, bodies wasting inside a crust of corrosion like shrimps in a shell of deep-fry. Ballast so badly washed out that ties were hanging from the rail rather than supporting it. Girders peeling and corrupted like German chocolate cake, the dark shavings, the miscellaneous crumble.

How modest—compared to the furious locomotive—a stretch of weedy track could seem, skirting a field of late sorghum. But without this track a train was ten thousand tons of ungovernable nothing. The will was in the track.

Everywhere Alfred went in the Erie Belt's hinterland he heard young Erie Belt employees telling one another, "Take it easy!"

"See ya later, Sam. Don't work too hard, now."

"Take it easy."

"You too, pal. Take it easy."

The phrase seemed to Alfred an eastern blight, a fitting epitaph for a once-great state, Ohio, that parasitic Teamsters had sucked nearly dry. Nobody in St. Jude would dare tell *him* to take it easy. On the high prairie where he'd grown up, a person who took it easy wasn't much of a man. Now came a new effeminate generation for whom "easygoing" was a compliment. Alfred heard Erie Belt track gangs yukking it up on company time, he saw flashily dressed clerks taking ten-minute breaks for coffee, he watched callow draftsmen smoke cigarettes with insinuating relish while a once-solid railroad fell to pieces all around them. "Take it easy" was the watchword of these superfriendly young men, the token of their overfamiliarity, the false reassurance that enabled them to ignore the filth they worked in.

The Midland Pacific, by contrast, was clean steel and white concrete. Crossties so new that blue creosote pooled in their grain. The applied science of vibratory tamping and prestressed rebar, motion detectors and welded rail. The Midpac was based in St. Jude and served a harder-working, less eastern region of the country. Unlike the Erie Belt, it took pride in its commitment to maintaining quality service on its branch lines. A thousand towns and small cities across the central tiers of states depended on the Midpac.

The more Alfred saw of the Erie Belt, the more distinctly he felt the Midland Pacific's superior size, strength, and moral vitality in his own limbs and carriage. In his shirt and tie and wing tips he nimbly took the catwalk over the Maumee River, forty feet above slag barges and turbid water, grabbed the truss's lower chord and leaned out upside down to whack the span's principal girder with his favorite whacking hammer, which he carried everywhere in his briefcase; scabs of paint and rust as big as sycamore leaves spiraled down into the river. A yard engine ringing its bell crept onto the span, and Alfred, who had no fear of heights, leaned into a hanger brace and planted his feet in the matchstick ties sticking out over the river. While the ties waggled and jumped he jotted on his clipboard a damning assessment of the bridge's competence.

Maybe some of the women drivers crossing the Maumee on the neighboring Cherry Street bridge saw him perched there, flat of belly and broad of shoulder, the wind winding his cuffs around his ankles, and maybe they felt, as Enid had felt the first time she'd laid eyes on him, that here was a *man*. Although he was oblivious to their glances, Alfred experienced from within what they saw from without. By day he felt like a man, and he showed this, you might even say flaunted it, by standing no-handedly on high narrow ledges, and working ten and twelve hours without a break, and cataloguing an eastern railroad's effeminacies.

Nighttime was a different matter. By night he lay awake on mattresses that felt made of cardboard and catalogued the faults of humanity. It seemed as if, in every motel he stayed in, he had neighbors who fornicated like there was no tomorrow—men of ill-breeding and poor discipline, women who chuckled and screamed. At 1 a.m. in Erie, Pennsylvania, a girl in the next room ranted and panted like a strumpet. Some slick, worthless fellow having his way with her. Alfred blamed the girl for taking it easy. He blamed the man for his easygoing confidence. He blamed both of them for lacking the consideration to keep their voices down. How could they never once stop to think of their neighbor, lying awake in the next room? He blamed God for allowing such people to exist. He blamed democracy for inflicting them on him. He blamed the motel's architect for trusting a single layer of cinder block to preserve the repose of paying customers. He blamed the motel management for not keeping in reserve a room for guests who suffered. He blamed the frivolous, easygoing townspeople of Washington, Pennsylvania, who had driven 150 miles for a high-school football championship game and filled every motel room in northwest Pennsylvania. He blamed his fellow guests for their indifference to the fornication, he blamed all of humanity for its insensitivity, and it was so unfair. It was unfair that the world could be so inconsiderate to a man who was so considerate to the world. No man worked harder than he, no man made a quieter motel neighbor, no man was more of a man, and yet the phonies of the world were allowed to rob him of sleep with their lewd transactions . . .

He refused to weep. He believed that if he heard himself weeping, at two in the morning in a smoke-smelling motel room, the world might end. If nothing else, he had discipline. The power to refuse: he had this.

But his exercising of it went unthanked. The bed in the next room thudded against the wall, the man groaning like a ham, the girl gasping in her ululations. And every waitress in every town had spherical mammaries insufficiently buttoned into a monogrammed blouse and made a point of leaning over him.

"More coffee, good-lookin'?"

"Ah, yes, please."

"You blushin', sweetheart, or is that the sun comin' up?"

"I will take the check now, thank you."

And in the Olmsted Hotel in Cleveland he surprised a porter and a maid lasciviously osculating in a stairwell. And the tracks he saw when he closed his eyes were a zipper that he endlessly unzipped, and the signals behind him turned from forbidding red to willing green the instant he passed them, and in a saggy bed in Fort Wayne awful succubuses descended on him, women whose entire bodies—their very clothes and smiles, the crossings of their legs—exuded invitation like vaginas, and up to the surface of his consciousness (do not soil the bed!) he raced the welling embolus of spunk, his eyes opening to Fort Wayne at sunrise as a scalding nothing drained into his pajamas: a victory, all things considered, for he'd denied the succubuses his satisfaction. But in Buffalo the trainmaster had a pinup of Brigitte Bardot on his office door, and in Youngstown Alfred found a filthy magazine beneath the motel telephone book, and in Hammond, Indiana, he was trapped on a siding while a freight train slid past him and varsity cheerleaders did splits on the ball field directly to his left, the blondest girl actually *bouncing* a little at the very bottom of her split, as if she had to *kiss* the cleat-chewed sod with her cotton-clad vulva, and the caboose rocking saucily as the train finally receded up the tracks: how the world seemed bent on torturing a man of virtue.

He returned to St. Jude in an executive car appended to an intercity freight run, and from Union Station he took the commuter local to the suburbs. In the blocks between the station and his house the last leaves were coming down. It was the season of hurtling, hurtling toward winter. Cavalries of leaf wheeled across the bitten lawns. He stopped in the street and looked at the house that he and a bank owned. The gutters were plugged with twigs and acorns, the mum beds were blasted. It occurred to him that his wife was pregnant again. Months were rushing him forward on their rigid track, carrying him closer to the day he'd be the father of three, the year he'd pay off his mortgage, the season of his death.

"I like your suitcase," Chuck Meisner said through the window of his commuter Fairlane, braking in the street alongside him. "For a second I thought you were the Fuller Brush man."

"Chuck," said Alfred, startled. "Hello."

"Planning a conquest. The husband's out of town forever."

Alfred laughed because there was nothing else for it. He and Chuck met in the street often, the engineer standing at attention, the banker relaxing at the wheel. Alfred in a suit and Chuck in golfwear. Alfred lean and flattopped. Chuck shiny-pated, saggy-breasted. Chuck worked easy hours at the branch he managed, but Alfred nonetheless considered him a friend. Chuck actually listened to what he said, seemed impressed with the work he did, and recognized him as a person of singular abilities.

"Saw Enid in church on Sunday," Chuck said. "She told me you'd been gone a week already."

"Eleven days I was on the road."

"Emergency somewhere?"

"Not exactly." Alfred spoke with pride. "I was inspecting every mile of track on the Erie Belt Railroad."

"Erie Belt. Huh." Chuck hooked his thumbs over the steering wheel, resting his hands on his lap. He was the most easygoing driver Alfred knew, yet also the most alert. "You do your job well, Al," he said. "You're a fantastic engineer. So there's got to be a reason why the Erie Belt."

"There is indeed," Alfred said. "Midpac's buying it."

The Fairlane's engine sneezed once in a canine way. Chuck had grown up on a farm near Cedar Rapids, and the optimism of his nature was rooted in the deep, well-watered topsoil of eastern Iowa. Farmers in eastern Iowa never learned not to trust the world. Whereas any soil that might have nurtured hope in Alfred had blown away in one or another west Kansan drought.

"So," Chuck said. "I imagine there's been a public announcement."

"No. No announcement."

Chuck nodded, looking past Alfred at the Lambert house. "Enid'll be happy to see you. I think she's had a hard week. The boys have been sick."

"You'll keep that information quiet."

"Al, Al, Al."

"I wouldn't mention it to anyone but you."

"Appreciate it. You're a good friend and a good Christian. And I've got about four holes' worth of daylight if I'm going to get that hedge pruned back."

The Fairlane inched into motion, Chuck steering it into his driveway with one index finger, as if dialing his broker.

Alfred picked up his suitcase and briefcase. It had been both spontaneous and the opposite of spontaneous, his disclosure. A spasm of goodwill and gratitude to Chuck, a calculated emission of the fury that had been building inside him for eleven days. A man travels two thousand miles but he can't take the last twenty steps without doing *something*—

And it did seem unlikely that Chuck would actually *use* the information—

Entering the house through the kitchen door, Alfred saw chunks of raw rutabaga in a pot of water, a rubber-banded bunch of beet greens, and some mystery meat in brown butcher paper. Also a casual onion that looked destined to be fried and served with—liver?

On the floor by the basement stairs was a nest of magazines and jelly glasses.

"Al?" Enid called from the basement.

He set down his suitcase and briefcase, gathered the magazines and jelly glasses in his arms, and carried them down the steps.

Enid parked her iron on the ironing board and emerged from the laundry room with butterflies in her stomach—whether from lust or from fear of Al's rage or from fear that she might become enraged herself she didn't know.

He set her straight in a hurry. "What did I ask you to do before I left?"

"You're home early," she said. "The boys are still at the Y."

"What is the one thing I asked you to do while I was gone?"

"I'm catching up on laundry. The boys have been sick."

"Do you remember," he said, "that I asked you to take care of the mess at the top of the stairs? That that was the one thing—*the one thing*—I asked you to do while I was gone?"

Without waiting for an answer, he went into his metallurgy lab and dumped the magazines and jelly glasses into a heavy-duty trash can. From the hammer shelf he took a badly balanced hammer, a crudely forged Neanderthal club that he hated and kept only for purposes of demolition, and methodically broke each jelly glass. A splinter hit his cheek and he swung more furiously, smashing the shards into smaller shards, but nothing could eradicate his transgression with Chuck Meisner, or the grass-damp triangles of cheerleading leotard, no matter how he hammered.

Enid listened from her station at the ironing board. She didn't care much for the reality of this moment. That her husband had left town eleven days ago without kissing her goodbye was a thing she'd halfway succeeded in forgetting. With the living Al absent, she'd alchemically transmuted her base resentments into the gold of longing and remorse. Her swelling womb, the pleasures of the fourth month, the time alone with her handsome boys, the envy of her neighbors all were colorful philtres over which she'd waved the wand of her imagination. Even as Al had come down the stairs she'd still imagined apologies, homecoming kisses, a bouquet of flowers maybe. Now she heard the ricochet of broken glass and glancing hammer blows on heavy-gauge galvanized iron, the frustrated shrieks of hard materials in conflict. The philtres may have been colorful but unfortunately (she saw now) they were chemically inert. Nothing had really changed.

It was true that Al had asked her to move the jars and magazines, and there was probably a word for the way she'd stepped around those jars and magazines for the last eleven days, often nearly stumbling on them; maybe a psychiatric word with many syllables or maybe a simple word like "spite." But it seemed to her that he'd asked her to do more than "one thing" while he was gone. He'd also asked her to make the boys three meals a day, and clothe them and read to them and nurse them in sickness, and scrub the kitchen floor and wash the sheets and iron his shirts, and do it all without a husband's kisses or kind words. If she tried to get credit for these labors of hers, however, Al simply asked her whose labors had *paid* for the house and food and linens? Never mind that his work so satisfied him that he didn't need her love, while her chores so bored her that she needed his love doubly. In any rational accounting, his work canceled her work.

Perhaps, in strict fairness, since he'd asked her to do "one thing" extra, she might have asked him to do "one thing" extra, too. She might have asked him to telephone her once from the road, for example. But he could argue that "someone's going to trip on those magazines and hurt themselves," whereas no one was going to trip over his not calling her from the road, no one was going to hurt themselves over that. And charging long-distance calls to the company was an abuse of his expense account ("You have my office number if there's an emergency"), and so a phone call cost the household quite a bit of money, whereas carrying junk into the basement cost it no money, and so she was always wrong, and it was demoralizing to dwell perpetually in the cellar of your wrongness, to wait perpetually for someone to take pity on you in your wrongness, and so it was no wonder, really, that she'd shopped for the Dinner of Revenge.

Halfway up the basement stairs, on her way to preparing this dinner, she paused and gave a sigh.

Alfred heard the sigh and suspected it had to do with "laundry" and "four months pregnant." However, his own mother had driven a team of plow horses around a twenty-acre field when she was eight months pregnant, so he was not exactly sympathetic. He gave his bleeding cheek a styptic dusting of ammonium aluminum sulfate.

From the front door of the house came a thumping of little feet and a mittened knocking, Bea Meisner dropping off her human cargo. Enid hurried on up the stairs to accept delivery. Gary and Chipper, her fifth-grader and her first-grader, had the chlorination of the Y about them. With their damp hair they looked riparian. Muskratty, beaverish. She called thanks to Bea's taillights.

As fast as they could without running (forbidden indoors), the boys proceeded to the basement, dropped their logs of sodden terry cloth in the laundry room, and found their father in his laboratory. It was in their nature to throw their arms around him, but this nature had been corrected out of them. They stood and waited, like company subordinates, for the boss to speak.

"So!" he said. "You've been swimming."

"I'm a Dolphin!" Gary cried. He was an unaccountably cheerful boy. "I got my Dolphin clip!"

"A Dolphin. Well, well." To Chipper, to whom life had offered mainly tragic perspectives since he was about two years old, the boss more gently said: "You, lad?"

"We used kickboards," Chipper said.

"He's a Tadpole," Gary said.

"So. A Dolphin and a Tadpole. And what special skills do you bring to the workplace now that you're a Dolphin?"

"Scissors kick."

"I wish I'd had a nice big swimming pool like that when I was growing up," the boss said, although for all he knew the pool at the Y was neither nice nor big. "Except for some muddy water in a cow pond I don't recall seeing water deeper than three feet until I saw the Platte River. I must have been nearly ten."

His youthful subordinates weren't following. They shifted on their feet, Gary still smiling tentatively as though hopeful of an upturn in the conversation, Chipper frankly gaping at the laboratory, which was forbidden territory except when the boss was in it. The air here tasted like steel wool.

Alfred regarded his two subordinates gravely. Fraternizing had always been a struggle for him. "Have you been helping your mother in the kitchen?" he said.

When a subject didn't interest Chipper, as this one didn't, he thought about girls, and when he thought about girls he felt a surge of hope. On the wings of this hope he floated from the laboratory and up the stairs.

"Ask me nine times twenty-three," Gary told the boss.

"All right," Alfred said. "What is nine times twenty-three?"

"Two hundred seven. Ask me another."

"What's twenty-three squared?"

In the kitchen Enid dredged the Promethean meat in flour and laid it in a Westinghouse electric pan large enough to fry nine eggs in tick-tacktoe formation. A cast aluminum lid clattered as the rutabaga water came abruptly to a boil. Earlier in the day a half package of bacon in the refrigerator had suggested liver to her, the drab liver had suggested a complement of bright yellow, and so the Dinner had taken shape. Un-fortunately, when she went to cook the bacon she discovered there were only three strips, not the six or eight she'd imagined. She was now struggling to believe that three strips would suffice for the entire family.

"What's *that*?" said Chipper with alarm.

"Liver 'n' bacon!"

Chipper backed out of the kitchen shaking his head in violent de-nial. Some days were ghastly from the outset; the breakfast oatmeal was studded with chunks of date like chopped-up cockroach; bluish swirls of inhomogeneity in his milk; a doctor's appointment after breakfast. Other days, like this one, did not reveal their full ghastliness till they were nearly over.

He reeled through the house repeating: "Ugh, horrible, ugh, horri-ble, ugh, horrible, ugh, horrible . . ."

"Dinner in five minutes, wash your hands," Enid called.

Cauterized liver had the odor of fingers that had handled dirty coins.

Chipper came to rest in the living room and pressed his face against the window, hoping for a glimpse of Cindy Meisner in her dining room. He had sat next to Cindy returning from the Y and smelled the chlorine on her. A sodden Band-Aid had clung by a few lingering bits of stickum to her knee.

Thukkety thukkety thukkety went Enid's masher round the pot of sweet, bitter, watery rutabaga.

Alfred washed his hands in the bathroom, gave the soap to Gary, and employed a small towel.

"Picture a square," he said to Gary.

Enid knew that Alfred hated liver, but the meat was full of health-bringing iron, and whatever Alfred's shortcomings as a husband, no one could say he didn't play by the rules. The kitchen was her domain, and he never meddled.

"Chipper, have you washed your hands?"

It seemed to Chipper that if he could only see Cindy again for one moment he might be rescued from the Dinner. He imagined being with her in her house and following her to her room. He imagined her room as a haven from danger and responsibility.

"Chipper?"

"You square A, you square B, and you add twice the product of A and B," Alfred told Gary as they sat down at the table.

"Chipper, you better wash your hands," Gary warned.

Alfred pictured a square:

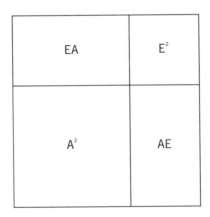

Figure 1. Large Square & Smaller Squares

"I'm sorry I'm a little short on bacon," Enid said. "I thought I had more."

In the bathroom Chipper was reluctant to wet his hands because he was afraid he would never get them dry again. He let the water run audibly while he rubbed his hands with a towel. His failure to glimpse Cindy through the window had wrecked his composure.

"We had high fevers," Gary reported. "Chipper had an earache, too."

Brown grease-soaked flakes of flour were impastoed on the ferrous lobes of liver like corrosion. The bacon also, what little there was of it, had the color of rust.

Chipper trembled in the bathroom doorway. You encountered a misery near the end of the day and it took a while to gauge its full extent. Some miseries had sharp curvature and could be negotiated readily. Others had almost no curvature and you knew you'd be spending hours turning the corner. Great whopping-big planet-sized miseries. The Dinner of Revenge was one of these.

"How was your trip," Enid asked Alfred because she had to sometime.

"Tiring."

"Chipper, sweetie, we're all sitting down."

"I'm counting to five," Alfred said.

"There's bacon, you like bacon," Enid sang. This was a cynical, expedient fraud, one of her hundred daily conscious failures as a mother.

"Two, three, four," Alfred said.

Chipper ran to take his place at the table. No point in getting spanked.

"Blessalor this foodier use nusta thy service make asair mindful neesa others Jesus name amen," Gary said.

A dollop of mashed rutabaga at rest on a plate expressed a clear yellowish liquid similar to plasma or the matter in a blister. Boiled beet greens leaked something cupric, greenish. Capillary action and the thirsty crust of flour drew both liquids under the liver. When the liver was lifted, a faint suction could be heard. The sodden lower crust was unspeakable.

Chipper considered the life of a girl. To go through life softly, to be a Meisner, to play in that house and be loved like a girl.

"You want to see my jail I made with Popsicle sticks?" Gary said.

"A jail, well well," Alfred said.

The provident young person neither ate his bacon immediately nor let it be soaked by the vegetable juices. The provident young person evacuated his bacon to the higher ground at the plate's edge and stored it there as an incentive. The provident young person ate his bite of fried onions, which weren't good but also weren't bad, if he needed a preliminary treat.

"We had a den meeting yesterday," Enid said. "Gary, honey, we can look at your jail after dinner."

"He made an electric chair," Chipper said. "To go in his jail. I helped."

"Ah? Well well."

"Mom got these huge boxes of Popsicle sticks," Gary said.

"It's the Pack," Enid said. "The Pack gets a discount."

Alfred didn't think much of the Pack. A bunch of fathers taking it easy ran the Pack. Pack-sponsored activities were lightweight: contests involving airplanes of balsa, or cars of pinewood, or trains of paper whose boxcars were books read.

(Schopenhauer: *If you want a safe compass to guide you through life . . . you cannot do better than accustom yourself to regard this world as a penitentiary, a sort of penal colony.*)

"Gary, say again what you are," said Chipper, for whom Gary was the glass of fashion. "Are you a Wolf?"

"One more Achievement and I'm a Bear."

"What are you now, though, a Wolf?"

"I'm a Wolf but basically I'm a Bear. All's I have to do now is Conversation."

"Conservation," Enid corrected. "All I have to do now is Conservation."

"It's not Conversation?"

"Steve Driblett made a gillateen but it didn't work," Chipper said.

"Driblett's a Wolf."

"Brent Person made a plane but it busted in half."

"Person is a Bear."

"Say broke, sweetie, not busted."

"Gary, what's the biggest firecracker?" Chipper said.

"M-80. Then cherry bombs."

"Wouldn't it be neat to get an M-80 and put it in your jail and blow it up?"

"Lad," Alfred said, "I don't see you eating your dinner."

Chipper was growing emceeishly expansive; for the moment, the Dinner had no reality. "Or *seven* M-80s," he said, "and you blew 'em all at once, or one after another, wouldn't it be neat?"

"I'd put a charge in every corner and then put extra fuse," Gary said. "I'd wind the fuses together and detonate them all at once. That's the best way to do it, isn't it, Dad. Separate the charges and put an extra fuse, isn't it. Dad?"

"Seven thousand hundred million M-80s," Chipper cried. He made explosive noises to suggest the megatonnage he had in mind.

"Chipper," Enid said with smooth deflection, "tell Dad where we're all going next week."

"The den's going to the Museum of Transport and I get to come, too," Chipper recited.

"Oh Enid." Alfred made a sour face. "What are you taking them there for?"

"Bea says it's very interesting and fun for kids."

Alfred shook his head, disgusted. "What does Bea Meisner know about transportation?"

"It's perfect for a den meeting," Enid said. "There's a real steam engine the boys can sit in."

"What they have," Alfred said, "is a thirty-year-old Mohawk from the New York Central. It's not an antique. It's not rare. It's a piece of junk. If the boys want to see what a *real* railroad is—"

"Put a battery and two electrodes on the electric chair," Gary said. "Put an M-80!"

"Chipper, no, you run a current and the *current* kills the prisoner."

"What's a current?"

A current flowed when you stuck electrodes of zinc and copper in a lemon and connected them.

What a sour world Alfred lived in. When he caught himself in mirrors it shocked him how young he still looked. The set of mouth of hemorrhoidal schoolteachers, the bitter permanent lip-pursing of arthritic men, he could taste these expressions in his own mouth sometimes, though he was physically in his prime, the souring of life.

He did therefore enjoy a rich dessert. Pecan pie. Apple brown Betty. A little sweetness in the world.

"They have two locomotives and a real caboose!" Enid said.

Alfred believed that the real and the true were a minority that the world was bent on exterminating. It galled him that romantics like Enid could not distinguish the false from the authentic: a poor-quality, flimsily stocked, profit-making "museum" from a real, honest railroad—

"You have to at least be a Fish."

"The boys are all excited."

"I could be a Fish."

The Mohawk that was the new museum's pride was evidently a romantic symbol. People nowadays seemed to resent the railroads for abandoning romantic steam power in favor of diesel. People didn't understand the first goddamned thing about running a railroad. A diesel locomotive was versatile, efficient, and low-maintenance. People thought the railroad owed them romantic favors, and then they bellyached if a train was slow. That was the way most people were—stupid.

(Schopenhauer: *Amongst the evils of a penal colony is the company of those imprisoned in it.*)

At the same time, Alfred himself hated to see the old steam engine pass into oblivion. It was a beautiful iron horse, and by putting the Mohawk on display the museum allowed the easygoing leisure-seekers of suburban St. Jude to dance on its grave. City people had no right to patronize the iron horse. They didn't know it intimately, as Alfred did. They hadn't fallen in love with it out in the northwest corner of Kansas where it was the only link to the greater world, as Alfred had. He despised the museum and its goers for everything they didn't know.

"They have a model railroad that takes up a whole room!" Enid said relentlessly.

And the goddamned model railroaders, yes, the goddamned hobby-ists. Enid knew perfectly well how he felt about these dilettantes and their pointless and implausible model layouts.

"A whole room?" Gary said with skepticism. "How big?"

"Wouldn't it be neat to put some M-80s on, um, on, um, on a model railroad bridge? Ker-PERSSSCHT! P'kow, p'kow!"

"Chipper, eat your dinner *now*," Alfred said.

"Big big big," Enid said. "The model is much much much much much bigger than the one your father bought you."

"*Now*," Alfred said. "Are you listening to me? Now."

Two sides of the square table were happy and two were not. Gary told a pointless, genial story about this kid in his class who had three rabbits while Chipper and Alfred, twin studies in bleakness, lowered their eyes to their plates. Enid visited the kitchen for more rutabaga.

"I know who not to ask if they want seconds," she said when she returned.

Alfred shot her a warning look. They had agreed for the sake of the boys' welfare never to allude to his own dislike of vegetables and certain meats.

"I'll take some," Gary said.

Chipper had a lump in his throat, a desolation so obstructive that he couldn't have swallowed much in any case. But when he saw his brother happily devouring seconds of Revenge, he became angry and for a moment understood how his entire dinner might be scarfable in no time, his duties discharged and his freedom regained, and he actually picked up his fork and made a pass at the craggy wad of rutabaga, tangling a morsel of it in his tines and bringing it near his mouth. But the rutabaga smelled carious and was already cold—it had the texture and tempera-ture of wet dog crap on a cool morning—and his guts convulsed in a spine-bending gag reflex.

"I *love* rutabaga," said Gary inconceivably.

"I could live on nothing but vegetables," Enid averred.

"More milk," Chipper said, breathing hard.

"Chipper, just hold your nose if you don't like it," Gary said.

Alfred put bite after bite of vile Revenge in his mouth, chewing quickly and swallowing mechanically, telling himself he had endured worse than this.

"Chip," he said, "take one bite of each thing. You're not leaving this table till you do."

"More milk."

"You will eat some dinner first. Do you understand?"

"Milk."

"Does it count if he holds his nose?" Gary said.

"More milk, please."

"That is *just* about enough," Alfred said.

Chipper fell silent. His eyes went around and around his plate, but he had not been provident and there was nothing on the plate but woe. He raised his glass and silently urged a very small drop of warm milk down the slope to his mouth. He stretched his tongue out to welcome it.

"Chip, put the glass down."

"Maybe he could hold his nose but then he has to eat *two* bites of things."

"There's the phone. Gary, you may answer it."

"What's for dessert?" Chipper said.

"I have some nice fresh *pineapple*."

"Oh for God's sake, Enid—"

"What?" She blinked innocently or faux-innocently.

"You can at least give him a cookie, or an Eskimo Pie, if he eats his dinner—"

"It's such sweet pineapple. It melts in your mouth."

"Dad, it's Mr. Meisner."

Alfred leaned over Chipper's plate and in a single action of fork removed all but one bite of the rutabaga. He loved this boy, and he put the cold, poisonous mash into his own mouth and jerked it down his throat with a shudder. "Eat that last bite," he said, "take one bite of the other, and you can have dessert." He stood up. "I will *buy* the dessert if necessary."

As he passed Enid on his way to the kitchen, she flinched and leaned away.

"Yes," he said into the phone.

Through the receiver came the humidity and household clutter, the warmth and fuzziness, of Meisnerdom.

"Al," Chuck said, "just looking in the paper here, you know, Erie Belt stock, uh. Five and five-eighths seems awfully low. You sure about this Midpac thing?"

"Mr. Replogle rode the motor car with me out of Cleveland. He indicated that the Board of Managers is simply waiting for a final report on track and structures. I'm going to give them that report on Monday."

"Midpac's kept this very quiet."

"Chuck, I can't recommend any particular course of action, and you're right, there are some unanswered questions here—"

"Al, Al," Chuck said. "You have a mighty conscience, and we all appreciate that. I'll let you get back to your dinner."

Alfred hung up hating Chuck as he would have hated a girl he'd been undisciplined enough to have relations with. Chuck was a banker and a thriver. You wanted to spend your innocence on someone worthy of it, and who better than a good neighbor, but no one could be worthy of it. There was excrement all over his hands.

"Gary: pineapple?" Enid said.

"Yes, please!"

The virtual disappearance of Chipper's root vegetable had made him a tad manic. Things were 1-1-1-looking up! He expertly paved one quadrant of his plate with the remaining bite of rutabaga, grading the yellow asphalt with his fork. Why dwell in the nasty reality of liver and beet greens when there was constructable a future in which your father had gobbled these up, too? Bring on the cookies! sayeth Chipper. Bring on the Eskimo Pie!

Enid carried three empty plates into the kitchen.

Alfred, by the phone, was studying the clock above the sink. The time was that malignant fiveishness to which the flu sufferer awakens after late-afternoon fever dreams. A time shortly after five which was a mockery of five. To the face of clocks the relief of order—two hands pointing squarely at whole numbers—came only once an hour. As every other moment failed to square, so every moment held the potential for fluish misery.

And to suffer like this for no reason. To know there was no moral order in the flu, no justice in the juices of pain his brain produced. The world nothing but a materialization of blind, eternal Will.

(Schopenhauer: *No little part of the torment of existence is that Time is continually pressing upon us, never letting us catch our breath but always coming after us, like a taskmaster with a whip.*)

"I guess you don't want pineapple," Enid said. "I guess you're buying your own dessert."

"Enid, drop it. I wish once in your life you would let something drop."

Cradling the pineapple, she asked why Chuck had called.

"We will talk about it later," Alfred said, returning to the dining room.

"Daddy?" Chipper began.

"Lad, I just did you a favor. Now you do me a favor and stop playing with your food and finish your dinner. *Right now.* Do you understand me? You will finish it right now, or there will be no dessert and no other privileges tonight or tomorrow night, and you will sit here until you do finish it."

"Daddy, though, can you—?"

"RIGHT NOW. DO YOU UNDERSTAND ME, OR DO YOU NEED A SPANKING?"

Tonsils release an ammoniac mucus when serious tears gather behind them. Chipper's mouth twisted this way and that. He saw the plate in front of him in a new light. It was as if the food were an unbearable companion whose company he had been sure that his connections higher up, the strings pullable on his behalf, would spare him. Now came the realization that he and the food were in it for the long haul.

Now he mourned the passing of his bacon, paltry though it had been, with a deep and true grief.

Curiously, though, he didn't outright cry.

Alfred retired to the basement with stamping and a slam.

Gary sat very quietly multiplying small whole numbers in his head.

Enid plunged a knife into the pineapple's jaundiced belly. She decided that Chipper was exactly like his father—at once hungry and impossible to feed. He turned food into shame. To prepare a square meal and then to see it greeted with elaborate disgust, to see the boy actually *gag* on his breakfast oatmeal: this stuck in a mother's craw. All Chipper wanted was milk and cookies, milk and cookies. Pediatrician said: "Don't give in. He'll get hungry eventually and eat something else." So Enid tried to be patient, but Chipper sat down to lunch and declared: "This smells like vomit!" You could slap his wrist for saying it, but then he said it with his face, and you could spank him for making faces, but then he said it with his eyes, and there were limits to correction—no way, in the end, to penetrate behind the blue irises and eradicate a boy's disgust.

Lately she had taken to feeding him grilled cheese sandwiches all day long, holding back for dinner the yellow and leafy green vegetables required for a balanced diet and letting Alfred fight her battles.

There was something almost tasty and almost sexy in letting the annoying boy be punished by her husband. In standing blamelessly aside while the boy suffered for having hurt her.

What you discovered about yourself in raising children wasn't always agreeable or attractive.

She carried two dishes of pineapple into the dining room. Chipper's head was bowed, but the son who loved to eat reached eagerly for his dish.

Gary slurped and aerated, wordlessly consuming pineapple.

The dogshit-yellow field of rutabaga; the liver warped by frying and so unable to lie flush with the plate; the ball of woody beet leaves collapsed and contorted but still entire, like a wetly compressed bird in an eggshell, or an ancient corpse folded over in a bog: the spatial relations among these foods no longer seemed to Chipper haphazard but were approaching permanence, finality.

The foods receded, or a new melancholy shadowed them. Chipper became less immediately disgusted; he ceased even to think about eating. Deeper sources of refusal were kicking in.

Soon the table was cleared of everything but his place mat and his plate. The light grew harsher. He heard Gary and his mother conversing on trivial topics as she washed and Gary dried. Then Gary's footsteps on the basement stairs. Metronomic thock of Ping-Pong ball. More desolate peals of large pots being handled and submerged.

His mother reappeared. "Chipper, just eat that up. Be a big boy now."

He had arrived in a place where she couldn't touch him. He felt nearly cheerful, all head, no emotion. Even his butt was numb from pressing on the chair.

"Dad means for you to sit there till you eat that. Finish it up now. Then your whole evening's free."

If his evening had been truly free he might have spent it entirely at a window watching Cindy Meisner.

"Noun adjective," his mother said, "contraction possessive noun. Conjunction conjunction stressed pronoun counterfactual verb pronoun I'd just gobble that up and temporal adverb pronoun conditional auxiliary infinitive—"

Peculiar how unconstrained he felt to understand the words that were spoken to him. Peculiar his sense of freedom from even that minimal burden of decoding spoken English.

She tormented him no further but went to the basement, where Alfred had shut himself inside his lab and Gary was amassing ("Thirty-seven, thirty-eight") consecutive bounces on his paddle.

"Tock tock?" she said, wagging her head in invitation.

She was hampered by pregnancy or at least the idea of it, and Gary could have trounced her, but her pleasure at being played with was so extremely evident that he simply disengaged himself, mentally multiplying their scores or setting himself small challenges like returning the ball to alternating quadrants. Every night after dinner he honed this skill of enduring a dull thing that brought a parent pleasure. It seemed to him a lifesaving skill. He believed that terrible harm would come to him when he could no longer preserve his mother's illusions.

And she looked so vulnerable tonight. The exertions of dinner and dishes had relaxed her hair's rolled curls. Little blotches of sweat were blooming through the cotton bodice of her dress. Her hands had been in latex gloves and were as red as tongues.

He sliced a winner down the line and past her, the ball running all the way to the shut door of the metallurgy lab. It bounced up and knocked on this door before subsiding. Enid pursued it carefully. What silence, what darkness, there was behind that door. Al seemed not to have a light on.

There existed foods that even Gary hated—Brussels sprouts, boiled okra—and Chipper had watched his pragmatic sibling palm them and fling them into dense shrubbery from the back doorway, if it was summer, or secrete them on his person and dump them in the toilet, if it was winter. Now that Chipper was alone on the first floor he could easily have disappeared his liver and his beet greens. The difficulty: his father would think that he had eaten them, and eating them was exactly what he was refusing now to do. Food on the plate was necessary to prove refusal.

He minutely peeled and scraped the flour crust off the top of the liver and ate it. This took ten minutes. The denuded surface of the liver was a thing you didn't want to see.

He unfolded the beet greens somewhat and rearranged them.

He examined the weave of the place mat.

He listened to the bouncing ball, his mother's exaggerated groans and her nerve-grating cries of encouragement ("Ooo, good one, Gary!"). Worse than spanking or even liver was the sound of someone else's Ping-Pong. Only silence was acceptable in its potential to be endless. The score in Ping-Pong bounced along toward twenty-one and then the game was over, and then two games were over, and then three were over, and to the people inside the game this was all right because fun had been had, but to the boy at the table upstairs it was not all right. He'd involved himself in the sounds of the game, investing them with hope to the extent of wishing they might never stop. But they did stop, and he was still at the table, only it was half an hour later. The evening devouring itself in futility. Even at the age of seven Chipper intuited that this feeling of futility would be a fixture of his life. A dull waiting and then a broken promise, a panicked realization of how late it was.

This futility had let's call it a flavor.

After he scratched his head or rubbed his nose his fingers harbored something. The smell of self.

Or again, the taste of incipient tears.

Imagine the olfactory nerves sampling themselves, receptors registering their own configuration.

The taste of self-inflicted suffering, of an evening trashed in spite, brought curious satisfactions. Other people stopped being real enough to carry blame for how you felt. Only you and your refusal remained. And like self-pity, or like the blood that filled your mouth when a tooth was pulled—the salty ferric juices that you swallowed and allowed yourself to savor—refusal had a flavor for which a taste could be acquired.

In the lab below the dining room Alfred sat with his head bowed in the darkness and his eyes closed. Interesting how eager he'd been to be alone, how hatefully clear he'd made this to everyone around him; and now, having finally closeted himself, he sat hoping that someone would come and disturb him. He wanted this someone to see how much he hurt. Though he was cold to her it seemed unfair that she was cold in turn to him: unfair that she could happily play Ping-Pong, shuffle around outside his door, and never knock and ask how he was doing.

Three common measures of a material's strength were its resistance to pressure, to tension, and to shearing.

Every time his wife's footsteps approached the lab he braced himself to accept her comforts. Then he heard the game ending, and he thought *surely* she would take pity on him now. It was the one thing he asked of her, the one thing—

(Schopenhauer: *Woman pays the debt of life not by what she does, but by what she suffers; by the pains of childbearing and care for the child, and by submission to her husband, to whom she should be a patient and cheering companion.*)

But no rescue was forthcoming. Through the closed door he heard her retreat to the laundry room. He heard the mild buzz of a transformer, Gary playing with the O-gauge train beneath the Ping-Pong table.

A fourth measure of strength, important to manufacturers of rail stock and machine parts, was hardness.

With unspeakable expenditure of will Alfred turned on a light and opened his lab notebook.

Even the most extreme boredom had merciful limits. The dinner table, for example, possessed an underside that Chipper explored by resting his chin on the surface and stretching his arms out below. At his farthest reach were baffles pierced by taut wire leading to pullable rings. Complicated intersections of roughly finished blocks and angles were punctuated, here and there, by deeply countersunk screws, little cylindrical wells with scratchy turnings of wood fiber around their mouths, irresistible to the probing finger. Even more rewarding were the patches of booger he'd left behind during previous vigils. The dried patches had the texture of rice paper or fly wings. They were agreeably dislodgable and pulverizable.

The longer Chipper felt his little kingdom of the underside, the more reluctant he became to lay eyes on it. Instinctively he knew that the visible reality would be puny. He'd see crannies he hadn't yet discovered with his fingers, and the mystery of the realms beyond his reach would be dispelled, the screw holes would lose their abstract sensuality and the boogers would shame him, and one evening, then, with nothing left to relish or discover, he just might die of boredom.

Elective ignorance was a great survival skill, perhaps the greatest.

Enid's alchemical lab beneath the kitchen contained a Maytag with a wringer that swung over it, twinned rubber rollers like enormous black lips. Bleach, bluing, distilled water, starch. A bulky locomotive of an iron, its power cord clad in a patterned knit fabric. Mounds of white shirts in three sizes.

To prepare a shirt for pressing she sprinkled it with water and left it rolled up in a towel. When it was thoroughly redampened she ironed the collar first and then the shoulders, working down.

During and after the Depression she'd learned many survival skills.

Her mother ran a boardinghouse in the basin between downtown St. Jude and the university. Enid had a gift for math, and so she not only washed sheets and cleaned toilets and served meals but also handled numbers for her mother. By the time she'd finished high school and the war had ended, she was keeping all the house's books, billing the boarders, and figuring the taxes. With the quarters and dollars she picked up on the side—wages from baby-sitting, tips from college boys and other long-term boarders—she paid for classes at night school, inching toward a degree in accounting which she hoped she would never have to use. Already two men in uniform had proposed to her, each of them a *rather* good dancer, but neither was clearly an earner and both still risked getting shot at. Her mother had married a man who didn't earn and died young. Avoiding such a husband was a priority with Enid. She intended to be comfortable in life as well as happy.

To the boardinghouse a few years after the war came a young steel engineer newly transferred to St. Jude to manage a foundry. He was a full-lipped thick-haired well-muscled boy in a man's shape and a man's suits. The suits were themselves luxuriantly pleated wool beauties. Once or twice every night, serving dinner at the big round table, Enid glanced over her shoulder and caught him looking, and made him blush. Al was Kansan. After two months he found courage to take her skating. They drank cocoa and he told her that human beings were born to suffer. He took her to a steel-company Christmas party and told her that the intelligent were doomed to be tormented by the stupid. He was a good dancer and a good earner, however, and she kissed him in the elevator. Soon they were engaged and they chastely rode a night train to McCook, Nebraska, to visit his aged parents. His father kept a slave whom he was married to.

Cleaning Al's room in St. Jude she found a much-handled volume of Schopenhauer with certain passages underlined. For example: *The pleasure in this world, it has been said, outweighs the pain; or, at any rate, there is an even balance between the two. If the reader wishes to see shortly whether this statement is true, let him compare the respective feelings of two animals, one of which is engaged in eating the other.*

What to believe about Al Lambert? There were the old-man things he said about himself and the young-man way he looked. Enid had chosen to believe the promise of his looks. Life then became a matter of waiting for his personality to change.

While she waited, she ironed twenty shirts a week, plus her own skirts and blouses.

Nosed in around the buttons with the iron's tip. Flattened the wrinkles, worked out the kinks.

Her life would have been easier if she hadn't loved him so much, but she couldn't help loving him. Just to look at him was to love him.

Every day she endeavored to cleanse the boys' diction, smooth out their manners, whiten their morals, brighten their attitudes, and every day she faced another pile of dirty crumpled laundry.

Even Gary was anarchic sometimes. He liked best to send the electric engine barreling into curves and derail it, see the black chunk of metal skid awkwardly and roll and spark in frustration. Second best was to place plastic cows and cars on the rail and engineer little tragedies.

What gave him the real techno boner, however, was a radio-controlled toy automobile, much advertised on television lately, that went *anywhere*. To avoid ambiguity he planned to make it the only item on his Christmas list.

From the street, if you paid attention, you could see the light in the windows dimming as Gary's train or Enid's iron or Alfred's experiments drained power off the grid. But how lifeless the house looked otherwise. In the lighted houses of the Meisners, of the Schumperts and the Persons and the Roots, people were clearly at home—whole families grouped around tables, young heads bent over homework, dens aflicker with TV, toddlers careening, a grandparent testing a tea bag's virtue with a third soaking. These were spirited, unselfconscious houses.

Whether anybody was home meant everything to a house. It was more than a major fact: it was the only fact.

The family was the house's soul.

The waking mind was like the light in a house.

The soul was like the gopher in his hole.

Consciousness was to brain as family was to house.

Aristotle: *Suppose the eye were an animal—sight would be its soul.*

To understand the mind you pictured domestic activity, the hum of related lives on varied tracks, the hearth's fundamental glow. You spoke of "presence" and "clutter" and "occupation." Or, conversely, of "vacancy" and "shutting down." Of "disturbance."

Maybe the futile light in a house with three people separately absorbed in the basement and only one upstairs, a little boy staring at a plate of cold food, was like the mind of a depressed person.

Gary was the first to tire of the basement. He surfaced and skirted the too-bright dining room, as if it held the victim of a sickening disfigurement, and went up to the second floor to brush his teeth.

Enid followed soon with seven warm white shirts. She, too, skirted the dining room. She reasoned that if the problem in the dining room was her responsibility then she was horrendously derelict in not resolving it, and a loving mother could never be so derelict, and she was a loving mother, so the responsibility must not have been hers. Eventually Alfred would surface and see what a beast he'd been and be very, very sorry. If he had the nerve to blame her for the problem, she could say: "You're the one who said he had to sit there till he ate it."

While she ran a bath she tucked Gary into bed. "Always be my little lion," she said.

"OK."

"Is he fewocious? Is he wicious? Is he my wicious wittle wion?"

Gary didn't answer these questions. "Mom," he said. "Chipper is still at the table, and it's almost nine."

"That's between Dad and Chipper."

"Mom? He really doesn't like those foods. He's not just pretending."

"I'm so glad you're a good eater," Enid said.

"Mom, it's not really fair."

"Sweetie, this is a phase your brother's going through. It's wonderful you're so concerned, though. It's wonderful to be so loving. Always be so loving."

She hurried to stop the water and immerse herself.

In a dark bedroom next door Chuck Meisner imagined, going

inside her, that Bea was Enid. As he chugged to ejaculation he was trading.

He wondered if any exchange had a market in Erie Belt options. Buy five thousand shares outright with thirty puts for a downside hedge. Or better, if someone offered him a rate, a hundred naked calls.

She was pregnant and trading up in cup size, A to B and eventually even C, Chuck guessed, by the time the baby came. Like some municipality's bond rating in a tailspin.

One by one the lights of St. Jude were going out.

And if you sat at the dinner table long enough, whether in punishment or in refusal or simply in boredom, you never stopped sitting there. Some part of you sat there all your life.

As if sustained and too-direct contact with time's raw passage could scar the nerves permanently, like staring at the sun.

As if too-intimate knowledge of any interior were necessarily harmful knowledge. Were knowledge that could never be washed off.

(How weary, how worn, a house lived in to excess.)

Chipper heard things and saw things but they were all in his head. After three hours, the objects surrounding him were as drained of flavor as old bubble gum. His mental states were strong by comparison and overwhelmed them. It would have taken an effort of will, a reawakening, to summon the term "place mat" and apply it to the visual field that he had observed so intensely that its reality had dissolved in the observing, or to apply the word "furnace" to the rustle in the ducts which in its recurrence had assumed the character of an emotional state or an actor in his imagination, an embodiment of Evil Time. The faint fluctuations in the light as someone ironed and someone played and someone experimented and the refrigerator cycled on and off had been part of the dream. This changefulness, though barely noticeable, had been a torment. But it had stopped now.

Now only Alfred remained in the basement. He probed a gel of ferroacetates with the electrodes of an ammeter.

A late frontier in metallurgy: custom-formation of metals at room temperature. The Grail was a substance which could be poured or molded but which after treatment (perhaps with an electrical current) had steel's superior strength and conductivity and resistance to fatigue. A substance easy like plastic and hard like metal.

The problem was urgent. A cultural war was being waged, and the forces of plastic were winning. Alfred had seen jam and jelly jars with plastic lids. Cars with plastic roofs.

Unfortunately, metal in its free state—a nice steel stake or a solid brass candlestick—represented a high level of order, and Nature was slatternly and preferred disorder. The crumble of rust. The promiscuity of molecules in solution. The chaos of warm things. States of disorder were vastly more likely to arise spontaneously than were cubes of perfect iron. According to the Second Law of Thermodynamics, much *work* was required to resist this tyranny of the probable—to force the atoms of a metal to behave themselves.

Alfred was sure that electricity was equal to this work. The current that came through the grid amounted to a borrowing of order from a distance. At power plants an organized piece of coal became a flatulence of useless warm gases; an elevated and self-possessed reservoir of water became entropic runoff wandering toward a delta. Such sacrifices of order produced the useful segregation of electrical charges that he put to work at home.

He was seeking a material that could, in effect, electroplate itself. He was growing crystals in unusual materials in the presence of electric currents.

It wasn't hard science but the brute probabilism of trial and error, a groping for accidents that he might profit from. One college classmate of his had already made his first million with the results of a chance discovery.

That he might someday not have to worry about money: it was a dream identical to the dream of being comforted by a woman, truly comforted, when the misery overcame him.

The dream of radical transformation: of one day waking up and finding himself a wholly different (more confident, more serene) kind of person, of escaping that prison of the given, of feeling divinely capable.

He had clays and gels of silicate. He had silicone putties. He had slushy ferric salts succumbing to their own deliquescence. Ambivalent acetylacetonates and tetracarbonyls with low melting points. A chunk of gallium the size of a damson plum.

The head chemist at the Midland Pacific, a Swiss Ph.D. bored into melancholy by a million measurements of engine-oil viscosity and Brinell hardness, kept Alfred in supplies. Their superiors were aware of the arrangement—Alfred would never have risked getting caught in something underhanded—and it was informally understood that if he ever came up with a patentable process, the Midpac would get a share of any proceeds.

Tonight something unusual was happening in the ferroacetate gel. His conductivity readings varied wildly, depending on where exactly he stuck the ammeter's probe. Thinking the probe might be dirty, he switched to a narrow needle with which he again poked the gel. He got a reading of no conductivity at all. Then he stuck the gel in a different place and got a high reading.

What was going on?

The question absorbed and comforted him and held the taskmaster at bay until, at ten o'clock, he extinguished the microscope's illuminator and wrote in his notebook: STAIN BLUE CHROMATE 2%. VERY VERY INTERESTING.

The moment he stepped from the lab, exhaustion hammered him. He fumbled to secure the lock, his analytic fingers suddenly thick and stupid. He had boundless energy for work, but as soon as he quit he could barely stand up.

His exhaustion deepened when he went upstairs. The kitchen and dining room were ablaze in light, and there appeared to be a small boy slumped over the dining-room table, his face on his place mat. The scene was so wrong, so sick with Revenge, that for a moment Alfred honestly thought the boy at the table was a ghost from his own childhood.

He groped for switches as if the light were a poison gas he had to stop the flow of.

In less hazardous dimness he gathered the boy in his arms and carried him upstairs. The boy had the weave of the place mat engraved on one cheek. He murmured nonsense. He was half-awake but resisting full consciousness, keeping his head down as Alfred undressed him and found pajamas in the closet.

Once the boy was in bed, in receipt of a kiss and fast asleep, an unguessable amount of time trickled through the legs of the bedside chair in which Alfred sat conscious of little but the misery between his temples. His tiredness hurt so much it kept him awake.

Or maybe he did sleep, for suddenly he was standing up and feeling marginally refreshed. He left Chipper's room and went to check on Gary.

Just inside Gary's door, reeking of Elmer's glue, was a jail of Popsicle sticks. The jail bore no relation to the elaborate house of correction that Alfred had imagined. It was a crude roofless square, crudely bisected. Its floor plan, in fact, was exactly the binomial square he'd evoked before dinner.

And this, this here in the jail's largest room, this bollixed knot of semisoft glue and broken Popsicle sticks was a—doll's wheelbarrow? Miniature step stool?

Electric chair.

In a mind-altering haze of exhaustion Alfred knelt and examined it. He found himself susceptible to the poignancy of the chair's having been made—to the pathos of Gary's impulse to fashion an object and seek his father's approval—and more disturbingly to the impossibility of squaring this crude object with the precise mental picture of an electric chair that he had formed at the dinner table. Like an illogical woman in a dream who was both Enid and not Enid, the chair he'd pictured had been at once completely an electric chair and completely Popsicle sticks. It came to him now, more forcefully than ever, that maybe *every* "real" thing in the world was as shabbily protean, underneath, as this electric chair. Maybe his mind was even now doing to the seemingly real hardwood floor on which he knelt exactly what it had done, hours earlier, to the unseen chair. Maybe a floor became truly a floor only in his mental reconstruction of it. The floor's nature was to some extent inarguable, of course; the wood definitely existed and had measurable properties. But there was a *second* floor, the floor as mirrored in his head, and he worried that the beleaguered "reality" that he championed was not the reality of an actual floor in a actual bedroom but the reality of a floor in his head which was idealized and no more worthy, therefore, than one of Enid's silly fantasies.

The suspicion that everything was relative. That the "real" and "authentic" might not be simply doomed but fictive to begin with. That his feeling of righteousness, of uniquely championing the real, was just a feeling. These were the suspicions that had lain in ambush in all those motel rooms. These were the deep terrors beneath the flimsy beds.

And if the world refused to square with his version of reality then it was necessarily an uncaring world, a sour and sickening world, a penal colony, and he was doomed to be violently lonely in it.

He bowed his head at the thought of how much strength a man would need to survive an entire life so lonely.

He returned the pitiful, unbalanced electric chair to the floor of the prison's largest room. As soon as he let go of the chair, it fell on its side. Images of hammering the jail to bits passed through his head, flashes of hiked-up skirts and torn-down underpants, images of shredded bras and outthrust hips, but came to nothing.

Gary was sleeping in perfect silence, the way his mother did. There was no hope that he'd forgotten his father's implicit promise to look at the jail after dinner. Gary never forgot anything.

Still, I am doing my best, Alfred thought.

Returning to the dining room, he noticed the change in the food on Chipper's plate. The well-browned margins of the liver had been carefully pared off and eaten, as had every scrap of crust. There was evidence as well that rutabaga had been swallowed; the small speck that remained was scored with tiny tine marks. And several beet greens had been dissected, the softer leaves removed and eaten, the woody reddish stems laid aside. It appeared that Chipper had taken the contractual one bite of each food after all, presumably at great personal cost, and had been put to bed without being given the dessert he'd earned.

On a November morning thirty-five years earlier Alfred had found a coyote's bloody foreleg in the teeth of a steel trap, evidence of certain desperate hours in the previous night.

There came an upwelling of pain so intense that he had to clench his jaw and refer to his philosophy to prevent its turning into tears.

(Schopenhauer: *Only one consideration may serve to explain the sufferings of animals: that the will to live, which underlies the entire world of phenomena, must in their case satisfy its cravings by feeding upon itself.*)

He turned off the last lights downstairs, visited the bathroom, and put on fresh pajamas. He had to open his suitcase to retrieve his toothbrush.

Into the bed, the museum of antique transports, he slipped beside Enid, settling as close to the far edge as he could. She was asleep in her sleep-feigning way. He looked once at the alarm clock, the radium jewelry on its two pointing hands—closer to twelve now than to eleven—and shut his eyes.

Came the question in a voice like noon: "What were you talking about with Chuck?"

His exhaustion redoubled. With his closed eyes he saw beakers and probes and the trembling needle of the ammeter.

"It sounded like the Erie Belt," Enid said. "Does Chuck know about that? Did you tell him?"

"Enid, I am very tired."

"I'm just surprised, that's all. Considering."

"It was an accident and I regret it."

"I just think it's interesting," Enid said, "that Chuck is allowed to make an investment that we're not allowed to make."

"If Chuck chooses to take unfair advantage of other investors, that's his business."

"A lot of Erie Belt shareholders would be happy to get five and three-quarters tomorrow. What's unfair about that?"

Her words had the sound of an argument rehearsed for hours, a grievance nursed in darkness.

"Those shares will be worth nine and a half dollars three weeks from now," Alfred said. "I know it and most people don't. That's unfair."

"You're smarter than other people," Enid said, "and you did better in school, and now you have a better job. That's unfair, too, isn't it? Shouldn't you make yourself stupid, to be completely fair?"

Chewing your own leg off was not an act to be undertaken lightly or performed halfway. At what point and by what process did the coyote make the decision to sink its teeth into its own flesh? Presumably there first came a period of waiting and weighing. But after that?

"I'm not going to argue with you," Alfred said. "Since you are awake, however, I want to know why Chip wasn't put to bed."

"You were the one who said he—"

"You came upstairs long before I did. It was not my intention that he sit there for five hours. You're using him against me, and I don't care for it one bit. He should have been put to bed at eight."

Enid simmered in her wrongness.

"Can we agree that this will not happen again?" Alfred said.

"We can agree."

"Well then. Let's sleep."

When it was very, very dark in the house, the unborn child could see as clearly as anyone. She had ears and eyes, fingers and a forebrain and a cerebellum, and she floated in a central place. She already knew the main hungers. Day after day the mother walked around in a stew of desire and guilt, and now the object of the mother's desire lay three feet away from her. Everything in the mother was poised to melt and shut down at a loving touch anywhere on her body.

There was a lot of breathing going on. A lot of breathing but no touching.

Sleep eluded even Alfred. Each sinusy gasp of Enid's seemed to pierce his ear the instant he was poised afresh to drop off.

After an interval that he judged to have lasted twenty minutes, the bed began to shake with poorly reined sobs.

He broke his silence, almost wailing: "What is it now?"

"Nothing."

"Enid, it is very, very late, and the alarm is set for six, and I am bone-weary."

She wept stormily. "You never kissed me goodbye!"

"I'm aware of that."

"Well, don't I have a right? A husband leaves his wife at home alone for two weeks?"

"This is water under the bridge. And frankly I've endured a lot worse."

"And then he comes home and doesn't even say hello? He just attacks me?"

"Enid, I have had a terrible week."

"And leaves the dinner table before dinner's over?"

"A terrible week and I am extraordinarily tired—"

"And locks himself in the basement for five hours? Even though he's supposedly very tired?"

"If you had had the week I had—"

"You didn't kiss me goodbye."

"Grow up! For God's sake! Grow up!"

"Keep your voice down!"

(Keep your voice down or the baby might hear.)

(Indeed *did* hear and was soaking up every word.)

"Do you think I was on a pleasure cruise?" Alfred demanded in a whisper. "Everything I do I do for you and the boys. It's been two weeks since I had a minute to myself. I believe I'm entitled to a few hours in the laboratory. You would not understand it, and you would not believe me if you did, but I have found something very interesting."

"Oh, very interesting," Enid said. Hardly the first time she'd heard this.

"Well it *is* very interesting."

"Something with commercial applications?"

"You never know. Look what happened to Jack Callahan. This could end up paying for the boys' education."

"I thought you said Jack Callahan's discovery was an accident."

"My God, listen to yourself. You tell me *I'm* negative, but when it's work that matters to *me*, who's negative?"

"I just don't understand why you won't even consider—"

"Enough."

"If the object is to make money—"

"Enough. Enough! I don't give a *damn* what other people do. I am not that kind of person."

Twice in church the previous Sunday Enid had turned her head and caught Chuck Meisner staring. She was a little fuller in the bust than usual, probably that was all. But Chuck had blushed both times.

"What is the reason you're so cold to me?" she said.

"There are reasons," Alfred said, "but I will not tell you."

"Why are you so unhappy? Why won't you tell me?"

"I will go to the grave before I tell you. To the grave."

"Oh, oh, oh!"

This was a *bad* husband she had landed, a bad, bad, bad husband who would never give her what she needed. Anything that might have satisfied her he found a reason to withhold.

And so she lay, a Tantala, beside the inert illusion of a feast. The merest finger anywhere would have. To say nothing of his split-plum lips. But he was useless. A wad of money stashed in a mattress and moldering and devaluing was what he was. A depression in the heartland had shriveled him the way it had shriveled her mother, who didn't understand that interest-bearing bank accounts were federally insured now, or that blue-chip stocks held for the long term with reinvested dividends might help provide for her old age. He was a bad investor.

But she was not. She'd even been known, when a room was very dark, to take a real risk or two, and she took one now. Rolled over and tickled his thigh with breasts that a certain neighbor had admired. Rested her cheek on her husband's ribs. She could feel him waiting for her to go away, but first she had to stroke the plain of his muscled belly, hover-gliding, touching hair but no skin. To her mild surprise she felt his his his coming to life at the approach of her fingers. His groin tried to dodge her but the fingers were more nimble. She could feel him growing to manhood through the fly of his pajamas, and in an access of pent-up hunger she did a thing he'd never let her do before. She bent sideways and took it into her mouth. It: the rapidly growing boy, the faintly urinary dumpling. In the skill of her hands and the swelling of her breasts she felt desirable and capable of anything.

The man beneath her shook with resistance. She freed her mouth momentarily. "Al? Sweetie?"

"Enid. What are you—?"

Again her open mouth descended on the cylinder of flesh. She held still for a moment, long enough to feel the flesh harden pulse by pulse against her palate. Then she raised her head. "We could have a little extra money in the bank—you think? Take the boys to Disneyland. You think?"

Back under she went. Tongue and penis were approaching an understanding, and he tasted like the inside of her mouth now. Like a chore and all the word implied. Perhaps involuntarily he kneed her in the ribs and she shifted, still feeling desirable. She stuffed her mouth and the top of her throat. Surfaced for air and took another big gulp.

"Even just to invest two thousand," she murmured. "With a four-dollar differential—ack!"

Alfred had come to his senses and forced the succubus away from him.

(Schopenhauer: *The people who make money are men, not women; and from this it follows that women are neither justified in having unconditional possession of it, nor fit persons to be entrusted with its administration.*)

The succubus reached for him again but he grabbed her wrist and with his other hand pulled her nightgown up.

Maybe the pleasures of a swing set, likewise of sky- and scuba diving, were tastes from a time when the uterus held you harmless from the claims of up and down. A time when you hadn't acquired the mechanics, even, to experience vertigo. Still luxuriated safely in a warm inland sea.

Only *this* tumble was scary, *this* tumble came accompanied by a rush of bloodborne adrenaline, as the mother appeared to be in some distress—

"Al, not sure it's a good idea, isn't, I don't think—"

"The book says there is nothing wrong—"

"Uneasy about this, though. Ooo. Really. Al?"

He was a man having lawful sexual intercourse with his lawful wife.

"Al, though, maybe not. So."

Fighting the image of the leotarded teenaged TWAT. And all the other CUNTS with their TITS and their ASSES that a man might want to FUCK, fighting it although the room was very dark and much was allowed in the dark.

"Oh, I'm so unhappy about this!" Enid quietly wailed.

Worst was the image of the little girl curled up inside her, a girl not much larger than a large bug but already a witness to such harm. Witness to a tautly engorged little brain that dipped in and out beyond the cervix and then, with a quick double spasm that could hardly be considered adequate warning, spat thick alkaline webs of spunk into her private room. Not even born and already drenched in sticky knowledge.

Alfred lay catching his breath and repenting his defiling of the baby. A last child was a last opportunity to learn from one's mistakes and make corrections, and he resolved to seize this opportunity. From the day she was born he would treat her more gently than he'd treated Gary or Chipper. Relax the law for her, indulge her outright, even, and never once force her to sit at the table after everyone was gone.

But he'd squirted such filth on her when she was helpless. She'd witnessed such scenes of marriage, and so of course, when she was older, she betrayed him.

What made correction possible also doomed it.

The sensitive probe that had given him readings at the top end of the red zone now read zero. He pulled away and squared his shoulders to his wife. Under the spell of the sexual instinct (as Arthur Schopenhauer called it) he'd lost sight of how cruelly soon he had to shave and catch the train, but now the instinct was discharged and consciousness of the remaining night's brevity weighed on his chest like #140 rail stock, and Enid had begun to cry again, as wives did when the hour was psychotically late and tampering with the alarm clock was not an option. Years ago, when they were first married, she'd sometimes cried in the wee hours, but then Alfred had felt such gratitude for the pleasure he'd stolen and the stabbing she'd endured that he never failed to ask why she was crying.

Tonight, notably, he felt neither gratitude nor the remotest obligation to quiz her. He felt sleepy.

Why did wives choose night to cry in? Crying at night was all very well if you didn't have to catch a train to work in four hours and if you hadn't, moments ago, committed a defilement in pursuit of a satisfaction whose importance now entirely escaped you.

Maybe it took all this—ten nights of wakefulness in bad motels followed by an evening on the emotional roller coaster and finally the run-outside-and-put-a-bullet-through-the-roof-of-your-mouth sucking and mewling noises of a wife trying to cry herself to sleep at two in the goddamned morning—to open his eyes to the fact that (a) sleep was a woman and (b) hers were comforts that he was under no obligation to refuse.

For a man who all his life had fought off extracurricular napping like any other unwholesome delight, the discovery was life-altering—no less momentous in its way than his discovery, hours earlier, of electrical anisotropism in a gel of networked ferroacetates. More than thirty years would pass before the discovery in the basement bore financial fruit; the discovery in the bedroom made existence chez Lambert more bearable immediately.

A Pax Somnis is descended on the household. Alfred's new lover soothed whatever beast was left in him. How much easier than raging or sulking he found it to simply close his eyes. Soon everybody understood that he had an invisible mistress whom he entertained in the family room on Saturday afternoon when his work week at the Midpac ended, a mistress he took along with him on every business trip and fell into the arms of in beds that no longer seemed uncomfortable in motel rooms that no longer seemed so noisy, a mistress he never failed to visit in the course of an evening's paperwork, a mistress with whom he shared a travel pillow after lunch on family summer trips while Enid lurchingly piloted the car and the kids in the back seat hushed. Sleep was the ideally work-compatible girl he ought to have married in the first place. Perfectly submissive, infinitely forgiving, and so respectable you could take her to church and the symphony and the St. Jude Repertory Theater. She never kept him awake with her tears. She demanded nothing and in return for nothing gave him everything he needed to do a long day's work. There was no mess in their affair, no romantic osculation, no leakages or secretions, no shame. He could cheat on Enid in

Enid's own bed without giving her a shred of legally admissible proof, and as long as he kept the affair private to the extent of not dozing at dinner parties Enid tolerated it, as sensible wives had always done, and so it was an infidelity for which as the decades passed there never seemed to come a reckoning . . .

"Psst! Asshole!"

With a jolt Alfred awakened to the tremor and slow pitching of the *Gunnar Myrdal.* Someone else was in the stateroom?

"Asshole!"

"Who's there?" he asked half in challenge, half in fear.

Thin Scandinavian blankets fell away as he sat up and peered into the semidarkness, straining to hear past the boundaries of his self. The partially deaf know like cellmates the frequencies at which their heads ring. His oldest companion was a contralto like a pipe organ's middle A, a clarion blare vaguely localized in his left ear. He'd known this tone, at growing volumes, for thirty years; it was such a fixture that it seemed it should outlive him. It had the pristine meaninglessness of eternal or infinite things. Was as real as a heartbeat but corresponded to no real thing outside him. Was a sound that nothing made.

Underneath it the fainter and more fugitive tones were active. Cirrus-like clusterings of very high frequencies off in deep stratosphere behind his ears. Meandering notes of almost ghostly faintness, as from a remote calliope. A jangly set of mid-range tones that waxed and waned like crickets in the center of his skull. A low, almost rumbling drone like a dilution of a diesel engine's blanket alldeafeningness, a sound he'd never quite believed was real—i.e., unreal—until he'd retired from the Midpac and lost touch with locomotives. These were the sounds his brain both created and listened to, was friendly with.

Outside of himself he could hear the psh, psh of two hands gently swinging on their hinges in the sheets.

And the mysterious rush of water all around him, in the *Gunnar Myrdal*'s secret capillaries.

And someone snickering down in the dubious space below the horizon of the bedding.

And the alarm clock pinching off each tick. It was three in the morning and his mistress had abandoned him. Now, when he needed her comforts more than ever, she went off whoring with younger sleepers. For thirty years she'd obliged him, spread her arms and opened her legs every night at ten-fifteen. She'd been the nook he sought, the womb. He could still find her in the afternoon or early evening, but not in a bed at night. As soon as he lay down he groped in the sheets and sometimes for a few hours found some bony extremity of hers to clutch. But reliably at one or two or three she vanished beyond any pretending that she still belonged to him.

He peered fearfully across the rust-orange carpeting to the Nordic blond wood lines of Enid's bed. Enid appeared to be dead.

The rushing water in the million pipes.

And the tremor, he had a guess about this tremor. That it came from the engines, that when you built a luxury cruise ship you damped or masked every sound the engines made, one after another, right down to the lowest audible frequency and even lower, but you couldn't go all the way to zero. You were left with this subaudible two-hertz shaking, the irreducible remainder and reminder of a silence imposed on something powerful.

A small animal, a mouse, scurried in the layered shadows at the foot of Enid's bed. For a moment it seemed to Alfred that the whole floor consisted of scurrying corpuscles. Then the mice resolved themselves into a single more forward mouse, horrible mouse, squishable pellets of excreta, habits of gnawing, heedless peeings—

"Asshole, asshole!" the visitor taunted, stepping from the darkness into a bedside dusk.

With dismay Alfred recognized the visitor. First he saw the dropping's slumped outline and then he caught a whiff of bacterial decay. This was not a mouse. This was the turd.

"Urine trouble now, he he!" the turd said.

It was a sociopathic turd, a loose stool, a motormouth. It had introduced itself to Alfred the night before and so agitated him that only Enid's ministrations, a blaze of electric light and Enid's soothing touch on his shoulder, had saved the night.

"Leave!" Alfred commanded sternly.

But the turd scurried up the side of the clean Nordic bed and relaxed like a Brie, or a leafy and manure-smelling Cabrales, on the covers. "Splat chance of that, fella." And dissolved, literally, in a gale of hilarious fart sounds.

To fear encountering the turd on his pillow was to summon the turd to the pillow, where it flopped in postures of glistening well-being.

"Get away, get away," Alfred said, planting an elbow in the carpeting as he exited the bed headfirst.

"No way, José," the turd said. "First I'm gonna get in your clothes."

"No!"

"Sure am, fella. Gonna get in your clothes and touch the upholstery. Gonna smear and leave a trail. Gonna stink so bad."

"Why? Why? Why would you do such a thing?"

"Because it's right for me," the turd croaked. "It's who I am. Put somebody else's comfort ahead of my own? Go hop in a toilet to spare somebody else's feelings? That's the kinda thing *you* do, fella. You got everything bass ackwards. And look where it's landed you."

"Other people ought to have more consideration."

"You oughtta have less. Me personally, I am opposed to all strictures. If you feel it, let it rip. If you want it, go for it. Dude's gotta put his own interests first."

"Civilization depends upon restraint," Alfred said.

"Civilization? Overrated. I ask you what's it ever done for me? Flushed me down the toilet! Treated me like shit!"

"But that's what you *are*," Alfred pleaded, hoping the turd might see the logic. "That's what a toilet is *for*."

"Who you calling shit here, asshole? I got the same rights as everybody else, don't I? Life, liberty, the pussuit of hotpussyness? That's what it says in the Constitution of the You Nighted—"

"That's not right," Alfred said. "You're thinking of the Declaration of Independence."

"Some old yellow piece a paper somewhere, what the ratass fuck do I care what exact paper? Tightasses like you been correcting every fucking word outta my mouth since I was yay big. You and all the constipated fascist schoolteachers and Nazi cops. For all I care the words are printed on a piece of fucking toilet paper. *I* say it's a free country, *I* am in the majority, and *you*, fella, are a minority. And so fuck you."

The turd had an attitude, a tone of voice, that Alfred found eerily familiar but couldn't quite place. It began to roll and tumble on his pillow, spreading a shiny greenish-brown film with little lumps and fibers in it, leaving white creases and hollows where the fabric was bunched. Alfred, on the floor by the bed, covered his nose and mouth with his hands to mitigate the stench and horror.

Then the turd ran up the leg of his pajamas. He felt its tickling mouselike feet.

"Enid!" he called with all the strength he had.

The turd was somewhere in the neighborhood of his upper thighs. Struggling to bend his rigid legs and hook his semifunctional thumbs on the waistband, he pulled the pajamas down to trap the turd inside the fabric. He suddenly understood that the turd was an escaped convict, a piece of human refuse that belonged in jail. That this was what jail was for: people who believed that they, rather than society, made the rules. And if jail did not deter them, they deserved death! Death! Drawing strength from his rage, Alfred succeeded in pulling the ball of pajamas from his feet, and with oscillating arms he wrestled the ball to the carpeting, hammering it with his forearms, and then wedged it deep between the firm Nordic mattress and the Nordic box spring.

He knelt, catching his breath, in his pajama top and adult diaper.

Enid continued to sleep. Something distinctly fairy-tale-like in her attitude tonight.

"Phlblaaatth!" the turd taunted. It had reappeared on the wall above Alfred's bed and hung precariously, as if flung there, beside a framed etching of the Oslo waterfront.

"God damn you!" Alfred said. "You belong in jail!"

The turd wheezed with laughter as it slid very slowly down the wall, its viscous pseudopods threatening to drip on the sheets below. "Seems to me," it said, "you anal retentive type personalities want *everything* in jail. Like, little kids, bad news, man, they pull your tchotchkes off your shelves, they drop food on the carpet, they cry in theaters, they miss the pot. Put 'em in the slammer! And *Polynesians*, man, they track sand in the house, get fish juice on the furniture, and all those pubescent chickies with their honkers exposed? Jail 'em! And how about ten to twenty, while we're at it, for every horny little teenager, I mean talk about insolence, talk about no restraint. And Negroes (sore topic, Fred?), I'm hearing rambunctious shouting and interesting grammar, I'm smelling liquor of the malt variety and sweat that's very rich and scalpy, and all that dancing and whoopee-making and singers that coo like body parts wetted with saliva and special jellies: what's a jail *for* if not to toss a Negro in it? And your Caribbeans with their spliffs and their potbelly toddlers and their like daily barbecues and ratborne hanta viruses and sugary drinks with pig blood at the bottom? Slam the cell door, eat the key. And the Chinese, man, those creepy-ass weird-name vegetables like homegrown dildos somebody forgot to wash after using, one-dollah, one-dollah, and those slimy carps and skinned-alive songbirds, and come on, like, puppy-dog soup and pooty-tat dumplings and female infants are national delicacies, and *pork bung*, by which we're referring here to the *anus* of a *swine*, presumably a sort of chewy and bristly type item, pork bung's a thing Chinks pay money for to *eat*? What say we just nuke all billion point two of 'em, hey? Clean that part of the world *up* already. And let's not forget about women generally, nothing but a trail of Kleenexes and Tampaxes everywhere they go. And your fairies with their doctor's-office lubricants, and your Mediterraneans with their whiskers and their garlic, and your French with their garter belts and raunchy cheeses, and your blue-collar ball-scratchers with their hot rods and beer belches, and your Jews with their circumcised putzes and gefilte fish like pickled turds, and your Wasps with their Cigarette boats and runny-assed polo horses and go-to-hell cigars? Hey, funny thing, Fred, the only people that don't belong in your jail are upper-middle-class northern European men. And you're on *my* case for wanting things *my* way?"

"What will it take to make you leave this room?" Alfred said.

"Loosen up the old sphincter, fella. Let it fly."

"I will never!"

"In that case I might pay a visit to your shaving kit. Have me a little episode o' diarrhea on your toothbrush. Drop a couple nice globbets in your shave cream and tomorrow a.m. you can lather up a rich brown foam—"

"Enid," Alfred said in a strained voice, not taking his eyes off the crafty turd, "I am having difficulties. I would appreciate your assistance."

His voice ought to have awakened her, but her sleep was Snow White–like in its depth.

"Enid *dahling*," the turd mocked in a David Niven accent, "I should *most* appreciate some assistance at your earliest *possible* convenience."

Unconfirmed reports from nerves in the small of Alfred's back and behind his knees indicated that additional turd units were in the vicinity. Turdish rebels snuffling stealthily about, spending themselves in trails of fetor.

"Food and pussy, fella," said the leader of the turds, now barely clinging to the wall by one pseudopod of fecal mousse, "is what it all comes down to. Everything else, and I say this in all modesty, is pure shit."

Then the pseudopod ruptured and the leader of the turds—leaving behind on the wall a small clump of putrescence—plunged with a cry of glee onto a bed that *belonged to Nordic Pleasurelines* and was due to be made in a few hours by a lovely young Finnish woman. Imagining this clean, pleasant housekeeper finding lumps of personal excrement spattered on the bedspread was almost more than Alfred could bear.

His peripheral vision was alive with writhing stool now. He had to hold things together, hold things together. Suspecting that a leak in the toilet might be the source of his trouble, he made his way on hands and knees into the bathroom and kicked the door shut behind him. Rotated with relative ease on the smooth tiles. Braced his back against the door and pushed his feet against the sink opposite him. He laughed for a moment at the absurdity of his situation. Here he was, an American executive sitting in diapers on the floor of a floating bathroom under siege by a squadron of feces. A person got the strangest notions late at night.

The light was better in the bathroom. There was a science of cleanliness, a science of looks, a science even of excretion as evidenced by the outsized Swiss porcelain eggcup of a toilet, a regally pedestaled thing with finely knurled levers of control. In these more congenial surroundings Alfred was able to collect himself to the point of understanding that the turdish rebels were figments, that to some extent he had been dreaming, and that the source of his anxiety was simply a drainage problem.

Unfortunately, operations were shut down for the night. There was no way to have a look personally at the rupture, nor any way to put a plumber's snake or video cam down there. Highly unlikely as well that a contractor could get a rig out to the site under conditions like these. Alfred wasn't even sure he could pinpoint his location on a map himself.

There was nothing for it but to wait until morning. Absent a full solution, two half-solutions were better than no solution at all. You tackled the problem with whatever you had in hand.

Couple of extra diapers: that ought to hold for a few hours. And here were the diapers, right by the toilet in a bag.

It was nearly four o'clock. There would be hell to pay if the district manager wasn't at his desk by seven. Alfred couldn't recollect the fellow's exact name, not that it mattered. Just call the office and whoever picked up the phone.

It was characteristic of the modern world, though, wasn't it, how slippery they made the goddamned tape on the diapers.

"Would you look at that," he said, hoping to pass off as philosophical amusement his rage with a treacherous modernity. The adhesive strips might as well have been covered with Teflon. Between his dry skin and his shakes, peeling the backing off a strip was like picking up a marble with two peacock feathers.

"Well, for goodness' sake."

He persisted in the attempt for five minutes and another five minutes. He simply couldn't get the backing off.

"Well, for goodness' sake."

Grinning at his own incapacity. Grinning in frustration and the overwhelming sense of being watched.

"Well, for goodness' sake," he said once more. This phrase often proved useful in dissipating the shame of small failures.

How changeful a room was in the night! By the time Alfred had given up on the adhesive strips and simply yanked a third diaper up his thigh as far as it would go, which regrettably wasn't far, he was no longer in the same bathroom. The light had a new clinical intensity; he felt the heavy hand of a more extremely late hour.

"Enid!" he called. "Can you help me?"

With fifty years of experience as an engineer he could see at a glance that the emergency contractor had botched the job. One of the diapers was twisted nearly inside out and a second had a mildly spastic leg sticking through two of its plies, leaving most of its absorptive capacity unrealized in a folded mass, its adhesive stickers adhering to nothing. Alfred shook his head. He couldn't blame the contractor. The fault was his own. Never should have undertaken a job like this under conditions like these. Poor judgment on his part. Trying to do damage control, blundering around in the dark, often created more problems than it solved.

"Yes, now we are in a fine mess," he said with a bitter smile.

And could this be liquid on the floor. Oh my Lord, there appeared to be some liquid on the floor.

Also liquid running in the *Gunnar Myrdal*'s myriad pipes.

"Enid, please, for God's sake. I am asking you for help."

No answer from the district office. Some kind of vacation everybody was on. Something about the color of a fall.

Liquid on the floor! Liquid on the floor!

So all right, though, they paid him to take responsibility. They paid him to make the hard calls.

He took a deep, bolstering breath.

In a crisis like this the first order of business was obviously to clear a path for the runoff. Forget about track repair, first you had to have a gradient or you risked a really major washout.

He noted grimly that he had nothing like a surveyor's transit, not even a simple plumb line. He'd have to eyeball it.

How the hell had he got stranded out here, anyway? Probably not even five in the morning yet.

"Remind me to call the district manager at seven," he said.

Somewhere, of course, a dispatcher had to be on duty. But then the problem was to find a telephone, and here a curious reluctance to raise his eyes above the level of the toilet made itself felt. Conditions in these parts were impossible. It could be midmorning by the time he found a telephone. And by that point.

"Uh! Such a lot of work," he said.

There appeared to be a slight depression in the shower stall. Yes, in fact, a preexisting culvert, maybe some old DOT road-building project that never got off the ground, maybe the Army Corps was involved somehow. One of those midnight serendipities: a real culvert. Still, he was looking at a hell of an engineering problem to relocate the operation to take advantage of the culvert.

"Not much choice, though, I'm afraid."

Might as well get at it. He wasn't getting any less tired. Think of the Dutch with their Delta Project. Forty years of battling the sea. Put things in perspective a little—one bad night. He'd endured worse.

Try to build some redundancy into the fix, that was the plan. No way he'd trust one little culvert to handle all the runoff. There could be a backup farther down the line.

"And then we're in trouble," he said. "Then we are in real trouble."

Could be a hell of a lot worse, in fact. They were lucky an engineer was right on site when the water broke through. Imagine if he hadn't been here, what a mess.

"Could have been a real disaster."

First order of business was to slap some sort of temporary patch on the leak, then tackle the logistical nightmare of rerouting the whole operation over the culvert, and then hope to hold things together until the sun came up.

"And see what we got."

In the faulty light he saw the liquid running one way across the floor and then reversing itself slowly, as if the horizontal had lost its mind.

"Enid!" he called with little hope as he commenced the sick-making work of stopping the leakage and getting himself back on track, and the ship sailed on.

Thanks to Aslan®—and to young Dr. Hibbard, an outstanding, high-caliber young man—Enid was having her first solid night's sleep in many months.

There were a thousand things she *wanted* from life, and since few were available at home with Alfred in St. Jude, she had forcibly channeled all her wanting into the numbered days, the mayfly lifetime, that the luxury cruise would last. For months the cruise had been her mind's safe parking space, the future that made her present bearable, and after her afternoon in New York had proved deficient in the fun department, she boarded the *Gunnar Myrdal* with her hungers redoubled.

Fun was being had buoyantly on every deck by cliques of seniors enjoying their retirement the way she wished Alfred would enjoy his. Although Nordic Pleasurelines was emphatically not a discount line, this cruise had been booked almost entirely by large groups such as the University of Rhode Island Alumni Association, American Hadassah of Chevy Chase (MD), the 85th Airborne ("Sky Devil") Division Reunion, and the Dade County (FL) Duplicate Bridge League, Senior Flight. Widows in excellent health guided one another by the elbow to special mustering places where name tags and information packets were distributed and the preferred token of mutual recognition was the glass-shattering scream. Already seniors intent on savoring every minute of precious cruise time were drinking the frozen cocktail du jour, a Lingonberry Lapp Frappe, from schooners that took two hands to handle safely. Others crowded the rails of lower decks, the ones sheltered from the rain, and scanned Manhattan for a face to wave goodbye to. A combo in the Abba Show Lounge was playing heavy-metal polka.

While Alfred had a final pre-dinner session in the bathroom, his third session inside an hour, Enid sat in the "B" Deck lounge and listened to the slow plant-and-drag of someone's walker-aided progress across the "A" Deck lounge above her.

Apparently the Duplicate League's cruise uniform was a T-shirt with the text: OLD BRIDGE PLAYERS NEVER DIE, THEY JUST LOSE THEIR FINESSE. Enid felt the joke did not bear heavy repetition.

She saw retirees *running*, actually lifting their feet off the ground, in the direction of the Lingonberry Lapp Frappe.

"Of course," she murmured, reflecting on how old everyone was, "I suppose who else could afford a cruise like this?"

The seeming dachshund that a man was pulling by a leash turned out to be a tank of oxygen mounted on roller-skate wheels and dressed in a pet sweater.

A very fat man walked by in a T-shirt that said TITANIC: THE BODY.

You'd spent a lifetime being waited for impatiently and now your impatient husband's minimum stay in a bathroom was fifteen minutes.

OLD UROLOGISTS NEVER DIE, THEY JUST PETER OUT.

Even on nights with a casual dress code, such as tonight, T-shirts were officially discouraged. Enid had put on a wool suit and asked Alfred to wear a tie, although given his handling of a soup spoon lately his neckties were little more than cannon fodder on dinner's front line. She'd made him pack a dozen. She was acutely conscious that Nordic Pleasurelines was deluxe. She expected—and had paid for, in part with her own money—*elegance*. Each T-shirt she saw was a specific small trampling of her fantasy and, hence, pleasure.

It rankled her that people richer than she were so often less worthy and attractive. More slobbish and louty. Comfort could be found in being poorer than people who were smart and beautiful. But to be less affluent than these T-shirted, joke-cracking fatsos—

"I am ready," Alfred announced, appearing in the lounge. He took Enid's hand for the ascent by elevator to the Søren Kierkegaard Dining Room. Holding his hand she felt married and, to that extent, grounded in the universe and reconciled to old age, but she couldn't help thinking how dearly she would have treasured holding his hand in the decades when he'd stridden everywhere a pace or two ahead of her. His hand was needy and subdued now. Even tremors of his that looked violent proved to be featherweight in feel. She could sense the hand's readiness to resume its paddling as soon as it was released, however.

Such travelers as were cruising without affiliation had been assigned to special dining tables for "floaters." To the delight of Enid, who relished cosmopolitan company provided it wasn't too snobbish, two of the "floaters" at her and Alfred's table were from Norway and two were from Sweden. Enid liked European countries small. One could learn an interesting Swedish custom or Norwegian fact without being made sensible of one's ignorance of German music, French literature, or Italian art. The usage of "skoal" was a good example. Likewise the fact that Norway was Europe's largest exporter of crude oil, as Mr. and Mrs. Nygren from Oslo were informing the table when the Lamberts claimed the last two seats.

Enid spoke first to her left-hand neighbor, Mr. Söderblad, a reassuringly ascoted and blue-blazered older Swede. "What's your impression of the ship so far?" she asked. "Is it really *super* authentic?"

"Well, it does seem to be floating," Mr. Söderblad said with a smile, "in spite of heavy seas."

Enid raised her voice to aid his comprehension. "I mean, is it AUTHENTICALLY SCANDINAVIAN?"

"Well, yes, of course," Mr. Söderblad said. "At the same time, everything in the world is more and more American, don't you think?"

"But you think this captures REALLY SUPER WELL," Enid said, "the flavor of a REAL SCANDINAVIAN SHIP?"

"Actually, it is better than most ships in Scandinavia. My wife and I are quite pleased so far."

Enid abandoned her inquiry unconvinced that Mr. Söderblad had grasped its import. It mattered to her that Europe be European. She'd visited the Continent five times on vacation and twice on business trips with Alfred, so about a dozen times altogether, and to friends planning tours of Spain or France she now liked to say, with a sigh, that she'd had her fill of the place. It drove her crazy, however, to hear her friend Bea Meisner affect the same indifference: "I'm so sick of flying to St. Moritz for my grandsons' birthdays," et cetera. Bea's dimwitted and unfairly gorgeous daughter Cindy had married an Austrian sports doctor, a von Somebody who'd garnered Olympic bronze in the giant slalom. That Bea continued to socialize at all with Enid amounted to a triumph of loyalty over divergent fortunes. But Enid never forgot that it was

Chuck Meisner's big investment in Erie Belt stock on the eve of the Midpac buyout that had helped fund their mansion in Paradise Valley. Chuck had become board chairman of his bank while Alfred stalled in the Midpac's second echelon and put his savings into inflation-prone annuities, so that even now the Lamberts could not afford Nordic Pleasurelines quality unless Enid dipped into private funds, which she did to escape going mad with envy.

"My best friend in St. Jude vacations at St. Moritz," she shouted, apropos essentially of nothing, in the direction of Mr. Söderblad's pretty wife. "Her Austrian son-in-law is tremendously successful and owns a chalet there!"

Mrs. Söderblad was like a precious-metal accessory somewhat scuffed and tarnished by Mr. Söderblad's use. Her lip gloss, hair color, eye shadow, and nail polish rang changes on a theme of platinum; her dinner dress was of silver lamé and afforded good views of sun-toasted shoulder and silicone augmentation. "St. Moritz is quite beautiful," she said. "I have performed many times in St. Moritz."

"YOU'RE A PERFORMER?" Enid shouted.

"Signe was a special entertainer," Mr. Söderblad said hastily.

"Those Alpine resorts can be terribly overpriced," the Norwegian woman, Mrs. Nygren, observed with a shiver. She had large round eyeglasses and a radial distribution of face wrinkles which together gave a mantislike impression. Visually she and the burnished Söderblad were mutual affronts. "On the other hand," she continued, "it is easy for us in Norway to be choosy. Even in certain of our city parks the skiing can be 'top-notch.' There is really nothing like it anywhere."

"Of course a distinction must be made," said Mr. Nygren, who was very tall and had ears like raw veal chops, "between the Alpine type of skiing and the cross-country, or Nordic, variety. Norway has produced outstanding Alpine skiers—I mention the name Kjetil Andre Aamodt with some confidence that it will 'ring a bell'—but it must be admitted that we have not always competed at the top level in this area. However, the cross-country, or Nordic, variety is quite a different story. There it is safe to say that we continue to gain more than our fair share of distinctions."

"Norwegians are fantastically boring," Mr. Söderblad said hoarsely in Enid's ear.

The other two "floaters" at the table, a handsome older couple named Roth from Chadds Ford, Pennsylvania, had done Enid the instinctive favor of engaging Alfred in conversation. Alfred's face was flushed with soup heat, the drama of a spoon, and also perhaps the effort of refusing to glance even once at the dazzling Söderbladian décolletage, while he explained to the Roths the mechanics of stabilizing an ocean liner. Mr. Roth, a brainy-looking man in a bow tie and eye-bloating horn-rims, was peppering him with discerning questions and assimilating the answers so raptly he appeared almost shocked.

Mrs. Roth was paying less attention to Alfred than to Enid. Mrs. Roth was a small woman, a handsome child in her mid-sixties. Her elbows barely cleared the tabletop. She had a white-flecked black pageboy and rosy cheeks and big blue eyes with which she was staring at Enid unabashedly, in the way of someone very smart or very stupid. Such a crushlike intensity of looking suggested hunger. Enid sensed immediately that Mrs. Roth would become her great friend on the cruise, or else her great rival, and so with something like coquetry she declined to speak to her or otherwise acknowledge her attention. As steaks were brought to the table and devastated lobsters taken away she repeatedly thrust and Mr. Söderblad repeatedly parried questions concerning his occupation, which appeared to involve the arms trade. She soaked up Mrs. Roth's blue-eyed gaze along with the envy that she imagined the "floaters" were provoking at other tables. She supposed that to the hoi polloi in their T-shirts the "floaters" looked extremely Continental. A touch of distinction here. Beauty, neckties, an ascot. A certain cachet.

"Sometimes I get so excited thinking about my morning coffee," Mr. Söderblad said, "I can't fall asleep at night."

Enid's hopes that Alfred might take her dancing in the Pippi Long-stocking Ballroom were dashed when he stood up and announced that he was going to bed. It wasn't even seven o'clock yet. Who ever heard of a grownup going to bed at seven in the evening?

"Sit down and wait for dessert," she said. "The desserts are supposed to be *divine*."

Alfred's unsightly napkin fell from his thighs to the floor. He seemed without inkling of how much he was embarrassing and disappointing her. "You stay," he said. "I've had enough."

And away across the Søren Kierkegaard broadloom he lurched, battling shifts in the horizontal which had grown more pronounced since the ship left New York Harbor.

Familiar waves of sorrow for all the fun she couldn't have with such a husband dampened Enid's spirits until it occurred to her that she now had a long evening to herself and no Alfred to spoil her fun.

She brightened, and brightened further when Mr. Roth departed for the Knut Hamsun Reading Room, leaving his wife at the table. Mrs. Roth switched seats to be closer to Enid.

"We Norwegians are great readers," Mrs. Nygren took the opportunity to remark.

"And great yakkers," Mr. Söderblad muttered.

"Public libraries and bookstores in Oslo are thriving," Mrs. Nygren informed the table. "I think it is *not* the same elsewhere. Reading is mostly in decline around the world. But not in Norway, hm. My Per is reading the complete works of John Galsworthy for the second time this autumn. In English."

"Nooo, Inga, nooo," Per Nygren whinnied. "Third time!"

"My God," said Mr. Söderblad.

"It's true." Mrs. Nygren looked at Enid and Mrs. Roth as though anticipating awe. "Each year Per reads one work by every winner of the Nobel Prize in Literature, and also the complete works of his favorite winner from his previous year's reading. And you see, each year the task becomes a bit more difficult, because there has been another winner, you see."

"It is a bit like raising the bar in a high jump," Per explained. "Every year a bit more challenging."

Mr. Söderblad, who by Enid's count was drinking his eighth cup of coffee, leaned close to her and said, "My God these people are boring!"

"It is safe to say that I have read more deeply into Henrik Pontoppidan than most," Per Nygren said.

Mrs. Söderblad tilted her head, smiling dreamily. "Do you know," she said, perhaps to Enid or to Mrs. Roth, "that until one hundred years ago Norway was a colony of Sweden?"

The Norwegians erupted like a batted hive.

"Colony!? Colony??"

"Oh, oh," Inga Nygren hissed, "I *think* there is a history here that our American friends deserve to—"

"This is a story of strategic alliances!" Per declared.

"By 'colony' what is the *exact* word in Swedish that you are groping for, *Mrs.* Söderblad? Since my English is obviously much stronger than yours, perhaps I can offer our American friends a more accurate translation, such as '*equal partner in a unified peninsular kingdom*'?"

"Signe," Mr. Söderblad observed wickedly to his wife, "I do believe you've hit a nerve." He raised a hand. "Waiter, refill."

"If one chooses as a vantage point the late ninth century," Per Nygren said, "and I suspect that even our Swedish friends will concede that the ascension of Harald the Blond is quite a reasonable 'hopping-off place' for our examination of the seesaw relationship of two great rival powers, or should I perhaps say *three* great powers, since Denmark as well plays a rather fascinating role in our story—"

"We'd love to hear it, but maybe another time," Mrs. Roth interrupted, leaning over to touch Enid's hand. "Remember we said seven o'clock?"

Enid was only briefly bewildered. She excused herself and followed Mrs. Roth into the main hall, where they encountered a crush of seniors and gastric aromas, disinfectant aromas.

"Enid, I'm Sylvia," said Mrs. Roth. "How do you feel about slot machines? I've had a physical craving all day."

"Oh, me too!" Enid said. "I think they're in the Stringbird Room."

"Strindberg, yes."

Enid admired quickness of mind but seldom credited herself with possessing it. "Thanks for the—you know," she said as she followed Sylvia Roth through the crush.

"Rescue. Don't mention it."

The Strindberg Room was packed with kibitzers, low-stakes blackjack players, and lovers of the slot. Enid couldn't remember when she'd had so much fun. The fifth quarter she dropped brought her three plums; as if so much fruit upset the bowels of her machine, specie gushed from its nether parts. She shoveled her take into a plastic bucket. Eleven quarters later it happened again: three cherries, a silver dump. White-haired players losing steadily at neighboring machines gave her dirty looks. I'm embarrassed, she told herself, although she wasn't.

Decades of insufficient affluence had made her a disciplined investor. From her winnings she set aside the amount of her initial investment. Half of every payoff she also salted away.

Her playing fund showed no sign of exhaustion, however.

"So, I've had my fix," Sylvia Roth said after nearly an hour, tapping Enid on the shoulder. "Shall we go hear the string quartet?"

"Yes! Yes! It's in the Greed Room."

"Grieg," said Sylvia, laughing.

"Oh, that is funny, isn't it? Grieg. I'm so stupid tonight."

"How much did you make? You seemed to be doing well."

"I'm not sure, I didn't count."

Sylvia smiled at her intently. "I think you did, though. I think you counted exactly."

"All right," Enid said, blushing because she was liking Sylvia so much. "It was a hundred thirty dollars."

A portrait of Edvard Grieg hung in a room of actual gilt ornateness that recalled the eighteenth-century splendor of Sweden's royal court. The large number of empty chairs confirmed Enid's suspicion that many of the cruise participants were low-class. She'd been on cruises where the classical concerts were SRO.

Although Sylvia seemed less than knocked dead by the musicians, Enid thought they were wonderful. They played, *from memory*, popular classical tunes such as "Swedish Rhapsody" and excerpts from *Finlandia* and *Peer Gynt*. In the middle of *Peer Gynt* the second violinist turned green and left the room for a minute (the sea really was a bit stormy, but Enid had a strong stomach and Sylvia had a patch) and then returned to his chair and managed to find his place again without, as it were, missing a beat. The twenty people in the audience shouted, "Bravo!"

At the elegant reception afterward Enid spent 7.7 percent of her gambling earnings on a cassette tape recorded by the quartet. She tried a complimentary glass of Spögg, a Swedish liqueur currently enjoying a $15 million marketing campaign. Spögg tasted like vodka, sugar, and horseradish, which in fact were its ingredients. As their fellow guests reacted to Spögg with looks of surprise and reproach, Enid and Sylvia fell to giggling.

"Special treat," Sylvia said. "Complimentary Spögg. Try some!"

"Yum!" Enid said in stitches, snorting for air. "Spögg!"

Then it was on to the Ibsen Promenade for the scheduled ten o'clock ice cream social. In the elevator it seemed to Enid that the ship was suffering not only from a seesaw motion but also from a yaw, as if its bow were the face of someone experiencing repugnance. Leaving the elevator, she almost fell over a man on his hands and knees like half a two-man prank involving shoving. On the back of his T-shirt was a punch line: THEY JUST LOSE THEIR AIM.

Enid accepted an ice cream soda from a food handler in a toque. Then she initiated an exchange of family data with Sylvia which quickly became an exchange more of questions than of answers. It was Enid's habit, when she sensed that family was not a person's favorite topic, to probe the sore relentlessly. She would sooner have died than admit that her own children disappointed her, but hearing of other people's disappointing children—their squalid divorces, their substance abuse, their foolish investments—made her feel better.

On the surface, Sylvia Roth had nothing to be ashamed of. Her sons were both in California, one in medicine and the other in computers, and both were married. Yet they seemed to be hot conversational sands to be avoided or crossed at a sprint. "Your daughter went to Swarthmore," she said.

"Yes, briefly," Enid said. "So, and *five* grandsons, though. My goodness. How old is the youngest?"

"He was two last month, and what about you?" Sylvia said. "Any grandkids?"

"Our oldest son, Gary, has three sons, but so, that's interesting, a five-year gap between the youngest and the next youngest?"

"Nearly six, actually, and your son in New York, I want to hear about him, too. Did you stop and see him today?"

"Yes, he made a lovely lunch but we didn't get down to see his office at the *Wall Street Journal* where he has a new job because the weather was bad, so, and do you get out much to California? To see your grandsons?"

Some spirit, a willingness to play the game, left Sylvia. She sat peering into her empty soda glass. "Enid, will you do me a favor?" she said finally. "Come upstairs and have a nightcap."

Enid's day had begun in St. Jude at five in the morning, but she never declined an attractive invitation. Upstairs in the Lagerkvist Taproom she and Sylvia were served by a dwarf in a horned helmet and leather jerkin who persuaded them to order cloudberry akvavit.

"I want to tell you something," Sylvia said, "because I have to tell someone on the ship, but you can't breathe a word of this to anyone. Are you good at keeping secrets?"

"It's one thing I do well."

"Then, good," Sylvia said. "Three days from now there's going to be an execution in Pennsylvania. So, and two days after that, on Thursday, Ted and I have our fortieth anniversary. And if you ask Ted, he'll tell you that's why we're on this cruise, for the anniversary. He'll tell you that, but it's not the truth. Or it's only a truth about Ted and not me."

Enid felt afraid.

"The man who's being executed," Sylvia Roth said, "killed our daughter."

"No."

The blue clarity of Sylvia's gaze made her seem a beautiful, lovable animal that was not, however, quite human. "Ted and I," she said, "are on this cruise because we have a problem with this execution. We have a problem with each other."

"No! What are you telling me?" Enid shuddered. "Oh, I can't stand to hear this! I can't stand to hear this!"

Sylvia quietly registered this allergy to her disclosure. "I'm sorry," she said. "It's not fair of me to ambush you. Maybe we should call it a night."

But Enid quickly regained her composure. She was determined not to miss becoming Sylvia's confidante. "Tell me everything you need to tell me," she said. "And I'll listen." She folded her hands in her lap like a good listener. "Go ahead. I'm listening."

"Then the other thing I have to tell you," Sylvia said, "is that I'm a gun artist. I draw guns. You really want to hear this?"

"Yes." Enid nodded eagerly and vaguely. The dwarf, she noticed, used a small ladder to fetch down bottles. "Interesting."

For many years, Sylvia said, she'd been an amateur printmaker. She had a sun-filled studio in her house in Chadds Ford, she had a cream-smooth lithography stone and a twenty-piece set of German woodblock chisels, and she belonged to a Wilmington art guild in whose semi-annual show, while her youngest child, Jordan, grew from a tomboy into an independent young woman, she'd sold decorative prints for prices like forty dollars. Then Jordan was murdered and for five years Sylvia printed, drew, and painted nothing but guns. Year after year only guns.

"Terrible terrible," Enid said with open disapproval.

The trunk of the wind-splintered tulip tree outside Sylvia's studio suggested stocks and barrels. Every human form sought to become a hammer, a trigger guard, a cylinder, a grip. There was no abstraction that couldn't be tracer fire, or the smoke of black powder, or a hollow-point's flowering. The body was worldlike in the repleteness of its possibilities, and just as no part of this little world was safe from a bullet's penetration, no form in the big world had no echo in a gun. Even a pinto bean was like a derringer, even a snowflake like a Browning on its tripod. Sylvia wasn't insane; she could force herself to draw a circle or sketch a rose. But what she hungered to draw was firearms. Guns, gun-fire, ordnance, projectiles. She spent hours capturing in pencil the pattern of gleam on nickel plating. Sometimes she also drew her hands and her wrists and forearms in what she guessed (for she had never held a gun) were appropriate grips for a .50 caliber Desert Eagle, a nine-millimeter Glock, a fully automatic M16 with a folding aluminum stock, and other exotic weapons from the catalogues that she kept in brown envelopes in her sun-drenched studio. She abandoned herself to her habit like a lost soul to its hellishly fitting occupation (although Chadds Ford, the subtle warblers that ventured up from the Brandywine, the scents of warm cattail and fermenting persimmon that October winds stirred out of nearby hollows, staunchly resisted being made a hell of); she was a Sisypha who every night destroyed her own creations—tore them up, erased them in mineral spirits. Kindled a merry fire in the living room.

"Terrible," Enid murmured again. "I can't think of a worse thing that could happen to a mother." She signaled to the dwarf for more cloudberry akvavit.

Some mysteries of her obsession, Sylvia said, were that she'd been raised as a Quaker and still went to meeting in Kennett Square; that the tools of Jordan's torture and murder had been one roll of nylon-reinforced "strapping" tape, one dish towel, two wire coat hangers, one General Electric Light 'n Easy electric iron, and one WMF twelve-inch serrated bread knife from Williams-Sonoma, i.e., no guns; that the killer, a nineteen-year-old named Khellye Withers, had turned himself in to the Philadelphia police without (again) a gun being unholstered; that with a husband who earned a huge late-career salary as Du Pont's vice president of Compliance, and a sport-utility vehicle so massive that a head-on crash with a VW Cabriolet might hardly have dented it, and a six-bedroom Queen Anne–style house into whose kitchen and pantry Jordan's entire Philadelphia apartment would have fit comfortably, Sylvia enjoyed a life of almost senseless ease and comfort in which her only task besides cooking for Ted, literally her only task, was to recover from Jordan's death; that she nevertheless often became so absorbed in rendering the tooling on a revolver butt or the veins in her arm that she had to drive crazily fast to avoid missing her thrice-weekly therapy with an M.D./Ph.D. in Wilmington; that by talking to the M.D./Ph.D., and by attending Wednesday-night sessions with other Parents of Victims of Violence and Thursday-night meetings with her Older Women's group, and by reading the poetry and novels and memoirs and insight books that her friends recommended, and by relaxing with yoga and horseback riding, and by volunteering as a physical therapist's assistant at Children's Hospital, she succeeded in working through her grief even as her compulsion to draw guns intensified; that she mentioned this compulsion to no one, not even to the M.D./Ph.D. in Wilmington; that her friends and advisers all constantly exhorted her to "heal" herself through her "art"; that by "art" they meant her decorative woodcuts and lithos; that when she happened to see an old woodcut of hers in the bathroom or guest bedroom of a friend she twisted her body with shame at the fraudulence; that when she saw guns on TV or in a movie she writhed in a similar way and for similar reasons; that she was secretly convinced, in other words, that she had become a real artist, a genuinely good artist of the gun; that it was the proof of this artistry that she destroyed at the end of each day; that she was convinced that Jordan, despite having earned a B.F.A. in painting and an M.A. in art therapy, and despite the encouragement and paid instruction in art she'd received for twenty years, had not been a good artist; that after achieving this objective view of her dead daughter she continued to draw guns and ammo; and that in spite of the rage and thirst for vengeance that her continuing obsession obviously betokened she had never once in five years drawn the face of Khellye Withers.

On the October morning when these mysteries impressed themselves on her en masse, Sylvia took the stairs to her studio after breakfast at a run. On a sheet of ivory Canson paper, and using a mirror so that it appeared to be her right hand, she drew her left hand with its thumb raised and fingers curled, sixty degrees behind full profile, a nearly full rear view. This hand she then filled with a snub-nose .38 revolver, expertly foreshortened, whose barrel penetrated a pair of smirking lips above which she penciled accurately, from memory, the taunting eyes of Khellye Withers, over the recent exhaustion of whose legal appeals few tears had been shed. And at that—a pair of lips, a pair of eyes—Sylvia had set down her pencil.

"It was time to move on," Sylvia said to Enid. "I saw it all of a sudden. That whether I liked it or not, the survivor and the artist was me, not her. We're all conditioned to think of our children as more important than us, you know, and to live vicariously through them. All of a sudden I was sick of that kind of thinking. I may be dead tomorrow, I said to myself, but I'm alive now. And I can live deliberately. I've paid the price, I've done the work, and I have nothing to be ashamed of.

"And when the event, the big change in your life, is simply an insight—isn't that a strange thing? That absolutely nothing changes except that you see things differently and you're less fearful and less anxious and generally stronger as a result: isn't it amazing that a completely invisible thing in your head can feel realer than anything you've experienced before? You see things more clearly and you *know* that you're seeing them more clearly. And it comes to you that this is what it means to love life, this is all anybody who talks seriously about God is ever talking about. Moments like this."

"Maybe one more?" Enid said to the dwarf, raising her glass. She was almost wholly not listening to Sylvia, but shaking her head and murmuring "Uh!" and "Oh!" while her consciousness stumbled through clouds of alcohol into such absurd realms of speculation as how the dwarf might feel against her hips and belly, embracing her. Sylvia turned out to be *very* intellectual, and Enid felt befriended under somewhat false pretenses, but while not listening she also had to listen, because she was missing certain key facts, such as whether Khellye Withers was black and whether Jordan had been brutally raped.

From her studio Sylvia had gone straight to a Wawa Food Market and bought one of every dirty magazine it had in stock. Nothing she found in the magazines was sufficiently hardcore, however. She needed to see the actual plumbing, the literal act. She returned to Chadds Ford and switched on the computer that her younger son had given her to foster closeness in their time of loss. Her e-mailbox contained a month's backlog of filial greetings that she ignored. In less than five minutes she located the goods she wanted—all it took was a credit card—and she moused through thumbnail views until she found the necessary angle on the necessary act with the necessary actors: black man performing oral sex on white man, camera shooting over left hip sixty degrees behind full profile, crescent of high values curving over buttock, knuckles of black fingers duskily visible in their probing on the dark side of this moon. She downloaded the image and viewed it at high resolution.

She was sixty-five years old and she'd never seen a scene like this. She'd fashioned images all her life and she'd never appreciated their mystery. Now here it was. All this commerce in bits and bytes, these ones and zeros streaming through servers at some midwestern university. So much evident trafficking in so much evident nothing. A population glued to screens and magazines.

She wondered: How could people respond to these images if images didn't secretly enjoy the same status as real things? Not that images were so powerful, but that the world was so weak. It could be vivid, certainly, in its weakness, as on days when the sun baked fallen apples in orchards and the valley smelled like cider, and cold nights when Jordan had driven to Chadds Ford for dinner and the tires of her Cabriolet had crunched on the gravel driveway; but the world was *fungible* only as images. Nothing got inside the head without becoming pictures.

And yet Sylvia was struck by the contrast between the online porn and her unfinished drawing of Withers. Unlike ordinary lust, which could be appeased by pictures or by pure imagination, the lust for revenge could not be tricked. The most graphic image couldn't satisfy it. This lust required the death of a specific individual, the termination of a specific history. As the menus said: NO SUBSTITUTIONS. She could draw her desire but not its fulfillment. And so she finally told herself the truth: she wanted Khellye Withers dead.

She wanted him dead despite her recent interview with the *Philadelphia Inquirer* in which she'd avowed that killing someone else's child wouldn't bring back her own. She wanted him dead despite the religious fervor with which her M.D./Ph.D. had forbidden her to interpret Jordan's death religiously—for example, as a divine judgment on her own liberal politics or liberal parenting or senseless affluence. She wanted him dead despite believing that Jordan's death had been a random tragedy and that redemption lay not in vengeance but in reducing the incidence of random tragedies nationwide. She wanted him dead despite imagining a society that provided jobs at a decent wage for young men like him (so that he would not have had to bind the wrists and ankles of his former art therapist and bully out of her the passwords for her bank card and credit cards), a society that stanched the flow of illegal drugs into urban neighborhoods (so that Withers could not have spent the stolen money on crack, and would have had more mental clarity when he returned to the apartment of his former art therapist, and would not have proceeded to smoke the rock and torture her, on and off, for thirty hours), a society in which young men had more to believe in than brand-name consumer goods (so that Withers would have fixated less insanely on his former art therapist's Cabriolet, and would have believed her when she insisted she'd lent the car to a friend for the weekend, and would have set less store by her possession of two sets of keys ("Couldn't get around that," he explained in his partially coerced but still legally admissible confession, "all the keys right there on the kitchen table, you know what I'm saying? Couldn't get my ass around that fact"), and would not have repeatedly applied the victim's Light 'n Easy iron to her bare skin and advanced the temperature setting from Rayon up through Cotton/Linen while demanding to know where she'd parked the Cabriolet, and would not have cut her throat in a panic when her friend came by on Sunday evening to return the car and her third set of keys), a society that once and for all put an end to the physical abuse of children (so that it would have been absurd for a convicted murderer to claim, in the sentencing phase of his trial, that his stepfather had burned him with an electric iron when he was little—though in the case of Withers, who had no burn scars to exhibit, such testimony seemed mainly to underscore the convict's own lack of imagination as a liar). She wanted him dead despite even her realization, in therapy, that his smirk had been a protective mask donned by a lonely boy surrounded by people who hated him, and that if she'd only smiled at him like a forgiving mother he might have laid aside his mask and wept with honest remorse. She wanted him dead despite knowing her desire would please conservatives for whom the phrase "personal responsibility" constituted permission to ignore social injustice. She wanted him dead despite being unable, for these political reasons, to attend the execution and to see with her own eyes the thing for which no image could substitute.

"But none of this," she said, "is why we're on this cruise."

"No?" Enid said as if awakening.

"No. We're here because Ted won't admit that Jordan was murdered."

"Is he . . . ?"

"Oh, he knows it," Sylvia said. "He just won't talk about it. He was very close to Jordan, closer in a lot of ways than he's ever been to me. And he grieved, I'll grant him that. He did grieve. He wept so much he could hardly move. But then one morning he was over it. He said that Jordan was gone and he wasn't going to live in the past. He said that starting on Labor Day he was going to forget she was a victim. And every day, as it got later in August, he reminded me that beginning after Labor Day he wouldn't admit that she was murdered. Ted's a very rational man. His view was that human beings have been losing children forever and that too much grieving is stupid and self-indulgent. He didn't care what happened to Withers, either. He said that following the trial was just another way of not getting over the murder.

"And so, on Labor Day, he said to me, 'It may seem strange to you, but I will never speak of her death again, and I want you to remember that I'm telling you this. Will you remember this, Sylvia? So you don't think I'm crazy later?' And I said, 'I don't like this, Ted, I don't accept this.' And he said he was sorry but he had to do it. And the next night when he got home from work I told him, I think it was, that Withers's lawyer was claiming his confession was coerced and the real killer was still at large. And Ted sort of grinned at me, in this way when he's pulling your leg, and he said, 'I don't know what you're talking about.' And so I actually said, 'I'm talking about the person who killed our daughter.' And he said, 'No one killed our daughter, I don't want to hear you say that again.' And I said, 'Ted, this is not going to work.' And he said, 'What's not going to work?' And I said, 'Your pretending Jordan isn't dead.' And he said, 'We had a daughter and we don't now and so I guess she's dead, but I'm warning you, Sylvia, you *do not* tell me she was killed, do you understand me?' And ever since then, Enid, no matter how hard I push, he's never dropped his pose. And I'll tell you, I'm an inch away from divorcing him. Always. Except he's so unfailingly dear to me otherwise. He never gets angry when I talk about Withers, he just gets bluff and laughs it off, like it's some peculiar idée fixe of mine. And I can see that he's like our cat dragging in a dead warbler. The *cat* doesn't know you don't like dead warblers. Ted wants me to be rational like he is, he thinks he's doing me a favor, and he takes me on all these trips and cruises, and everything's fine except that for him the most terrible thing in our life didn't happen and for me it did."

"So did it happen?" Enid said.

Sylvia drew her head back, shocked. "Thank you," she said although Enid had posed the question because she was momentarily confused, not because she wanted to do Sylvia a favor. "Thank you for being honest enough to ask me that. I do feel crazy sometimes. All my work is in my head. I'm moving around a million little pieces of nothing, a million thoughts and feelings and memories inside my head, day after day, for years, there's this enormous scaffolding and planning, like I'm building a cathedral of toothpicks inside my head. And it doesn't even help to keep a diary, because I can't make the words on the page have any effect on my brain. As soon as I write a thing down I leave it behind. It's like dropping pennies over the side of a boat. And so I'm doing all this mental work without any possibility of external support, except for these slightly dowdy people in my Wednesday and Thursday groups, and meanwhile my own husband is pretending that the whole *point* of all this huge interior work—namely, that my daughter was murdered—isn't real. And so, more and more, literally the only beacons I still have in my life, my only north and south and east and west, are my emotions.

"And Ted's right on top of that, he thinks our culture attaches too much importance to feelings, he says it's out of control, it's not computers that are making everything virtual, it's mental health. Everyone's trying to correct their thoughts and improve their feelings and work on their relationships and parenting skills instead of just getting married and raising children like they used to, is what Ted says. We've bumped up to the next level of abstraction because we have too much time and money, is what he says, and he refuses to be a part of it. He wants to eat 'real' food and go to 'real' places and talk about 'real' things like business and science. So he and I don't really agree at all anymore on what's important in life.

"And he foxed my therapist, Enid. I had her to dinner so she could take a look at him, and you know those dinners the magazines say you shouldn't make for company, where you're in the kitchen for twenty minutes before every course? I made one of those, a risotto milanese and then pan-fried steaks with a two-stage reduction, and my therapist was out in the dining room the whole time quizzing Ted. And when I saw her the next day she said his condition was very common in men, he appeared to have dealt with his grief enough to function, and she believed he wasn't going to change and it was up to me now to accept this.

"And you know, I'm not supposed to let myself think magical or religious thoughts, but one thought I can't escape is that this crazy thirst for revenge I've had for all these years isn't really my own. It's Ted's. He won't deal with it himself, and somebody's got to deal with it, so I do, like I'm a surrogate mother except I'm not carrying a baby, I'm carrying emotions. Maybe if Ted had taken more responsibility for his feelings, and been less in a hurry to go back to work at Du Pont, I would have stayed just like I always was, and sold my woodcuts at the guild every Christmas. Maybe it was Ted's being so rational and businesslike that pushed me over the edge. And so maybe the moral of this long story which you've been a total dear to listen to, Enid, is that I can't stop finding a moral to the story no matter how hard I try not to."

To Enid at this moment came a vision of rain. She saw herself in a house with no walls; to keep the weather out, all she had was tissue. And here came the rain from the east, and she tacked up a tissue version of Chip and his exciting new job as a reporter. Here it came from the west, and the tissue was how handsome and intelligent Gary's boys were and how much she loved them. Then the wind shifted, and she *ran* to the north side of the house with such shreds of tissue as Denise afforded: how she'd married too young but was older and wiser now and enjoying great success as a restaurateur and hoping to meet the right young man! And then the rain came blasting up from the south, the tissue disintegrating even as she insisted that Al's impairments were very mild and he'd be fine if he'd just work on his attitude and get his drugs adjusted, and it rained harder and harder, and she was so tired, and all she had was tissue—

"Sylvia?" she said.

"Yes?"

"I need to tell you something. It's about my husband."

Eager, perhaps, to repay the favor of listening, Sylvia nodded with encouragement. But suddenly she reminded Enid of Katharine Hepburn. In Hepburn's eyes there had been a blank unconsciousness of privilege that made a once-poor woman like Enid want to kick her patrician shins with the hardest-toed pumps at her disposal. It would be a mistake, she felt, to confess anything to this woman.

"Yes?" Sylvia prompted.

"Nothing. I'm sorry."

"No, say."

"Nothing, really, just that I *must* get to bed. There's certainly lots to do tomorrow!"

She rose unsteadily and let Sylvia sign for the drinks. They rode an elevator in silence. Too-precipitous intimacy had left in its wake a kind of dirty awkwardness. When Sylvia stepped out at the Upper Deck level, however, Enid followed. She couldn't bear to be seen by Sylvia as a "B" Deck sort of person.

Sylvia stopped by the door of a large outside stateroom. "Where's your room?"

"Just down the hall here," Enid said. But this pretense, she saw, was unsustainable. Tomorrow she would have to pretend she'd been confused.

"Good night, then," Sylvia said. "Thanks again for listening."

She waited with a gentle smile for Enid to move on. But Enid didn't move on. She looked around uncertainly. "I'm sorry. What deck is this?"

"This is the Upper."

"Oh dear, I'm on the wrong deck. I'm sorry."

"Don't be sorry. Do you want me to walk you down?"

"No, I got confused, I see now, this is the Upper Deck and I'm supposed to be on a lower deck. A much lower deck. So, I'm sorry."

She turned away but still she didn't leave. "My husband . . ." She shook her head. "No, our son, actually. We didn't have lunch with him today. That's what I wanted to tell you. He met us at the airport and we were supposed to have lunch with him and his friend, but they just—*left*, I don't understand it, and he never came back, and we still don't know where he went. So, anyway."

"That is peculiar," Sylvia agreed.

"So, I don't want to bore you—"

"No no no, Enid, shame on you."

"I just wanted to straighten that out, and now I'm off to bed, so, and I'm *so* glad we met! There's a lot to do tomorrow. So. We'll see you at breakfast!"

Before Sylvia could stop her, Enid sidled up the corridor (she needed surgery on her hip but imagine leaving Al at home alone while she was in the hospital, just imagine) castigating herself for blundering down a hall she didn't belong on and blurting out shameful nonsense about her son. She veered to a cushioned bench and slumped and did, now, burst into tears. God had given her the imagination to weep for the sad strivers who booked the most el-cheapo "B" Deck inside state-rooms on a luxury cruise ship; but a childhood without money had left her unable to stomach, herself, the $300 per person it cost to jump one category up; and so she wept for herself. She felt that she and Al were the only intelligent people of her generation who had managed not to become rich.

Here was a torture that the Greek inventors of the Feast and the Stone had omitted from their Hades: the Blanket of Self-Deception. A lovely warm blanket as far as it covered the soul in torment, *but it never quite covered everything*. And the nights were getting cold now.

She considered returning to Sylvia's room and fully unburdening herself.

But then, through her tears, she saw a sweet thing beneath the bench beside her.

It was a ten-dollar bill. Folded once. Very sweet.

With a glance up the corridor, she reached down. The texture of engraving was delicious.

Feeling restored, she descended to the "B" Deck. Background music whispered in the lounge, something perky with accordions. She imagined she heard her name bleated, distantly, as she fitted her key card in the lock and pushed on her door.

She encountered resistance and pushed harder.

"Enid," Alfred bleated from the other side.

"Shh, Al, what on earth?"

Life as she knew it ended with her squeeze through the half-open door. Diurnality yielded to a raw continuum of hours. She found Alfred naked with his back to the door on a layer of bedsheets spread on sections of morning paper from St. Jude. Pants and a sport coat and a tie were laid out on his bed, which he'd stripped to the mattress. The excess bedding he'd piled on the other bed. He continued to call her name even after she'd turned on a light and occupied his field of vision. Her immediate aim was to quiet him and get some pajamas on him, but this took time, for he was terribly agitated and not finishing his sentences, not even making his verbs and nouns agree in number and person. He believed that it was morning and he had to bathe and dress, and that the floor by the door was a bathtub, and that the handle was a faucet, and that nothing worked. Still he insisted on doing everything his way, which led to a pushing and pulling, an actual blow to her shoulder. He raged and she wept and abused him. He managed with his madly flopping hands to unbutton his pajama top as fast she could button it. She'd never heard him use the words "t**d" or "c**p," and the fluency with which he used them now illuminated years of prior silent usage in his head. He unmade her bed while she tried to remake his. She begged him to sit still. He cried that it was very late and he was very confused. Even now she couldn't help loving him. Maybe especially now. Maybe she'd known all along, for fifty years, that there was this little boy in him. Maybe all the love she'd given Chipper and Gary, all the love for which in the end she'd got so little in return, had merely been practice for this most demanding of her children. She soothed and berated him and silently cursed his addling medications for an hour or more, and finally he was asleep and her travel clock showed 5:10 and 7:30 and he was running his electric shaver. Not having gone properly under, she felt fine getting up and fine dressing and catastrophically bad going to breakfast, her tongue like a dust mop, her head like something on a spit.

Even for a big ship the sea this morning was poor footing. The re-gurgitative splats outside the Kierkegaard Room were almost rhythmic, a kind of music of chance, and Mrs. Nygren informatively brayed about the evils of caffeine and the quasi-bicamerality of the Storting, and the Söderblads arrived damp from intimate Swedish exertions, and some-how Al proved equal to conversation with Ted Roth. Enid and Sylvia resumed relations stiffly, their emotional muscles pulled and aching from last night's overuse. They talked about the weather. An activities coordinator named Suzy Ghosh came by with orientative tidings and registration forms for the afternoon's outings in Newport, Rhode Is-land. With a bright smile and anticipatory noises Enid signed up for a tour of the town's historic homes, and then watched in dismay as every-one else but the Norwegian social lepers passed along the clipboard without registering. "Sylvia!" she chid, her voice shaking, "you're not going on the tour?" Sylvia glanced at her bespectacled husband, who nodded like McGeorge Bundy green-lighting ground troops for Viet-nam, and for a moment her blue eyes seemed to look inward; appar-ently she had that ability of the enviable, of the non-midwestern, of the moneyed, to assess her desires without regard to social expectations or moral imperatives. "OK, yes, good," she said, "maybe I will." Ordinar-ily Enid would have squirmed at the hint of charity here, but she was waiving the oral exam for gift horses today. She needed all the charity she could get. And so on up the day's steep incline she labored, availing herself of a complimentary half-session of Swedish massage, watching coastal leaves senesce from the Ibsen Promenade, and downing six ibuprofens and a quart of coffee to prepare for her afternoon in charm-ing and historic Newport! In which freshly rain-laundered port of call Alfred announced that his feet hurt too much to venture ashore, and Enid made him promise not to nap or he wouldn't sleep at night, and she laughingly (for how could she admit that it was life and death?) im-plored Ted Roth to keep him awake, and Ted replied that getting the Nygrens off the ship ought to help with that.

Smells of sun-warmed creosote and cold mussels, of boat fuel and football fields and drying kelp, an almost genetic nostalgia for things

maritime and things autumnal, beset Enid as she limped from the gang-
way toward the tour bus. The day was dangerously beautiful. Big gusts
and related clouds and a fierce lion of a sun blew the gaze around, agi-
tating Newport's white clapboard and mown greens, making them un-
seeable straight on. "Folks," the tour guide urged, "just sit back and
drink it in." But that which can be drunk can also drown. Enid had slept
for six of the previous fifty-five hours, and even as Sylvia thanked her
for inviting her along she found she had no energy for touring. The
Astors and the Vanderbilts, their pleasure domes and money: she was
sick of it. Sick of envying, sick of herself. She didn't understand antiques
or architecture, she couldn't draw like Sylvia, she didn't read like Ted,
she had few interests and no expertise. A capacity for love was the only
true thing she'd ever had. And so she tuned out the tour guide and
heeded the October angle of the yellow light, the heart-mangling inten-
sities of the season. In the wind pushing waves across the bay she could
smell night's approach. It was coming at her fast: mystery and pain and
a strange yearning sense of *possibility*, as though heartbreak were a thing
to be sought and moved toward. On the bus between Rosecliff and the
lighthouse, Sylvia offered Enid a cell phone so she could give Chip a
call. Enid declined, since cell phones ate dollars and she thought a person might incur charges simply by touching one, but she made this
statement: "It's been years, Sylvia, since we had a relationship with him.
I don't think he tells us the truth about what he's doing with his life. He
said once he was working for the *Wall Street Journal.* Maybe I misheard
him, but I think that's what he said, but I don't think that's really where
he's working. I don't know what he does for a living really. You must
think it's awful of me to complain about this, when you've had things so
much worse." In Sylvia's insistence that it wasn't awful, not at all, Enid
glimpsed how she might confess an even more shameful thing or two,
and how this exposure to the public elements might, while painful, offer
solace. But like so many phenomena that were beautiful at a distance—
thunderheads, volcanic eruptions, the stars and planets—this alluring
pain proved, at closer range, to be inhuman in its scale. From Newport
the *Gunnar Myrdal* sailed east into sapphire vapors. The ship felt stifling

to Enid after an afternoon's exposure to big skies and the tanker-size playpens of the superwealthy, and though she won sixty more dollars in the Stringbird Room she felt like a lab animal caged with other lever-yanking animals amid the mechanized blink and burble, and bedtime came early, and when Alfred began to stir she was already awake listening to the anxiety bell ringing with such force that her bed frame vibrated and her sheets were abrasive, and here was Alfred turning on lights and shouting, and a next-door neighbor banging on the wall and shouting back, and Alfred stock-still listening with his face twisted in paranoid psychosis and then whispering conspiratorially that he'd seen a t**d run between the beds, and then the making and unmaking of said beds, the application of a diaper, the application of a second diaper to address some hallucinated exigency, and the balking of his nerve-damaged legs, and the bleating of the word "Enid" until he nearly wore it out, and the woman with the rawly abraded name sobbing in the dark with the worst despair and anxiety she'd ever felt until finally—like an overnight traveler arriving at a train station differing from the dismal ones before it only in the morning twilight, the small miracles of restored visibility: a chalky puddle in a gravel parking lot, the steam twisting from a sheet-metal chimney—she was brought to a decision.

On her map of the ship, at the stern end of the "D" Deck, was the universal symbol of aid for those in need. After breakfast she left her husband in conversation with the Roths and made her way to this red cross. The physical thing corresponding to the symbol was a frosted-glass door with three words lettered on in gold leaf. "Alfred" was the first word and "Infirmary" was the third; the sense of the middle word was lost in the shadows cast by "Alfred." She studied it fruitlessly. No. Bel. Nob-Ell. No Bell.

All three words retreated as the door was pulled open by a muscular young man with a name tag pinned to a white lapel: Mather Hibbard, M.D. He had a large, somewhat coarse-skinned face like the face of the Italian-American actor people loved, the one who once starred as an angel and another time as a disco dancer. "Hi, how are you this morning?" he said, showing pearly teeth. Enid followed him through a vestibule into the inner office, where he directed her to the chair by his desk.

"I'm Mrs. Lambert," she said. "Enid Lambert in B11. I was hoping you could help me."

"I hope so, too. What seems to be the problem?"

"I'm having some trouble."

"Mental trouble? Emotional trouble?"

"Well, it's my husband—"

"Excuse me. Stop? Stop?" Dr. Hibbard ducked a little and smiled impishly. "You say *you're* having the trouble?"

His smile was adorability itself. It took hostage that part of Enid that melted at the sight of seal pups and kittens, and it refused to release her until, somewhat grudgingly, she'd smiled back. "My trouble," she said, "is my husband and my children—"

"Sorry again, Edith. Time out?" Dr. Hibbard ducked very low, put his hands on his head, and peered up from between his arms. "We need to be clear: *you* are the one having trouble?"

"No. *I'm* fine. But everyone else in my—"

"Are you anxious?"

"Yes, but—"

"Not sleeping?"

"Exactly. You see, my husband—"

"Edith? You said Edith?"

"Enid. Lambert. L-A-M-B—"

"Enith, what's four times seven with three taken away?"

"What? Oh. Well, twenty-five."

"And, what day of the week is it today?"

"Today is Monday."

"And, what historic Rhode Island resort town did we visit yesterday?"

"Newport."

"And, are you currently taking medication for depression, anxiety, bipolar disorder, schizophrenia, epilepsy, parkinsonism, or any other psychiatric or neurologic disorder?"

"No."

Dr. Hibbard nodded and sat up straight, rolled open a deep drawer in the console behind him, and withdrew a handful of rattling plastic-

and-foil packages. He counted off eight of them and set them on his desk in front of Enid. They had an expensive sheen she didn't like the looks of.

"This is an excellent new medication that will help you enormously," Hibbard recited in a monotone. He winked at her.

"Excuse me?"

"Have we misunderstood each other? I believe you said, 'I am having trouble.' And mentioned anxiety and sleep disturbance?"

"Yes, but what I meant was that my husband—"

"Husband, right. Or wife. It's often the less inhibited spouse that comes to see me. In fact a crippling fear of asking for Aslan is the condition for which Aslan is most commonly indicated. The drug exerts a remarkable blocking effect on 'deep' or 'morbid' shame." Hibbard's smile was like a fresh dent in soft fruit. He had a puppy's lush eyelashes, a head that invited stroking. "This interests you?" he said. "I have your full attention?"

Enid lowered her eyes and wondered if people ever died of sleep loss. Taking her silence for assent, Hibbard continued: "We think of a classic CNS depressant such as alcohol as suppressing 'shame' or 'inhibitions.' But the 'shameful' admission that a person spills under the influence of three martinis doesn't lose its shamefulness in the spilling; witness the deep remorse that follows when the martinis have worn off. What's happening on the molecular level, Edna, when you drink those martinis, is that the ethanol interferes with the reception of excess Factor 28A, i.e., the 'deep' or 'morbid' shame factor. But the 28A is not metabolized or properly reabsorbed at the receptor site. It's kept in temporary unstable storage at the transmitter site. So when the ethanol wears off, the receptor is *flooded* with 28A. Fear of humiliation and the craving for humiliation are closely linked: psychologists know it, Russian novelists know it. And this turns out to be not only 'true' but really *true*. True at the molecular level. Anyway, Aslan's effect on the chemistry of shame is entirely different from a martini's. We're talking complete annihilation of the 28A molecules. Aslan's a fierce predator."

Evidently it was Enid's turn to speak now, but she'd missed a cue somewhere. "Doctor," she said, "I'm sorry, but I haven't slept and I'm a little confused."

The doctor frowned adorably. "Confused? Or *confused*?"

"Excuse me?"

"You've told me you are 'having trouble.' You're carrying one hundred fifty U.S. dollars in cash or traveler's checks. Based on your clinical responses I've diagnosed subclinical dysthymia with no observable dementia, and I'm providing you, free of charge, with eight SampLpaks of Aslan 'Cruiser,' each containing three thirty-milligram capsules, so that you may comfortably enjoy the remainder of your cruise and afterward follow the recommended thirty-twenty-ten step-down program. However, Elinor, I must warn you right away that if you are *confused*, as opposed to merely confused, it may compel me to alter my diagnosis, which may well jeopardize your access to the Aslan."

Here Hibbard raised his eyebrows and whistled a few bars of a melody that his faux-disingenuous smile robbed the tune of.

"I'm not confused," Enid said. "My husband is confused."

"If by 'confused' you mean *confused* then let me express the sincere hope that you intend the Aslan for your own use and not your husband's. Where dementia is present, Aslan is strongly contraindicated. Officially, therefore, I must insist that you use the medication only as directed and only under my strict supervision. In practice, though, I'm not naïve. I understand that such a powerful, relief-bringing medication, a medication not yet available on the mainland, often finds its way into other hands."

Hibbard whistled a few more tuneless bars, a cartoon of someone minding his own business, while studying Enid to be sure he was amusing her.

"My husband gets strange at night, sometimes," she said, averting her eyes. "Very agitated and difficult, and I can't sleep then. I'm dead tired all day and so upset. And there's so much I want to *do*."

"Aslan will help you," Hibbard assured her in a more sober voice. "A lot of travelers consider it a more important investment even than cancellation insurance. With all the money you've paid for the privilege of being here, Enith, you have a right to feel your best at every moment. A quarrel with your spouse, anxiety about a pet you've left behind, a perceived snub where none was intended: you can't afford these bad feelings. Think of it this way. If Aslan prevents you from missing just one prepaid Pleasurelines activity due to your subclinical dysthymia, it has paid for itself, by which I mean that your flat-fee consultation with me, at the end of which you'll receive eight complimentary SampLpaks of thirty-milligram Aslan 'Cruiser,' has paid for itself."

"What is Ashland?"

Someone knocked on the outside door and Hibbard shuddered as if to clear his head. "Edie, Eden, Edna, Enid, excuse me one moment. I'm beginning to understand that you really are *confused* about the state-of-the-global-art psychopharmacology that Pleasurelines is proud to make available to its discerning clientele. I see you need a bit more explanation than most of our cruisers, and if you'll excuse me for just one moment . . ."

Hibbard took eight SampLpaks of Aslan from his console, actually troubled to lock the console and pocket the key, and stepped into the vestibule. Enid heard his murmur and the husky voice of an older man replying, "Twenty-five," "Monday," and "Newport." In less than two minutes the doctor returned, carrying some traveler's checks.

"Is this really all right, what you're doing?" Enid asked. "I mean, legally?"

"Good Q, Enid, but guess what: it's wonderfully legal." He examined one of the checks somewhat absently and then tucked them all into his shirt pocket. "Excellent question, though. Really ace Q. Professional ethics prevent me from selling the drugs I prescribe, so I'm confined to dispensing free samples, which luckily conforms to Pleasurelines' own *tutto è incluso* policy. Regrettably, since Aslan has yet to receive full American regulatory approval, and since most of our cruisers are American, and since Aslan's designer and maker, Farmacopea S.A., therefore has no incentive to provide me with complimentary samples sufficient to the extraordinary demand, I do find it necessary to purchase the complimentary samples in bulk. Hence my consulting fee, which might otherwise strike some as inflated."

"What's the actual cash value of the eight sample packs?" Enid asked.

"Being complimentary and strictly not for resale, they have no actual cash value, Eartha. If you're asking what it costs me to provide this service to you free of charge, the answer is about eighty-eight dollars, U.S."

"Four dollars a pill!"

"Correct. Full dosage for patients of ordinary sensitivity is thirty milligrams per day. In other words, one caplet. Four dollars a day to feel great: most cruisers consider it a bargain."

"And tell me, though, what it is? Ashram?"

"Aslan. Named, I'm told, for a mythical creature in ancient mythology. Mithraism, sun-worshippers, and so forth. I'd be making it up if I told you any more. But my understanding is Aslan was a great benign Lion."

Enid's heart leaped in its cage. She took a SampLpak from the desk and examined the pills through the bubbles of hard plastic. Each tawny-gold caplet was scored twice for ease of splitting and emblazoned with a many-rayed sun—or was it the silhouetted head of a richly maned lion? ASLAN® Cruiser™ was the label.

"What's it do?" she said.

"Absolutely nothing," Hibbard replied, "if you are in perfect mental health. However, let's face it, who is?"

"Oh, and if you're not?"

"Aslan provides state-of-the-art factor regulation. The best medications now approved for American use are like two Marlboros and a rum-and-Coke, by comparison."

"It's an antidepressant?"

"Crude term. 'Personality optimizer' is the phrase I prefer."

"And 'Cruiser'?"

"Aslan optimizes in sixteen chemical dimensions," Hibbard said patiently. "But guess what. Optimal for a person enjoying a luxury cruise isn't optimal for a person functioning in the workplace. The chemical differences are pretty subtle, but if you're capable of fine control, why not offer it? Besides Aslan 'Basic,' Farmacopea sells eight custom blends. Aslan 'Ski,' Aslan 'Hacker,' Aslan 'Performance Ultra,' Aslan 'Teen,' Aslan 'Club Med,' Aslan 'Golden Years,' and I'm forgetting what? Aslan 'California.' Very popular in Europe. The plan is to bring the number of blends up to twenty within two years. Aslan 'Exam Buster,' Aslan 'Courtship,' Aslan 'White Nights,' Aslan 'Reader's Challenge,' Aslan 'Connoisseur Class,' yada yada yada. American regulatory approval would accelerate the process, but I'm not holding my breath. If you're asking what's specific to 'Cruiser'? Mainly that it switches your anxiety to the Off position. Turns that little dial right down to zero. Aslan 'Basic' won't do that, because to function day to day a moderate anxiety level is desirable. I'm on 'Basic' right now, for example, because I'm working."

"How—"

"Less than one hour. That's the glory of it. The action is effectively instantaneous. That's compared with up to four weeks for some of the dinosaurs they're still using Stateside. Go on Zoloft today and you're lucky to feel better a week from Friday."

"No, but how do I refill the prescription at home?"

Hibbard looked at his watch. "What part of the country are you from, Andie?"

"The Midwest. St. Jude."

"OK. Your best bet's going to be Mexican Aslan. Or, if you have friends vacationing in Argentina or Uruguay, you might work something out with them. Obviously, if you like the medication and you want total ease of access, Pleasurelines hopes you'll take another cruise."

Enid pulled a scowl. Dr. Hibbard was very handsome and charismatic, and she liked the idea of a pill that would help her enjoy the cruise and take better care of Alfred, but the doctor seemed to her a trifle glib. Also, her name was Enid. E-N-I-D.

"You're really, really, really sure this will help me?" she said. "You're really super certain this is the best thing for me?"

"I 'guarantee' it," Hibbard said with a wink.

"What does 'optimize' mean, though?" Enid said.

"You'll feel emotionally more resilient," Hibbard said. "More flexible, more confident, happier with yourself. Your anxiety and oversensitivity will disappear, as will any morbid concern about the opinion of others. Anything you're ashamed of now—"

"Yes," Enid said. "Yes."

" 'If it comes up, I'll talk about it; if not, why mention it?' That will be your attitude. The vicious bipolarity of shame, that rapid cycling between confession and concealment—this is a complaint of yours?"

"I think you understand me."

"Chemicals in your brain, Elaine. A strong urge to confess, a strong urge to conceal: What's a strong urge? What else can it be but chemicals? What's memory? A chemical change! Or maybe a structural change, but guess what. Structures are made of proteins! And what are proteins made of? Amines!"

Enid had the dim worry that her church taught otherwise—something about Christ being both a hunk of flesh hanging from a cross and also the Son of God—but questions of doctrine had always seemed to her forbiddingly complex, and Reverend Anderson at their church had such a kindly face and often in his sermons told jokes or quoted *New Yorker* cartoons or secular writers such as John Updike, and he never did anything disturbing like telling the congregation that it was damned, which would have been absurd since everyone at the church was so friendly and nice, and then, too, Alfred had always pooh-poohed her faith and it was easier just to stop believing (if in fact she ever had believed) than to try to beat Alfred in a philosophical argument. Now Enid believed that when you were dead you were really dead, and Dr. Hibbard's account of things was making sense to her.

Nevertheless, being a tough shopper, she said: "I'm just a dumb old midwesterner, so, but changing your personality doesn't sound right to me." She made her face long and sour to be sure her disapproval wasn't overlooked.

"What's wrong with change?" Hibbard said. "Are you happy with the way you feel right now?"

"Well, no, but if I'm a different person after I take this pill, if I'm *different*, that can't be right, and—"

"Edwina, I'm completely sympathetic. We all have irrational attachments to the particular chemical coordinates of our character and temperament. It's a version of the fear of death, right? I don't know what it will be like not to be me anymore. But guess what. If 'I'm' not around to tell the difference, then what do 'I' really care? Being dead's only a problem if you know you're dead, which you never do because you're dead!"

"But it sounds like the drug makes everybody the same."

"Uh-uh. Beep-beep. Wrong. Because guess what: two people can have the same personality and still be individuals. Two people with the same IQ can have completely different knowledge and memories. Right? Two very affectionate people can have completely different objects of affection. Two identically risk-averse individuals may be avoiding completely different risks. Maybe Aslan does make us a little more alike, but guess what, Enid. We're all still individuals."

The doctor unleashed an especially lovable smile, and Enid, who calculated that he was netting $62 per consultation, decided that she'd now received her money's worth of his time and attention, and she did what she'd known she would do since she first laid eyes on the sunny, leonine caplets. She reached into her purse and from the Pleasurelines envelope that held her slot winnings she took a handful of cash and counted out $150.

"All joy of the Lion," Hibbard said with a wink as he slid the stack of SampLpaks across his desk. "Do you need a bag for that?"

With a pounding heart Enid made her way to the bow of the "B" Deck. After the nightmare of the previous day and nights she again had a concrete thing to look forward to; and how sweet the optimism of the person carrying a newly scored drug that she believed would change her head; how universal the craving to escape the givens of the self. No exertion more strenuous than raising hand to mouth, no act more violent than swallowing, no religious feeling, no faith in anything more mystical than cause and effect was required to experience a pill's transformative blessings. *She couldn't wait to take it.* She treaded on air all the way to B11, where happily she saw no sign of Alfred. As if to acknowledge the illicit nature of her mission, she threw the dead bolt on the hall door. Further locked herself inside the bathroom. Raised her eyes to their reflected twins and, on a ceremonial impulse, returned their gaze as she hadn't in months or maybe years. Pushed one golden Aslan through the foil backing of its SampLpak. Placed it on her tongue and swallowed it with water.

For a few minutes she brushed and flossed, a bit of oral housekeeping to pass the time. Then with a shudder of cresting exhaustion she went to her bed to lie and wait.

Golden sunlight fell across the blankets in her windowless room.

He nuzzled her palm with his warm velvet snout. He licked her eyelids with a tongue both sandpapery and slick. His breath was sweet and gingery.

When she came awake the cool halogen lighting in the stateroom wasn't artificial anymore. It was the cool light of sun from behind a momentary cloud.

I've taken the medication, she told herself. I've taken the medication. I've taken the medication.

Her new emotional flexibility received a bold challenge the next morning when she rose at seven and discovered Alfred curled up fast asleep in the shower stall.

"Al, you're lying in the shower," she said. "This is not the place to sleep."

Having awakened him, she began to brush her teeth. Alfred opened undemented eyes and took stock. "Ugh, I am stiff stiff," he said.

"What on earth are you doing in there?" Enid gurgled through a fluoride foam, brushing merrily away.

"Got all turned around in the night," he said. "I had such dreams."

She found that in the arms of Aslan she had new reserves of patience for the wrist-straining wiggle-waggle brushstroke her dentist recommended for the sides of her molars. She watched with low to medium interest as Alfred achieved full uprightness through a multi-stage process of propping, levering, hoisting, bracing, and controlled tipping. A lunatic dhoti of bunched and shredded diapers hung from his loins. "Look at this," he said, shaking his head. "Would you look at this."

"I had the most wonderful night's sleep," she answered.

"And how are our floaters this morning?" roving activities coordinator Suzy Ghosh asked the table in a voice like hair in a shampoo commercial.

"We didn't sink last night, if that's what you mean," said Sylvia Roth.

The Norwegians quickly monopolized Suzy with a complicated inquiry regarding lap swimming in the larger of the *Gunnar Myrdal's* pools.

"Well, well, Signe," Mr. Söderblad remarked to his wife at an indiscreet volume, "this is indeed a great surprise. The Nygrens have a lengthy question for Miss Ghosh this morning."

"Yes, Stig, they do always seem to have a lengthy question, don't they? They are very thorough people, our Nygrens."

Ted Roth spun half a grapefruit like a potter, stripping out its flesh. "The story of carbon," he said, "is the story of the planet. You're familiar with the greenhouse effect?"

"It's triple tax-free," Enid said.

Alfred nodded. "I am familiar with the greenhouse effect."

"You have to actually physically clip the coupons, which sometimes I forget," Enid said.

"The earth was very hot four billion years ago," said Dr. Roth. "The atmosphere was unbreathable. Methane, carbon dioxide, hydrogen sulfide."

"Of course at our age income matters more than growth."

"Nature hadn't learned to break down cellulose. When a tree fell, it lay on the ground and got buried by the next tree that fell. This was the Carboniferous. The earth a lush riot. And in the course of millions and millions of years of trees falling on trees, almost all the carbon got taken from the air and buried underground. And there it stayed until yesterday, geologically speaking."

"Lap swimming, Signe. Do you suppose that this is similar to lap dancing?"

"Some people are disgusting," said Mrs. Nygren.

"What happens to a log that falls today is that funguses and microbes digest it, and all the carbon goes back into the sky. There can never be another Carboniferous. Ever. Because you can't ask Nature to unlearn how to biodegrade cellulose."

"It's called Orfic Midland now," Enid said.

"Mammals came along when the world cooled off. Frost on the pumpkin. Furry things in dens. But now we have a very clever mammal that's taking all the carbon from underground and putting it back into the atmosphere."

"I think we own some Orfic Midland ourselves," Sylvia said.

"As a matter of fact," Per Nygren said, "we, too, own Orfic Midland."

"Per would know," said Mrs. Nygren.

"I daresay he would," said Mr. Söderblad.

"Once we burn up all the coal and oil and gas," said Dr. Roth, "we'll have an antique atmosphere. A hot, nasty atmosphere that no one's seen for three hundred million years. Once we've let the carbon genie out of its lithic bottle."

"Norway has superb retirement benefits, hm, but I also supplement my national coverage with a private fund. Per checks the price of each stock in the fund every morning. There are quite a number of American stocks. How many, Per?"

"Forty-six at present," Per Nygren said. "If I am not mistaken, 'Orfic' is an acronym for the Oak Ridge Fiduciary Investment Corporation. The stock has maintained its value quite well and pays a handsome dividend."

"Fascinating," said Mr. Söderblad. "Where is my coffee?"

"But, Stig, do you know," said Signe Söderblad, "I am quite sure we also have this stock, Orfic Midland."

"We own a great many stocks. I can't remember every name. At the same time, too, the print in the newspaper is very tiny."

"The moral of the story is don't recycle plastic. Send your plastic to a landfill. Get that carbon underground."

"If it had been up to Al, we'd still have every penny in passbook savings."

"Bury it, bury it. Stopper the genie in the bottle."

"I happen to have an eye condition that makes it painful for me to read," said Mr. Söderblad.

"Oh, really?" said Mrs. Nygren acidly. "What is the medical name of this condition?"

"I like a cool autumn day," said Dr. Roth.

"Then again," said Mrs. Nygren, "I suppose that to learn the condition's name would itself necessitate painful reading."

"This is a small planet."

"There is *lazy* eye, of course, but to have two *lazy* eyes at once—"

"That is not really possible," said Mr. Nygren. "The 'lazy eye' syndrome, or amblyopia, is a condition in which one eye assumes the work of the other. Therefore, if one eye is lazy, the other is by definition—"

"Per, shut up," said Mrs. Nygren.

"Inga!"

"Waiter, refill."

"Imagine the Uzbek upper middle class," said Dr. Roth. "One of the families had the same Ford Stomper we have. In fact the only difference between our upper middle class and their upper middle class was that none of them, not even the richest family in town, had indoor plumbing."

"I am aware," said Mr. Söderblad, "that as a nonreader I am morally inferior to all Norwegians. I accept this."

"Flies like around something four days dead. Bucket of ashes that you sprinkle in the hole. Even the little way you can see down into it is farther than you want to. And a glittering Ford Stomper parked in their driveway. And they're videotaping us videotaping them."

"At the same time, in spite of my disability, I do manage to enjoy a pleasure or two in life."

"How empty, though, Stig, our pleasures must be," said Signe Söderblad, "compared to those of the Nygrens."

"Yes, they do seem to experience the deep and lasting pleasures of the mind. At the same time, Signe, this is a very flattering dress you are wearing this morning. Even Mr. Nygren has been admiring this dress, in spite of the deep and lasting pleasures he finds elsewhere."

"Per, come along," said Mrs. Nygren. "We are being insulted."

"Stig, did you hear? The Nygrens have been insulted and are leaving us."

"It is a great pity. They are such fun to be with."

"Our children are all easterners now," Enid said. "Nobody seems to like the Midwest anymore."

"Biding my time here, fella," said a familiar voice.

"The cashier at the Du Pont executive dining room was an Uzbek girl. I've probably seen Uzbeks at the IKEA store in Plymouth Meeting. These aren't extraterrestrials we're talking about. Uzbeks wear bifocals. They fly on planes."

"We're stopping in Philadelphia on the way home so we can eat at her new restaurant. It's called the Generator?"

"Enid, my gosh, that's *her* place? Ted and I were there two weeks ago."

"It's a small world," Enid said.

"We had a terrific dinner. Really memorably good."

"So in effect we've spent six thousand dollars to be reminded of what a pit toilet smells like."

"I'll never forget it," Alfred said.

"And are grateful for that pit toilet! In terms of the actual benefits of foreign travel. In terms of what TV and books can't give you. In terms of what you can only experience firsthand. Take away the pit toilet and we'd feel like we'd wasted six thousand dollars."

"Shall we go rot our brains on the Sun Deck?"

"Oh, Stig, let's. I am intellectually exhausted."

"Thank God for poverty. Thank God for driving on the left side of the road. Thank God for Babel. Thank God for strange voltages and oddly shaped plugs." Dr. Roth lowered his glasses and peered over them, observing the Swedish exodus. "I note in passing that every dress that woman owns is designed for quick removal."

"I've never seen Ted so eager to get to breakfast," Sylvia said. "And lunch. And dinner."

"Stunning northern scenery," Roth said. "Isn't that what we're here for?"

Alfred lowered his eyes uncomfortably. A little fishbone of prudery was stuck in Enid's throat as well. "Do you think he really has an eye problem?" she managed to say.

"His eye is excellent in at least one respect."

"Ted, though, stop."

"That the Swedish bombshell is a stale cliché is itself a stale cliché."

"Please stop."

The retired vice president of Compliance pushed his glasses back up his nose and turned to Alfred. "I wonder if we're depressed because there's no frontier anymore. Because we can't pretend anymore there's a place no one's been. I wonder if aggregate depression is on the rise, worldwide."

"I feel so wonderful this morning. Slept so well."

"Lab rats become listless in overcrowded conditions."

"You do, Enid, seem transformed. Just tell me this isn't related to that doctor on the 'D' Deck. I hear stories."

"Stories?"

"The so-called cyber frontier," said Dr. Roth, "but where's the wilderness?"

"A drug called Aslan," Sylvia said.

"Aslan?"

"The so-called space frontier," said Dr. Roth, "but I like this earth. It's a good planet. There's a scarcity of atmospheric cyanide, sulfuric acid, ammonia. Which is a boast by no means every planet can make."

"Grandmother's little helper, I think they call it."

"But even in your big quiet house you feel crowded if there's a big quiet house at the antipodes and every point in between."

"All I ask is a little privacy," Alfred said.

"No beach between Greenland and the Falklands that isn't threatened with development. No acre uncleared."

"Oh dear, what time is it?" Enid said. "We don't want to miss that lecture."

"Sylvia's different. She likes the hubbub at the docks."

"I do like the hubbub," Sylvia said.

"Gangways, portholes, stevedores. She likes the blast of the horn. To me this is a floating theme park."

"You have to put up with a certain amount of fantasy," Alfred said. "It can't be helped."

"Uzbekistan didn't agree with my stomach," Sylvia said.

"I like all the waste up here," said Dr. Roth. "Good to see such vast useless mileage."

"You romanticize poverty."

"I beg your pardon?"

"We've traveled in Bulgaria," Alfred said. "I don't know about Uzbekistan, but we've traveled in China. Everything, as far as you could see from the railroad—if it were up to me, I'd tear it all down. Tear it down and start over. The houses don't have to be pretty, just make them solid. Get the plumbing indoors. A good concrete wall and a roof that doesn't leak—that's what these people need. Sewers. Look at the Germans, what they did to rebuild. There's a model of a country."

"Wouldn't want to eat a fish out of the Rhine, though. If I could even find a fish in it."

"That's a lot of environmentalist nonsense."

"Alfred, you're too smart a man to call it nonsense."

"I am in need of a bathroom."

"Al, when you're done, why don't you take a book outside and read for a while. Sylvia and I are going to the investment lecture. You just sit. In the sun. And relax relax relax."

He had good days and bad days. It was as if when he lay in bed for a night certain humors pooled in the right or wrong places, like marinade around a flank steak, and in the morning his nerve endings either had enough of what they needed or did not; as if his mental clarity might depend on something as simple as whether he'd lain on his side or on his back the night before; or as if, more disturbingly, he were a damaged transistor radio which after a vigorous shaking might function loud and clear or spew nothing but a static laced with unconnected phrases, the odd strain of music.

Still, even the worst morning was better than the best night. In the morning every process *quickened*, speeding his meds to their destinations: the canary-yellow spansule for incontinence, the small pink

Tums-like thing for the shakes, the white oblong to discourage nausea, the wan blue tablet to squelch hallucinations from the small pink Tums-like thing. In the morning the blood was crowded with commuters, the glucose peons, lactic and ureic sanitation workers, hemoglobinous de-liverymen carrying loads of freshly brewed oxygen in their dented vans, the stern foremen like insulin, the enzymic middle managers and exec-utive epinephrine, leukocyte cops and EMS workers, expensive consul-tants arriving in their pink and white and canary-yellow limos, everyone riding the aortal elevator and dispersing through the arteries. Before noon the rate of worker accidents was tiny. The world was newborn.

He had energy. From the Kierkegaard Room he lopingly careened through a red-carpeted hallway that had previously vouchsafed him a comfort station but this morning seemed all business, no M or W in sight, just salons and boutiques and the Ingmar Bergman Cinema. The problem was that his nervous system could no longer be relied on for an accurate assessment of his need to go. At night his solution was to wear protection. By day his solution was to visit a bathroom hourly and al-ways to carry his old black raincoat in case he had an accident to hide. The raincoat had the added virtue of offending Enid's romantic sensi-bilities, and his hourly stops the added virtue of lending structure to his life. Simply holding things together—simply keeping the ocean of night terrors from breaching the last bulkhead—was his ambition now.

Throngs of women were streaming toward the Longstocking Ball-room. A strong eddy in their current swept Alfred into a hallway lined with the staterooms of onboard lecturers and entertainers. At the end of this hall a men's room beckoned.

An officer in epaulets was using one of the two urinals. Afraid of failing to perform under scrutiny, Alfred entered a stall and slid the bolt and found himself face to face with an ordure-strafed toilet which fortu-nately said nothing, merely stank. He exited and tried the next stall, but here something did scurry on the floor—a mobile turd, ducking for cover—and he didn't dare enter. In the meantime the officer had flushed, and as he turned from his urinal Alfred recognized his blue cheeks and rose-tinted eyeglasses, his pudenda-pink lips. Hanging from his still-open zipper was twelve inches or more of limp tan tubing. A yellow grin opened between his blue cheeks. He said, "I left a little treasure in your bed, Mr. Lambert. To replace the one I took."

Alfred reeled out of the bathroom and fled up a staircase, higher and higher, up seven flights to the open air of the Sports Deck. Here he found a bench in hot sunlight. From the pocket of his raincoat he took a map of Canada's maritime provinces and tried to fix himself within a grid, identify some landmarks.

Three old men in Gore-Tex parkas were standing at the rail. Their voices were inaudible one moment and fully distinct the next. Apparently the wind had pockets in its fluid mass, small spaces of stillness through which a sentence or two might find a way.

"Here's a fellow with a map," a man said. He came over to Alfred looking happy in the way of all men in the world except Alfred. "Excuse me, sir. What do you reckon we're looking at up here on the left?"

"That is the Gaspé Peninsula," Alfred answered firmly. "There should be a large town coming up around the bend."

"Thank you very much."

The man returned to his companions. As if the ship's location mattered to them greatly, as if only the quest for this information had brought them to the Sports Deck to begin with, all three immediately departed for a lower deck, leaving Alfred alone on top of the world.

The protective sky was thinner in this country of northern water. Clouds ran in packs resembling furrows in a field, gliding along beneath the sky's enclosing dome, which was noticeably low. One approached Ultima Thule here. Green objects had red coronas. In the forests that stretched west to the limit of visibility, as in the purposeless rushing of the clouds, as in the air's supernal clarity, there was nothing local.

Odd to glimpse infinity precisely in a finite curve, eternity precisely in the seasonal.

Alfred had recognized the blue-cheeked man in the bathroom as the man from Signals, as betrayal personified. But the blue-cheeked man from Signals couldn't possibly afford a luxury cruise, and this worried him. The blue-cheeked man came from the distant past but was walking and talking in the present, and the turd was a creature from the night but was afoot in broad daylight, and this worried him a lot.

According to Ted Roth, holes in the ozone layer started at the poles. It was during the long Arctic night that the earth's shell first weakened, but once the shell was punctured the damage spread outward, encroaching even on the sunny tropics—even the equator—and soon no spot on the globe was safe.

Meanwhile an observatory in the far nether regions had sent out a feeble signal, an ambiguous message.

Alfred received the signal and wondered what to do about it. He felt shy of bathrooms now, but he couldn't very well drop his trousers out here in the open. The three men might return at any moment.

Beyond a protective railing to his right was a collection of thickly painted planes and cylinders, two navigational spheres, an inverted cone. Since he was not afraid of heights, nothing prevented him from ignoring the strongly worded warning in four languages, squeezing past the railing, and stepping out onto the sandpapery metal surface to seek, as it were, a tree to pee behind. He was high above everything and invisible.

But too late.

Both legs of his trousers were very soaked, the left leg nearly to his ankle. Warm-cold wetness all over everything.

And where a town should have appeared on the coast, the land instead was dropping away. Gray waves marched across strange waters, and the tremor of the engines became more labored, less easy to ignore. The ship either had not reached the Gaspé Peninsula or had already passed it. The data he'd transmitted to the men in parkas was faulty. He was lost.

And from the deck immediately below him came a windborne giggle. It came again, a trilling squeal, a northern lark.

He edged away from the spheres and cylinders and leaned out past the outer railing. A few yards farther astern was a small "Nordic" sunbathing area, sequestered behind cedar fencing, and a man standing where no passenger was permitted to stand could see right over the fencing and behold Signe Söderblad, her chill-stippled arms and thighs and belly, the plump twin cloudberries into which a suddenly gray winter sky had drawn her nipples, the quaking ginger fur between her legs.

The day world floated on the night world and the night world tried to swamp the day world and he worked and worked to keep the day world watertight. But there had been a grievous breach.

Came another cloud then, larger, denser, that turned the gulf below it to a greenish black. Ship and shadow in collision.

And shame and despair—

Or was it the wind catching the sail of his raincoat?

Or was it the ship's pitching?

Or the tremor in his legs?

Or the corresponding tremor of the engines?

Or a fainting spell?

Or vertigo's standing invitation?

Or the relative warmth of open water's invitation to someone soaked and freezing in the wind?

Or was he leaning, deliberately, to glimpse again the gingery mons?

"How fitting it is," said internationally noted investment counselor Jim Crolius, "to be talking money on a Nordic Pleasurelines Luxury Fall Color Cruise. Folks, it's a beautiful sunny morning, isn't it?"

Crolius was speaking from a lectern beside an easel on which the title of his talk—"Surviving the Corrections"—was written in purple ink. His question brought murmurs of assent from the first few rows in front of him, the people who'd arrived early for good seats. Someone up there even said: "Yes, *Jim!*"

Enid felt ever so much better this morning, but a few atmospheric disturbances still lingered in her head, for example a squall now consisting of (a) resentment of the women who'd come to the Longstocking Ballroom absurdly early, as if the potential lucrativeness of Jim Crolius's advice might somehow decline with one's distance from him, and (b) particular resentment of the pushy New York kind of woman who elbowed in ahead of everyone to establish a first-name relationship with a lecturer (she was sure that Jim Crolius could see right through their presumption and hollow flattery, but he might be too polite to ignore them and focus on less pushy and more deserving midwestern women such as Enid), and (c) intense irritation with Alfred for having stopped in a bathroom *twice* on the way to breakfast, which had prevented her from leaving the Kierkegaard Room early and securing a good front-row seat herself.

Almost as soon as the squall had gathered it disappeared, however, and the sun shone strongly again.

"Well, I hate to break it to you folks in the back," Jim Crolius was saying, "but from where *I* stand, up here by the windows, I can see some clouds on the horizon. Those could be friendly little white clouds. Or they could be dark rain clouds. Appearances can be deceiving! From where I stand I may think I see a safe course ahead, but I'm no expert. I may be piloting the ship straight into a reef. Now, you wouldn't want to sail on a ship without a captain, would you? A captain who's got all the maps and gadgets, all the bells and whistles, the whole nine yards. Right? You got your radar, you got your sonar, you got your Global Positioning System," Jim Crolius was counting off each instrument on his fingers. "You got your satellites up in outer space! It's all pretty technical. But somebody's got to have that information, or we could all be in big trouble. Right? This is a *deep* ocean. This is your *life*. So what I'm saying is you may not want to master all that technical stuff personally, all the bells and whistles, the whole nine yards. But you better hope you've got a good captain when you go cruising the high seas of high finance."

There was applause from the front rows.

"He must literally think we're eight years old," Sylvia Roth whispered to Enid.

"This is just his introduction," Enid whispered back.

"Now, another way this is fitting," Jim Crolius continued, "is that we're here to see the changing leaves. The year has its rhythms—winter, spring, summer, fall. The whole thing is cyclical. You got your upswings in the spring, you got your downturns in the fall. It's just like the market. Cyclical business, right? You can have a bull market for five, ten, even fifteen years. We've seen it in our lifetime. But we've also seen corrections. I may look like I'm just a kid, but I've even seen a genuine market *break* in my lifetime. Scary stuff. Cyclical business. People, we've got a lot of green out there right now. It's been a long, glorious summer. In fact, let me see a show of hands here, how many of you are paying for this cruise, either entirely or in part, on the strength of your investments?"

Forest of raised hands.

Jim Crolius nodded with satisfaction. "Well, folks, I hate to break it to you, but those leaves are starting to turn. No matter how green things are for you right now, it's not going to survive the winter. Of course, every year is different, every cycle's different. You never know exactly when that green is going to turn. But we're here, every one of us, because we're foresighted people. Every person in this room has proved to me she's a smart investor, just by virtue of being here. You know why? *Because it was still summer when you left home.* Every person in this room had the foresight to know that something was going to change on this cruise. And the question we all have—I'm speaking in metaphors here—the question is: Will all that glorious green out there turn to glorious gold? Or will it all just wither on the branch in the winter of our discontent?"

The Longstocking Ballroom was electric with excitement now. There were murmurs of "Marvelous! Marvelous!"

"More matter and less art," Sylvia Roth said dryly.

Death, Enid thought. He was talking about death. And all the people clapping were so *old*.

But where was the sting of this realization? Aslan had taken it away.

Jim Crolius turned now to the easel and flipped over the first of its big newsprint pages. The second page was headed WHEN THE CLIMATE CHANGES, and the categories—Funds, Bonds, Common Stock, etc.— drew a gasp from the front row out of all proportion to the informational content. For an instant it seemed to Enid as if Jim Crolius were doing a technical market analysis of the kind that her broker in St. Jude had told her never to pay attention to. Discounting the minimal effects of wind drag at low velocities, something "plummeting" (a thing of value "plunging" in a "free fall") experienced an acceleration due to gravity of 32 feet per second squared, and, acceleration being the second-order derivative of distance, the analyst could integrate once over the distance the object had fallen (roughly 30 feet) to calculate its velocity (42 feet per second) as it passed the center of a window 8 feet tall, and assuming a 6-foot-long object, and also assuming for simplicity's sake a constant velocity over the interval, derive a figure of approximately four-tenths of a second of full or partial visibility. Four-tenths of a second wasn't much. If you were looking aside and mentally adding up the hours until the execution of a young killer, all that registered was something dark flashing by. But if you happened to be gazing directly at the window in question and you happened as well to be feeling unprecedentedly calm, four-tenths of a second was more than enough time to identify the falling object as your husband of forty-seven years; to notice that he was wearing the *awful* black raincoat which had lost its shape and should never have been worn in public but which he'd willfully packed for the trip and willfully carried with him everywhere; to experience not only the certainty that something terrible had happened but also a peculiar sense of intrusion, as if you were witnessing an event that nature had never intended you to witness, like the impact of a meteorite or the copulation of whales; and even to observe the expression on your husband's face, to register its almost youthful beauty, its peculiar serenity, for who could have anticipated the grace with which the raging man would fall?

He was remembering the nights he'd sat upstairs with one or both of his boys or with his girl in the crook of his arm, their damp bath-smelling heads hard against his ribs as he read aloud to them from *Black Beauty* or *The Chronicles of Narnia*. How his voice alone, its palpable resonance, had made them drowsy. These were evenings, and there were hundreds of them, maybe thousands, when nothing traumatic enough to leave a scar had befallen the nuclear unit. Evenings of plain vanilla closeness in his black leather chair; sweet evenings of doubt between the nights of bleak certainty. They came to him now, these forgotten counterexamples, because in the end, when you were falling into water, there was no solid thing to reach for but your children.

THE GENERATOR

ROBIN PASSAFARO was a Philadelphian from a family of troublemakers and true believers. Robin's grandfather and her uncles Jimmy and Johnny were all unreconstructed Teamsters; the grandfather, Fazio, had served under the Teamsters boss Frank Fitzsimmons as a national vice president and had run the biggest Philly local and mishandled the dues of its 3,200 members for twenty years. Fazio had survived two racketeering indictments, a coronary, a laryngectomy, and nine months of chemotherapy before retiring to Sea Isle City on the Jersey coast, where he still hobbled out onto a pier every morning and baited his crab traps with raw chicken.

Uncle Johnny, Fazio's eldest son, got along well on two kinds of disability ("chronic and severe lumbar pain," the claim forms stated), his seasonal cash-only house-painting business, and his luck or talent as an online day trader. Johnny lived near Veterans Stadium with his wife and their youngest daughter in a vinyl-sided row house that they'd expanded until it filled their tiny lot, from the sidewalk to the rear property line; a flower garden and a square of Astroturf were on the roof.

Uncle Jimmy ("Baby Jimmy") was a bachelor and the site manager for IBT Document Storage, a cinder-block mausoleum that the International Brotherhood of Teamsters, in more optimistic times, had built on the industrial banks of the Delaware and later, because only three (3) loyal Teamsters had ever opted for interment in its thousand fireproof vaults, converted into a long-term repository for corporate and legal paper. Baby Jimmy was famous in local NA circles for having hooked himself on methadone without ever trying heroin.

Robin's father, Nick, was Fazio's middle child and the only Passafaro of his generation who never got with the Teamster program. Nick was the family brain and a committed Socialist; the Teamsters with their Nixonian and Sinatran allegiances were anathema to him. Nick married an Irish girl and pointedly moved out to racially integrated Mount Airy and embarked on a career of teaching high-school social studies in the city district, daring principals to fire him for his ebullient Trotskyism.

Nick and his wife, Colleen, had been told that they were infertile. They adopted a year-old boy, Billy, a few months before Colleen became pregnant with Robin—the first of three daughters. Robin was a teenager before she learned that Billy was adopted, but her earliest emotional memories from childhood, she told Denise, were of feeling helplessly *privileged.*

There was probably a good diagnostic label for Billy, corresponding to abnormal EEG waveforms or troubled red nodules or black lacunae on his CAT scan and to hypothetical causes like severe neglect or cerebral trauma in his preadoptive infancy; but his sisters, Robin especially, knew him simply as a terror. Billy soon figured out that no matter how cruel he was to Robin, she would always blame herself. If she lent him five dollars, he made fun of her for thinking he would pay it back. (If she complained to her father, Nick just gave her another five.) Billy chased her with the grasshoppers whose legs he'd clipped the ends off, the frogs he'd bathed in Clorox, and he told her—he meant it as a joke—"I hurt them because of you." He put turds of mud in Robin's dolls' underpants. He called her Cow Clueless and Robin No-Breast. He stuck her forearm with a pencil and broke the lead off deep. The day after a new bicycle of hers disappeared from the garage, he turned up with a good pair of black roller skates that he said he'd found on Germantown Avenue and that he used to rocket around the neighborhood in the months while she was waiting for another bike.

Their father, Nick, had eyes for every injustice in the First and Third Worlds except those of which Billy was the author. By the time Robin started high school, Billy's delinquency had driven her to padlock her closet, stuff Kleenex in the keyhole of her bedroom door, and sleep with her wallet beneath her pillow; but even these measures she took more sadly than angrily. She had little to complain of and she knew it. She and her sisters were poor and happy in their big falling-down house on Phil-Ellena Street, and she went to a good Quaker high school and then to an excellent Quaker college, both on full scholarships, and she married her college boyfriend and had two baby girls, while Billy was going down the tubes.

Nick had taught Billy to love politics, and Billy had repaid him by taunting him with the epithet *bourgeois liberal, bourgeois liberal*. When this failed to incense Nick sufficiently, Billy befriended the other Passafaros, who were predisposed to love any traitor in the family traitor's family. After Billy was arrested on his second felony charge and Colleen threw him out of the house, his Teamster relatives gave him something of a hero's welcome. It was a while before he fully wore it out.

He lived for a year with his Uncle Jimmy, who well into his fifties felt happiest among like-minded adolescents with whom he could share his large collections of guns and knives, Chasey Lain videos, and Warlords III and Dungeonmaster paraphernalia. But Jimmy also worshipped Elvis Presley at a shrine in one corner of his bedroom, and Billy, who never got it through his head that Jimmy wasn't joking about Elvis, finally desecrated the shrine in some grievous and irreversible manner that Jimmy afterward refused to talk about, and was put out on the street.

From there Billy drifted into the radical underground scene in Philly—that Red Crescent of bomb-makers and Xeroxers and zinesters and punks and Bakuninites and minor vegan prophets and orgoneblanket manufacturers and women named Afrika and amateur Engels biographers and Red Army Brigade émigrés that stretched from Fishtown and Kensington in the north, over through Germantown and West Philly (where Mayor Goode had firebombed the good citizens of MOVE), and down into blighted Point Breeze. It was an odd Philly Phact that a non-negligible fraction of the city's crimes were committed with political consciousness. After Frank Rizzo's first mayoralty nobody could pretend that the city police force was clean or impartial; and since, in the estimation of Red Crescent denizens, all cops were murderers or, at the very least, ipso facto accessories to murder (witness MOVE!), any crime of violence or wealth redistribution to which a cop might object could be justified as a legitimate action in a long-running dirty war. This logic by and large eluded local judges, however. The young anarchist Billy Passafaro over the years drew ever more severe sentences for his crimes—probation, community service, experimental penal boot camp, and finally the state pen at Graterford. Robin and her father often argued about the justice of these sentences, Nick stroking his Lenin-like goatee and asserting that, although not a violent man himself, he was not opposed to violence in the service of ideals, Robin challenging him to specify what political ideal, exactly, Billy had advanced by stabbing a Penn undergrad with a broken pool cue.

The year before Denise met Robin, Billy was released on parole and attended a ribbon-cutting ceremony for a Community Computing Center in the poor near-north neighborhood of Nicetown. One of the many policy coups of Mayor Goode's popular two-term successor was the commercial exploitation of the city's public schools. The mayor had shrewdly cast the deplorable neglect of the schools as a business opportunity ("Act Fast, Be Part of Our Message of Hope," his letters said), and the N—— Corporation had responded to his pitch by assuming responsibility for the city's severely underfunded school athletic programs. Now the mayor had midwifed a similar arrangement with the W—— Corporation, which was donating to the city of Philadelphia sufficient units of its famous Global Desktop to "empower" every classroom in the city, plus five Community Computing Centers in blighted northern and western neighborhoods. The agreement granted W—— the exclusive right to employ for promotional and advertising purposes all classroom activities within the school district of Philadelphia, including but not limited to all Global Desktop applications. Critics of the mayor alternately denounced the "sellout" and complained that W—— was donating its slow and crash-prone Version 4.0 Desktops to the schools and its nearly useless Version 3.2 technology to the Community Computing Centers. But the mood in Nicetown on that September afternoon was buoyant. The mayor and W——'s twenty-eight-year-old corporate-image vice president, Rick Flamburg, joined hands on big shears to cut ribbon. Local politicians of color said *children* and *tomorrow*. They said *digital* and *democracy* and *history*.

Outside the white tent, the usual crowd of anarchists, eyed warily by a police detail that was later criticized as having been too small, openly carried banners and placards and privately, in the pockets of their cargo pants, carried powerful bar magnets with which they hoped, amid the cake-eating and punch-drinking and confusion, to erase much data from the center's new Global Desktops. Their banners said REFUSE IT and COMPUTERS ARE THE OPPOSITE OF REVOLUTION and THIS HEAVEN GIVES ME MIGRAINE. Billy Passafaro, neatly shaved and wearing a short-sleeve white button-down, carried a four-foot length of two-by-four on which he'd written WELCOME TO PHILADELPHIA!! When the official ceremonies ended and the scene became more appealingly anarchic, Billy edged into the crowd, smiling and holding aloft his message of goodwill, until he was close enough to the dignitaries that he could swing the two-by-four like a baseball bat and break Rick Flamburg's skull. Three further blows demolished Flamburg's nose, jaw, collarbone, and most of his teeth before the mayor's bodyguard tackled Billy and a dozen cops piled on.

Billy was lucky the tent was too crowded for the cops to shoot him. He was also lucky, given the obvious premeditation of his crime and the politically awkward shortage of white inmates on death row, that Rick Flamburg didn't die. (Less clear was whether Flamburg himself, an unmarried Dartmouth grad whom the attack left palsied, disfigured, slurred of speech, blind in one eye, and prone to incapacitating headaches, felt lucky about this.) Billy was indicted for attempted murder, first-degree assault, and assault with a deadly weapon. He categorically rejected any plea agreement and chose to represent himself in court, dismissing as "accommodationist" both his court-appointed counsel and the old Teamster attorney who offered to bill his family fifty an hour.

To the surprise of nearly everyone but Robin, who had never doubted her brother's intelligence, Billy mounted an articulate self-defense. He argued that the mayor's "sale" of the children of Philadelphia into the "technoslavery" of the W—— Corporation represented a "clear and present public danger" to which he'd been justified in responding violently. He denounced the "unholy connivance" of American business and American government. He compared himself to the Minutemen at Lexington and Concord. When Robin, much later, showed Denise the trial transcript, Denise imagined bringing Billy and her brother Chip together over dinner and listening while they compared notes about "the bureaucracy," but this dinner would have to wait until Billy had served seventy percent of his twelve-to-eighteen-year sentence at Graterford.

Nick Passafaro had taken a leave of absence and loyally attended his son's trial. Nick went on TV and said everything you'd expect from an old red: "Once a day the victim's black, and there's silence; once a year the victim's white, and there's an outcry," and "My son will pay dearly for his crime, but W—— will never pay for its crimes," and "The Rick Flamburgs of the world have made billions selling phony violence to America's children." Nick concurred in most of Billy's courtroom arguments and was proud of his performance, but after the photos of Flamburg's injuries were introduced in court, he began to lose his grip. The deep V-shaped indentations in Flamburg's cranium, nose, jaw, and clavicle spoke to a savagery of exertion, a madness, that didn't square well with idealism. Nick stopped sleeping as the trial progressed. He stopped shaving and lost his appetite. At Colleen's insistence, he saw a psychiatrist and came home with medications, but even then he woke her in the night. He shouted, "I won't apologize!" He shouted, "It's a war!" Eventually his dosages were upped, and in April the school district retired him.

Because Rick Flamburg had worked for the W—— Corporation, Robin felt responsible for all of this.

Robin had become the Passafaro ambassador to Rick Flamburg's family, showing up at the hospital until Flamburg's parents had spent their anger and suspicion and recognized that she was not her brother's keeper. She sat by Flamburg and read *Sports Illustrated* to him. She walked alongside his walker as he shuffled up a corridor. On the night of the second of his reconstructive surgeries, she took his parents to dinner and listened to their (frankly boring) stories about their son. She told them how quick Billy had been, how in fourth grade he'd already had the spelling and handwriting skills to forge a plausible note excusing him from school, and what a fund of dirty jokes and important reproductive information he was, and how it felt to be a smart girl and see your equally smart brother make himself more stupid by the year, as if specifically to avoid becoming a person like you: how mysterious it all was and how sorry she felt about what he'd done to their son.

On the eve of Billy's trial, Robin invited her mother to go to church. Colleen had been confirmed as a Catholic, but she hadn't taken communion in forty years; Robin's own church experience was confined to weddings and funerals. Nevertheless, on three consecutive Sundays, Colleen agreed to be picked up in Mount Airy and driven to her childhood parish, St. Dymphna's, in North Philly. Leaving the sanctuary on the third Sunday, Colleen told Robin, in the faint brogue she'd retained all her life, "That'll do for me, thanks." After that, Robin went by herself to mass at St. Dymphna's and, by and by, to confirmation classes.

Robin could afford the time for these good works and acts of devotion because of the W—— Corporation. Her husband, Brian Callahan, was the son of a local small-time manufacturer and had grown up comfortably in Bala-Cynwyd, playing lacrosse and developing sophisticated tastes in expectation of inheriting his father's small specialty-chemical company. (Callahan *père* in his youth had profitably developed a compound that could be thrown into Bessemer converters and patch their cracks and ulcers while their ceramic walls were still hot.) Brian had married the prettiest girl in his college class (in his opinion, this was Robin), and soon after graduation he'd become president of High Temp Products. The company was housed in a yellow-brick building in an industrial park near the Tacony-Palmyra Bridge; by coincidence, its nearest living commercial neighbor was IBT Document Storage. The cerebral drain of running High Temp Products being minimal, Brian spent his executive afternoons noodling around with computer code and Fourier analysis, blasting on his presidential boom box certain cult California bands to which he was partial (Fibulator, Thinking Fellers Union, the Minutemen, the Nomatics), and writing a piece of software that in the fullness of time he quietly patented, quietly found a VC backer for, and one day, on the advice of this backer, quietly sold to the W—— Corporation for $19,500,000.

Brian's product, called Eigenmelody, processed any piece of recorded music into an eigenvector that distilled the song's tonal and melodic essence into discrete, manipulable coordinates. An Eigen-melody user could select a favorite Moby song, and Eigenmelody would spectroanalyze her choice, search a recorded-music database for songs with similar eigenvectors, and produce a list of kindred sounds that the user might otherwise have never found: the Au Pairs, Laura Nyro, Thomas Mapfumo, Pokrovsky's wailing version of *Les Noces*. Eigen-melody was parlor game, musicological tool, and record-sales-enhancer rolled into one. Brian had worked enough kinks out of it that the behe-moth of W——, belatedly scrambling for a piece of the online music-distribution action, came running to him with a big wad of monopoly money in its outstretched hand.

It was characteristic of Brian, who hadn't mentioned the impending sale to Robin, that on the evening of the day the deal went through he didn't breathe a word of it until the girls were in bed in their modest yuppie row house near the Art Museum and he and she were watching a *Nova* show about sunspots.

"Oh, by the way," Brian said, "neither of us ever has to work again."

It was characteristic of Robin—her excitability—that on receiving this news she laughed until she got the hiccups.

Alas, there was justice in Billy's old epithet for Robin: Cow Clue-less. Robin was under the impression that she already had a good life with Brian. She lived in her town house, grew vegetables and herbs in her little back yard, taught "language arts" to ten- and eleven-year-olds at an experimental school in West Philly, sent her daughter Sinéad to an excellent private elementary school on Fairmount Avenue and her daughter Erin to the preschool program at Friends' Select, bought soft-shell crabs and Jersey tomatoes at the Reading Terminal Market, took weekends and Augusts at Brian's family's house at Cape May, socialized with old friends who had children of their own, and burned off enough sexual energy with Brian (she ideally liked it *daily*, she told Denise) to keep her halfway calm.

Cow Clueless was therefore shocked by Brian's next question. He asked her where she thought they should live. He said he was thinking of Northern California. He was also thinking of Provence, New York, and London.

"We're happy here," Robin said. "Why go someplace where we don't know anybody and everybody's a millionaire?"

"Climate," Brian said. "Beauty, safety, culture. Style. None of which are Philly's long suit. I'm not saying let's move. I'm just saying tell me if there's anyplace you'd like to go, even for a summer."

"I like it here."

"So we'll stay here," he said. "Until you feel like going someplace else."

She was naïve enough, she told Denise, to think this ended the discussion. She had a good marriage, stably founded on childrearing, eating, and sex. It was true that she and Brian had different class backgrounds, but High Temp Products wasn't exactly E. I. Du Pont de Nemours, and Robin, holding degrees from two elite schools, wasn't your typical proletarian. Their few real differences came down to style, and these differences were mostly invisible to Robin, because Brian was a good husband and a nice guy and because, in her cow innocence, Robin couldn't imagine that style had anything to do with happiness. Her musical tastes ran to John Prine and Etta James, and so Brian played Prine and James at home and saved his Bartók and Defunkt and Flaming Lips and Mission of Burma for blasting on his boom box at High Temp. That Robin dressed like a grad student in white sneakers and a purple nylon shell and oversized round wireframes of a kind last worn by fashionable people in 1978 didn't altogether disappoint Brian, because he alone among men got to see her naked. That Robin was high-strung and had a penetrating screechy voice and a kookaburra laugh seemed, likewise, a small price to pay for a heart of gold and an eye-popping streak of lechery and a racing metabolism that kept her movie-actress thin. That Robin never shaved her armpits and too seldom washed her glasses—well, she was the mother of Brian's children, and as long as he could play his music and tinker with his tensors by himself, he didn't mind indulging in her the anti-style that liberal women of a certain age wore as a badge of feminist identity. This, at any rate, was how Denise imagined Brian had solved the problem of style until the money from W—— came rolling in.

(Denise, though only three years younger than Robin, could not conceive of wearing a purple nylon parka or failing to shave her armpits. She didn't even *own* white sneakers.)

Robin's first concession to her new wealth was to spend the summer house-hunting with Brian. She'd grown up in a big house and she wanted her girls to grow up in one, too. If Brian needed twelve-foot ceilings and four baths and mahogany details throughout, she could live with that. On the sixth of September they signed a contract on a grand brownstone on Panama Street, near Rittenhouse Square.

Two days later, with all the strength in his prison-built shoulders, Billy Passafaro welcomed W——'s corporate-image vice president to Philadelphia.

What Robin needed to know and couldn't find out, in the weeks following the attack, was whether, by the time he lettered his message on a two-by-four, Billy had learned of Brian's windfall and knew which company she and Brian owed their sudden wealth to. The answer mattered, mattered, mattered. However, it was pointless to ask Billy. She knew she wouldn't get the truth from Billy, she'd get whatever answer he believed would hurt her worst. Billy had made it abundantly clear to Robin that he would never stop sneering at her, never address her as a peer, until she could prove to him that her life was as fucked-up and miserable as his. And it was precisely this totemic role she seemed to play for him, precisely the fact that he'd singled her out as the arche-typical possessor of the happy normal life he couldn't have, that made her feel as if *hers* were the head he'd swung for when he brained Rick Flamburg.

Before the trial she asked her father if he'd told Billy that Brian had sold Eigenmelody to W——. She didn't want to ask him, but she couldn't not. Nick, because he gave Billy money, was the only person in the family still in regular communication with him. (Uncle Jimmy had promised to shoot the desecrator of his shrine, the little prick nephew, if he ever showed his little prick Elvis-hating face again, and eventually Billy had stolen once too often from everybody else; even Nick's parents, Fazio and Carolina, who had long insisted that there was nothing wrong with Billy but, in Fazio's words, "attentive deficiency disorder," no longer let their grandson inside their Sea Isle City house.)

Nick unfortunately grasped the import of Robin's question right away. Choosing his words carefully, he replied that, no, he didn't recall saying anything to Billy.

"It's better if you just tell me the truth, Dad," Robin said.

"Well . . . I . . . I don't think there's any connection there . . . uh, Robin."

"Maybe it wouldn't make me feel guilty. Maybe it would just piss me off."

"Well . . . Robin . . . those . . . those feelings often amount to the same thing anyway. Guilt, anger, same thing . . . right? But don't you worry about Billy."

She hung up wondering whether Nick was trying to protect her from her guilt, trying to protect Billy from her anger, or simply spacing out under the strain. She suspected it was a combination of all three. She suspected that during the summer her father had mentioned Brian's windfall to Billy and that father and son had then traded snidenesses and bitternesses about the W—— Corporation and bourgeois Robin and leisure-class Brian. She suspected this, if nothing else, because of how badly Brian and her father got along. Brian was never as outspoken with his wife as he was with Denise ("Nick's the worst kind of coward," he remarked to her once), but he made no secret of hating Nick's bad-boy disquisitions on the uses of violence and his teeth-sucking satisfaction with his so-called socialism. Brian liked Colleen well enough ("She sure got a raw deal in *that* marriage," he remarked to Denise) but shook his head and left the room whenever Nick began holding forth. Robin didn't let herself imagine what her father and Billy had said about her and Brian. But she was pretty sure that things were said and that Rick Flamburg had paid the price. Nick's response to the trial photographs of Flamburg lent further credence to this view.

During the trial, as her father fell apart, Robin studied the catechism at St. Dymphna's and made two further claims on Brian's new money. First she quit her job at the experimental school. She was no longer satisfied to work for parents paying $23,000 a year per child (although, of course, she and Brian were paying nearly that much to school Sinéad and Erin). And then she embarked on a philanthropic project. In a badly blighted section of Point Breeze, less than a mile south of their new house, she bought a vacant city block with a single derelict row house standing on one corner. She also bought five truck-loads of humus and good liability insurance. Her plan was to hire local teenagers at minimum wage, teach them the rudiments of organic gar-dening, and let them share the profits from whatever vegetables they could sell. She threw herself into her Garden Project with a manic in-tensity that was scary even by Robin standards. Brian found her awake at her Global Desktop at 4 a.m., tapping both feet and comparing vari-eties of turnip.

With a different contractor coming to Panama Street every week to make improvements, and with Robin disappearing into a utopist sink of time and energy, Brian reconciled himself to remaining in the dismal city of his childhood. He decided to have some fun of his own. He began eating lunch at the good restaurants of Philadelphia, one after another, and comparing each to his current favorite, Mare Scuro. When he was sure that he still liked Mare Scuro best, he called the chef and made a proposal.

"The first truly cool restaurant in Philly," he said. "The kind of place that makes a person say, 'Hey, *I* could live in Philly—if I had to.' I don't care if anybody else actually feels that way. I just want a place that makes *me* feel that way. So whatever they're paying you now, I will double. And then you go to Europe and eat for a couple of months at my expense. And then come back and design and operate a truly cool restaurant."

"You're going to lose vast amounts of money," Denise replied, "if you don't find an experienced partner or an exceptionally good man-ager."

"Tell me what to do, and I'll do it," Brian said.

" 'Double,' you said?"

"You've got the best place in the city."

" 'Double' is intriguing."

"So say yes."

"Well, it might happen," Denise said. "But you're still probably going to lose vast amounts of money. You're certainly overpaying your chef."

Denise had always had trouble saying no when she felt wanted in the right way. Growing up in suburban St. Jude, she'd been kept at safe distances from anybody who might have wanted her in this way, but after she finished high school she worked for a summer in the Signal Department of the Midland Pacific Railroad, and here, in a big sunny room with twin rows of drafting tables, she became acquainted with the desires of a dozen older men.

The brain of the Midland Pacific, the temple of its soul, was a Depression-era limestone office building with rounded rooftop crenellations like the edges of a skimpy waffle. Higher-order consciousness had its cortical seat in the boardroom and executive dining room on the sixteenth floor and in the offices of the more abstract departments (Operations, Legal, Public Relations) whose vice presidents were on fifteen. Down at the reptile-brain bottom of the building were billing, payroll, personnel, and data storage. In between were mid-level skill functions such as Engineering, which encompassed bridges, track, buildings, and signals.

The Midland Pacific lines were twelve thousand miles long, and for every signal and every wire along the way, every set of red and amber lights, every motion detector buried in ballast, every flashing cantilever crossing guard, every agglomeration of timers and relays housed in a ventless aluminum shed, there were up-to-date circuit diagrams in one of six heavy-lidded filing tanks in the tank room on the twelfth floor of headquarters. The oldest diagrams were drawn freehand in pencil on vellum, the newest with Rapidograph pens on preprinted Mylar blanks.

The draftsmen who tended these files and liaised with the field engineers who kept the railroad's nervous system healthy and untangled were Texan and Kansan and Missourian natives: intelligent, uncultured, twangy men who'd come up the hard way from no-skill jobs in signal gangs, chopping weeds and digging postholes and stringing wire until, by virtue of their aptitude with circuits (and also, as Denise later realized, by virtue of being white), they'd been singled out for training and advancement. None had more than a year or two of college, most only high school. On a summer day when the sky got whiter and the grass got browner and their former gangmates were battling heatstroke in the field, the draftsmen were happy indeed to sit in cushioned roller chairs in air so cool they all kept cardigans handy in their personal drawers.

"You'll find that some of the men take coffee breaks," Alfred told Denise in the pink of the rising sun, as they drove downtown on her first morning. "I want you to know they're not paid to take coffee breaks. I expect you not to take coffee breaks yourself. The railroad is doing us a favor by hiring you, and it's paying you to work eight hours. I want you to remember that. If you apply yourself with the same energy you brought to your schoolwork and your trumpet-playing, you'll be remembered as a great worker."

Denise nodded. To say she was competitive was to put it mildly. In the high-school band there had been two girls and twelve boys in the trumpet section. She was in the first chair and boys were in the next twelve. (In the last chair was a part-Cherokee girl from downstate who hit middle C instead of high E and helped cast that pall of dissonance that shadows every high-school band.) Denise had no great passion for music, but she loved to excel, and her mother believed that bands were good for children. Enid liked the discipline of bands, the upbeat normality, the patriotism. Gary in his day had been an able boy trumpeter and Chip had (briefly, honkingly) attempted the bassoon. Denise, when her time came, asked to follow in Gary's footsteps, but Enid didn't think that little girls and trumpets matched. What matched little girls was flutes. But there was never much satisfaction for Denise in competing with girls. She'd insisted on the trumpet, and Alfred had backed her up, and eventually it had dawned on Enid that rental fees could be avoided if Denise used Gary's old trumpet.

Unlike sheet music, unfortunately, the signal diagrams that Denise was given to copy and file that summer were unintelligible to her. Since she couldn't compete with the draftsmen, she competed with the boy who'd worked in Signals the previous two summers, Alan Jamborets, the corporation counsel's son; and since she had no way to gauge Jamborets's performance, she worked with an intensity that she was certain *nobody* could match.

"Denise, whoa, God, damn," Laredo Bob, a sweating Texan, said while she was cutting and collating blueprints.

"What?"

"You gonna burn yourself out going that fast."

"Actually, I enjoy it," she said. "Once I'm in the rhythm."

"Thing is, though," Laredo Bob said, "you can leave some of that for tomorrow."

"I don't enjoy it *that* much."

"OK, well, but y'all take a coffee break now. You hear me?"

Draftsmen were yipping as they trotted toward the hallway.

"Coffee time!"

"Snack cart's here!"

"Coffee time!"

She worked with undiminished speed.

Laredo Bob was the low man to whom drudge work fell when there was no summer help to relieve him. Laredo Bob ought to have to been chagrined that Denise—in full view of the boss—was performing in half an hour certain clerical tasks to which he liked to devote whole mornings while he chewed up a Swisher Sweet cigar. But Laredo Bob believed that character was destiny. To him Denise's work habits were simply evidence that she was her daddy's daughter and that soon enough she would be an executive just like her daddy while he, Laredo Bob, would go on performing clerical tasks at the speed you'd expect from somebody fated to perform them. Laredo Bob further believed that women were angels and men were poor sinners. The angel he was married to revealed her sweet, gracious nature mainly by forgiving his tobacky habit and feeding and clothing four children on a single small-ish income, but he was by no means surprised when the Eternal Feminine turned out to have supernatural abilities in the area of labeling and alphabetically sorting thousand-count boxes of card-mounted microform. Denise seemed to Laredo Bob an all-around marvelous and purty creature. Before long he began singing a rockabilly chorus ("Denise-uh-why-you-done, what-you-did?") when she arrived in the morning and when she returned from her lunch break in the little treeless city park across the street.

The chief of draftsmen, Sam Beuerlein, told Denise that next summer they would have to pay her not to come to work, since she was doing the work of two this summer.

A grinning Arkansan, Lamar Parker, who wore enormous thick glasses and had precancers on his forehead, asked her if her daddy had told her what a rascally, worthless crew the men of Signals were.

"Just worthless," Denise said. "He never said rascally."

Lamar cackled and puffed on his Tareyton and repeated her remark in case the men around him hadn't heard it.

"Heh-heh-heh," the draftsman named Don Armour muttered with unpleasant sarcasm.

Don Armour was the only man in Signals who seemed not to love Denise. He was a solidly built, short-legged Vietnam vet whose cheeks, close-shaved, were nearly as blue and glaucous as a plum. His blazers were tight around his massive upper arms; drafting tools seemed toy-sized in his hand; he looked like a teenager stuck at a first-grader's desk. Instead of resting his feet on the ring of his high wheeled chair, like everyone else, he let his feet dangle, his toe-tips dragging on the floor. He draped his upper body across the drafting surface, bringing his eyes to within inches of his Rapidograph pen. After working for an hour like this, he went limp and pressed his nose into Mylar or buried his face in his hands and moaned. His coffee breaks he often passed pitched forward like a murder victim, his forehead on his table, his plastic aviator glasses in his fist.

When Denise was first introduced to Don Armour, he looked away and gave her a dead-fish handshake. When she worked at the far end of the drafting room, she could hear him murmuring things while the men around him chuckled; when she was close to him he kept silent and smirked fiercely at his tabletop. He reminded her of the smartasses who haunted the back rows of classrooms.

She was in the women's room one morning in July when she heard Armour and Lamar outside the bathroom door by the drinking fountain where Lamar rinsed out his coffee mugs. She stood by the door and strained to hear.

"Remember we thought old Alan was a crazy worker?" Lamar said.

"I'll say this for Jamborets," Don Armour said. "He was a hell of a lot easier on the eyes."

"Hee hee."

"Hard to get much work done with somebody as good-looking as Alan Jamborets walking around all day in little skirts."

"Alan was a pretty boy, all right."

There was a groan. "I swear to God, Lamar," Don Armour said, "I'm this close to filing a complaint with OSHA. This is cruel and un-usual. Did you see that skirt?"

"I seen it. But shush now."

"I'm going crazy."

"This is a seasonal problem, Donald. It's like to take care of itself in two months."

"If the Wroths don't fire me first."

"Say, what makes you so sure this merger's going through?"

"I sweated eight years in the field to get to this office. It's about time something else came along and fucked things up."

Denise was wearing a short electric-blue thrift-store skirt that in truth she was surprised was in compliance with her mother's Islamic female dress code. To the extent that she accepted the idea that Lamar and Don Armour had been talking about *her*—and the idea did have an undeniable strange headache-like residency status in her brain —she felt all the more keenly snubbed by Don. She felt as if he were having a party *in her own house* without inviting her.

When she returned to the drafting room, he cast a skeptical eye around the room, sizing up everyone but her. As his gaze skipped past her, she felt a curious need to push her fingernails into the quick or to pinch her own nipples.

It was the season of thunder in St. Jude. The air had a smell of Mexican violence, of hurricanes or coups. There could be morning thunder from unreadably churning skies, ominous dull reports from south-county municipalities that nobody you knew had ever been to. And lunch-hour thunder from a solitary anvil wandering through otherwise semi-fair skies. And the more serious thunder of midafternoon, as solid sea-green waves of cloud rolled up in the southwest, the sun shining all the brighter locally and the heat bearing down more urgently, as if aware that time was short. And the great theater of a good dinnertime blowout, storms crowded into the fifty-mile radius of the radar's sweep like big spiders in a little jar, clouds booming at each other from the sky's four corners, and wave upon wave of dime-sized raindrops arriving like plagues, the picture in your window going blackand-white and fuzzy, trees and houses lurching in the flashes of lightning, small kids with swimsuits and drenched towels running home headlong, like refugees. And the drumming late at night, the rolling caissons of summer on the march.

And every day the St. Jude press carried rumblings of an impending merger. The Midpac's importunate twin-brother suitors, Hillard and Chauncy Wroth, were in town talking to three unions. The Wroths were in Washington countering Midpac testimony before a Senate subcommittee. The Midpac had reportedly asked the Union Pacific to be its white knight. The Wroths defended their postacquisitional restructuring of the Arkansas Southern. The Midpac's spokesman begged all concerned St. Judeans to write or call their congressmen . . .

Denise was leaving the building for lunch under partly cloudy skies when the top of a utility pole a block away from her exploded. She saw bright pink and felt the blast of thunder on her skin. Secretaries ran screaming through the little park. Denise turned on her heel and took her book and her sandwich and her plum back up to the twelfth floor, where every day two tables of pinochle formed. She sat down by the windows, but it seemed pretentious or unfriendly to be reading *War and Peace*. She divided her attention between the crazy skies outside and the card game nearest her.

Don Armour unwrapped a sandwich and opened it to a slice of bologna on which the texture of bread was lithographed in yellow mustard. His shoulders slumped. He wrapped the sandwich up again loosely in its foil and looked at Denise as if she were the latest torment of his day.

"Meld sixteen."

"Who made this mess?"

"Ed," Don Armour said, fanning cards, "you gotta be careful with those bananas."

Ed Alberding, the most senior draftsman, had a body shaped like a bowling pin and curly gray hair like an old lady's perm. He was blinking rapidly as he chewed banana and studied his cards. The banana, peeled, lay on the table in front of him. He broke off another dainty bite.

"Awful lot of potassium in a banana," Don Armour said.

"Potassium's good for you," Lamar said from across the table.

Don Armour set his cards down and regarded Lamar gravely. "Are you joking? Doctors use potassium to induce cardiac arrest."

"Ol' Eddie eats two, three bananas every day," Lamar said. "How's that heart of yours feelin', Mr. Ed?"

"Let's just play the hand here, boys," Ed said.

"But I'm terribly concerned about your health," Don Armour said.

"You tell too many lies, mister."

"Day after day I see you ingesting toxic potassium. It's my duty as a friend to warn you."

"Your trick, Don."

"Put a card down, Don."

"And in return all I get," Armour said in an injured tone, "is suspicion and denial."

"Donald, you in this game or just keepin' that seat warm?"

"Of course, if Ed were to keel over dead of cardiac arrest, due to acute long-term potassium poisoning, that would make me fourth highest in seniority and secure me a place in Little Rock with the Arkansas Southern slash Midland Pacific, so why am I even mentioning this? Please, Ed, eat my banana, too."

"Hee hee, watch your mouth," Lamar said.

"Gentlemen, I believe these tricks are all mine."

"Son of a gun!"

Shuffle, shuffle. Slap, slap.

"Ed, you know, they got computers down in Little Rock," Don Armour said, never glancing at Denise.

"Uh-oh," Ed said. "Computers?"

"You go down there, I'm warning you, they're going to make you learn to use one."

"Eddie'll be asleep with angels before he learns computers," Lamar said.

"I beg to differ," Don said. "Ed's going to go to Little Rock and learn computer drafting. He's going to make somebody else sick to their stomach with his bananas."

"Say, Donald, what makes you so sure you ain't going to Little Rock yourself?"

Don shook his head. "We'd spend two, three thousand dollars less a year if we lived in Little Rock, and pretty soon I'd be making a couple thousand a year more. It's cheap down there. Patty could work maybe half days, let the girls have a mother again. We could buy some land in the Ozarks before the girls got too old to enjoy it. Someplace with a pond. You think anybody's gonna let that happen to me?"

Ed was sorting his cards with the nervous twitches of a chipmunk. "What do they need computers for?" he said.

"To replace useless old men with," Don said, his plum face splitting open with an unkind smile.

"Replace us?"

"Why do you think the Wroths are buying *us* out and not the other way around?"

Shuffle, shuffle. Slap, slap. Denise watched the sky stick forks of lightning into the salad of trees on the Illinois horizon. While her head was turned, there was an explosion at the table.

"Jesus Christ, Ed," Don Armour said, "why don't you just go ahead and lick those before you put them down?"

"Easy there, Don," said Sam Beuerlein, the chief of draftsmen.

"Am I alone in this turning my stomach?"

"Easy. Easy."

Don threw his cards down and shoved off in his rolling chair so violently that the praying-mantis drafting light creaked and swayed. "Laredo," he called, "come take my cards. I gotta get some banana-free air."

"Easy."

Don shook his head. "It's say it now, Sam, or go crazy when the buyout happens."

"You're a smart man, Don," Beuerlein said. "You'll land on your feet no matter what."

"I don't know about smart. I'm not half as smart as Ed. Am I, Ed?"

Ed's nose twitched. He tapped the table with his cards impatiently.

"Too young for Korea, too old for *my* war," Don said. "That's what I call smart. Smart enough to get off the bus and cross Olive Street every morning for twenty-five years without getting hit by a car. Smart enough to get back on it every night. That's what counts for smart in this world."

Sam Beuerlein raised his voice. "Don, now, you listen to me. You go take a walk, you hear? Go outside and cool down. When you get back, you may decide you owe Eddie an apology."

"Meld eighteen," Ed said, tapping the table.

Don pressed his hand into the small of his back and limped up the aisle, shaking his head. Laredo Bob came over with egg salad in his mustache and took Don's cards.

"No need for apologies," Ed said. "Let's just play the hand here, boys."

Denise was leaving the women's room after lunch when Don Armour stepped off the elevator. He had a shawl of rain marks on his shoulders. He rolled his eyes at the sight of Denise, as if at some fresh persecution.

"What?" she said.

He shook his head and walked away.

"What? What?"

"Lunch hour's over," he said. "Aren't you supposed to be working?"

Each wiring diagram was labeled with the name of the line and the milepost number. The Signal Engineer hatched plans for corrections, and the draftsmen sent paper copies of the diagrams into the field, highlighting additions in yellow pencil and subtractions in red. The field engineers then did the work, often improvising their own fixes and shortcuts, and sent the copies back to headquarters torn and yellowed and greasily fingerprinted, with pinches of red Arkansas dust or bits of Kansas weed chaff in their folds, and the draftsmen recorded the corrections in black ink on the Mylar and vellum originals.

Through the long afternoon, as the perch-belly white of the sky turned the color of a fish's flanks and back, Denise folded the thousands of offprints she'd cut in the morning, six copies of each in the prescribed folds that fit in the field engineer's binder. There were signals at mileposts 16.2 and 17.4 and 20.1 and 20.8 and 22.0 and so on up to the town of New Chartres at 74.35, the end of the line.

On the way out to the suburbs that night she asked her father if the Wroths were going to merge the railroad with the Arkansas Southern.

"I don't know," Alfred said. "I hope not."

Would the company move to Little Rock?

"That seems to be their intention, if they get control."

What would happen to the men in Signals?

"I'd guess some of the more senior ones would move. The younger ones—probably laid off. But I don't want you talking about this."

"I won't," Denise said.

Enid, as on every other Thursday night for the last thirty-five years, had dinner waiting. She'd stuffed green peppers and was abubble with enthusiasm about the coming weekend.

"You'll have to take the bus home tomorrow," she told Denise as they sat down at the table. "Dad and I are going to Lake Fond du Lac Estates with the Schumperts."

"What is Lake Fond du Lac Estates?"

"It is a boondoggle," Alfred said, "that I should have known better than to get involved with. However, your mother wore me down."

"Al," Enid said, "there are *no strings attached.* There is *no pressure* to go to any of the seminars. We can spend the whole weekend doing anything we want."

"There's bound to be pressure. The developer can't keep giving away free weekends and not try to sell some lots."

"The brochure said *no* pressure, *no* expectation, *no* strings attached."

"I am dubious," Alfred said.

"Mary Beth says there's a wonderful winery near Bordentown that we can tour. And we can all swim in Lake Fond du Lac! And the brochure says there are paddleboats and a gourmet restaurant."

"I can't imagine a Missouri winery in mid-July is going to be appealing," Alfred said.

"You just have to get in the *spirit* of things," Enid said. "The Dribletts went last October and had so much fun. Dale said there was no pressure at all. Very little pressure, he said."

"Consider the source."

"What do you mean?"

"A man who sells coffins for a living."

"Dale's no different than anybody else."

"I said I am dubious. But I will go." Alfred added, to Denise: "You can take the bus home. We'll leave a car here for you."

"Kenny Kraikmeyer called this morning," Enid told Denise. "He wondered if you're free on Saturday night."

Denise shut one eye and widened the other. "What did you say?"

"I said I thought you were."

"You *what*?"

"I'm sorry. I didn't realize you had plans."

Denise laughed. "My only plan at the moment is to not see Kenny Kraikmeyer."

"He was very polite," Enid said. "You know, it doesn't hurt to go on one date if somebody takes the trouble to ask you. If you don't have fun, you don't have to do it again. But you ought to start saying yes to *somebody*. People will think nobody's good enough for you."

Denise set down her fork. "Kenny Kraikmeyer literally turns my stomach."

"Denise," Alfred said.

"That's not right," Enid said, her voice trembling. "That's not something I want to hear you saying."

"OK, I'm sorry I said that. But I'm not free on Saturday. Not for

Kenny Kraikmeyer. Who, if he wants to go out, might consider asking *me*."

It occurred to Denise that Enid would probably enjoy a weekend with Kenny Kraikmeyer at Lake Fond du Lac, and that Kenny would probably have a better time there than Alfred would.

After dinner she biked over to the oldest house in the suburb, a high-ceilinged cube of antebellum brick across the street from the boarded-up commuter rail station. The house belonged to the high-school drama teacher, Henry Dusinberre, who'd left his campy Abyssin-ian banana and gaudy crotons and tongue-in-cheek potted palms in his favorite student's care while he spent a month with his mother in New Orleans. Among the bordelloish antiques in Dusinberre's parlor were twelve ornate champagne glasses, each with an ascending column of air bubbles captured in its faceted crystal stem, that he allowed only Denise, of all the young thespians and literary types who gravitated to his liquor on Saturday nights, to drink from. ("Let the little beasts use plastic cups," he would say as he arranged his wasted limbs in his calf-skin club chair. He had fought two rounds against a cancer now offi-cially in remission, but his glossy skin and protuberant eyes suggested that all was not well oncologically. "Lambert, extraordinary creature," he said, "sit here where I can see you in profile. Do you realize the Japanese would worship you for your neck? *Worship* you.") It was in Dusinberre's house that she'd tasted her first raw oyster, her first quail egg, her first grappa. Dusinberre steeled her in her resolve not to suc-cumb to the charms of any (his phrase) "pimpled adolescents." He bought dresses and jackets on approval in antique stores, and if they fit Denise he let her keep them. Fortunately, Enid, who wished that Denise would dress more like a Schumpert or a Root, held vintage clothing in such low esteem that she actually believed that a spotless embroidered yellow satin party dress with buttons of tiger-eye agate had cost Denise (as she claimed) ten dollars at the Salvation Army. Over Enid's bitter objections she'd worn this dress to her senior prom with Peter Hicks, the substantially pimpled actor who'd played Tom to her Amanda in *The Glass Menagerie*. Peter Hicks, on prom night, had been invited to join her and Dusinberre in drinking from the rococo champagne glasses, but Peter was driving and stuck with his plastic cup of Coke.

After she watered the plants, she sat in Dusinberre's calfskin chair and listened to New Order. She wished she felt like dating someone, but the boys she respected, like Peter Hicks, didn't move her romantically, and the rest were in the mold of Kenny Kraikmeyer, who, though bound for the Naval Academy and a career in nuclear science, fancied himself a hipster and collected Cream and Jimi Hendrix "vinyl" (his word) with a passion that God had surely intended him to bring to building model submarines. Denise was a little worried by the degree of her revulsion. She didn't understand what made her so *very* mean. She was unhappy to be so mean. There seemed to be something wrong with the way she thought about herself and other people.

Whenever her mother pointed this out, though, she had no choice but to nuke her.

The next day she was taking her lunch hour in the park, sunning herself in one of the tiny sleeveless tops that her mother was unaware she wore to work beneath her sweaters, when Don Armour appeared from nowhere and dropped onto the bench beside her.

"You're not playing cards," she said.

"I'm going crazy," he said.

She returned her eyes to her book. She could feel him looking at her body pointedly. The air was hot but not so hot as to account for the heat on his side of her face.

He took his glasses off and rubbed his eyes. "This is where you come and sit every day."

"Yes."

He wasn't good-looking. His head seemed too large, his hair was thinning, and his face had the dusky nitrite red of a wiener or bologna, except where his beard made it blue. But she recognized an amusement, a brightness, an animal sadness in his expression; and the saddle curves of his lips were inviting.

He read the spine of her book. "Count Leo Tolstoy," he said. He shook his head and laughed silently.

"What?"

"Nothing," he said. "I'm just trying to imagine what it's like to be you."

"What do you mean?"

"I mean beautiful. Smart. Disciplined. Rich. Going to college. What's it like?"

She had a ridiculous impulse to answer him by touching him, to let him feel what it was like. There was no other way, really, to answer.

She shrugged and said she didn't know.

"Your boyfriend must feel very lucky," Don Armour said.

"I don't have a boyfriend."

He flinched as if this were difficult news. "I find that puzzling and surprising."

Denise shrugged again.

"I had a summer job when I was seventeen," Don said. "I worked for an old Mennonite couple that had a big antique store. We used this stuff called Magic Mixture—paint thinner, wood alcohol, acetone, tung oil. It would clean up the furniture without stripping it. I'd breathe it all day and come home flying. Then around midnight I'd get this wicked headache."

"Where'd you grow up?"

"Carbondale. Illinois. I had this idea that the Mennonites were underpaying me, in spite of the free highs. So I started borrowing their pickup at night. I had a girlfriend who needed rides. I crashed the pickup, which was how the Mennonites found out I'd been using it, and my then-stepdad said if I enlisted in the Marines he would deal with the Mennonites and their insurance company, otherwise I was on my own with the cops. So I joined the Marines in the middle of the sixties. It just seemed like the thing to do. I've got a real knack for timing."

"You were in Vietnam."

Don Armour nodded. "If this merger goes through, I'm back to where I was when I was discharged. Plus three kids and another set of skills that no one wants."

"How old are your kids?"

"Ten, eight, and four."

"Does your wife work?"

"She's a school nurse. She's at her parents' in Indiana. They've got five acres and a pond. Nice for the girls."

"Are you taking some vacation?"

"Two weeks next month."

Denise had run out of questions. Don Armour sat bent over with his hands pressed flat between his knees. He sat like this for a long time. From the side, she could see his trademark smirk wearing through his impassivity; he seemed like a person who would always make you pay for taking him seriously or showing concern. Finally Denise stood up and said she was going inside, and he nodded as if this were a blow he'd been expecting.

It didn't occur to her that Don Armour was smiling in embarrassment at the obviousness of his play for her sympathies, the staleness of his pickup lines. It didn't occur to her that his performance at the pinochle table the day before had been staged for her benefit. It didn't occur to her that he'd guessed she was eavesdropping in the bathroom and had let himself be overheard. It didn't occur to her that Don Armour's fundamental mode was self-pity and that he might, in his self-pity, have hit on many girls before her. It didn't occur to her that he was already plotting—had been plotting since he first shook hands with her—how to get into her skirt. It didn't occur to her that he averted his eyes not simply because her beauty caused him pain but because Rule #1 in every manual advertised at the back of men's magazines ("How to Make Her WILD for You—Every Time!") was *Ignore Her*. It didn't occur to her that the differences of class and circumstance that were causing her discomfort might be, for Don Armour, a provocation: that she might be an object he desired for its luxury, or that a fundamentally self-pitying man whose job was in jeopardy might take a variety of satisfactions in bedding the daughter of his boss's boss's boss. None of this occurred to Denise then or after. She was still feeling responsible ten years later.

What she was aware of, that afternoon, were the problems. That Don Armour wanted to put his hands on her but couldn't was a problem. That through an accident of birth she had *everything* while the man who wanted her had so much less—this lack of parity—was a *big* problem. Since she was the one who had everything, the problem was clearly hers to solve. But any word of reassurance she could give him, any gesture of solidarity she could imagine making, felt condescending.

She experienced the problem intensely in her body. Her surfeit of gifts and opportunities, in comparison to Don Armour's, manifested itself as a physical botheration—a dissatisfaction that pinching the sensitive parts of herself might address but couldn't fix.

After lunch she went to the tank room, where the originals of all signal tracings were stored in six heavy-lidded steel tanks resembling elegant Dumpsters. Over the years, the big cardboard folders in the tanks had become overloaded, collecting lost tracings in their bulging lower depths, and Denise had been given the satisfying task of restoring order. Draftsmen visiting the tank room worked around her while she relabeled folders and unearthed long-lost vellums. The biggest tank was so deep that she had to lie on her stomach on the tank beside it, her bare legs on cold metal, and dive in with both arms to reach the bottom. She dropped the rescued tracings on the floor and reached in for more. When she surfaced for air she became aware that Don Armour was kneeling by the tank.

His shoulders were muscled like an oarsman's and stretched his blazer tight. She didn't know how long he'd been here or what he'd been looking at. Now he was examining an accordion-pleated vellum, a wiring plan for a signal tower at Milepost 101.35 on the McCook line. It had been drawn freehand by Ed Alberding in 1956.

"Ed was a kid when he drew this. It's a beautiful thing."

Denise climbed down from the tank, smoothed her skirt, and dusted herself off.

"I shouldn't be so hard on Ed," Don said. "He's got talents I'll never have."

He seemed to be thinking less about Denise than she'd been thinking about him. He uncrumpled another tracing, and she stood looking down at a boyish whorl of his pencil-gray hair. She took a step closer and leaned a little closer yet, eclipsing her view of him with her chest.

"You're kind of in my light," he said.

"Do you want to have dinner with me?"

He sighed heavily. His shoulders slumped. "I'm supposed to drive to Indiana for the weekend."

"OK."

"But let me think about it."

"Good. Think about it."

She sounded cool, but her knees were unsteady as she made her way to the women's room. She locked herself in a stall and sat and worried while, outside, the elevator bell faintly chimed and the afternoon snack cart came and went. Her worrying had no content. Her eyes simply alighted on something, the chrome bolt on the door of the stall or a square of tissue on the floor, and the next thing she knew, she'd been staring at it for five minutes and had thought about nothing. Nothing. Nothing.

She was cleaning up the tank room, five minutes before day's end, when Don Armour's broad face loomed up at her shoulder, his eyelids drooping sleepily behind his glasses. "Denise," he said. "Let me take you to dinner."

She nodded quickly. "OK."

In a rough neighborhood, mostly poor and black, just north of downtown was an old-fashioned soda shop and diner that Henry Dusinberre and his student thespians patronized. Denise had appetite for nothing more than iced tea and french fries, but Don Armour ordered a hamburger platter and a milk shake. His posture, she noticed, was a frog's. His head sank into his shoulders as he bent to the food. He chewed slowly, as if with irony. He cast bland smiles around the room, as if with irony. He pushed his glasses up his nose with fingers whose nails, she noticed, were bitten to the pink.

"I would never come to this neighborhood," he said.

"These couple of blocks are pretty safe."

"See, for you, that's true," he said. "A place can sense if you understand trouble. If you don't understand it, you get left alone. My problem is I understand it. If I had come to a street like this when I was your age, something ugly would have happened."

"I don't see why."

"It's just the way it was. I would look up, and suddenly there would be three strangers who hated my guts. And I hated theirs. This is a world you can't even see if you're an effective and happy person. A person like you walks right through it. It's waiting for someone like me to come along so I can have the shit beat out of me. It's had me picked out from a mile away."

Don Armour drove a big American sedan similar to Denise's mother's, only older. He piloted it patiently onto an artery and headed west at a low speed, amusing himself by slouching at the wheel ("I'm slow; my car is bad") while other drivers roared by on the left and right.

Denise directed him to Henry Dusinberre's house. The sun was still shining, low in the west above the plywood-eyed train station, when they mounted the stairs to Dusinberre's porch. Don Armour looked up at the surrounding trees as if even the trees were somehow better, more expensive, in this suburb. Denise had her hand on the screen door before she realized that the door behind it was open.

"Lambert? Is that you?" Henry Dusinberre came out of the gloom of his parlor. His skin was waxier than ever, his eyes more protuberant, and his teeth seemed larger in his head. "My mother's doctor sent me home," he said. "He wanted to wash his hands of me. I think he's had enough of *death*."

Don Armour was retreating toward his car, head down.

"Who's the incredible hulk?" Dusinberre said.

"A friend from work," Denise said.

"Well, you can't bring him in. I'm sorry. I won't have hulks in the house. You'll have to find someplace else."

"Do you have food? Are you all right here?"

"Yes, run along. I feel better already, being back. That doctor and I were mutually embarrassed by my health. Apparently, child, I'm quite without white blood cells. The man was shaking with fear. He was convinced that I was going to die *right there in his office*. Lambert, I felt so sorry for him!" A dark hole of mirth opened in the sick man's face. "I tried to explain to him that my white-blood-cell needs are entirely nugatory. But he seemed intent on regarding me as a medical curiosity. I had lunch with Mother and took a taxi to the airport."

"You're sure you're OK."

"Yes. Go, with my blessing. Be foolish. But not in my house. Go."

It was unwise to be seen with Don Armour at her house before dark, with observant Roots and curious Dribletts coming and going on the street, so she directed him to the elementary school and led him into the field of grass behind it. They sat amid the electronic menagerie of bug sounds, the genital intensity of certain fragrant shrubs, the fading heat of a nice July day. Don Armour put his arms around her belly, his chin on her shoulder. They listened to the dull pops of small-bore fireworks.

In her house after dark, in the frost of its air-conditioning, she tried to move him quickly toward the stairs, but he tarried in the kitchen, he lingered in the dining room. She was pierced by the unfairness of the impression that the house was obviously making. Although her parents weren't wealthy, her mother so yearned for a certain kind of elegance and had worked so hard to achieve it that to Don Armour the house *looked* like the house of rich people. He seemed reluctant to tread on the carpeting. He stopped and took proper note, as possibly no one else ever had, of the Waterford goblets and candy dishes that Enid kept on display in the breakfront. His eyes fell on each object, the music boxes, the Parisian street scenes, the matching and beautifully upholstered furniture, as they'd fallen on Denise's body—was it just today? Today at lunch?

She put her large hand in his larger hand, knitted her fingers into his, and pulled him toward the stairs.

In her bedroom, on his knees, he planted his thumbs on her hip-bones and pressed his mouth to her thighs and then to her whatever; she felt returned to a childhood world of Grimm and C. S. Lewis where a touch could be transformative. His hands made her hips into a woman's hips, his mouth made her thighs into a woman's thighs, her whatever into a cunt. These were the advantages of being wanted by someone older—to feel less like an ungendered marionette, to be given a guided tour of the state of her morphology, to have its usefulness elucidated by a person for whom it was just the ticket.

Boys her own age wanted *something*, but they didn't seem to know exactly what. Boys her own age wanted approximately. Her function—

the role she'd played on more than one lousy date—was to help them learn more specifically what they wanted, to unbutton her shirt and give them suggestions, to (as it were) flesh out their rather rudimentary ideas.

Don Armour wanted her minutely, inch by inch. She appeared to make brilliant sense to him. Simply possessing a body had never much helped her, but seeing it as a thing that she herself might want—imagining herself as Don Armour on her knees, desiring the various parts of herself—made her possession of it more forgivable. She had what the man expected to find. There was no anxiety to his location and appreciation of each feature.

When she unhooked her bra, Don bowed his head and shut his eyes.

"What is it?"

"A person could die of how beautiful you are."

This she liked, yes.

Her feeling when she took him in her hands was a preview of her feeling a few years later, as a young cook, when she handled her first truffles, her first foie gras, her first sacs of roe.

On her eighteenth birthday her theater friends had given her a hollowed-out Bible containing a nip of Seagram's and three candy-colored condoms, which came in handy now.

Don Armour's head, looming above her, was a lion's head, a jack-o'-lantern. When he came, he roared. His subsiding sighs overtook one another, overlapped almost. Oh, oh, oh, oh. She'd never heard anything like it.

There was blood in proportion to her pain, which had been fairly bad, and in reverse proportion to her pleasure, which had been mainly in her head.

In the dark, after she'd grabbed a dirty towel from the laundry basket in the hall closet, she pumped her fist at having achieved non-virginity before she left for college.

Less wonderful was the presence of a large and somewhat bloody man in her bed. It was a single bed, the only bed she'd ever slept in, and she was very tired. This perhaps explained why she made a fool of herself by standing in the middle of her room, with a towel wrapped around her, and unexpectedly weeping.

She loved Don Armour for getting up and wrapping his arms around her and not minding that she was a child. He put her to bed, found a pajama top for her, helped her into it. Kneeling by the bed, he drew the sheet up over her shoulder and stroked her head as she had to assume he often stroked his daughters' heads. He did this until she was nearly asleep. Then the theater of his stroking expanded into regions that she had to assume were off-limits with his daughters. She tried to stay half-asleep, but he came at her more insistently, more scratchily. Everything he did either tickled or hurt, and when she made so bold as to whimper, she had her first experience of a man's hands pressing on her head, pushing her southward.

Thankfully, when he was done, he didn't try to spend the night. He left her room and she lay utterly still, straining to hear what he was doing and whether he was coming back. Finally—she may have dozed —she heard the click of the front door's latch and the whinny of his big car's starter.

She slept until noon and was showering in the downstairs bathroom shower stall, trying to comprehend what she'd done, when she heard the front door again. Heard voices.

She madly rinsed her hair, madly toweled off, and burst out of the bathroom. Her father was lying down in the den. Her mother was rinsing out the insulated picnic hamper in the kitchen sink.

"Denise, you didn't eat *any* of the dinner I left you!" Enid cried. "It doesn't look like you've touched a single thing."

"I thought you guys were coming back tomorrow."

"Lake Fond du Lac was not what we expected," Enid said. "I don't know what Dale and Honey were thinking. It was a big nothing."

At the bottom of the stairs were two overnight bags. Denise ran past them and up to her bedroom, where condom wrappers and bloody linens were visible from the doorway. She closed the door behind her.

The rest of her summer was ruined. She was absolutely lonely both at work and at home. She hid the bloody sheet and the bloody towel in her closet and despaired of dealing with them. Enid was naturally surveillant and had myriad idle synapses to devote to such tasks as noticing when her daughter had her period. Denise hoped to come forward apologetically with the ruined towel and sheet at the appropriate time, two weeks hence. But Enid had brainpower to spare for the counting of linens.

"I'm missing one of my *good* monogrammed bath towels."

"Oh, shoot, I left it at the pool."

"Denise, why you took a *good* monogrammed bath towel, when we have so many other towels . . . And then, of all the towels to lose! Did you call the pool?"

"I went back and looked."

"Those are very expensive towels."

Denise never made mistakes like the one she was claiming to have made. The injustice would have rankled less if it had served a greater pleasure—if she could have gone to Don Armour and laughed about it and sought his consolation. But she didn't love him and he didn't love her.

At work now the friendliness of the other draftsmen was suspect; it all seemed liable to lead to fucking. Don Armour was too embarrassed, or discreet, to even meet her eyes. He spent his days in a torpor of unhappiness with the Wroth brothers and unfriendliness to everyone around him. There was nothing left for Denise at work but work, and now its dullness was a burden, now she hated it. By the end of a day, her face and neck hurt from holding back tears and working at speeds that only a person working happily could maintain without discomfort.

This, she told herself, was what happened when you acted on an impulse. She was amazed that she'd given all of two hours' thought to her decision. She'd taken a liking to Don Armour's eyes and mouth, she'd determined that she owed him the thing he wanted—and this was all she remembered thinking. A dirty and appealing possibility had occurred to her (I could lose my virginity *tonight*), and she'd leaped at the chance.

She was too proud to admit to herself, let alone to Don Armour, that he wasn't what she wanted. She was too inexperienced to know she simply could have said, "Sorry—big mistake." She felt a responsibility to give him more of what he wanted. She expected that an affair, if you took the trouble to start it, went on for quite a while.

She suffered for her reluctance. The first week in particular, while she worked herself up to proposing to Don Armour that they get together again on Friday night, her throat ached steadily for hours on end. But she was a trouper. She saw him on the next three Fridays, telling her parents that she was dating Kenny Kraikmeyer. Don Armour took her to dinner at a strip-mall family restaurant and then back to his flimsy little house in a tornado-alley exurb, one of fifty small towns that St. Jude in its endless sprawl was swallowing. His house embarrassed him to the point of loathing. No houses in Denise's suburb had ceilings so low or hardware so cheap, or doors too light to slam properly, or window sashes and window tracks made of plastic. To soothe her lover and shut him up on the topic ("your life vs. mine") that she least enjoyed, and also to fill some hours that would otherwise have passed awkwardly, she pulled him down on the Hide-A-Bed in his junk-swamped basement and brought her perfectionism to bear on a whole new world of skills.

Don Armour never said how he'd explained to his wife his cancellation of their weekend plans in Indiana. Denise couldn't stand to ask one question about his wife.

She endured criticism from her mother for another mistake that she would never have made: failing to soak a bloody sheet immediately in cold water.

On the first Friday of August, moments after Don Armour's two-week vacation started, he and Denise doubled back into the office and locked themselves in the tank room. She kissed him and put his hands on her tits and tried to work his fingers for him, but his hands wanted to be on her shoulders; they wanted to press her to her knees.

His stuff got up into her nasal passages.

"Are you coming down with a cold?" her father asked her a few minutes later, while they were driving past the city limits.

At home, Enid gave her the news that Henry Dusinberre ("your friend") had died at St. Luke's on Wednesday night.

Denise would have felt even guiltier if she hadn't visited Dusinberre in his house as recently as Sunday. She'd found him in the grip of an intense irritation with his next-door neighbor's baby. "I'm doing without white blood cells," he said. "You'd think they could shut their goddamn windows. My God, that infant has lungs! I suspect they're proud of those lungs. I suspect it's like those bikers who disconnect their mufflers. Some spurious, savage token of manhood." Dusinberre's skull and bones were pushing ever closer to his skin. He discussed the cost of mailing a three-ounce package. He told Denise a meandering, incorrect story about an "octoroon" to whom he'd briefly been engaged. ("If I was surprised that she was only seventh-eighths white, imagine her surprise that I was only one-eighth straight.") He spoke of his lifelong crusade on behalf of fifty-watt lightbulbs. ("Sixty's too bright," he said, "and forty is too dim.") For years, he'd lived with death and kept it in its place by making it trivial. He still managed a reasonably wicked laugh, but in the end the struggle to hold fast to the trivial proved as desperate as any other. When Denise said goodbye and kissed him, he seemed not to apprehend her personally. He smiled with downcast eyes, as if he were a special child whose beauty was to be admired and whose tragic situation pitied.

She never saw Don Armour again either.

On Monday, August 6, after a summer of give and take, Hillard and Chauncy Wroth reached agreement with the principal rail workers' unions. The unions had made substantial concessions for the promise of less paternalistic, more innovative management, thus sweetening the Wroths' $26/share tender offer for the Midland Pacific with a potential near-term savings of $200 million. The Midpac's board of managers wouldn't vote officially for another two weeks, but the conclusion was foregone. With chaos looming, a letter came down from the president's office accepting the resignations of all summer employees, effective Friday, August 17.

Since there were no women (besides Denise) in the drafting room, her co-workers prevailed on the Signal Engineer's secretary to bake a farewell cake. It came out on her last afternoon of work. "I reckon it's a major victory," Lamar said, munching, "that we finally made you take a coffee break."

Laredo Bob dabbed at his eyes with a handkerchief the size of a pillowcase.

Alfred passed along a compliment in the car that night.

"Sam Beuerlein," he said, "tells me you're the greatest worker he's ever seen."

Denise said nothing.

"You made a deep impression on those men. You opened their eyes to the kind of work a girl can do. I didn't tell you this before, but I had the feeling the men were dubious about getting a girl for the summer. I think they expected a lot of chattering and not much substance."

She was glad of her father's admiration. But his kindness, like the kindness of the draftsmen who weren't Don Armour, had become inaccessible to her. It seemed to fall upon her body, to refer to it somehow; and her body rebelled.

Denise-uh-why-you-done, what-you-did?

"Anyhow," her father said, "now you've had a taste of life in the real world."

Until she actually got to Philadelphia, she'd looked forward to going to school near Gary and Caroline. Their big house on Seminole Street was like a home without home's sorrows, and Caroline, whose beauty could make Denise breathless with the sheer privilege of speaking to her, was always good for reassurance that Denise had every right to be driven crazy by her mother. By the end of her first semester of college, though, she found that she was letting Gary leave three messages on her telephone for every message she returned. (Once, just once, there was a message from Don Armour which she likewise did not return.) She found herself declining Gary's offers to pick her up at her dorm and return her after dinner. She claimed she had to study, and then, instead of studying, she watched TV with Julia Vrais. It was a hat trick of guilt: she felt bad for lying to Gary, worse for blowing off her work, and worst of all for distracting Julia. Denise could always pull an all-nighter, but Julia was useless after ten o'clock. Julia had no motor and no rudder. Julia could not explain why her fall schedule consisted of Intro Italian, Intro Russian, Eastern Religion, and Music Theory; she accused Denise of having had unfair outside help in choosing her balanced academic diet of English, history, philosophy, and biology.

Denise for her part was jealous of the college "men" in Julia's life. Initially both she and Julia had been *besieged*. An inordinate number of the junior and senior "men" who banged their trays down beside them in the dining hall were from New Jersey. They had middle-aged faces and megaphonic voices with which they compared math curricula or reminisced about that time they went to Rehoboth Beach and got so wasted. They had only three questions for Julia and Denise: (1) *What's your name?* (2) *What dorm are you in?* and (3) *Do you want to come to our party on Friday?* Denise was amazed by the rudeness of this summary exam and no less amazed by Julia's fascination with these Teaneck natives with monster digital wristwatches and merging eyebrows. Julia wore the heads-up look of a squirrel convinced that somebody has stale bread in his pocket. Leaving a party, she would shrug and tell Denise: "He's got drugs, so I'm going with him." Denise began to spend Friday nights studying by herself. She acquired a rep as an ice queen and possible lesbian. She lacked Julia's ability to melt at the windowside chorusing of her name at three in the morning by the entire college soccer team. "I'm so embarrassed," Julia would moan, in an agony of happiness, as she peered around the lowered blind. The "men" outside the window had no idea how happy they were making her and therefore, in Denise's strict undergraduate judgment, did not deserve to have her.

Denise spent the next summer in the Hamptons with four of her dissolute college hallmates and lied to her parents about every aspect of her situation. She slept on a living-room floor and made good money as a dishwasher and prep drone at the Inn at Quogue, working elbow to elbow with a pretty girl from Scarsdale named Suzie Sterling and falling in love with the life of a cook. She loved the crazy hours, the intensity of the work, the beauty of the product. She loved the deep stillness that underlay the din. A good crew was like an elective family in which everyone in the little hot world of the kitchen stood on equal footing, and every cook had weirdnesses concealed in her past or in his character, and even in the midst of the most sweaty togetherness each family member enjoyed *privacy* and *autonomy*: she loved this.

Suzie Sterling's father, Ed, had given Suzie and Denise several lifts into Manhattan before the night in August when Denise was biking home and almost rode right into him where he stood, by his BMW, smoking a Dunhill and hoping that she might come by alone. Ed Sterling was an entertainment lawyer. He pleaded inability to live without Denise. She hid her (borrowed) bike in some bushes by the road. That the bike was stolen by the time she came back for it the next day, and that she swore to its owner that she'd chained it to the usual post, ought to have given her fair warning of the territory she was entering. But she was excited by what she did to Sterling, by the dramatic hydraulic physiology of his desire, and when she returned to school in September she decided that a liberal-arts college did not compare well to a kitchen. She didn't see the point of working hard on papers that only a professor ever saw; she wanted an audience. She also resented that the college was making her feel guilty about her privileges while granting certain lucky identity groups plenary indulgences from guilt. She felt guilty enough already, thank you. Almost every Sunday she took the cheap slow proletarian combo of SEPTA and New Jersey Transit to New York. She put up with Ed Sterling's paranoid one-way telephone communications and his last-minute postponements and his chronic distraction and his jaw-taxing performance anxieties and her own shame at being taken to cheap ethnic restaurants in Woodside and Elmhurst and Jackson Heights so as not to be seen by anyone Sterling knew (because, as he told her often—running both hands through his mink-thick hair—he knew *everybody* in Manhattan). While her lover teetered closer to utter freakout and inability to see her anymore, Denise ate Uruguayan T-bones, Sino-Colombian tamales, thumbnail crayfish in red Thai curry, and alder-smoked Russian eels. Beauty or excellence, as typified for her by memorable food, could redeem almost any humiliation. But she never stopped feeling guilty about the bike. Her insistence that she'd chained it to the usual post.

The third time she got involved with a man twice her age, she married him. She was determined not to be a squishy liberal. She'd quit school and worked to save money for a year, had taken six months in France and Italy, and had returned to Philly to cook at a thronged fish-

and-pasta place off Catharine Street. As soon as she'd picked up some skills, she offered her services at Café Louche, which was then the most exciting place in town. Emile Berger hired her on the spot, on the basis of her knife work and her looks. Within a week, he was complaining to her about the borderline competence of every person in his kitchen except her and him.

Arrogant, ironic, devoted Emile became her asylum. She felt infinitely adult with him. He said he'd had enough of marriage his first time around, but he obligingly took Denise to Atlantic City and (in the words of the Barbera D'Alba she'd been drunk on when she proposed to him) *made an honest woman of her*. At Café Louche they worked like partners, experience flowing from his head into hers. They sneered at their pretentious old rival, Le Bec-Fin. They impulse-bought a three-story town house on Federal Street, in a mixed black and white and Vietnamese neighborhood near the Italian Market. They talked about flavor the way Marxists talked about revolution.

When Emile had finally taught her everything he would ever teach her, she tried to teach *him* a thing or two—like, let's freshen up the menu, how about, let's maybe try that with a vegetable stock and a little bit of cumin, how about—and ran smack into that wall of irony and ironclad opinion that she'd loved as long as she was on the happy side of it. She felt more skilled and ambitious and *hungry* than her white-haired husband. She felt as if, while working and sleeping and working and sleeping, she'd aged so rapidly that she'd passed Emile and caught up with her parents. Her circumscribed world of round-the-clock domestic and workplace togetherness seemed to her identical to her parents' universe of two. She had old-person aches in her young hips and knees and feet. She had scarred old-person hands, she had a dry old-person vagina, she had old-person prejudices and old-person politics, she had an old-person dislike of young people and their consumer electronics and their diction. She said to herself: "I'm too young to be so old." Whereupon her banished guilt came screaming back up out of its cave on vengeful wings, because Emile was as devoted to her as ever, as faithful to his unchanging self, and she was the one who'd insisted they get married.

By amicable agreement she left his kitchen and signed on with a competitor, Ardennes, which needed a sous-chef and which, in her opinion, was superior to Café Louche in all things except the art of being excellent without seeming to try. (Unperspiring virtuosity was undeniably Emile's great gift.)

At Ardennes she conceived a desire to strangle the young woman who prepped and held down *garde manger*. The woman, Becky Hemerling, was a culinary-institute grad with wavy blond hair and a petite flat body and fair skin that turned scarlet in the kitchen heat. Everything about Becky Hemerling sickened Denise—her C.I.A. education (Denise was an autodidact snob), her overfamiliarity with more senior cooks (especially with Denise), her vocal adoration of Jodie Foster, the stupid fish-and-bicycle texts on her T-shirts, her overuse of the word "fucking" as an intensifier, her self-conscious lesbian "solidarity" with the "latinos" and "Asians" in the kitchen, her generalizations about "right-wingers" and "Kansas" and "Peoria," her facility with phrases like "men and women of color," the whole bright aura of entitlement that came of basking in the approval of educators who wished that they could be as marginalized and victimized and free of guilt as she was. *What is this person doing in my kitchen?* Denise wondered. Cooks were not supposed to be political. Cooks were the mitochondria of humanity; they had their own separate DNA, they floated in a cell and powered it but were not really *of* it. Denise suspected that Becky Hemerling had chosen the cooking life to make a political point: to be one tough chick, to hold her own with the guys. Denise loathed this motivation all the more for harboring a speck of it herself. Hemerling had a way of looking at her that suggested that she (Hemerling) knew her better than she knew herself—an insinuation at once infuriating and impossible to refute. Lying awake beside Emile at night, Denise imagined squeezing Hemerling's neck until her blue, blue eyes bugged out. She imagined pressing her thumbs into Hemerling's windpipe until it cracked.

Then one night she fell asleep and dreamed that she was strangling Becky and that Becky didn't mind. Becky's blue eyes, in fact, invited further liberties. The strangler's hands relaxed and traveled up along Becky's jawline and past her ears to the soft skin of her temples. Becky's lips parted and her eyes fell shut, as if in bliss, as the strangler stretched her legs out on her legs and her arms out on her arms . . .

Denise couldn't remember being sorrier to wake from a dream.

"If you can have this feeling in a dream," she said to herself, "it must be possible to have it in reality."

As her marriage foundered—as she became for Emile one more flashy trend-chasing crowd-pleaser from Ardennes, and as he became for her the parent she betrayed with every word she spoke or swallowed—she took comfort in the idea that her trouble with Emile was his gender. This idea dulled the edge of her guilt. It got her through the terrible Announcement she had to make, it got Emile out the door, it propelled her through an incredibly awkward first date with Becky Hemerling. She glommed on to the belief that she was gay, she held it close and thereby spared herself just enough guilt that she could let Emile be the one to leave the house, she could live with buying him out and staying, she could allow him that moral advantage.

Unfortunately, as soon as he was gone, Denise had second thoughts. She and Becky enjoyed a lovely and instructive honeymoon and then began to fight. And fight, and fight. Their fighting life, like the sex life that so briefly preceded it, was a thing of ritual. They fought about why they were fighting so much, whose fault it was. They fought in bed late at night, they drew on unguessed reservoirs of something like libido, they were hungover from fighting in the morning. They fought their little brains out. Fought fought fought. Fought on the stairway, fought in public, fought on car seats. And although they got off regularly—climaxed in red-faced screaming fits, slammed doors, kicked walls, collapsed in wet-faced paroxysms—the lust for combat was never gone for long. It bound them together, overcame their mutual dislike. As a lover's voice or hair or curving hip keeps triggering the need to stop everything and fuck, so Becky had a score of provocations that reliably sent Denise's heart rate through the roof. The worst was her contention that Denise, at heart, was a liberal collectivist pure lesbian and was simply unaware of it.

"You're so unbelievably alienated from yourself," Becky said. "You are *obviously* a dyke. You *obviously* always were."

"I'm not anything," Denise said. "I'm just me."

She wanted above all to be a private person, an independent individual. She didn't want to belong to any group, let alone a group with bad haircuts and strange resentful clothing issues. She didn't want a label, she didn't want a lifestyle, and so she ended where she'd started: wanting to strangle Becky Hemerling.

She was lucky (from a guilt-management perspective) that her divorce was in the works before she and Becky had their last, unsatisfying fight. Emile had moved to Washington to run the kitchen at the Hotel Belinger for a ton of money. The Weekend of Tears, when he returned to Philly with a truck and they divided their worldly goods and packed up his share of them, was long past by the time Denise decided, in reaction to Becky, that she wasn't a lesbian after all.

She left Ardennes and became chef at Mare Scuro, a new Adriatic seafood place. For a year she turned down every guy who asked her for a date, not just because she wasn't interested (they were waiters, purveyors, neighbors) but because she dreaded being seen in public with a man. She dreaded the day Emile found out (or the day she had to tell him, lest he find out accidentally) that she'd fallen for another man. It was better to work hard and see nobody. Life, in her experience, had a kind of velvet luster. You looked at yourself from one perspective and all you saw was weirdness. Move your head a little bit, though, and everything looked reasonably normal. She believed she couldn't hurt anybody as long as she was only working.

On a bright morning in May, Brian Callahan came by her house on Federal Street in his old Volvo station wagon, which was the color of pistachio ice cream. If you were going to buy an old Volvo, pale green was the color to get, and Brian was the kind of person who wouldn't buy a vintage car in any but the best color. Now that he was rich, of course, he could have had any car he wanted custom-painted. But, like Denise, Brian was the kind of person who considered this cheating.

When she got in the car, he asked if he could blindfold her. She looked at the black bandanna he was holding. She looked at his wedding ring.

"Trust me," he said. "It's worth being surprised by."

Even before he'd sold Eigenmelody for $19.5 million, Brian had moved through the world like a golden retriever. His face was meaty and less than handsome, but he had winning blue eyes and sandy hair and little-boy freckles. He looked like what he was—a former Haverford lacrosse player and basically decent man to whom nothing bad had ever happened and whom you therefore didn't want to disappoint.

Denise let him touch her face. She let his big hands get in her hair and tie the knot, let him disable her.

The wagon's engine sang of the work involved in propelling a chunk of metal down a road. Brian played a track from a girl-group album on his pullout stereo. Denise liked the music, but this was no surprise. Brian seemed intent on playing and saying and doing nothing that she didn't like. For three weeks he'd been phoning her and leaving low-voiced messages. ("Hey. It's me.") She could see his love coming like a train, and she liked it. Was vicariously excited by it. She didn't mistake this excitement for attraction (Hemerling, if she'd done nothing else, had made Denise suspicious of her feelings), but she couldn't help rooting for Brian in his pursuit of her; and she'd dressed, this morning, accordingly. The way she'd dressed was hardly even fair.

Brian asked her what she thought of the song.

"Eh." She shrugged, testing the limits of his eagerness to please. "It's OK."

"I'm fairly stunned," he said. "I was pretty sure you'd love this."

"Actually I do love it."

She thought: *What is my problem?*

They were on bad road with stretches of cobblestone. They crossed railroad tracks and an undulating stretch of gravel. Brian parked. "I bought the option on this site for a dollar," he said. "If you don't like it, I'm out a buck."

She put her hand to the blindfold. "I'm going to take this off."

"No. We're almost there."

He gripped her arm in a legitimate way and led her across warm gravel and into shadow. She could smell the river, feel the quiet of its nearness, its sound-swallowing liquid reach. She heard keys and a padlock, the squawk of heavy-duty hinges. Cold industrial air from a pent-up reservoir flowed over her bare shoulders and between her bare legs. The smell was of a cave with no organic content.

Brian led her up four flights of metal stairs, unpadlocked another door, and led her into a warmer space where the reverb had train-station or cathedral grandeur. The air tasted of dry molds that fed on dry molds that fed on dry molds.

When Brian unblinded her, she knew immediately where she was. The Philadelphia Electric Company in the seventies had decommissioned its dirty-coal power plants—majestic buildings, like this one just south of Center City, that Denise slowed down to admire whenever she drove by. The space was bright and vast. The ceiling was sixty feet up, and Chartres-like banks of high windows punctuated the northern and southern walls. The concrete floor had been serially repatched and deeply gouged by materials even harder than itself; it was more like a terrain than a floor. In the middle of it were the exoskeletal remains of two boiler-and-turbine units that looked like house-size crickets stripped of limbs and feelers. Eroded black electromotive oblongs of lost capability. At the river end of the space were giant hatches where the coal had come in and the ashes had gone out. Traces of absent chutes and ducts and staircases brightened the smoky walls.

Denise shook her head. "You can't put a restaurant in here."

"I was afraid you'd say that."

"You're going to lose your money before I have a chance to lose it myself."

"I might get some bank funding, too."

"Not to mention the PCBs and asbestos we're inhaling as we speak."

"There you're wrong," Brian said. "This place wouldn't be available if it qualified for Superfund money. Without Superfund money, PECO can't afford to tear it down. It's too clean."

"Bummer for PECO." She approached the turbines, loving the space regardless of its suitability. The industrial decay of Philadelphia, the rotting enchantments of the Workshop of the World, the survival of mega ruins in micro times: she recognized the mood from having been born into a family of older people who kept mothballed wool and iron things in ancient boxes in the basement. She'd gone to school in a bright modernity and come home every day to an older, darker world.

"You can't heat it, you can't cool it," she said. "It's a utility-bill nightmare."

Brian, retriever, watched her intently. "My architect says we can run a floor along the entire south wall of windows. Come out about fifty feet. Glass it in on the other three sides. Put the kitchen underneath. Steam-clean the turbines, hang some spots, and let the main space just be itself."

"This is so totally a money pit."

"Notice there aren't any pigeons," Brian said. "No puddles."

"But figure a year for the permits, another year to build, another year to get inspected. That's a long time to pay me for nothing."

Brian replied that he was aiming for a February opening. He had architect friends and contractor friends, and he foresaw no trouble with "L&I"—the dreaded city office of Licenses and Inspections. "The commissioner," he said, "is a friend of my dad's. They golf every Thursday."

Denise laughed. Brian's ambition and competence, to use a word of her mother's, "tickled" her. She looked up at the arching tops of the windows. "I don't know what kind of food you think is going to work in here."

"Something decadent and grand. That's your problem to solve."

When they returned to the car, the greenness of which was of a piece with the weeds around the empty gravel lot, Brian asked if she'd made plans for Europe. "You should take at least two months," he said. "I have an ulterior motive here."

"Yes?"

"If you go, then I can go for a couple of weeks myself. I want to eat what you eat. I want to hear how you think."

He said this with disarming self-interest. Who wouldn't want to travel in Europe with a pretty woman who knew her food and wine? If you, not he, were the lucky devil who got to do it, he would be as delighted for you as he expected you, now, to be delighted for him. This was his tone.

The part of Denise that suspected she might have better sex with Brian than she'd had with other men, the part of her that recognized her own ambition in him, agreed to take six weeks in Europe and connect with him in Paris.

The other, more suspicious part of her said: "When am I going to meet your family?"

"How about next weekend? Come out and see us at Cape May."

Cape May, New Jersey, consisted of a core of overdecorated Victorians and fashionably shabby bungalows surrounded by new printed-circuit tracts of vile boom. Naturally, being Brian's parents, the Callahans owned one of the best old bungalows. Behind it was a pool for early-summer weekends when the ocean was cold. Here Denise, arriving late on a Saturday afternoon, found Brian and his daughters lounging while a mouse-haired woman, covered with sweat and rust, attacked a wrought-iron table with a wire brush.

Denise had expected Brian's wife to be ironic and stylish and something of a knockout. Robin Passafaro was wearing yellow sweat pants, an MAB paint cap, a Phillies jersey of unflattering redness, and terrible glasses. She wiped her hand on her sweats and gave it to Denise. Her greeting was squeaky and oddly formal: "It's very nice to meet you." She went immediately back to work.

I don't like you either, Denise thought.

Sinéad, a skinny pretty girl of ten, was sitting on the diving board with a book in her lap. She waved carefully at Denise. Erin, a younger and chunkier girl wearing headphones, was hunched over a picnic table with a scowl of concentration. She gave a low whistle.

"Erin's learning birdcalls," Brian said.

"Why?"

"Basically, we have no idea."

"Magpie," Erin announced. "Queg-queg-queg-queg?"

"This might be a good time to put that away," Brian said.

Erin peeled off her headphones, ran to the diving board, and tried to bounce her sister off it. Sinéad's book nearly went into the soup. She snagged it with an elegant hand. "Dad—!"

"Honey, it's a diving board, not a reading board."

There was a coked-up fast-forwardness to Robin's brushing. Her work seemed pointed and resentful and it set Denise's nerves on edge. Brian, too, sighed and considered his wife. "Are you almost done with that?"

"Do you want me to stop?"

"That would be nice, yes."

"OK." Robin dropped the brush and moved toward the house. "Denise, can I get you something to drink?"

"Glass of water, thanks."

"Erin, listen," Sinéad said. "I'll be a black hole and you be a red dwarf."

"I want to be a black hole," Erin said.

"No, I'm the black hole. The red dwarf runs around in circles and gradually gets sucked in by powerful gravitational forces. The black hole sits here and reads."

"Do we collide?" Erin said.

"Yes," Brian interposed, "but no information about the event ever reaches the outside world. It's a perfectly silent collision."

Robin reappeared in a black one-piece swimsuit. With a gesture just short of rude, she gave Denise her water.

"Thank you," Denise said.

"You're welcome!" Robin said. She took off her glasses and dove into the deep end. She swam underwater while Erin circled the pool and emitted shrieks appropriate to a dying M- or S-class star. When Robin surfaced at the shallow end she looked naked in her semi-blindness. She looked more like the wife Denise had imagined—hair pouring in rivers down her head and shoulders, her cheekbones and dark eyebrows gleaming. As she left the pool, water beaded on the hemming of her suit and streamed through the untended hairs of her bikini line.

An old unresolved confusion gathered like asthma in Denise. She felt a need to get away and cook.

"I stopped at the necessary markets," she told Brian.

"It doesn't seem fair to put our guest to work," he said.

"On the other hand, I offered, and you're paying me."

"There is that, yes."

"Erin, now you be a pathogen," Sinéad said, slipping into the water, "and I'll be a leukocyte."

Denise made a simple salad of red and yellow cherry tomatoes. She made quinoa with butter and saffron, and halibut steaks with a color guard of mussels and roasted peppers. She was nearly done before she thought to peer under the foil coverings of several containers in the refrigerator. Here she found a tossed salad, a fruit salad, a platter of cleaned ears of corn, and a pan of (could it be?) pigs in blankets?

Brian was drinking a beer by himself on the deck.

"There's a dinner in the fridge," Denise told him. "There's already a dinner."

"Yikes," Brian said. "Robin must have—I guess when the girls and I were out fishing."

"Well, there's a whole dinner there. I just made a second whole dinner." Denise laughed, really angry. "Do you guys not communicate?"

"No, in fact, this was not our most communicative day. Robin had some work at the Garden Project that she wanted to stay and do. I had to kind of drag her over here."

"Well, fuck."

"Look," Brian said, "we'll have your dinner now, and we can have hers tomorrow. This is totally my fault."

"I guess!"

She found Robin on the other porch, cutting Erin's toenails. "I just realized," she said, "that I've been making dinner and you already made it. Brian didn't tell me."

Robin shrugged. "Whatever."

"No, I'm really sorry about this, though."

"Whatever," Robin said. "The girls are excited that you're cooking."

"I'm sorry."

"Whatever."

At dinner Brian prodded his shy progeny to answer Denise's questions. Each time she caught the girls staring at her, they lowered their eyes and reddened. Sinéad in particular seemed to know the right way to want her. Robin ate quickly with her head down and declared the food "tasty." It wasn't clear how much her unpleasantness was aimed at Brian and how much at Denise. She went to bed soon after the girls, and in the morning she had already left for mass when Denise got up.

"Quick question," Brian said, pouring coffee. "How would you feel about driving me and the girls back to Philly tonight? Robin wants to get back to the Garden Project early."

Denise hesitated. She felt positively shoved by Robin into Brian's arms.

"Not a problem if you don't want to," he said. "She's willing to take a bus and leave us the car."

A *bus*? A *bus*?

Denise laughed. "Sure, no, I'll drive you." She added, echoing Robin: "Whatever!"

At the beach, as the sun burned off the metallic morning coastal clouds, she and Brian watched Erin veer through the surf while Sinéad dug a shallow grave.

"I'll be Jimmy Hoffa," Sinéad said, "and you guys be the Mob."

They worked to inter the girl in sand, smoothing the cool curves of her burial mound, thumping the hollows of the living body underneath. The mound was geologically active and was experiencing little quakes, webs of fissure spreading where Sinéad's belly rose and fell.

"I'm just now putting it together," Brian said, "that you were married to Emile Berger."

"Do you know him?"

"Not personally, but I knew Café Louche. Ate there often."

"That was us."

"Two awfully big egos in a little kitchen."

"Yuh."

"Do you miss him?"

"My divorce is the great unhappiness of my life."

"That's an answer," Brian said, "but not to my question."

Sinéad was destroying her sarcophagus slowly from within, toes wriggling into daylight, a knee erupting, pink fingers sprouting from moist sand. Erin flung herself into a slurry of sand and water, picked herself up, and flung herself back down.

I could get to like these girls, Denise thought.

At home that night she called her mother and listened, as she did every Sunday, to Enid's litany of Alfred's sins against a healthy attitude, against a healthful lifestyle, against doctors' orders, against circadian orthodoxies, against established principles of daytime verticality, against commonsense rules regarding ladders and staircases, against all that was fun-loving and optimistic in Enid's nature. After fifteen grueling minutes Enid concluded, "Now, and how are you?"

Since her divorce, Denise had resolved to tell her mother fewer lies, and so she made herself come clean about her enviable travel plans. She omitted only the fact that she would travel in France with someone else's husband; this fact already radiated trouble.

"Oh, I wish I could go with you!" Enid said. "I so love Austria."

Denise manfully offered: "Why don't you take a month and come over?"

"Denise, there's no way could I leave Dad by himself."

"He can come, too."

"You know what he says. He's given up on land tours. He has too much trouble with his legs. So, you just go and have a wonderful time *for* me. Say hello to my favorite city! And be sure and visit Cindy Meisner. She and Klaus have a chalet in St. Moritz and a huge, elegant apartment in Vienna."

To Enid, Austria meant "The Blue Danube" and "Edelweiss." The music boxes in her living room, with their floral and Alpine marquetry, all came from Vienna. Enid was fond of saying that her mother's mother had been "Viennese," because this was a synonym, in her mind, for "Austrian," by which she meant "of or relating to the Austro-Hungarian Empire"—an empire that at the time of her grandmother's birth had encompassed lands from north of Prague to south of Sarajevo. Denise, who as a girl had had a massive crush on Barbra Streisand in *Yentl* and who as a teenager had steeped herself in I. B. Singer and Sholem Aleichem, once badgered from Enid an admission that the grandmother in question might in fact have been Jewish. Which, as she pointed out in triumph, would make both her and Enid Jewish by direct matrilineal descent. But Enid, quickly backpedaling, said that no, no, her grandmother had been *Catholic*.

Denise had a professional interest in certain flavors from her grandmother's cooking—country ribs and fresh sauerkraut, gooseberries and whortleberries, dumplings, trouts, and sausages. The culinary problem was to make central European heartiness palatable to Size 4 Petites. The Titanium Card crowd didn't want Wagnerian slabs of Sauerbraten, or softballs of Semmelknödel, or alps of Schlag. This crowd might, however, eat sauerkraut. If ever there was a food for chicks with toothpick legs: low-fat and high-flavor and versatile, ready to fall in bed with pork, with goose, with chicken, with chestnuts, ready to take a raw plunge with mackerel sashimi or smoked bluefish . . .

Severing her last ties with Mare Scuro, she flew to Frankfurt as a salaried employee of Brian Callahan with a no-limit American Express card. In Germany she drove a hundred miles an hour and was tailgated by cars flashing their high beams. In Vienna she looked for a Vienna that didn't exist. She ate nothing that she couldn't have done better herself; one night she had Wiener schnitzel and thought, yes, this is Wiener schnitzel, uh huh. Her idea of Austria was way more vivid than Austria itself. She went to the Kunsthistorisches Museum and the Philharmonic; she reproached herself for being a bad tourist. She got so bored and lonely that she finally called Cindy von Kippel (née Meisner) and accepted an invitation to dinner at her seventeen-room apartment on the Ringstraße.

Cindy had gone thick around the middle and looked, Denise thought, far worse than she had to. Her features were lost in foundation, rouge, and lipstick. Her black silk pants were roomy in the hips and tight at the ankles. Brushing cheeks and weathering the tear-gas attack of Cindy's perfume, Denise was surprised to detect bacterial breath.

Cindy's husband, Klaus, had yard-wide shoulders, narrow hips, and a butt of fascinating tininess. The von Kippel living room was half a block long and furnished with gilt chairs in sociability-killing formations. Ancestral Watteauery hung on the walls, as did Klaus's Olympic bronze medal, mounted and framed, beneath the largest chandelier.

"What you see here is merely a replica," Klaus told Denise. "The original medal is in safe storage."

On a Louis XIV–ish sideboard was a plate of bread disks, a mangled smoked fish with the consistency of chunk canned tuna, and a not-large piece of Emmentaler.

Klaus took a bottle from a silver bucket and poured Sekt with a flourish. "To our culinary pilgrim," he said, raising a glass. "Welcome to the holy city of Wien."

The Sekt was sweet and overcarbonated and remarkably much like Sprite.

"It's so neat you're here!" Cindy cried. She snapped her fingers frantically, and a maid hurried in through a side door. "Annerl, hun," Cindy said in a more babyish voice, "remember I said use the rye bread, not the white bread?"

"Yis, madam," the middle-aged Annerl said.

"So it's sort of too late now, because I meant this white bread for later, but I really wish you'd take this back and bring us the rye bread instead! And then maybe send someone out for more white bread for later!" Cindy explained to Denise: "She's so so sweet, but so so silly. Aren't you, Annerl? Aren't you a silly thing?"

"Yis, madam."

"Well, you know what it's like, you're a chef," Cindy told Denise as Annerl exited. "It's probably even worse for you, the stupidity of people."

"The *arrogance* and stupidity," Klaus said.

"Tell somebody what to do," Cindy said, "and they just go do something else, it's so frustrating! So frustrating!"

"My mother sends her greetings," Denise said.

"Your mom is so neat. She was always so nice to me. Klaus, you know the tiny, tiny little house my family used to live in (a long time ago, when I was a tiny, tiny little girl), well, Denise's parents were our neighbors. My mom and her mom are still good friends. I guess your folks are still in their little old house, right?"

Klaus gave a harsh laugh and turned to Denise. "Do you know what I rilly *hate* about St. Jude?"

"No," Denise said. "What do you really hate about St. Jude?"

"I rilly hate the phony democracy. The people in St. Jude pretend they're all alike. It's all very *nice*. Nice, nice, nice. But the people are not all alike. Not at all. There are class differences, there are race differences, there are enormous and decisive economic differences, and yet nobody's honest in this case. Everybody pretends! Have you noticed this?"

"Do you mean," Denise said, "like the differences between my mom and Cindy's mom?"

"No, I don't know your mother."

"Klaus, actually!" Cindy said. "Actually you did meet her. Three Thanksgivings ago, at the open house. Remember?"

"Well, you see, everybody's the same," Klaus explained. "That's what I'm telling you. How can you distinguish the people when everybody pretends to be the same?"

Annerl came back with the dismal plate and different bread.

"Here, try some of this fish," Cindy urged Denise. "Isn't this champagne wonderful? Really different! Klaus and I used to drink it drier, but then we found this, and we love it."

"There's a *snob appeal* to the dry," Klaus said. "But those who rilly know their Sekt know this emperor, this *Extra-Trocken*, is quite naked."

Denise crossed her legs and said, "My mother tells me you're a doctor."

"Yah, sports medicine," Klaus said.

"All the best skiers come to Klaus!" Cindy said.

"This is how I repay my debt to society," Klaus said.

Though Cindy begged her to stay, Denise escaped from the Ringstraße before nine and escaped from Vienna the next morning, heading east across the haze-white valley of the middle Danube. Conscious of spending Brian's money, she worked long days, walking Budapest sector by sector, taking notes at every meal, checking out bakeries and tiny stalls and cavernous restaurants rescued from the brink of terminal neglect. She traveled as far east as Ruthenia, the birthplace of

Enid's father's parents, now a trans-Carpathian smidgen of the Ukraine. In the landscapes she traversed there was no trace of shtetl. No Jews to speak of in any but the largest cities. Everything as durably, drably Gentile as she'd reconciled herself to being. The food, by and large, was coarse. The Carpathian highlands, everywhere scarred with the stab wounds of coal and pitchblende mining, looked suitable for burying lime-sprinkled bodies in mass graves. Denise saw faces that resembled her own, but they were closed and prematurely weathered, not a word of English in their eyes. She had no roots. This was not her country.

She flew to Paris and met Brian in the lobby of the Hôtel des Deux Îles. In June he'd spoken of bringing his whole family, but he'd come alone. He was wearing American khakis and a very wrinkled white shirt. Denise was so lonely she almost jumped into his arms.

What kind of idiot, she wondered, *lets her husband go to Paris with a person like me?*

They ate dinner at La Cuillère Curieuse, a Michelin two-star establishment that in Denise's opinion was trying too hard. She didn't want raw yellowtail or papaya confit when she came to France. On the other hand, she was plenty sick of goulash.

Brian, deferring to her judgment absolutely, made her choose the wine and order both dinners. Over coffee she asked him why Robin hadn't come along to Paris.

"It's the first zucchini harvest at the Garden Project," he said with uncharacteristic bitterness.

"Travel is a chore for some people," Denise said.

"It didn't use to be for Robin," Brian said. "We used to take great trips, all over the West. And now that we can really afford it, she doesn't want to go. It's like she's on strike against money."

"It must be a shock, suddenly having so much."

"Look, I just want to have fun with it," Brian said. "I don't want to be a different person. But I'm not going to wear sackcloth, either."

"Is that what Robin is doing?"

"She hasn't been happy since the day I sold the company."

Let's get an egg timer, Denise thought, and see how long this marriage lasts.

She waited in vain, as they walked the length of the quai after dinner, for Brian to brush her hand with his. He kept looking at her hopefully, as if to be sure she had no objection to his stopping at this store window or veering down that side street. He had a happy canine way of seeking approval without seeming insecure. He described his plans for the Generator as if it were a party that he was almost certain she would enjoy. Clearly convinced, in the same way, that he was doing a Good Thing that she wanted, he backed away from her hygienically when they parted for the night in the lobby of the Deux Îles.

She endured ten days of his affability. Toward the end she couldn't stand to see herself in mirrors, her face seemed to her so ravaged, her tits so droopy, her hair such a frizzball, her clothes so traveled-out. She was, basically, *shocked* that this unhappy husband was resisting her. Even though he had good reason to resist her! He being the father of two lovely girls! And she being, after all, his paid employee! She respected his resistance, she believed that this was how adults should behave; and she was extremely unhappy about it.

She bent her will to the task of not feeling overweight and starving herself. It didn't help that she was sick of lunch and dinner and wanted only picnics. Wanted baguettes, white peaches, dry chèvre, and coffee. She was sick of watching Brian enjoy a meal. She hated Robin for having a husband she could trust. She hated Robin for her rudeness at Cape May. She cursed Robin in her head, called Robin a cunt and threatened to fuck her husband. Several nights, after dinner, she considered violating her own twisted ethics and putting the moves on Brian (because surely he would defer to her judgment; surely, given permission, he would jump up on her bed and pant and grin and lick her hand), but she was finally too demoralized by her hair and clothes. She was ready to go home.

Two nights before they left, she knocked on Brian's door before dinner and he pulled her into his room and kissed her.

He'd given no warning of his change of heart. She visited the confessor in her head and was able to say, "Nothing! I did nothing! I knocked on the door, and next thing I know, he's on his knees."

On his knees, he pressed her hands to his face. She looked at him as she'd looked at Don Armour long ago. His desire brought cool topical relief to the dryness and crackedness, the bodywide distress, of her person. She followed him to bed.

Naturally, being good at everything, Brian knew how to kiss. He had the oblique style she liked. She murmured ambiguously: "I love your taste." He put his hands everywhere she'd expected him to put them. She unbuttoned his shirt as the woman does at a certain point. She licked his nipple in the nodding, firm way of a grooming cat. She put a practiced, curled hand on the lump in his pants. She was beautifully, avidly adulterous and she knew it. She embarked on buckle work, on hook and button projects, on elastic-band labors, until there began to swell inside her, hardly noticeable and then suddenly distinct, and then not merely distinct but increasingly painful in its pressure on her peritoneum and eyeballs and arteries and meninges, a body-sized, Robin-faced balloon of *wrongness*.

Brian's voice was in her ear. He was asking the protection question. He'd mistaken her discomfort for transports, her squirming for an invitation. She clarified by rolling out of bed and crouching in a corner of the hotel room. She said she couldn't.

Brian sat up on the bed and made no reply. She stole a glance and confirmed that his endowment was per expectation for the man who had everything. She suspected that she wouldn't soon forget the sight of this dick. Would be seeing it when she closed her eyes, at inconvenient times, in far-fetched contexts.

She apologized to him.

"No, you're right," Brian said, deferring to her judgment. "I feel terrible. I've never done anything like this."

"See, I have," she said, lest he think her merely timid. "More than once. And I don't want to anymore."

"No, of course, you're right."

"If you weren't married— If I weren't your employee—"

"Listen, I'm dealing with it. I'm going in the bathroom now. I'm dealing with it."

"Thank you."

Part of her thought: *What is my problem?*

Another part of her thought: *For once in my life, I'm doing the right thing.*

She spent four nights by herself in Alsace and flew home from Frankfurt. She was shocked when she went to see the progress that Brian's team had made at the Generator in her absence. The building-within-a-building was already framed out, the concrete subfloors poured. She could see what the effect would be: a bright bubble of modernity in a twilight of monumental industry. Although she had faith in her cooking, the grandness of the space made her nervous. She wished that she'd insisted on an ordinary plain space in which her food could shine alone. She felt seduced and suckered somehow—as if, unbeknownst to her, Brian had been competing with her for the world's attention. As if, all along, in his affable way, he'd been angling to make the restaurant his, not hers.

She was haunted, just as she'd feared, by the afterimage of his dick. She felt gladder and gladder that she hadn't let him put it in her. Brian had every advantage that she had, plus many of his own. He was male, he was rich, he was a born insider; he wasn't hampered by Lambert weirdnesses or strong opinions; he was an *amateur* with nothing to lose but throwaway money, and to succeed all he needed was a good idea and somebody else (namely her) to do the hard work. How lucky she'd been, in that hotel room, to recognize him as her adversary! Two more minutes and she would have disappeared. She would have become another facet of his really fun life, her beauty reflecting on his irresistibility, her talents redounding to his restaurant's glory. How lucky she'd been, how lucky.

She believed that if, when the Generator opened, reviewers paid more attention to the space than to the food, she would *lose* and Brian would *win*. And so she worked her ass off. She convection-roasted country ribs to brownness and cut them thin, along the grain, for presentation, reduced and darkened the kraut gravy to bring out its nutty, earthy, cabbagy, porky flavor, and arted up the plate with twin testicular new potatoes, a cluster of Brussels sprouts, and a spoon of stewed white beans that she lightly spiked with roasted garlic. She invented luxurious new white sausages. She matched a fennel relish, roasted potatoes, and good bitter wholesome rapini with fabulous pork chops that she bought direct from a sixties holdover organic farmer who did his own butchering and made his own deliveries. She took the guy to lunch and visited his farm in Lancaster County and met the hogs in question, examined their eclectic diet (boiled yams and chicken wings, acorns and chestnuts) and toured the soundproofed room where they were slaughtered. She extracted commitments from her old crew at Mare Scuro. She took former colleagues out on Brian's AmEx and sized up the local competition (most of it reassuringly undistinguished) and sampled desserts to see if anybody's pastry chef was worth stealing. She staged one-woman late-night forcemeat festivals. She made sauerkraut in five-gallon buckets in her basement. She made it with red cabbage and with shredded kale in cabbage juice, with juniper berries and black peppercorns. She hurried along the fermentation with hundred-watt bulbs.

Brian still called her every day, but he didn't take her driving in his Volvo anymore, he didn't play her music. Behind his polite questions she sensed a waning interest. She recommended an old friend of hers, Rob Zito, to manage the Generator, and when Brian took the two of them to lunch, he stayed for half an hour. He had an appointment in New York.

One night Denise called him at home and instead got Robin Passafaro. Robin's clipped phrases—"OK," "Whatever," "Yes," "I'll tell him," "OK"—so irritated Denise that she deliberately kept her on the line. She asked how the Garden Project was going.

"Fine," Robin said. "I'll tell Brian you called."

"Could I come over sometime and see it?"

Robin replied with naked rudeness: "Why?"

"Well," Denise said, "it's something Brian talks about" (this was a lie; he rarely mentioned it), "it's an interesting project" (in fact, it sounded utopian and crackpot), "and, you know, I love vegetables."

"Uh huh."

"So maybe some Saturday afternoon or something."

"Whenever."

A moment later Denise slammed the phone down in its cradle. She was angry, among other things, at how fake she'd sounded to herself. "I could have fucked your husband!" she said. "And I chose not to! So how about a little friendliness?"

Maybe, if she'd been a better person, she would have left Robin alone. Maybe she wanted to make Robin like her simply to deny her the satisfaction of disliking her—to win that contest of esteem. Maybe she was just picking up the gauntlet. But the desire to be liked was real. She was haunted by the feeling that Robin had been in the hotel room with her and Brian; by that bursting sensation of Robin's presence inside her body.

On the last Saturday of baseball season she cooked at home for eight hours, shrink-wrapping trout, juggling half a dozen kraut salads, and pairing the pan juices of sautéed kidneys with interesting spirits. Late in the day she went for a walk and, finding herself going west, crossed Broad Street into the ghetto of Point Breeze, where Robin had her Project.

The weather was fine. Early autumn in Philadelphia brought smells of fresh seawater and tidewater, gradual abatements in temperature, a quiet abdication of control by the humid air masses that had held the onshore breeze at bay all summer. Denise passed an old woman in a housecoat standing watch while two dusty men unloaded Acme groceries from a corroded Pinto's hatchback. Cinderblock was the material of choice over here for blinding windows. There were fire-gutted LUNC ONETTEs and P ZER As. Friable houses with bedsheet curtains. Expanses of fresh asphalt that seemed to seal the neighborhood's fate more than promise renewal.

Denise didn't care if she saw Robin. Almost better, in a way, to score the point subtly—to let Robin find out from Brian that she'd taken the trouble to walk by the Project.

She came to a block within whose chain-link confines were small hills of mulch and large piles of wilted vegetation. At the far corner of the block, behind the only house left standing on it, somebody was working rocky soil with a shovel.

The front door of the solitary house was open. A black girl of college age was sitting at a desk that also contained a vastly ghastly plaid sofa and a wheeled blackboard on which a column of names (Lateesha,

Latoya, Tyrell) was followed by columns of HOURS TO DATE and DOL-LARS TO DATE.

"Looking for Robin," Denise said.

The girl nodded at the open rear door of the house. "She's in back."

The garden was raw but peaceful. Not much seemed to have been grown here besides squashes and their cousins, but the patches of vine were extensive, and the smells of mulch and dirt, and the onshore autumn breeze, were full of childhood memory.

Robin was shoveling rubble into a makeshift sieve. She had thin arms and a hummingbird metabolism and took many fast small bites of rubble instead of fewer big ones. She was wearing a black bandanna and a very dirty T-shirt with the text QUALITY DAYCARE: PAY NOW OR PAY LATER. She seemed neither surprised nor pleased to see Denise.

"This is a big project," Denise said.

Robin shrugged, holding the shovel with both hands as if to stress that she felt interrupted.

"Do you want some help?" Denise said.

"No. The kids were supposed to do this, but there's a game over at the river. I'm just cleaning up."

She whacked the rubble in the sieve to urge some dirt through. Caught in the mesh were fragments of brick and mortar, gobs of roofing tar, ailanthus limbs, petrified cat shit, Baccardi and Yuengling labels with backings of broken glass.

"So what did you grow?" Denise said.

Robin shrugged again. "Nothing that would impress you."

"Well, like what?"

"Like zucchini and pumpkins."

"I cook with both of those."

"Yeah."

"Who's the girl?"

"I have a couple of half-time assistants that I pay. Sara's a junior at Temple."

"And who are the kids who were supposed to be here?"

"Neighborhood kids between twelve and sixteen." Robin took off her glasses and rubbed sweat from her face with a dirty sleeve. Denise had forgotten, or had never noticed to begin with, what a pretty mouth she had. "They get minimum wage plus vegetables, plus a share of any money we make."

"Do you subtract expenses?"

"That would discourage them."

"Right."

Robin looked away, across the street, at a row of dead buildings with rusting sheet-metal cornices. "Brian says you're very competitive."

"Oh really?"

"He said he wouldn't want to arm-wrestle you."

Denise winced.

"He said he wouldn't want to be the other chef in the kitchen with you."

"No danger of that," Denise said.

"He said he wouldn't want to play Scrabble with you."

"Uh huh."

"He said he wouldn't want to play Trivial Pursuit with you."

OK, OK, Denise thought.

Robin was breathing hard. "Anyway."

"Yeah, anyway."

"Here's why I didn't go to Paris," Robin said. "I thought Erin was too young. Sinéad was having fun at art camp, and I had tons of work here."

"I understood that."

"And you guys were going to be talking about food all day. And Brian said it was business. So."

Denise raised her eyes from the dirt but couldn't quite look Robin in the eye. "It was business."

Robin, her lip trembling, said, "Whatever!"

Above the ghetto a fleet of copper-bottomed clouds, Revere Ware clouds, had withdrawn to the northwest. It was the moment when the blue backdrop of the sky grayed to the same value as the stratus formations in front of it, when night light and day light were in equilibrium.

"You know, I'm not really into guys," Denise said.

"Pardon me?"

"I said I don't sleep with men anymore. Since I got divorced."

Robin frowned as if this made no sense to her at all. "Does Brian know that?"

"I don't know. Not from my telling him."

Robin thought this over for a moment and then began to laugh. She said, "Hee hee hee!" She said, "Ha ha ha!" Her laugh was full-throated and embarrassing and, at the same time, Denise thought, lovely. It echoed off the rusty-corniced houses. "Poor Brian!" she said. "Poor Brian!"

Robin immediately became more cordial. She put down her shovel and gave Denise a tour of the garden—"my little enchanted kingdom" she called it. Finding that she had Denise's interest, she risked enthusiasm. Here was a new asparagus patch, here two rows of young pear and apple trees that she hoped to espalier, here the late crops of sunflowers, acorn squash, and kale. She'd planted only sure winners this summer, hoping to hook a core group of local teenagers and reward them for the thankless infrastructural work of preparing beds, running pipes, adjusting drainages, and connecting rain barrels to the roof of the house.

"This is basically a selfish project," Robin said. "I always wanted a big garden, and now the whole inner city's going back to farmland. But the kids who really need to be out working with their hands and learning what fresh food tastes like are the ones who aren't doing it. They're latchkey kids. They're getting high, they're having sex, or they're stuck in some classroom until six with a computer. But they're also at an age when it's still fun to play in the dirt."

"Though possibly not as much fun as sex or drugs."

"Maybe not for ninety percent of kids," Robin said. "I just want there to be something for the other ten percent. Some alternative that doesn't involve computers. I want Sinéad and Erin to be around kids who aren't like them. I want them to learn how to work. I want them to know that work isn't just pointing and clicking."

"This is very admirable," Denise said.

Robin, mistaking her tone, said, "Whatever."

Denise sat on the plastic skin of a bale of peat moss while Robin washed up and changed her clothes. Maybe it was because she could count on one hand the autumn Saturday evenings that she'd spent out-side a kitchen since she was twenty, or maybe because some sentimental part of her was taken in by the egalitarian ideal that Klaus von Kippel found so phony in St. Jude, but the word she wanted to apply to Robin Passafaro, who had lived in urban Philly all her life, was "midwestern." By which she meant *hopeful* or *enthusiastic* or *community-spirited*.

She didn't care so much, after all, about being liked. She found her-self liking. When Robin came out and locked the house, Denise asked if she had time for dinner.

"Brian and his dad took the girls to see the Phillies," Robin said. "They'll come home full of stadium food. So, sure. We can have din-ner."

"I have stuff in my kitchen," Denise said. "Do you mind?"

"Anything. Whatever."

Typically, if a chef invited you to dinner, you considered yourself lucky and you hastened to show it. But Robin seemed determined not to be impressed.

Night had fallen. The air on Catharine Street smelled like the last weekend of baseball. Walking east, Robin told Denise the story of her brother, Billy. Denise had already heard the story from Brian, but parts of Robin's version were new to her.

"So wait," she said. "Brian sold his company to W——, and then Billy attacked one of W——'s vice presidents, and you think there's a connection?"

"God, yes," Robin said. "That's what's so horrible."

"Brian didn't mention that part."

Shrillness came pouring out of Robin. "I can't believe it! That's the whole *point*. God! It is so, so, so like him not to mention that part. Be-cause that part might actually make things hard for him, you know, the way things are hard for me. It might get in the way of his fun time in Paris, or his lunch date with Harvey Keitel, or whatever. I can't believe he didn't mention it."

"Explain to me what the problem is?"

"Rick Flamburg's disabled for life," Robin said. "My brother is in jail for the next ten or fifteen years, this horrible company is corrupting the city schools, my father is on anti-psychotics, and Brian is like, hey, look what W—— just did for us, let's move to Mendocino!"

"But you didn't do anything wrong," Denise said. "You're not responsible for any of those other things."

Robin turned and looked straight into her. "What's life for?"

"I don't know."

"I don't either. But I don't think it's about winning."

They marched along in silence. Denise, to whom winning did matter, grimly noted that, on top of all his other luck, Brian had married a woman of principle and spirit.

She further noted, however, that Robin didn't seem particularly loyal.

Denise's living room contained little more than it had after Emile had emptied it three years earlier. In their contest of self-denials, on the Weekend of Tears, Denise had had the double advantage of feeling guiltier than Emile and of having already agreed to take the house. In the end she'd succeeded in making Emile take practically every joint possession that she liked or valued and many others that she didn't like but could have used.

The emptiness of the house had disgusted Becky Hemerling. It was *cold*, it was *self-hating*, it was *a monastery*.

"Nice and spare," Robin commented.

Denise sat her down at the half Ping-Pong table that served as her kitchen table, opened a fifty-dollar wine, and proceeded to feed her. Denise had seldom had to struggle with her weight, but she would have blimped out in a month if she'd eaten like Robin. She watched in awe as her guest, elbows flying, devoured two kidneys and a homemade sausage, tried each of the kraut salads, and spread butter on her third healthy wedge of artisanal rye bread.

She herself had the butterflies and ate hardly anything.

"St. Jude is one of my favorite saints," Robin said. "Did Brian tell you I've been going to church?"

"He mentioned it, yes."

"I'm sure he did. I'm sure he was very understanding and patient!" Robin's voice was loud and her face red with wine. Denise felt a constriction in her chest. "Anyway, one of the great things about being Catholic is you get to have saints, like St. Jude."

"Patron saint of hopeless causes?"

"Exactly. What's a church for if not lost causes?"

"I feel this way about sports teams," Denise said. "That the winners don't need your help."

Robin nodded. "*You* know what I mean. But if you live with Brian you start feeling like there's something wrong with losers. Not that he'll actually criticize you. He'll always be very understanding and patient and loving. Brian's great! Nothing wrong with Brian! It's just that he'd rather root for a winner. And I'm not really a winner like that. And I don't really want to be."

Denise would never have talked about Emile like this. She wouldn't do it even now.

"See, but you *are* that kind of winner," Robin said. "That's why I frankly sort of saw you as my potential replacement. I saw you as next in line."

"Nope."

Robin made her self-consciously delighted sounds. She said, "Hee hee hee!"

"In Brian's defense," Denise said, "I don't think he needs you to be Brooke Astor. I think he'd settle for bourgeois."

"I can live with being bourgeois," Robin said. "A house like this is what I want. I love that your kitchen table is half a Ping-Pong table."

"It's yours for twenty bucks."

"Brian's wonderful. He's the person I wanted to spend my life with, he's the father of my kids. *I'm* the problem. *I'm* the one who's not getting with the program. *I'm* the one who's going to confirmation class. Listen, do you have a jacket? I'm freezing."

The low candles were spilling wax in the October draft. Denise fetched her favorite jean jacket, a discontinued Levi's product with a woolen lining, and noticed how large it looked on Robin's smaller arms, how it engulfed her thinner shoulders, like a letter jacket on a ballplayer's girlfriend.

The next day, wearing the jacket herself, she found it softer and lighter than she remembered. She pulled on the collar and hugged herself with it.

No matter how hard she worked that fall, she had more free time and a more flexible schedule than she'd had in many years. She began to drop by the Project with food from her kitchen. She went over to Brian and Robin's house on Panama Street, found Brian away, and stayed for an evening. A few nights later, when Brian came home and found her baking madeleines with the girls, he acted as if he'd seen her in his kitchen a hundred times.

She had a lifetime of practice at arriving late in a family of four and being loved by all. Her next conquest on Panama Street was Sinéad, the serious reader, the little fashion plate. Denise took her shopping on Saturdays. She bought her costume jewelry, an antique Tuscan jewelry case, mid-seventies disco and proto-disco albums, old illustrated books about costumes, Antarctica, Jackie Kennedy, and shipbuilding. She helped Sinéad select larger, brighter, lesser gifts for Erin. Sinéad, like her father, had impeccable taste. She wore black jeans and corduroy miniskirts and jumpers, silver bangles, and strings of plastic beads even longer than her very long hair. In Denise's kitchen, after shopping, she peeled potatoes immaculately or rolled out simple doughs while the cook contrived lagniappes for a child's palate: wedges of pear, strips of homemade mortadella, elderberry sorbet in a doll-size bowl of elderberry soup, lambsmeat ravioli Xed with mint-charged olive oil, cubes of fried polenta.

On the rare occasions, like weddings, when Robin and Brian still went out together, Denise baby-sat the girls at Panama Street. She taught them how to make spinach pasta and how to tango. She listened to Erin recite the U.S. presidents in order. She joined Sinéad in raiding drawers for costumes.

"Denise and I will be ethnologists," Sinéad said, "and, Erin, you can be a Hmong person."

As she watched Sinéad work out with Erin how a Hmong woman might comport herself, as she watched her dance to Donna Summer with her lazy half-bored minimalism, barely lifting her heels from the floor, faintly rolling her shoulders and letting her hair slide and sift across her back (Erin all the while throwing epileptic fits), Denise loved not only the girl but the girl's parents for whatever childrearing magic they'd brought to bear on her.

Robin was less impressed. "Of course they love *you*," she said. "You're not trying to comb the tangles out of Sinéad's hair. You're not arguing for twenty minutes about what constitutes 'making the bed.' You never see Sinéad's math scores."

"They're not good?" the smitten baby-sitter said.

"They're appalling. We may threaten not to let her see you if they don't improve."

"Oh, don't do that."

"Maybe you'd like to do some long division with her."

"I'll do anything."

One Sunday in November, while the family of five was walking in Fairmount Park, Brian remarked to Denise, "Robin's really warmed to you. I wasn't sure she would."

"I like Robin a lot," Denise said.

"I think at first she felt a little intimidated by you."

"She had good reason to. Didn't she?"

"I never told her anything."

"Well, thank you for that."

It didn't escape Denise that the qualities that would have enabled Brian to cheat on Robin—his sense of entitlement, his retrieverish conviction that whatever he was doing was the Good Thing We All Want—would also make it easy to cheat on him. Denise could feel herself becoming an extension of "Robin" in Brian's mind, and since "Robin" had permanent status as "great" in Brian's estimation, neither she nor "Denise" required further thought or worry on his part.

Brian seemed to put similarly absolute faith in Denise's friend Rob Zito to oversee the Generator. Brian kept himself reasonably well informed, but mainly, as the weather got colder, he was absent. Denise briefly wondered if he'd fallen for another female, but the new darling turned out to be an independent filmmaker, Jerry Schwartz, who was noted for his exquisite taste in sound-track music and his skill at repeatedly finding funding for red-ink art-house projects. ("A film best enjoyed," *Entertainment Weekly* said of Schwartz's mopey slasher flick *Moody Fruit*, "with both eyes closed.") A fervent admirer of Schwartz's sound tracks, Brian had swooped down like an angel with a crucial fifty thou just as Schwartz began principal photography on a modern-dress *Crime and Punishment* in which Raskolnikov, played by Giovanni Ribisi, was a young anarchist and rabid audiophile living underground in North Philadelphia. While Denise and Rob Zito were making hardware and lighting decisions at the Generator, Brian joined Schwartz and Ribisi et al. on location at soulful ruins in Nicetown, and swapped CDs with Schwartz from identical zippered CD carrying cases, and ate dinner at Pastis in New York with Schwartz and Greil Marcus or Stephen Malkmus.

Without realizing it, Denise had let herself imagine that Brian and Robin had no sex life anymore. So on New Year's Eve, when she and four couples and a mob of children gathered at the house on Panama Street and she saw Brian and Robin necking in the kitchen after midnight, she pulled her coat from the bottom of the coat pile and ran from the house. For more than a week she was too ripped up to call Robin or see the girls. She had a thing for a straight woman who was married to a man whom she herself might have liked to marry. It was a reasonably hopeless case. And St. Jude gave and St. Jude took away.

Robin ended Denise's moratorium with a phone call. She was screeching mad. *"Do you know what Jerry Schwartz's movie is about?"*

"Uh, Dostoevsky in Germantown?"

"You know it. How come *I* didn't know it? Because he *kept* it from me, because he knew what I would think!"

"We're talking about a Giovanni-Ribisi-as-wispily-bearded-Raskolnikov type of thing," Denise said.

"My husband," Robin said, "has put fifty thousand dollars, *which he got from the W—— Corporation*, into a movie about a North Philly anarchist who splits two women's skulls and goes to jail for it! He's getting off on how *cool* it is to hang out with Giovanni Ribisi, and Jerry Schwartz, and Ian What's His Face, and Stephen Whoever, while my

North Philly anarchist *brother*, who really *did* split somebody's skull—"

"No, I get it," Denise said. "There's a definite want of sensitivity there."

"I don't even think so," Robin said. "I think he's deeply pissed off with me and he doesn't even know it."

From that day forward, Denise became a stealthy advocate of infidelity. She learned that by defending Brian's minor insensitivities she could spur Robin to more serious accusations with which she then reluctantly concurred. She listened and she listened. She took care to understand Robin better than anyone else ever had. She plied Robin with the questions Brian wasn't asking: about Billy, about her dad, about church, about her Garden Project plans, about the half-dozen teenagers who'd caught the gardening bug and were coming back next summer, about the romantic and academic travails of her young assistants. She attended Seed Catalogue Night at the Project and put faces to the names of Robin's favorite kids. She did long division with Sinéad. She nudged conversations in the direction of movie stars or popular music or high fashion, the sorest topics in Robin's marriage. To the untrained ear, she sounded as if she were merely advocating closer friendship; but she had seen Robin eat, she knew this woman's hunger.

When a sewer-line problem delayed the opening of the Generator, Brian took the opportunity to attend the Kalamazoo Film Festival with Jerry Schwartz, and Denise took the opportunity to hang out with Robin and the girls for five nights running. The last of these nights found her agonizing in the video store. She finally settled on *Wait Until Dark* (disgusting male menaces resourceful Audrey Hepburn, whose coloration happens to resemble Denise Lambert's) and *Something Wild* (kinky, gorgeous Melanie Griffith liberates Jeff Daniels from a dead marriage). The very titles, when she arrived at Panama Street, made Robin blush.

Between movies, after midnight, they drank whiskey on the living-room sofa, and in a voice that even for her was unusually squeaky Robin asked permission to ask Denise a personal question. "How often, in, like, a week," she said, "did you and Emile fool around?"

"I'm not the person to ask about what's normal," Denise answered. "I've mainly seen normal in the rearview mirror."

"I know. I know." Robin stared intensely at the blue TV screen. "But, what did you *think* was normal?"

"I guess, at the time, I had the sense," Denise said, telling herself *large number, say a large number*, "that maybe three times a week might be normal."

Robin sighed loudly. A square inch or two of her left knee rested against Denise's right knee. "Just tell me what you think is normal," she said.

"I think for some people, once a day feels right."

Robin spoke in a voice like an ice cube compressed between molars. "I might like that. That doesn't sound bad to me."

A numbing and prickling and burning broke out on the engaged portion of Denise's knee.

"I take it that's not how things are."

"Like twice a MONTH," Robin said through her teeth. "Twice a MONTH."

"Do you think Brian's seeing somebody?"

"I don't know what he does. But it doesn't involve me. And I just feel like such a freak."

"You're not a freak. You're the opposite."

"So what's the other movie?"

"*Something Wild.*"

"OK, whatever. Let's watch it."

For the next two hours Denise mainly paid attention to her hand, which she'd laid on the sofa cushion within easy reach of Robin's. The hand wasn't comfortable there, it wanted to be retracted, but she didn't want to give up hard-won territory.

When the movie ended they watched TV, and then they were silent for an impossibly long time, five minutes or a year, and still Robin didn't take the warm, five-fingered bait. Denise would have welcomed some pushy male sexuality right around now. In hindsight, the week and a half she'd waited before Brian grabbed her had passed like a heartbeat.

At 4 a.m., sick with tiredness and impatience, she stood up to leave. Robin put on her shoes and her purple nylon parka and walked her to her car. Here, at last, she seized Denise's hand in both of hers. She rubbed Denise's palm with her dry, grown-woman thumbs. She said she was glad that Denise was her friend.

Stay the course, Denise enjoined herself. *Be sisterly.*

"I'm glad, too," she said.

Robin produced the spoken cackle that Denise had come to recognize as pure distilled self-consciousness. She said, "Hee hee hee!" She looked at Denise's hand, which she was kneading nervously in hers now. "Wouldn't it be ironic if I was the one who cheated on Brian?"

"Oh God," Denise said involuntarily.

"Don't worry." Robin made a fist around Denise's index finger and squeezed it hard, in spasms. "I'm totally joking."

Denise stared at her. *Are you even listening to what you're saying? Are you aware of what you're doing to my finger?*

Robin pressed the hand to her mouth now and bit down on it with lip-cushioned teeth, sort of softly gnawed on it, and then dropped it and skittered away. She bounced from one foot to the other. "So I'll see you."

The next day, Brian came back from Michigan and put an end to the house party.

Denise flew to St. Jude for a long Easter weekend, and Enid, like a toy piano with one working note, spoke every day of her old friend Norma Greene and Norma Greene's tragic involvement with a married man. Denise, to change the subject, observed that Alfred was livelier and sharper than Enid portrayed him in her letters and Sunday calls.

"He pulls himself together when you're in town," Enid countered. "When we're alone, he's impossible."

"When you're alone, maybe you're too focused on him."

"Denise, if you lived with a man who slept in his chair all day—"

"Mother, the more you nag, the more he resists."

"You don't see it, because you're only here for a few days. But I know what I'm talking about. And I don't know what I'm going to do."

If I lived with a person who was hysterically critical of me, Denise thought, I would sleep in a chair.

Back in Philly, the kitchen at the Generator was finally available. Denise's life returned to near-normal levels of madness as she assembled and trained her crew, invited her pastry-chef finalists to compete head to head, and solved a thousand problems of delivery, scheduling, production, and pricing. As a piece of architecture, the restaurant was every bit as stunning as she'd feared, but for once in her career she'd prepared a menu properly and had twenty winners on it. The food was a three-way conversation between Paris and Bologna and Vienna, a Continental conference call with her own trademark emphasis on flavor over flash. Seeing Brian again in person, rather than imagining him through Robin's eyes, she remembered how much she liked him. She awoke, to an extent, from her dreams of conquest. As she fired up the Garland and drilled her line and sharpened her knives, she thought: *An idle brain is the Devil's workshop.* If she had been working as hard as God intended her to work, she would never have had time to chase someone's wife.

She went into full avoidance mode, working 6 a.m. to midnight. The more days she spent free of the spell that Robin's body and body heat and hunger cast on her, the more willing she was to admit how little she liked Robin's nervousness, and Robin's bad haircut and worse clothes, and Robin's rusty-hinge voice, and Robin's forced laughter, her whole profound *uncoolness*. Brian's benign neglect of his wife, his hands-off attitude of "Yeah, Robin's great," made more sense now to Denise. Robin *was* great; and yet, if you were married to her, you might need some time away from her incandescent energy, you might enjoy a few days by yourself in New York, and Paris, and Sundance . . .

But the damage had been done. Denise's case for infidelity had apparently been compelling. With a persistence the more irritating for the shyness and apologies that accompanied it, Robin began to seek her out. She came to the Generator. She took Denise to lunch. She called Denise at midnight and chattered about the mildly interesting things that Denise had long pretended to be extremely interested in. She caught Denise at home on a Sunday afternoon and drank tea at the half Ping-Pong table, blushing and hee-heeing.

And part of Denise was thinking, as the tea went cold: *Shit, she's really into me now.* This part of her considered, as if it were an actual threat of harm, the exhausting circumstance: *She wants sex every day.* This same part of her was thinking also: *My God, the way she eats.* And: *I am not a "lesbian."*

At the same time, another part of her was literally awash in desire. She'd never seen so objectively what an illness sex was, what a collection of bodily symptoms, because she'd never been remotely as sick as Robin made her.

During a lull in the chatter, beneath a corner of the Ping-Pong table, Robin gripped Denise's tastefully shod foot between her own knobby, white, purple-and-orange-accented sneakers. A moment later she leaned forward and seized Denise's hand. Her blush looked life-threatening.

"So," she said. "I've been thinking."

The Generator opened on May 23, exactly a year after Brian began paying Denise her inflated salary. The opening was delayed a final week so that Brian and Jerry Schwartz could attend the festival at Cannes. Every night, while he was away, Denise repaid his generosity and his faith in her by going to Panama Street and sleeping with his wife. Her brain might feel like the brain of a questionable calf's head at a Ninth Street "discount" butcher, but she was never as tired as she initially believed. One kiss, one hand on the knee, awakened her body to itself. She felt haunted, animated, revved, by the ghost of every coital encounter she'd ever nixed in her marriage. She shut her eyes against Robin's back and pillowed her cheek between her shoulder blades, her hands supporting Robin's breasts, which were round and flat and strangely light; she felt like a kitten with two powder puffs. She dozed for a couple of hours and then scraped herself out of the sheets, opened the door that Robin had locked against surprise visits from Erin or Sinéad, and crept down and out into the damp Philly dawn and shivered violently.

Brian had placed strong cryptic ads for the Generator in the local weeklies and monthlies and had put the buzz out through his network, but 26 covers on the first day of lunch and 45 that night did not exactly tax Denise's kitchen. The glassed-in dining room, suspended in a blue Cherenkov glow, sat 140; she was ready for 300-cover evenings. Brian and Robin and the girls came to dinner on a Saturday and stopped briefly in the kitchen. Denise did a good impression of being at ease with the girls, and Robin, looking great in red lipstick and a little black dress, did a good impression of being Brian's wife.

Denise fixed things as well as she could with the authorities in her head. She reminded herself that Brian had dropped to his knees in Paris; that she was doing nothing worse than playing by his rules; that she'd waited for Robin to make the first move. But moral hair-splitting could not explain her complete, dead absence of remorse. In conversation with Brian she was distracted and thick-headed. She caught the meaning of his words at the last moment, as if he were speaking French. She had reason to seem strung out, of course—she routinely slept four hours a night, and before long the kitchen was running at full throttle—and Brian, distracted by his film projects, was every bit as easy to deceive as she'd anticipated. But "deceive" wasn't even the word. "Dissociate" was more like it. Her affair was like a dream life unfolding in that locked and soundproofed chamber of her brain where, growing up in St. Jude, she'd learned to hide desires.

Reviewers descended on the Generator in late June and came away happy. The *Inquirer* invoked matrimony: the "wedding" of a "completely unique" setting with "serious and seriously delicious food" from the "perfectionist" Denise Lambert for a "must-have" experience that "single-handedly" put Philadelphia on the "map of cool." Brian was ecstatic but Denise was not. She thought the language made the place sound crappy and middlebrow. She counted four paragraphs about architecture and decor, three paragraphs about nothing, two about service, one about wine, two about desserts, and only seven about her food.

"They didn't mention my sauerkraut," she said, angry nearly to the point of tears.

The reservation line rang day and night. She needed to *work*, to *work*. But Robin called her at midmorning or midafternoon on the executive chef's line, her voice pinched with shyness, her cadences syncopated with embarrassment: "So—I was wondering—do you think— could I see you for a minute?" And instead of saying no, Denise kept saying yes. Kept delegating or delaying sensitive inventory work, tricky preroastings, and necessary phone calls to purveyors to slip away and meet Robin in the nearest strip of park along the Schuylkill. Sometimes they just sat on a bench, discreetly held hands, and, although non-work conversations during work hours made Denise *extremely impatient*, discussed Robin's guilt and her own dissociated lack of it, and what it meant to be doing what they were doing, how exactly it had come to pass. But soon the talking tapered off. Robin's voice on the executive chef's line came to signify *tongue*. She didn't say more than a word or two before Denise tuned out. Robin's tongue and lips continued to form the instructions demanded by the day's exigencies, but in Denise's ear they were already speaking that other language of up and down and round and round that her body intuitively understood and autonomously obeyed; sometimes she melted so hard at the sound of this voice that her abdomen caved in and she doubled over; for the next hour-plus there was nothing in the world but tongue, no inventory or buttered pheasants or unpaid purveyors; she left the Generator in a buzzing hypnotized state of poor reflexes, the volume of the world's noise lowered to near zero, other drivers luckily obeying basic traffic laws. Her car was like a tongue gliding down the melty asphalt streets, her feet like twin tongues licking pavement, the front door of the house on Panama Street like a mouth that swallowed her, the Persian runner in the hall outside the master bedroom like a tongue beckoning, the bed in its cloak of comforter and pillows a big soft tongue begging to be depressed, and then.

This was all, safe to say, new territory. Denise had never wanted anything, certainly not sex, like this. Simply coming, when she was married, had come to seem like a laborious but occasionally necessary kitchen chore. She cooked for fourteen hours and routinely fell asleep in street clothes. The last thing she wanted late at night was to follow a complicated and increasingly time-consuming recipe for a dish she was too tired to enjoy in any case. Prep time a minimum fifteen minutes. Even after that, the cooking was seldom straightforward. The pan overheated, the heat was too high, the heat was too low, the onions refused to caramelize or burned immediately and stuck; you had to set the pan aside to cool off, you had to start over after painful discussion with the now angry and anguished sous-chef, and inevitably the meat got tough and stringy, the sauce lost its complexity in the repeated dilutions and deglazings, and it was *so fucking late,* and your eyes were burning, and OK, with enough time and effort you could fairly reliably get the sucker plated, but by then it was something you might hesitate to serve your floor personnel; you simply bolted it ("OK, there," you thought, "I came") and fell asleep with an ache. And it was *so* not worth the effort. But she'd made the effort every week or two because her coming mattered to Emile and she felt guilty. Him she could please as adroitly and unfailingly (and, before long, as unthinkingly) as she clarified consommé; and what pride, what pleasure, she took in the exercise of her skills! Emile, however, seemed to believe that without a few shudders and semi-willed sighs on her part the marriage would be in trouble, and although later events proved him one-hundred-percent correct, she couldn't help feeling, in the years before she clapped eyes on Becky Hemerling, enormous guilt and pressure and resentment on the O front.

Robin was prêt-à-manger. You didn't need a recipe, you didn't need prep, to eat a peach. Here was the peach, boom, here was the payoff. Denise had had intimations of ease like this with Hemerling, but only now, at the age of thirty-two, did she *get* what all the fuss was about. Once she got it, there was trouble. In August the girls went to camp and Brian went to London, and the executive chef of the hottest new restaurant in the region would get out of a bed only to find herself down on some carpet, would dress only to find herself undressing, would come as close to escape as the entry hall and then find herself coming with her back to the front door; jelly-kneed and slit-eyed, she dragged herself back to a kitchen to which she'd promised to return in forty-five minutes. And this was not good. The restaurant was suffering. There was gridlock on the line, delays on the floor. Twice she had to strike entrées from the menu because the kitchen, doing without her, had run out of prep time. And still she went AWOL in the middle of the second evening rush. She drove through Crack Haven and down Junk Row and past Blunt Alley to the Garden Project, where Robin had a blanket. Most of the garden was mulched and limed and planted now. Tomatoes had grown up inside bald tires outfitted with cylinders of gutter screen. And the searchlights and wing lights of landing jets, and the smog-stunted constellations, and the radium glow from the watch glass of Veterans Stadium, and the heat lightning over Tinicum, and the moon to which filthy Camden had given hepatitis as it rose, all these compromised urban lights were reflected in the skins of adolescent eggplants, young peppers and cukes and sweet corn, pubescent cantaloupes. Denise, naked in the middle of the city, rolled off the blanket into night-cool dirt, a sandy loam, freshly turned. She rested a cheek in it, pushed her Robiny fingers down into it.

"God, stop, stop," Robin squeaked, "that's our new lettuce."

Then Brian was home and they started taking stupid chances. Robin explained to Erin that Denise hadn't felt well and had needed to lie down in the bedroom. There was a feverish episode in the pantry at Panama Street while Brian read E. B. White aloud not twenty feet away. Finally, a week before Labor Day, there came a morning in the director's office at the Garden Project when the weight of two bodies on Robin's antique wooden desk chair snapped its back off. They were laughing when they heard Brian's voice.

Robin jumped up and unlocked the door and opened it in one motion, to conceal that it had been locked. Brian was holding a basket of speckled green erections. He was surprised—but delighted, as always—to see Denise. "What's going on in there?"

Denise knelt by Robin's desk, her shirt untucked. "Robin's chair broke," she said. "I'm licking a take at Robin's chair."

"I asked Denise if she could fix it!" Robin squeaked.

"What are you doing here?" Brian asked Denise, very curious.

"I had the same thought you had," she said. "Zucchini."

"Sara said nobody was here."

Robin was edging away. "I'll go talk to her. She should know when I'm here."

"How did Robin break that?" Brian asked Denise.

"I don't know," she said. She had the bad child's impulse to cry when caught red-handed.

Brian picked up the top half of the chair. He had never specifically reminded Denise of her father, but she was pierced now by the resemblance to Alfred in his intelligent sympathy for the broken object. "This is good oak," he said. "Weird it should just suddenly break."

She rose from her knees and wandered into the hall, stuffing shirt into pants as she went. She kept wandering until she was outside and got into her car. She drove up Bainbridge Street to the river. Pulled up to a galvanized guardrail and killed the engine by letting out the clutch, let the car lurch into the guardrail and bounce back dead, and now, finally, she broke down and cried about the broken chair.

Her head was clearer when she returned to the Generator. She saw that she was in the weeds on every front. There were unanswered phone messages from a food writer at the *Times*, from an editor at *Gourmet*, and from the latest restaurateur hoping to steal Brian's chef. A thousand dollars' worth of unrotated duck breasts and veal chops had gone bad in the walk-in. Everybody in the kitchen knew and nobody had told her that a needle had turned up in the employee bathroom. The pastry chef claimed to have left Denise a pair of handwritten notes, presumably salary-related, that Denise had no memory of seeing.

"Why is nobody ordering country ribs?" Denise asked Rob Zito. "Why are the waiters not pushing my phenomenally delicious and unusual country ribs?"

"Americans don't like sauerkraut," Zito said.

"The hell they don't. I've seen my reflection in the plates coming back when people order it. I've counted my eyelashes."

"It's possible we get some German nationals in here," Zito said. "German passport-holders may be responsible for those clean plates."

"Is it possible you don't like sauerkraut yourself?"

"It's an interesting food," Zito said.

She didn't hear from Robin and she didn't call her. She gave the *Times* an interview and let herself be photographed, she stroked the pastry chef's ego, she stayed late and bagged up the spoiled meats in privacy, she fired the dishwasher who'd tied off in the john, and every lunch and every dinner she dogged the line and troubleshot.

On Labor Day: deadness. She made herself leave her office and went walking in the empty hot city, bending her steps, in her loneliness, toward Panama Street. She had a liquid Pavlovian response when she saw the house. The brownstone façade was still a face, the door still a tongue. Robin's car was in the street but Brian's wasn't; they'd gone to Cape May. Denise rang the bell, although she could already tell, from a dustiness around the door, that nobody was home. She let herself in with the dead-bolt key on which she'd written "R/B." She walked up two flights to the parental bedroom. The house's expensive retrofitted central air conditioner was doing its job, the cool canned-smelling air contending with Labor Day sunbeams. As she lay down on the unmade parental bed, she remembered the smell and the quiet of the St. Judean summer afternoons when she would be left alone in the house and could be, for a couple of hours, as weird as she wanted. She brought herself off. She lay on the snarled sheets, a slice of sunlight falling on her chest. She took a second helping of herself and stretched her arms luxuriantly. Beneath a parental pillow, she scratched her hand on the foil corner of something like a condom wrapper.

It was a condom wrapper. Torn and empty. She actually whimpered as she pictured the penetrative act it attested to. She actually clutched her head.

She scrambled out of the bed and smoothed her dress across her hips. She scanned the sheets for other sickening surprises. Well, of course a married couple had sex. Of course. But Robin had told her that she wasn't on the Pill, she'd said that she and Brian no longer fooled around enough to bother; and all summer long Denise had seen and tasted and smelled no trace of a husband on her lover's body, and so she'd let herself forget the obvious.

She knelt at the wastebasket by Brian's dresser. She stirred Kleenexes, ticket stubs, and segments of floss and found another condom wrapper. Hatred of Robin, hatred and jealousy, were coming on like a migraine. She went into the master-bedroom bathroom and found two more wrappers and a knotted rubber in the can beneath the sink.

She actually hit her temples with her fists. She heard the breath in her teeth as she ran down the stairs and let herself out into the late afternoon. The temperature was ninety and she was shivering. Weirdness,

weirdness. She hiked back to the Generator and let herself in at the loading dock. She inventoried oils and cheeses and flours and spices, drew up meticulous order sheets, left twenty voice-mail messages in a wry and articulate and civilized voice, did her e-mail chores, fried herself a kidney on the Garland, chased it with a single shot of grappa, and called a cab at midnight.

Robin showed up in the kitchen unannounced the next morning. She was wearing a big white shirt that appeared to have been Brian's. Denise's stomach flipped at the sight of her. She led her back to the executive chef's office and shut the door.

"I can't do this anymore," Robin said.

"Good, neither can I, so."

Robin's face was all blotch. She scratched her head and scrunched up her nose with tic-like incessancy and pushed on the bridge of her glasses. "I haven't been to church since June," she said. "Sinéad's caught me in about ten different lies. She wants to know why you're never around. I don't even know half the kids turning up at the Project lately. Everything's a mess, and I just can't *do* it anymore."

Denise choked out a question: "How's Brian?"

Robin blushed. "He doesn't know anything. He's the same as always. You know—he likes you, he likes me."

"I bet."

"Things have gotten weird."

"Well, and I've got a lot of work here, so."

"Brian never did anything bad to me. He didn't deserve this."

Denise's phone rang and she let it ring. Her head felt close to cracking open. She couldn't stand to hear Robin say Brian's name.

Robin raised her face to the ceiling, pearls of tear beading in her lashes. "I don't know what I came for. I don't know what I'm saying. I'm just feeling really, really bad and incredibly alone."

"Get over it," Denise said. "That's what I'm going to do."

"Why are you being so cold?"

"Because I'm a cold person."

"If you'd call me, or say you loved me—"

"Get over it! For God's sake! Get over it! Get over it!"

Robin gave her a beseeching look; but really, even if the matter of the condoms were somehow cleared up, what was Denise supposed to do? Quit working at the restaurant that was making her a star? Go live in the ghetto and be one of Sinéad and Erin's two mommies? Start wearing big sneakers and cooking vegetarian?

She knew she was telling herself lies, but she didn't know which of the things in her head were the lies and which were the truth. She stared at her desk until Robin yanked open the door and fled.

The next morning the Generator made the front page of the *New York Times* food section, below the fold. Beneath the headline ("Generating Buzz by the Megawatt") was *a photograph of Denise*, the interior and exterior architectural shots having been relegated to page 6, where *her country ribs and sauerkraut* could also be seen. This was better. This was more like it. By noon she'd been offered a guest appearance on the Food Channel and a permanent monthly column in *Philadelphia*. She bypassed Rob Zito and instructed the reservation girl to start overbooking by forty seats an evening. Gary and Caroline called separately with congratulations. She dressed down Zito for refusing a weekend reservation to the local NBC-affiliate anchorwoman, she let herself abuse him a little bit, it felt good.

Expensive people of a sort formerly scarce in Philadelphia were three-deep at the bar when Brian came by with a dozen roses. He hugged Denise and she lingered in his arms. She gave him a little bit of what men liked.

"We need more tables," she said. "Three fours and a six at a minimum. We need a full-time reservationist who knows how to screen. We need better parking-lot security. We need a pastry chef with more imagination and less attitude. Also think about replacing Rob with somebody from New York who can handle the kind of customer profile we're going to get."

Brian was surprised. "You want to do that to Rob?"

"He wouldn't push my ribs and sauerkraut," Denise said. "The *Times* liked my ribs and sauerkraut. I say fuck him if he can't do the job."

The hardness in her voice brought a glow to Brian's eyes. He seemed to like her like this.

"Whatever you think," he said.

Late Saturday night she joined Brian and Jerry Schwartz and two cheekboned blondes and the lead singer and the lead guitarist from one of her favorite bands for drinks on the little railed-in aerie that Brian had rigged on the roof of the Generator. The night was warm and the bugs along the river were nearly as loud as the Schuylkill Expressway. Both blondes were talking on their phones. Denise accepted a cigarette from the guitarist, who was hoarse from a gig, and let him examine her scars.

"Holy shit, your hands are worse than mine."

"The job," she said, "consists of tolerating pain."

"Cooks do notoriously abuse their substances."

"I like a drink at midnight," she said. "Two Tylenols when I get up at six."

"Nobody's tougher than Denise," Brian bragged unattractively over the antennae of the blondes.

The guitarist responded by sticking his tongue out, holding his cigarette like an eyedropper, and lowering the coal into the glistening cleft. The sizzle was loud enough to distract the blondes from their phoning. The taller one squealed and spoke the guitarist's name and said he was insane.

"Well, but I'm wondering what substances you've ingested," Denise said.

The guitarist applied cold vodka directly to the burn. The taller blonde, unhappy with his performance, answered, "Klonopin and Jameson's and whatever that is now."

"Well, and a tongue is wet," Denise said, extinguishing her own cigarette on the tender skin behind her ear. She felt like she'd taken a bullet in the head, but she flicked the dead cigarette toward the river casually.

The aerie got very quiet. Her weirdness was showing as she didn't use to let it show. Because she didn't have to—because she could have trimmed a rack of lamb now or had a conversation with her mother—she produced a strangled scream, a comical sound, to reassure her audience.

"Are you OK?" Brian asked her later in the parking lot.

"I've burned myself worse by accident."

"No, I mean are you *OK*? That was a little scary to watch."

"You're the one who bragged about my toughness, thanks."

"I'm trying to say I feel bad about that."

She was awake in pain all night.

A week later she and Brian hired the former manager of the Union Square Cafe and fired Rob Zito.

A week after that the mayor of Philadelphia, the junior senator from New Jersey, the CEO of the W—— Corporation, and Jodie Foster were in the restaurant.

A week after that, Brian took Denise home after work and she invited him inside. Over the same fifty-dollar wine she'd once served his wife, he asked if she and Robin had had a falling-out.

Denise pursed her lips and shook her head. "I've just gotten very busy."

"That's what I thought. I figured it didn't have anything to do with you. Robin's pissed off with everything lately. Especially with anything that has to do with me."

"I miss hanging out with the girls," Denise said.

"Believe me, they miss you," Brian said. He added, with a slight stammer, "I'm—thinking of moving out."

Denise said she was sorry to hear it.

"The sackcloth business is out of control," he said, pouring. "She's been going to *nightly* mass for the last three weeks. I didn't even know there was such a thing. And I literally can't say a word about the Generator without setting off an explosion. She, meanwhile, is talking about home-schooling the girls. She's decided our house is too big. She wants to move into the Project house and home-school the girls and maybe a couple of the Project kids. 'Rasheed'? 'Marilou'? Which, what a great place for Sinéad and Erin to grow up, a brownfield in Point Breeze. We're verging over into the loony, a little bit. I mean, Robin is great. She believes in better things than I believe in. I'm just not sure I love her anymore. I feel like I'm arguing with Nicky Passafaro. It's Class Hatred II, the Sequel."

"Robin is full of guilt," Denise said.

"She's verging on being an irresponsible parent."

Denise found breath to ask: "Would you want to take the girls, if it came to that?"

Brian shook his head. "I'm not sure, if it came to that, that Robin would actually want custody. I could see her giving up everything."

"Don't bet on it."

Denise thought of Robin brushing Sinéad's hair and suddenly— keenly, terribly—missed her crazy yearnings, her excesses and accesses, her innocence. A switch was flipped and Denise's brain became a passive screen on which was projected a highlight reel of all that was excellent in the person she'd driven away. She reappreciated the least of Robin's habits and gestures and distinguishing marks, her preference for scalded milk in her coffee, and the off-color cap on the front tooth that her brother had broken with a rock, and the way she put her head down like a goat and butted Denise with love.

Denise, pleading exhaustion, made Brian leave. Early the next morning a tropical depression slid up the seaboard, a humid hurricane- like disturbance that set trees thrashing moodily and water spilling over curbs. Denise left the Generator in the hands of her sous and took the train to New York to bail out her feckless brother and entertain her par- ents. In the stress of lunch, as Enid repeated verbatim her narrative of Norma Greene, Denise didn't notice any change in herself. She had a still-working old self, a Version 3.2 or a Version 4.0, that deplored the deplorable in Enid and loved the lovable in Alfred. Not until she was at the pier and her mother kissed her and a quite different Denise, a Ver- sion 5.0, nearly put her tongue in the pretty old woman's mouth, nearly ran her hands down Enid's hips and thighs, nearly caved in and prom- ised to come at Christmas for as long as Enid wanted, did the extent of the correction she was undergoing reveal itself.

She sat on a southbound train while rain-glazed local platforms flashed by at intercity speed. Her father at the lunch table had looked insane. And if he was losing his mind, it was possible that Enid had not been exaggerating her difficulties with him, possible that Alfred really was a mess who pulled himself together for his children, possible that Enid wasn't entirely the embarrassing nag and pestilence that Denise for twenty years had made her out to be, possible that Alfred's problems went deeper than having the wrong wife, possible that Enid's problems did not go much deeper than having the wrong husband, possible that Denise was more like Enid than she had ever dreamed. She listened to the pa-thum-pa-thum-pa-thump of wheels on track and watched the October sky darken. There might have been hope for her if she could have stayed on the train, but it was a short ride to Philly, and then she was back at work and had no time to think about anything until she went to the Axon road show with Gary and surprised herself by defending not only Alfred but Enid as well in the arguments that followed.

She could not remember a time when she had loved her mother.

She was soaking in her bathtub around nine o'clock that night when Brian called and invited her to dinner with him and Jerry Schwartz, Mira Sorvino, Stanley Tucci, a Famous American Director, a Famous British Author, and other luminaries. The Famous Director had just finished shooting a film in Camden, and Brian and Schwartz had roped him into a private screening of *Crime and Punishment and Rock and Roll*.

"It's my night off," Denise said.

"Martin says he'll send his driver," Brian said. "I'd be grateful if you came. My marriage is over."

She put on a black cashmere dress, ate a banana to avoid seeming hungry at dinner, and rode with the director's driver up to Tacconelli's, the storefront pizzeria in Kensington. A dozen famous and semifamous people, plus Brian and the simian, round-shouldered Jerry Schwartz, had taken over three tables at the rear. Denise kissed Brian on the mouth and sat down between him and the Famous British Author, who appeared to have an evening's worth of cricket- and darts-related wit with which he wished to regale Mira Sorvino. The Famous Director told Denise he'd had her country ribs and sauerkraut and loved them, but she changed the subject as fast as she could. She was clearly there as Brian's date; the movie people weren't interested in either of them. She put her hand on Brian's knee, as if consolingly.

"Raskolnikov in headphones, listening to Trent Reznor while he whacks the old lady, is so perfect," the very least famous person at the table, a college-age intern of the director, gushed to Jerry Schwartz.

"Actually, it's the Nomatics," Schwartz corrected with devastating lack of condescension.

"Not Nine Inch Nails?"

Schwartz lowered his eyelids and shook his head minimally. "Nomatics, 1980, 'Held in Trust.' Later covered with insufficient attribution by that person whose name you just mentioned."

"Everybody steals from the Nomatics," Brian said.

"They suffered on the cross of obscurity so that others might enjoy eternal fame," Schwartz said.

"What's their best record?"

"Give me your address, I'll make you a CD," Brian said.

"It's all brilliant," Schwartz said, "until 'Thorazine Sunrise.' That was when Tom Paquette quit, but the band didn't realize it was dead until two albums later. Somebody had to break that news to them."

"I suppose that a country that teaches creationism in its schools," the Famous British Author remarked to Mira Sorvino, "may be forgiven for believing that baseball does not derive from cricket."

It occurred to Denise that Stanley Tucci had directed and starred in her favorite restaurant movie. She happily talked shop with him, resenting the beautiful Sorvino a little less and enjoying, if not the company itself, then at least her own lack of intimidation by it.

Brian drove her home from Tacconelli's in his Volvo. She felt entitled and attractive and well aerated and alive. Brian, however, was angry.

"Robin was supposed to be there," he said. "I guess you could call it an ultimatum. But she'd agreed to go to dinner with us. She was going to take some tiny, minimal interest in what I'm doing with my life, even if I knew she'd deliberately dress like a grad student to make me uncomfortable and prove her point. And then I was going to spend next Saturday at the Project. That was the agreement. And then this morning she decides she's going to march against the death penalty instead. I'm no fan of the death penalty. But Khellye Withers is not my idea of a poster boy for leniency. And a promise is a promise. I didn't see that one fewer candle in the candlelight vigil was going to make much difference. I said she could miss one march for my sake. I said, why don't I write a check to the ACLU, whatever size you want. Which didn't go over so well."

"Writing checks, no, not good," Denise said.

"I realized that. But things got said that are going to be hard to unsay. I frankly don't have a lot of interest in unsaying them."

"You never know," Denise said.

Washington Avenue between the river and Broad was lonely at eleven on a Monday evening. Brian appeared to be experiencing his first real disappointment in life, and he couldn't stop talking. "Remember when you said if I weren't married and you weren't my employee?"

"I remember."

"Does that still hold?"

"Let's go in and have a drink," Denise said.

Which was how Brian came to be sleeping in her bed at nine-thirty the next morning when her doorbell rang.

She was still full of the alcohol that had fueled completion of the picture of weirdness and moral chaos that her life seemed bent on being. Beneath her soddenness, though, an agreeable fizz of celebrity lingered from the night before. It was stronger than anything she felt for Brian.

The doorbell rang again. She got up and put on a maroon silk robe and looked out the window. Robin Passafaro was standing on the stoop. Brian's Volvo was parked across the street.

Denise considered not answering the door, but Robin wouldn't be looking for her here if she hadn't already tried the Generator.

"It's Robin," she said. "Stay here and be quiet."

Brian in the morning light still wore his pissed-off expression of the night before. "I don't care if she knows I'm here."

"Yeah, but I do."

"Well, my car's right across the street."

"I'm aware of that."

She, too, felt strangely pissed off with Robin. All summer, betraying Brian, she'd never felt anything like the contempt she felt for his wife as she descended the stairs now. Annoying Robin, stubborn Robin, screeching Robin, hooting Robin, styleless Robin, clueless Robin.

And yet, the moment she opened the door, her body recognized what it wanted. It wanted Brian on the street and Robin in her bed.

Robin's teeth were chattering, though the morning wasn't cold. "Can I come in?"

"I'm about to go to work," Denise said.

"Five minutes," Robin said.

It seemed impossible that she hadn't seen the pistachio-colored wagon across the street. Denise let her into the front hall and closed the door.

"My marriage is over," Robin said. "He didn't even come home last night."

"I'm sorry."

"I've been praying for my marriage, but I get distracted by the thought of you. I'm kneeling in church and I start thinking about your body."

Dread settled on Denise. She didn't exactly feel guilty—the egg timer on an ailing marriage had run out; at worst she'd hurried the clock along—but she was sorry that she'd wronged this person, sorry she'd competed. She took Robin's hands and said, "I want to see you and I want to talk to you. I don't like what's happened. But I have to go to work now."

The telephone rang in the living room. Robin bit her lip and nodded. "OK."

"Can we meet at two?" Denise said.

"OK."

"I'll call you from work."

Robin nodded again. Denise let her out and shut the door and released five breaths' worth of air.

"*Denise, it's Gary, I don't know where you are, but call me when you get this, there's been an accident, Dad fell off the cruise ship, he fell about eight stories, I just talked to Mom—*"

She ran to the phone and picked up. "Gary."

"I tried you at work."

"Is he alive?"

"Well, he shouldn't be," Gary said. "But he is."

Gary was at his best in emergencies. The qualities that had infuriated her the day before were a comfort now. She *wanted* him to know it all. She *wanted* him to sound pleased with his own calm.

"They apparently towed him for a mile in forty-five–degree water before the ship could stop," Gary said. "They've got a helicopter coming to take him to New Brunswick. But his back is not broken. His heart is still working. He's able to speak. He's a tough old guy. He could be fine."

"How's Mom?"

"She's concerned that the cruise is being delayed while the helicopter comes. Other people are being inconvenienced."

Denise laughed with relief. "Poor Mom. She wanted this cruise so badly."

"Well, I'm afraid her cruising days with Dad are over."

The doorbell rang again. Immediately there was a pounding on the door as well, a pounding and a kicking.

"Gary, hang on one second."

"What's going on?"

"Let me call you right back."

The doorbell rang so long and hard it changed its tone, went flat and a little hoarse. She opened the door to a trembling mouth and eyes bright with hatred.

"Get out of my way," Robin said, "because I don't want to touch any part of you."

"I made a really bad mistake last night."

"Get out of my way!"

Denise stood aside, and Robin headed up the stairs. Denise sat in the only chair in her penitential living room and listened to the shouting. She was struck by how seldom in her childhood her parents, that other married couple in her life, that other incompatible pair, had shouted at each other. They'd held their peace and let the proxy war unfold inside their daughter's head.

Whenever she was with Brian she would pine for Robin's body and sincerity and good works and be repelled by Brian's smug coolness, and whenever she was with Robin she would pine for Brian's good taste and like-mindedness and wish that Robin would notice how sensational she looked in black cashmere.

Easy for you guys, she thought. *You can split in two.*

The shouting stopped. Robin came running down the stairs and went on out the front door without slowing.

Brian followed a few minutes later. Denise had expected Robin's disapproval and could handle it, but from Brian she was hoping for a word of understanding.

"You're fired," he said.

———

FROM: Denise3@cheapnet.com
TO: exprof@gaddisfly.com
SUBJECT: Let's maybe try a little harder next time

Lovely to see you on Saturday. I really appreciated your effort to hurry back and help me out.

Since then, Dad's fallen off the cruise ship and been pulled out of icy water with a broken arm, a dislocated shoulder, a detached retina, short-term memory loss, and possibly a mild stroke, he and Mom have been helicoptered to New Brunswick, I've been fired from the best job I may ever have, and Gary and I have learned about a new medical technology that I feel certain you would agree is horrifying and dystopic and malignant except that it's good for Parkinson's and can maybe help Dad.

Other than that, not much to report.

Hope all's well wherever the fuck you are. Julia says Lithuania and expects me to believe it.

FROM: exprof@gaddisfly.com
TO: Denise3@cheapnet.com
SUBJECT: Re: "Let's maybe try a little harder next time"

Business opportunity in Lithuania. Julia's husband, Gitanas, is paying me to produce a profit-making website. It's actually a lot of fun and not unlucrative.

All your favorite high-school groups are on the radio here. Smiths, New Order, Billy Idol. A blast from the past. I saw an old man kill a horse with a shotgun on a street near the airport. I'd been on Baltic soil for maybe fifteen minutes. Welcome to Lithuania!

Talked to Mom this morning, got the whole story, made my apologies, so don't worry about that.

I'm sorry about your job. To be honest, I'm stunned. I can't believe anyone would fire you.

Where are you working now?

FROM: Denise3@cheapnet.com
TO: exprof@gaddisfly.com
SUBJECT: Holiday responsibilities

Mom says you won't commit to coming home for Christmas, and she expects me to believe it. But I'm thinking no way could you talk to a woman who's just had the highlight of her year truncated by an accident, and who otherwise has a shitty life with a semi-disabled man, and who hasn't gotten to be at home for Christmas since like Dan Quayle's vice presidency, and who *survives* by looking forward to things, and who loves Christmas the way other people love sex, and who's seen you for all of forty-five minutes in the last three years: I'm thinking no way could you have told this woman, nope, sorry, staying in Vilnius.

(Vilnius!)

Mom must have misunderstood you. Please clarify.

Since you ask, I'm not working anywhere. Subbing a little at Mare Scuro but otherwise sleeping until two in the afternoon. If this continues, I may have to do some therapeutic thing of the sort that will horrify you. Got to regain my appetite for shopping and other non-free consumer pleasures.

The last thing I heard about Gitanas Misevicious was that he'd given Julia two black eyes. But whatever.

FROM: exprof@gaddisfly.com
TO: Denise3@cheapnet.com
SUBJECT: Re: "Holiday responsibilities"

I intend to get to St. Jude as soon as I make some money. Maybe even by Dad's birthday. But Christmas is hell, you know that. There's no worse time. You can tell Mom I'll come early in the new year.

Mom says that Caroline and the boys will be in St. Jude for Christmas. Can this be true?

Don't not take a psychotropic on my account.

FROM: Denise3@cheapnet.com
TO: exprof@gaddisfly.com
SUBJECT: "The only thing I hurt was my dignity"

Nice try, but no, sorry, I insist that you come for Christmas.

I've been talking to Axon, and the plan is to give Dad six months of Corecktall beginning right after New Year's, and to let him and Mom stay with me while that's going on. (Helpfully, my life is in ruins, so it's easy to make myself available.) The only way this scenario won't happen is if Axon's medical staff decides that Dad has non-drug-related dementia. He admittedly seemed pretty shaky when he was in New York, but he's been sounding good on the phone. "All I hurt when I fell was my dignity," etc. They took the cast off his arm a week early.

Anyway, he's probably going to be with me in Philly for his birthday, and for the rest of the winter and spring too, and so Christmas is the time for you to come to St. Jude, and so please don't argue with me anymore, just do it.

I eagerly (but with confidence) await confirmation that you will be there.

P.S. Caroline, Aaron, and Caleb are not coming. Gary's coming with Jonah and flying back to Philly at noon on the 25th.

P.P.S. Don't worry, I say NO to drugs.

FROM: exprof@gaddisfly.com
TO: Denise3@cheapnet.com
SUBJECT: Re: "The only thing I hurt was my dignity"

I saw a man shot six times in the stomach last night. A paid hit in a club called Musmiryte. It had nothing to do with us, but I wasn't happy to see it.

It's not clear to me why I'm required to come to St. Jude on some specific date. If Mom and Dad were my children, whom I'd created out of nothing without asking their permission, I could understand being responsible for them. Parents have an overwhelming Darwinian hard-wired genetic stake in their children's welfare. But children, it seems to me, have no corresponding debt to their parents.

Basically, I have very little to say to these people. And I don't think they want to hear what I do have to say.

Why don't I plan to see them when they're in Philadelphia? That sounds more fun anyway. That way all nine of us can get together, instead of just six of us.

FROM: Denise3@cheapnet.com
TO: exprof@gaddisfly.com
SUBJECT: A serious flaming from your pissed-off sister

My god you sound self-pitying.

I'm saying come for MY sake. For MY sake. And also for YOUR OWN sake, because I'm sure it's very cool and interesting and adult-feeling to watch somebody get shot in the stomach, but you only have two parents, and if you miss your time with them now you won't get another chance.

I'll admit it: I'm a mess.

I will tell you—because I want to tell someone—even though you never told me why YOU got fired—that I was fired for sleeping with my boss's wife.

So, what do you think *I* have to say to "these people"? What do you think my little Sunday chats with Mom are like these days?

You owe me $20,500. How's THAT for a debt?

Buy the fucking ticket. I'll reimburse you.

I love you and I miss you. Don't ask me why.

FROM: Denise3@cheapnet.com
TO: exprof@gaddisfly.com
SUBJECT: Remorse

I'm sorry I flamed you. The last line is the only one I meant. I don't have the right temperament for e-mail. Please write back. Please come for Christmas.

FROM: Denise3@cheapnet.com
TO: exprof@gaddisfly.com
SUBJECT: Worry

Please, please, please don't talk about people getting shot and then do the silence thing to me.

FROM: Denise3@cheapnet.com
TO: exprof@gaddisfly.com
SUBJECT: Only six more shopping days before Christmas!

Chip? Are you there? Please write or call.

Global Warming Enhances Value
of Lithuania Incorporated

VILNIUS, OCTOBER 30. With world ocean levels rising by more than an inch per year and millions of cubic meters of ocean beach eroded daily, the European Council on Natural Resources this week warned that Europe could face "catastrophic" shortages of sand and gravel by the end of the decade.

"Throughout history, mankind has regarded sand and gravel as inexhaustible resources," said ECNR chairman Jacques Dormand. "Sadly, our overreliance on greenhouse-gas-producing fossil fuels will leave many central European countries, including Germany, at the mercy of sand-and-gravel cartel states, particularly sand-rich Lithuania, if they wish to continue with basic road-building and construction."

Gitanas R. Misevičius, founder and CEO of Lithuania's Free Market Party Company, compared the impending European sand-and-gravel crisis to the oil crisis of 1973. "Back then," Misevičius said, "tiny oil-rich countries like Bahrain and Brunei were the mice that roared. Tomorrow, Lithuania."

Chairman Dormand described the pro-Western, pro-business Free Market Party Company as "currently the only political movement in Lithuania willing to deal fairly and responsibly with Western capital markets.

"Our misfortune," Dormand said, "is that most of Europe's reserve sand-and-gravel capacity is in the hands of Baltic nationalists beside whom Muammar Gadhafi looks like Charles de Gaulle. I scarcely exaggerate in saying that the future economic stability of the EC is in the hands of a few brave Eastern capitalists like Mr. Misevičius . . ."

The beauty of the Internet was that Chip could post whole-cloth fabrications without troubling to check even his spelling. Reliability on the Web was ninety-eight percent a function of how slick and cool your site looked. Although Chip personally wasn't fluent in Web, he was an American under forty, and Americans under forty were exquisite judges of what was slick and cool and what was not. He and Gitanas went to a pub called Prie Universiteto and hired five young Lithuanians in Phish and R.E.M. T-shirts for thirty dollars a day plus millions of worthless stock options, and for a month Chip rode these slang-slinging Webheads mercilessly. He made them study American sites like nbci.com and Oracle. He told them to do it like *this*, to make it look like *this*.

Lithuania.com was officially launched on November 5. A high-res banner—DEMOCRACY PAYS HANDSOME DIVIDENDS—unfurled to the accompaniment of sixteen joyful bars of the "Dance of the Coachmen and

Grooms" in *Petrushka*. Side by side, in a rich blue graphical space below the banner, were a black-and-white **Before** picture ("Socialist Vilnius") of shell-scarred façades and shattered lindens on the Gedimino Prospektas and a luscious color **After** photograph ("Free-Market Vilnius") of a honey-lit harborside development of boutiques and bistros. (The development was actually in Denmark.) For a week Chip and Gitanas had stayed up late drinking beer and composing the other pages, which promised investors the various eponyms and inseminatory privileges from Gitanas's original bitter posting and also, according to the level of financial commitment,

- time-shares in ministerial beachside villas at Palanga!
- pro rata mineral rights and logging rights to all national parklands!
- appointment of selected local magistrates and judges!
- blanket 24-hour-a-day parking privileges in perpetuity in the Old City of Vilnius!
- fifty-percent discount on selected rentals of Lithuanian national troops and armaments on a sign-up basis, except during wartime!
- no-hassle adoptions of Lithuanian girl babies!
- discretionary immunity from left-turn-on-red prohibitions!
- inclusion of the investor's likeness on commemorative stamps, collector's-item coins, microbrewery beer labels, bas-relief chocolate-covered Lithuanian cookies, Heroic Leader trading cards, printed wrapping tissue for holiday clementines, etc.!
- honorary Doctorate of Humane Letters from Vilnius University, founded in 1578!
- "no-questions-asked" access to wiretaps and other state-security apparatus!
- the legally enforceable right, whilst on Lithuanian soil, to such titles and honorifics as "Your Lordship" and "Your Ladyship" and "Your Grace," with non-use by service

personnel punishable by public flogging and up to sixty days in jail!

- last-minute "bumping" privileges for train and plane seats, reserved-seating cultural events, and table reservations at participating five-star restaurants and nightclubs!
- "top-of-the-list" priority for liver, heart, and cornea transplants at Vilnius's famed Antakalnis Hospital!
- no-limit hunting and fishing licenses, plus off-season privileges in national game reserves!
- your name in block letters on the side of large boats!
- etc., etc.!

The lesson that Gitanas had learned and that Chip was now learning was that the more patently satirical the promises, the lustier the influx of American capital. Day after day Chip churned out press releases, make-believe financial statements, earnest tracts arguing the Hegelian inevitability of a nakedly commercial politics, gushing eyewitness accounts of Lithuania's boom-economy-in-the-making, slow-pitch questions in online investment chat rooms, and line-drive-home-run answers. If he got flamed for his lies or his ignorance, he simply moved to another chat room. He wrote text for the stock certificates and for the accompanying brochure ("Congratulations—You Are Now a Free-Market Patriot of Lithuania") and had them sumptuously printed on cotton-rich stock. He felt as if, finally, here in the realm of pure fabrication, he'd found his métier. Exactly as Melissa Paquette had promised him long ago, it was a gas to start a company, a gas to see the money flowing in.

A reporter for *USA Today* e-mailed to ask: "Is this for real?"

Chip e-mailed back: "It's for real. The for-profit nation-state, with a globally dispersed citizenry of shareholders, is the next stage in the evolution of political economy. 'Enlightened neotechnofeudalism' is blossoming in Lithuania. Come see for yourself. I can guarantee you a minimum ninety minutes' face time with G. Misevičius."

There was no reply from *USA Today*. Chip worried that he'd overplayed his hand; but weekly gross receipts were topping forty thousand dollars. The money came in the form of bank drafts, credit-card numbers, e-cash encryption keys, wire transfers to Crédit Suisse, and hundred-dollar bills in airmail envelopes. Gitanas plowed much of the money into his ancillary enterprises, but, per agreement, he did double Chip's salary as profits rose.

Chip was living rent-free in the stucco villa where the commander of the Soviet garrison had once eaten pheasants and drunk Gewürztraminers and chatted with Moscow on secure phone links. The villa had been stoned and looted and tagged with triumphant graffiti in the fall of 1990, and had then stood derelict until the VIPPPAKJRIINPB17 was voted out of power and Gitanas was recalled from the UN. Gitanas had been attracted to the shattered villa by its unbeatable price (it was free), by its outstanding security arrangements (including an armored tower and a U.S.-embassy-quality fence), and by the opportunity to sleep in the bedroom of the very commander who'd had him tortured for six months in the old Soviet barracks next door. Gitanas and other Party members had worked weekends with trowels and scrapers to restore the villa, but the Party had disbanded altogether before the job was finished. Now half the rooms stood vacant, the floors splashed with broken glass. As throughout the Old City, heat and hot water originated at a mammoth Central Boiler Facility and dissipated much vigor in the long trip, via buried pipes and leaky risers, to the showers and radiators of the villa. Gitanas had set up offices for the Free Market Party Company in the former grand ballroom, claimed the master bedroom for himself, installed Chip in the former aide-de-camp's suite on the third floor, and let the young Webheads crash where they pleased.

Although Chip was still paying the rent on his New York apartment and the monthly minimum on his Visa bills, he felt agreeably affluent in Vilnius. He ordered from the top of menus, shared his booze and cigarettes with those less fortunate, and never looked at the prices in the natural food store near the university where he bought his groceries.

True to Gitanas's word, there were plenty of underage girls in heavy makeup available at the bars and pizzerias, but by leaving New York and escaping from "The Academy Purple," Chip seemed to have lost his need to fall in love with adolescent strangers. Twice a week he and Gitanas visited the Club Metropol and, after a massage and before a sauna, had their needs efficiently gratified on the Metropol's indifferently clean foam cushions. Most of the Metropol's female clinicians were in their thirties and led daytime lives that revolved around child care, or parent care, or the university's International Journalism program, or the making of art in political hues that nobody would buy. Chip was surprised by how willing these women were, while they dressed and fixed their hair, to speak to him like a human being. He was struck by how much pleasure they seemed to take in their daytime lives, how blah their night work was by contrast, how altogether meaningless; and since he himself had begun to take active pleasure in his daytime work, he became, with each therapeutic (trans)act(ion) on the massage mat, a little more adept at putting his body in its place, at putting sex in its place, at understanding what love was and wasn't. With each prepaid ejaculation he rid himself of another ounce of the hereditary shame that had resisted fifteen years of sustained theoretical attack. What remained was a gratitude that he expressed in the form of two hundred percent tips. At two or three in the morning, when the city lay oppressed by a darkness that seemed to have fallen weeks earlier, he and Gitanas returned to the villa through high-sulfur smoke and snow or fog or drizzle.

Gitanas was Chip's real love in Vilnius. Chip particularly liked how much Gitanas liked him. Everywhere the two men went, people asked if they were brothers, but the truth was that Chip felt less like a sibling of Gitanas than like his girlfriend. He felt much like Julia: perpetually feted, lavishly treated, and almost wholly dependent on Gitanas for favors and guidance and basic necessities. He sang for his supper, like Julia. He was a valued employee, a vulnerable and delightful American, an object of amusement and indulgence and even mystery; and what a great pleasure it was, for a change, to be the pursued one—to have qualities and attributes that somebody else so wanted.

All in all, he found Vilnius a lovely world of braised beef and cabbage and potato pancakes, of beer and vodka and tobacco, of comradeship, subversive enterprise, and pussy. He liked a climate and a latitude that substantially dispensed with daylight. He could sleep extremely late and still rise with the sun, and very soon after breakfast the time came for an evening pick-me-up of coffee and a cigarette. His was partly a student life (he'd always loved a student life) and partly a life in the fast lane of dot-com start-ups. From a distance of four thousand miles, everything he'd left behind in the U.S. looked manageably small—his parents, his debts, his failures, his loss of Julia. He felt so much better on the work front and sex front and friendship front that for a while he forgot what misery tasted like. He resolved to stay in Vilnius until he'd earned enough money to pay down his debts to Denise and to his credit-card issuers. He believed that as few as six months would suffice for this.

How wholly typical it was of his luck, then, that before he could enjoy even two good months in Vilnius, both his father and Lithuania fell apart.

Denise in her e-mails had been hectoring Chip about Alfred's health and insisting that Chip come to St. Jude for Christmas, but a trip home in December held little attraction. He suspected that if he abandoned the villa, even for a week, something stupid would prevent him from returning. A spell would be broken, a magic lost. But Denise, who was the steadiest person he knew, finally sent him an e-mail in which she sounded downright desperate. Chip skimmed the message before he realized that he shouldn't have looked at it at all, because it named the sum he owed her. The misery whose taste he thought he'd forgotten, the troubles that had seemed small from a distance, filled his head again.

He deleted the e-mail and immediately regretted it. He had a dreamlike semi-memory of the phrase *fired for sleeping with my boss's wife*. But this was such an unlikely phrase, coming from Denise, and his eye had brushed over it so quickly, that he couldn't fully credit the memory. If his sister was on her way out as a lesbian (which, come to think of it, would make sense of several aspects of Denise that had always puzzled him), then she could certainly now use the support of her Foucaultian older brother, but Chip wasn't ready to go home yet, and so he assumed that his memory had deceived him and that her phrase had referred to something else.

He smoked three cigarettes, dissolving his anxiety in rationalizations and counteraccusations and a fresh resolve to stay in Lithuania until he could pay his sister the $20,500 that he owed her. If Alfred lived with Denise until June, this meant that Chip could stay in Lithuania for another six months and still keep his promise of an all-family reunion in Philadelphia.

Lithuania, unfortunately, was rattling down the road toward anarchy.

Through October and November, despite the global financial crisis, a veneer of normalcy had adhered to Vilnius. Farmers still brought to market poultry and livestock for which they were paid in litai that they then spent on Russian gasoline, on domestic beer and vodka, on stonewashed jeans and Spice Girls sweatshirts, on pirated *X Files* videos imported from economies even sicker than Lithuania's. The truckers who distributed the gasoline and the workers who distilled the vodka and the kerchiefed old women who sold the Spice Girls sweatshirts out of wooden carts all bought the farmers' beef and chicken. The land produced, the litai circulated, and in Vilnius, at least, the pubs and clubs stayed open late.

But the economy wasn't simply local. You could give litai to the Russian petroleum exporter who supplied your country with gasoline, but this exporter was within his rights to ask which Lithuanian goods or services, exactly, he might care to spend his litai on. It was easy to buy litai at the official rate of four per dollar. Hard, however, to buy a dollar for four litai! In a familiar paradox of depression, goods became scarce *because* there were no buyers. The harder it was to find aluminum foil or ground beef or motor oil, the more tempting it became to hijack truckloads of these commodities or to muscle in on their distribution. Meanwhile public servants (notably the police) continued to draw fixed salaries of irrelevant litai. The underground economy soon learned to price a precinct captain as unerringly as it priced a box of lightbulbs.

Chip was struck by the broad similarities between black-market Lithuania and free-market America. In both countries, wealth was concentrated in the hands of a few; any meaningful distinction between private and public sectors had disappeared; captains of commerce lived in a ceaseless anxiety that drove them to expand their empires ruthlessly; ordinary citizens lived in ceaseless fear of being fired and ceaseless confusion about which powerful private interest owned which formerly public institution on any given day; and the economy was fueled largely by the elite's insatiable demand for luxury. (In Vilnius, by November of that dismal autumn, five criminal oligarchs were responsible for employing thousands of carpenters, bricklayers, craftsmen, cooks, prostitutes, barkeeps, auto mechanics, and bodyguards.) The main difference between America and Lithuania, as far as Chip could see, was that in America the wealthy few subdued the unwealthy many by means of mind-numbing and soul-killing entertainments and gadgetry and pharmaceuticals, whereas in Lithuania the powerful few subdued the unpowerful many by threatening violence.

It warmed his Foucaultian heart, in a way, to live in a land where property ownership and the control of public discourse were so obviously a matter of who had the guns.

The Lithuanian with the most guns was an ethnic Russian named Victor Lichenkev, who had parlayed the cash liquidity of his heroin and Ecstasy near-monopoly into absolute control of the Bank of Lithuania after the bank's previous owner, FrendLeeTrust of Atlanta, had catastrophically misjudged consumer appetite for its Dilbert MasterCards. Victor Lichenkev's cash reserves enabled him to arm a five-hundred-man private "constabulary" which in October boldly surrounded the Chernobyl-type nuclear reactor at Ignalina, 120 kilometers northeast of Vilnius, that supplied three-quarters of the nation's electricity. The siege gave Lichenkev excellent leverage in negotiating his purchase of the country's largest utility from the rival oligarch who himself had bought it on the cheap during the great privatization. Overnight, Lichenkev gained control of every litas flowing from every electric meter in the country; but, fearing that his Russian heritage might provoke nationalist animosity, he took care not to abuse his new power. As a gesture of goodwill, he slashed electricity prices by the fifteen percent that the previous oligarch had been overcharging. On the resulting wave of popularity, he chartered a new political party (the Cheap Power for the People Party) and fielded a slate of parliamentary candidates for the mid-December national elections.

And still the land produced and the litai circulated. A slasher flick called *Moody Fruit* opened at the Lietuva and the Vingis. Lithuanian drolleries issued from Jennifer Aniston's mouth on *Friends*. City workers emptied concrete-clad garbage receptacles on the square outside St. Catherine's. But every day was darker and shorter than the day before.

As a global player, Lithuania had been fading since the death of Vytautas the Great in 1430. For six hundred years the country was passed around among Poland, Prussia, and Russia like a much-recycled wedding present (the leatherette ice bucket; the salad tongs). The country's language and a memory of better times survived, but the main fact about Lithuania was that it wasn't very large. In the twentieth century, the Gestapo and SS could liquidate 200,000 Lithuanian Jews and the Soviets could deport another quarter-million citizens to Siberia without attracting undue international attention.

Gitanas Misevičius came from a family of priests and soldiers and bureaucrats near the Belorussian border. His paternal grandfather, a local judge, had failed a Q&A session with the new Communist administrators in 1940 and had been sent to the gulag, along with his wife, and never heard from again. Gitanas's father owned a pub in Vidiskés and gave aid and comfort to the partisan resistance movement (the so-called Forest Brothers) until hostilities ceased in '53.

A year after Gitanas was born, Vidiskés and eight surrounding municipalities were emptied by the puppet government to clear the way for the first of two nuclear power plants. The fifteen thousand people thus displaced ("for reasons of safety") were offered housing in a brand-new, fully modern small city, Khrushchevai, that had been erected hastily in the lake country west of Ignalina.

"Kind of bleak-looking, all cinderblock, no trees," Gitanas told Chip. "My dad's new pub had a cinderblock bar, cinderblock booths, cinderblock shelves. The socialist planned economy in Belorussia had made too many cinderblocks and was giving them away for nothing. Or so we were told. Anyway, we all move in. We got our cinderblock beds and our cinderblock playground equipment and our cinderblock park benches. The years go by, I'm ten years old, and suddenly everybody's mom or dad's got lung cancer. I mean *everybody's*. Well, and then my dad's got a lung tumor, and finally the authorities come and take a look at Khrushchevai, and lo and behold, we got a radon problem. Serious radon problem. Really fucking disastrous radon problem, actually. Because it turns out those cinderblocks are mildly radioactive! And radon is pooling in every closed room in Khrushchevai. Especially rooms like a pub, with not a lot of air, where the owner sits all day and smokes cigarettes. Like for instance my dad does. Well, Belorussia, which is our sister socialist republic (and which, by the way, we Lithuanians used to *own*), Belorussia says it's really sorry. There must have somehow been some pitchblende in those cinderblocks, says Belorussia. Big mistake. Sorry, sorry, sorry. So we all move out of Khrushchevai, and my dad dies, horribly, at ten minutes after midnight on the day after his wedding anniversary, because he doesn't want my mom remembering his death on their wedding date, and then thirty years go by, and Gorbachev steps down, and finally we get to take a look in those old archives, and what do you know? There was no weird glut of cinderblock due to poor planning. There was no snafu in the five-year plan. There was a deliberate strategy of recycling very-low-grade nuclear waste in building materials. On the theory that the cement in cinderblock renders the radioisotopes harmless! But the Belorussians had Geiger counters, and that was the end of that happy dream of harmlessness, and so a thousand trainloads of cinderblock got sent to us, who had no reason to suspect that anything was wrong."

"Ouch," Chip said.

"It's beyond ouch," Gitanas said. "It killed my dad when I was eleven. And my best friend's dad. And hundreds of other people, over the years. And everything made sense. There was always an enemy with a big red target on his back. There was a big evil daddy U.S.S.R. that we all could hate, until the nineties."

The platform of the VIPPPAKJRIINPB17, which Gitanas helped found after Independence, consisted of one very broad and heavy plank: the Soviets must pay for raping Lithuania. For a while, in the nineties, it was possible to run the country on pure hatred. But soon other parties emerged with platforms which, while giving revanchism its due, also sought to move beyond it. By the end of the nineties, after the VIPP-PAKJRIINPB17 lost its last seat in the Seimas, all that remained of the party was its half-renovated villa.

Gitanas tried to make political sense of the world around him and could not. The world had made sense when the Red Army was illegally detaining him, asking him questions that he refused to answer, and slowly covering the left side of his body with third-degree burns. After Independence, though, politics had lost its coherence. Even as simple and vital an issue as Soviet reparations to Lithuania was bedeviled by the fact that during World War II the Lithuanians themselves had helped persecute the Jews and by the fact that many of the people now running the Kremlin were themselves former anti-Soviet patriots who deserved reparations nearly as much as the Lithuanians did.

"What do I do now," Gitanas asked Chip, "when the invader is a system and a culture, not an army? The best future I can hope now for my country is that someday it looks more like a second-rate country in the West. More like everybody else, in other words."

"More like Denmark, with its attractive harborside bistros and boutiques," Chip said.

"How Lithuanian we all felt," Gitanas said, "when we could point to the Soviets and say: *No, we're not like that.* But to say, *No, we are not free-market, no, we are not globalized*—this doesn't make me feel Lithuanian. This makes me feel stupid and Stone Age. So how do I be a patriot now? What *positive* thing do I stand for? What is the *positive* definition of my country?"

Gitanas continued to reside in the semiderelict villa. He offered the aide-de-camp's suite to his mother, but she preferred to stay in her apartment outside Ignalina. As was de rigueur for all Lithuanian officials of that era, especially for revanchists like himself, he acquired a piece of formerly Communist property—a twenty percent stake in Sucrosas, the beet-sugar refinery that was Lithuania's second-largest single-site employer—and lived fairly comfortably as a retired patriot on the dividends.

For a time, like Chip, Gitanas glimpsed salvation in the person of Julia Vrais: in her beauty, in her American path-of-least-resistance quest for pleasure. Then Julia ditched him on a Berlin-bound jet. Hers was the latest betrayal in a life that had come to seem a numbing parade of betrayals. He was screwed by the Soviets, screwed by the Lithuanian electorate, and screwed by Julia. Finally he was screwed by the IMF and World Bank, and he brought a forty-year load of bitterness to the joke of Lithuania Incorporated.

Hiring Chip to run the Free Market Party Company was the first good decision he'd made in a long time. Gitanas had gone to New York to find a divorce lawyer and possibly to hire a cheap American actor, somebody middle-aged and failing, whom he could install in Vilnius to reassure such callers and visitors as Lithuania Incorporated might attract. He could hardly believe that a man as young and talented as Chip was willing to work for him. He was only briefly dismayed that Chip had been sleeping with his wife. In Gitanas's experience, *everyone* eventually betrayed him. He appreciated that Chip had accomplished his betrayal before they even met.

As for Chip, the inferiority he felt in Vilnius as a "pathetic American" who spoke neither Lithuanian nor Russian, and whose father hadn't died of lung cancer at an early age, and whose grandparents hadn't disappeared into Siberia, and who'd never been tortured for his ideals in an unheated military-prison cell, was offset by his competence as an employee and by the memory of certain extremely flattering contrasts that Julia used to draw between him and Gitanas. In pubs and clubs, where the two men often didn't bother to deny that they were brothers, Chip had the sensation of being the more successful of the two.

"I was a pretty good deputy prime minister," Gitanas said gloomily. "I'm not a very good criminal warlord."

Warlord, indeed, was a somewhat glorified term for Gitanas's line of work. He was exhibiting signs of failure with which Chip was all too familiar. He spent an hour worrying for every minute he spent doing. Investors around the globe were sending him gaudy sums that he deposited in his Crédit Suisse account every Friday afternoon, but he couldn't decide whether to use the money "honestly" (i.e., to buy seats in Parliament for the Free Market Party Company) or to commit fraud unabashedly and pour his ill-gotten hard currency into even less legitimate businesses. For a while he sort of did both and sort of did neither. Finally his market research (which he conducted by quizzing drunken strangers in bars) persuaded him that, in the current economic climate, even a Bolshevik had a better chance of attracting votes than a party with "Free Market" in its name.

Abandoning any notion of staying legit, Gitanas hired bodyguards. Soon Victor Lichenkev asked his spies: Why is this has-been patriot Misevičius bothering with protection? Gitanas had been far safer as an undefended has-been patriot than he was as the commander of ten strapping Kalashnikov-toting youths. He was obliged to retain more bodyguards, and Chip, for fear of getting shot, stopped leaving the compound without an escort.

"You're not in danger," Gitanas assured him. "Lichenkev might want to kill me and take over the company for himself. But you're the goose with the golden ovaries."

The back of Chip's neck nonetheless prickled with vulnerability when he went out in public. On the night of Thanksgiving in America he watched two of Lichenkev's men elbow through the crowd at a sticky-floored club called Musmiryté and put six holes in the abdomen of a red-haired "wine and spirits importer." That Lichenkev's men had walked past Chip without harming him did go to prove Gitanas's point. But the body of the "wine and spirits importer" looked every bit as soft, in comparison to bullets, as Chip had always feared a body was. Bad overloads of current flooded the dying man's nerves. Violent convulsions, hidden stores of galvanic energy, immensely distressing electrochemical outcomes, had clearly lain latent in his wiring all his life.

Gitanas showed up at Musmiryté half an hour later. "My problem," he mused, looking at the bloodstains, "is it's easier for me to be shot than to shoot."

"There you go again, running yourself down," Chip said.

"I'm good at enduring pain, bad at inflicting it."

"Seriously. Don't be so hard on yourself."

"Kill or be killed. It's not an easy concept."

Gitanas had tried to be aggressive. As a criminal warlord, he did have one fine asset: the cash generated by the Free Market Party Company. After Lichenkev's forces had surrounded the Ignalina reactor and coerced the sale of Lithuanian Electric, Gitanas sold his lucrative stake in Sucrosas, emptied the coffers of the Free Market Party Company, and bought a controlling interest in the principal cellular phone-service provider in Lithuania. The company, Transbaltic Wireless, was the only utility in his price range. He gave his bodyguards 1,000 domestic minutes per month, plus free voice mail and caller ID, and put them to work monitoring calls on Lichenkev's many Transbaltic cell phones. When he learned that Lichenkev was about to dump his entire position in the National Tannery and Livestock Products and Byproducts Corporation, Gitanas was able to short his own shares. The move netted him a bundle but proved fatal in the long run. Lichenkev, tipped off to the monitoring of his phones, switched service to a more secure regional system operated out of Riga. Then he turned around and attacked Gitanas.

On the eve of the December 20 elections, an electrical substation "accident" selectively blacked out the switching center of Transbaltic Wireless and six of its transceiver towers. A mob of angry young Vilniusian cell phone users with shaved heads and goatees attempted to storm Transbaltic's offices. Transbaltic's management called for help on ordinary copper-wire lines; the "police" responding to the call joined the mob in looting the office and laying siege to its treasury until the arrival of three vanloads of "police" from the only precinct that Gitanas could afford to pay off. After a pitched battle, the first group of "police" retreated, and the remaining "police" dispersed the mob.

Through Friday night and into Saturday morning the company's technical staff scrambled to repair the Brezhnev-era emergency generator that provided backup power to the switching center. The generator's main transfer bus was badly corroded, and when the senior supervisor jiggled it to test its integrity he snapped if off at the base. Working to reattach it in the light of candles and flashlights, the supervisor then burned a hole in the primary induction coil with his welding torch, and given the political instabilities surrounding the election there were no other gas-powered AC generators to be had at any price in Vilnius (and certainly no three-phase generators of the kind for which the switching center had been retrofitted for no better reason than that an old Brezhnev-era three-phase generator was available for cheap), and meanwhile electrical-parts suppliers in Poland and Finland were reluctant, given the political instabilities, to ship anything into Lithuania without first receiving payment in hard Western currency, and so a country whose citizens, like so many of their Western counterparts, had simply disconnected their copper-wire telephones when cell phones became cheap and universal was plunged into a communications silence of nineteenth-century proportions.

On a very gloomy Sunday morning, Lichenkev and his slate of smugglers and hit men on the Cheap Power for the People Party ticket claimed 38 of the 141 seats in the Seimas. But the Lithuanian President, Audrius Vitkunas, a charismatic and paranoid arch-nationalist who hated Russia and the West with equal passion, refused to certify the election results.

"Hydrophobic Lichenkev and his mouth-frothing hellhounds will not intimidate me!" Vitkunas shouted in a televised address on Sunday evening. "Localized power failures, a near-total breakdown in the communications network of the capital and its environs, and the presence of roving heavily armed 'constabularies' of Lichenkev's hired mouth-frothing lickspittle hellhounds do not *inspire confidence* that yesterday's voting reflects the stubborn will and immense good sense of the great and glorious immortal Lithuanian People! I will not, I cannot, I must not, I durst not, I shall not certify these scum-flecked, maggot-riddled, tertiary-syphilitic national parliamentary election results!"

Gitanas and Chip watched the address on the television in the former ballroom at the villa. Two bodyguards quietly played Dungeonmaster in a corner of the room while Gitanas translated for Chip the richer nuggets of Vitkunasian rhetoric. The peaty light of the year's shortest day had faded in the casement windows.

"I got a real bad feeling about this," Gitanas said. "I got a feeling Lichenkev wants to gun down Vitkunas and take his chances with whoever replaces him."

Chip, who was doing his best to forget that Christmas was four days away, had no wish to hang on in Vilnius only to be driven out a week after the holiday. He asked Gitanas if he'd thought about emptying the Crédit Suisse account and leaving the country.

"Oh, sure." Gitanas was wearing his red motocross jacket and hugging himself. "I think about shopping at Bloomingdale's every day. I think about the big tree at Rockefeller Center."

"Then what's keeping you?"

Gitanas scratched his scalp and smelled his fingernails, blending the aroma of scalp with the skin-oil smells from around his nose, taking obvious comfort in sebum. "If I leave," he said, "and the trouble blows over, then where am I? I'm fucked three ways. I'm not employable in America. As of next month, I'm not married to an American. And my mom's in Ignalina. What do I got in New York?"

"We could run this thing in New York."

"They got laws there. They'd shut us down in a week. I'm fucked three ways."

Toward midnight Chip went upstairs and inserted himself between his thin, cold East Bloc sheets. His room smelled of damp plaster, cigarettes, and strong synthetic shampoo fragrances such as pleased the Baltic nose. His mind was aware of its own racing. He didn't fall into sleep but skipped off it, again and again, like a stone on water. He kept mistaking the streetlight in his window for the light of day. He went downstairs and realized that it was already late afternoon on Christmas Eve; he had the oversleeper's panicked sense of having fallen behind, of lacking information. His mother was making Christmas Eve dinner in the kitchen. His father, youthful in a leather jacket, was sitting in the ballroom in the dim late light and watching the *CBS Evening News with Dan Rather*. Chip, to be friendly, asked him what the news was.

"Tell Chip," Alfred told Chip, whom he didn't recognize, "there's trouble in the East."

Real daylight came at eight. A shouting in the street woke him up.

His room was cold but not freezing; a smell of warm dust came off the radiator—the city's Central Boiler Facility still functioning, the social order still intact.

Through the branches of the spruce trees outside his window he saw a crowd of several dozen men and women in bulky overcoats milling outside the fence. A dusting of snow had fallen in the night. Two of Gitanas's security men, the brothers Jonas and Aidaris—big blond fellows with semiautomatics on straps—were parleying through the bars of the front gate with a pair of middle-aged women whose brassy hair and red faces, like the heat in Chip's radiator, gave evidence of ordinary life's persistence.

Downstairs the ballroom echoed with emphatic televised Lithuanian declarations. Gitanas was sitting exactly where Chip had left him the night before, but his clothes were different and he appeared to have slept.

The gray morning light and the snow on the trees and the peripheral sense of disarray and breakup recalled the end of an academic fall term, the last day of exams before the Christmas break. Chip went to the kitchen and poured Vitasoy Delite Vanilla soy milk on a bowl of Barbara's All-Natural Shredded Oats Bite Size cereal. He drank some of the viscous German organic black-cherry juice that he'd lately been enjoying. He made two mugs of instant coffee and took them to the ballroom, where Gitanas had turned off the TV and was sniffing his fingernails again.

Chip asked him what the news was.

"All my bodyguards ran away except Jonas and Aidaris," Gitanas said. "They took the VW and the Lada. I doubt they're coming back."

"With protectors like this, who needs attackers?" Chip said.

"They left us the Stomper, which is a crime magnet."

"When did this happen?"

"Must have been right after President Vitkunas put the Army on alert."

Chip laughed. "When did *that* happen?"

"Early this morning. Everything in the city is apparently still functioning—except, of course, Transbaltic Wireless," Gitanas said.

The mob in the street had swelled. There were perhaps a hundred people now, holding aloft cell phones that collectively produced an eerie, angelic sound. They were playing the sequence of tones that signified SERVICE INTERRUPTION.

"I want you to go back to New York," Gitanas said. "We'll see what happens here. Maybe I'll come, maybe I won't. I gotta see my mother for Christmas. Meantime, here's your severance."

He tossed Chip a thick brown envelope just as multiple thuds were sounding on the villa's outer walls. Chip dropped the envelope. A rock crashed through a window and bounced to a stop by the television set. The rock was four-sided, a broken corner of granite cobblestone. It was coated with fresh hostility and seemed faintly embarrassed.

Gitanas dialed the "police" on the copper-wire line and spoke wearily. The brothers Jonas and Aidaris, fingers on triggers, came in through the front door, followed by cold air with a sprucey Yule flavor. The brothers were cousins of Gitanas; this was presumably why they hadn't deserted with the others. Gitanas put down the phone and conferred with them in Lithuanian.

The brown envelope contained a meaty stack of fifty- and hundred-dollar bills.

Chip's feeling from his dream, his belated realization that the holiday had come, was persisting in the daylight. None of the young Webheads had reported to work today, and now Gitanas had given him a present, and snow was clinging to the boughs of spruces, and carolers in bulky coats were at the gate . . .

"Pack your bags," Gitanas said. "Jonas will take you to the airport."

Chip went upstairs with an empty head and heart. He heard guns banging on the front porch, the ting-a-ling of ejected casings, Jonas and Aidaris firing (he hoped) at the sky. Jingle bells, jingle bells.

He put on his leather pants and leather coat. Repacking his bag connected him to the moment of unpacking it in early October, completed a loop of time and pulled a drawstring that made the twelve intervening weeks disappear. Here he was again, packing.

Gitanas was smelling his fingers, his eyes on the news, when Chip returned to the ballroom. Victor Lichenkev's mustaches went up and down on the TV screen.

"What's he saying?"

Gitanas shrugged. "That Vitkunas is mentally unfit, et cetera. That Vitkunas is mounting a putsch to reverse the legitimate will of the Lithuanian people, et cetera."

"You should come with me," Chip said.

"I'm gonna go see my mother," Gitanas said. "I'll call you next week."

Chip put his arms around his friend and squeezed him. He could smell the scalp oils that Gitanas in his agitation had been sniffing. He felt as if he were hugging himself, feeling his own primate shoulder blades, the scratch of his own woolen sweater. He also felt his friend's gloom—how not-there he was, how distracted or shut down—and it made him, too, feel lost.

Jonas beeped the horn on the gravel drive outside the front door.

"Let's meet up in New York," Chip said.

"OK, maybe." Gitanas pulled away and wandered back to the television.

Only a few stragglers remained to throw rocks at the Stomper as Jonas and Chip roared through the open gate. They drove south out of the city center on a street lined with forbidding gas stations and brown-walled, traffic-scarred buildings that seemed happiest and most themselves on days, like this one, when the weather was raw and the light was poor. Jonas spoke very little English but managed to exude tolerance toward Chip, if not friendliness, while keeping his eyes on the rearview mirror. Traffic was extremely sparse this morning, and sport-utility vehicles, those workhorses of the warlord class, attracted unhealthy attention in times of instability.

The little airport was mobbed with young people speaking the languages of the West. Since the Quad Cities Fund had liquidated Lietuvos Avialinijos, other airlines had taken over some of the routes, but the curtailed flight schedule (fourteen departures a day for a capital of Europe) wasn't equipped to handle loads like today's. Hundreds of

British, German, and American students and entrepreneurs, many of their faces familiar to Chip from his pub-crawling with Gitanas, had converged on the reservation counters of Finnair and Lufthansa, Aeroflot and LOT Polish Airlines.

Doughty city buses were arriving with fresh loads of foreign nationals. As far as Chip could see, none of the counter lines were moving at all. He tallied the flights on the Outbound board and chose the airline, Finnair, with the most departures.

At the end of the very long Finnair line were two American college girls in bell-bottom jeans and other Sixties Revival wear. The names on their luggage were Tiffany and Cheryl.

"Do you have tickets?" Chip asked.

"For tomorrow," Tiffany said. "But things looked kinda nasty, so."

"Is this line moving?"

"I don't know. We've only been here ten minutes."

"It hasn't moved in ten minutes?"

"There's only one person at the counter," Tiffany said. "But it's not like there's some other, better Finnair counter someplace else, so."

Chip was feeling disoriented and had to steel himself not to hail a cab and return to Gitanas.

Cheryl said to Tiffany: "So my dad's like, you've got to sublet if you're going to Europe, and I'm like, I promised Anna she could stay there weekends when there's home games so she can sleep with Jason, right? I can't take a promise *back*—right? But my dad's getting like all bottom-line, and I'm like, hello, it's *my* condominium, right? You bought it for *me*, right? I didn't know I was going to have some stranger, you know, who, like, *fries* things on the stove, and sleeps in my bed?"

Tiffany said: "That is so-gross."

Cheryl said: "And uses my pillows?"

Two more non-Lithuanians, a pair of Belgians, joined the line behind Chip. Simply not to be the last in line brought some relief. Chip, in French, asked the Belgians to watch his bag and hold his place. He went to the men's room, locked himself in a stall, and counted the money Gitanas had given him.

It was $29,250.

It upset him somehow. It made him afraid.

A voice on a bathroom speaker announced, in Lithuanian and then Russian and then English, that LOT Polish Airlines Flight #331 from Warsaw had been canceled.

Chip put twenty hundreds in his T-shirt pocket, twenty hundreds in his left boot, and returned the rest of the money to the envelope, which he hid inside his T-shirt, against his belly. He wished that Gitanas hadn't given him the money. Without money, he'd had a good reason to stay in Vilnius. Now that he had no good reason, a simple fact which the previous twelve weeks had kept hidden was stripped naked in the fecal, uric bathroom stall. The simple fact was that he was afraid to go home.

No man likes to see his cowardice as clearly as Chip could see his now. He was angry at the money and angry at Gitanas for giving it to him and angry at Lithuania for falling apart, but the fact remained that he was afraid to go home, and this was nobody's fault but his.

He reclaimed his place in the Finnair line, which hadn't moved at all. Airport speakers were announcing the cancellation of Flight #1048 from Helsinki. A collective groan went up, and bodies surged forward, the head of the line blunting itself against the counter like a delta.

Cheryl and Tiffany kicked their bags forward. Chip kicked his bag forward. He felt returned to the world and he didn't like it. A kind of hospital light, a light of seriousness and inescapability, fell on the girls and the baggage and the Finnair personnel in their uniforms. Chip had nowhere to hide. Everyone around him was reading a novel. He hadn't read a novel in at least a year. The prospect frightened him nearly as much as the prospect of Christmas in St. Jude. He wanted to go out and hail a cab, but he suspected that Gitanas had already fled the city.

He stood in the hard light until the hour was 2:00 and then 2:30— early morning in St. Jude. While the Belgians watched his bag again, he waited in a different line and made a credit-card phone call.

Enid's voice was slurred and tiny. "Wello?"

"Hi, Mom, it's me."

Her voice trebled instantly in pitch and volume. "Chip? Oh, Chip! Al, it's Chip! It's Chip! Chip, where are you?"

"I'm at the airport in Vilnius. I'm on my way home."

"Oh, wonderful! Wonderful! Wonderful! Now, tell me, when do you get here?"

"I don't have a ticket yet," he said. "Things are sort of falling apart here. But tomorrow afternoon sometime. Wednesday at the latest."

"Wonderful!"

He hadn't been prepared for the joy in his mother's voice. If he'd ever known that he could bring joy to another person, he'd long since forgotten it. He took care to steady his own voice and keep his word count low. He said that he would call again as soon as he was at a better airport.

"This is wonderful news," Enid said. "I'm so happy!"

"OK, then, I'll see you soon."

Already the great Baltic winter night was shouldering in from the north. Veterans from the front of the Finnair line reported that the rest of the day's flights were sold out and that at least one of these flights was likely to be canceled, but Chip hoped that by flashing a couple of hundreds he could secure those "bumping privileges" that he'd lampooned on lithuania.com. Failing that, he would buy somebody's ticket for lots of cash.

Cheryl said: "Oh my God, Tiffany, the StairMaster is so-totally *butt-building*."

Tiffany said: "Only if you, like, stick it out."

Cheryl said: "Everybody sticks it out. You can't help it. Your legs get tired."

Tiffany said: "Duh! It's a StairMaster! Your legs are *supposed* to get tired."

Cheryl looked out a window and asked, with withering undergraduate disdain: "Excuse me, why is there a *tank* in the middle of the runway?"

A minute later the lights went out and the phones went dead.

ONE LAST CHRISTMAS

DOWN IN THE BASEMENT, at the eastern end of the Ping-Pong table, Alfred was unpacking a Maker's Mark whiskey carton filled with Christmas-tree lights. He already had prescription drugs and an enema kit on the table. He had a sugar cookie freshly baked by Enid in a shape suggestive of a terrier but meant to be a reindeer. He had a Log Cabin syrup carton containing the large colored lights that he'd formerly hung on the outdoor yews. He had a pump-action shotgun in a zippered canvas case, and a box of twenty-gauge shells. He had rare clarity and the will to use it while it lasted.

A shadowy light of late afternoon was captive in the window wells. The furnace was cycling on often, the house leaking heat. Alfred's red sweater hung on him in skewed folds and bulges, as if he were a log or a chair. His gray wool slacks were afflicted with stains that he had no choice but to tolerate, because the only other option was to take leave of his senses, and he wasn't quite ready to do that.

Uppermost in the Maker's Mark carton was a very long string of white Christmas lights coiled bulkily around a wand of cardboard. The string stank of mildew from the storeroom beneath the porch, and when he put the plug into an outlet he could see right away that all was not well. Most of the lights were burning brightly, but near the center of the spool was a patch of unlit bulbs—a substantia nigra deep inside the tangle. He unwound the spool with veering hands, paying the string out on the Ping-Pong table. At the very end of it was an unsightly stretch of dead bulbs.

He understood what modernity expected of him now. Modernity expected him to drive to a big discount store and replace the damaged string. But the discount stores were mobbed at this time of year; he'd be in line for twenty minutes. He didn't mind waiting, but Enid wouldn't let him drive the car now, and Enid did mind waiting. She was upstairs flogging herself through the home stretch of Christmas prep.

Much better, Alfred thought, to stay out of sight in the basement, to work with what he had. It offended his sense of proportion and economy to throw away a ninety-percent serviceable string of lights. It offended his sense of himself, because he was an individual from an age of individuals, and a string of lights was, like him, an individual thing. No matter how little the thing had cost, to throw it away was to deny its value and, by extension, the value of individuals generally: to willfully designate as trash an object that you knew wasn't trash.

Modernity expected this designation and Alfred resisted it.

Unfortunately, he didn't know how to fix the lights. He didn't understand how a stretch of fifteen bulbs could go dead. He examined the transition from light to darkness and saw no change in the wiring pattern between the last burning bulb and the first dead one. He couldn't follow the three constituent wires through all their twists and braidings. The circuit was semiparallel in some complex way he didn't see the point of.

In the old days, Christmas lights had come in short strings that were wired serially. If a single bulb burned out or even just loosened in its socket, the circuit was broken and the entire string went dark. One of the season's rituals for Gary and Chip had been to tighten each little brass-footed bulb in a darkened string and then, if this didn't work, to replace each bulb in turn until the dead culprit was found. (What joy the boys had taken in the resurrection of a string!) By the time Denise was old enough to help with the lights, the technology had advanced. The wiring was parallel, and the bulbs had snap-in plastic bases. A single faulty light didn't affect the rest of the community but identified itself instantly for instant replacement . . .

Alfred's hands were rotating on his wrists like the twin heads of an eggbeater. As well as he could, he advanced his fingers along the string, squeezing and twisting the wires as he went—and the dark stretch reignited! The string was complete!

What had he done?

He smoothed out the string on the Ping-Pong table. Almost immediately, the faulty segment went dark again. He tried to revive it by squeezing it and patting it, but this time he had no luck.

(You fitted the barrel of the shotgun into your mouth and you reached for the switch.)

He reexamined the braid of olive-drab wires. Even now, even at this extremity of his affliction, he believed he could sit down with pencil and paper and reinvent the principles of basic circuitry. He was certain, for the moment, of his ability to do this; but the task of puzzling out a parallel circuit was far more daunting than the task, say, of driving to a discount store and waiting in line. The mental task required an inductive rediscovery of basic precepts; it required a rewiring of his own cerebral circuitry. It was truly marvelous that such a thing was even thinkable—that a forgetful old man alone in his basement with his shotgun and his sugar cookie and his big blue chair could spontaneously regenerate organic circuitry complex enough to understand electricity—but the *energy* that this reversal of entropy would cost him vastly exceeded the energy available to him in the form of his sugar cookie. Maybe if he ate a whole box of sugar cookies all at once, he could relearn parallel circuitry and make sense of the peculiar three-wire braiding of these infernal lights. But oh, my God, a person got so tired.

He shook the string and the dead lights came on again. He shook it and shook it and they didn't go out. By the time he'd coiled the string back onto the makeshift spool, however, the deep interior was dark again. Two hundred bulbs were burning bright, and modernity insisted that he junk the whole thing.

He suspected that somewhere, somehow, this new technology was stupid or lazy. Some young engineer had taken a shortcut and failed to anticipate the consequences that he was suffering now. But because he didn't understand the technology, he had no way to know the nature of the failure or to take steps to correct it.

And so the goddamned lights made a victim of him, and there wasn't a goddamned thing he could do except go out and *spend*.

You were outfitted as a boy with a will to fix things by yourself and with a respect for individual physical objects, but eventually some of your internal hardware (including such mental hardware as this will and this respect) became obsolete, and so, even though many other parts of you still functioned well, an argument could be made for junking the whole human machine.

Which was another way of saying he was tired.

He fitted the cookie into his mouth. Chewed carefully and swallowed. It was hell to get old.

Fortunately, there were thousands of other lights in the Maker's Mark box. Alfred methodically plugged in each bunch. He found three shorter strings in good working order, but all the rest were either inexplicably dead or were so old that the light was faint and yellow; and three shorter strings wouldn't cover the whole tree.

At the bottom of the box he found packages of replacement bulbs, carefully labeled. He found strings that he'd spliced back together after excising faulty segments. He found old serial strings whose broken sockets he'd hot-wired with drops of solder. He was amazed, in retrospect, that he'd had time to do all this repair work amid so many other responsibilities.

Oh, the myths, the childish optimism, of the fix! The hope that an object might never have to wear out. The dumb faith that there would always be a future in which he, Alfred, would not only be alive but have enough energy to make repairs. The quiet conviction that all his thrift and all his conservator's passion would have a point, later on: that someday he would wake up transformed into a wholly different person with infinite energy and infinite time to attend to all the objects that he'd saved, to keep it all working, to keep it all together.

"I ought to pitch the whole damn lot of it," he said aloud.

His hands wagged. They always wagged.

He took the shotgun into his workshop and leaned it against the laboratory bench.

The problem was insoluble. There he'd been, in extremely cold salty water, his lungs half-full and his heavy legs cramping and his shoulder useless in its socket, and all he would have had to do was nothing. Let go and drown. But he kicked, it was a reflex. He didn't like the depths and so he kicked, and then down from above had rained orange flotation devices. He'd stuck his working arm through a hole in one of them just as a really serious combination of wave and undertow—the

Gunnar Myrdal's wake—sent him into a gargantuan wash-and-spin. All he would have had to do then was let go. And yet it was clear, even as he was nearly drowning there in the North Atlantic, that in the *other* place there would be no objects whatsoever: that this miserable orange flotation device through which he'd stuck his arm, this fundamentally inscrutable and ungiving fabric-clad hunk of foam, would be a GOD in the objectless world of death toward which he was headed, would be the SUPREME I-AM-WHAT-I-AM in that universe of unbeing. For a few minutes, the orange flotation device was the only object he had. It was his last object and so, instinctively, he loved it and pulled it close.

Then they hauled him out of the water and dried him off and wrapped him up. They treated him like a child, and he reconsidered the wisdom of surviving. There was nothing wrong with him except his one-eyed blindness and his non-working shoulder and a few other small things, but they spoke to him as if he were an idiot, a lad, a demented person. In their phony solicitude, their thinly veiled contempt, he saw the future that he'd chosen in the water. It was a nursing-home future and it made him weep. He should have just drowned.

He shut and locked the door of the laboratory, because it all came down to privacy, didn't it? Without privacy there was no point in being an individual. And they would give him no privacy in a nursing home. They would be like the people on the helicopter and not leave him be.

He undid his pants, took out the rag that he kept folded in his underwear, and peed into a Yuban can.

He'd bought the gun a year before his retirement. He'd imagined that retirement would bring that radical transformation. He'd imagined himself hunting and fishing, imagined himself back in Kansas and Nebraska on a little boat at dawn, imagined a ridiculous and improbable life of recreation for himself.

The gun had a velvety, inviting action, but soon after he bought it, a starling had broken its neck on the kitchen window while he was eating lunch. He hadn't been able to finish eating, and he'd never fired the gun.

The human species was given dominion over the earth and took the opportunity to exterminate other species and warm the atmosphere and

generally ruin things in its own image, but it paid this price for its privileges: that the finite and specific animal body of this species contained
a brain capable of conceiving the infinite and wishing to be infinite
itself.

There came a time, however, when death ceased to be the enforcer
of finitude and began to look, instead, like the last opportunity for radical transformation, the only plausible portal to the infinite.

But to be seen as the finite carcass in a sea of blood and bone chips
and gray matter—to inflict that version of himself on other people—
was a violation of privacy so profound it seemed it would outlive him.

He was also afraid that it might hurt.

And there was a very important question that he still wanted answered. His children were coming, Gary and Denise and maybe even
Chip, his intellectual son. It was possible that Chip, if he came, could
answer the very important question.

And the question was:

The question was:

Enid hadn't felt ashamed at all, not the tiniest bit, when the warning
horns were sounding and the *Gunnar Myrdal* was shuddering with the
reversal of its thrusters and Sylvia Roth was pulling her through the
crowded Pippi Longstocking Ballroom, crying, "Here's his wife, let us
through!" It hadn't embarrassed Enid to see Dr. Hibbard again as he
knelt on the shuffleboard deck and cut the wet clothes off her husband
with dainty surgical clippers. Not even when the assistant cruise director who was helping her pack Alfred's bags found a yellowed diaper in
an ice bucket, not even when Alfred cursed the nurses and orderlies on
the mainland, not even when the face of Khellye Withers on the TV in
Alfred's hospital room reminded her that she hadn't said a comforting
word to Sylvia on the eve of Withers's execution, did she feel shame.

She returned to St. Jude in such good spirits that she was able to
call Gary and confess that, rather than sending Alfred's notarized
patent-licensing agreement to the Axon Corporation, she'd hidden it in
the laundry room. After Gary had given her the disappointing news that
five thousand dollars was probably a reasonable licensing fee after all,

she went to the basement to retrieve the notarized agreement and couldn't find it in its hiding place. Strangely unembarrassed, she called Schwenksville and asked Axon to send her a duplicate set of contracts. Alfred was puzzled when she presented him with these duplicates, but she waved her hands and said, well, things get lost in the mail. Dave Schumpert again served as notary, and she was feeling quite all right until she ran out of Aslan and nearly died of shame.

Her shame was crippling and atrocious. It mattered to her now, as it hadn't a week earlier, that a thousand happy travelers on the *Gunnar Myrdal* had witnessed how peculiar she and Alfred were. Everyone on the ship had understood that the landing at historic Gaspé was being delayed and the side trip to scenic Bonaventure Island was being canceled because the palsied man in the awful raincoat had gone where nobody was supposed to go, because his wife had selfishly enjoyed herself at an investment lecture, because she'd taken a drug so bad that no doctor in America could legally prescribe it, because she didn't believe in God and she didn't respect the law, because she was horribly, unspeakably *different* from other people.

Night after night she lay awake, suffered shame, and pictured the golden caplets. She was ashamed of lusting for these caplets, but she was also convinced that only they could bring relief.

In early November she took Alfred to the Corporate Woods Medical Complex for his bimonthly neurological checkup. Denise, who'd signed Alfred up for Axon's Phase II testing of Corecktall, had been asking Enid if he seemed "demented." Enid referred the question to Dr. Hedgpeth during his private interview with her, and Hedgpeth replied that Alfred's periodic confusion did suggest early Alzheimer's or Lewy-body dementia—at which point Enid interrupted to ask whether possibly Alfred's dopamine-boosters were causing his "hallucinations." Hedgpeth couldn't deny that this was possible. He said the only sure way to rule out dementia would be to put Alfred in the hospital for a ten-day "drug holiday."

Enid, in her shame, didn't mention to Hedgpeth that she was leery of hospitals now. She didn't mention that there had been some raging and some thrashing and some cursing in the Canadian hospital, some overturning of Styrofoam water pitchers and of wheeled IV-drip stands, until Alfred was sedated. She didn't mention that Alfred had requested that she shoot him before she put him in a place like that again.

Nor, when Hedgpeth asked how she was holding up, did she mention her little Aslan problem. Fearing that Hedgpeth would recognize her as a weak-willed, wild-eyed substance-craver, she didn't even ask him for an alternative "sleep aid." However, she did mention that she wasn't sleeping well. She stressed this, in fact: *not sleeping well at all*. But Hedgpeth merely suggested that she try a different bed. He suggested Tylenol PM.

It seemed unfair to Enid, as she lay in the dark beside her snoring husband, that a drug legally purchasable in so many other countries should be unavailable to her in America. It seemed unfair that many of her friends had "sleep aids" of the sort that Hedgpeth had failed to offer her. How cruelly scrupulous Hedgpeth was! She could have gone to a different doctor, of course, and asked for a "sleep aid," but this other doctor would surely wonder why her own doctors weren't giving her the drugs.

Such was her situation when Bea and Chuck Meisner departed for six weeks of winter family fun in Austria. The day before the Meisners left, Enid had lunch with Bea at Deepmire and asked her to do her a favor in Vienna. She pressed into Bea's hands a slip of paper on which she'd copied information from an empty SampLpak—*ASLAN 'Cruiser' (rhadamanthine citrate 88%, 3-methyl-rhadamanthine chloride 12%)*—with the annotation *Temporarily unavailable in U.S., I need 6 months supply*.

"Now, don't bother if it's any trouble," she told Bea, "but if Klaus could write you a prescription, it would be so much easier than my doctor trying to get something from overseas, so, anyway, I hope you have a wonderful time in my favorite country!"

Enid couldn't have asked such a shameful favor of anyone but Bea. Even Bea she dared to ask only because (a) Bea was a tiny bit dumb, and (b) Bea's husband had once upon a time made his own shameful insider purchase of Erie Belt stock, and (c) Enid felt that Chuck had never properly thanked or compensated Alfred for that inside information.

No sooner had the Meisners flown away, however, than Enid's shame mysteriously abated. As if an evil spell had worn off, she began to sleep better and think less about the drug. She brought her powers of selective forgetfulness to bear on the favor she'd asked of Bea. She began to feel like herself again, which was to say: optimistic.

She bought two tickets for a flight to Philadelphia on January 15. She told her friends that the Axon Corporation was testing an exciting new brain therapy called Corecktall and that Alfred, because he'd sold his patent to Axon, was eligible for the tests. She said that Denise was being a doll and offering to let her and Alfred stay in Philadelphia for as long as the testing lasted. She said that, no, Corecktall was not a laxative, it was a revolutionary new treatment for Parkinson's disease. She said that, yes, the name was confusing, but it was not a laxative.

"Tell the people at Axon," she told Denise, "that Dad has some mild symptoms of hallucination which his doctor says are *probably drug-related*. Then, see, if Corecktall helps him, we can take him off the medication, and the hallucinations will probably stop."

She told not only her friends but everybody else she knew in St. Jude, including her butcher, her broker, and her mailman, that her grandson Jonah was coming for the holidays. Naturally she was disappointed that Gary and Jonah were staying for just three days and were leaving at noon on Christmas, but plenty of fun could be packed into three days. She had tickets for the Christmasland light show and *The Nutcracker*; tree-trimming, sledding, caroling, and a Christmas Eve church service were also on the bill. She dug out cookie recipes that she hadn't used in twenty years. She laid in eggnog.

On the Sunday before Christmas she awoke at 3:05 a.m. and thought: *Thirty-six hours*. Four hours later she got up thinking: *Thirty-two hours*. Late in the day she took Alfred to the street-association Christmas party at Dale and Honey Driblett's, sat him down safely with Kirby Root, and proceeded to remind all her neighbors that her favorite grandson, who'd been *looking forward all year* to a Christmas in St. Jude, was arriving tomorrow afternoon. She located Alfred in the Dribletts' downstairs bathroom and argued with him unexpectedly about his supposed constipation. She took him home and put him to bed, erased the argument from her memory, and sat down in the dining room to knock off another dozen Christmas cards.

Already the wicker basket for incoming greetings contained a four-inch stack of cards from old friends like Norma Greene and new friends like Sylvia Roth. More and more senders Xeroxed or word-processed their Christmas notes, but Enid was having none of this. Even if it meant being late with them, she'd undertaken to handwrite a hundred notes and hand-address nearly two hundred envelopes. Besides her standard Two-Paragraph Note and her four-paragraph Full Note, she had a boilerplate Short Note:

> Loved our cruise to see the autumn color in New England and maritime Canada. Al took an unexpected "swim" in the Gulf of St. Lawrence but is feeling "ship-shape" again! Denise's super-deluxe new restaurant in Phila. was written up in the NY Times. Chip continued work at his NYC law firm and pursued investments in Eastern Europe. We enjoyed a wonderful visit from Gary and our "precocious" youngest grandson Jonah. Hoping the whole family will be in St. Jude for Christmas—a *heavenly* treat for me! Love to you all—

It was ten o'clock and she was shaking the cramp from her writing hand when Gary called from Philadelphia.

"Looking forward to seeing the two of you in seventeen hours!" Enid sang into the telephone.

"Some bad news here," Gary said. "Jonah's been throwing up and has a fever. I don't think I can take him on the plane."

This camel of disappointment balked at the needle's eye of Enid's willingness to apprehend it.

"See how he feels in the morning," she said. "Kids get twenty-four-hour bugs, I bet he'll be fine. He can rest on the plane if he needs to. He can go to bed early and sleep late on Tuesday!"

"Mother."

"If he's really sick, Gary, I understand, he can't come. But if he gets over his fever—"

"Believe me, we're all disappointed. Especially Jonah."

"No need to make any decision right this minute. Tomorrow is a completely new day."

"I'm warning you it will probably just be me."

"Well, but, Gary, things could look very, very different in the morning. Why don't you wait and make your decision then, and surprise me. I bet everything's going to work out fine!"

It was the season of joy and miracles, and Enid went to bed full of hope.

Early the next morning she was awakened—*rewarded*—by the ringing of the phone, the sound of Chip's voice, the news that he was coming home from Lithuania within forty-eight hours and the family would be complete on Christmas Eve. She was humming when she went downstairs and pinned another ornament on the Advent calendar that hung on the front door.

For as long as anyone could remember, the Tuesday ladies' group at the church had raised money by manufacturing Advent calendars. These calendars were not, as Enid would hasten to tell you, the cheap windowed cardboard items that you bought for five dollars in a cellophane sleeve. They were beautifully hand-sewn and reusable. A green felt Christmas tree was stitched to a square of bleached canvas with twelve numbered pockets across the top and another twelve across the bottom. On each morning of Advent your children took an ornament from a pocket—a tiny rocking horse of felt and sequins, or a yellow felt turtledove, or a sequin-encrusted toy soldier—and pinned it to the tree. Even now, with her children all grown, Enid continued to shuffle and distribute the ornaments in their pockets every November 30. Only the ornament in the twenty-fourth pocket was the same every year: a tiny plastic Christ child in a walnut shell spray-painted gold. Although Enid generally fell far short of fervor in her Christian beliefs, she was devout about this ornament. To her it was an icon not merely of the Lord but of her own three babies and of all the sweet baby-smelling babies of the world. She'd filled the twenty-fourth pocket for thirty years, she knew very well what it contained, and still the anticipation of opening it could take her breath away.

"It's wonderful news about Chip, don't you think?" she asked Alfred at breakfast.

Alfred was shoveling up his hamster-pellet All-Bran and drinking his morning drink of hot milk and water. His expression was like a perspectival regression toward a vanishing point of misery.

"*Chip* will be here *tomorrow*," Enid repeated. "Isn't that wonderful news? Aren't you happy?"

Alfred consulted with the soggy mass of All-Bran on his wandering spoon. "Well," he said. "If he comes."

"He said he'd be here tomorrow afternoon," Enid said. "Maybe, if he's not too tired, he can go to *The Nutcracker* with us. I still have six tickets."

"I am dubious," Alfred said.

That his comments actually pertained to her questions—that in spite of the infinity in his eyes he was participating in a finite conversation—made up for the sourness in his face.

Enid had pinned her hopes, like a baby in a walnut shell, on Corecktall. If Alfred proved to be too confused to participate in the testing, she didn't know what she was going to do. Her life therefore bore a strange resemblance to the lives of those friends of hers, Chuck Meisner and Joe Person in particular, who were "addicted" to monitoring their investments. According to Bea, Chuck's anxiety drove him to check quotes on his computer two or three times an hour, and the last time Enid and Alfred had gone out with the Persons, Joe had made Enid *frantic* by cell-phoning three different brokers from the restaurant. But she was the same way with Alfred: painfully attuned to every hopeful upswing, forever fearful of a crash.

Her freest hour of the day came after breakfast. Every morning, as soon as Alfred had downed his cup of hot milky water, he went to the basement and focused on evacuation. Enid wasn't welcome to speak to him during this peak hour of his anxiety, but she could leave him to his own devices. His colonic preoccupations were a madness but not the kind of madness that would disqualify him for Corecktall.

Outside the kitchen window, snowflakes from an eerily blue-clouded sky drifted through the twigs of an unthriving dogwood that had been planted (this really dated it) by Chuck Meisner. Enid mixed and refrigerated a ham loaf for later baking and assembled a salad of bananas, green grapes, canned pineapple, marshmallows, and lemon Jell-O. These foods, along with twice-baked potatoes, were official St. Jude favorites of Jonah's and were on the menu for tonight.

For months she'd imagined Jonah pinning the Christ child to the Advent calendar on the morning of the twenty-fourth.

Elated by her second cup of coffee, she went upstairs and knelt by the old cherrywood dresser of Gary's where she kept gifts and party favors. She'd finished her Christmas shopping weeks ago, but all she'd bought for Chip was a sale-priced brown-and-red Pendleton wool bathrobe. Chip had forfeited her goodwill several Christmases ago by sending her a used-looking cookbook, *Foods of Morocco*, wrapped in aluminum foil and decorated with stick-on pictures of coat hangers with red slashes through them. Now that he was coming home from Lithuania, however, she wanted to reward him to the full extent of her gift budget. Which was:

Alfred: no set amount
Chip, Denise: $100 each, plus grapefruit
Gary, Caroline: $60 each, maximum, plus grapefruit
Aaron, Caleb: $30 each, maximum
Jonah (this year only): no set amount

Having paid $55 for the bathrobe, she needed $45 worth of additional gifts for Chip. She rummaged in the dresser drawers. She rejected the vases in shopworn boxes from Hong Kong, the many matching bridge decks and score pads, the many thematic cocktail napkins, the really neat and really useless pen-and-pencil sets, the many travel alarm clocks that folded up or beeped in unusual ways, the shoehorn with a telescoping handle, the inexplicably dull Korean steak knives, the cork-bottomed bronze coasters with locomotives engraved on their faces, the ceramic 5×7 picture frame with the word "Memories" in glazed lavender script, the onyx turtle figurines from Mexico, and the cleverly boxed kit of ribbon and wrapping paper called The Gift of Giving. She weighed the suitability of the pewter candle snuffer and the Lucite salt-shaker cum pepper grinder. Recalling the paucity of Chip's home furnishings, she decided that the snuffer and the shaker/grinder would do just fine.

In the season of joy and miracles, while she wrapped, she forgot about the urine-smelling laboratory and its noxious crickets. She was able not to care that Alfred had put up the Christmas tree at a twenty-degree tilt. She could believe that Jonah was feeling just as healthy this morning as she was.

By the time she'd finished her wrapping, the light in the gull-plumage winter sky had a midday angle and intensity. She went down to the basement, where she found the Ping-Pong table buried under green strings of lights, like a chassis engulfed by kudzu, and Alfred seated on the floor with electrician's tape, pliers, and extension cords.

"Damn these lights!" he said.

"Al, what are you doing on the floor?"

"These goddamned cheap new lights!"

"Don't *worry* about them. Just leave them. Let Gary and Jonah do that. Come upstairs and have lunch."

The flight from Philadelphia was due in at one-thirty. Gary was going to rent a car and be at the house by three, and Enid intended to let Alfred sleep in the meantime, because tonight she would have reinforcements. Tonight, if he got up and wandered, she wouldn't be the only one on duty.

The quiet in the house after lunch was of such density that it nearly stopped the clocks. These final hours of waiting ought to have been the perfect time to write some Christmas cards, a win-win occasion in which either the minutes would fly by or she would get a lot of work done; but time could not be cheated in this way. Beginning a Short Note, she felt as if she were pushing her pen through molasses. She lost track of her words, wrote *took an unexpected "swim" in an unexpected "swim,"* and had to throw the card away. She stood up to check the kitchen clock and found that five minutes had passed since she'd last checked. She arranged an assortment of cookies on a lacquered wooden holiday plate. She set a knife and a huge pear on a cutting board. She shook a carton of eggnog. She loaded the coffeemaker in case Gary wanted coffee. She sat down to write a Short Note and saw in the blank whiteness of the card a reflection of her mind. She went to the window and peered out at the bleached zoysia lawn. The mailman, struggling with holiday volumes, was coming up the walk with a mighty bundle that he pushed through the slot in three batches. She pounced on the mail and sorted wheat from chaff, but she was too distracted to open the cards. She went down to the blue chair in the basement.

"Al," she shouted, "I think you should get up."

He sat up haystack-haired and empty-eyed. "Are they here?"

"Any minute. Maybe you want to freshen up."

"Who's coming?"

"Gary and Jonah, unless Jonah's too sick."

"Gary," Alfred said. "And Jonah."

"Why don't you take a *shower*?"

He shook his head. "No showers."

"If you want to be stuck in that tub when they get here—"

"I think I'm entitled to a bath, after the work I've done."

There was a nice shower stall in the downstairs bathroom, but Alfred had never liked to stand while bathing. Since Enid now refused to help him get out of the upstairs tub, he sometimes sat there for an hour, the water cold and soap-gray at his haunches, before he contrived to extricate himself, because he was so stubborn.

He had bathwater running in the upstairs bathroom when the long-awaited knock finally came.

Enid rushed to the front door and opened it to the vision of her handsome elder son alone on the front stoop. He was wearing his calf-skin jacket and holding a carry-on suitcase and a paper shopping bag. Sunlight, low and polarized, had found a way around the clouds, as it often did near the end of a winter day. Flooding the street was the preposterous golden indoor light with which a minor painter might illuminate the parting of the Red Sea. The bricks of the Persons' house, the blue and purple winter clouds, and the dark green resinous shrubs were all so falsely vivid as to be not even pretty but alien, foreboding.

"Where's Jonah?" Enid cried.

Gary came inside and set his bags down. "He still has a fever."

Enid accepted a kiss. Needing a moment to collect herself, she told Gary to bring his other suitcase in while he was at it.

"This is my only suitcase," he informed her in a courtroom kind of voice.

She stared at the tiny bag. "That's all you brought?"

"Look, I know you're disappointed about Jonah—"

"How high was his fever?"

"A hundred this morning."

"A hundred is not a high fever!"

Gary sighed and looked away, tilting his head to align it with the axis of the listing Christmas tree. "Look," he said. "Jonah's disappointed. I'm disappointed. You're disappointed. Can we leave it at that? We're all disappointed."

"It's just that I'm all ready for him," Enid said. "I made his favorite dinner—"

"I specifically warned you—"

"I got tickets for Waindell Park tonight!"

Gary shook his head and walked toward the kitchen. "So we'll go to the park," he said. "And then tomorrow Denise is here."

"Chip too!"

Gary laughed. "What, from Lithuania?"

"He called this morning."

"I'll believe that when I see it," Gary said.

The world in the windows looked less real than Enid would have liked. The spotlight of sunshine coming in under the ceiling of cloud was the dream light of no familiar hour of the day. She had an intimation that the family she'd tried to bring together was no longer the family she remembered—that this Christmas would be nothing at all like the Christmases of old. But she was doing her best to adjust to the new reality. She was suddenly *very* excited that Chip was coming. And since Jonah's wrapped gifts would now be going to Philadelphia with Gary, she needed to wrap some travel alarm clocks and pen-and-pencil sets for Caleb and Aaron to reduce the contrast in her giving. She could do this while she waited for Denise and Chip.

"I have so many cookies," she told Gary, who was washing his hands fastidiously at the kitchen sink. "I have a pear that I can slice, and some of that dark coffee that you kids like."

Gary sniffed her dish towel before he dried his hands with it.

Alfred began to bellow her name from upstairs.

"Uch, Gary," she said, "he's stuck in the tub again. You go help him. I won't do it anymore."

Gary dried his hands extremely thoroughly. "Why isn't he using the shower like we talked about?"

"He says he likes to sit down."

"Well, tough luck," Gary said. "This is a man whose gospel is taking responsibility for yourself."

Alfred bellowed her name again.

"Go, Gary, help him," she said.

Gary, with ominous calm, smoothed and straightened the folded dish towel on its rack. "Here are the ground rules, Mother," he said in the courtroom voice. "Are you listening? These are the ground rules. For the next three days, I will do anything you want me to do, except deal with Dad in situations he shouldn't be in. If he wants to climb a ladder and fall off, I'm going to let him lie on the ground. If he bleeds to death, he bleeds to death. If he can't get out of the bathtub without my help, he'll be spending Christmas in the bathtub. Have I made myself clear? Apart from that, I will do anything you want me to do. And then, on Christmas morning, you and he and I are going to sit down and have a talk—"

"*ENID*." Alfred's voice was amazingly loud. "*SOMEBODY'S AT THE DOOR!*"

Enid sighed heavily and went to the bottom of the stairs. "Al, it's *Gary*."

"Can you help me?" came the cry.

"Gary, go see what he wants."

Gary stood in the dining room with folded arms. "Did I not make my ground rules clear?"

Enid was remembering things about her elder son which she liked to forget when he wasn't around. She climbed the stairs slowly, trying to work a knot of pain out of her hip.

"Al," she said, entering the bathroom, "I can't help you out of the tub, you have to figure that out yourself."

He was sitting in two inches of water with his arm extended and his fingers fluttering. "Get that," he said.

"Get what?"

"That bottle."

His bottle of Snowy Mane hair-whitening shampoo had fallen to the floor behind him. Enid knelt carefully on the bath mat, favoring her hip, and put the bottle in his hands. He massaged it vaguely, as though seeking purchase or struggling to remember how to open it. His legs were hairless, his hands spotted, but his shoulders were still strong.

"I'll be damned," he said, grinning at the bottle.

Whatever heat the water had begun with had dissipated in the December-cool room. There was a smell of Dial soap and, more faintly, old age. Enid had knelt in this exact spot thousands of times to wash her children's hair and rinse their heads with hot water from a 1½-quart saucepan that she brought up from the kitchen for that purpose. She watched her husband turn the shampoo bottle over in his hands.

"Oh, Al," she said, "what are we going to do?"

"Help me with this."

"All right. I'll help you."

The doorbell rang.

"There it is again."

"Gary," Enid called, "see who that is." She squeezed shampoo into her palm. "You've got to start taking showers instead."

"Not steady enough on my feet."

"Here, wet your hair." She paddled a hand in the tepid water, to give Alfred the idea. He splashed some on his head. She could hear Gary talking to one of her friends, somebody female and chipper and St. Judean, Esther Root maybe.

"We can get a stool for the shower," she said, lathering Alfred's hair. "We can put a strong bar in there to hold on to, like Dr. Hedgpeth said we should. Maybe Gary can do that tomorrow."

Alfred's voice vibrated in his skull and on up through her fingers: "Gary and Jonah got in all right?"

"No, just Gary," Enid said. "Jonah has a high, high fever and terrible vomiting. Poor kid, he's much too sick to fly."

Alfred winced in sympathy.

"Lean over now and I'll rinse."

If Alfred was trying to lean forward, it was evident only from a trembling in his legs, not from any change in his position.

"You need to do *much* more stretching," Enid said. "Did you ever look at that sheet from Dr. Hedgpeth?"

Alfred shook his head. "Didn't help."

"Maybe Denise can teach you how to do those exercises. You might like that."

She reached behind her for the water glass from the sink. She filled it and refilled it at the bathtub's tap, pouring the hot water over her husband's head. With his eyes squeezed shut he could have been a child.

"You'll have to get yourself out now," she said. "I won't help you."

"I have my own method," he said.

Down in the living room Gary was kneeling to straighten the crooked tree.

"Who was at the door?" Enid said.

"Bea Meisner," he said, not looking up. "There's a gift on the mantel."

"Bea Meisner?" A late flame of shame flickered in Enid. "I thought they were staying in Austria for the holiday."

"No, they're here for one day and then going to La Jolla."

"That's where Katie and Stew live. Did she bring anything?"

"On the mantel," Gary said.

The gift from Bea was a festively wrapped bottle of something presumably Austrian.

"Anything else?" Enid said.

Gary, clapping fir needles from his hands, gave her a funny look. "Were you expecting something else?"

"No, no," she said. "There was a silly little thing I asked her to get in Vienna, but I'm sure she forgot."

Gary's eyes narrowed. "What silly little thing?"

"Oh, nothing, just, nothing." Enid examined the bottle to see if anything was attached to it. She'd survived her infatuation with Aslan, she'd done the work necessary to forget him, and she was by no means sure she wanted to see the Lion again. But the Lion still had power over her. She had a sensation from long ago, a pleasurable apprehension of a lover's return. It made her miss how she used to miss Alfred.

She chided: "Why didn't you invite her in?"

"Chuck was waiting in their Jaguar," Gary said. "I gather they're making the rounds."

"Well." Enid unwrapped the bottle—it was a Halb-Trocken Austrian champagne—to be sure there was no hidden package.

"That is an extremely sugary-looking wine," Gary said.

She asked him to build a fire. She stood and marveled as her competent gray-haired son walked steadily to the woodpile, returned with a load of logs on one arm, deftly arranged them in the fireplace, and lit a match on the first try. The whole job took five minutes. Gary was doing nothing more than function the way a man was supposed to function, and yet, in contrast to the man Enid lived with, his capabilities seemed godlike. His least gesture was glorious to watch.

Along with her relief at having him in the house, though, came the awareness of how soon he would leave again.

Alfred, wearing a sport coat, stopped in the living room and visited with Gary for a minute before repairing to the den for a high-decibel dose of local news. His age and his stoop had taken two or three inches off his height, which not long ago had been the same as Gary's.

While Gary, with exquisite motor control, hung the lights on the tree, Enid sat by the fire and unpacked the liquor cartons in which she kept her ornaments. Everywhere she'd traveled she'd spent the bulk of her pocket money on ornaments. In her mind, while Gary hung them, she traveled back to a Sweden populated by straw reindeers and little red horses, to a Norway whose citizens wore authentic Lapp reindeer-skin boots, to a Venice where all the animals were made of glass, to a dollhouse Germany of enameled wood Santas and angels, to an Austria of wooden soldiers and tiny Alpine churches. In Belgium the doves of peace were made of chocolate and wrapped decoratively in foil, and in France the gendarme dolls and artiste dolls were impeccably dressed, and in Switzerland the bronze bells tinkled above overtly religious mini-crèches. Andalusia was atwitter with gaudy birds; Mexico jangled with its painted tin cutouts. On the high plateaux of China, the noise-less gallop of a herd of silk horses. In Japan, the Zen silence of its lacquered abstractions.

Gary hung each ornament as Enid directed. He was seeming different to her—calmer, more matoor, more deliberate—until she asked him to do a little job for her tomorrow.

"Installing a bar in the shower is not a 'little job,'" he replied. "It would have made sense a year ago, but it doesn't now. Dad can use the bathtub for another few days until we deal with this house."

"It's still four weeks before we fly to Philadelphia," Enid said. "I want him to get in the habit of using the shower. I want you to buy a stool and put a bar in there tomorrow, so it's done."

Gary sighed. "Are you thinking you and Dad can actually stay in this house?"

"If Corecktall helps him—"

"Mother, he's being evaluated for dementia. Do you honestly believe—"

"For *non-drug-related* dementia."

"Look, I don't want to puncture your bubble—"

"Denise has it all set up. We have to try it."

"So, and then what?" Gary said. "He's miraculously cured, and the two of you live here happily ever after?"

The light in the windows had died entirely. Enid didn't understand why her sweet, responsible oldest child, with whom she'd felt such a bond from his infancy onward, became so *angry*, now, when she came to him in need. She unwrapped a Styrofoam ball that he'd decorated with fabric and sequins when he was nine or ten. "Do you remember this?"

Gary took the ball. "We made these in Mrs. Ostriker's class."

"You gave it to me."

"Did I?"

"You said you'd do anything I asked tomorrow," Enid said. "This is what I'm asking."

"All right! All right!" Gary threw his hands in the air. "I'll buy the stool! I'll install the bar!"

After dinner he took the Olds from the garage, and the three of them went to Christmasland.

From the back seat Enid could see the undersides of clouds catching urban light; the patches of clear sky were darker and riddled with stars. Gary piloted the car down narrow suburban roads to the limestone gates of Waindell Park, where a long queue of cars, trucks, and minivans was waiting to enter.

"Look at all the cars," Alfred said with no trace of his old impatience.

By charging admission to Christmasland, the county helped defray the cost of mounting this annual extravaganza. A county park ranger took the Lamberts' ticket and told Gary to extinguish all but his parking lights. The Olds crept forward in a line of darkened vehicles that had never looked more like animals than they did now, collectively, in their humble procession through the park.

For most of the year, Waindell was a tired place of burnt grass, brown ponds, and unambitious limestone pavilions. In December, by day, it looked its very worst. Garish cables and utilitarian power lines crisscrossed the lawns. Armatures and scaffolds were exposed in their flimsiness, their provisionality, their metallic knobbiness of joint. Hundreds of trees and shrubs were draped in light strings, limbs sagging as if hammered by a freezing rain of glass and plastic.

By night the park was Christmasland. Enid drew breath sharply as the Olds crept up a hill of light and across a landscape made luminous. Just as the beasts were said to speak on Christmas Eve, so the natural order of the suburbs seemed overturned here, the ordinarily dark land alive with light, the ordinarily lively road dark with crawling traffic.

The mild gradients of Waindell's slopes and the intimacy of its ridgelines' relations with the sky were midwestern. So, it seemed to Enid, were the hush and patience of the drivers; so were the isolated close-knit frontier communities of oaks and maples. She'd spent the last eight Christmases exiled in the alien East, and now, at last, she felt at home. She imagined being buried in this landscape. She was happy to think of her bones resting on a hillside such as this.

There came scintillant pavilions, luminous reindeer, pendants and necklaces of gathered photons, electro-pointillist Santa Claus faces, a glade of towering glowing candy canes.

"Lot of work involved here," Alfred commented.

"Well, I'm sorry Jonah couldn't come after all," Gary said, as if, until now, he had not been sorry.

The spectacle was nothing more than lights in darkness, but Enid was speechless. So often credulity was asked of you, so seldom could you summon it absolutely, but here at Waindell Park she could. Somebody had set out to delight all comers, and Enid was delighted. And tomorrow Denise and Chip came, tomorrow was *The Nutcracker*, and on Wednesday they would take the Christ baby from its pocket and pin the walnut cradle to the tree: she had so much to look forward to.

In the morning, Gary drove over to Hospital City, the close-in suburb where St. Jude's big medical centers were concentrated, and held his breath among the eighty-pound men in wheelchairs and the five-hundred-pound women in tentlike dresses who clogged the aisles of Central Discount Medical Supply. Gary hated his mother for sending him here, but he recognized how lucky he was in comparison to her, how free and advantaged, and so he set his jaw and kept maximum distance from the bodies of these locals who were loading up on syringes and rubber gloves, on butterscotch bedside candies, on absorptive pads in every imaginable size and shape, on jumbo 144-packs of get-well cards and CDs of flute music and videos of visualization exercises and disposable plastic hoses and bags that connected to harder plastic interfaces sewn into living flesh.

Gary's problem with illness in aggregate, aside from the fact that it involved large quantities of human bodies and that he didn't like human bodies in large quantities, was that it seemed to him low-class. Poor people smoked, poor people ate Krispy Kreme doughnuts by the dozen. Poor people were made pregnant by close relatives. Poor people practiced poor hygiene and lived in toxic neighborhoods. Poor people with their ailments constituted a subspecies of humanity that thankfully remained invisible to Gary except in hospitals and in places like Central Discount Medical. They were a dumber, sadder, fatter, more resignedly suffering breed. A Diseased underclass that he really, really liked to keep away from.

However, he'd arrived in St. Jude feeling guilty about several circumstances that he'd concealed from Enid, and he'd vowed to be a good son for three days, and so in spite of his embarrassment he pushed through the crowds of the lame and halt, entered Central Discount Medical's vast furniture showroom, and looked for a stool for his father to sit on while he showered.

A full-symphonic version of the most tedious Christmas song ever written, "Little Drummer Boy," dripped from hidden speakers in the showroom. The morning outside the showroom's plate-glass windows was brilliant, windy, cold. A sheet of newsprint wrapped itself around a parking meter with erotic-looking desperation. Awnings creaked and automotive mud flaps shivered.

The wide array of medical stools and the variety of afflictions to which they attested might have upset Gary had he not been able to make aesthetic judgments.

He wondered, for example, why beige. Medical plastic was usually beige; at best, a sickly gray. Why not red? Why not black? Why not teal?

Maybe the beige plastic was intended to ensure that the furniture be used for medical purposes only. Maybe the manufacturer was afraid that, if the chairs were too handsome, people would be tempted to buy them for nonmedical purposes.

There was a problem to avoid, all right: too many people wanting to buy your product!

Gary shook his head. The idiocy of these manufacturers.

He picked out a sturdy, low aluminum stool with a wide beige seat. He selected a heavy-duty (beige!) gripping bar for the shower. Marveling at the gouge-level pricing, he took these items to the checkout counter, where a friendly midwestern girl, possibly evangelical (she had a brocade sweater and feather-cut bangs), showed the bar codes to a laser beam and remarked to Gary, in a downstate drawl, that these aluminum chairs were really a super product. "So lahtweight, practically indestructible," she said. "Is it for your mom or your dad?"

Gary resented invasions of his privacy and refused the girl the satisfaction of an answer. He did, however, nod.

"Our older folks get shaky in the shower at a certain point. Guess it happens to us all, eventually." The young philosopher swiped Gary's AmEx through a groove. "You home for the holidays, helpin' out a little bit?"

"You know what these stools would really be good for," Gary said, "would be to hang yourself. Don't you think?"

Life drained from the girl's smile. "I don't know about that."

"Nice and light—easy to kick away."

"Sign this, please, sir."

He had to fight the wind to push the Exit door open. The wind had teeth today, it bit right through his calfskin jacket. It was a wind unchecked by any serious topography between the Arctic and St. Jude.

Driving north toward the airport, with the low sun mercifully behind him, Gary wondered if he'd been cruel to the girl. Possibly he had. But he was under stress, and a person under stress, it seemed to him, had a right to be strict in the boundaries he established for himself— strict in his moral accounting, strict about what he would and wouldn't do, strict about who he was and who he wasn't and whom he would and wouldn't talk to. If a perky, homely evangelical girl insisted on talking, he had a right to choose the topic.

He was aware, nevertheless, that if the girl had been more attractive, he might have been less cruel.

Everything in St. Jude strove to put him in the wrong. But in the months since he'd surrendered to Caroline (and his hand had healed nicely, thank you, with hardly a scar), he'd reconciled himself to being the villain in St. Jude. When you knew in advance that your mother would consider you the villain no matter what you did, you lost your incentive to play by her rules. You asserted your own rules. You did whatever it took to preserve yourself. You pretended, if need be, that a healthy child of yours was sick.

The truth about Jonah was that he'd freely chosen not to come to St. Jude. This was in accordance with the terms of Gary's surrender to Caroline in October. Holding five nonrefundable plane tickets to St. Jude, Gary had told his family that he wanted everyone to come along with him for Christmas, but that *nobody would be forced to go*. Caroline and Caleb and Aaron had all instantly and loudly said no thank you; Jonah, still under the spell of his grandmother's enthusiasm, declared that he would "very much like" to go. Gary never actually promised Enid that Jonah was coming, but he also never warned her that he might not.

In November Caroline bought four tickets to see the magician Alain Gregarius on December 22 and another four tickets for *The Lion King* in New York City on December 23. "Jonah can come along if he's here," she explained, "otherwise Aaron or Caleb can bring a friend." Gary wanted to ask why she hadn't bought tickets for the week *after* Christmas, which would have spared Jonah a difficult choice. Ever since the October surrender, however, he and Caroline had been enjoying a second honeymoon, and although it was understood that Gary, as a dutiful son, would be going to St. Jude for three days, a shadow fell on his domestic bliss whenever he made reference to the trip. The more days that elapsed without mention of Enid or Christmas, the more Caroline seemed to want him, the more she included him in her private jokes with Aaron and Caleb, and the less depressed he felt. Indeed, the topic of his depression hadn't come up once since the morning of Alfred's fall. Silence on the topic of Christmas seemed a small price to pay for such domestic harmony.

And for a while the treats and attention that Enid had promised Jonah in St. Jude seemed to outweigh the attractions of Alain Gregarius and *The Lion King*. Jonah mused aloud at the dinner table about Christmasland and the Advent calendar that Grandma talked so much about; he ignored, or didn't see, the winks and smiles that Caleb and Aaron were exchanging. But Caroline more and more openly encouraged the older boys to laugh at their grandparents and to tell stories about Alfred's cluelessness ("He called it Intendo!") and Enid's puritanism ("She asked what the show was *rated*!") and Enid's parsimony ("There were two green beans and she wrapped them up in foil!"), and Gary, since his surrender, had begun to join in the laughter himself ("Grandma is funny, isn't she?"), and finally Jonah became self-conscious about his plans. At the age of eight, he fell under the tyranny of Cool. First he ceased to bring up Christmas at the dinner table, and then when Caleb with his trademark semi-irony asked if he was looking forward to *Christmasland*, Jonah replied, in an effortfully wicked voice, "It's probably really *stupid*."

"Lots of fat people in big cars driving around in the dark," Aaron said.

"Telling each other how *wunnerful* it is," Caroline said.

"Wunnerful, wunnerful," Caleb said.

"You shouldn't make fun of your grandmother," Gary said.

"They're not making fun of *her*," Caroline said.

"Right, we're not," Caleb said. "It's just that people are funny in St. Jude. Aren't they, Jonah?"

"People certainly are very large there," Jonah said.

On Saturday night, three days ago, Jonah had thrown up after dinner and gone to bed with a mild fever. By Sunday evening, his color and appetite were back to normal, and Caroline played her final trump. For Aaron's birthday, earlier in the month, she'd bought an expensive computer game, *God Project II*, in which players designed and operated organisms to compete in a working ecosystem. She hadn't allowed Aaron and Caleb to start the game until classes ended, and now, when they finally did start, she insisted that they let Jonah be Microbes, because Microbes, in any ecosystem, had the most fun and never lost.

By bedtime on Sunday, Jonah was entranced with his team of killer bacteria and looked forward to sending them into battle the next day. When Gary woke him on Monday morning and asked if he was coming to St. Jude, Jonah said he'd rather stay home.

"It's your choice," Gary said. "But it would mean a lot to your grandma if you came."

"What if it's not fun, though?"

"There's never a guarantee that something's going to be fun," Gary said. "But you'll make Grandma happy. That's one thing I can guarantee."

Jonah's face clouded. "Can I think about it for an hour?"

"OK, one hour. But then we have to pack and go."

The end of the hour found Jonah deeply immersed in *God Project II*. One strain of his bacteria had blinded eighty percent of Aaron's small hoofed mammals.

"It's OK not to go," Caroline assured Jonah. "Your personal choice is what matters here. This is your vacation."

Nobody will be forced to go.

"I'll say it one more time," Gary said. "Your grandma is really looking forward to seeing you."

To Caroline's face there came a desolation, a deep tearful stare, reminiscent of the troubles in September. She rose without a word and left the entertainment room.

Jonah's answer came in a voice not much louder than a whisper: "I think I'm going to stay here."

If it had still been September, Gary might have seen in Jonah's decision a parable of the crisis of moral duty in a culture of consumer choice. He might have become depressed. But he'd been down that road now and he knew there was nothing for him at the end of it.

He packed his bag and kissed Caroline. "I'll be happy when you're back," she said.

In a strict moral sense Gary knew he hadn't done anything wrong. He'd never promised Enid that Jonah was coming. It was simply to spare himself an argument that he'd lied about Jonah's fever.

Similarly, to spare Enid's feelings, he hadn't mentioned that in the six business days since the IPO, his five thousand shares of Axon Corporation stock, for which he'd paid $60,000, had risen in value to $118,000. Here again, he'd done nothing wrong, but given the pitiful size of Alfred's patent-licensing fee from Axon, concealment seemed the wisest policy.

The same also went for the little package Gary had zipped into the inside pocket of his jacket.

Jets were dropping from the bright sky, happy in their metal skins, while he jockeyed through the crush of senior traffic converging at the airport. The days before Christmas were the St. Jude airport's finest hour—its raison d'être, almost. Every garage was full and every walkway thronged.

Denise was right on time, however. Even the airlines conspired to protect her from the embarrassment of a late arrival or an inconvenienced brother. She was standing, per family custom, at a little-used gate on the departure level. Her overcoat was a crazy garnet woolen thing with pink velvet trim, and something about her head seemed different to Gary—more makeup than usual, maybe. More lipstick. Each time he'd seen Denise in the last year (most recently at Thanksgiving), she'd looked more emphatically unlike the person he'd always imagined that she would grow up to be.

When he kissed her, he smelled cigarettes.

"You've become a smoker," he said, making room in the trunk for her suitcase and shopping bag.

Denise smiled. "Unlock the door, I'm freezing."

Gary flipped open his sunglasses. Driving south into glare, he was nearly sideswiped while merging. Road aggression was encroaching in St. Jude; traffic no longer moved so sluggishly that an eastern driver could pleasurably slalom through it.

"I bet Mom's happy Jonah's here," Denise said.

"As a matter of fact, Jonah is not here."

Her head turned sharply. "You didn't bring him?"

"He got sick."

"I can't believe it. You didn't bring him!"

She seemed not to have considered, even for a moment, that he might be telling the truth.

"There are five people in my house," Gary said. "As far as I know, there's only one in yours. Things are more complicated when you have multiple responsibilities."

"I'm just sorry you had to get Mom's hopes up."

"It's not my fault if she chooses to live in the future."

"You're right," Denise said. "It's not your fault. I just wish it hadn't happened."

"Speaking of Mom," Gary said, "I want to tell you a very weird thing. But you have to promise not to tell her."

"What weird thing?"

"Promise you won't tell her."

Denise so promised, and Gary unzipped the inner pocket of his jacket and showed her the package that Bea Meisner had given him the day before. The moment had been fully bizarre: Chuck Meisner's Jaguar in the street, idling amid cetacean puffs of winter exhaust, Bea Meisner standing on the Welcome mat in her embroidered green loden coat while she dug from her purse a seedy and much-handled little packet, Gary setting down the wrapped bottle of champagne and taking delivery of the contraband. "This is for your mother," Bea had said. "But you must tell her that Klaus says to be very careful with this. He didn't want to give it to me at all. He says it can be very, very addictive, which is why I only got a little bit. She wanted six months, but Klaus would only give me one. So you tell her to be sure and talk to her doctor. Maybe, Gary, you should even hold on to it until she does that. Anyway, have a wonderful Christmas"—here the Jaguar's horn beeped—"and give our best love to everyone."

Gary recounted this to Denise while she opened the packet. Bea had folded up a page torn from a German magazine and taped it shut. On one side of the page was a bespectacled German cow promoting ultrapasteurized milk. Inside were thirty golden pills.

"My God." Denise laughed. "Mexican A."

"Never heard of it," Gary said.

"Club drug. Very young-person."

"And Bea Meisner is delivering it to Mom at our front door."

"Does Mom know you took it?"

"Not yet. I don't even know what this stuff does."

Denise reached over with her smoky fingers and put a pill near his mouth. "Try one."

Gary jerked his head away. His sister seemed to be on some drug herself, something stronger than nicotine. She was greatly happy or greatly unhappy or a dangerous combination of the two. She was wearing silver rings on three fingers and a thumb.

"Is this a drug you've tried?" he said.

"No, I stick with alcohol."

She folded up the packet and Gary took control of it again. "I want to make sure you're with me on this," he said. "Do you agree that Mom should not be receiving illegal addictive substances from Bea Meisner?"

"No," Denise said. "I don't agree. She's an adult and she can do what she wants. And I don't think it's fair to take her pills without telling her. If you don't tell her, I will."

"Excuse me, I believe you promised not to," Gary said.

Denise considered this. Salt-splashed embankments were flying past.

"OK, maybe I promised," she said. "But why are you trying to run her life?"

"I think you'll see," he said, "that the situation is out of hand. I think you'll see that it's about time somebody stepped in and ran her life."

Denise didn't argue with him. She put on shades and looked at the towers of Hospital City on the brutal south horizon. Gary had hoped to find her more cooperative. He already had one "alternative" sibling and he didn't need another. It frustrated him that people could so happily drop out of the world of conventional expectations; it undercut the pleasure he took in his home and job and family; it felt like a unilateral rewriting, to his disadvantage, of the rules of life. He was especially galled that the latest defector to the "alternative" was not some flaky Other from a family of Others or a class of Others but his own stylish and talented sister, who as recently as September had excelled in conventional ways that his friends could read about in the *New York Times*. Now she'd quit her job and was wearing four rings and a flaming coat and reeking of tobacco . . .

Carrying the aluminum stool, he followed her into the house. He compared her reception by Enid to the reception he'd received the day before. He took note of the duration of the hug, the lack of instant criticism, the smiles all around.

Enid cried: "I thought maybe you'd run into Chip at the airport and all three of you would be coming home!"

"That scenario is implausible in eight different ways," Gary said.

"He told you he'd be here today?" Denise said.

"This afternoon," Enid said. "Tomorrow at the latest."

"Today, tomorrow, next April," Gary said. "Whatever."

"He said there was some trouble in Lithuania," Enid said.

While Denise went to find Alfred, Gary fetched the morning *Chronicle* from the den. In a box of international news sandwiched between lengthy features ("New 'Peticures' Make Dogs 'Red in Claw'" and "Are Ophthalmologists Overpaid?—Docs Say No, Optometrists Say Yes") he located a paragraph about Lithuania: *civil unrest following disputed parliamentary elections and attempted assassination of President Vitkunas . . . three-fourths of the country without electricity . . . rival paramilitary groups clashing on the streets of Vilnius . . . and the airport—*

"The airport is closed," Gary read aloud with satisfaction. "Mother? Did you hear me?"

"He was already at the airport yesterday," Enid said. "I'm sure he got out."

"Then why hasn't he called?"

"He was probably running to catch a flight."

At a certain point Enid's capacity for fantasy became physically painful to Gary. He opened his wallet and presented her with the receipt for the shower stool and safety bar.

"I'll write you a check later," she said.

"How about now, before you forget."

Muttering and soughing, Enid complied with his wishes.

Gary examined the check. "Why is this dated December twenty-six?"

"Because that's the soonest you could possibly deposit it in Philadelphia."

Their skirmishing continued through lunch. Gary slowly drank a beer and slowly drank a second, relishing the distress that he was causing Enid as she told him for a third time and a fourth time that he'd better get started on that shower project. When he finally stood up from the table, it occurred to him that his impulse to run Enid's life was the logical response to her own insistence on running his.

The safety shower bar was a fifteen-inch length of beige enamel pipe with flanged elbows at each end. The stubby screws included in the package might have sufficed to attach the bar to plywood but were useless with ceramic tile. To secure the bar, he would have to run six-inch bolts through the wall into the little closet behind the shower.

Down in Alfred's workshop, he was able to find masonry bits for the electric drill, but the cigar boxes that he remembered as cornucopias of useful hardware seemed mainly to contain corroded, orphaned screws and strike plates and toilet-tank fittings. Certainly no six-inch bolts.

Departing for the hardware store, wearing his I'm-a-jerk smile, he noticed Enid at the dining-room windows, peering out through a sheer curtain.

"Mother," he said. "I think it's important not to get your hopes up about Chip."

"I just thought I heard a car door in the street."

Fine, go ahead, Gary thought as he left the house, *fixate on whoever isn't here and oppress whoever is.*

On the front walk he passed Denise, who was returning from the supermarket with groceries. "I hope you're letting Mom pay for those," he said.

His sister laughed in his face. "What difference does it make to you?"

"She's always trying to get away with things. It burns me up."

"So redouble your vigilance," Denise said, proceeding toward the house.

Why, exactly, had he been feeling guilty? He'd never promised to bring Jonah on the trip, and although he was currently ahead by $58,000 on his Axon investment he'd worked hard for those shares and he'd taken all the risk, and Bea Meisner herself had urged him not to give Enid the addictive drug; so why had he felt guilty?

As he drove, he imagined the needle on his cranial-pressure gauge creeping clockwise. He was sorry he'd offered his services to Enid. Given the brevity of his visit, it was stupid to spend the afternoon on a job she should have paid a handyman to do.

At the hardware store, he stood in the checkout line behind the fattest and slowest people in the central tier of states. They'd come to buy marshmallow Santas, packages of tinsel, venetian blinds, eight-dollar blow-dryers, and holiday-theme pot-holders. With their bratwurst fingers they dug for exact change in tiny purses. White cartoon puffs of steam shot out of Gary's ears. All the fun things he could be doing instead of waiting half an hour to buy six six-inch bolts assumed ravishing form in his imagination. He could be visiting the Collector's Room at the Museum of Transport gift shop, or sorting out the old bridge and track drawings from his father's early career at the Midland Pacific, or searching the under-porch storeroom for his long-missing O-gauge model railroad equipment. With the lifting of his "depression," he'd developed a new interest, hobbylike in its intensity, in framable and collectible railroad memorabilia, and he could happily have spent the whole day—the whole week!—pursuing it . . .

Back at the house, as he was heading up the walk, he saw the sheer curtains part, his mother peering out again. Inside, the air was steamy and dense with the smell of foods that Denise was baking, simmering, and browning. Gary gave Enid the receipt for the bolts, which she regarded as the token of hostility that it was.

"You can't afford four dollars and ninety-six cents?"

"Mother," he said. "I'm doing the work like I promised. But this is not my bathroom. This is not my safety bar."

"I'll get the money for you later."

"You might forget."

"Gary, I will get the money for you *later*."

Denise, in an apron, followed this exchange from the kitchen doorway with laughing eyes.

When Gary made his second trip to the basement, Alfred was snoring in the big blue chair. Gary proceeded into the workshop, and here he was stopped in his tracks by a new discovery. A shotgun in a canvas case was leaning against the lab bench. He didn't remember having seen it here earlier. Could he have somehow failed to notice it? Ordinarily the gun was kept in the under-porch storeroom. He was sorry indeed to see that it had moved.

Do I let him shoot himself?

The question was so clear in his mind that he almost spoke it out loud. And he considered. It was one thing to intervene on behalf of Enid's safety and confiscate her drugs; there was life and hope and pleasure worth saving in Enid. The old man, however, was kaput.

At the same time, Gary had no wish to hear a gunshot and come down and wade into the gore. He didn't want his mother to go through this, either.

And yet, horrible though the mess would be, it would be followed by a huge quantum uptick in the quality of his mother's life.

Gary opened the box of shells on the bench and saw that none were missing. He wished that someone else, not he, had noticed that Alfred had moved the gun. But his decision, when it came, was so clear in his mind that he did speak it out loud. Into the dusty, uric, non-reverberative silence of the laboratory he said: "If that's what you want, be my guest. I ain't gonna stop you."

Before he could drill holes in the shower, he had to clear the shelves of the little bathroom closet. This in itself was a substantial job. Enid had saved, in a shoe box, every cotton ball she'd ever taken from a bottle of aspirin or prescription medication. There were five hundred or a thousand cotton balls. There were petrified half-squeezed tubes of ointment. There were plastic pitchers and utensils (in colors even worse, if possible, than beige) from Enid's admissions to the hospital for foot surgery, knee surgery, and phlebitis. There were dear little bottles of Mercurochrome and Anbesol that had dried up sometime in the 1960s. There was a paper bag that Gary quickly, for the sake of his composure, threw to the back of a high shelf because it appeared to contain ancient menstrual belts and pads.

The daylight was fading by the time he had the closet empty and was ready to drill six holes. It was then that he discovered that the old masonry bits were as dull as rivets. He leaned into the drill with all his weight, the tip of the bit turned bluish-black and lost its temper, and the old drill began to smoke. Sweat came pouring down his face and chest.

Alfred chose this moment to step into the bathroom. "Well, look at this," he said.

"You got some pretty dull masonry bits here," Gary said, breathing heavily. "I should have bought some new ones while I was at the store."

"Let me see," Alfred said.

It hadn't been Gary's intention to attract the old man and the agitated twin fingered animals that were his advance guard. He shied from the incapacity and greedy openness of these hands, but Alfred's eyes were fixed on the drill now, his face bright with the possibility of solving a problem. Gary relinquished the drill. He wondered how his father could even see what he was holding, the drill shook so violently. The old man's fingers crawled around its tarnished surface, groping like eyeless worms.

"You got it on Reverse," he said.

With the ridged yellow nail of his thumb, Alfred pushed the polarity switch to Forward and handed the drill back to Gary, and for the first time since his arrival, their eyes met. The chill that ran through Gary was only partly from his cooling sweat. The old man, he thought, still had a few lights on upstairs. Alfred, indeed, looked downright happy: happy to have fixed a thing and even happier, Gary suspected, to have proved that he was smarter, in this tiny instance, than his son.

"We can see why I'm not an engineer," Gary said.

"What's the project?"

"I'm putting in this bar to hold on to. Are you going to use the shower if we put a stool and a bar in here?"

"I don't know what they have planned for me," Alfred said as he was leaving.

That was your Christmas present, Gary told him silently. *Flipping that switch was your present from me.*

An hour later he had the bathroom back together and was in a fully nasty mood again. Enid had second-guessed his siting of the bar, and Alfred, when Gary invited him to try the new stool, had announced that he preferred a bath.

"I've done my part and now I'm done," Gary said in the kitchen, pouring liquor. "Tomorrow I have a few things that *I* want to do."

"It's a wonderful improvement in the bathroom," Enid said.

Gary poured heavily. Poured and poured.

"Oh, Gary," she said, "I thought we might open that champagne Bea brought us."

"Oh, let's not," said Denise, who had baked a stollen, a coffee cake, and two loaves of cheese bread and was preparing, if Gary was not mistaken, a dinner of polenta and braised rabbit. Safe to say it was the first time this kitchen had ever seen a rabbit.

Enid returned to hovering by the dining-room windows. "I'm worried that he isn't calling," she said.

Gary joined her by the window, his glial cells purring with the first sweet lubrication of his drink. He asked if she was familiar with Occam's razor.

"Occam's razor," he said with cocktail sententiousness, "invites us to choose the simpler of two explanations for a phenomenon."

"Well, what's your point," Enid said.

"My point," he said, "is that it's possible that Chip hasn't called you because of something complicated that we know nothing about. Or it could be because of something very simple and well known to us, namely, his incredible irresponsibility."

"He *said* he was coming and he *said* he would call," Enid answered flatly. "He said, I'm coming *home*."

"All right. Fine. Stand at the window. It's your choice."

Because he was expected to drive to *The Nutcracker*, Gary couldn't do as much drinking as he might have wished before dinner. He therefore did quite a bit more as soon as the family came home from the ballet and Alfred headed upstairs, practically at a run, and Enid bedded down in the den with the intention of letting her children handle any problems in the night. Gary drank scotch and checked in with Caroline. He drank scotch and searched the house for Denise and found no sign of her. From his own room he fetched his Christmas packages and arranged them under the tree. He was giving everybody the same gift: a leather-bound copy of the All-Time Lambert Two Hundred album. He'd pushed hard to get all the printing done in time for the holiday, and now that the album was complete, he planned to dismantle the darkroom, spend some of his Axon profits, and build a model-railroad setup on the second floor of the garage. It was a hobby that he'd chosen for himself, rather than having it chosen for him, and as he laid his scotchy head on the cold pillow and turned out the light in his old St. Judean bedroom, he was gripped by an ancient excitement at the prospect of running trains through mountains of papier-mâché, across high Popsicle-stick trestles . . .

He dreamed ten Christmases in the house. He dreamed of rooms and people, rooms and people. He dreamed that Denise was not his sister and was going to murder him. His only hope was the shotgun in the basement. He was examining this shotgun, making sure that it was loaded, when he felt an evil presence behind him in the workshop. He turned around and didn't recognize Denise. The woman he saw was some other woman whom he had to kill or be killed by. And there was no resistance in the shotgun's trigger; it dangled, limp and futile. The gun was on Reverse, and by the time he got it on Forward, she was coming to kill him—

He woke up needing to pee.

The darkness in his room was relieved only by the glow of the digital clock radio, whose face he didn't check because he didn't want to know how early it still was. He could dimly see the loaf of Chip's old bed by the opposite wall. The silence of the house felt momentary and unpeaceful. Recently fallen.

Honoring this silence, Gary eased himself out of bed and crept toward the door; and here the terror struck him.

He was afraid to open the door.

He strained to hear what was happening outside it. He thought he could hear vague shiftings and creepings, faraway voices.

He was afraid to go to the bathroom because he didn't know what he would find there. He was afraid that if he left his room he would find the wrong person, his mother maybe, or his sister or his father, in his bed when he came back.

He was convinced that people were moving in the hallway. In his clouded, imperfect wakefulness, he connected the Denise who'd disappeared before he went to bed to the Denise-like phantom who was trying to kill him in his dream.

The possibility that this phantom killer was even now lurking in the hall seemed only ninety percent fantastical.

It was safer all around, he thought, to stay in his room and pee into one of the decorative Austrian beer steins on his dresser.

But what if his tinkling attracted the attention of whoever was creeping around outside his door?

Moving on tiptoe, he took a beer stein into the closet that he'd shared with Chip ever since Denise was given the smaller bedroom and the boys were put together. He pulled the closet door shut after him, crowded up against the dry-cleaned garments and the bursting Nordstrom bags of miscellany that Enid had taken to storing here, and relieved himself into the beer stein. He lipped a fingertip over the rim so that he could feel if he was going to overflow it. Just when the warmth of rising urine had reached this fingertip, his bladder finally emptied. He lowered the stein to the closet floor, took an envelope from a Nordstrom bag, and covered the mouth of the receptacle.

Quietly, quietly, then, he left the closet and returned to his bed. As he was swinging his legs off the floor, he heard Denise's voice. It was so distinct and conversational that she might have been in the room with him. She said, "Gary?"

He tried not to move, but the bedsprings creaked.

"Gary? Sorry to bother you. Are you awake?"

He had little choice now but to get up and open the door. Denise was right outside it, wearing white flannel pajamas and standing in a shaft of light from her own bedroom. "Sorry," she said. "Dad's been calling for you."

"Gary!" came Alfred's voice from the bathroom by her room.

Gary, heart thudding, asked what time it was.

"I have no idea," she said. "He woke me up calling Chip's name. Then he started calling yours. But not mine. I think he's more comfortable with you."

Cigarettes on her breath again.

"Gary? Gary!" came the call from the bathroom.

"Fuck this," Gary said.

"It could be his medication."

"Bullshit."

From the bathroom: "Gary!"

"Yeah, Dad, OK, I'm coming."

Enid's bodiless voice floated up from the bottom of the stairs. "Gary, help your father."

"Yeah, Mom. I'm all over it. You just go back to sleep."

"What does he want?" Enid said.

"Just go back to bed."

Out in the hall he could smell the Christmas tree and the fireplace. He tapped on the bathroom door and opened it. His father was standing in the bathtub, naked from the waist down, with nothing but psychosis in his face. Until now, Gary had seen faces like this mainly at the bus stops and the Burger King bathrooms of central Philadelphia.

"Gary," Alfred said, "they're all over the place." The old man pointed at the floor with a trembling finger. "Do you see him?"

"Dad, you're hallucinating."

"Get him! Get him!"

"You're hallucinating and it's time to get out of the tub and go back to bed."

"Do you see them?"

"You're hallucinating. Go back to bed."

This went on for a while, ten or fifteen minutes, before Gary was able to lead Alfred out of the bathroom. A light was burning in the master bedroom, and several unused diapers were spread out on the floor. It seemed to Gary that his father was having a dream while he was awake, a dream as vivid as Gary's own dream about Denise, and that the awakening that he, Gary, had accomplished in half a second was taking his father half an hour.

"What is 'hallucinate'?" Alfred said finally.

"It's like you're dreaming when you're awake."

Alfred winced. "I'm concerned about this."

"Well. Rightly so."

"Help me with the diaper."

"Yes, all right," Gary said.

"I'm concerned that something is wrong with my thoughts."

"Oh, Dad."

"My head doesn't seem to work right."

"I know. I know."

But Gary himself was infected, there in the middle of the night, by his father's disease. As the two of them collaborated on the problem of the diaper, which his father seemed to regard more as a lunatic conversation piece than as an undergarment to be donned, Gary, too, had a sensation of things dissolving around him, of a night that consisted of creepings and shiftings and metamorphoses. He had the sense that there were many more than two people in the house beyond the bedroom door; he sensed a large population of phantoms that he could glimpse only dimly.

Alfred's polar hair was hanging in his face when he lay down. Gary pulled the blanket up over his shoulder. It was hard to believe that he'd been fighting with this man, taking him seriously as an adversary, three months ago.

His clock radio showed 2:55 when he returned to his room. The house was quiet again, Denise's door closed, the only sound an eighteen-wheeler on the expressway half a mile away. Gary wondered why his room smelled—faintly—like somebody's cigarette breath.

But maybe it wasn't cigarette breath. Maybe it was that Austrian beer stein full of piss that he'd left on the closet floor!

Tomorrow, he thought, *is for me. Tomorrow is Gary's Recreation Day. And then on Thursday morning we're going to blow this house wide open. We're going to put an end to this charade.*

After Brian Callahan had fired Denise, she'd carved herself up and put the pieces on the table. She told herself a story about a daughter in a family so hungry for a daughter that it would have eaten her alive if she hadn't run away. She told herself a story about a daughter who, in her desperation to escape, had taken refuge in whatever temporary shelters she could find—a career in cooking, a marriage to Emile Berger, an old-person's life in Philadelphia, an affair with Robin Passafaro. But naturally these refuges, chosen in haste, proved unworkable in the long run. By trying to protect herself from her family's hunger, the daughter accomplished just the opposite. She ensured that when her family's hunger reached its peak her life would fall apart and leave her without a spouse, without kids, without a job, without responsibilities, without a defense of any kind. It was as if, all along, she'd been conspiring to make herself available to nurse her parents.

Meanwhile her brothers had conspired to make themselves unavailable. Chip had fled to Eastern Europe and Gary had placed himself under Caroline's thumb. Gary, it was true, did "take responsibility" for his parents, but his idea of responsibility was to bully and give orders. The burden of listening to Enid and Alfred and being patient and understanding fell squarely on the daughter's shoulders. Already Denise could see that she would be the only child in St. Jude for Christmas dinner and the only child on duty in the weeks and months and years after that. Her parents had better manners than to ask her to come and live with them, but she knew that this was what they wanted. As soon as she'd enrolled her father in Phase II testing of Corecktall and offered to house him, Enid had unilaterally ceased hostilities with her. Enid had never again mentioned her adulterous friend Norma Greene. She'd never asked Denise why she'd "quit" her job at the Generator. Enid was in trouble, her daughter was offering to help, and so she could no longer afford the luxury of finding fault. And now the time had come, according to the story that Denise told herself about herself, for the chef to carve herself up and feed the pieces to her hungry parents.

Lacking a better story, she almost bought this one. The only trouble was she didn't recognize herself in it.

When she put on a white blouse, an antique gray suit, red lipstick, and a black pillbox hat with a little black veil, then she recognized herself. When she put on a sleeveless white T-shirt and boy's jeans and tied her hair back so tightly that her head ached, she recognized herself. When she put on silver jewelry, turquoise eye shadow, corpse-lip nail polish, a searing pink jumper, and orange sneakers, she recognized herself as a living person and was breathless with the happiness of living.

She went to New York to appear on the Food Channel and visit one of those clubs for people like herself who were starting to Figure It Out and needed practice. She stayed with Julia Vrais in Julia's outstanding apartment on Hudson Street. Julia reported that in the discovery phase of her divorce proceedings she'd learned that Gitanas Misevičius had paid for this apartment with funds embezzled from the Lithuanian government.

"Gitanas's lawyer claims it was an 'oversight,' " Julia told Denise, "but I find that hard to believe."

"Does this mean you're going to lose the apartment?"

"Well, no," Julia said, "in fact this makes it more likely that I'll get to keep it without paying anything. But still, I feel so awful! My apartment rightfully belongs to the people of Lithuania!"

The temperature in Julia's extra bedroom was about ninety. She gave Denise a foot-thick down comforter and asked if she wanted a blanket, too.

"Thanks, this looks like plenty," Denise said.

Julia gave her flannel sheets and four pillows with flannel cases. She asked how Chip was doing in Vilnius.

"It sounds like he and Gitanas are the best of friends."

"I hate to think what the two of them are saying about me," Julia mused happily.

Denise said that it wouldn't surprise her if Chip and Gitanas avoided the topic altogether.

Julia frowned. "Why wouldn't they talk about me?"

"Well, you did painfully dump both of them."

"But they could talk about how much they hate me!"

"I don't think anybody could hate you."

"Actually," Julia said, "I was afraid *you'd* hate me for breaking up with Chip."

"No, I never had anything at stake there."

Clearly relieved to hear this, Julia confided to Denise that she was now being dated by a lawyer, nice but bald, with whom Eden Procuro had set her up. "I feel safe with him," she said. "He's so confident in restaurants. And he's got tons of work, so he's not always after me for, you know, favors."

"Really," Denise said, "the less you tell me about things with you and Chip, the happier I'll be."

When Julia then asked if Denise was seeing anybody, it shouldn't have been so hard to tell her about Robin Passafaro, but it was very hard. Denise didn't want to make her friend uncomfortable, didn't want to hear her voice go small and soft with sympathy. She wanted to soak up Julia's company in its familiar innocence, and so she said, "I'm seeing nobody."

Nobody except, the next night, at a sapphic pasha's den two hundred steps from Julia's apartment, a seventeen-year-old just off the bus from Plattsburgh, New York, with a drastic hairstyle and twin 800s on her recent SATs (she carried the official ETS printout like a certificate of sanity or possibly of madness) and then, the night after that, a religious-studies major at Columbia whose father (she said) operated the largest sperm bank in Southern California.

This accomplished, Denise went to a midtown studio and taped her guest appearance on *Pop Food for Now People*, making lambsmeat ravioli and other Mare Scuro standards. She met with some of the New Yorkers who'd tried to hire her away from Brian—a couple of Central Park West trillionaires seeking a feudal relationship with her, a Munich banker who believed she was the Weißwurst Messiah who could restore German cooking to its former glory in Manhattan, and a young restaurateur, Nick Razza, who impressed her by itemizing and breaking down each of the meals he'd eaten at Mare Scuro and the Generator. Razza came from a family of purveyors in New Jersey and already owned a popular mid-range seafood grill on the Upper East Side. Now he wanted to jump into the Smith Street culinary scene in Brooklyn with a restaurant that starred, if possible, Denise. She asked him for a week to think it over.

On a sunny fall Sunday afternoon she took the subway out

to Brooklyn. The borough seemed to her a Philadelphia rescued by adjacency to Manhattan. In half an hour she saw more beautiful, interesting-looking women than she saw in half a year in South Philly. She saw their brownstones and their nifty boots.

Returning home by Amtrak, she regretted having hidden for so long in Philadelphia. The little subway station under City Hall was as empty and echoing as a battleship in mothballs; every floor and wall and beam and railing was painted gray. Heartbreaking the little train that finally pulled up, after fifteen minutes, with a population of riders who in their patience and isolation were less like commuters than like emergency-room supplicants. Denise surfaced from the Federal Street station among sycamore leaves and burger wrappers racing in waves down the Broad Street sidewalk, swirling up against the pissy façades and barred windows and scattering among the Bondo-fendered cars that were parked at the curb. The urban vacancy of Philadelphia, the hegemony of wind and sky here, struck her as enchanted. As Narnian. She loved Philadelphia the way she loved Robin Passafaro. Her heart was full and her senses were sharp, but her head felt liable to burst in the vacuum of her solitude.

She unlocked the door of her brick penitentiary and collected her mail from the floor. Among the twenty people who'd left messages on her machine were Robin Passafaro, breaking her silence to ask if Denise might like to have a "little chat," and Emile Berger, politely informing her that he'd accepted Brian Callahan's offer of the job of executive chef at the Generator and was moving back to Philadelphia.

At this news from Emile, Denise kicked the tiled south wall of her kitchen until she was afraid she'd broken her toe. She said, "I've got to get out of here!"

But getting out was not so easy. Robin had had a month to cool off and conclude that if sleeping with Brian was a sin then she was guilty of it also. Brian had rented a loft for himself in Olde City, and Robin, as Denise had suspected, was dead set on keeping custody of Sinéad and Erin. To strengthen her case, she stayed put in the big house on Panama Street and rededicated herself to motherhood. But she was free during school hours and all day on Saturday when Brian took the girls out, and on mature reflection she decided that these free hours might best be spent in Denise's bed.

Denise still couldn't say no to the drug of Robin. She still wanted Robin's hands on her and at her and around her and inside her, that prepositional smorgasbord. But there was something in Robin, probably her propensity to blame herself for harms that other people inflicted on her, that invited betrayal and abuse. Denise went out of her way to smoke in bed now, because cigarette smoke irritated Robin's eyes. She dressed to the hilt when she met Robin for lunch, she did her best to highlight Robin's dowdiness, and she held the gaze of anyone, female or male, who turned to look at her. She visibly winced at the volume of Robin's voice. She behaved like an adolescent with a parent except that an adolescent couldn't help rolling her eyes whereas Denise's contempt was a deliberate, calculated form of cruelty. She shushed Robin angrily when they were in bed and Robin began to hoot self-consciously. She said, "Keep your voice down. Please. *Please.*" Exhilarated by her own cruelty, she stared at Robin's Gore-Tex raingear until Robin was provoked to ask why. Denise said, "I'm just wondering if you're ever tempted to be *slightly* less uncool." Robin replied that she was never going to be cool and so she might as well be comfortable. Denise allowed her lip to curl.

Robin was eager to bring her lover back into contact with Sinéad and Erin, but Denise, for reasons that she herself could only halfway fathom, refused to see the girls. She couldn't imagine looking them in the eye; the very thought of four-girl domesticity sickened her.

"They adore you," Robin said.

"I can't do it."

"Why *not?*"

"Because I don't feel like it. That's why."

"All right. Whatever."

"How long is 'whatever' going to be your word? Are you ever going to retire it? Or is it your word for life?"

"Denise, they *adore* you," Robin squeaked. "They miss you. And you used to love to see them."

"Well, I'm not in a kid kind of mood. I don't know if I'll ever be, frankly. So please stop asking me."

By now most people would have got the message; most people would have cleared out and never come back. But Robin, it transpired, had a taste for cruel treatment. Robin said, and Denise believed her, that she would never have left Brian if Brian hadn't left her. Robin liked to be licked and stroked within a micron of coming and then abandoned and made to beg. And Denise liked to do this to her. Denise liked to get out of bed and get dressed and go downstairs while Robin waited for sexual release, because she wouldn't cheat and touch herself. Denise sat in the kitchen and read a book and smoked until Robin, humiliated, trembling, came down and begged. Denise's contempt then was so pure and so strong, it was almost better than sex.

And so it went. The more Robin agreed to be abused, the more Denise enjoyed abusing her. She ignored Nick Razza's phone messages. She stayed in bed until two in the afternoon. Her social cigarette habit bloomed into craving. She indulged fifteen years' accumulated laziness; she lived on her savings account. Every day, she considered all the work she had to do to prepare the house for her parents' arrival—putting a handle in the shower, carpeting the staircases, buying furniture for the living room, finding a better kitchen table, moving her bed down from the third floor and setting it up in the guest room—and concluded that she lacked the energy. Her life consisted of waiting for the ax to fall. If her parents were coming for six months, there was no point in starting something else. She had to get all her slacking-off done now.

What exactly her father thought about Corecktall was difficult to know. The one time she asked him directly, on the phone, he didn't answer.

"AL?" Enid prompted. "Denise wants to know HOW YOU FEEL ABOUT CORECKTALL."

Alfred's voice was sour. "You'd think they could have found a better name than that."

"It's a completely different spelling," Enid said. "Denise wants to know if you're EXCITED ABOUT THE TREATMENT."

Silence.

"Al, tell her how excited you are."

"I find that my affliction gets a little worse every week. I can't see that another drug is going to make much difference."

"Al, it's not a drug, it's a radical new therapy that uses your patent!"

"I've learned to put up with a certain amount of optimism. So, we will stick to the plan."

"Denise," Enid said, "I can do *lots* to help out. I can make *all* the meals and do *all* the laundry. I think it will be a great adventure! It's so wonderful that you're offering."

Denise couldn't imagine six months with her parents in a house and a city she was done with, six months of invisibility as the accommodating and responsible daughter that she could barely pretend to be. She'd made a promise, however; and so she took her rage out on Robin.

On the Saturday night before Christmas she sat in her kitchen and blew smoke at Robin while Robin maddened her by trying to cheer her up.

"You're giving them a great gift," Robin said, "by inviting them to stay with you."

"It would be a gift if I weren't a mess," Denise said. "But you should only offer what you can actually deliver."

"You can deliver it," Robin said. "I'll help you. I can spend mornings with your dad, and give your mom a break, and you can go off by yourself, and do whatever you want. I'll come three or four mornings a week."

To Denise Robin's offer only made the prospect of those mornings bleaker and more suffocating.

"Do you not understand?" she said. "I hate this house. I hate this city. I hate my life here. I hate family. I hate home. I'm ready to *leave*. *I'm not a good person*. And it only makes it worse to pretend I am."

"I think you're a good person," Robin said.

"I treat you like garbage! Have you not noticed?"

"It's because you're so unhappy."

Robin came around the table and tried to lay a hand on her; Denise elbowed it aside. Robin tried again, and this time Denise caught her squarely in the cheek with the knuckles of her open hand.

Robin backed away, her face crimson, as if she were bleeding on the inside. "You hit me," she said.

"I'm aware of that."

"You hit me rather hard. Why did you do that?"

"Because I don't want you here. I don't want to be part of your life. I don't want to be part of anybody's life. I'm sick of watching myself be cruel to you."

Interconnecting flywheels of pride and love were spinning behind Robin's eyes. It was a while before she spoke. "OK, then," she said. "I'll leave you alone."

Denise did nothing to stop her from leaving, but when she heard the front door close she understood that she'd lost the only person who could have helped her when her parents came to town. She'd lost Robin's company, her comforts. Everything she'd spurned a minute earlier she wanted back.

She flew to St. Jude.

On her first day there, as on the first day of every visit, she warmed to her parents' warmth and did whatever her mother asked her to. She waved off the cash Enid tried to give her for the groceries. She refrained from commenting on the four-ounce bottle of rancid yellow glue that was the only olive oil in the kitchen. She wore the lavender synthetic turtleneck and the matronly gold-plate necklace that were recent gifts from her mother. She effused, spontaneously, about the adolescent ballerinas in *The Nutcracker*, she held her father's gloved hand as they crossed the regional theater's parking lot, she loved her parents more than she'd ever loved anything; and the minute they were both in bed she changed her clothes and fled the house.

She paused in the street, a cigarette on her lip, a matchbook (*Dean & Trish ♦ June 13, 1987*) trembling in her fingers. She hiked to the field behind the grade school where she and Don Armour had once sat and smelled cattails and verbena; she stamped her feet, rubbed her hands, watched the clouds occult the constellations, and took deep fortifying breaths of selfhood.

Later in the night, she undertook a clandestine operation on her mother's behalf, entering Gary's bedroom while he was occupied with

Alfred, unzipping the inside pocket of his leather jacket, replacing the Mexican A with a handful of Advils, and spiriting Enid's drug away to a safer place before she finally, good daughter, fell asleep.

On her second day in St. Jude, as on the second day of every visit, she woke up angry. The anger was an autonomous neurochemical event; no stopping it. At breakfast she was tortured by every word her mother said. Browning the ribs and soaking the sauerkraut according to ancestral custom, rather than in the modern style she'd developed at the Generator, made her angry. (So much grease, such sacrifice of texture.) The bradykinetic languor of Enid's electric stove, which hadn't bothered her the day before, made her angry. The hundred-and-one refrigerator magnets, puppy-dog sentimental in their iconography and so feeble in their pull that you could scarcely open the door without sending a snapshot of Jonah or a postcard of Vienna swooping to the floor, filled her with rage. She went to the basement to get the ancestral ten-quart Dutch oven, and the clutter in the laundry-room cabinets made her furious. She dragged a trash can in from the garage and began to fill it with her mother's crap. This was arguably helpful to her mother, and so she went at it with abandon. She threw away the Korean barfle-berries, the fifty most obviously worthless plastic flowerpots, the assortment of sand-dollar fragments, and the sheaf of silver-dollar plants whose dollars had all fallen off. She threw away the wreath of spray-painted pinecones that somebody had ripped apart. She threw away the brandy-pumpkin "spread" that had turned a snottish gray-green. She threw away the Neolithic cans of hearts of palm and baby shrimps and miniature Chinese corncobs, the turbid black liter of Romanian wine whose cork had rotted, the Nixon-era bottle of Mai Tai mix with an oozing crust around its neck, the collection of Paul Masson Chablis carafes with spider parts and moth wings at the bottom, the profoundly corroded bracket for some long-lost wind chimes. She threw away the quart glass bottle of Vess Diet Cola that had turned the color of plasma, the ornamental jar of brandied kumquats that was now a fantasia of rock candy and amorphous brown gunk, the smelly thermos whose broken inner glass tinkled when she shook it, the mildewed half-peck produce basket full of smelly yogurt cartons, the hurricane lanterns sticky with oxidation and brimming with severed moth wings, the lost empires of florist's clay and florist's tape that hung together even as they crumbled and rusted . . .

At the very back of the closet, in the cobwebs behind the bottom shelf, she found a thick envelope, not old-looking, with no postage on it. The envelope was addressed to the Axon Corporation, 24 East Industrial Serpentine, Schwenksville, PA. The return addressee was Alfred Lambert. The words SEND CERTIFIED were also on the face.

Water was running in the little half-bathroom by her father's laboratory, the toilet tank refilling, faint sulfurous odors in the air. The door to the lab was ajar and Denise knocked on it.

"Yes," Alfred said.

He was standing by the shelves of exotic metals, the gallium and bismuth, and buckling his belt. She showed him the envelope and told him where she'd found it.

Alfred turned it over in his shaking hands, as if an explanation might magically occur to him. "It's a mystery," he said.

"Can I open it?"

"You may do as you wish."

The envelope contained three copies of a licensing agreement dated September 13, signed by Alfred, and notarized by David Schumpert.

"What is this doing on the floor of the laundry-room closet?" Denise said.

Alfred shook his head. "You'd have to ask your mother."

She went out to the bottom of the stairs and raised her voice. "Mom? Can you come down here for a second?"

Enid appeared at the top of the stairs, wiping her hands on a dish towel. "What is it? Can't you find the pot?"

"I found the pot, but can you come down here?"

Alfred, in the lab, was holding the Axon documents loosely, not reading them. Enid appeared in the doorway with guilt on her face. "What?"

"Dad wants to know why this envelope was in the laundry-room closet."

"Give me that," Enid said. She snatched the documents from Alfred and crumpled them in her fist. "This has all been taken care of. Dad signed another set of agreements and they sent us a check right away. This is nothing to worry about."

Denise narrowed her eyes. "I thought you said you'd sent these in. When we were in New York, at the beginning of October. You said you'd sent these in."

"I thought I had. But they were lost in the mail."

"In the *mail*?"

Enid waved her hands vaguely. "Well, that's where I thought they were. But I guess they were in the closet. I must have set a stack of mail down there, when I was going to the post office, and then this fell down behind. You know, I can't keep track of every last thing. Sometimes things get lost, Denise. I have a big house to take care of, and sometimes things get lost."

Denise took the envelope from Alfred's workbench. "It says 'Send Certified.' If you were at the post office, how did you not notice that something you needed to send Certified was missing? How did you not notice that you weren't filling out a Certified Mail slip?"

"Denise." Alfred's voice had an angry edge. "That's enough now."

"I don't know what happened," Enid said. "It was a busy time for me. It's a complete mystery to me, and let's just leave it that way. Because it doesn't *matter*. Dad got his five thousand dollars just fine. It doesn't *matter*."

She further crumpled the licensing agreements and left the laboratory.

I'm developing Garyitis, Denise thought.

"You shouldn't be so hard on your mother," Alfred said.

"I know. I'm sorry."

But Enid was exclaiming in the laundry room, exclaiming in the Ping-Pong–table room, returning to the workshop. "Denise," she cried, "you've got the whole closet completely torn up! What on earth are you doing in there?"

"I'm throwing food away. Food and other rotten junk."

"All right, but why now? We have the whole weekend if you want to help me clean some closets out. It's wonderful if you want to help me. But not *today*. Let's not get into it *today*."

"It's bad food, Mom. If you leave it long enough, it turns to poison. Anaerobic bacteria will kill you."

"Well, get it cleaned up now, and let's do the rest on the weekend. We don't have time for that today. I want you to work on dinner so it's all ready and you don't have to think about it, and then I *really* want you to help Dad with his exercises, like you said you would!"

"I will do that."

"Al," Enid shouted, leaning past her, "Denise wants to help you with your exercises after lunch!"

He shook his head as if with disgust. "As you wish."

Stacked up on one of the old family bedspreads that had long served as a dropcloth were wicker chairs and tables in early stages of scraping and painting. Lidded coffee cans were clustered on an open section of newspaper; a gun in a canvas case was by the workbench.

"What are you doing with the gun, Dad?" Denise said.

"Oh, he's been meaning to sell that for years," Enid said. "AL, ARE YOU EVER GOING TO SELL THAT GUN?"

Alfred seemed to run this sentence through his brain several times in order to extract its meaning. Very slowly, he nodded his head. "Yes," he said. "I will sell the gun."

"I hate having it in the house," Enid said as she turned to leave. "You know, he never used it. Not once. I don't think it's ever been fired."

Alfred came smiling at Denise, making her retreat toward the door. "I will finish up in here," he said.

Upstairs it was Christmas Eve. Packages were accumulating beneath the tree. In the front yard the nearly bare branches of the swamp white oak swung in a breeze that had shifted to more snow-threatening directions; the dead grass snagged dead leaves.

Enid was peering out through the sheer curtains again. "Should I be worried about Chip?"

"I would worry that he's not coming," Denise said, "but not that he's in trouble."

"The paper says rival factions are fighting for control of central Vilnius."

"Chip can take care of himself."

"Oh, here," Enid said, leading Denise to the front door, "I want you to hang the last ornament on the Advent calendar."

"Mother, why don't you do that."

"No, I want to see you do it."

The last ornament was the Christ baby in a walnut shell. Pinning it to the tree was a task for a child, for someone credulous and hopeful, and Denise could now see very clearly that she'd made a program of steeling herself against the emotions of this house, against the saturation of childhood memory and significance. She *could not* be the child to perform this task.

"It's your calendar," she said. "You should do it."

The disappointment on Enid's face was disproportionately large. It was an ancient disappointment with the refusal of the world in general and her children in particular to participate in her preferred enchantments. "I guess I'll ask Gary if he'll do it," she said with a scowl.

"I'm sorry," Denise said.

"I remember you used to love pinning on the ornaments, when you were a little girl. You used to *love* it. But if you don't want to do it, you don't want to do it."

"Mom." Denise's voice was unsteady. "Please don't make me."

"If I'd known it would seem like such a chore," Enid said, "I never would have asked you."

"Let me watch you do it!" Denise pleaded.

Enid shook her head and walked away. "I'll ask Gary when he gets back from shopping."

"I'm so sorry."

She went outside and sat on the front steps smoking. The air had a disturbed southern snowy flavor. Down the street Kirby Root was winding pine rope around the post of his gas lamp. He waved and she waved back.

"When did you start smoking?" Enid asked her when she came inside.

"About fifteen years ago."

"I don't mean to criticize," Enid said, "but it's a terrible habit for your health. It's bad for your skin, and frankly, it's not a pleasant smell for others."

Denise, with a sigh, washed her hands and began to brown the flour for the sauerkraut gravy. "If you're going to come and live with me," she said, "we need to get some things clear."

"I said I wasn't criticizing."

"One thing we need to be clear about is that I'm having a hard time. For example, I didn't quit the Generator. I was fired."

"Fired?"

"Yes. Unfortunately. Do you want to know why?"

"No!"

"Are you sure?"

"Yes!"

Denise, smiling, stirred more bacon grease into the bottom of the Dutch oven.

"Denise, I promise you," her mother said, "we will not be in your way. You just show me where the supermarket is, and how to use your washer, and then you can come and go as you please. I know you have your own life. I don't want to disrupt anything. If I could see any other way to get Dad into that program, believe me, I would do it. But Gary never invited us, and I don't think Caroline would want us anyway."

The bacon fat and the browned ribs and the boiling kraut smelled good. The dish, as prepared in this kitchen, bore little relation to the high-art version that she'd plated for a thousand strangers. The Generator's ribs and the Generator's monkfish had more in common than the Generator's ribs and these homemade ribs had. You thought you knew what food was, you thought it was elemental. You forgot how much restaurant there was in restaurant food and how much home was in homemade.

She said to her mother: "Why aren't you telling me the story of Norma Greene?"

"Well, you got so angry with me last time," Enid said.

"I was mainly mad at Gary."

"My only concern is that you not be hurt like Norma was. I want to see you happy and settled."

"Mom, I'm never going to get married again."

"You don't know that."

"Yes, in fact, I do know that."

"Life is full of surprises. You're still very young and very darling."

Denise put more bacon fat into the pot; there was no reason to hold back now. She said, "Are you listening to me? I'm quite certain that I will never get married again."

But a car door had slammed in the street and Enid was running into the dining room to part the sheer curtains.

"Oh, it's Gary," she said, disappointed. "Just Gary."

Gary breezed into the kitchen with the railroad memorabilia that he'd bought at the Museum of Transport. Obviously refreshed by a morning to himself, he was happy to indulge Enid by pinning the Christ baby to the Advent calendar; and, as quickly as that, Enid's sympathies shifted away from her daughter and back to her son. She crowed about the beautiful job that Gary done in the downstairs shower and what a *huge* improvement the stool there represented. Denise miserably finished the dinner preparations, assembled a light lunch, and washed a mountain of dishes while the sky in the windows turned fully gray.

After lunch she went to her room, which Enid had finally redecorated into near-perfect anonymity, and wrapped presents. (She'd bought clothes for everyone; she knew what people liked to wear.) She uncrumpled the Kleenex that contained thirty sunny caplets of Mexican A and considered wrapping them up as a gift for Enid, but she had to respect the limits of her promise to Gary. She balled the caplets back into the Kleenex, slipped out of her room and down the stairs, and stuffed the drug into the freshly vacated twenty-fourth pocket of the Advent calendar. Everybody else was in the basement. She was able to glide back upstairs and shut herself in her room as if she'd never left.

When she was young, when Enid's mother had browned the ribs in the kitchen and Gary and Chip had brought home their unbelievably beautiful girlfriends and everybody's idea of a good time was to buy Denise a lot of presents, this had been the longest afternoon of the year.

An obscure natural law had forbidden whole-family gatherings before nightfall; people had scattered to wait in separate rooms. Sometimes, as a teenager, Chip had taken mercy on the last child in the house and played chess or Monopoly with her. When she got a little older, he'd brought her along to the mall with his girlfriend of the moment. There was no greater bliss for her at ten and twelve than to be so included: to take instruction from Chip in the evils of late capitalism, to gather couturial data on the girlfriend, to study the length of the girlfriend's bangs and the height of her heels, to be left alone for an hour at the bookstore, and then to look back, from the top of the hill above the mall, on the silent slow choreography of traffic in the faltering light.

Even now it was the longest afternoon. Snowflakes a shade darker than the snow-colored sky had begun to fall in quantity. Their chill found its way past the storm windows, it skirted the flows and masses of furnace-heated air from the registers, it came right at your neck. Denise, afraid of getting sick, lay down and pulled a blanket over herself.

She slept hard, with no dreams, and awoke—where? what time? what day?—to angry voices. Snow had webbed the corners of the windows and frosted the swamp white oak. There was light in the sky but not for long.

Al, Gary went to ALL that trouble—

I never asked him to!

Well, can't you try it at least once? After all the work he did yesterday?

I am entitled to a bath if I want to take a bath.

Dad, it's only a matter of time before you fall on the stairs and break your neck!

I am not asking anyone for help.

You're damn right you're not! Because I have forbidden Mom—forbidden her—to go anywhere near that bathtub—

Al, please, just try the shower—

Mom, forget it, let him break his neck, we'd all be better off—

Gary—

The voices were coming closer as the contretemps moved up the stairs. Denise heard her father's heavy tread pass her door. She put her glasses on and opened the door just as Enid, slow on her bad hip, reached the top of the stairs. "Denise, what are you doing?"

"I took a nap."

"Go talk to your father. Tell him it's important that he try the shower that Gary did so much work on. He'll listen to *you*."

The depth of her sleep and the manner of her awakening had put Denise out of phase with external reality; the scene in the hall and the scene in the hall windows had faint antimatter shadows; sounds were at once too loud and barely audible. "Why—" she said. "Why are we making an issue of this today?"

"Because Gary's leaving tomorrow and I want him to see if the shower's going to work for Dad."

"And tell me again what's wrong with the bath?"

"He gets stuck. And he's so bad on the stairs."

Denise closed her eyes, but this substantially worsened the phase-sync problem. She opened them.

"Oh, plus, and Denise," Enid said, "you haven't worked with him on his exercises yet like you promised!"

"Right. I'll do that."

"Do it now, before he gets cleaned up. Here, I'll get you the sheet from Dr. Hedgpeth."

Enid limped back down the stairs, and Denise raised her voice. "Dad?"

No answer.

Enid came halfway up the stairs and pushed through the rails of the banister a violet sheet of paper ("MOBILITY IS GOLDEN") on which stick figures illustrated seven stretching exercises. "Really teach him," she said. "He gets impatient with me, but he'll listen to you. Dr. Hedgpeth keeps asking if Dad's doing his exercises. It's very important that he really learn these. I had no idea you were sleeping all this time."

Denise took the instruction sheet into the master bedroom and found Alfred in the doorway of his closet, naked from the waist down.

"Whoa, Dad, sorry," she said, retreating.

"What is it?"

"We need to work on your exercises."

"I'm already undressed."

"Just put some pajamas on. Loose clothing is better anyway."

It took her five minutes to calm him down and stretch him out on his back on the bed in his wool shirt and his pajama bottoms; and here at last the truth came pouring out.

The first exercise required that Alfred take his right knee in his hands and draw it toward his chest, and then do the same with his left knee. Denise guided his wayward hands to his right knee, and although she was dismayed by how rigid he was getting, he was able, with her help, to stretch his hip past ninety degrees.

"Now do your left knee," she said.

Alfred put his hands on his right knee again and pulled it toward his chest.

"That's great," she said. "But now try it with your left."

He lay breathing hard and did nothing. He wore the expression of a man suddenly remembering disastrous circumstances.

"Dad? Try it with your left knee."

She touched his left knee, to no avail. In his eyes she saw a desperate wish for clarification and instruction. She moved his hands to his left knee, and the hands immediately fell off. Possibly his rigidity was worse on the left side? She put his hands back on his knee and helped him raise it.

If anything, he was more flexible on the left.

"Now you try it," she said.

He grinned at her, breathing like someone very scared. "Try what."

"Put your hands on your left knee and lift it."

"Denise, I've had enough of this."

"You'll feel a lot better if you can do a little stretching," she said. "Just do what you just did. Put your hands on your left knee and raise it."

The smile she gave him came reflected back as confusion. His eyes met hers in silence.

"Which is my left?" he said.

She touched his left knee. "This one."

"And what do I do?"

"Put your hands on it and pull it toward your chest."

His eyes wandered anxiously, reading bad messages on the ceiling.

"Dad, just concentrate."

"There's not much point."

"OK." She took a deep breath. "OK, let's leave that one and try the second exercise. All right?"

He looked at her as if she, his only hope, were sprouting fangs and antlers.

"So in this one," she said, trying to ignore his expression, "you cross your right leg over your left leg, and then let both legs fall to the right as far as they can go. I like this exercise," she said. "It stretches your hip flexor. It feels really good."

She explained it to him two more times and then asked him to raise his right leg.

He lifted both legs a few inches off the mattress.

"Just your right leg," she said gently. "And keep your knees bent."

"Denise!" His voice was high with strain. "There's no point!"

"Here," she said. "Here." She pushed on his feet to bend his knees. She lifted his right leg, supporting it by the calf and thigh, and crossed it over his left knee. At first there was no resistance, and then, all at once, he seemed to cramp up violently.

"*Denise.*"

"Dad, just relax."

She already knew that he was never coming to Philadelphia. But now a tropical humidity was rising off him, a tangy almost-smell of letting go. The pajama fabric on his thigh was hot and wet in her hand, and his entire body was trembling.

"Oh, shoot," she said, releasing his leg.

Snow was swirling in the windows, lights appearing in the neighbors' houses. Denise wiped her hand on her jeans and lowered her eyes to her lap and listened, her heart beating hard, to the labored breathing of her father and the rhythmic rustling of his limbs on the bedspread. There was an arc of soak on the bedspread near his crotch and a longer capillary-action reach of wetness down one leg of his pajamas. The initial almost-smell of fresh piss had resolved, as it cooled in the underheated room, into an aroma quite definite and pleasant.

"I'm sorry, Dad," she said. "Let me get you a towel."

Alfred smiled up at the ceiling and spoke in a less agitated voice. "I lie here and I can see it," he said. "Do you see it?"

"See what?"

He pointed vaguely skyward with one finger. "Bottom on the bottom. Bottom on the bottom of the bench," he said. "Written there. Do you see it?"

Now she was confused and he wasn't. He cocked an eyebrow and gave her a canny look. "You know who wrote that, don't you? The fuh. The fuh. Fellow with the you know."

Holding her gaze, he nodded significantly.

"I don't understand what you're talking about," Denise said.

"Your friend," he said. "Fellow with the blue cheeks."

The first one percent of comprehension was born at the back of her neck and began to grow to the north and to the south.

"Let me get a towel," she said, going nowhere.

Her father's eyes rolled up toward the ceiling again. "He wrote that on the bottom of the bench. Bommunnuthuh. Bottomofthebench. And I lie there and I can see it."

"Who are we talking about?"

"Your friend in Signals. Fellow with the blue cheeks."

"You're confused, Dad. You're having a dream. I'm going to get a towel."

"See, there was never any point in saying anything."

"I'm getting a towel," she said.

She crossed the bedroom to the bathroom. Her head was still in the nap that she'd been taking, and the problem was getting worse. She was falling further out of sync with the waveforms of reality that constituted towel-softness, sky-darkness, floor-hardness, air-clearness. Why this talk of Don Armour? Why now?

Her father had swung his legs out of bed and peeled off his pajama bottoms. He extended his hand for the towel when she returned. "I'll clean this mess up," he said. "You go help your mother."

"No, I'll do it," she said. "You take a bath."

"Just give me the rag. It's not your job."

"Dad, take a bath."

"It was not my intention to involve you in this."

His hand, still extended, flopped in the air. Denise averted her eyes from his offending, wetting penis. "Stand up," she said. "I'm going to take the bedspread off."

Alfred covered his penis with the towel. "Leave that to your mother," he said. "I told her Philadelphia's a lot of nonsense. I never intended to involve you in any of this. You have your own life. Just have fun and be careful."

He remained seated on the edge of the bed, his head bowed, his hands like large empty fleshy spoons on his lap.

"Do you want me to start the bathwater?" Denise said.

"I nuh-nunnunnunn-unh," he said. "Told the fellow he was talking a lot of nonsense, but what can you do?" Alfred made a gesture of self-evidence or inevitability. "Thought he was going to Little Rock. You guh. I said! Gotta have seniority. Well, that's a lot of nonsense. I told him to get the hell out." He gave Denise an apologetic look and shrugged. "What else could I do?"

Denise had felt invisible before, but never like this. "I'm not sure what you're saying," she said.

"Well." Alfred made a vague gesture of explanation. "He told me to look under the bench. Simple as that. Look under the bench if I didn't believe him."

"What bench?"

"It was a lot of nonsense," he said. "Simpler for everybody if I just quit. You see, he never thought of that."

"Are we talking about the railroad?"

Alfred shook his head. "Not your concern. It was never my intention to involve you in any of this. I want you to go and have fun. And *be careful*. Tell your mother to come up here with a rag."

With this, he launched himself across the carpeting and shut the bathroom door behind him. Denise, to be doing something, stripped the bed and balled everything up, including her father's wet pajamas, and carried it downstairs.

"How's it going up there!" Enid asked from her Christmas-card station in the dining room.

"He wet the bed," Denise said.

"Oh my word."

"He doesn't know his left leg from his right."

Enid's face darkened. "I thought maybe he'd listen better to you."

"Mother, *he doesn't know his left leg from his right.*"

"Sometimes the medication—"

"Yeah! Yeah!" Denise's voice was plangent. "The medication!"

Having silenced her mother, she proceeded to the laundry room to sort and soak the linens. Here Gary, all smiles, accosted her with an O-gauge model railroad engine in his hands.

"I found it," he said.

"Found what."

Gary seemed hurt that Denise hadn't been paying close attention to his desires and activities. He explained that half of his childhood model-railroad set—"the important half, with the cars and the transformer"—had been missing for decades and presumed lost. "I just took the entire storeroom apart," he said. "And where do you think I found it?"

"Where."

"Guess," he said.

"At the bottom of the rope box," she said.

Gary's eyes widened. "How did you know that? I've been looking for *decades.*"

"Well, you should have asked me. There's a smaller box of railroad stuff inside the big rope box."

"Well, anyway." Gary shuddered to accomplish a shift of focus away from her and back to him. "I'm glad I had the satisfaction of finding it, although I wish you'd told me."

"I wish you'd asked!"

"You know, I'm having a great time with this railroad stuff. There are some truly neat things that you can buy."

"Good! I'm happy for you!"

Gary marveled at the engine he was holding. "I never thought I'd see this again."

When he was gone and she was alone in the basement, she went to Alfred's laboratory with a flashlight, knelt among the Yuban cans, and examined the underside of the bench. There, in shaggy pencil, was a heart the size of a human heart:

She slumped onto her heels, her knees on the stone-cold floor. *Little Rock. Seniority. Simpler if I just quit.*

Absently, she raised the lid of a Yuban can. It was full to the brim with lurid orange fermented piss.

"Oh boy," she said to the shotgun.

As she ran up to her bedroom and put on her coat and gloves, she felt sorriest about her mother, because no matter how often and how bitterly Enid had complained to her, she'd never got it through her head that life in St. Jude had turned into such a nightmare; and how could you permit yourself to breathe, let alone laugh or sleep or eat well, if you were unable to imagine how hard another person's life was?

Enid was at the dining-room curtains again, looking out for Chip.

"Going for a walk!" Denise called as she closed the front door behind her.

Two inches of snow lay on the lawn. In the west the clouds were breaking up; violent eye-shadow shades of lavender and robin's-egg blue marked the cutting edge of the latest cold front. Denise walked down the middle of tread-marked twilit streets and smoked until the nicotine had dulled her distress and she could think more clearly.

She gathered that Don Armour, after the Wroth brothers had

bought the Midland Pacific and commenced their downsizing of it, had failed to make the cut for Little Rock and had gone to Alfred and complained. Maybe he'd threatened to brag about his conquest of Alfred's daughter or maybe he'd asserted his rights as a quasi member of the Lambert family; either way, Alfred had told him to go to hell. Then Alfred had gone home and examined the underside of his workbench.

Denise believed that there had been a scene between Don Armour and her father, but she hated to imagine it. How Don Armour must have loathed himself for crawling to his boss's boss's boss and trying to beg or blackmail inclusion in the railroad's move to Little Rock; how betrayed Alfred must have felt by this daughter who'd won such praise for her work habits; how dismally the entire intolerable scene must have turned on the insertion of Don Armour's dick into this and that guilty, unexcited orifice of hers. She hated to think of her father kneeling beneath his workbench and locating that penciled heart, hated the idea of Don Armour's drecky insinuations entering her father's prudish ears, hated to imagine how keenly it offended a man of such discipline and privacy to learn that Don Armour had been roaming and poking through his house at will.

It was never my intention to involve you in this.

Well, and sure enough: her father had resigned from the railroad. He'd saved her privacy. He'd never breathed a word of any of this to Denise, never given any sign of thinking less of her. For fifteen years she'd tried to pass for a perfectly responsible and careful daughter, and he'd known all along that she was not.

She thought there might be comfort in this idea if she could manage to keep it in her head.

As she left her parents' neighborhood, the houses got newer and bigger and boxier. Through windows with no mullions or fake plastic mullions she could see luminous screens, some giant, some miniature. Evidently every hour of the year, including this one, was a good hour for staring at a screen. Denise unbuttoned her coat and turned back, taking a shortcut through the field behind her old grade school.

She'd never really known her father. Probably nobody had. With his shyness and his formality and his tyrannical rages he protected his interior so ferociously that if you loved him, as she did, you learned that you could do him no greater kindness than to respect his privacy.

Alfred, likewise, had shown his faith in her by taking her at face value: by declining to pry behind the front that she presented. She'd felt happiest with him when she was publicly vindicating his faith in her: when she got straight A's; when her restaurants succeeded; when reviewers loved her.

She understood, better than she would have liked to, what a disaster it had been for him to wet the bed in front of her. Lying on a stain of fast-cooling urine was not the way he wished to be with her. They only had one good way of being together, and it wasn't going to work much longer.

The odd truth about Alfred was that love, for him, was a matter not of approaching but of keeping away. She understood this better than Chip and Gary did, and so she felt a particular responsibility for him.

To Chip, unfortunately, it seemed that Alfred cared about his children only to the degree that they succeeded. Chip was so busy feeling misunderstood that he never noticed how badly he himself misunderstood his father. To Chip, Alfred's inability to be tender was the proof that Alfred didn't know, or care, who he was. Chip couldn't see what everyone around him could: that if there was anybody in the world whom Alfred did love purely for his own sake, it was Chip. Denise was aware of not delighting Alfred like this; they had little in common beyond formalities and achievements. Chip was the one whom Alfred had called for in the middle of the night, even though he knew Chip wasn't there.

I made it as clear to you as I could, she told her idiot brother in her head as she crossed the snowy field. *I can't make it any clearer.*

The house to which she returned was full of light. Gary or Enid had swept the snow from the front walk. Denise was scuffing her feet on the hemp mat when the door flew open.

"Oh, it's you," Enid said. "I thought it might be Chip."

"No. Just me."

She went in and pried her boots off. Gary had built a fire and was sitting in the armchair closest to it, a stack of old photo albums at his feet.

"Take my advice," he told Enid, "and forget about Chip."

"He must be in some sort of trouble," Enid said. "Otherwise he would have called."

"Mother, he's a sociopath. Get it through your head."

"You don't know a thing about Chip," Denise said to Gary.

"I know when somebody refuses to pull his weight."

"I just want us all to be together!" Enid said.

Gary let out a groan of tender sentiment. "Oh, Denise," he said. "Oh, oh. Come and see this baby girl."

"Maybe another time."

But Gary crossed the living room with the photo album and foisted it on her, pointing at the photo image on a family Christmas card. The chubby, mop-headed, vaguely Semitic little girl in the picture was Denise at about eighteen months. There was not a particle of trouble in her smile or in the smiles of Chip and Gary. She sat between them on the living-room sofa in its pre-reupholstered instantiation; each had an arm around her; their clear-skinned boy faces nearly touched above her own.

"Is that a cute little girl?" Gary said.

"Oh, how darling," Enid said, crowding in.

From the center pages of the album fell an envelope with a Registered Mail sticker. Enid snatched it up and took it to the fireplace and fed it directly to the flames.

"What was that?" Gary said.

"Just that Axon business, which is taken care of now."

"Did Dad ever send half the money to Orfic Midland?"

"He asked me to do it but I haven't yet. I'm so swamped with insurance forms."

Gary laughed as he went upstairs. "Don't let that twenty-five hundred burn any holes in your pocket."

Denise blew her nose and went to peel potatoes in the kitchen.

"Just in case," Enid said, joining her, "be sure there's enough for Chip. He said this afternoon at the latest."

"I think it's officially evening now," Denise said.

"Well, I want a *lot* of potatoes."

All of her mother's kitchen knives were butter-knife dull. Denise resorted to a carrot scraper. "Did Dad ever tell you why he didn't go to Little Rock with Orfic Midland?"

"No," Enid said emphatically. "Why?"

"I just wondered."

"He told them yes, he was going. And, Denise, it would have made *all* the difference for us financially. It would have nearly doubled his pension, just those two years. We would have been in so much better shape now. He told me he was going to do it, he agreed it was the right thing, and then he came home three nights later and said he'd changed his mind and quit."

Denise looked into the eyes semireflected in the window above the sink. "And he never told you why."

"Well, he couldn't stand those Wroths. I assumed it was a personality clash. But he never talked about it with me. You know—he never tells me anything. He just decides. Even if it's a financial disaster, it's his decision and it's final."

Here came the waterworks. Denise let potato and scraper fall into the sink. She thought of the drugs she'd hidden in the Advent calendar, she thought they might stop her tears long enough to let her get out of town, but she was too far from where they were stashed. She'd been caught defenseless in the kitchen.

"Sweetie, what is it?" Enid said.

For a while there was no Denise in the kitchen, just mush and wetness and remorse. She found herself kneeling on the rag rug by the sink. Little balls of soaked Kleenex surrounded her. She was reluctant to raise her eyes to her mother, who was sitting beside her on a chair and feeding her dry tissues.

"So many things you think are going to matter," Enid said with a new sobriety, "turn out not to matter."

"Some things still matter," Denise said.

Enid gazed bleakly at the unpeeled potatoes by the sink. "He's not going to get better, is he."

Denise was happy to let her mother think that she'd been crying about Alfred's health. "I don't think so," she said.

"It's probably not the medication, is it."

"It probably isn't."

"And there's probably no point in going to Philadelphia," Enid said, "if he can't follow instructions."

"You're right. There probably isn't."

"Denise, what are we going to do?"

"I don't know."

"I knew something was wrong this morning," Enid said. "If you'd found that envelope three months ago, he would have exploded at me. But you saw today. He didn't do a thing."

"I'm sorry I put you on the spot there."

"It didn't even matter. He didn't even know."

"I'm sorry anyway."

The lid on a pot of white beans boiling on the stove began to rattle. Enid stood up to reduce the heat. Denise, still kneeling, said, "I think there's something in the Advent calendar for you."

"No, Gary pinned the last ornament."

"In the 'twenty-four' pocket. There might be something for you."

"Well, what?"

"I don't know. You might go check, though."

She heard her mother make her way to the front door and then return. Although the pattern of the rag rug was complex, she thought she would soon have it memorized from staring.

"Where did these come from?" Enid said.

"I don't know."

"Did you put them there?"

"It's a mystery."

"You must have put them there."

"No."

Enid set the pills on the counter, took two steps away from them, and frowned at them severely. "I'm sure whoever put these there meant well," she said. "But I don't want them in my house."

"That's probably a good idea."

"I want the real thing or I don't want anything."

With her right hand Enid herded the pills into her left hand. She dumped them into the garbage grinder, turned on water, and ground them up.

"What's the real thing?" Denise said when the noise subsided.

"I want us all together for one last Christmas."

Gary, showered and shaved and dressed in his aristocratic style, entered the kitchen in time to catch this declaration.

"You'd better be willing to settle for four out of five," he said, opening the liquor cabinet. "What's wrong with Denise?"

"She's upset about Dad."

"Well, it's about time," Gary said. "There's plenty to be upset about."

Denise gathered up the Kleenex balls. "Pour me a lot of whatever you're having," she said.

"I thought we could have Bea's champagne tonight!" Enid said.

"No," Denise said.

"No," Gary said.

"We'll save it and see if Chip comes," Enid said. "Now, what's taking Dad so long upstairs?"

"He's not upstairs," Gary said.

"Are you sure?"

"Yes, I'm sure."

"Al?" Enid shouted. "*AL?*"

Gases snapped in the neglected fire in the living room. White beans simmered on moderate heat; the registers breathed warm air. Out in the street somebody's tires were spinning on snow.

"Denise," Enid said. "Go see if he's in the basement."

Denise didn't ask "Why me?" although she wanted to. She went to the top of the basement stairs and called her father. The basement lights were on, and she could hear a cryptic faint rustling from the workshop.

She called again: "Dad?"

There was no answer.

Her fear, as she descended the stairs, was like a fear from the unhappy year of her childhood when she'd begged for a pet and received a cage containing two hamsters. A dog or a cat might have harmed Enid's fabrics, but these young hamsters, a pair of siblings from a litter at the Driblett residence, were permitted in the house. Every morning, when Denise went to the basement to give them pellets and change their water, she dreaded to discover what new deviltry they'd hatched in the night for her private spectation—maybe a nest of blind, wriggling, incest-crimson offspring, maybe a desperate pointless wholesale rearrangement of cedar shavings into a single great drift beside which the two parents were trembling on the bare metal of the cage's floor, looking bloated and evasive after eating all their children, which couldn't have left an agreeable aftertaste, even in a hamster's mouth.

The door to Alfred's workshop was shut. She tapped on it. "Dad?"

Alfred's reply came immediately in a strained, strangled bark: "Don't come in!"

Behind the door something hard scraped on concrete.

"Dad? What are you doing?"

"I said don't come in!"

Well, she'd seen the gun and she was thinking: Of course it's me down here. She was thinking: And I have no idea what to do.

"Dad, I have to come in."

"Denise—"

"I'm coming in," she said.

She opened the door to brilliant lighting. In a single glance she took in the old paint-spattered bedspread on the floor, the old man on his back with his hips off the ground and his knees trembling, his wide eyes fixed on the underside of the workbench while he struggled with the big plastic enema apparatus that he'd stuck into his rectum.

"Whoops, sorry!" she said, turning away, her hands raised.

Alfred breathed stertorously and said nothing more.

She pulled the door partway shut and filled her lungs with air. Upstairs the doorbell was ringing. Through the walls and the ceiling she could hear footsteps approaching the house.

"That's him, that's him!" Enid cried.

A burst of song—"It's Beginning to Look a Lot Like Christmas"— punctured her illusion.

Denise joined her mother and brother at the front door. Familiar faces were clustered around the snowy stoop, Dale Driblett, Honey Driblett, Steve and Ashley Driblett, Kirby Root with several daughters and buzz-cut sons-in-law, and the entire Person clan. Enid corralled Denise and Gary and hugged them closer, bouncing on her toes with the spirit of the moment. "Run and get Dad," she said. "He loves the carolers."

"Dad's busy," Denise said.

For the man who'd taken care to protect her privacy and who had only ever asked that his privacy be respected, too, wasn't the kindest course to let him suffer by himself and not compound his suffering with the shame of being witnessed? Hadn't he, with every question that he'd ever failed to ask her, earned the right to relief from any uncomfortable question she might want to ask him now? Like: *What's with the enema, Dad?*

The carolers seemed to be singing straight at her. Enid was swaying to the tune, Gary had easy tears in his eyes, but Denise felt like the intended audience. She would have liked to stay there with the happier side of her family. She didn't know what it was about difficulty that made such a powerful claim on her allegiance. But as Kirby Root, who directed the choir at Chiltsville Methodist, led a segue into "Hark, the Herald Angels Sing," she began to wonder if respecting Alfred's privacy wasn't a little bit too easy. He wanted to be left alone? Well, how nice for her! She could go back to Philadelphia, live her own life, and be doing exactly what he wanted. He was embarrassed to be seen with a plastic squirter up his ass? Well, how convenient! She was pretty goddamned embarrassed herself!

She extricated herself from her mother, waved to the neighbors, and returned to the basement.

The workshop door was ajar, as she'd left it. "Dad?"

"Don't come in!"

"I'm sorry," she said, "but I have to come in."

"I never intended to involve you in this. Not your worry."

"I know. But I have to come in anyway."

She found him in much the same position, with an old beach towel wadded up between his legs. Kneeling among the shit smells and piss smells, she rested a hand on his quaking shoulder. "I'm sorry," she said.

His face was covered with sweat. His eyes glittered with madness. "Find a telephone," he said, "and call the district manager."

Chip's great revelation had come at about six o'clock on Tuesday morning, as he was walking in near-perfect darkness down a road surfaced with Lithuanian gravel, between the tiny hamlets of Neravai and Miškiniai, a few kilometers from the Polish border.

Fifteen hours earlier, he'd reeled out of the airport and had nearly been run over by Jonas, Aidaris, and Gitanas as they veered to the curb in their Ford Stomper. The three men had been on their way out of Vilnius when they'd heard the news of the airport's closing. Pulling a U-turn on the road to Ignalina, they'd returned to rescue the pathetic American. The Stomper's rear cargo area was fully constipated with luggage and computers and telephone equipment, but by bungee-cording two suitcases to the roof they made room for Chip and his bag.

"We'll get you to a small checkpoint," Gitanas said. "They're putting roadblocks on all the big roads. They salivate when they see Stompers."

Jonas had then driven at unsafe speeds on suitably awful roads west of Vilnius, skirting the towns of Jieznas and Alytus. The hours had passed in darkness and jostling. At no point did they see a working streetlight or a law-enforcement vehicle. Jonas and Aidaris listened to Metallica in the front seat while Gitanas pressed buttons on his cell phone in the forlorn hope that Transbaltic Wireless, of which he was still nominally the controlling shareholder, had managed to restore power to its transceiver station in the midst of a national blackout and the mobilization of Lithuania's armed forces.

"This is a calamity for Vitkunas," Gitanas said. "Mobilizing just makes him look more Soviet. Troops in the street and no electricity: this will not endear your government to the Lithuanian people."

"Is anybody actually shooting at people?" Chip asked.

"No, it's mostly posturing. A tragedy rewritten as a farce."

Toward midnight the Stomper rounded a sharp curve near Lazdijai, the last sizable town before the Polish frontier, and passed a three-Jeep convoy heading in the opposite direction. Jonas accelerated on the corduroy road and conferred with Gitanas in Lithuanian. The glacial moraine in this region was rolling but unforested. It was possible to look back and see that two of the Jeeps had turned around and commenced pursuit of the Stomper. It was likewise possible, if you were in the Jeeps, to see Jonas making a sharp left onto a gravel road and speeding alongside the whiteness of a frozen lake.

"We'll outrun 'em," Gitanas assured Chip approximately two seconds before Jonas, encountering an elbow curve, rolled the Stomper off the road.

We're having an accident, Chip thought while the vehicle was airborne. He experienced huge retroactive affection for good traction, low centers of gravity, and non-angular varieties of momentum. There was time for quiet reflection and gritting of teeth and then no time at all, just blow after blow, noise upon noise. The Stomper tried out several versions of the vertical—ninety, two-seventy, three-sixty, one-eighty—and finally came to rest on its left side with its engine dead and its lights still burning.

Chip's hips and chest felt seriously bruised by his lap and shoulder belts. Otherwise he seemed to be in one piece, as did Jonas and Aidaris.

Gitanas had been thrown around and bludgeoned by loose luggage. He was bleeding from wounds on his chin and forehead. He spoke to Jonas urgently, apparently telling him to cut the lights, but it was too late. There was a sound of great downshifting on the road behind them. The pursuing Jeeps pulled up at the elbow curve, and uniformed men in ski masks piled out.

"Police in ski masks," Chip said. "I'm struggling to put a positive construction on this."

The Stomper had crashed in a frozen-over marsh. In the intersecting high beams of two Jeeps, eight or ten masked "officers" surrounded it and ordered everybody out. Chip, pushing open the door above him, felt like a Jack emerging from its box.

Jonas and Aidaris were relieved of their weapons. The contents of the vehicle were methodically dumped on the crusty snow and broken reeds that covered the ground. A "policeman" pressed the muzzle of a rifle into Chip's cheek, and Chip received a one-word order that Gitanas translated: "He's inviting you to take your clothes off."

Death, that overseas relation, that foul-breathed remittance man, had suddenly appeared in the immediate neighborhood. Chip was quite afraid of the gun. His hands shook and lost feeling; it took the entire sum of his will to apply them to the task of unzipping and unbuttoning himself. Apparently he'd been singled out for this humiliation because of the quality of the leather goods he was wearing. Nobody seemed to care about Gitanas's red motocross jacket or Jonas's denim. But ski-masked "policemen" gathered round and fingered the fine grain of Chip's pants and coat. Puffing frost through O-shaped mouth holes with their weirdly decontexualized lips, they tested the flexure of his left boot's sole.

A cry went up when a wad of U.S. currency fell from the boot. Again the gun muzzle was in Chip's cheek. Chilly fingers discovered the big envelope of cash under his T-shirt. The "police" examined his wallet as well but didn't steal his litai or his credit cards. Dollars were all they wanted.

Gitanas, with blood congealing on several quadrants of his head, lodged a protest with the captain of the "police." The ensuing argument, in which Gitanas and the captain repeatedly gestured at Chip and used the words "dollars" and "American," ended when the captain pointed a pistol at Gitanas's bloody forehead and Gitanas raised his hands to concede that the captain had a point.

Chip's sphincter had meanwhile dilated nearly to the degree of unconditional surrender. It seemed very important to contain himself, however, and so he stood in his socks and underwear and pressed his butt cheeks together as well as he could with his shaking hands. Pressed and pressed and fought the spasms manually. He didn't care how ridiculous this looked.

The "police" were finding much to steal from the luggage. Chip's bag was emptied on the snowy ground and his belongings picked through. He and Gitanas looked on while the "police" shredded the Stomper's upholstery, tore up its floor, and located Gitanas's reserves of cash and cigarettes.

"What exactly is the pretext here?" Chip said, still shivering violently but winning the really important battle.

"We're accused of smuggling currency and tobacco," Gitanas said.

"And who's accusing us?"

"I'm afraid they're what they seem to be," Gitanas said. "In other words, national police in ski masks. There's kind of a Mardi Gras atmosphere in the country tonight. Kind of an anything-goes type of spirit."

It was 1 a.m. when the "police" finally roared away in their Jeeps. Chip and Gitanas and Jonas and Aidaris were left with frozen feet, a smashed-up Stomper, wet clothes, and demolished luggage.

On the plus side, Chip thought, I didn't shit myself.

He still had his passport and the $2,000 that the "police" had failed to locate in his T-shirt pocket. He also had gym shoes, some loose-fitting jeans, his good tweed sport coat, and his favorite sweater, all of which he hurried to put on.

"This pretty much ends my career as a criminal warlord," Gitanas commented. "I have no further ambitions in that direction."

Using cigarette lighters, Jonas and Aidaris were inspecting the Stomper's undercarriage. Aidaris delivered the verdict in English for Chip's benefit: *"Truck fucked up."*

Gitanas offered to walk with Chip to the border crossing on the road to Sejny, fifteen kilometers to the west, but Chip was painfully aware that if his friends hadn't circled back to the airport they would probably be safe now with their relatives in Ignalina, their vehicle and their cash reserves intact.

"Eh," Gitanas said with a shrug. "We might have got shot on the road to Ignalina. Maybe you saved our life."

"Truck fucked up," Aidaris repeated with spite and delight.

"So I'll see you in New York," Chip said.

Gitanas sat down on a seventeen-inch computer monitor with a stove-in screen. He carefully felt his bloody forehead. "Yeah, right. New York."

"You can stay in my apartment."

"I'll think about it."

"Let's just do it," Chip said somewhat desperately.

"I'm a Lithuanian," Gitanas said.

Chip felt more hurt, more disappointed and abandoned, than the situation called for. However, he contained himself. He accepted a road map, a cigarette lighter, an apple, and the Lithuanians' sincere good wishes and set off in the darkness.

Once he was alone, he felt better. The longer he walked, the more he appreciated the comfort of his jeans and gym shoes as hiking gear, relative to his boots and leather pants. His tread was lighter, his stride freer; he was tempted to start skipping down the road. How pleasant to be out walking in these gym shoes!

But this was not his great revelation. His great revelation came when he was a few kilometers from the Polish border. He was straining to hear whether any of the homicidal farm dogs in the surrounding darkness might be unleashed, he had his arms outstretched, he was feeling more than a little ridiculous, when he remembered Gitanas's remark: *tragedy rewritten as a farce.* All of a sudden he understood why nobody, including himself, had ever liked his screenplay: he'd written a thriller where he should have written farce.

Faint morning twilight was overtaking him. In New York he'd honed and polished the first thirty pages of "The Academy Purple" until his memory of them was nearly eidetic, and now, as the Baltic sky brightened, he bore down with a mental red pencil on his mental reconstruction of these pages, made a little trim here, added emphasis or hyperbole there, and in his mind the scenes became what they'd wanted to be all along: ridiculous. The tragic BILL QUAINTENCE became a comic fool.

Chip picked up his pace as if hurrying toward a desk at which he could begin to revise the script immediately. He came over a rise and saw the blacked-out Lithuanian town of Eisiskès and, farther in the distance, beyond the frontier, some outdoor lights in Poland. Two dray horses, straining their heads over a barbed-wire fence, nickered at him optimistically.

He spoke out loud: "Make it *ridiculous*. Make it *ridiculous*."

Two Lithuanian customs officials and two "policemen" manned the tiny border checkpoint. They handed Chip's passport back to him without the bulky stack of litai that he'd filled it with. For no discernible reason except petty cruelty, they made him sit in an overheated room for several hours while cement mixers and chicken trucks and bicyclists came and went. It was late morning before they let him walk over into Poland.

A few kilometers down the road, in Sejny, he bought zlotys and, using the zlotys, lunch. The shops were well stocked, it was Christmastime. The men of the town were old and looked a lot like the Pope.

Rides in three trucks and a city taxi got him to the Warsaw airport by noon on Wednesday. The improbably apple-cheeked personnel at the LOT Polish Airlines ticket counter were delighted to see him. LOT had added extra holiday flights to its schedule to accommodate the tens of thousands of Polish guest workers returning to their families from the West, and many of the westbound flights were underbooked. All the red-cheeked counter girls wore little hats like drum majorettes. They took cash from Chip, gave him a ticket, and told him *Run*.

He ran to the gate and boarded a 767 that then sat on the runway for four hours while a possibly faulty instrument in the cockpit was examined and finally, reluctantly, replaced.

The flight plan was a great-circle route to the great Polish city of Chicago, nonstop. Chip kept sleeping in order to forget that he owed Denise $20,500, was maxed out on his credit cards, and now had neither a job nor any prospect of finding one.

The good news in Chicago, after he'd cleared Customs, was that two rental-car companies were still doing business. The bad news, which he learned after standing in line for half an hour, was that people with maxed-out credit cards could not rent cars.

He went down the list of airlines in the phone book until he found one—Prairie Hopper, never heard of it—that had a seat on a St. Jude flight at seven the next morning.

By now it was too late to call St. Jude. He chose an out-of-the-way patch of airport carpeting and lay down on it to sleep. He didn't understand what had happened to him. He felt like a piece of paper that had once had coherent writing on it but had been through the wash. He felt roughened, bleached, and worn out along the fold lines. He semi-dreamed of disembodied eyes and isolated mouths in ski masks. He'd lost track of what he wanted, and since who a person was was what a person wanted, you could say that he'd lost track of himself.

How strange, then, that the old man who opened the front door at nine-thirty in St. Jude the next morning seemed to know exactly who he was.

A holly wreath was on the door. The front walk was edged with snow and evenly spaced broom marks. The midwestern street struck the traveler as a wonderland of wealth and oak trees and conspicuously use-less space. The traveler didn't see how such a place could exist in a world of Lithuanias and Polands. It was a testament to the insulatory effectiveness of political boundaries that power didn't simply arc across the gap between such divergent economic voltages. The old street with its oak smoke and snowy flat-topped hedges and icicled eaves seemed precarious. It seemed mirage-like. It seemed like an exceptionally vivid memory of something beloved and dead.

"Well!" Alfred said, his face blazing with joy, as he took Chip's hand in both of his. "Look who's here!"

Enid tried to elbow her way into the picture, speaking Chip's name, but Alfred wouldn't let go of his hand. He said it twice more: "Look who's here! Look who's here!"

"Al, let him come in and close the door," Enid said.

Chip was balking at the doorway. The world outside was black and white and gray and swept by fresh, clear air; the enchanted interior was dense with objects and smells and colors, humidity, large personalities. He was afraid to enter.

"Come in, come in," Enid squeaked, "and shut the door."

To protect himself from spells, he privately spoke an incantation: *I'm staying for three days and then I'm going back to New York, I'm finding a job, I'm putting aside five hundred dollars a month, minimum, until I'm out of debt, and I'm working every night on the script.*

Invoking this charm, which was all he had now, the paltry sum of his identity, he stepped through the doorway.

"My word, you're scratchy and smelly," Enid said, kissing him. "Now, where's your suitcase?"

"It's by the side of a gravel road in western Lithuania."

"I'm just happy you're home safely."

Nowhere in the nation of Lithuania was there a room like the Lambert living room. Only in this hemisphere could carpeting so sumptuously woolen and furniture so big and so well made and so opulently upholstered be found in a room of such plain design and ordinary situation. The light in the wood-framed windows, though gray, had a prairie optimism; there wasn't a sea within six hundred miles to trouble the atmosphere. And the posture of the older oak trees reaching toward this sky had a jut, a wildness and entitlement, predating permanent settlement; memories of an unfenced world were written in the cursive of their branches.

Chip apprehended it all in a heartbeat. The continent, his homeland. Scattered around the living room were nests of opened presents and little leavings of spent ribbon, wrapping-paper fragments, labels. At the foot of the fireside chair that Alfred always claimed for himself, Denise was kneeling by the largest nest of presents.

"Denise, look who's here," Enid said.

As if out of obligation, with downcast eyes, Denise rose and crossed the room. But when she'd put her arms around Chip and he'd squeezed her in return (her height, as always, surprised him), she wouldn't let go. She *clung* to him—kissed his neck, fastened her eyes on him, and thanked him.

Gary came over and embraced Chip awkwardly, his face averted. "Didn't think you were going to make it," he said.

"Neither did I," Chip said.

"Well!" Alfred said again, gazing at him in wonder.

"Gary has to leave at eleven," Enid said, "but we can all have breakfast together. You get cleaned up, and Denise and I will start breakfast. Oh, this is *just* what I wanted," she said, hurrying to the kitchen. "This is the best Christmas present I've ever had!"

Gary turned to Chip with his I'm-a-jerk face. "There you go," he said. "Best Christmas present she's ever had."

"I think she means having all five of us together," Denise said.

"Well, she'd better enjoy it in a hurry," Gary said, "because she owes me a discussion and I'm expecting payment."

Chip, detached from his own body, trailed after it and wondered what it was going to do. He removed an aluminum stool from the downstairs bathroom shower. The blast of water was strong and hot. His impressions were fresh in a way that he would either remember all his life or instantly forget. A brain could absorb only so many impressions before it lost the ability to decode them, to put them in coherent shape and order. His nearly sleepless night on a patch of airport carpeting, for example, was still very much with him and begging to be processed. And now here was a hot shower on Christmas morning. Here were the familiar tan tiles of the stall. The tiles, like every other physical constituent of the house, were suffused with the fact of their ownership by Enid and Alfred, saturated with an aura of belonging to this family. The house felt more like a body—softer, more mortal and organic—than like a building.

Denise's shampoo had the pleasing, subtle scents of late-model Western capitalism. In the seconds it took Chip to lather his hair, he forgot where he was. Forgot the continent, forgot the year, forgot the time of day, forgot the circumstances. His brain in the shower was piscine or amphibian, registering impressions, reacting to the moment. He wasn't far from terror. At the same time, he felt OK. He was hungry for breakfast and thirsty, in particular, for coffee.

With a towel around his waist he stopped in the living room, where Alfred leaped to his feet. The sight of Alfred's suddenly aged face, its disintegration-in-progress, its rednesses and asymmetries, cut Chip like a bullwhip.

"Well!" Alfred said. "That was quick."

"Can I borrow some clothes of yours?"

"I will leave that to your judgment."

Upstairs in his father's closet the ancient shaving kits, shoehorns, electric razors, shoe trees, and tie rack were all in their accustomed places. They'd been on duty here each hour of the fifteen hundred days since Chip had last been in this house. For a moment he was angry (how could he not be?) that his parents had never moved anywhere. Had simply stayed here waiting.

He took underwear, socks, wool slacks, a white shirt, and a gray cardigan to the room that he'd shared with Gary in the years between Denise's arrival in the family and Gary's departure for college. Gary had an overnight bag open on "his" twin bed and was packing it.

"I don't know if you noticed," he said, "but Dad's in bad shape."

"No, I noticed."

Gary put a small box on Chip's dresser. It was a box of ammunition—twenty-gauge shotgun shells.

"He had these out with the gun in the workshop," Gary said. "I went down there this morning and I thought, better safe than sorry."

Chip looked at the box and spoke instinctively. "Isn't that kind of Dad's own decision?"

"That's what I was thinking yesterday," Gary said. "But if he wants to do it, he's got other options. It's supposed to be down near zero tonight. He can go outside with a bottle of whiskey. I don't want Mom to find him with his head blown off."

Chip didn't know what to say. He silently dressed in the old man's clothes. The shirt and pants were marvelously clean and fit him better than he would have guessed. He was surprised, when he put the cardigan on, that his hands did not begin to shake, surprised to see such a young face in the mirror.

"So what have you been doing with yourself?" Gary said.

"I've been helping a Lithuanian friend of mine defraud Western investors."

"Jesus, Chip. You don't want to be doing that."

Everything else in the world might be strange, but Gary's condescension galled Chip exactly as it always had.

"From a strictly moral viewpoint," Chip said, "I have more sympathy for Lithuania than I do for American investors."

"You want to be a Bolshevik?" Gary said, zipping up his bag. "Fine, be a Bolshevik. Just don't call *me* when you get arrested."

"It would never occur to me to call you," Chip said.

"Are you fellas about ready for breakfast?" Enid sang from halfway up the stairs.

A holiday linen tablecloth was on the dining table. In the center was an arrangement of pinecones, white holly and green holly, red candles, and silver bells. Denise was bringing food out—Texan grapefruit, scrambled eggs, bacon, and a stollen and breads that she'd baked.

Snow cover boosted the strong prairie light.

Per custom, Gary sat alone on one side of the table. On the other side, Denise sat by Enid and Chip by Alfred.

"Merry, merry, merry Christmas!" Enid said, looking each of her children in the eye in turn.

Alfred, head down, was already eating.

Gary also began to eat, rapidly, with a glance at his watch.

Chip didn't remember the coffee being so drinkable in these parts.

Denise asked him how he'd gotten home. He told her the story, omitting only the armed robbery.

Enid, with a scowl of judgment, was following every move of Gary's. "Slow *down*," she said. "You don't have to leave until eleven."

"Actually," Gary said, "I said quarter to eleven. It's past ten-thirty, and we have some things to discuss."

"We're finally all together," Enid said. "Let's just relax and enjoy it."

Gary set his fork down. "*I've* been here since Monday, Mother, waiting for us all to be together. Denise has been here since Tuesday morning. It's not my fault if Chip was too busy defrauding American investors to get here on time."

"I just explained why I was late," Chip said. "If you were listening."

"Well, maybe you should have left a little earlier."

"What does he mean, defrauding?" Enid said. "I thought you were doing computer work."

"I'll explain it to you later, Mom."

"No," Gary said. "Explain it to her now."

"Gary," Denise said.

"No, sorry," Gary said, throwing down his napkin like a gauntlet. "I've had it with this family! I'm done waiting! I want some answers *now*."

"I was doing computer work," Chip said. "But Gary's right, strictly speaking, the intent was to defraud American investors."

"I don't approve of that at all," Enid said.

"I know you don't," Chip said. "Although it's a little more complicated than you might—"

"What is so complicated about obeying the law?"

"Gary, for God's sake," Denise said with a sigh. "It's Christmas?"

"And you're a thief," Gary said, wheeling on her.

"What?"

"You know what I'm talking about. You sneaked into somebody's room and you took a thing that didn't belong—"

"Excuse me," Denise said hotly, "I *restored* a thing that was stolen from its rightful—"

"Bullshit, bullshit, bullshit!"

"Oh, I'm not sitting here for this," Enid wailed. "Not on Christmas morning!"

"No, Mother, sorry, you're not going anywhere," Gary said. "We're going to sit here and have our little talk *right now*."

Alfred gave Chip a complicit smile and gestured at the others. "You see what I have to put up with?"

Chip arranged his face in a facsimile of comprehension and agreement.

"Chip, how long are you here for?" Gary said.

"Three days."

"And, Denise, you're leaving on—"

"Sunday, Gary. I'm leaving on Sunday."

"So what's going to happen on Monday, Mom? How are you going to make this house work on Monday?"

"I'll think about that when Monday comes."

Alfred, still smiling, asked Chip what Gary was talking about.

"I don't know, Dad."

"You really think you're going to go to Philadelphia?" Gary said. "You think Corecktall's going to fix all this?"

"No, Gary, I don't," Enid said.

Gary didn't seem to hear her answer. "Dad, here, do me a favor," he said. "Put your right hand on your left shoulder."

"Gary, stop it," Denise said.

Alfred leaned close to Chip and spoke confidentially. "What's he asking?"

"He wants you to put your right hand on your left shoulder."

"That's a lot of nonsense."

"Dad?" Gary said. "Come on, right hand, left shoulder."

"*Stop it,*" Denise said.

"Let's go, Dad. Right hand, left shoulder. Can you do that? You want to show us how you follow simple instructions? Come on! *Right hand. Left shoulder.*"

Alfred shook his head. "One bedroom and a kitchen is all we need."

"Al, I don't *want* one bedroom and a kitchen," Enid said.

The old man pushed his chair away from the table and turned once more to Chip. He said, "You can see it's not without its difficulties."

As he stood up, his leg buckled and he pitched to the floor, dragging his plate and place mat and coffee cup and saucer along with him. The crash might have been the last bar of a symphony. He lay on his side amid the ruins like a wounded gladiator, a fallen horse.

Chip knelt down and helped him into a sitting position while Denise hurried to the kitchen.

"It's quarter to eleven," Gary said as if nothing unusual had happened. "Before I leave, here's a summary. Dad is demented and incontinent. Mom can't have him in this house without a lot of help, which she says she doesn't want even if she could afford it. Corecktall is obviously not an option, and so what I want to know is what you're going to do. *Now*, Mother. I want to know *now*."

Alfred rested his shaking hands on Chip's shoulders and gazed in wonder at the room's furnishings. Despite his agitation, he was smiling.

"My question," he said. "Is who owns this house? Who takes care of all of this?"

"You own it, Dad."

Alfred shook his head as if this didn't square with the facts as he understood them.

Gary was demanding an answer.

"I guess we'll have to try the drug holiday," Enid said.

"Fine, try that," Gary said. "Put him in the hospital, see if they ever let him out. And while you're at it, you might take a drug holiday yourself."

"Gary, she got rid of it," Denise said from the floor, where she'd knelt with a sponge. "She put it in the Disposall. So just lay off."

"Well, I hope you learned your lesson there, Mother."

Chip, in the old man's clothes, wasn't able to follow this conversation. His father's hands were heavy on his shoulders. For the second time in an hour, somebody was *clinging* to him, as if he were a person of substance, as if there were something to him. In fact, there was so little to him that he couldn't even say whether his sister and his father were mistaken about him. He felt as if his consciousness had been shorn of all identifying marks and transplanted, metempsychotically, into the body of a steady son, a trustworthy brother . . .

Gary had dropped into a crouch beside Alfred. "Dad," he said, "I'm sorry it had to end this way. I love you and I'll see you again soon."

"Well. Yurrr vollb. Yeaugh," Alfred replied. He lowered his head and looked around with rank paranoia.

"And *you*, my feckless sibling." Gary spread his fingers, clawlike, on top of Chip's head in what he apparently meant as a gesture of affection. "I'm counting on you to help out here."

"I'll do my best," Chip said with less irony than he'd aimed for.

Gary stood up. "I'm sorry I ruined your breakfast, Mom. But I, for one, feel better for having got this off my chest."

"Why you couldn't have waited till after the holiday," Enid muttered.

Gary kissed her cheek. "Call Hedgpeth tomorrow morning. Then call me and tell me what the plan is. I'm going to monitor this closely."

It seemed unbelievable to Chip that Gary could simply walk out of the house with Alfred on the floor and Enid's Christmas breakfast in ruins, but Gary was in his most rational mode, his words had a formal hollowness, his eyes were evasive as he put on his coat and gathered up his bag and Enid's bag of gifts for Philadelphia, because he was afraid. Chip could see it clearly now, behind the cold front of Gary's wordless departure: his brother was afraid.

As soon as the front door had closed, Alfred made his way to the bathroom.

"Let's all be happy," Denise said, "that Gary got that off his chest and feels so much better now."

"No, he's right," Enid said, her eyes resting bleakly on the holly centerpiece. "Something has to change."

After breakfast the hours passed in the sickishness, the invalid waiting, of a major holiday. Chip in his exhaustion had trouble staying warm, but his face was flushed with the heat from the kitchen and the smell of baking turkey that blanketed the house. Whenever he entered his father's field of vision, a smile of recognition and pleasure spread over Alfred's face. This recognition might have had the character of mistaken identity if it hadn't been accompanied by Alfred's exclamation of Chip's name. Chip seemed *beloved* to the old man. He'd been arguing with Alfred and deploring Alfred and feeling the sting of Alfred's disapproval for most of his life, and his personal failures and his political views were, if anything, more extreme than ever now, and yet it was Gary who was fighting with the old man, it was Chip who brightened the old man's face.

At dinner he took the trouble to describe in some detail his activities in Lithuania. He might as well have been reciting the tax code in a monotone. Denise, normally a paragon of listening, was absorbed in helping Alfred with his food, and Enid had eyes only for her husband's deficiencies. She flinched or sighed or shook her head at every spilled bite, every non sequitur. Alfred was quite visibly making her life a hell now.

I'm the least unhappy person at this table, Chip thought.

He helped Denise wash the dishes while Enid spoke to her grand-sons on the telephone and Alfred went to bed.

"How long has Dad been like this?" he asked Denise.

"Like this? Just since yesterday. But he wasn't great before that."

Chip put on a heavy coat of Alfred's and took a cigarette outside. The cold was deeper than any he'd experienced in Vilnius. Wind rattled the thick brown leaves still clinging to the oaks, those most conservative of trees; snow squeaked beneath his feet. *Near zero tonight*, Gary had said. *He can go outside with a bottle of whiskey.* Chip wanted to pursue the important question of suicide while he had a cigarette to enhance his mental performance, but his bronchi and nasal passages were so trau-matized by cold that the trauma of smoke barely registered, and the ache in his fingers and ears—the damned rivets—was fast becoming un-bearable. He gave up and hurried inside just as Denise was leaving.

"Where are you going?" Chip asked.

"I'll be back."

Enid, by the fire in the living room, was gnawing at her lip with naked desolation. "You haven't opened your presents," she said.

"Maybe in the morning," Chip said.

"I'm sure I didn't get you anything you'll like."

"It's nice you got me anything."

Enid shook her head. "This wasn't the Christmas I'd hoped for. Suddenly Dad can't do a thing. Not one single thing."

"Let's give him a drug holiday and see if that helps."

Enid might have been reading bad prognoses in the fire. "Will you stay for a week and help me take him to the hospital?"

Chip's hand went to the rivet in his earlobe as to a talisman. He felt like a child out of Grimm, lured into the enchanted house by the warmth and the food; and now the witch was going to lock him in a cage, fatten him up, and eat him.

He repeated the charm he'd invoked at the front door. "I can only stay three days," he said. "I've got to start working right away. I owe Denise some money that I need to pay her back."

"Just a *week*," the witch said. "Just a week, until we see how things go in the hospital."

"I don't think so, Mom. I've got to go back."

Enid's bleakness deepened, but she didn't seem surprised by his refusal. "I guess this is my responsibility, then," she said. "I guess I always knew it would be."

She retired to the den, and Chip put more logs on the fire. Cold drafts were finding ways through the windows, faintly stirring the open curtains. The furnace was running almost constantly. The world was colder and emptier than Chip had realized, the adults had gone away.

Toward eleven, Denise came inside reeking of cigarettes and looking two-thirds frozen. She waved to Chip and tried to go straight upstairs, but he insisted that she sit by the fire. She knelt and bowed her head, sniffling steadily, and put her hands out toward the embers. She kept her eyes on the fire as if to ensure that she not look at him. She blew her nose on a wet shred of Kleenex.

"Where'd you go?" he said.

"Just on a walk."

"Long walk."

"Yuh."

"You sent me some e-mails that I deleted before I really read them."

"Oh."

"So what's going on?" he said.

She shook her head. "Just everything."

"I had almost thirty thousand dollars in cash on Monday. I was going to give you twenty-four thousand of it. But then we got robbed by uniformed men in ski masks. Implausible as that may sound."

"I want to forgive that debt," Denise said.

Chip's hand went to the rivet again. "I'm going to start paying you a minimum of four hundred a month until the principal and interest are paid off. It's my top priority. Absolute highest priority."

His sister turned and raised her face to him. Her eyes were bloodshot, her forehead as red as a newborn's. "I said I forgive the debt. You owe me nothing."

"Appreciate it," he said quickly, looking away. "But I'm going to pay you anyway."

"No," she said. "I'm not going to take your money. I forgive the debt. Do you know what 'forgive' means?"

In her peculiar mood, with her unexpected words, she was making Chip anxious. He pulled on the rivet and said, "Denise, come on. Please. At least show me the respect of letting me pay you back. I realize I've been a shit. But I don't want to be a shit all my life."

"I want to forgive that debt," she said.

"Really. Come on." Chip smiled desperately. "You've got to let me pay you."

"Can you stand to be forgiven?"

"No," he said. "Basically, no. I can't. It's better all around if I pay you."

Still kneeling, Denise bent over and tucked in her arms and made herself into an olive, an egg, an onion. From within this balled form came a low voice. "Do you understand what a huge favor you'd be doing me if you would let me forgive the debt? Do you understand that it's hard for me to ask this favor? Do you understand that coming here for Christmas is the only other favor I've ever asked you? Do you understand that I'm not trying to insult you? Do you understand that I never doubted that you wanted to pay me back, and I know I'm asking you to do something very hard? Do you understand that I wouldn't ask you to do something so hard if I didn't really, really, really need it?"

Chip looked at the trembling balled human form at his feet. "Tell me what's wrong."

"I'm having trouble on numerous fronts," she said.

"This is a bad time to talk about the money, then. Let's forget it for a while. I want to hear what's bothering you."

Still balled up, Denise shook her head emphatically, once. "I need you to say yes here, now. Say 'Yes, thank you.'"

Chip made a gesture of utter bafflement. It was near midnight and his father had begun to thump around upstairs and his sister was curled up like an egg and begging him to accept relief from the principal torment of his life.

"Let's talk about it tomorrow," he said.

"Would it help if I asked you for something else?"

"Tomorrow, OK?"

"Mom wants somebody here next week," Denise said. "You could stay a week and help her. That would be a huge relief for me. I'm going to die if I stay past Sunday. I will literally cease to exist."

Chip was breathing hard. The door of the cage was closing on him fast. The sensation he'd had in the men's room at the Vilnius Airport, the feeling that his debt to Denise, far from being a burden, was his last defense, returned to him in the form of dread at the prospect of its being forgiven. He'd lived with the affliction of this debt until it had assumed the character of a neuroblastoma so intricately implicated in his cerebral architecture that he doubted he could survive its removal.

He wondered if the last flights east had left the airport or whether he might still escape tonight.

"How about we split the debt in half?" he said. "So I only owe you ten. How about we both stay here till Wednesday?"

"Nope."

"If I said yes," he said, "would you stop being so weird and lighten up a little?"

"First say yes."

Alfred was calling Chip's name from upstairs. He was saying, "Chip, can you help me?"

"He calls your name even when you're not here," Denise said.

The windows shook in the wind. When had it happened that his parents had become the children who went to bed early and called down for help from the top of the stairs? When had this happened?

"Chip," Alfred called. "I don't understand this blanket. CAN YOU HELP ME?"

The house shook and the storms rattled and the draft from the window nearest Chip intensified; and in a gust of memory he remembered the curtains. He remembered when he'd left St. Jude for college. He remembered packing the hand-carved Austrian chessmen that his parents had given him for his high-school graduation, and the six-volume Sandburg biography of Lincoln that they'd given him for his eighteenth birthday, and his new navy-blue blazer from Brooks Brothers ("It makes you look like a handsome young doctor!" Enid hinted), and great stacks of white T-shirts and white jockey underpants and white long johns, and a fifth-grade school picture of Denise in a Lucite frame, and the very same Hudson Bay blanket that Alfred had taken as a freshman to the University of Kansas four decades earlier, and a pair of leather-clad wool mittens that likewise dated from Alfred's deep Kansan past, and a set of heavy-duty thermal curtains that Alfred had bought for him at Sears. Reading Chip's college orientation materials, Alfred had been struck by the sentence *New England winters can be very cold*. The curtains he'd bought at Sears were of a plasticized brown-and-pink fabric with a backing of foam rubber. They were heavy and bulky and stiff. "You'll appreciate these on a cold night," he told Chip. "You'll be surprised how much they cut down drafts." But Chip's freshman roommate was a prep-school product named Roan McCorkle who would soon be leaving thumbprints, in what appeared to be Vaseline, on the fifth-grade photo of Denise. Roan laughed at the curtains and Chip laughed, too. He put them back in the box and stowed the box in the basement of the dorm and let it gather mold there for the next four years. He had nothing against the curtains personally. They were simply curtains and they wanted no more than what any curtains wanted—to hang well, to exclude light to the best of their ability, to be neither too small nor too large for the window that it was their task in life to cover; to be pulled this way in the evening and that way in the morning; to stir in the breezes that came before rain on a summer night; to be much used and little noticed. There were numberless hospitals and retirement homes and budget motels, not just in the Midwest but in the East as well, where these particular brown rubber-backed curtains could have had a long and useful life. It wasn't their fault that they didn't belong in a dorm room. They'd betrayed no urge to rise above their station; their material and patterning contained not a hint of unseemly ambition. They were what they were. If anything, when he finally dug them out on the eve of graduation, their virginal pinkish folds turned out to be rather *less* plasticized and homely and Sears-like than he remembered. They were nowhere near as shameful as he'd thought.

"I don't understand these blankets," Alfred said.

"All right," Chip told Denise as he started up the stairs. "If it makes you feel better, I won't pay you back."

The question was: How to get out of this prison?

The big black lady, the mean one, the bastard, was the one he had to keep an eye on. She intended to make his life a hell. She stood at the far end of the prison yard throwing him significant glances to remind him that she hadn't forgotten him, she was still in hot pursuit of her vendetta. She was a lazy black bastard and he said so at a shout. He cursed the bastards, black and white, all around him. Goddamned sneaky bastards with their pinheaded regulations. EPA bureaucrats, OSHA functionaries, insolent so-and-sos. They were keeping their distance now, sure, because they knew he was onto them, but just let him nod off for one minute, just let him let his guard down, and watch what they would do to him. They could hardly wait to tell him he was nothing. They could hardly wait to show their disrespect. That fat black bastard, that nasty black bitch over there, held his eye and nodded across the white heads of the other prisoners: *I'm gonna get you.* That's what her nod said to him. And nobody else could see what she was doing to him. All the rest were timid useless strangers talking nonsense. He'd said hello to one of the fellows, asked him a simple question. The fellow didn't even understand English. It ought to have been simple enough, ask a simple question, get a simple answer, but evidently not. He was on his own now, he was by himself in a corner; and the bastards were out to get him.

He didn't understand where Chip was. Chip was an intellectual and had ways of talking sense to these people. Chip had done a good job yesterday, better than he could have done himself. Asked a simple question, got a simple answer, and then explained it in a way that a man could understand. But there was no sign of Chip now. Inmates semaphoring one another, waving their arms like traffic cops. Just try giving a simple order to these people, just try it. They pretended you didn't exist. That fat bastard black woman had them all scared witless. If she figured out that the prisoners were on his side, if she found out they'd aided him in any way, she'd make them pay. Oh, she had that look. She had that *I'm gonna make you hurt* look. And he, at this point in his life, he'd had just about enough of this insolent black type of woman, but what could you do? It was a prison. It was a public institution. They'd throw anybody in here. White-haired women semaphoring. Hairless fairies touching toes. But why *him*, for God's sake? Why *him*? It made him weep to be thrown into a place like this. It was hell to get old even without being persecuted by that waddling black so-and-so.

And here she came again.

"Alfred?" Sassy. Insolent. "You gonna let me stretch your legs now?"

"You're a goddamned bastard!" he told her.

"I is what I is, Alfred. But I know who my parents are. Now why don't you put your hands down, nice and easy, and let me stretch your legs and help you feel better."

He lunged as she came at him, but his belt had got stuck in the chair, in the chair somehow, in the chair. Got stuck in the chair and he couldn't move.

"You keep that up, Alfred," the mean one said, "and we're gonna have to take you back to your room."

"Bastard! Bastard! Bastard!"

She pulled an insolent face and went away, but he knew that she'd be back. They always came back. His only hope was to get his belt free of the chair somehow. Get himself free, make a dash, put an end to it. Bad design to build a prison yard this many stories up. A man could see clear to Illinois. Big window right there. Bad design if they meant to house prisoners here. From the look of the glass it was thermal pane, two layers. If he hit it with his head and pitched forward he could make it. But first he had to get the goddamned belt free.

He struggled with its smooth nylon breadth in the same way over and over. There was a time when he'd encountered obstacles philosophically but that time was past. His fingers were as weak as grass when he tried to work them under the belt so he could pull on it. They bent like soft bananas. Trying to work them under the belt was so *obviously and utterly hopeless*—the belt had such overwhelming advantages of toughness and tightness—that his efforts soon became merely a pageant of spite and rage and incapacity. He caught his fingernails on the belt and then *flung* his arms apart, letting his hands bang into the arms of his captivating chair and painfully ricochet this way and that way, because he was so goddamned angry—

"Dad, Dad, Dad, whoa, calm down," the voice said.

"Get that bastard! Get that bastard!"

"Dad, whoa, it's me. It's Chip."

Indeed, the voice was familiar. He looked up at Chip carefully to make sure the speaker really was his middle child, because the bastards would try to take advantage of you any way they could. Indeed, if the speaker had been anybody in the world but Chip, it wouldn't have paid to trust him. Too risky. But there was something in Chipper that the bastards couldn't fake. You looked at Chipper and you knew he'd never lie to you. There was a sweetness to Chipper that nobody else could counterfeit.

As his identification of Chipper deepened toward certainty, his breathing leveled out and something like a smile pushed through the other, warring forces in his face.

"Well!" he said finally.

Chip pulled another chair over and gave him a cup of ice water for which, he realized, he was thirsty. He took a long pull on the straw and gave the water back to Chip.

"Where's your mother?"

Chip set the cup on the floor. "She woke up with a cold. I told her to stay in bed."

"Where's she living now?"

"She's at home. Exactly where she was two days ago."

Chip had already explained to him why he had to be here, and the explanation had made sense as long as he could see Chip's face and hear his voice, but as soon as Chip was gone the explanation fell apart.

The big black bastard was circling the two of them with her evil eye.

"This is a physical-therapy room," Chip said. "We're on the eighth floor of St. Luke's. Mom had her foot operation here, if you remember that."

"That woman is a bastard," he said, pointing.

"No, she's a physical therapist," Chip said, "and she's been trying to help you."

"No, look at her. Do you see the way she's? Do you see it?"

"She's a physical therapist, Dad."

"The what? She's a?"

On the one hand, he trusted the intelligence and assurance of his intellectual son. On the other hand, the black bastard was giving him the Eye to warn him of the harm she intended to do him at her earliest opportunity; there was a grand malevolence to her manner, plain as day. He couldn't begin to reconcile this contradiction: his belief that Chip was absolutely right and his conviction that that bastard absolutely wasn't any physicist.

The contradiction opened into a bottomless chasm. He stared into its depths, his mouth hanging open. A warm thing was crawling down his chin.

And now some bastard's hand was reaching for him. He tried to slug the bastard and realized, in the nick of time, that the hand belonged to Chip.

"Easy, Dad. I'm just wiping your chin."

"Ah God."

"Do you want to sit here a little, or do you want to go back to your room?"

"I leave it to your discretion."

This handy phrase came to him all ready to be spoken, neat as you please.

"Let's go back, then." Chip reached behind the chair and made adjustments. Evidently the chair had casters and levers of enormous complexity.

"See if you can get my belt unhooked," he said.

"We'll go back to the room, and then you can walk around."

Chip wheeled him out of the yard and up the cellblock to his cell.

He couldn't get over how luxurious the appointments were. Like a first-class hotel room except for the bars on the bed and the shackles and the radios, the prisoner-control equipment.

Chip parked him near the window, left the room with a Styrofoam pitcher, and returned a few minutes later in the company of a pretty little girl in a white jacket.

"Mr. Lambert?" she said. She was pretty like Denise, with curly black hair and wire glasses, but smaller. "I'm Dr. Schulman. You may remember we met yesterday."

"Well!" he said, smiling wide. He remembered a world where there were girls like this, pretty little girls with bright eyes and smart brows, a world of hope.

She placed a hand on his head and bent down as if to kiss him. She scared the hell out of him. He almost hit her.

"I didn't mean to scare you," she said. "I just want to look in your eye. Is that all right with you?"

He turned to Chip for reassurance, but Chip himself was staring at the girl.

"Chip!" he said.

Chip took his eyes off her. "Yeah, Dad?"

Well, now that he'd attracted Chip's attention, he had to say something, and what he said was this: "Tell your mother not to worry about the mess down there. I'll take care of all that."

"OK. I'll tell her."

The girl's clever fingers and soft face were all around his head. She asked him to make a fist, she pinched him and prodded him. She was talking like the television in somebody else's room.

"Dad?" Chip said.

"I didn't hear."

"Dr. Schulman wants to know if you'd prefer 'Alfred' or 'Mr. Lambert.' What would you rather she called you?"

He grinned painfully. "I'm not following."

"I think he prefers 'Mr. Lambert,' " Chip said.

"Mr. Lambert," said the little girl, "can you tell me where we are?"

He turned again to Chip, whose expression was expectant but unhelpful. He pointed toward the window. "That's Illinois in that direction," he said to his son and to the girl. Both were listening with great interest now, and he felt he should say more. "There's a window," he said, "which . . . if you get it open . . . would be what I want. I couldn't get the belt undone. And then."

He was failing and he knew it.

The little girl looked down on him kindly. "Can you tell me who our President is?"

He grinned, it was an easy one.

"Well," he said. "She's got so much stuff down there. I doubt she'd even notice. We ought to pitch the whole lot of it."

The little girl nodded as if this were a reasonable answer. Then she held up both her hands. She was pretty like Enid, but Enid had a wedding ring, Enid didn't wear glasses, Enid had lately gotten older, and he probably would have recognized Enid, although, being far more familiar to him than Chip, she was that much harder to see.

"How many fingers am I holding up?" the girl asked him.

He considered her fingers. As far as he could tell, the message they were sending was Relax. Unclench. Take it easy.

With a smile he let his bladder empty.

"Mr. Lambert? How many fingers am I holding up?"

The fingers were there. It was a beautiful thing. The relief of irresponsibility. The less he knew, the happier he was. To know nothing at all would be heaven.

"Dad?"

"I should know that," he said. "Can you believe I'd forget a thing like that?"

The little girl and Chip exchanged a look and then went out into the corridor.

He'd enjoyed unclenching, but after a minute or two he felt clammy. He needed to change his clothes now and he couldn't. He sat in his mess as it chilled.

"Chip?" he said.

A stillness had fallen on the cellblock. He couldn't rely on Chip, he was always disappearing. He couldn't rely on anybody but himself.

With no plan in his head and no power in his hands he attempted to loosen the belt so he could take his pants off and dry himself. But the belt was as maddening as ever. Twenty times he ran his hands along its length and twenty times he failed to find a buckle. He was like a person of two dimensions seeking freedom in a third. He could search for all eternity and never find the goddamned buckle.

"Chip!" he called, but not loudly, because the black bastard was lurking out there, and she would punish him severely. "Chip, come and help me."

He would have liked to remove his legs entirely. They were weak and restless and wet and trapped. He kicked a little and rocked in his unrocking chair. His hands were in a tumult. The less he could do about his legs, the more he swung his arms. The bastards had him now, he'd been betrayed, and he began to cry. If only he'd known! If only he'd known, he could have taken steps, he'd had the gun, he'd had the bottomless cold ocean, if only he'd known.

He swatted a pitcher of water against the wall, and finally somebody came running.

"Dad, Dad, Dad. What's wrong?"

Alfred looked up at his son and into his eyes. He opened his mouth, but the only word he could produce was "I—"

I—

I have made mistakes—

I am alone—

I am wet—

I want to die—

I am sorry—

I did my best—

I love my children—

I need your help—

I want to die—

"I can't be here," he said.

Chip crouched on the floor by the chair. "Listen," he said. "You have to stay here another week so they can monitor you. We need to find out what's wrong."

He shook his head. "No! You have to get me out of here!"

"Dad, I'm sorry," Chip said, "but I can't take you home. You have to stay here for another week at least."

Oh, how his son tried his patience! By now Chip should have understood what he was asking for without being told again.

"I'm saying put an end to it!" He banged on the arms of his captivating chair. "You have to help me put an end to it!"

He looked at the window through which he was ready, at last, to throw himself. Or give him a gun, give him an ax, give him anything, but get him out of here. He had to make Chip understand this.

Chip covered his shaking hands with his own.

"I'll stay with you, Dad," he said. "But I can't do that for you. I can't put an end to it like that. I'm sorry."

Like a wife who had died or a house that had burned, the clarity to think and the power to act were still vivid in his memory. Through a window that gave onto the next world, he could still see the clarity and see the power, just out of reach, beyond the window's thermal panes. He could see the desired outcomes, the drowning at sea, the shotgun blast, the plunge from a height, so near to him still that he refused to believe he'd lost the opportunity to avail himself of their relief.

He wept at the injustice of his sentence. "For God's sake, Chip," he said loudly, because he sensed that this might be his last chance to liberate himself before he lost all contact with that clarity and power and it was therefore crucial that Chip understand *exactly* what he wanted. "I'm asking for your help! You've got to get me out of this! You have to put an end to it!"

Even red-eyed, even tear-streaked, Chip's face was full of power and clarity. Here was a son whom he could trust to understand him as he understood himself; and so Chip's answer, when it came, was absolute. Chip's answer told him that this was where the story ended. It ended with Chip shaking his head, it ended with him saying: "I can't, Dad. I can't."

THE
CORRECTIONS

THE CORRECTION, when it finally came, was not an overnight bursting of a bubble but a much more gentle letdown, a year-long leakage of value from key financial markets, a contraction too gradual to generate headlines and too predictable to seriously hurt anybody but fools and the working poor.

It seemed to Enid that current events in general were more muted or insipid nowadays than they'd been in her youth. She had memories of the 1930s, she'd seen firsthand what could happen to a country when the world economy took its gloves off; she'd helped her mother pass out leftovers to homeless men in the alley behind their roominghouse. But disasters of this magnitude no longer seemed to befall the United States. Safety features had been put in place, like the squares of rubber that every modern playground was paved with, to soften impacts.

Nevertheless, the markets did collapse, and Enid, who hadn't dreamed that she would ever be *glad* that Alfred had locked their assets up in annuities and T-bills, weathered the downturn with less anxiety than her high-flying friends. Orfic Midland did, as threatened, terminate her traditional health insurance and force her into an HMO, but her old neighbor Dean Driblett, with the stroke of a pen, bless his heart, upgraded her and Alfred to DeeDeeCare Choice Plus, which allowed her to keep her favorite doctors. She still had major non-reimbursable monthly nursing-home expenses, but by scrimping she was able to pay the bills with Alfred's pension and Railroad Retirement benefits, and meanwhile her house, which she owned outright, continued to appreciate. The simple truth was that, although she wasn't rich, she also wasn't poor. Somehow this truth had eluded her during the years of her anxiety and uncertainty about Alfred, but as soon as he was out of the house and she'd caught up on her sleep, she saw it clearly.

She saw everything more clearly now, her children in particular.

When Gary returned to St. Jude with Jonah a few months after the catastrophic Christmas, she had nothing but fun with them. Gary still wanted her to sell the house, but he could no longer argue that Alfred was going to fall down the stairs and kill himself, and by then Chip had done many of the jobs (wicker-painting, waterproofing, gutter-cleaning, crack-patching) which, as long as they'd been neglected, had been Gary's other good argument for selling the house. He and Enid did bicker about money, but this was recreational. Gary hounded her for the $4.96 that she still "owed" him for six six-inch bolts, and she countered by asking, "Is that a new watch?" He conceded that, yes, Caroline had given him a new Rolex for Christmas, but more recently he'd taken a nasty little bath on a biotech IPO whose shares he couldn't sell before June 15, and anyway, there was a principle at stake here, Mother, a principle. But Enid refused, on principle, to give him the $4.96. She enjoyed knowing that she would go to her grave refusing to pay for those six bolts. She asked Gary which biotech stock, exactly, he'd taken the bath on. Gary said never mind.

After Christmas Denise moved to Brooklyn and went to work at a new restaurant, and in April she sent Enid a plane ticket for her birthday. Enid thanked her and said she couldn't make the trip, she couldn't possibly leave Alfred, it would not be right. Then she went and enjoyed four wonderful days in New York City. Denise looked so much happier than she had at Christmas that Enid chose not to care that she still didn't have a man in her life or any discernible desire to get one.

Back in St. Jude, Enid was playing bridge at Mary Beth Schumpert's one afternoon when Bea Meisner began to vent her Christian disapproval of a famous "gay" actress.

"She's a *terrible* role model for young people," Bea said. "I think if you make an evil choice in your life, the least you can do is not brag about it. Especially when they have all these new programs that can help people like that."

Enid, who was Bea's partner for that rubber and was already annoyed by Bea's failure to respond to an opening two-bid, mildly commented that she didn't think "gays" could help being "gay."

"Oh, no, it's definitely a choice," Bea said. "It's a weakness and it starts in adolescence. There's no question about that. All the experts agree."

"I loved that thriller her girlfriend made with Harrison Ford," Mary Beth Schumpert said. "What was it called?"

"I don't believe it's a choice," Enid insisted quietly. "Chip said an interesting thing to me once. He said that with so many people hating 'gays' and disapproving of them, why would anybody choose to be 'gay' if they could help it? I thought that was really an interesting perspective."

"Well, no, it's because they want special rights," Bea said. "It's because they want to have 'gay pride.' That's why so many people don't like them, even apart from the immorality of what they're doing. They can't just make an evil choice. They have to brag about it, too."

"I can't remember the last time I saw a really good movie," said Mary Beth.

Enid was no champion of "alternative" lifestyles, and the things she disliked about Bea Meisner she'd disliked for forty years. She couldn't have said why this particular bridge-table conversation made her decide that she no longer needed to be friends with Bea Meisner. Nor could she have said why Gary's materialism and Chip's failures and Denise's childlessness, which had cost her countless late-night hours of fretting and punitive judgment over the years, distressed her so much less once Alfred was out of the house.

It made a difference, certainly, that all three of her kids were helping out. Chip in particular seemed almost miraculously transformed. After Christmas, he stayed with Enid for six weeks, visiting Alfred every day, before returning to New York. A month later he was back in St. Jude, minus his awful earrings. He proposed that he extend his visit to a length that delighted and astonished Enid until it emerged that he'd got himself involved with the chief neurology resident at St. Luke's Hospital.

The neurologist, Alison Schulman, was a kinky-haired and rather plain-looking Jewish girl from Chicago. Enid liked her well enough, but she was mystified that a successful young doctor wanted anything to do with her semi-employed son. The mystery deepened in June when

Chip announced that he was moving to Chicago to commence an immoral cohabitation with Alison, who had joined a group practice in Skokie. Chip neither confirmed nor denied that he had no real job and no intention of paying his fair share of household expenses. He claimed to be working on a screenplay. He said that "his" producer in New York had "loved" his "new" version and asked for a rewrite. His only gainful employment, however, as far as Enid knew, was part-time substitute teaching. Enid did appreciate that he drove to St. Jude from Chicago once a month and spent several long days with Alfred; she loved having a child of hers back in the Midwest. But when Chip informed her that he was going to be the father of twins with a woman he wasn't even married to, and when he then invited Enid to a wedding at which the bride was *seven months pregnant* and the groom's current "job" consisted of rewriting his screenplay for the fourth or fifth time and the majority of the guests not only were extremely Jewish but seemed *delighted* with the happy couple, there was certainly no shortage of material for Enid to find fault with and condemn! And it didn't make her proud of herself, it didn't make her feel good about her nearly fifty years of marriage, to think that if Alfred had been with her at the wedding, she *would* have found fault and she *would* have condemned. If she'd been sitting beside Alfred, the crowd bearing down on her would surely have seen the sour look on her face and turned away, would surely not have lifted her and her chair off the ground and carried her around the room while the klezmer music played, and she would surely not have loved it.

The sorry fact seemed to be that life without Alfred in the house was better for everyone but Alfred.

Hedgpeth and the other doctors, including Alison Schulman, had kept the old man at St. Luke's through January and into February, lustily billing Orfic Midland's soon-to-be-former health insurer while they explored every conceivable avenue of treatment, from ECT to Haldol. Alfred was finally discharged with a diagnosis of parkinsonism, dementia, depression, and neuropathy of the legs and urinary tract. Enid felt morally obliged to offer to care for him at home, but her children, thank God, wouldn't hear of it. Alfred was installed in the Deepmire Home, a long-term care facility adjacent to the country club, and

Enid undertook to visit him every day, to keep him well dressed, and to bring him homemade treats.

She was glad, if nothing else, to have his body back. She'd always loved his size, his shape, his smell, and he was much more available now that he was restrained in a geri chair and unable to formulate coherent objections to being touched. He let himself be kissed and didn't cringe if her lips lingered a little; he didn't flinch if she stroked his hair.

His body was what she'd always wanted. It was the rest of him that was the problem. She was unhappy before she went to visit him, unhappy while she sat beside him, and unhappy for hours afterward. He'd entered a phase of deep randomness. Enid might arrive and find him sunk deeply in a funk, his chin on his chest and a cookie-sized drool spot on his pants leg. Or he might be chatting amiably with a stroke victim or a potted plant. He might be unpeeling the invisible piece of fruit that occupied his attention hour after hour. He might be sleeping. Whatever he was doing, though, he wasn't making sense.

Somehow Chip and Denise had the patience to sit and converse with him about whatever demented scenario he inhabited, whatever train wreck or incarceration or luxury cruise, but Enid couldn't tolerate the least error. If he mistook her for her mother, she corrected him angrily: "Al, it's *me*, Enid, your wife of *forty-eight years*." If he mistook her for Denise, she used the very same words. She'd felt Wrong all her life and now she had a chance to tell him how Wrong *he* was. Even as she was loosening up and becoming less critical in other areas of life, she remained strictly vigilant at the Deepmire Home. She had to come and tell Alfred that he was wrong to dribble ice cream on his clean, freshly pressed pants. He was wrong not to recognize Joe Person when Joe was nice enough to drop in. He was wrong not to look at snapshots of Aaron and Caleb and Jonah. He was wrong not to be excited that Alison had given birth to two slightly underweight but healthy baby girls. He was wrong not to be happy or grateful or even remotely lucid when his wife and daughter went to enormous trouble to bring him home for Thanksgiving dinner. He was wrong to say, after that dinner, when they returned him to the Deepmire Home, "Better not to leave here than to have to come back." He was wrong, if he could be so lucid as to produce a sentence like that, not to be lucid at any other time. He was wrong to attempt to hang himself with bedsheets in the night. He was wrong to hurl himself against a window. He was wrong to try to slash his wrist with a dinner fork. Altogether he was wrong about so many things that, except for her four days in New York and her two Christmases in Philadelphia and her three weeks of recovery from hip surgery, she never failed to visit him. She had to tell him, while she still had time, how wrong he'd been and how right she'd been. How wrong not to love her more, how wrong not to cherish her and have sex at every opportunity, how wrong not to trust her financial instincts, how wrong to have spent so much time at work and so little with the children, how wrong to have been so negative, how wrong to have been so gloomy, how wrong to have run away from life, how wrong to have said no, again and again, instead of yes: she had to tell him all of this, every single day. Even if he wouldn't listen, she had to tell him.

He'd been living at the Deepmire Home for two years when he stopped accepting food. Chip took time away from parenthood and his new teaching job at a private high school and his eighth revision of the screenplay to visit from Chicago and say goodbye. Alfred lasted longer after that than anyone expected. He was a lion to the end. His blood pressure was barely measurable when Denise and Gary flew into town, and still he lived another week. He lay curled up on the bed and barely breathed. He moved for nothing and responded to nothing except to shake his head emphatically, once, if Enid tried to put an ice chip in his mouth. The one thing he never forgot was how to refuse. All of her correction had been for naught. He was as stubborn as the day she'd met him. And yet when he was dead, when she'd pressed her lips to his forehead and walked out with Denise and Gary into the warm spring night, she felt that nothing could kill her hope now, nothing. She was seventy-five and she was going to make some changes in her life.